THE GARDENER

Charles Reeza

Cover photograph and design by Charles Reeza

Portions of this work were first published online: July 2013

First E-book Edition: Sept 2015
Second E-book Edition: Nov 2017
ASIN: B015RS47MQ

First Paperback Edition: Dec 2017
ISBN: 978-0-692-98854-1

If an offense come out of the truth, better is it that the offense come than that the truth be concealed.

—Thomas Hardy, Tess of the D'Urbervilles

1

I'm not rich.

Yeah, I make decent money, and I don't have a mortgage on the house. My parents left it to me after dying sooner than any of us would have liked. You always think those things happen to other people, but . . . that was a couple of years ago and it costs money to maintain an old house. The heating bills are terrible.

Don't get me wrong, I love the house. We moved here when I was a kid and they put a lot of work into it. My mother refinished the woodwork and hung wallpaper while my father collected tools and learned how to fix things. The house became more impressive and more comfortable year after year. But there was always more to do. Dad asked me to help with the yard work. We planted trees and hedges that enclosed the back yard. We cultivated flower beds all around the house. My parents saw how much I enjoyed it, so they bought me books about gardening and let me decide what to plant. They called me the gardener.

I like perennials. Annuals are fine, too, but they're not much of challenge. With perennials, I need to guess how the combination of soil, sunlight and water will affect them from one year to the next. I document the changes and adjust things the next year. It takes a lot of patience. Some plants don't thrive while others get bigger than expected and overshadow the rest. I happen to like plants that assert themselves that way. I give them what they need to get as big as possible, and they give me what I want when they bloom. I don't talk to them or anything. I'm not crazy. But I spend a lot of time with my plants.

I was a quiet kid. Now I call myself an introvert, but back then I didn't know what that was. My parents worried about me not having friends, but they weren't very social either. I got along with people in high school. No one bothered me. I was on the swimming team for a couple of years and ran cross country after that. I liked running in the woods. Sometimes I'd hang out with another kid, but I preferred books. I looked forward to being alone at the end of the school day.

There were a few girls who liked me. I managed to frustrate them with my friendly, clueless demeanor until they moved on. I knew what I liked when I looked at other boys, but I maintained a safe distance. I didn't take risks. I smiled at jokes about "queers." This was before things got better for kids like me. My fear was justified.

I carefully chose a date for the senior prom. She was a nice girl, as quiet as me, who seemed to get it. I thought we had a good time, but she had a tear in her eye when I shook her hand and said good night. I went home and read an article about soil analysis, trying not to feel guilty. I knew I should have skipped the prom.

College was difficult, though I was an excellent student. Freshmen had to live on campus, and I was never comfortable there. The dormitory was like a greenhouse full of young men ripening in the testosterone-rich atmosphere. Some guys liked to walk around half-naked, displaying their impressive bodies casually. I wondered if they knew others might feel envy, or insecurity, or lust. I was plagued by uncomfortable urges.

One day, as I brushed my teeth in a room full of sinks and mirrors, I furtively watched the reflection of a reflection of a large athlete who was shaving the thick muscles of his chest. As he rinsed and flexed them for his own approval, he caught me staring into his mirror. My heart jumped. My eyes darted around, looking for a safe place to land. Without speaking or turning around, he removed the towel from his waist and used it to dry his chest. With a trace of a smile, he shifted his stance to accentuate the impressive shape of his ass. Terrified, I scurried out of the room and found a safe place to masturbate.

For the rest of the year, whenever I was near that guy, he stood a little too close, lingering long enough for me to feel his heat. I remember being pressed against him on a crowded elevator, close enough to see his chest hadn't been shaved recently, and I was aroused. He looked down at me as if he knew, and was pleased, but he never acknowledged it. I distanced myself from other students, spending more time in the library and less time in the dorm. I was the quiet guy whose name you couldn't remember. I ran every day but never joined a team. I focused on my classes.

I was relieved when I could live off campus and commute to school. My parents fixed up an apartment above their garage to give me, or them, more privacy. Before automobiles were common, the garage was a coach house with servants' quarters on the upper level. I liked the apartment and felt safer there. I could maintain my garden and use student loans for tuition instead of rent.

My attention to detail helped me in science and mathematics and eventually led me to accounting. I never thought about doing something related to gardening. A profession with a reliable salary and benefits offered more security. Accounting would do. Graduate school followed college. I excelled, got along, and kept my nose to the grindstone. Next thing I knew I was a CPA with a decent job and my own cubicle. I could even say I didn't live with my parents, sort of.

Lakeport is a small city. I knew people wondered about me. I saw the curious looks and heard comments about that nice young man who doesn't have a girlfriend. It didn't help that my parents were Catholic. They never asked me, and I never told. It was easier that way. Besides, what was there to talk about? Private thoughts and feelings could stay private. It would be different if I had a "friend," but I didn't. Gays with money could risk being open about it, but I'm not rich. I never did anything to fuel gossip, hinder my career, or threaten my security.

My interest in gardening never faded. One spring, Dave, the owner of my favorite nursery, offered me an unusual peony that was shipped in from a southern state. He knew the kind of plants I liked, but warned me it might not thrive in this climate. "I'll give it to you for ten bucks if you want it." Loving a bargain, I accepted the challenge. I took it home and found a sunny spot behind the house, planted it in rich, fertile soil and gave it a good soaking. That's when the sheriff's car pulled into the driveway. "Your parents . . . a car accident . . . I'm sorry . . ."

The safe life I had so carefully cultivated was permanently altered by one unpredictable event. I noticed the sympathy and kindness people offered, but I was numb. I found comfort in my routines, pushed through the days and embraced the grindstone. The seasons presented a yearlong drama about life and death in the private theater of my garden. I watched it alone. Then I watched it again.

I moved back into the house, donated my parents clothing and rearranged the furniture. I learned to cook and never had guests. I rented the apartment above the coach house to carefully screened tenants who respected my privacy and were rarely seen. The extra income helped. There were property taxes to pay, and the utilities, and a car payment. I got a promotion at the accounting firm - an office and a little more money. I worked a lot. And I had the garden. The garden kept me busy.

One December, my tenant told me she was being transferred to Chicago. She needed to move in January, the worst time of year to find a new tenant. I was not pleased. I told her I would try to find someone, but she had to keep paying the rent until an acceptable replacement was found. She was surprised I wouldn't let her out of the lease. *Business is business,* I thought. *I can't afford to be flexible.* Grudgingly, I advertised the apartment with a lengthy list of rules and restrictions to discourage undesirable applicants. I took the extra step of putting a "For Rent" sign in front of the house even though I couldn't fit all my rules on it. Silently cursing my departing tenant, I trudged through the snow and into the house.

While making coffee the following Saturday morning, I saw someone standing on the snowy driveway looking up at the coach house. It wasn't my tenant – she was out of town. It was a young man. I eyed him suspiciously. *Salesman? Jehovah's Witness? Burglar?* I didn't like visitors. *Go away!* He saw me in the window and raised his hand in a cautious wave. *Crap.* I moved toward the back door, crammed my feet into some shoes and put on a coat. He was about to walk up the back steps, so I exited the house, closing the door behind me before he could rush in and rob me. "Can I help you?"

"Hi. Yeah, I saw the sign. About the apartment?"

"Oh. Right."

"Is it still available?"

"Well, I'm currently reviewing two applicants." It was a lie I told prospective tenants.

"Am I too late? Could I still apply in case the others don't take it?"

"That depends . . ."

"It looks great! What a great house!"

"Thanks, but . . ."

"Must be a lot of work to keep this up. I hope you have someone to help with all the chores." He smiled.

I squinted. *Not much more than a kid.* "We manage." Another lie. I didn't want him to know I was alone.

"So, could I apply? I need a place, and I can walk to work from here. I've been looking for a while and this is the first place I've seen. I'd appreciate any . . ."

"Where do you work?"

"I'm a waiter at the hotel, the Harbor View." Hotel, restaurant, bar, health club. Thirty-six rooms with views of the harbor. Smells like fish.

"How long have you been there?"

"A couple of months. I just moved here, but I'm working hard, and my boss says . . ."

"I'm pretty sure the other two applicants will qualify. They seem very solid. I'd give you an application, but I wouldn't want you to get your hopes up." *I'm not renting to some kid with a shitty job.*

"I understand, sir. If it's not too much trouble, I'd still like to apply. I wouldn't want to miss out on a wonderful place like this because I didn't fill out a form. I could help with whatever . . ."

"I can't show you the apartment today. My tenant is out of town and I didn't get permission . . ."

"That's okay, I'm sure it's fine. I like old buildings." The kid wasn't going away. He looked so eager, with his rosy cheeks and bright eyes. I had to get rid of him somehow.

"All right, let me get the form and you can bring it back . . ."

"Or I could fill it out here to save time. Then I won't have to disturb you again." He had a point.

"I guess you could, uh . . ." It occurred to me I had to let him in my house. "Um . . ." He gave me a curious look. *He seems innocent enough, but when you let down your guard . . .* "Uh . . ." I was taking way too long. I turned away to hide my embarrassment, but it looked like I was going into the house. He stepped forward. I got flustered and reached for the doorknob. *Too late now - I have to let him in. Dammit!* He followed me inside and closed the door behind him. I left my shoes on the doormat. "Wait here." I rushed into the adjacent room where I kept the application forms. *Hurry, before he steals something!* When I returned, he was standing on the doormat in his stocking feet.

"I don't want to get snow on your floor. Nice kitchen."

"Okay. Yes. I mean, thank you." I was uneasy. *When was the last time I had someone in the house? Was it after the funeral?* "Uh . . . you could sit at the table. I'll get a pen." I took off my coat and hung it on the back of a chair. He stepped into the kitchen and did the same. *Taller than I realized. Six-one? Six-two?* I gave him a pen as he sat down.

I remembered the coffee I was making. *No wonder I'm so irritable. I suppose I'll have to offer him a cup. It would be rude not to.* I assessed him more closely while he filled out the application. Cheap flannel shirt, worn jeans, dark hair and a trace of dark stubble on his jaw. *He doesn't smell, but I can't rent to a hobo.* My inner voice was a real bitch.

"Do you want some coffee?" I poured a cup for myself.

"No, thanks, I don't want to trouble you."

I guess I wasn't listening. I poured him a cup. "Milk? Sugar?" I set them on the table.

"Um, okay. Sugar, please." He put three heaping scoops into his mug. "Thank you."

"You like it sweet." I absentmindedly pulled open a tin of cookies and set it on the table.

"I'm still getting used to city coffee. The first time I had a Starbucks I felt like a jackrabbit. This is good." He continued with the application. "I don't have a paycheck with me, is that okay? I make most of my money from tips anyway." When he looked up, I was reminded of someone at my college. One of those guys I stayed away from.

"It doesn't matter. Write down your monthly income." I pushed the tin of cookies closer. He took the hint and picked one out. *Why am I feeding him?* I suppose he looked hungry. Despite his broad shoulders, his waist was narrow. *He'll find another place.*

"I think that's everything. Do you want to check it?" I reviewed the application while he drank his coffee and ate another cookie. His name was Sam Engel.

"Is your legal name Samuel?"

"Um, it's Samson." His green eyes shifted. "My parents were into the Bible, but I prefer Sam." His cheeks flushed. *It's a shame I'll have to reject him.*

"Okay. I'll call you if the other applicants don't follow through."

Sam got up and took his coat off the chair. "I appreciate it . . . um . . . I don't know your name."

"I'm sorry, it's Adam. Adam Evans." I reached out to shake his hand. *Big, warm hand.* It felt good, so I pulled away.

"Okay, Adam, I'll wait to hear from you. I hope . . . I guess I shouldn't say I hope the others change their minds, but . . . let me get my shoes on."

As he bent to pull on his boots, I noticed the way his jeans fit. "Thanks for coming, Sam." I was surprised I said that. I couldn't have meant it.

"Thanks for your hospitality." He continued to talk as he stepped onto the porch. "I feel like I should . . . would you mind . . . I could shovel your sidewalk before I go." Now he seemed flustered. "You've been . . . to thank you for the coffee, I mean."

"That's not necessary. I have a snow blower."

"No, I'll use the shovel. No problem, it's the least I can do. I'll put it back when I'm done. Thanks again!" He was on his way before I could object. *Dammit! Why is he being so nice?* I wanted to be annoyed, but I wasn't looking forward to dealing with the snow that had fallen overnight.

I poured myself another cup of coffee and watched him from the front window. He scooped up big mounds of wet snow and tossed them aside, one after another, without slowing down. He finished in half the time it would have taken me, even when I was his age. I was impressed. Then he started on the driveway. *That can't be done with a shovel. It's too much.* I considered telling him to stop, but Sam kept going at the same pace until he was finished. *Huh . . . strong kid.* He left the shovel outside the back door, as promised. As he jogged down the street toward the harbor, I felt something. I think it was anxiety. *Too much coffee, maybe.*

Almost a week later, on another snowy day, I came home from work to find the snow had already been removed from my sidewalks and driveway. I immediately thought of the young man, Sam, and my heart skipped a beat. *Will he ambush me behind the house?* When I pulled up to the garage there was no sign of him. I found a note stuck in the back door. "Hi Adam - Wondering if you rented the apartment yet. Starting my shift at the restaurant, so I couldn't wait for you. Hope you call, Sam." *Shit, he's persistent.* I was hoping he would find another place so I wouldn't have to turn him down.

I did my usual background check on him, but there was nothing to find. He was only twenty years old, with no credit history and no public records. I even registered on Facebook to see if he was on there, but he wasn't. I quickly deleted my account before anyone could "friend" me. His only references were the manager and a chef at the Harbor View. I hadn't called because Sam's pay wasn't high enough. The rent was about two-thirds of his monthly earnings, and I used a strict rent-to-income ratio when selecting my tenants. That's what I would have to tell him, even though no one else had called about the apartment.

I was surprised by a knock at the back door. *Now what?* It was my departing tenant. I opened the door and barked, "Is there a problem?" I immediately regretted my unfriendly tone and sheepishly invited her to step inside.

"What a pretty kitchen. I wondered what it looked like in here. I heard you have someone to rent the apartment. That's great!" My jaw dropped. "Sam was here to shovel the snow. He said there were two other applicants before him? I was afraid you wouldn't find anyone."

"Uh, that's . . ."

"What a nice guy! I hope you don't mind that I showed him the place. You could have shown him while I was out of town, but I know how you are about the rules."

"I'm not renting to him."

"Oh . . . I'm sorry. Did you accept one of the other applicants?"

Crap! I had to lie again. "The other applicants changed their minds."

"Okay, so . . . what about Sam?" She sounded suspicious.

"His income is too low."

She knit her brow. "It is? He was so excited about it. He offered to buy some of the furniture I'm not taking to Chicago. He had cash, but I told him I needed to talk to you first. Are you . . . or is he . . ."

I was irritated. "This is a big misunderstanding. I told him I would review his application, but he doesn't make enough money."

"But you're paying him to shovel snow. Wouldn't that cover part of the rent? And I wouldn't mind having him as a neighbor, if you know what I mean." She moved her eyebrows.

I did not know what she meant. *What's with the eyebrows?* "I'm not paying him to shovel . . . listen, I need to clear this up with him. I'm sorry for the confusion, but I'll let you know when I have a new tenant." She tilted her head and squinted, but I practically shoved her out the door before she could ask any more questions.

I started pacing, thinking about what to do. *I'll go down to the restaurant and tell him to fuck off! Wait, that's too strong . . . he's just a kid who got carried away. I'll be firm with him and he'll understand. Do I have to pay him for shoveling the snow? Crap!* Muttering and fuming, I grabbed my coat and headed downtown. *I'm not giving up my rental income! She'll have to keep paying until I find someone else. Business is business!* My stomach was growling by the time I stomped through the door of the Harbor View Restaurant.

"Good evening, sir, will you be dining alone this evening?"

"I'm looking for Sam. I think he's working tonight."

"He is here tonight, but there aren't any tables left in his section. I would be happy to serve you at one of my tables." The waiter stared straight into my eyes until I looked away, feeling awkward.

"I wasn't planning to eat." *How should I do this?* "All right, give me the corner table."

"That's one of Cheryl's tables," he huffed. "Suit yourself."

What's with the attitude? I chose a spot where I could see the whole dining room. A moment later, buxom Cheryl arrived with a menu.

"Hi, handsome. You here alone tonight?"

"Yes." *What did she call me?*

"I hope to make your evening enjoyable. Can I start you off with something from the bar?"

"No, I'll have fish. That smell . . . whatever it is . . . I'll have that."

"You mean our fish fry? Excellent choice, sir." There was sarcasm in her voice. "Would you like coleslaw or a tossed salad?"

"Whatever. A salad." I saw Sam come out of the kitchen with a huge tray of food on one hand. He didn't see me, occupied as he was.

"What kind of dressing?"

"Yes." I was distracted. "Do you know when Sam will have a break? I need to talk to him."

"Oh, you're here for Sam, huh?" Her smile was crooked. "Stand in line, honey. My tips have gone down since he got here. Sweet guy, though. Do you want anything to drink?"

"Just water." I was focused on Sam, hoping to catch his eye. "Could you tell him I'd like to talk when he has a chance?"

"Okay, I'll let him know. But cool your jets – it might be a while."

I sat back and watched Sam work. He was dressed in black, with the sleeves of his shirt turned up to his elbows. His pants were . . . snug. He distributed plates to a group of customers, and all their eyes were on him. *What could he be saying?* He lightly touched a woman's shoulder before nodding his head and retreating to the kitchen. No one at the table looked down until he was gone. *Hmm . . . must be a good waiter.*

I was still watching when Cheryl brought water, a salad, and a basket of bread. "Did you let Sam know I'm here?"

"Wow, you've got it bad." I blinked at her. "I'll tell him in a minute, but what's your story? Are you a friend of his?"

"No, of course not. He was interested in an apartment I'm renting and . . ."

"Oh, you're *that* guy. Adam, right? It's been 'Adam this' and 'Adam that' all week."

"No . . . that must be someone else. I need to . . ."

"You have the Victorian house on Eden Place. The one with all the flowers in the summer? I wondered who lived there."

What? Why is he telling people about me? It's no one's business!

"Let me get your fish, hon. I'll tell him you're here."

Exasperated, I picked up a fork and stabbed the salad to death, angrily shoving it in my mouth. *What's this dressing? I didn't order this.* While I buttered a roll, Cheryl whispered in Sam's ear and gestured toward me. His face lit up as he glanced in my direction, but he was busy with another table. Again, I noticed his smooth interactions with the customers who gazed up at him. His gestures were graceful, his smile sincere.

I became aware of my heartbeat. My eyes traveled from Sam's dark, wavy hair to the squareness of his jaw, the wide shoulders, narrow waist, and the shape of his butt in those snug black pants. My face grew warm. An unexpected thought rose from the sudden pressure in my groin to my conscious mind. *Holy shit, he's hot!* My heart pounded.

Cheryl returned with the fish while my mouth was hanging open. "He's a fine-looking man, isn't he? I wish he'd move into my apartment."

She walked away before I realized what she had seen in me. I tore my eyes away from Sam and looked down at my food. *How could I be so careless? People must be staring.* I rearranged my food with trembling hands. I took a few deep breaths to calm myself down, then tasted the fried fish. The warmth felt good in my belly. I ate quickly, trying to organize my thoughts. *I'll be direct and businesslike. It doesn't matter what he looks like, he can't afford the apartment. Be rational about this, and everything will be fine.*

"Adam, it's great to see you!" Sam approached, smiling, and seemed to tower over me. "Do you mind if I sit? I only have a few minutes."

"Yeah, sure, have a seat." I wiped my mouth with a napkin.

He laid his thick forearms on the table, leaning toward me with an eager expression. I couldn't look him in the eye. His open collar revealed fine, dark hair on his chest. "Did you get my note?"

"Yes." I cleared my throat and swallowed hard. "Um . . . when can you move in?"

2

I wasn't comfortable with my decision to let Sam rent the apartment. It was risky in more ways than one, and risk was something I avoided. I agreed to reduce his rent in exchange for some chores I was happy to be rid of. He earned extra money by shoveling snow for a few other homeowners and businesses in town, so his income was higher than I thought. He bought enough furniture from the previous tenant to make the apartment functional, and moved in with only a backpack and a large duffel bag. He had been living in a room at the Harbor View since he began working there. My coach house was his first apartment.

Sam turned out to be reliable, and I was continually impressed by his willingness to work hard. One weekend, late in the winter, we were hit by a storm that dumped nearly a foot of wet snow between midnight and noon on Sunday. Before it even stopped falling, Sam was out there with the shovel. I stuck my head out the back door and told him he should use the snow blower. "No thanks, I like the exercise!" He attacked a long snow drift that was half his height, effortlessly tossing big scoops of snow over his shoulder. He was a strong, handsome young man. My mind wandered into uncomfortable territory.

I swept those thoughts aside by focusing on the pot of chili I was making. I felt guilty about Sam working so hard outside while I was in my cozy house. *Maybe I should give him some chili. That would be nice, I think.* 'Nice' didn't come naturally to me; it required effort.

When he came up the driveway to stow the shovel, I opened the back door again, despite the knot in my guts. "Hey, um . . . I'm making chili. I'll give you some when you're done . . . you know . . . if you want it." *I bet he hates chili.*

He looked surprised, but he smiled. "Wow, Adam, that's . . . awesome. I'll get back as soon as I can."

"It won't be done for a while. You should slow down before you pull . . . a thing . . . in your . . . whatever."

"Don't worry, I'm stronger than I look. I'll see you later." Still smiling, he jogged away.

I regretted being so suspicious when we first met. I couldn't ask for a more polite, quiet tenant. As far as I could tell, he never had visitors. He didn't have a car, so I didn't know when he was coming or going. There were nights when I suspected he was sleeping elsewhere. *None of my business.* He probably had a girlfriend, or several. I was completely focused on my studies at his age. Not that I wanted a girlfriend. Or any friend. Sam was a nice guy. I must have seen that when I impulsively offered him the apartment.

Around five-thirty I heard a knock at the back door. *Is that him already?* There he was, looking fresh and eager. "How did you finish so fast?" I gestured for him to enter. "You must be worn out."

"No, I'm fine. It was great exercise. Your chili smells fantastic."

"It'll be ready in a few minutes." I went to the stove and stirred the large pot. I was planning to put half of it in another container so I could hand it to him at the door. When I turned around, Sam had removed his coat, his wet boots were on the door mat, and he had stepped into the kitchen. He was expecting to eat with me. His cheeks were red from the cold. He wore jeans and a gray sweatshirt with a damp patch of perspiration on his chest. He was taller and broader than I remembered. *Why do I keep forgetting that?* Suddenly the room felt humid. *I guess it wouldn't kill me to let him eat here.* "Would you like something to drink?"

"Just water, thanks. I worked up a thirst."

I handed him an empty glass and pointed at the faucet. "Help yourself."

"Thanks again for inviting me." He filled the glass and drank it quickly. He filled it again. "I don't get many home cooked meals anymore. I eat at the restaurant when I'm working." He drank the second glass of water more slowly. "I'm still learning how to cook for myself."

I was cutting a loaf of French bread into thick slices. "You work harder than most people your age. I'm impressed." *Do I know anyone else his age? No.*

"I grew up on a farm, so that's normal for me. Besides, I need the money." He paused. "You work long hours. What do you do?"

I wasn't planning to talk about myself, but that's what happens when you start a conversation. "I'm an accountant." I set the bread on the table. "Have a seat."

"Oh, wow. You must be smart to be an accountant. Do you like it?"

"Um . . . it pays the bills." *Am I smart?* I was more aware of my weaknesses than my strengths. I ladled chili into two bowls and set them on the table. "Be careful, it's hot." I sat down across from him.

"Thanks, this looks great." He leaned forward to blow steam away from his bowl, smiled boyishly, and tasted the chili. "Mmm."

"I hope it's not too spicy."

As he swallowed another spoonful, his eyes grew wider. "Oh!" He grabbed his glass and gulped half of the water. He paused, then drank again.

"Oops," I grimaced. I was the only one who had ever eaten my chili. I had no idea it was so powerful. "Are you all right?"

"Yeah," he squeaked, and got up to refill his glass. "I'll get used to it." He wiped a couple of tears from his eyes and sat down to eat again. "I like it." Sam was so polite.

"Okay, if you're telling the truth, there's plenty more." I relaxed a little and inquired about his background. Sam was an only child, like me. His parents' farm was in Sorek County in the northern part of the state. They were religious people with high expectations for him. "Loving, but strict," he said. "We didn't see eye to eye, so I had to leave." He stopped there.

When he asked me about the house and how long I had owned it, I mentioned my parents' death. I rarely talked about that, but it explained how I could afford to live in such a large house by myself. Feeling awkward, I offered more chili. "Have as much as you'd like."

Sam's appetite turned out to be as impressive as his work ethic. "I'm sorry I'm eating like a horse, but it's so good." Apparently, he got used to the spices. "I'm sure my parents don't miss feeding me. They complained about it all the time." When he finished, he sat back and patted his stomach. "That feels good. Thank you so much." He stretched his long arms toward the ceiling, knit his fingers together and brought his hands behind his head. I caught myself wondering what he would look like with his shirt off, and I was uncomfortable. I stood up to collect the dishes.

"Let me help." He brought the glassware to the sink and stood beside me, close enough for his hip and thigh to touch mine. I pulled away and Sam quickly took a step in the other direction.

"I can clean up," I said. "You must be tired."

"Not really." He looked sheepish. An awkward pause hung in the air.

My heart was beating harder than usual. I didn't know what to say, so I wanted him to go. A long-ignored voice inside me wanted something else, but it wasn't loud enough yet. I blurted out the dumbest question that popped into my head. "Do you have a girlfriend, Sam?"

There was another awkward silence. "Um, no, I don't have a girlfriend. Do you?"

Naturally my question would lead to the subject I least wanted to discuss. "No, I don't have a girlfriend." My face was hot.

"Why not? You're good looking, you have an excellent job and this great house. I think you'd be a catch."

"Oaf! Nah." I hated compliments, especially from someone like him. I stared into the sink and retrieved a line I had used in the past. "I'm not cut out for relationships. I like being alone."

"Yeah, I know what you mean. I like being alone, too. But I get lonely sometimes. Don't you?"

I found it hard to believe he would ever be lonely. *Please! He could have anyone he wants.* My options were irrelevant. I pulled out another stock phrase I often used. "At my age, there's not much point in thinking about it."

"At your age? You make it sound like you're an old man. How old are you?"

I continued washing the dishes. "Thirty-two."

He made a face. "That's all? You're still young. Why do you talk like you're old?" His questions were getting bolder, more familiar. He leaned against the counter, looking at me curiously.

I didn't know what to say. I knew I wasn't old, but thought of myself that way. His questions were making me squirm, making me think about why I lived like this. *If I keep thinking about it, I might . . . I need to stop this.* "Listen, I'm getting tired. Would you mind?"

"You want me to go? Okay . . . I'm sorry I made you uncomfortable." He moved toward the door.

I rubbed my hands on the dish towel. "I'm not uncomfortable. Just tired." *A blatant lie.*

Sam's disbelief was all over his face, but he didn't express it. He was too nice for that. He thanked me again for the meal while he put on his boots. He stood up and faced me with a serious expression. "Adam . . . I want you to know I'm gay. Okay?"

What? My intestines did a somersault. *No!* It had not registered on my fucked-up radar that Sam might be gay. And he was coming out to me! I thought these things only happened . . . somewhere else.

"The main reason I had to leave my parents' farm was because they couldn't accept it. I made up my mind, from then on, I would always be honest about it. So I wanted to tell you." He turned, took his coat from the hook and put it on without looking at me.

"Uh, okay. That's fine. I, uh . . . thanks for telling me. It must be difficult . . ."

His eyes met mine. "Yeah, it is." He opened the door and stepped outside.

I wanted to say something else. *Say something!* I went after him and did the best I could. "Sam . . . I'm glad you're . . . I mean, I'm glad you're here. You're . . . you're a good person." My voice cracked.

"Thanks, Adam. That's nice. Good night." He walked across the driveway to the coach house. It was snowing again.

I closed the door with my back and slid down to the floor. I rarely cried, even when I was alone, but the floodgates were opened that night. I cried and cried without knowing why. Not yet, anyway. Eventually it subsided. I scolded myself for losing control and pulled myself together.

I kept reviewing my conversation with Sam, regretting things I'd said and a few things I hadn't. I cleaned up the kitchen and headed upstairs to my bedroom, exhausted. Reluctantly, I looked in the mirror as I undressed. *Am I good looking?* I thought of myself as average in every way. Brownish hair, bluish eyes, five-ten, runner's build, with an extra ten pounds since I hadn't been running as much. No deformities, nothing missing. My face? I don't know . . . it seemed ordinary to me.

I took one last look. *Well . . . you're not repulsive.* It was probably the nicest thing I had ever said to myself.

I turned off the lights and went to the window. There was a light on in the coach house. I sent a silent *good night* to Sam, closed the curtains and crawled into bed.

3

I saw very little of Sam for a few weeks. He'd lift a hand in my direction when he was coming or going. I waved back with self-conscious enthusiasm. I didn't want to appear uncomfortable, though I was. And I hoped he wouldn't think it was because he was gay, even if it was freaking me out. He seemed more dangerous because of it. I was always uncomfortable around handsome men, as if they could read my mind and discover my hidden desires. *Then what?* I assumed they would beat me up, I suppose. Or laugh at me. But Sam was different. He made me nervous for other reasons.

I accepted Sam as a tenant because he was stunningly handsome. I was afraid that if I let down my guard, and if he wanted to, Sam could manipulate me. My head was spinning with anxiety about how to behave around him. I had to be in control. I wanted him to like me, but didn't want to seem too interested. I knew I wouldn't have a chance with a guy who looked like that, and with our age difference. *I'm not stupid!* If I could live in my college dormitory for a year without being called a fag, I could control myself around one hot guy. *I can be accepting and supportive from a distance . . . like a cool uncle. Yeah.* That was my plan.

The snowstorm on the day we ate chili together was the last major snowfall of the winter. There were still a few patches of snow in shady places where Sam piled it extra high, but spring had arrived. Crocus and snowdrops were blooming around the edges of my garden. Anxious to start gardening, I drove past local nurseries like a stalker. It was too early to plant anything, they didn't have any plants yet, and I didn't need any more plants. That didn't stop me.

One sunny Saturday, I decided it was safe to put away the snow shovel and the bag of salt. I opened the half of the garage my tenants used if they had a car. Sam didn't have a car, but I discovered he was using the space. A weight bench was set up in the middle of the floor with metal plates and dumbbells neatly arranged around the edges. I wondered how he moved all that iron in there. My heart skipped a beat when I heard him coming down the stairs from his apartment. *I didn't know he was home!* I turned to see him dressed in soft cotton shorts and a gray t-shirt that hung on his form in wonderful ways. Not that I was looking.

"Hey, I hope you don't mind me putting this equipment in here. I should have asked first."

"No, you shouldn't have. *Wait, that came out wrong!* I mean, you shouldn't have asked, not that you shouldn't have put it in here. You don't have to ask, is what I mean. *Do I sound nervous?* It's your space. It comes with the apartment, so . . . unless you're cooking meth in here, it's fine."

Sam's eyebrows went up a little. "I'm not cooking meth."

Shit! "I was kidding. My sense of humor is . . ."

"I know, Adam." Sam smiled. *Did his eyes just twinkle?*

I awkwardly waived an arm in his direction. "You've been working out . . . it looks like . . . because of the weights, I mean. Not because you look . . ." *Shut up! Idiot!*

"I just started. I don't really know what I'm doing." He rubbed his chest with one hand. "I'm glad I ran into you. I wanted to ask . . . I don't know if you'll want to, but . . . could I make dinner for you some evening? To thank you for . . . I'm not much of a cook, but . . . you know, in return for your hospitality?"

"That's not necessary." Sam's face fell. "But I'd like to come . . . to join you . . . for dinner in your apartment." *No! Wrong! Mistake!* My brain and my mouth were no longer cooperating.

"Great! How about tomorrow? Are you free?"

I visualized the vast white space of my social calendar. "I think tomorrow would work. I can do that." *Danger! Danger!* "Um, do you want me to bring anything?" *Stop! Don't do this!*

He waved his hand. "I'll take care of everything. Come over around six o'clock." He beamed. "I'm so glad you . . . I was afraid you might . . . I'm . . ."

Abort! Abort! "Okay then, six o'clock tomorrow. Good. Let me put away the shovel and the salt and I'll be out of your way." *Run! Fast!*

"I'll get that." He leapt past me to pick up the bag of salt with one hand. It was a fifty-pound bag, almost full, but he lifted it as if it weighed a pound. I noticed the way his biceps filled his shirt sleeve and looked away quickly. He stowed the items and brushed his hands against each other. I stood there like a dummy. Sam hesitated. "I think I'll work out before I go to the restaurant."

"Yes, of course, I'll see you tomorrow." I turned, nearly tripping over my own feet, and scurried away like a chipmunk. I locked myself in the house as if Sam would come after me. *What have you done, you fool? So much for keeping your distance!* My thoughts were all over the place. *How did he trick me into having dinner with him?* My heart thumped, *what have I done, what have I done, what have I done?*

I had to calm down, to stop thinking. *What to do? What will work?* I needed relief from the tension. Masturbation was the cure for all kinds of stress. *Yeah, that's it!* I ran up to my bedroom and flopped onto the bed for a few minutes of vigorous distraction. I didn't think of Sam at all.

A short while later, everything seemed more manageable.

* * *

The next day, I woke up full of energy. The sun was out again, so I decided to clean up my flower beds. I opened the garden shed and brought out my tools, a wheelbarrow, and work gloves. I strapped on my iPod, put in my ear buds and chose an album of Bach harpsichord concertos. I was truly fired up. I spent several hours tidying the perennial borders and hauling debris to the compost pile. I often lost track of time in the garden because it didn't feel like work. While kneeling next to the peony I planted the day my parents died, a shadow passed over me. I raised my head and saw Sam. From my perspective, he looked like a giant with the sun behind him. I pulled out my ear buds.

"Hey, Adam."

"Hi. Hey." *Stand up? No, stay down. Dammit!*

"What are you working on?" He was wearing shorts again. His legs had a perfect distribution of dark hair and his feet looked good in leather sandals. I forced myself to picture a dead bird I'd found near the hedge.

"I'm cleaning up the garden for spring." *Kneeling in front of him is weird. I should stand.*

"Are all these areas planted with different things? Are they all flowers?"

"Yeah, mostly. Some ferns, but most of my plants have flowers." *I'll stand now. No, I won't. Fuck.*

He squatted next to me and looked at the red shoots growing among the dead stems. "What's this one?"

I was distracted by his thighs. *Look away!* "That's a peony. It's supposed to have big white flowers, but I haven't seen any so far. Nothing but leaves for the last few years."

"Huh. Maybe you'll have better luck this year." He rose to his towering height again. "I'm kinda nervous about dinner tonight. Did I mention the food might be terrible?"

"I like terrible food . . . no I don't, that was dumb." *God, I hate myself!* "It'll be fine, Sam."

"Okay. I'm . . . never mind. I'll see you later."

"Yeah. What time is it?"

"About four o'clock." He walked toward the coach house.

I watched his backside until he glanced back at me, then I scolded myself for looking. I gathered my tools, put them in the shed, and went in the house to take a shower. And I jacked off. I was feeling the urge more often lately. *Probably because it's spring. Yeah, that's it.*

I took a bottle of wine to dinner because it didn't feel right to go empty-handed. I had butterflies in my stomach as I climbed the stairs. *I must be hungry.* Sam came to the door wearing faded jeans and a snug white polo shirt. My knees wobbled, and I forgot to say hello.

He took the bottle of wine. "Thanks - I didn't think of that. I'm not old enough to buy it, so it's a good thing . . ."

"Crap! I shouldn't have brought that." *Idiot!*

"That's okay, you can drink it. I'll have iced tea so you won't get in trouble."

Get in trouble?!

"I'll get a glass . . . wait, I don't have a cork screw."

"It's a screw top bottle. Cheap and easy."

He smiled. "That's good to know." When he opened the cupboard, I was surprised to see a whole shelf full of junk food, bags of candy, and a box from a doughnut shop. "This meal won't be anything fancy. I'm still learning to . . . I told you that already. The chef at the restaurant showed me some basics, but I'm not good at it." He handed me a tumbler filled with my cheap wine. "Sorry I don't have a wine glass."

"It's fine, thanks. What did you make?"

"Salad, lemon chicken, and broccoli." He lifted his iced tea. "Cheers!"

I took a gulp of wine. He stood a little closer than I preferred, so I had to look up at him. I looked down to see what shoes he was wearing - flat leather sandals. I looked up again.

"What?"

"You seem . . . taller."

"It's funny you said that. They measured me at work the other day and I was six-four. I thought I was six-three. I hope I'm not still growing."

"Why were they measuring you?" Another swallow of wine drowned my curiosity about his other dimensions.

"They want me to start working as a personal trainer in the health club. They were taking my stats to show me how it's done."

"Was that . . . were you trying . . ." I drained my glass. "I didn't know you did . . . personal training."

"No, I wasn't planning to be a trainer. I thought I would need a degree, but the manager said I have what it takes, the right personality and . . . other stuff." He crossed his arms over his chest. "I guess because I'm in pretty good shape."

"You certainly are . . . a hard worker." I caught myself that time. "I'm sure you'll be great."

"Thanks, Adam. You're . . . you . . . want more wine? The chicken should be ready." His hand shook as he filled my glass and gestured toward the table. I sat down and watched him get the food, the way his polo shirt fit . . . and the jeans . . . his long, thick arms. I sighed loud enough to make him glance at me, but I'm sure my expression was innocent. *Who wouldn't want him to be their trainer?* Sam was a living, breathing advertisement for vigorous exercise.

He put a bowl of salad on the table along with a loaf of crusty bread, then brought out a steaming pan full of chicken breasts and broccoli and set it on a straw mat. I could smell the lemon. "Wow, you made enough for an army." A slight exaggeration, but there were eight chicken breasts.

"You've seen how much I can eat. Help yourself." I took a modest portion of everything. Sam took twice as much. While we ate, he told me about his new job at the Harbor View Health Club. He would continue as a waiter for a few shifts each week while putting in most of his hours as a trainer. "The club pays better, and I'll get health insurance, but I won't get tips like I do in the restaurant."

"Oh, you'll get tips."

"What do you mean? They didn't mention that."

"I'm just saying, you'll probably get tips because people like . . . because you're so . . . helpful, or whatever."

"Okay, cool. The customers at the restaurant are generous. It's great, but I don't get it."

Seriously? Has he looked in the mirror lately?

"How's the food?"

I wasn't sure what to say. The salad was foolproof and the broccoli was okay, but the chicken was dry and hard to swallow, so I drank my wine faster than I should have. "It's good," I lied.

He emptied the wine bottle into my glass. "Are you sure? Don't you think the chicken is dry?" He was looking me square in the face. I had to summon my best acting skills.

"No, it's got the lemon . . . and . . . what is the other flavor in there?"

A slow smile formed a dimple on one side of his mouth. "Is it chicken? Is that what you taste?"

"Yeah, the chicken. It's very . . ." I had nothing.

Now he was grinning. "It's pretty bad, isn't it? You're such a liar."

Busted. "I'm sorry, Sam, I can't eat this." I felt bad, but he wasn't offended.

"That's okay. I'll eat it." He stabbed the remainder of my chicken with his fork and moved it to his own plate. "I don't like it either, but I can't afford to waste food." Even with his extra income from odd jobs, he must have been struggling financially. But he always paid his rent on time.

I took more salad and bread and watched Sam eat. I couldn't linger for long on any part of him because it was all too appealing – the veins in his arms, those bulky shoulders, a glimpse of chest hair, and his green eyes. I had to think about something else. "I suppose you won't get as many meals at the restaurant."

"We'll see. The chef likes to feed me. My coworkers call me 'Hoover' because I eat like a vacuum cleaner. I smile and keep eating."

I liked the nickname. "You probably won't use your weights downstairs if you're working out at the health club all day."

"No, I'll still use them because I'd rather not lift at the club. I did for a while, but the regulars there are too competitive. They always want to know how much

I'm lifting, and I'm not into that. I bought those weights from a guy who was moving to California."

"Were you lifting more than the other guys?" I probably sounded a little too interested.

Sam looked down as he loaded up his plate again. "I wasn't competing with them, but I wasn't losing." He didn't elaborate.

That bottle of wine gave me courage to be direct. "You're very strong, aren't you?" It was more of a statement than a question.

He blushed. "Yeah."

"How strong?"

"I don't know. How would I answer that?"

Dumb question. "Have you always been strong?"

"I guess." He paused without looking up from his plate. "When I was a kid, my father told me it was a gift from God. Like Samson, the guy in the Bible they named me after. I knew I was stronger than other kids, but I didn't see it as a gift."

"Why not? It's useful, isn't it?"

"Sure, I suppose. But it was one more thing that made me different from everyone else. I never understood why they thought strength was a gift from God, but the other thing - being gay - was an 'abomination.' It doesn't make sense."

I tried to lighten things up. "It makes you a gifted snow shoveler."

"Great. I'm gay and I can move snow. Best gifts ever." He smiled crookedly. On top of his more visible attributes, Sam was smart, and he had a sense of humor. I liked him. I enjoyed his company. I wouldn't say that about most people.

I had an idea . . . a bad one, probably, but the wine was talking. "Hey, would you be interested in helping with a few projects around here? In return, I'm thinking . . . maybe I could cook for you? I'll buy the food in exchange for your work, so your budget won't be so tight. I cook for myself anyway, so on days when you're not at the restaurant you could eat what I make . . . pick it up, or . . . well, you probably wouldn't want to eat with me."

He looked surprised. "That would be great, but I don't know . . . how much would it cost to feed me? I eat a lot more than you do."

"I'd take that into account. Believe me, I'd get my money's worth. There's so much work to be done on this property, it might not be fair to you."

"No, no! It would be great for me, don't get me wrong, I love the idea if you're comfortable with . . . you know . . . I can't believe you would do this for me." For a moment, I thought he might cry. He looked away. "Coffee . . . do you want coffee? I have decaf or regular."

"Sure. Regular is fine. After a whole bottle of wine, I could probably use it."

He stood up. "Sorry about the chicken. Did you get enough to eat? I know I did." He slipped a hand under his polo shirt and patted his tight stomach.

The sound of skin hitting skin aroused me. "Yeah, I had plenty. I'm good."

"Can you show me how much coffee to use? I don't want to screw it up."

I followed him to the counter near the sink where he had filters and two bags of ground coffee next to the obviously new, inexpensive coffee maker. "This reminds me of all the coffee I made in this kitchen when I was a student." I opened the bag of regular coffee and looked for a spoon.

"You used to live here?" He filled the carafe with water.

"Yeah, I was . . . twenty years old, about your age, when I moved in here. My parents fixed it up for me." I scooped coffee into the filter.

Sam moved closer to fill the coffee maker. One side of his body connected with mine as it had several weeks ago in my kitchen. Not wanting to offend him again, I stayed in place. He was surprisingly warm. Human contact was so foreign to me, any aspect of it could be a surprise. I liked it, but it was also uncomfortable. When he finished pouring the water and pulled away, I missed the warmth. He replaced the pot, pressed the switch, and we were silent for a moment.

"I didn't realize this used to be your apartment. I'm trying to picture you at age twenty." He squinted. "Hmm, not much different than you look now."

I smiled shyly and blushed. I think I was doing well under the circumstances. Thanks to a bottle of cheap wine.

We sat at the table and drank coffee while I told him about projects I had in mind for the garden and the house. Sam listed all the practical skills he learned from his father and talked as though he wanted to get started tomorrow. I asked what foods he liked. He couldn't think of anything he didn't like, so I reminded him of my spicy chili.

He laughed. "I liked your chili! I wasn't lying like you did about my chicken." When he tipped his mug to drink the last swallow of coffee, a single drop fell onto his white shirt over his left pectoral. I watched it bleed into the fabric near the outline of his nipple. He must have noticed where I was looking. "Are you staring at my boobs?"

I knew Sam was joking, but it startled me. Suddenly I felt sober. "You dripped coffee on your shirt." I pointed to the spot.

He looked down at it, pulling his shoulders back and pushing his chest out. "Crap!" He grabbed a napkin and pressed it against his chest.

My guilt and anxiety kicked in. "I should go." I pushed my chair back and stood.

He stopped fussing over his shirt. "Already? Are you sure?" He got up as I moved toward the door. "I guess it's getting late."

"I have to go to work in the morning."

"I know. I need to go to the health club tomorrow for orientation with the head trainer, and I have the evening shift in the restaurant."

"I don't want to keep you. Thanks for dinner."

"Adam . . . when do you want to start our new arrangement?"

"Oh . . . yeah. Are you sure you want to do that? You're not obligated . . ."

"I do, yeah. Why? Are you having second thoughts?"

Sort of. "No, I need help around here. That's why I suggested it." *No other reason.*

"I'd like to help you."

I paused. "How about Tuesday? Can you give me your work schedule?"

"Sure." He hesitated. "Do you mind if I eat with you?"

My heart thumped. "No. It makes no difference to me, but it's probably easier."

He moved one step closer. "I like . . . talking to you."

"Hah," I scoffed. "Suit yourself. I'm usually in a bad mood, so . . . you've been warned."

"I'll risk it." He opened the door for me. "Thanks for coming, I'm glad we can be friends."

"Yeah, sure." *Friends? Is that okay?*

He waited for me to walk down the stairs. "Good night, Adam."

"Good night, Sam." My inner voice warned me, *you can't be friends with him, he's your tenant! It's too risky! Things will get messy! What will people think?*

I told the voice to shut the fuck up.

4

On Monday after work I went shopping at the gigantic grocery store on the outskirts of town. I rarely shopped there, but it made more sense if I would be cooking for two – or three, considering Sam's appetite. In the meat department, I picked up roasts, packs of ground beef and chicken, whole hams and bags of frozen fish fillets. I had an unused chest freezer in the basement that would come in handy. Boxes of pasta, canned goods, cartons of soup stock, and blocks of cheese all went into the cart. I could start baking again without worrying about stuffing a whole cake in my mouth. Unlike Sam, I had to watch my weight. My cart was full by the time I got to the produce department, so I would have to buy fruit and vegetables at the market closer to home.

At the checkout, I watched the total of my purchases climb toward an amount that made my throat constrict, unaccustomed as I was to spending money. I cracked open my wallet and pulled out a credit card as shiny as it was the day it arrived two years earlier. I handed it to the fat young cashier with black lipstick. "I hope this works. I've never used it."

She slashed it through her card reader as if she were plunging a dagger into my chest. With one cheerful blip, the machine made me poorer. "Sign in the box," she croaked. I did as I was told, then forced myself to smile in case she was thinking of killing me. No wonder I rarely went out.

Hauling the food home and putting it in the pantry was a lot of work. I had to evict a few spiders from shelves that had been empty since my parents were around. I half-expected bats to fly out of there. Filling it with food seemed to put life in the house again. When I was finished, I assembled a pan of lasagna and baked a lemon pound cake for the following night. I enjoyed cooking with someone else in mind, and Sam was certainly on my mind.

It took us a few weeks to get into our new routine. He cleaned up the lawnmower and cut the grass every week. I never allowed anyone to work in my private paradise before, but I asked him to remove the overgrown brush between the trees and hedges around the perimeter of the garden. I told him about the bulbs that were blooming and what they needed to look their best. There were clumps of fragrant hyacinths, mobs of daffodils, and a long row of multicolored Dutch irises along the south side of the house. I had a circular bed of enormous tulips on the front lawn. I said we would have to dig those up in the summer and plant new ones in the fall so they would be just as impressive next year. He looked at me to see if I was serious. *Why wouldn't I be serious?* I showed him how to prune the undergrowth on the lilac bush that was already displaying large purple blooms.

I was proud of it. No ordinary, average-sized, pale lilac would have satisfied me. It had to be big.

When we ate dinner together, I could tell Sam was getting more relaxed around me. He stretched his long limbs and draped himself over his chair like a big cat. Unfortunately, the more relaxed he was, the more tightly I had to wind my internal spring to keep myself from sprouting a huge erection. I bought tighter underwear. I started masturbating before he arrived to relieve the tension, but always had another round in the chamber by the time he left. I hadn't jacked off that much since high school.

He told me about his work as a personal trainer. He knew very little about physical fitness and exercise techniques before he got his job at the Harbor View. The staff at the health club assumed, based on his appearance and the amount of weight he was lifting, that he had been working out for years. In fact, the only exercise he was familiar with was farm labor. But he had enough charm and intelligence to bluff his way through and learn quickly. He certainly knew enough to satisfy the many women who were signing up for his services.

During a meal of baked ham with macaroni and cheese, he told me how some women touched him and made assumptions about what he might want to do with them for a little extra money. He told them he was gay, despite the objections of the manager who worried that it would reduce traffic at the club. Fortunately, most of the women were content to remain in his presence and ogle him without touching, a concession I understood perfectly.

I was drinking wine dispensed from a box in my refrigerator, so I asked Sam if he had similar issues with any male customers. He blushed. "I'm sorry, forget I asked."

"No, it's all right." He paused. "I've had guys come on to me. Some of them are creepy and I have no problem telling them to switch to another trainer. Some of them are attractive." He looked up to see my reaction.

"Go on." I was imitating my high school guidance counselor.

"I'm a horny twenty-year-old, and sometimes I want to do more than jerk off. So, I've done stuff . . . or they did stuff to me. Sometimes it was nice . . . some of it was gross. There's never much conversation. If they want to see me again, they only talk about sex and what they want to do. Like . . . I'm not a real person . . . know what I mean?"

"Uh huh." I had nothing else to offer, so I put the last slice of ham on his plate.

"You know . . . I wish I knew a gay man with more experience . . . someone who could give me advice." He looked at me.

"Yeah, that would be nice, wouldn't it?" I took a big swallow of wine.

There was a long silence while Sam finished eating. He carefully set the knife and fork on his plate before speaking again. "Adam . . . is there anything you could say that might help me?"

I looked at him. I didn't let his handsome face frighten me. I really looked this time. "Help you with what?"

"Can you help me feel more comfortable about being gay?"

I thought about it, then answered with a question of my own. "Do you seriously think I know anything about that?"

He sighed heavily. "But why aren't you comfortable? Why won't you tell me?"

"It's not you, Sam. I haven't told anyone. Ever." My face was hot.

"Seriously? But you know I know, right? Doesn't that make it easier?"

"You would think so, but no." My voice cracked. "I tried to tell you when you told me about yourself, but it wouldn't come out."

"So, do it now. Just say it."

I wanted to refill my wine glass, but it wasn't an appropriate time. "All right . . . I'm gay." My heart pounded. "I'm gay. I've been gay forever. Gay, gay, gay!" I waited for something bad to happen. I stared at the floor and waited. The earth didn't shake, the planet still turned, the sky stayed in place. I raised my head.

Sam took a deep breath and let it out. "Thank you, I know it wasn't easy."

"No, it wasn't." I rubbed a single tear into my face before it could fall. For me, there was no sense of relief. I wasn't there yet. It felt like I had exposed myself to a new set of risks.

We continued to talk for a while, tentatively. I admitted I was a virgin and would be useless as a mentor. He was surprised. I thought he would have a lot of sexual experience, but he only mentioned a few recent encounters and an awkward attempt with a friend back home who rejected him. Sam wanted a real relationship, not just sex, no matter how long he had to wait for the right person. I thought, sadly, that his idealistic notions would eventually be ground into dust, but I didn't want to discourage him. "You'll find someone."

He asked if I ever thought about having a boyfriend. My honest answer was, "No." If he had asked whether I thought about having sex, my answer would have been different, but that didn't mean I was doing anything about it. I repeated my old excuse about not being cut out for a relationship. I still believed it.

The conversation was exhausting, so I started clearing away the dishes and changed the subject. "By the way, are you okay with the food I'm making? I don't want to sabotage your workouts."

"Yeah, I love your cooking. I don't think it matters what I eat. The nutritionist at the club asked me about my diet, and when I told her what I've been eating, she said I would get fat instead of gaining muscle. She brought out this thing that measures body fat . . ." He lifted the front of his t-shirt. My eyes must have expanded like little balloons. He had the classic six-pack of a marble Adonis, but with a jagged line of dark hair leading into his pants. I covered my soft belly with my arms.

Sam went on talking, obviously unaware of the effect he had on me. "She grabbed a fold of skin like this, and measured. She couldn't believe how lean I was." Sam moved his fingers over the flexed muscles, then slapped his stomach a couple times with his open hand. "I told her, 'That's what old fashioned home cooking can do for you.' I gained some weight, though, so it must be muscle. They told me it would be hard for a guy my height, but my legs are getting bigger. My jeans are tighter."

I prayed my tight underwear wouldn't burst. "So, that's . . . you're doing . . . well, then. Good." I filled the sink with hot, soapy water. We took turns washing and drying the dishes, and it was my turn to wash. "I could make healthier food."

"No, I like the food you make. It's like my mom's cooking."

"I'm using my mom's recipes. When I was younger, I ran every day and I could eat like this, but I've gained a few pounds recently."

"No, you haven't, you look good."

"Uff," I sputtered. *I wish he would stop patronizing me. I thought he was nicer than that.* "Trust me, I've gained weight." I handed him a washed platter. "It wouldn't hurt to listen to the nutritionist."

He groaned. "I don't want to be hungry all the time. I feel so good after I leave here. Does it cost too much? If that's it, I can . . ."

"No, I didn't say I would cook less food. You can eat as much as you want, and it's not about money. In fact, it'll probably cost more to eat healthier. If I cut down on fat and carbs and add more protein, I could lose weight and you could . . . you know . . . gain muscle."

"Oh. Okay." He was quiet for a minute. "You think I need more muscle?"

"No, I'm just saying . . . for your job . . . it sounds like they want you to be muscular . . . to set an example for the members . . . give them something to aim for . . . know what I mean?" I tried to sound indifferent, and I attempted a joke. "Besides, while you're looking for Mr. Right, you know how fussy the gays can be."

"Okay." He looked thoughtful. "I appreciate the advice." He seemed awfully serious. *He knows I'm joking, right?*

After the dishes were put away, Sam moved toward the door. "Adam, I know you're not comfortable with it yet, but . . . I'm honored to be the first person you came out to."

"Oh." *Am I 'out' now?* He was right; I wasn't comfortable with it.

"It means a lot to me, seriously."

I guess it meant something to me, too, because I choked up and muttered, "Arble urg gruph." I was unable to speak real words under certain circumstances. Sam stepped forward and wrapped his arms around me in an unexpected hug. "Urg!" My face pressed against his chest while he squeezed me hard enough to provide a chiropractic adjustment. I awkwardly patted his broad back as if I were burping a gassy baby.

He released me and stepped back. "I'm sorry, you probably don't hug much, do you?"

"Nawr." I crossed my arms and stared at the floor.

"It wasn't so bad, was it?"

I shrugged. "Murf."

"Okay then. Thanks for dinner."

"'Kay." I glanced up. "Night."

Later, in bed, I hugged my pillow and remembered the warmth and smell of Sam's body.

5

The week before Memorial Day, one of the few co-workers I talked to on a regular basis stopped in my office. Donna Gilson was middle-aged and happily married, with kids in high school. I felt comfortable joking with her in a way I never would have with the single women in the office. Plus, she was wickedly sarcastic. I liked that. She asked if I had plans for the weekend. I rolled my eyes and claimed I would be busy.

"That's right, you'll be rushing from one social event to the next."

"I have a lot to do around the house and I want to plant a few things in my garden."

"If you plant any more flowers, you'll start drawing tourists."

God, I hope not! "I prefer plants to people. It's just the way I am."

"Seriously, Adam, it wouldn't kill you to make a brief appearance at a barbecue." She lowered her voice. "There are people around here who are very interested in you."

"What are you talking about? Why would anyone be interested in me?"

"They want to harvest your organs." She said this with a straight face. "Are you dense? Some of these women are betting on which one of them will go out with you first. Whatever you're doing with your diet or exercise, keep it up. You're looking even better lately."

I looked at her like she had two heads. "Whess ya mot?!" My gibberish again. *I gained weight! How is that better?* I had been making healthier meals for a few weeks, I stopped drinking wine, and I started running again, but it wasn't enough. I dismissed her claims. "I don't want to hear your nonsense."

"You don't even want to know who they are, do you?" She cocked an eyebrow. "If that's not what you're into, the young guy they hired in the tax department has his eye on you, too."

"Oaf! Noggle!" It was hard to tell whether she was being serious or sarcastic, but I was alarmed. There was a new guy who looked very good in his fitted dress shirts, so I avoided him. He complimented my neckties a few times. *Could he have been . . .? Nah! Nope.* Didn't believe it. "Don't you have any work to do, Donna?"

She sighed. "Okay, it's your life. If you're happy . . . good for you. But I think you're living in a plastic bubble. You need to get out of there occasionally." Beneath the sarcasm, she cared about me. I gave her a disinterested look before she rolled her eyes and went away.

The weekend couldn't come soon enough. There were lots of things to do, and Sam only had to work one shift at the restaurant on Saturday. He planned to start repainting my garden shed. I had to plant dahlias and several flats of annuals to fill in where the spring bulbs had faded. It was an exciting time for me because many of my perennials were growing and blooming.

On Friday after work, I walked around the property with Sam, discussing my plans and showing off the plants that were at their peak. On the south side of the house I had trellises supporting five distinct types of clematis vines. He was impressed by the six-inch blooms. "You like big flowers, don't you?"

"Yes, I do."

"Speaking of which, do I look bigger to you?" It was an odd segue. Sam straightened up and waited for my assessment.

He looked great, but I wasn't planning to say anything. I didn't want to sound like the creepy guys at the gym. I offered a bland affirmation. "That t-shirt looks small on you. You'll have to buy new clothes soon." In truth, I couldn't look at him for long without getting an erection.

"Yeah, I'm doing pretty well. That high-protein diet is helping. You look good, too, Adam."

"Myek," I said, in the language of my discomfort. *I wish people would stop saying that!* We continued our tour around the house. There were bouquets of multicolored Columbines blooming in between the larger plants. Sam squatted in front of them to have a closer look. I admired the V-shape of his torso as his t-shirt stretched tightly across his back.

He examined the flowers carefully. "I like these. They're not big, but they're interesting . . . kind of complicated. Even the leaves are complex." I looked at the Columbine. *Huh - he's right.* I liked them well enough, but never gave them the credit they deserved.

We arrived at my struggling peony. For the first time, it had three flower buds with ants crawling over them. It was encouraging, but still frustrating. The other peonies were loaded with buds that would become big soft flowers in shades of pink and red. This one would be white if it ever bloomed. "Did I tell you when I planted this, Sam?"

"I don't think so."

"It was the day my parents died. Right before I found out about the accident." Without a word, Sam put his hand on my shoulder and left it there. I didn't mind. For some reason, it brought tears to my eyes. It had been three years already, but I guess it was . . . I don't know . . . it was nice. I turned my head and brushed the tears away. "The sun's going down, we should have dinner. I want to get an early start tomorrow." He followed me into the house.

We had a salad of cold shrimp and black beans with chopped tomatoes, peppers and cucumbers. Sam loved it and ate until he sat back with a contented smile and one hand on his flat belly. He was still long and lean, but his body was thicker, and his muscles were more defined. "Are people at the health club impressed with your workout results?"

"Um, they're surprised, mostly. I made a lot of progress pretty fast."

"Oh? How much?"

"I've gained about twenty pounds, but I was skinny when I got here."

"Twenty pounds? And none of it is fat?"

"That was their reaction. They asked me if I was on steroids, but I would never do that. I told them how much I eat, and they see me eating there every day. They still don't believe it."

"Wait, you eat at the restaurant every day?"

"Yeah, I told you the chef likes me." He looked apprehensive. "You're not angry, are you?"

"No, of course not, but . . ." My mind was already somewhere else.

He blushed. "I make my own breakfast." As if I were scolding him for not cooking his own meals. "I can eat less if it bothers you."

I snapped out of my trance. "No, no, it doesn't bother me. But how can you eat like that and not get fat? I'm so fucking jealous! Sorry, I shouldn't swear."

"You can swear, Adam, I'm not a child."

"You don't know how foul I can be."

"I don't care about that. Am I doing what you want? Is this okay?"

"Of course. Why wouldn't it be okay?"

"I don't know, I'm never sure . . . I don't know what people think of me."

"Don't worry about that. Who cares what people think?"

"Well . . . some opinions matter more than others." I was too preoccupied with my own insecurities to really hear him.

We cleared the table and washed the dishes with minimal conversation. As we finished, Sam asked, "Will I ever get to see the rest of the house?"

I was stunned.

"I know you're a private person, but I've been coming here for a few months and I've never been past the kitchen. I like old houses. I'm wondering what it looks like inside."

I have no social skills. None! "I'm sorry, I'm such an idiot. Of course you can see the house. Come on, I'll give you a tour."

"Okay, I'm glad I asked. I thought maybe you didn't trust me." I wished that wasn't the reason, but it was something like that. I hadn't let people in for so long, I forgot it was the normal thing to do.

I led him into the small room adjacent to the kitchen that I used as an office. It was functional, but nothing special. I continued into the dining room and pressed the push-button light switch, illuminating the brass chandelier with hand painted glass shades. There was a massive walnut table with eight chairs my mother reupholstered, and built-in china cabinets on either side of the large windows. Sam was impressed.

I walked through the columned archway at the other side of the dining room and pushed another switch, lighting up the living room, the most impressive room in the house. It was filled with Victorian furniture and other things my parents collected, like the blue and white vases on the mahogany mantel. I pulled the chain on a stained-glass floor lamp. Sam took it all in. “Beautiful.”

Another arched doorway led into the front entrance hall. The wealthy businessman who built the house in the 1880s spared no expense in its construction. “Adam, this is awesome!” The floor was made of English encaustic tiles and the staircase was carved oak, with dozens of beautifully crafted spindles. There were stained glass windows around the door.

The room on the other side of the entrance hall had a marble mantelpiece and was furnished with a flat screen TV, a contemporary leather sofa and matching chairs. “This is where I watch TV, obviously.” I pointed to the back of the room. "That door leads to a small bathroom and then back to the kitchen.”

"Very nice. What’s upstairs?”

“Um . . . I’ll show you.” I ascended the stairs with an uneasy feeling. *Should I show him my bedroom? Will it be weird?* The second floor was divided into two identical suites of rooms on either side of the stairs. At the top, I went to the right, to my rooms. I decided to make it a quick tour. There was a smaller dressing room at the back of the house and a large bedroom with a window bay at the front of the house. *Good thing I always make my bed.*

Probably sensing my discomfort, Sam did not linger in my bedroom, but complimented the elaborate Gothic Revival furniture my parents bought for themselves. It was my favorite furniture in the house. Back in the dressing room, he peered out the window at the coach house. "This is the window I see from my apartment."

"I guess so," I briskly led him back into the hall. "Here’s the bathroom. It's the only one up here, but it's big." On each side of the room there were matching marble sinks with shiny brass hardware and beveled mirrors on the walls. My parents had moved the claw-footed bathtub into a corner and added a walk-in shower lined with black and white tile matching the original mosaic tile on the floors and walls.

"And across the hall is my library." I led him to the suite that was mine when I was younger. The back room held a motley collection of things from my childhood, and the front room was lined with book cases.

Sam's eyes grew large. "So many books! Have you read all of them?”

“Most of them. Some belonged to my parents.”

"I love to read, but my parents didn't want me to. They thought books were for daydreamers, except the Bible." He ran his fingers over the bindings, looking at the titles.

"You can borrow something, if you want. You might not like my taste in literature." I preferred serious novels with unhappy endings.

Sam pulled out *Tess of the d'Urbervilles* by Thomas Hardy. "Is this good?" he asked.

"It's one of my favorites, but . . ."

"I'll give it a try. Thanks." He looked happy. As we retraced our steps through the other room, he noticed some old toys on a shelf in the corner. He picked up a shirtless G.I. Joe action figure. "What's this?"

I cringed. "Oh, that old thing? What's that doing there?"

He raised an eyebrow while examining the hyper-muscular plastic doll.

I confessed, "I liked his body, okay?"

"I can see why." He was enjoying my embarrassment, so I had to smile. He put it back on the shelf and we headed down the stairs. "Thanks for giving me the tour. I'm very impressed."

"Let me show you the basement, too. There's some junk down there I'll need help with." I led him back through the kitchen and down the basement stairs. This was my father's domain. The work benches full of tools were still neatly organized but covered with dust because I was not as handy as he had been. Sam was like a kid in a toy store, eager to use as many of the tools as possible.

I redirected him to an area of the basement I called "the junkyard." My father was a pack rat, always reluctant to throw things away. There were piles of scrap lumber, rusty pipes, and an old washing machine. Also, a cast-iron radiator that was removed when the kitchen was remodeled. It was so heavy I could barely move it an inch.

"I'd like to clear this out. There's a scrap dealer who'll pick up the metal stuff if I put it outside, but I don't know if we should do it this weekend."

"It won't take long." He bent over the washing machine.

"Not now . . . don't try to . . ."

He picked it up.

"Don't hurt yourself!"

"I won't." He set it down and looked at me like I was overreacting.

"Oh, I forgot . . . the strength thing."

"Yeah, this is when it comes in handy." He squatted in front of the radiator.

"Please don't try to lift that, Sam."

He put his hands on either end. "I need to see how heavy it is."

"It's too heavy. I can't even . . ."

He bent his knees and picked up the radiator like I would lift a box of books. His limbs exploded into segments of hard muscle. He was straining, but not a lot. He set it down with a loud clunk.

Oh, fuck! His strength turned me on in a big way, and I wasn't wearing my tightest underwear. *Shit, this will be awkward.*

But Sam wasn't looking at me, and he wasn't trying to show off. He was casual about it. "Find out when the scrap guy can come, and I'll take this stuff outside. What about that wood?"

"Wood?" I crossed my legs like a child with a full bladder. "I don't know, whatever."

He finally looked at me. "Are you okay?"

"I didn't think you could lift something like that."

"Why? I told you I was strong."

"I know, but how much does that thing weigh?"

"I don't know, what difference does it make? You think it's weird, don't you?"

"No! It's awesome, it'll make things easier." I turned away to hide my erection.

"Okay . . . are you sure you're all right?"

"Yeah, I need to use the bathroom. I should have gone earlier."

"Oh, then I'll get out of here so you can go." He hurried up the stairs ahead of me, giving me an eye-level view of his butt. This did not help my condition.

I spoke quickly. "First thing tomorrow we'll go to the nursery and pick up the stuff I ordered, okay?"

"Okay, thanks Adam." He was always thanking me.

I locked the door and hobbled through the house in need of relief. Believe it or not, I had a rule against masturbating on the first floor. I had a lot of rules. I waited until I was upstairs to free myself from my pants. The light in Sam's apartment drew me toward the window. His blinds were open, and I saw him walk across the room, pull off his shirt, and pace back and forth like a restless tiger. His body was everything I imagined it to be. I grabbed my erection and ejaculated immediately. I sank to my knees, deflating like a leaky balloon.

So much for self-control. Having Sam around would be more difficult than I thought.

6

The next day I woke up to sunlight and the sound of a lawnmower. I rolled out of bed and stretched, then cursed the soft flesh around my waist. I did this every morning. I went to the bay window and cautiously peered through the sheer curtains. Sam was mowing the lawn, shirtless. I sighed. *Why did I do this to myself?*

It was warm enough to wear shorts and a t-shirt for the first time that year. After eating my breakfast of high fiber cereal and low-fat yogurt, I went out the back door and BAM! Sam suddenly came around the corner of the house and collided with me. He caught me by the shoulders before I fell. "Shit! I didn't know you were out here!"

"Uff." My face was covered with sweat from his naked chest. I wiped it with my hand and rubbed it on my shirt.

"Did I get sweat on you? Here, use this." He offered me the t-shirt hanging from his back pocket. I wiped my face and gave it back. He quickly put it on, allowing me a quick view of his armpits and sculpted torso. "I'm sorry, are you okay?"

"I'm fine. You startled me. I wasn't . . . I didn't . . ."

"I'm embarrassed."

"Don't be."

"I only took off my shirt to cut the grass and I was . . ."

"It's fine. You live here, you should be comfortable." I took a deep breath and moved on. "So . . . we're going to Dave's Nursery to pick up a load of stuff. Are you ready?"

"Could I take a quick shower and grab breakfast before we head out? Twenty minutes, tops."

"Sure, go ahead." He bounded up the stairs to his apartment. I sniffed the front of my shirt. It smelled like him, which was not unpleasant at all. I sniffed it again before finding something to do while I was waiting.

A short while later, Sam came bouncing down the stairs with wet hair, neatly combed. I pointed at his face. "You've got something there."

He touched his chin and looked at his hand. "That's powdered sugar." He rubbed at it. "Is it gone?"

"Yeah." But he had a handsome stubble on his jaw. "Powdered sugar?"

"Doughnuts for breakfast."

"Seriously? You work at a health club." I shook my head.

"Come on, I like doughnuts, okay? Don't hassle me."

"Hey, it's your life. I'm not your mom."

"You were starting to sound like her."

"All right, let's go." Despite my economy sedan personality, I drove a small pickup truck so I could haul plants and gardening supplies. It never seemed so small as it did with Sam as a passenger. He moved his seat all the way back so he had enough legroom and rested his arm in the open window. I compared my legs to his and felt my testicles shrink. *Why did I wear shorts?*

Sam leaned his head out the window to enjoy the rush of fresh air. "Where did you say we're going?"

"Dave's Nursery. I've been going there since I was a teenager. Dave finds the plants I like . . . the giant lilac, all the clematis, my hydrangeas. I want to tell him I finally have buds on that peony. He's a good guy."

"He must be if you like him."

"What does that mean?"

"I'm just saying . . . you don't seem to like a lot of people. Nothing wrong with that. Merely an observation."

I had no response. It was true.

Memorial Day weekend is very busy for garden centers and Dave's Nursery was packed. That's why I placed my order in advance. Dave saw me coming and waved. No matter how busy he was, Dave took time to talk with me.

"Adam, where have you been? You're usually bugging the hell out of me by this time of year."

I smiled and shook his hand. "I thought I'd give you a break. I've been shopping at the Garden Mart instead."

"What? I hate that fucking place!"

"I'm kidding, Dave, calm down." He knew I would never shop there.

He looked at Sam. "Who's this?"

"This is my tenant, Sam. He's been helping me with yard work and stuff."

Sam offered his hand. "Pleased to meet you."

Dave measured him with his eyes, then shook his hand. "What are they feeding you kids these days?"

"A lot, I guess."

I said, "Mostly doughnuts."

Sam shot me a look. Dave noticed and looked back and forth between the two of us. "You know, I offered Adam a job when he was about your age, but he said he was too busy with school. I think he was lazy." Sam smiled.

"I forgot about that. I couldn't work for you, Dave. You're too mean."

"You bet I am!" He winked. "So, what can I sell you, Adam? I'm counting on you to keep me in business."

"I'm here to pick up the annuals I ordered, and I'll take a cubic yard of mulch."

"Okay, have the kid fill your truck with mulch while you come inside to get your flats."

I dangled my keys over Sam's palm. "Do you have a driver's license?"

"Yeah, Adam, I'm not sixteen." I pointed at the mulch bins and told him what I wanted. He jogged away while we watched him go.

Dave made a face. "You trust him?"

"Yeah, he's a responsible kid . . . man . . . guy, or whatever." I shifted gears. "Do you have anything new I might like?"

"I have a perennial hibiscus that's right up your alley. Huge flowers, like something out of science fiction. I'll show you."

"Sounds good. By the way, the peony you sold me a few years ago finally has buds."

"The white peony. I remember . . . that was the day your parents . . ."

"Yep, that's the one."

His expression was serious. "That's good to hear. I wasn't sure it would make it."

I squirmed. "It's just a plant, Dave."

"You know what I mean, kiddo." He wasn't talking about the plant. My throat tightened as he put his hand on my back and led me into the greenhouse.

Dave was right about the hibiscus - I wanted it. He asked an employee to bring it to the checkout along with my flats of annuals, then excused himself, saying he had something else to do. I stopped to look at organic pesticides. While the cashier totaled my order, I saw Dave and Sam talking next to my truck. It looked like Dave was lecturing while Sam nodded. If I hadn't been paying for my stuff, I would have gone out there.

Their conversation was over by the time I pulled my cart to the parking lot. Sam loaded the truck while Dave took me aside. "You know I could use a guy like Sam around here. I can't do all the heavy work I used to do." Dave had aged, but he still looked fit. "You should think about letting him work for me."

Letting him? "It's not up to me, Dave. Sam can do what he wants."

"Okay . . . but talk to him about it, would you?" Then he spoke louder so Sam could hear. "And I expect to see you back here next weekend! You must have a few square inches where you could cram in another plant."

I got into the truck and had to pull the driver's seat forward from where Sam had moved it. He was quiet as we merged into the traffic on the street. "So, what was that about?"

"What?"

"I saw you talking to Dave. What did he say?"

"Nothing. I mean, he offered me a job."

"Yeah? What did you say?"

"I told him I had a job."

"You don't sound excited. It was a nice offer."

"Yeah, but I would need a car to get here." True, but he was strangely reticent.

"What else did he say?"

"That was it."

I didn't believe him. "It seemed like there was more to it than . . ."

"He said I should be careful with you."

I bristled. "You should be careful with me? What does that mean?"

"He said, 'I'm glad you and Adam are friends, but be careful with him.'"

"Why? What does he think I'll do to you?" My temper flared. "I can't believe he would say that! Like I can't be trusted with . . ."

"That's not what he meant."

"Why would he try to turn you against me?"

"Adam . . . that's not . . ."

"No matter how long you know people, they can still stab you in the back!"

"Adam, stop! That's not what he meant! Forget it. I shouldn't have told you."

"He doesn't know me as well as he thinks he does!"

"ADAM! Dave is your friend! Okay? He's not your enemy - he's your friend!" He shook his head. "You're lucky you have any friends at all!"

That shut me up. I was seething, but quiet. We drove in silence for what seemed like ages.

"I'm sorry, Adam."

"No, I'm sorry." I wasn't sorry.

"I shouldn't have said that . . . it was too harsh."

"I appreciate your honesty." I didn't like it at all.

He sighed heavily. "Adam, you've been good to me. You're a good friend. I don't want anything to get in the way of that. I appreciate everything you've done for me, and I like being with you. Even when you're like this."

Well . . . all right. "I know it's difficult to . . . I'm difficult."

He didn't disagree.

I cleared my throat. "I'm sorry I got angry. I don't want things to be awkward between us." The words weren't coming out easily. "I was looking forward to this weekend."

"Yeah? Me too."

"You were?" My voice cracked.

He paused to look at me. "Yes, Adam. I like to spend time with you. You treat me like a real person . . . like an adult."

"You are a real person. You're an adult." I pulled into my driveway and shut off the engine.

"But not everyone treats me that way. So . . . are we cool?"

"Yeah, we're okay." I couldn't say 'cool.' It didn't apply to me.

We got out of the truck and walked around to the tailgate. I found the courage to say more than I usually would. "Sam . . . thank you for helping me." I looked him in the eye. He moved toward me, but I held up one hand. "Please don't hug me." He retreated. "Now . . . I'll go the house for a few minutes, and when I come back, we'll start working, okay?"

"Okay, take your time. I'll unload the truck."

* * *

After shoving most of my feelings back to wherever I kept them, I found Sam standing in front of the garden shed surveying its deteriorated condition. He launched right into work talk. "So, what's the plan for this?"

"It needs to be scraped and painted. It hasn't been done for years." The shed was built around the same time as the house, and it had an architectural style - Stick Victorian, to be precise.

"It needs more than paint. It's a nice little building. With a few repairs, it could be beautiful."

"I'm not good at fixing things. That was my dad's hobby."

"Well, I need to earn my food. Can I tell you what I would do with it?" He showed me what he could fix, and suggested paint colors to match the house and highlight the trim. I told him to restore the shed the way he thought it should be done, and he was very happy. Sam was extra cute when he was happy, and I wanted to keep him that way if I could. I invited him to get whatever tools he needed from the basement.

"Awesome! I'll take everything out of the shed to clean it, but I'll put it all back before I go to the restaurant this afternoon."

"Good, I don't even know what's in there anymore." I took the gardening tools I needed to plant the annuals in the front yard while he worked on the shed.

"Can I take off my shirt again?"

"You don't need to ask. Make yourself comfortable."

"You can take yours off, too." The corner of his mouth was turned up.

"I don't need your permission!"

"I'm just saying . . . it wouldn't bother me."

"Okay, thanks!" If I didn't know better, I would have thought he was flirting. *As if!* I dismissed the idea immediately. I usually worked with my shirt off in warm weather, but I felt more self-conscious with Sam around. I didn't want to compare my body to his. However, I didn't want him to think I was uncomfortable either. A brief argument in my head resulted in a decision to take off my t-shirt, exposing my soft, pale torso to sunlight.

I turned on my iPod and queued up Ella Fitzgerald's *Cole Porter Songbook.* Soon I was transported to the inner world where I preferred to live, while plugging plants into every open space in the flower beds. I was oblivious to my surroundings until I glanced up and caught Sam peering around the shrub at the corner of the house. He quickly pulled his head out of sight. *What the hell?* I went back to work, keeping one eye on the shrub. After a few moments, Sam was there again. *Is he afraid to interrupt me? Maybe he thinks I'm still angry.*

I looked up and pretended to be startled. He acted like he was just coming around the corner. His narrow waist and broad chest made me regret taking my shirt off. I pulled out my ear buds.

"Adam, look what I found." It was a rusty iron weathervane in the form of an angel blowing a trumpet. "I think this was on the roof of the shed, on top of a cupola that was in there."

"I remember seeing this when I was a kid." I furtively examined Sam's nipples.

"There's a bunch of shingles, too. Enough to cover the roof."

His abs looked like stones. "What did you say? I was looking at the thing."

"Come in the back for a minute, I'll show you." I followed him, watching the muscles in his legs. The contents of the shed were spread out on the grass, including several bundles of wood shingles and a weather-beaten cupola.

"Maybe my dad was planning to restore the shed, but never got around to it."

"That's what I thought." He picked up some wooden scrolls that looked like the trim on the house. "I bet these were attached to the eaves - like this." He stretched to hold one of the pieces under the edge of the roof.

I liked what I was seeing . . . and what he was showing me. It was nice to think he could complete a project my father started. "This is great, Sam. Can you put the cupola back on the roof?"

"Yeah, no problem. And the wood shingles will look a lot better than what's on there." He lifted one of the bundles, turning his biceps into a hard ball.

I redirected my thoughts. "We should break for lunch. Do you want a sandwich? Or several?"

"Sure, I could eat."

"You keep working, I'll make them."

"Yes, master," he teased.

"I'll be watching!" That was true, of course.

I took out a pound of lean roast beef and a loaf of sourdough bread. I mixed mayonnaise and horseradish to spread on the sandwiches – two for him and one for me. We ate at a small table on the porch, shirtless. I tried not to feel inferior. I should have warned Sam about the horseradish. It brought tears to his eyes and beads of sweat to his forehead, but he kept eating and said he liked it.

After lunch, he started scraping the shed. He was strong enough to remove layers of paint with a few strokes, exposing the clean wood underneath. I paused to watch the rippling muscles in his back, then walked away before my fantasies led to another awkward situation.

I was still angry that Dave told Sam to be careful with me, but my lustful thoughts made me wonder if his warning was fair. If Sam had any idea how many times I masturbated to mental images of him, he would certainly look for a new place to live. The last thing he needed was another guy perving on him. He got enough of that at the health club. He deserved better. I told myself, *I will not be a perv, I will not be a perv . . .*

After planting all the annuals, I found Sam picking stray paint chips off his sweaty chest and abs. *Is the universe testing me?* He needed to get ready for work, so I offered to put everything back in the shed. I arranged the garden tools, clay pots, fertilizers and insecticides, and stacked the bundles of shingles next to the shed. The cupola wasn't huge, but I couldn't lift it. I left it where it was.

Sam came down the stairs in the black clothes he wore at the restaurant, reminding me of the day I went there to reject his application. Freshly showered and shaved, he was impossibly handsome. Without a break in his stride, he picked up the cupola, holding it away from his body so his clothes wouldn't get dirty, and put it next to the shingles. "I should get going. What's the plan for tomorrow?"

"Um . . . sleep as late as you want, and we'll figure it out in the morning."

"Okay, see you tomorrow." He jogged down the driveway and turned toward the harbor.

I wanted to go to my bedroom to relieve some tension, but I felt guilty about objectifying Sam. Instead, I chose to channel my sexual energy into a healthy run through the woods nearby. Then I jacked off in the shower.

It was still early evening and the house seemed too quiet as I wandered through the rooms and thought about dusting the furniture. I opened the refrigerator. I closed it, wishing I still had wine in the house. I sat down at the kitchen table for a few minutes, but it felt lonely.

I decided to watch something from my collection of movies. I found Roman Polanski's *Tess*, a film version of the novel Sam borrowed from my library. I put the DVD in the player and stretched out on the leather couch to watch the young heroine's life get destroyed, first by seduction, and later, by love. As Tess woke up on the slab at Stonehenge surrounded by the police who would arrest her for murder, I fell asleep.

7

Lakeport is one of those places with a church on a hill in the center of it. It was the Catholic church where my parents went to mass. I stopped going during my first year of college and never went back, but I liked the way the Gothic Revival building capped off the picture-perfect view of the town. And the church bells were nice. They were ringing when I woke up on the couch. *Must be Sunday.* I grabbed the TV remote to shut off the annoying blue screen and half-remembered a dream about being arrested. I rubbed my face. *I'm too boring to get arrested.*

Coffee made it possible for me to think about how to spend the next two days. I needed groceries, but I still had mulch in the bed of my truck. I glanced out the window and saw Sam's side of the garage was open. *Was there a burglar, or is he working out?* I went outside to check.

"Sam?"

I heard a thump and felt a vibration in the pavement. "Yeah, I'm in here!" The morning sun made it difficult to see into the dark garage. Sam came to the doorway wearing a snug tank top, looking more muscular than ever.

"Holy . . . wow!" *Shut your face!*

"What?"

"Nothing! It's . . . you look . . . um, I didn't realize how big . . ."

"I'm pumped from lifting. Why? Am I too . . . should I stop?"

"Stop? No, I didn't mean to interrupt your workout."

"You didn't, I'm done." He covered his biceps with his hands. "Do you need me to do something?"

"I'm sorry, I shouldn't have . . . why did I come out here? Oh, yeah, could you unload the mulch from the truck? No hurry. You can pile it over there."

He nodded and looked . . . serious? Sad? I couldn't interpret his expression.

"Okay. I'm going . . ." I pointed my thumb toward the porch. "Thanks." I fled from the awkwardness back into the house, poured another cup of coffee, and hyper-analyzed every second of our interaction. All the anxious voices in my head agreed: *He thinks I'm a creep, like those guys at the gym.* I knocked my forehead against the table. *Dammit, Adam, you suck at life.*

I felt a little better after breakfast and a shower. I forced myself to go back outside. Sam was sweeping the last of the mulch out of my truck. He had changed into a baggy t-shirt with sleeves down to his elbows. *Of course.* "Thanks for doing that, Sam. It's great to have your help around here."

"You're welcome. It's great to be here." He sounded sincere, but I had my doubts.

"Do you want to keep working on the shed today? I'll weed and mulch the flower beds."

"Okay, but I'll need paint for the shed."

"Oh yeah. Maybe we should get that before we do anything else." There was a big home improvement store nearby that was open on Sundays. I locked the house and we headed out in the truck.

Eventually Sam broke the silence. "I started reading *Tess of the d'Urbervilles.* I like it."

"Yeah? I watched the film version last night while you were at work. How far did you get?"

"I finished the part where her baby dies. It's sad so far, but I like the way he writes. It made me think about life on the farm. Hey, do you think Tess wanted to have sex with Alec, or do you think he raped her? It wasn't clear, was it?"

"Oh, man, I remember having this discussion in English Lit class in college. I said it was rape, but a lot of girls in my class thought she wanted him to seduce her. That surprised me. I mean, he was wealthy, and she was poor, and she worked on his estate . . . he took advantage of her. That's rape in my book."

"I know, but there was a lot that happened before that. The scene where she eats the strawberry from his hand? I think she wanted him. Sometimes people are afraid to admit what they want. Right?"

Hmm. Are we still talking about Tess? "We'll see what you think when you finish the book."

In the paint department, we chose a color that was a close match for the house, and another color to highlight the architectural details of the shed. We also picked up a quart of black enamel for the weathervane. While Sam was chatting with the guy mixing our paint, two neatly dressed older men looked at Sam, then winked at me and nodded approvingly. *What the hell?* I didn't acknowledge them. *Go away! I hate strangers!*

We put the paint in our cart and walked through the store. Sam pointed to a set of outdoor furniture. "You should have something like that in the yard for when you have guests." I stared at him blankly. *Guests?* He cracked a smile and bumped my shoulder with his fist. "I'm messing with you."

"Wow. You're funny." I sat down in one of the patio chairs. He settled into a big wicker armchair. "I could have guests if I wanted to."

"Like who?"

Dammit! I should have known he would ask. "Like . . . friends . . . from work."

"You have friends at work?"

"One . . . maybe."

"What's his name?"

"Her name is Donna, and the other day she was telling me about all the people who are interested in me and wanted me to come to their barbecues this weekend."

Sam leaned forward. "You had invitations? Why aren't you going?"

"No one expects me to come. They invite everyone, I never go."

"Then who did she say is interested in you?"

"Uff! It's stupid, I shouldn't have brought it up."

"Come on, tell me."

"Ach! I've never noticed, but Donna claims there are women trying to go out with me. And . . ." I hesitated.

"And?"

I whispered, "There's a cute guy in the tax department." I blushed furiously.

"Oh." He sat back. "Are you interested in him?"

"No! I don't even know if Donna was serious. She's hard to read."

"What does he look like?"

Part of me wanted to brag a little. "He's blond, handsome, a little taller than me but more streamlined, like a swimmer. He wears these fitted dress shirts that show off his body. And he graduated from one of the top accounting schools, so he must be smart."

"Uh huh." Sam looked away. I would have introduced them, though Sam was a hundred degrees hotter than that guy. I couldn't understand why he didn't have a boyfriend.

I stood up. "Should I buy one of these grills?"

He muttered, "I guess we're changing the subject." He joined me in front of a large kettle grill.

"My dad used to have one of these. They're not too expensive. We could grill steaks tomorrow."

"It's your money."

I thought he would be more enthusiastic. "I'm not usually impulsive . . ."

"That's for sure."

". . . but I'm doing it! There's one in a box. Could you carry that?"

Sam glared at me and whispered, "I'm not carrying that through the store! I'll put it on a cart like everyone else." He stomped off.

Jeez! What got into him? He was joking with me a minute ago.

He came back with a platform cart for the grill. "Are we done now?"

"Yeah, I suppose." I grabbed a bag of charcoal and we headed toward the checkout area, past the counter where they make keys. "Could we stop here so I can have my house key copied for you?"

"What?"

"I want a copy of my key so you can have one. It won't take long."

"You're giving me a key to your house?"

"Yeah. Do I need to talk louder?"

"Uh . . . that's a big deal, Adam."

"Why? It'll be easier if you need to get tools from the basement while I'm at work. Besides, if you wanted to rob me, I think you would have done it by now."

He took a deep breath and squinted for a long moment. "Fine! Go ahead!" He moved to the other side of the aisle and stood there looking very annoyed.

What is wrong with him? I walked to the counter and told the young woman what I wanted. I watched the machine make a copy of my key. As the girl gave it to me in a little envelope, her gaze traveled over my shoulder, her eyes grew bigger and her mouth opened. Sam was standing behind me. That's how people looked at him.

In the parking lot, he asked me to help him lift the grill into the back of the truck. I knew he didn't need help, but I obliged. When we climbed into the cab, he spoke firmly. "I don't want people to see how strong I am, okay? When we're in public, please don't ask me to lift or carry anything you couldn't lift."

"Oh. Is that why you were so annoyed?"

"You noticed I was annoyed? Great! That's a hopeful sign!" His tone was unusually sarcastic.

"I don't understand . . ."

"Of course you don't."

"Look, I know I can be . . . I don't know . . . Donna called me "dense" the other day."

"That's IT!" He startled me by raising his voice. "That's EXACTLY right! You're DENSE! It's the perfect word for you. Donna must be a good friend if she told you that."

I was stunned. "What am I missing?"

He took another deep breath, obviously trying to stay calm. "Adam, there are things happening around you that you don't see. Like the people who are attracted to you. How do you not see that?"

"I can't . . . I'm not interested, so . . . I don't know!"

"Maybe you don't want to see it. Maybe you're afraid."

Me? Afraid? Hmm. "I suppose . . . it's possible."

"I'm sure you don't do it on purpose, but it's frustrating."

"Okay." I didn't understand why he was so concerned about my co-workers' feelings. "I'm sorry."

"I'll deal with it. Somehow." He rolled down the window and stuck his elbow through the opening. "We should go, we're wasting the weekend."

"It's not a waste of time. I've never had anyone tell me what I'm like. I could use more of that. Thank you."

"Any time."

"Oh, this is yours." I pulled the little envelope from my shirt pocket and gave him the key.

"Thank you." His tone was softer now. "You have no idea how much this means to me, do you?"

Ugh! I'm going to be dense again. "I'm not sure. I know I trust you. I don't think I've ever trusted anyone as much as you."

Sam covered his eyes with his hand.

Crap, I must have said the wrong thing.

"That's good, Adam." His voice was wobbly. "You got it right this time."

I breathed a sigh of relief. Even though I didn't understand how I got it right, I was glad I did. I started the truck and we drove home in silence.

* * *

Back at the house, Sam lifted the grill off the truck by himself and set it near the back porch. "Do you want me to put this together?"

"Yes, please. Thanks for offering." I handed him the cans of paint. "I think I should go to the grocery store before I get messed up in the garden. How many steaks do you think you can eat?"

"That's the wrong question to ask. How many steaks will fit on the grill?"

"Ah, good point. Let's have the steaks tomorrow. We could order pizza tonight. I shouldn't eat any, but you can."

"Why don't you buy some wine? You should relax and forget about your diet."

"I don't want to gain any more . . ."

"You're not fat, Adam."

"Mebbly tulu." Gibberish, every time.

"Could you buy some ice cream? I love ice cream."

This was unusual. Sam never asked for anything for himself. I didn't hesitate. "What flavor?"

"I like them all. And thank you for your cooking and the groceries. I don't want you to think I take it for granted."

"Well, that's our arrangement."

"It's more than an arrangement, Adam. You're very generous with me."

"I'll be back in a little while." I wanted to get out of there before we had another emotional talk.

At the high-end grocery store near the center of town, I stopped at the deli counter to get pita wraps for our lunch. I picked up three thick porterhouse steaks, and spinach and strawberries to make a salad. In the liquor aisle, after a few minutes of hesitation, I chose a box of Shiraz. The cheapest one.

I passed over the half-gallons of ice cream and focused on the premium brands. I hadn't tried them because they were surprisingly expensive and shockingly caloric, but if Sam wanted ice cream, that was different. Rather than deciding which flavors to buy, I took a pint of each. It was a lot of ice cream. A woman shopping nearby said, "You must be having a rough day."

"It's not for me, it's for a friend."

She tilted her head. "Okay, sweetie."

On my way to the checkout I picked up a small watermelon for my dessert.

When I got home, Sam helped me unpack the groceries. He saw all the ice cream and gushed about my alleged generosity again. He certainly liked to talk about his feelings. "What are the strawberries for?"

"I'll use them in a salad for dinner tomorrow."

"Okay, just checking." He smiled like he'd made a joke, but I didn't get it.

Then it dawned on me - our conversation about Tess being seduced with a strawberry. *I hope he doesn't think I would try something like that.* I thought of our awkward encounter outside the garage that morning. *I should say something.* I brought it up while we ate the pita wraps.

"You know, I agree that I can be dense, so . . . this morning when I came out to the garage . . . was I making you uncomfortable?"

"No. I mean, it wasn't you. I was feeling . . . insecure, I guess."

Insecure? Sam? "It's okay to tell me if I'm being weird."

He shook his head and went quiet for a few minutes. All I heard was chewing until, "I didn't want to say anything yet, but . . . I don't know how much longer I'll be working at the Harbor View."

"Why?"

"Last night the manager asked me how much I eat at the restaurant. I'm not sure what he heard, but he was angry."

"Crap."

"He questioned the chef about inventory control and profit margins and stuff. Now I'm afraid he'll get fired because of me." He was getting agitated. "How could I be so stupid?"

"You're not stupid."

"If I get fired, I won't be able to pay the rent!"

"Do you think he'll fire you?"

"Why wouldn't he?"

"Maybe it's not that bad."

"Someone at the health club complained about me, too. Probably because I wouldn't do what they wanted."

"Shit."

"Yeah, and if I lose this job, you'll have to kick me out of the apartment and I won't have anywhere to go!"

"No, calm down Sam."

“I’m fucking up everything! I’m such a fucking idiot!”

“Stop it! Maybe you should quit before you get fired."

"What? I can't quit!"

"Dave offered you a job, you can work for him."

"I have no way to get there!"

My mind started spinning. "Um . . . you can take my truck."

"What are you talking about? How will you get to work?”

"I guess . . . I'll buy a new truck. I was thinking of getting a bigger one."

“No! You can't give me your truck!"

"I'll sell it to you. You can make payments. It's getting old, so you can have it for whatever its worth."

"Still, I can’t afford it, and I won’t take advantage of you like that."

"You wouldn’t be! I’m offering it. Let me help you.”

“You’re too generous, Adam.”

“Come on! No one has ever said that about me. Besides, I would be taking most of your income. How generous is that?”

"Oh.” He stopped to think. He took a big bite from his pita wrap and chewed. "Are you sure you can afford a new truck?"

"I haven't even touched the insurance settlement I got after my parents died."

"I don't want you to spend that money to help me."

"I won’t spend five-hundred-thousand on a truck."

"Five hundred . . . thousand? Like . . . half a million dollars?"

"That makes it sound like more than it is. I’m not rich, but I can afford to buy a new truck."

Sam shook his head. "Financial stuff makes me uncomfortable. I pay cash for everything. I don’t even have a bank account. I'm afraid . . . "

"Don't be afraid, I'm an accountant.” Like that made me a superhero. “Everything will be fine." I got up to clear the table.

He thought about it for a few more minutes while he swallowed the last of his lunch. "You wouldn’t mind if I worked for Dave?"

"It's up to you, but I've thought about what you said. I know he's a friend."

Sam stood up suddenly. "I don't care what you say . . . I'm gonna hug the shit out of you." He grabbed me and squeezed. My feet left the floor, so I wrapped my arms around his back and held on. “Thank you, Adam.”

He let me go and I cleared my throat. "You say 'thank you' about a hundred times a day."

"Too bad. You’ll have to deal with it."

"I'm not getting anything done. Let's get to work."

* * *

We spent the rest of the afternoon working on our separate projects. Every now and then I looked at him, or he looked at me. We took off our shirts again, and I was okay with it. I was always so self-conscious and self-critical. I assumed guys like Sam - men who looked like that - were supremely self-confident, and untouched by insecurity. I was wrong. I thought nothing could be more attractive than complete self-assurance, but I discovered a deeper beauty in a man who doubted himself. Sam was not one of those distant gods. He was a vulnerable human being.

By the time the sun was touching the western horizon, Sam had stripped the old shingles off the roof of the garden shed, reattached the cupola, and put a first coat of paint on the whole building. Watching him carry that cupola up a ladder made me question the laws of physics, but there it was on the roof, waiting to be crowned with the weathervane.

I complimented his work and asked what he wanted on the pizza. He didn't hesitate. "Cheese, sausage, mushrooms, onions and black olives." I liked it when he told me what he wanted because I could give it to him. I wished I could be that decisive about food and other things. In the past, I had eaten the same meals every day because it was easier than thinking about what I really wanted. It protected me from the delicious things I shouldn't eat.

Sam returned to his apartment to take a shower. I went upstairs to do the same after calling to order two large pizzas. I asked for salads to quiet my guilt about eating a forbidden food. I put on a clean pair of jeans and, for some reason, I spent a few minutes choosing a shirt that brought out the blue in my eyes. I descended the stairs in the gathering darkness and turned on the lights in the living room and dining room. In the kitchen, I made a pitcher of iced tea for Sam, cracked open my new box of Shiraz and filled a glass. It was a strongly flavored wine with a spicy finish that warmed my insides.

I heard a polite knock at the back door. "Come on in, Sam! The door's unlocked." He entered wearing the polo shirt he wore when I had dinner in his apartment. It was tighter now and barely met the top of his jeans. The white fabric contrasted with his golden tan skin. He was so handsome.

"You look good in blue, Adam. You should wear it more often."

"Thanks."

"Wow, you said 'thanks' to a compliment. Usually it's some other language."

“No, it’s not.” He was right. Something within me had shifted. "I was thinking we could eat in the dining room for a change. Could you bring the iced tea?" I picked up my box of wine and led the way.

“You're living dangerously tonight! A change of routine, a box of wine . . ."

"Yeah . . . who knows what might happen next?" I smiled at him over my shoulder. The front doorbell rang. "Could you get some plates and forks while I pay the guy?" I went to the entrance hall and pulled open the heavy paneled door I rarely used. A bright-eyed young man with a scruffy beard held our food. I took it from him and turned to set the pizzas down, but Sam was there to take them. The pizza guy looked at us and smiled. He was cute. He told me the total and wrote something on the receipt while I counted out enough bills to include a generous tip.

"Thanks, man! See ya." He handed me the receipt and trotted back to his car. After closing the door, I looked at the receipt and saw a scribbled phone number and his name, Scott. I showed it to Sam. "Is this what I think it is?"

"Yep! That'll happen to you more often if you keep wearing blue."

I blushed. "It's probably for you, you're closer to his age."

Sam shook his head. "You don't see what other people see. Come on, let's eat, this smells great!" He headed for the dining room and added, "Maybe the guy wanted a threesome." My face burned a little hotter.

We sat at one end of the big oak table with the pizza boxes and the salads and the beverages spread out before us. I grabbed a roll of paper towels from the kitchen to clean our hands and faces. I ate a little of my salad, but the pizza was so good, I stuck with that and the Shiraz, which I enjoyed immensely. Sam ate more noisily than usual, smacking his lips and moaning with satisfaction whenever he bit into another slice of pizza. He certainly was a "Hoover."

Not one to stay quiet for long, Sam started teasing me again. "Did you keep that guy's number? Will you call him?"

"No! I mean, yes I have his number, but no, I won't call him." I looked at him like he was crazy.

"Why don't you throw it away then?" He scanned the table for the receipt, then saw the edge of it sticking out of my shirt pocket. He reached out to grab it, but I clamped my hand over my pocket before he could get to it. He grinned and chewed. "Seems like you want to hang on to that."

Busted! "Well, I don't get attention from a cute young guy every day."

"Uh huh."

"I'll keep it as a trophy. Unless you want to call him." I hated to think Sam wasn't out there looking for the right guy. *What a waste.*

"I don't want to call him. But don't you ever think about . . . you know . . . some no-strings-attached sex?"

"There are always strings. Besides, I wouldn't have a clue about what to do or how to do it. I'd have a panic attack just thinking about it."

"Come on, you could figure it out."

"No, I'd probably throw up on the guy before I got anywhere. That's a mood killer."

"Maybe you would do better than you think."

"Nah, it's easier to stick with my right hand."

"I know what you mean. Are you finishing your salad?"

"No, go ahead." I filled my wine glass again and watched the muscles in Sam's arms while he ate. "Are you leaving room for dessert?"

He knew I was kidding. He crunched loudly on a big forkful of salad and chewed it with his mouth open while he looked me in the eyes. It was strangely sexy.

I stirred from my chair and stacked the empty pizza boxes. "I'll get the ice cream. What flavor do you want?"

He threw his arms in the air like he'd won a race. "Surprise me, dude! I'm open to anything!"

God, he's adorable. I left the boxes on the kitchen table and opened the freezer to get a pint of ice cream. I grabbed the one in front - strawberry - and set it on the counter to soften while I bent over to lift the watermelon I bought. As I stood up I could feel the effects of the wine and had to steady myself. I cut off one end of the melon and decided I would eat it with a spoon, right from the rind. I pulled the lid off the ice cream and peeled off the plastic liner. I jabbed one spoon into the ice cream and another in the watermelon and went back to the dining room.

Sam had pulled out his chair so he could sit with his legs crossed, facing my chair across the corner of the table. He was bobbing his head to some internal music.

"Have you been sampling my wine?"

"No, I'm just happy." He continued smiling and bobbing his head as he watched me come around the table. "You got a problem with that?"

I snorted. "No! I like seeing you happy." I handed him the ice cream. He looked at it like it was a pot of gold, then he looked at what I had.

"You're eating watermelon? What the . . ."

"Don't hassle me! I don't have your metabolism."

"All right, but you don't know what you're missing." He ran his spoon around the top edge of the carton, collecting the softest ice cream first. He put the spoon in his mouth, closed his eyes and moaned. "Mmmmmmm."

I scooped out a piece of watermelon. "I was thinking, Sam, would you like to meet the guy at work I told you about?"

He knit his brow. "You mean the swimmer tax guy? Why would I want to meet him?"

"He's pretty hot. You might like him."

"If he's so hot, why don't you take him? Apparently, he'd like that. Besides, he's probably too smart for me."

"What?! That's ridiculous. No one's too smart for you."

He was kneading the sides of the ice cream carton to soften its contents. "I don't have a degree."

"So? That doesn't mean you aren't smart. I can't believe some of the things you say. There isn't anyone you're not good enough for." I gathered some watermelon seeds on my spoon and discarded them on a paper towel.

Sam put a big spoonful of ice cream in his mouth and savored it. "You should try this - it's so creamy." He scooped more out of the carton. "But, seriously, Adam, why wouldn't you give the hot guy a chance? You'd probably have a lot in common."

"Maybe, but he's not the type I would go for . . . if I were interested in a relationship, which I'm not." The watermelon wasn't as sweet as I hoped, but I kept eating it.

"Why do you say that? What do you think a relationship would be like? What would be so bad about it?"

I set aside the watermelon and picked up my wine glass. "It wouldn't be bad, I just wouldn't be good at it. I'd have to make compromises and change the way I do things. I'd have to share." I rolled my eyes at the idea.

"Taste this, Adam. You won't believe how good it is." Sam held a spoonful of his strawberry ice cream in front of my face. I hesitated. "Don't worry, you won't catch anything from me. Take it before it drips." I opened my mouth and accepted it, closing my lips over the spoon. He pulled it out slowly and waited for my reaction.

"Mmm. That is good!" It tasted like sin.

"I knew you would like it." He put the spoon in his mouth and licked it clean. "So . . . you were saying?"

"Yeah, relationships. I don't think I could tolerate the everyday interaction - putting up with someone's moods and listening to their problems. You know what I'm like. Can you imagine someone trying to live with all my quirks and annoying habits?"

"Yeah." He swallowed another spoonful of ice cream. "Do you want more of this?"

"Sure." I leaned forward and opened my mouth even though it took him a moment to fill the spoon. I closed my lips tighter this time to get all the ice cream. He had to tug a little harder to get his spoon back. I swallowed and continued talking. "Another tricky part would be trusting someone else to hold up their end of things . . . financially, and, like, taking care of the house and stuff . . . all the maintenance that should be divided equally."

"You mean like we do?" He continued eating.

"Yes, exactly! If it were someone like you, it would be easy." He held up another spoonful of ice cream and I opened wide to take it. "It would be hard to find someone I could trust like that."

Sam waited a minute before he replied, "But I'm right here."

It took me a while to absorb what he said. "Yeah, but . . . we're not in a . . . relationship." The taste of strawberries lingered in my mouth.

"We're not?" He looked at me patiently.

I felt a thump in my chest. "No. There's more to a relationship than . . ."

He spoke carefully. "There *could* be more to it."

My heart was beating like crazy. I felt hot. "But . . . no. Maybe if I were younger . . ."

"Why would you have to be younger?"

I was afraid to continue, but I did. "Because you're too . . . at your age . . . you wouldn't be . . ."

He looked in my eyes. "I would, Adam. I am."

My mind reeled. I hadn't seen what was happening right in front of me, inside of me. I was already in the middle of something I didn't believe was possible. *How could it . . . How could I?*

Sam leaned forward and spoke softly. "I know this is scary for you, Adam, but you don't have to do anything."

I wasn't breathing normally. "But you're not . . . are you . . . attracted to me?"

"Yes. Very."

I covered my face with my hands. I felt like I would have another breakdown, as I did when Sam told me he was gay. I couldn't maintain my defenses any longer. The wall had been breached. There were so many feelings at once, I thought I would explode into pieces. You might think I should have been happy, but you don't live in my head.

Above all else, I was frightened. Or was I excited? I wasn't sure if I knew the difference. It was unfamiliar territory, and I didn't like being lost. I wanted to be safe. My whole life had been built for safety, and this was not safe. Worse yet, it was all my own doing! I had allowed it . . . no, I *welcomed* it into my life! *I can't even trust myself anymore!*

Unaccustomed as I was to expressing even the most basic feelings, I had no idea what to do with this wave of emotion. I cried. I sobbed. Sam knelt beside my chair and gently rubbed my back.

I don't know how long it lasted. Long enough. Eventually I regained some sense of control, but I had no idea what to do next. Sam knew. "You should go to bed, Adam, you're exhausted. I'll clean up and turn out the lights and lock the door when I leave."

"Okay." I stood up and headed for the stairs.

"Come over to my place for breakfast in the morning. I'm good at making breakfast - I promise. Whatever time you wake up will be fine."

"Okay." I went up the stairs.

"Good night."

"Night."

I shuffled into my dressing room. I didn't bother to turn on the light or close the door. I pushed my shoes off, unbuttoned my shirt and dropped it on the floor. The same with my jeans, my underwear, and my socks. I pulled back the covers on my bed and slid under them, turning on my side and pulling my knees toward my chest. I heard dishes being washed and cabinet doors closing. Then the clicking of light switches. The door latched, the lock clicked. And the faint sound of footsteps.

8

Ten hours later I was awake. I must have slept soundly for part of the night, but I tossed and turned a lot and cried off and on. As exhausted as I was, I couldn't stop thinking about how oblivious I had been. I recalled interactions I had with people over the years, things that were said, or small gestures that seemed odd to me. Once I recognized the things I had missed, I began to question everything.

I also started a lengthy process that was too much for me to understand at the time. I was grieving. Not for my parents, but for all the lost opportunities, for all my willful blindness, for my stunted courage, for the blocked affection, for the feeling of being touched, for the lost friendships . . . for all those years. That's why I cried. And I would be crying about it for quite a while before I was finished.

In many ways, it was easier to obsess about the past than to think about the present, about the night before, and about how things might change because Sam was attracted to me. I had been totally focused on controlling and hiding my sexual attraction to Sam. Meanwhile, I had made him so much a part of my life that it shocked me to see it. How could my intentions be so estranged from my behavior? It boggled my mind. Now, my feelings about Sam were so overwhelming, I thought I would burst if I focused on them for more than a moment. How could I look at him or talk to him? How could I function while feeling so out of control, so vulnerable?

I considered hiding out in my bedroom for a few months until Sam went away, but now that he had a key it wasn't a viable option. *How did I let that happen?* I knew he was expecting me for breakfast, so I slid out of bed to see if the laws of gravity still applied since the world had been turned upside down. Sure enough, my feet stayed on the floor. At least some things were the same. I picked up my scattered clothing and headed to the bathroom.

I showered but decided not to shave. *It's a holiday.* I felt more nervous as I got dressed. Again, I took my time choosing a shirt. *What's up with that?* I settled on a yellow polo I hadn't worn in years because it seemed too flashy. It looked good with my jeans. I looked good. *Hey, wait a minute! Who are you talking about?* I ran my hand over the scruff on my chin and noticed the sun had given my complexion a healthy glow. I liked the way I looked.

Part of me wanted to delay going over to the coach house, but it was nearly nine o'clock and I knew Sam was an early riser. I tried to remember the last time I felt so nervous. My mind flashed back to the time in college when that muscular athlete caught me looking at him while he shaved his chest. At the time, I failed to recognize an invitation from a beautiful and seemingly unattainable man. Would I react the same way today? No . . . today would be different. I wanted it to be different. I forced myself to move.

I walked down the stairs and through the house, noticing how Sam had cleaned things up the night before. My hand trembled as I unlocked the door. A minute later I was going up the stairs to his apartment, hoping I wouldn't embarrass myself in one of the many ways I had already imagined. *This must be what a first date feels like.* I took a deep breath and knocked on his door. I heard footsteps, then the door opened.

"Good morning, come on in." Sam was wearing plaid shorts and a green t-shirt. He looked great, as always. The apartment smelled like bacon. "I don't know why, but I was afraid you might not come." He paused and waited for me to say something.

" . . . " I opened my mouth, but nothing came out. I was thrilled to be there with him and I wanted to turn around and run and I wanted to touch him or pass out or maybe I would cry again, and I shouldn't have come but I never wanted to leave! My eyes must have communicated something like that.

"You look nervous. And you look good in yellow. Did you put that on for me? No, I'm kidding. But if you did, it's working. And I like the stubble. I talk too much when I'm nervous, but I'm guessing you're the opposite."

I nodded.

"Yeah? I couldn't sit still while I was waiting for you."

I took a deep breath. "I had to force myself to walk over here . . . but I'm glad I did."

"I'm glad you're here. Let's try to make this as normal as possible. Would you like to make coffee? I haven't made any yet. I didn't want to get more restless."

"I don't function well without caffeine." I found the filters and coffee. "I could make it half-decaf."

"That's good. Did you sleep all right?" He cracked eggs into a bowl.

"Off and on. My mind was spinning." I went to the sink to get water.

"I was afraid of that. I didn't sleep well either."

"Were you . . . worried?"

"Yeah. I thought . . . I hoped . . . well, never mind. It's too soon to get into that."

"Please tell me, Sam. I don't want to waste any more time on things I might be clueless about."

"Okay, last night . . . I didn't expect you to react like that. I knew you would be uncomfortable, but I guess . . . I thought you might be . . . happier."

"Oh, Sam." I hadn't considered what he would think of my reaction. I was glad he told me, but it made me sad to hear it. "You think I wasn't happy? Oh, my God. My feelings are so messed up, and I'm not good at talking about this stuff like you are, but . . ."

"I know. It's too soon. I shouldn't have said anything." He beat the eggs with a fork.

"No, Sam, stop letting me off the hook like that! I need to learn how to do this." I rubbed my face with my hands. "I need to think for a minute. I need caffeine." I watched the coffee dribbling into the pot. "I need to . . ." Then it hit me. I needed to stop thinking and *do* something.

Sam continued beating eggs. Without a word, I slipped my arms around his chest and hugged him from behind. He flinched a little, probably shocked that I would initiate physical contact. I pressed my face against his back. He put his arms over mine and I listened to his heart beat. I was in no hurry to let go.

"That says a lot, Adam. You can take your time finding the right words." He patted the back of my hand. "Let's have breakfast. I'm hungrier than usual." I released him. He looked over his shoulder and smiled.

While I drank coffee, Sam scrambled the eggs and transferred them to a bowl. He opened the oven and brought out a tray full of thin pancakes and crisply cooked bacon. Obviously, he had been cooking before I arrived. "That smells wonderful. I'm impressed."

"Thanks. I know how to cook a few things. These are buttermilk pancakes, but not the thick ones they serve in restaurants. My mom used to make these on Sundays." He set the tray on the table and brought orange juice and maple syrup. I piled food on my plate like I did when I was a teenager. I knew it would please him. It was all good.

Once the caffeine kicked in, I was ready to talk. "Sam, this won't surprise you, but I've been living a very safe, carefully controlled life."

"I did notice that."

"When I agreed to let you rent this apartment . . . it was risky for me."

"I know, my income wasn't as high as it should have been."

"I told myself that was the biggest issue, but it wasn't."

"I'm too young, right? You thought I would wreck the place."

"No, you probably won't guess the real reason. You've been a great tenant, by the way."

"Oh, you had me worried for a minute."

"Sam . . . do you know how good looking you are?"

"Uh . . . I guess so." He blushed. "I mean . . . I get compliments, but, doesn't everyone?"

"Probably not as many as you get. I suppose it's a matter of taste, but in my eyes, Sam . . ." My chest was tight. "I don't know how else to put this . . . you are so fucking hot . . . it feels dangerous to be near you." I got that out without choking.

Sam stared at me with his mouth open. I waited. I was sure he would say something, but he didn't.

I continued. "So . . . I let you move in here even though I feel out of control around you."

Sam blinked a few times. "But you hardly ever look at me. I keep trying to get your attention, and you're always looking away. I thought you didn't . . . I thought you weren't . . ."

"Wait . . . you thought I wasn't attracted to you? You've got to be kidding! I was trying to hide it, but it wasn't easy."

"Why would you hide it? You knew I was gay . . . why?"

"You're so much younger and better looking. I didn't want to offend you. I was afraid you would leave."

"I . . . I don't understand this at all. I can't believe . . . all this time . . ."

"I told you I was messed up! It seems stupid now, but I thought you would leave if you found out. When you told me about the creepy guys at the gym who flirted with you . . . I thought I would be like those guys."

"What? You're not like them at all! Why would you think that? If I thought you were creepy, I never would've moved in here, Adam!"

I took a deep breath, attempting to unclench my body. The conversation wasn't as warm and fuzzy as I had hoped. I tried to zero in on the stuff that would make my behavior understandable. "Sam, try to put yourself in my head . . . I don't think I'm anything special, and along comes this incredibly hot younger guy who couldn't possibly be interested in me, but he's so . . . kind, and smart, and funny . . . and so nice to be with . . . and I was so lonely . . ." That's where I started to lose it. I had never admitted to myself how lonely I was.

We were quiet for a while until I pulled myself together. "Sam, once you were here and I realized how much I liked you . . . and I mean the person you are, not just the way you look . . . I didn't want to lose you. So, I tried to keep you as a friend. Do you understand?"

He appeared to be lost in thought. "Yeah. Yeah, that makes sense. I couldn't figure out all the mixed signals. It was like that from the first time I came here. Do you remember when I filled out the application form for the apartment?"

"Yes. I wasn't very friendly, was I?"

"You were an asshole."

"Oh."

"I wanted the apartment, so I wouldn't go away. And . . . this is such a little thing, but . . . do you remember offering me coffee?"

"Yeah."

"I said, 'No,' but you gave it to me anyway and brought out cookies. I thought it was interesting that you were pretty much telling me to go away at the same time you were making me feel at home. I was hooked."

"Hooked?"

"I made up my mind I would get to know you. Even if I didn't get the apartment, I would have found another reason to come back. That's why I offered to shovel your snow before I left."

"Because you thought I was . . . interesting?"

"It didn't hurt that you're so fu- . . . good looking, I mean." He blushed.

"What were you about to say?"

"No, forget it. It's bad."

"Now you have to tell me, or it'll drive me crazy. Come on."

He groaned. "Fuckable. You're fuckable. I'm sorry." He covered his face with his hands.

It was so unexpected. And coming from him! *Sam thinks I'm "fuckable!" That's awesome!*

He peeked through his fingers and saw me grinning. "You're not offended?"

"No. I'm surprised but . . . thank you?"

"Yeah, it's a compliment, Adam. So, anyway, when you came to see me at the restaurant, I wasn't sure what to expect."

"I was planning to reject your application."

"You were?"

"I rehearsed a whole speech."

"What changed your mind?"

"Well, I'm not proud of this, but I took a good look at you, and I . . . wasn't in control of myself anymore." I glanced up, embarrassed.

"You rented to me because of the way I look?"

"It was so impulsive. Completely out of character for me."

"Do you regret it?"

"Oh, God no! It was the best decision I ever made."

Sam smiled. "I never would have guessed you felt that way. You seemed nervous, but I thought you were shy."

"Yeah, that too."

He paused to think. "That's why you were different. Other guys were so focused on the way I look, but they didn't care about getting to know me. I didn't know if you were attracted to me. I felt like I had to win you over."

"So, it was a good thing I was so repressed?"

He laughed. "I wouldn't go that far, but it's an interesting point. I don't know how I would have reacted if I knew you thought I was 'so fucking hot.' If you had known I thought you were fuckable, would it have made a difference?"

"I would've had a massive stroke." This was only a slight exaggeration. I liked hearing the 'f' word again, but it made me nervous. I wasn't ready to talk about sex with Sam. "This is still overwhelming. Maybe I shouldn't have had coffee."

"We can change the subject if you want."

I jumped right on that. "You haven't finished your breakfast. Are you feeling okay?"

He looked at the food left on the table and seemed surprised as well. "I got distracted." He picked up his fork. "It's because you were talking about your feelings. It's like seeing a flying pig."

"Oh, shut up!" I laughed. "You'll be sorry you cracked open my shell. I've got thirty years of repressed emotions in here."

He grinned. "That's terrifying."

* * *

As usual, we washed the dishes together. I wanted to go back to our comfortable routines, but I knew something should change. I wasn't sure how to proceed. "Sam, if we're already in a relationship . . . what is it?"

"I was thinking about that, too. We're friends. That's a good place to start."

"Yeah, but it's more complicated. You're my tenant, and we have this arrangement, and maybe you'll buy my truck. It's like a business relationship, too."

"Huh . . . I never thought of it that way. You're more of a business guy. For me, it got complicated when it looked more and more like we were dating, but without any romance or sex."

"Uh . . . how did it look like we were dating?"

"We eat together several times a week and talk about personal stuff. We spend most of our free time together. We're doing chores together and running errands together. And yesterday, when you gave me the key to your house, that was the kicker."

"I still don't understand why that means so much."

"Adam, when two people are dating, exchanging keys usually means they're moving to the next level, like a committed relationship."

"Oh. Oh! Now I get it." *Finally.* "No wonder you were so frustrated with me."

"Thank you."

"But, we are, aren't we?"

"We are what?"

"Moving to the next level, wherever that is."

"I hope so. I wasn't sure if you were ready for that."

"Probably not, but I want it. You'll have to be patient with me."

"You make it sound like I'm the expert here. I'm not sure how to do this either. And I'm afraid you'll shut down again if I do the wrong thing." He finished washing the skillet and set it in the drying rack. "You said you didn't want to risk losing me. I feel the same way, plus I have a lot more to lose if things don't go well. Have you thought about that?"

I was very good at worst case scenarios, but I never thought about consequences for anyone but myself. *Am I that selfish?* Sam had a lot to lose, and I could shut down at the drop of a hat. "You're right. You must be pretty brave to want a relationship with me."

He shrugged. "It's a good thing you're so damned cute." He gave my butt a gentle pat.

I jumped as though I'd been shocked with a cattle prod. "Hey! Watch it! I'm not wearing my tight underwear."

"Your what?"

"Dammit! I shouldn't have said that." I let out a heavy sigh. "I wear tight underwear to keep . . . things . . . under control when I'm with you." I waited for him to laugh.

"I'm glad I'm not the only one."

"Huh?"

"I wear compression shorts." He pulled up one leg of his plaid shorts to reveal his muscular thigh encased in tight black Lycra.

I couldn't look for more than a moment, and I didn't want to think about what was going on under there. "Okay then!" I clapped my hands together. "We should plan our day."

Sam leaned against the counter, crossed his arms and smiled. Part of me wanted to jump on him and figure things out while I tore his clothes off, but I was already way outside of my comfort zone, and there were things to do.

I tried to stay focused. "As much as I'd like to stay here and . . . whatever . . . I was thinking you should go to the nursery and talk to Dave about the job he offered you."

"Would he be there on a holiday?"

"Yeah, this is a busy weekend for him. You can take the truck. Do you remember how to get there?"

"I think so, but why don't you come along?"

"No, you should do this by yourself. I don't need to be involved. Besides, I think I need to be away from you for a little while. I'm feeling . . . too much . . . I don't know . . . come and get the keys, okay?"

"You're not having that stroke you mentioned, are you?"

"No, I'm fine. We'll talk more later. And talk, and talk, and talk . . . " I rolled my eyes comically.

"Hey, you're the one doing most of the talking today. But seriously, whenever you need a break from me, just say so. Sometimes I need one, too."

I doubted he was that attracted to me, but it was nice of him to say it. I retrieved the keys from the house and sent him on his way. As he drove off, I thought, *I just let someone take my truck. Who the fuck am I?*

There was no point in pretending I would get anything else done before masturbating, so I ran upstairs. A short while later, I was good to go. *Isn't sex grand?*

* * *

The thought of buying a new truck was stuck in my head. Typically, I would do a lot of research before making such a big purchase, but I knew there were Memorial Day sales on new vehicles. And my next-door neighbor was the widow of one of the bigger car dealers in town. Her son ran the dealership now, but she inherited the business. *Could she get me a discount?* She was always nice to me. I used to swim in her beautiful in-ground pool until . . . I don't know when I stopped, or why I stopped. *I'll see if she's around.*

The weather was as warm and sunny as it had been all weekend. I peeked through the hedge separating my garden from Mrs. O'Neill's back yard. Luckily, she was sitting on her terrace reading the newspaper. I squeezed through a gap at the end of the hedge and waved. "Hello, Mrs. O'Neill."

"Adam! You scamp, you almost gave me a heart attack."

"I'm sorry, I didn't mean to startle you."

"Well, I'm happy to see you nonetheless. Come here and give me some sugar!" Mrs. O'Neill was born in the South and retained many of its charming mannerisms. She offered her cheek for me to kiss. "My oh my! You get more handsome every year. Please sit down. Would you like some tea?"

"No, thank you. I drank a boatload of coffee." I sat down in one of her comfortable patio chairs.

"I haven't seen you in ages, dear. Where have you been hiding?"

"Over there behind the hedge. The house and the garden keep me very busy."

"And you do such a wonderful job. It's a gift to the entire neighborhood." Her warmth and sincere affection touched my heart. "I'm so pleased to see you have help now."

"You mean Sam, my tenant? Yes, he's been a godsend." Thinking of him made me smile.

She reached over and put her hand on top of mine. "Sweetheart, you'll have to forgive the impertinence of an old woman, but I hope he's more than a tenant." Her expression was sympathetic.

I was shocked. "I don't . . . what do you mean?" *She knows I'm gay? She knows about Sam?!*

"Oh, honey! There's no need to be coy with me. Many years ago, I fell in love with a sensitive young man much like yourself, and I received a heartbreaking education in the ways of the world. Things have changed a great deal since then, but not nearly enough when it comes to the variations of love."

I sputtered. "Is it . . . are we . . . obvious?" *Am I the last person to know out about me and Sam?!*

"I don't know, dear. My eyes have been well-trained to see things that may be invisible to others. I believe people see what they want to see. Fortunately, I can see a great deal from my bedroom window." She pointed to a large window on the second floor of her spacious house. It had an excellent view of my enclosed garden.

Once again, my head was spinning. *Enough already!*

She continued in her melodious southern drawl. "That young man is the loveliest addition you've made to your garden in a long while, Adam. And I love what he's doing to that old shed. Wherever did you find him?"

"He found me. He showed up one day to ask about the apartment."

"Ah, serendipity! What would our lives be like without it?"

"Lonely."

She smiled knowingly. "I do hope he can hold an intelligent conversation."

"Ha! I can barely keep up with him."

"Oh, that's wonderful, darling." She beamed at me. "Now, I hate to chase you away so soon, but I'm playing bridge this afternoon with a bunch of old ladies who depend on me for scandalous remarks. Was there a reason for your visit today, or did you only want to give me a thrill?"

I felt guilty about my reason for coming over. "I hate to bring this up, but . . . I'm in the market for a new pickup truck and I . . ."

"I hope you weren't planning to pay full price, because I won't hear of it."

"Everything is on sale this weekend . . ."

"That won't do, I'm afraid. Go over to the dealership and I'll make a phone call before you get there. Ask for Clarence. He's one of our senior salesmen and a very dear friend of mine."

"Shouldn't I talk to your son?"

"Edward? Oh, heavens no! He would steal a handbag from a woman in a wheelchair. You must talk to Clarence. I'll make sure he gives you a deal that will make steam come out of Edward's ears."

"Are you sure that's a good idea?"

"Honey, nothing would give me more pleasure! But I will ask for one favor in return for my assistance with your purchase."

"Absolutely. Anything you need."

"You and your young man must join me for lunch one day soon, and bring your bathing suits. You've been neglecting that swimming pool as much as you've been neglecting me, and I won't stand for it any longer." Her expression made it clear this should not be taken lightly.

"We would be happy to come, Mrs. O'Neill. And I'm sorry I haven't been visiting. I've been neglecting a lot of things. I know you'll love Sam as much as I . . . I mean, you'll get along like a house on fire."

Her eyes twinkled. "Please call me Flora, honey. I think we're beyond formalities."

"Thank you . . . Flora." I felt surprisingly close to her. I had forgotten how long and how well she knew me. There weren't many people who knew me at all. "Can I ask you something else?"

"Certainly. What is it?"

"What happened to the man you fell in love with when you were young? Did you keep in touch with him?"

"Of course, dear. I married him. It was Mr. O'Neill." I wasn't expecting that, and didn't know what to say. "Don't look so surprised, sweetie! That was ages ago. Marriage was different for men and women of my generation. I gave him a respectable way to hide his proclivities, and he gave me nearly everything I wanted. He was a terrible rascal, but I did love him so. And we always had good conversations." She smiled. "Now I really must go."

"Okay. Thank you so much." I stood up and gave her another kiss. "I'll talk to you soon about lunch."

As I walked away, I felt a deep sense of gratitude followed by another wave of regret for the way I had been shutting people out of my life. I shed a few tears.

* * *

A short while later, Sam returned from his trip to Dave's Nursery. Dave had been happy to see him, and his job offer was generous. "I didn't have to negotiate at all. He offered me a little more than I'm making at the Harbor View for forty hours a week plus overtime during the busy season. And during the winter he runs a snow plowing service. Did you know about that?"

"I remember seeing one of his trucks with a plow blade on it. Did you tell him you've done snow removal already?"

"Yeah . . . it backfired a little. It turns out I stole one of his customers, but he got over it. He said, 'You've got some balls, kid! I like that!'" Sam did a pretty good impersonation of Dave. "I have a feeling he'll run me ragged, though. He's intense."

"It would take an awful lot to wear you out."

"I don't know . . . between you and Dave I might be headed for an early grave."

"Yeah, right! We have another errand to run. You can drive." On the way to the car dealership I told him about our neighbor and her invitation. Sam was happy to hear we could use her swimming pool. I pictured him standing in the sunlight, dripping wet. "I'm looking forward to that, too."

Clarence, the salesman Mrs. O'Neill told me to see, was a gregarious white-haired gentleman who welcomed us warmly and showed us the available pickup trucks. I narrowed it down to two basic models with similar features, one silver and one dark blue. Clarence said silver wouldn't show dirt as much as darker colors, but Sam bent down and whispered in my ear, "You look good in blue."

After a brief test drive, I went to Clarence's office to complete the paperwork for my shiny blue pickup truck. The price he gave me was so low I thought he'd made an error. He assured me, "Flora was very clear it should be dealer cost, and not a penny more. I'm glad she told Ed about it herself. I didn't want to deliver that message."

Flora's only son, Edward O'Neill, was not someone to be trifled with. He was active in local politics and had a reputation for asserting his influence in unsavory ways. I didn't want to be on his radar. I felt uneasy about the great deal I was getting, but it was too late to get out of it. I signed all the paperwork and handed over the largest check I had ever written.

When I apologized to Clarence for not providing him with a commission on the sale of the truck, he reassured me. "Don't worry about it. Flora and I go way back. She takes care of me, and I take care of her." He winked. Confused, I smiled a little. He nodded to clarify what he meant. *Oh, come on! Am I the only person in town who's not getting laid?*

We shook hands and I made a beeline for the door where Sam was leaning against the new truck outside the showroom. A booming voice behind me said, "Wait a minute! Are you Adam?" I turned to see Ed O'Neill coming toward me. *Shit!* "I'm Big Ed O'Neill." He called himself "Big Ed" in his advertisements. Big enough to be intimidating, he extended his hand to shake mine.

"Yes, I've seen your picture in the ads." My hand was swallowed up in his big sweaty mitt. "I've lived next door to your mother since I was . . ."

He didn't let me finish. "My mother has a soft heart. She's elderly and frail." His grip was painfully tight, and his expression was menacing. "I thought her neighbors would understand that." I tried to pull my hand away from him, but he was sending a message and wouldn't let go. "I hate to think some opportunistic little shit would take advantage of her kindness by. . ."

"Adam?" Sam was behind me. "Are you ready to go?"

Ed loosened his grip enough for me to pull my hand away. It was obvious he hurt me. Sam stepped forward and extended his hand. "We haven't met. I'm Samson." I was surprised he used his given name. He gripped Ed's hand. "You owe Adam an apology." The hostile, condescending look on Ed's face turned to surprise, then worry. He found himself on the receiving end of a much stronger handshake. "Apologize."

"I . . . I misunderstood the situation." His eyes bulged in his sweaty, red face. "I'm sure my mother appreciates your friendship, Adam. I'm sorry." Sam let go. Ed grunted, stumbled a bit, and cradled his injured hand.

"Nice meeting you. Let's go, Adam."

I turned and walked quickly to my truck. "What did you do?"

"I gave him a taste of his own medicine. Show me your hand." He gently examined it.

"We can't afford to have an enemy like him! What were you thinking?!"

"He was already your enemy, Adam. I balanced things out." He seemed calm, but there was something under the surface I hadn't seen before . . . something fierce. "It doesn't look like he broke anything. How does it feel?"

"It hurts, but I'll live." I took a deep breath to settle myself down, then whispered, "That was fuckin' awesome! Let's get out of here." He smiled, and we went to our separate vehicles. As I drove home, I thought about Sam's quiet power and how protective he had been. I played the scene over and over in my mind. It was uncomfortable to drive with a full boner.

* * *

I felt like it had been a very long day, but it was only mid-afternoon. My days were never this busy. I liked the way things were going, but it was a lot to absorb. Sam pulled into the driveway and parked the old truck in front of his garage space. He got out and walked around my new truck to find me waiting for him. "The truck looks great, Adam. Excellent choice."

"Thanks for helping me choose the color. And thanks for . . . the other thing. I've never . . . no one has ever . . . I mean, it was . . ."

"Hey . . . nobody messes with my landlord." There was a sparkle in his eye.

"You know, I was about to kick his ass when you stepped in. It's a good thing you did."

"I know. It would've been ugly."

I was glad we had the same sense of humor. “So, what do you want to do this afternoon?"

"You're asking me? You're the boss man."

"Come on, you're not my slave."

He raised an eyebrow and lowered his voice. "I could be if you're into that."

"Stop it! Jeez! I have enough trouble controlling myself around you." I squirmed and did a little dance as if I needed to pee.

"You're not the only one! I didn't have a chance to jack off after breakfast like you did."

"How do you know what I . . ."

"It was so obvious!"

"Could we discuss this in the house, please?"

"No, I need to go take care of myself. I'll come back when I'm done. It won't take long, believe me."

"Fine . . . take care of . . . whatever." I went straight into the house while Sam went up to his apartment. It may sound absurd, but with my anxiety and my complete lack of sexual experience, we weren't going to start fucking like porn stars.

I had done enough gardening for the weekend, and the day's events were still spinning in my head. I needed to slow down and relax, so I made a pot of coffee. I wanted to be with Sam, whether we were working, or talking, or being quiet together. I never wanted to talk to anyone as much as I liked talking with him, even when it made me anxious. When we were together, I felt more . . . alive, I guess.

I gathered the ingredients for dinner. I scrubbed a few potatoes and prepared them for the grill before Sam came in the back door. I glanced over my shoulder. "That was quick. Do you feel better now?"

"Yes, I do." He stood close behind me. "Adam, you know I wouldn't hurt you, right?"

"Yeah. Why?"

"This will probably be uncomfortable, but I think it'll be good for us."

Uh oh. "Okay."

"Let me bring your hand behind your back." He gently positioned my arm, then pulled me against himself so my hand was pinned against his crotch. I stiffened. "It's okay, try to relax." His lips were very close to my ear. He draped his other arm over my body and cupped my package in his hand. "You know I have a penis, I know you have a penis, and we get excited when we're around each other, right?" I nodded. "We don't need to be embarrassed about it. It's a good thing. Just because our dicks get hard doesn't mean we need to do something with them."

"Okay." He was right about how uncomfortable this would make me.

"So, if one of us has an erection when we're together, nothing bad will happen."

Clearly, he hadn't given this enough thought. "What if we're in a public place?"

"Well . . . that could be embarrassing, but I wouldn't do anything to make it happen when we're in public."

"You don't have to do anything, Sam. You could just be standing there. That's why I never look at you for more than a few seconds."

"It can't be that bad."

"It is, though. I haven't been this horny since I was a teenager."

I could feel the shape of his penis against my hand. "Come on, you're exaggerating."

"No, I'm not! Like, the other night when we were in the basement and you picked up the radiator. Remember, I told you I needed to pee?"

"You mean . . . you got excited because I lifted something?"

"Hell yes! Your strength is such a huge turn-on for me, I can barely stand it." His erection was becoming more prominent. "And you look better every week . . . the way your white polo shirt fits you now is . . . you're so fucking sexy . . . and at the end of a meal when you . . ."

"Okay, okay, slow down Adam . . ." He let go of me and backed away. When I turned around, he had his hand over a very prominent tent in his shorts. "Damn, what did you do to me?" He squirmed and winced.

My eyes were glued to his predicament. "Do you want some privacy?"

"No . . . give me a minute." He turned his back and leaned against the wall on the other side of the room. "This never happened to me before. Listening to you talk about me like that . . ."

I was erect, but more comfortable. I adjusted myself in my pants while I had a long look at Sam's butt. It was good to see him struggling with his arousal. He always seemed to be in control of himself, while I felt out of control. "So . . . what were you saying about not being embarrassed by our erections?"

He laughed quietly. "Okay, you're right." He turned to face me again. The tent in his shorts was still visible. "Go ahead, stare at it if you want to."

I grinned. "Can I touch it again?"

"No. Not today." His face was red.

"I'm going to write in my diary, 'Today I touched Sam's boner for the first time."

He closed his eyes and shook his head, smiling. "You'll make it bigger if you keep talking like that."

"I can't wait!"

"All right, smart ass, you asked for it!" He made a sudden move in my direction.

"No! Careful with that thing! You'll break it!" I tried to evade him, but he caught me as I turned away. He pulled me into his chest and held me. I stopped struggling. My heart was beating rapidly . . . *thump thump thump thump.* It wasn't fear . . . *thump thump thump* . . . or anxiety . . . *thump, thump, thump* . . . I was excited. . . *thump* . . . *thump* . . . *thump. That's what it feels like!*

Sam tightened his embrace and nuzzled my neck. "I'm so happy, Adam."

A surge of emotion kept me from speaking right away. We stood like that, listening to each other breathe, until I could say, "Me too, Sam."

He didn't let go. "So, what's the plan for the rest of the day?"

"I don't know. I thought we could relax until dinner. Do you want some coffee?"

"Don't you want me to work on the shed?"

"No, you have all summer to do that. It's a holiday."

Sam released me. I turned as he raised his arms into a big stretch. I observed the lengthening of his body, the expansion of his chest, and the trail of hair on his exposed belly. I watched, and he knew I was watching. He lowered his arms and rested his hands on his narrow waist. "I'll have some coffee. Maybe I could read more of that book. I like the way things are going for Tess now that she met a decent guy."

I filled two mugs. "You mean Angel Clare? Yeah. Isn't that a great name for a character?"

"It certainly fits him. Do you want me to go back to my apartment to read?"

I wanted him closer to me. "You could read in the living room if you want. Or wherever."

"Okay, I'll get the book." As he went out the door he added, "You should have some chairs in the garden, don't you think?"

"I suppose I could." He took the stairs to his apartment two at a time, then trotted back down with the book in his hand. I knew Tess, and Sam, would be disappointed in Angel Clare, but I couldn't tell him that now. *I should have given him a different book.*

I pointed to his coffee mug and the sugar bowl next to it. He scooped three heaping teaspoons into the mug and stirred. "I'll have to move my weights out of the garage so I can park the truck in there. I don't have room for them in the apartment. Maybe I should sell them."

I wasn't thrilled with that idea. "Don't you want to work out anymore?"

"Yeah, I enjoy it, but . . ."

"You can put them in the basement. Use them whenever you want."

"That would be perfect. Thanks. I can show you how to use them, too, if you're interested."

"Maybe. We'll see." A wave of insecurity swept over me as I thought about my body next to his. I was tired of it. *He'll get tired of it.* "Sam, I wish . . . I'm sorry I'm so nervous about everything. I know it's not easy for you."

"It's fine. I think things are going well."

"Okay. Good." I believed him, for the moment. My fear of disappointing him would be difficult to shake. *Wouldn't it be easier to get it over with?* If ever there was a reason to overcome my fears, it was the young man standing before me. As he sipped his coffee, I remembered something from our conversation that morning. I opened a cabinet and pulled out a tin, like I did on that winter day when he showed up in my driveway. "Cookies?" Despite the challenges I would face, I wanted Sam in my life.

He smiled. "Nice move. Thanks."

"You can take that in the other room. Read your book. Whatever."

"Do you want help with dinner?"

"No, I'll take care of it. You made breakfast."

"Okay. I'll be in the living room." He tucked the book under his arm and ventured into the part of the house that had been off limits to everyone but me for far too long.

9

With a glass of Shiraz dispensed from the box I had opened the night before, I went to my computer to look up instructions for grilling steaks. I relied on the internet to teach me how to do new things. I jotted down a few notes and went outside to light the grill.

Cooking, like gardening, is an activity that helps clear the noise out of my head. It gives me something to do but doesn't require all my attention. I had time to think about why, when something more wonderful than I could have imagined was happening in my life, I felt more afraid than happy. *What am I afraid of?* The answer was . . . pretty much everything.

I was afraid of public erections, of saying or doing something embarrassing in front of Sam, of exposing my flawed body to someone who was physically perfect, of being rejected, and then feeling like I couldn't live without him. I was afraid I would surrender control of my life and he would hurt me or even destroy me, financially, emotionally, or physically. So, basically, I was putting my life at risk. *Is that all? What's the big deal?* Fortunately, I had a well-developed rational mind to beat my stupid feelings into submission. And the denial. Denial helped.

One thing that puzzled me had to do with Sam's physical strength. When I thought about how easily Sam could control me or hurt me, I wasn't afraid - I was aroused. As someone who opted for safety in every area of his life, it made no sense. Nevertheless, I was always attracted to men who were bigger and stronger than me. It seemed strange that what I had so carefully avoided in my life - feeling defenseless, vulnerable, and out of control - turned my sexual crank more than anything else.

Dinner was almost ready, except for the steaks. I stepped quietly into the dining room to find Sam stretched out in the middle of the living room rug, reading. His book was on the floor, illuminated by a patch of sunlight. I paused for a few moments to appreciate the scene. When he turned a page, I said, "Hey."

He looked up. "Hey. How long have you been there?"

"A few minutes. You can sit on the furniture, you know."

"Yeah, I tried it. It's nice to look at, but not very comfortable. For me, at least."

"How do you want your steak cooked?"

"Rare, or medium rare is fine."

"Could you set the table?"

"Sure. Are we eating in the dining room?"

"I think so. It worked for us last night, didn't it?"

"It certainly did."

A short while later we were cutting into beautifully charred porterhouse steaks, baked potatoes and a salad I made from spinach, strawberries, and balsamic vinaigrette. I had another glass of wine but made that my limit for the evening. The steak was delicious. "I'm glad I bought the grill. Good thing I was feeling impulsive."

"I'll say. This is awesome. You should be impulsive more often."

"Pfft, no kidding. I hope I can keep it going."

Sam smiled. "It's not always good to be impulsive, though. Sometimes you need to be extra cautious."

"I don't know. I've been doing that for so long, I can't think of anything I feel like being cautious about right now."

Sam paused for a minute before saying, "I can."

"Oh? What's that?"

"Well . . . I think we should get tested. For sexually transmitted diseases."

My mind went off in ten different directions.

"You know I've been with other guys. I think it would be good to do it before we . . . you know . . . move forward." His face was red. It must not have been easy to bring this up.

I was surprised I hadn't thought of it, though the possibility of sexual activity had only come up the night before. "Um, you're right. I would feel more comfortable knowing you're . . . healthy. But I've never been with anyone, so why do I need to get tested?"

"I know, and I believe you, Adam. But there are some things we should be extra careful about. This is one of them."

"Sam, you know I'm not the type of person who would have casual sex."

"The 'type of person?' You mean, like me? Do you think you're better than me because you're a virgin? I wouldn't brag about that at your age."

Ouch! "I didn't mean it that way! I'm embarrassed to be a virgin, but it's also why I don't need to get tested."

"Is it really too much to ask, Adam?" He paused and took a deep breath. "Think about it . . . would you want to be with someone who let you get away with not being tested?" He chomped on a large chunk of meat and chewed it angrily.

I had to let that sink in. He was right on several levels. I couldn't trust someone who would be careless about safety. This was one of those moments when I realized Sam was so much more than what he appeared to be. He was smart, he had principles, and he had the courage to stand up to me when I was being a dick. I conceded. "I'm sorry. You're right, I'll get tested."

"Thank you." I took a bite of steak but kept looking at him. "What? Why are you looking at me like that?"

"I'm impressed. You were right, and you stood up to me. I like that."

"Good, because I'll keep doing it." He was still annoyed.

I waited a few beats. "Your integrity is giving me a boner."

It made him smile. "Shut up! Everything gives you a boner."

"Everything about *you* does."

He shook his head and kept eating.

After a few minutes of quiet, I asked him how far he got in *Tess of the D'Urbervilles.*

"Tess was wondering whether to tell Angel about her past with Alec, that she's not a virgin. She's afraid he'll reject her, but she wrote a letter about it and slipped it under his door. I'm anxious to see how he reacts to it. Don't tell me what happens."

"I won't." I was anxious to see how Sam would react to it. "There's a lot of tension in that relationship, isn't there? Kind of like our relationship." It dawned on me at the same time I said it.

Sam nodded. "She worries about whether she's good enough for him, if he'll still want her if he knows the truth about her. It's familiar. I suppose everyone's afraid of being rejected for some reason or another."

I still found it hard to believe Sam worried about being rejected, especially by someone like me. "While I was making dinner, I was figuring out what makes me nervous when I'm with you. I thought about the difference between fear and excitement, or . . . how they're alike."

"What do you mean? How are they alike?" He put another steak on his plate.

"Well, for example, I loved roller coasters when I was a kid. The bigger and scarier they were, the more I liked them. They felt dangerous, so it was exciting. And when I was older, I liked scary movies for the same reason. Those feelings weren't that different from what I felt last night when you told me . . . what you told me."

"That I'm attracted to you?"

"Yeah. It's happening now. My heart is beating faster, and I'm breathing differently. You know what I mean? It makes me think I'm afraid, but . . . maybe I forgot what it feels like to be excited. I used to enjoy that feeling."

"Hmm." He nodded. "I like that. It makes sense. When was the last time you were on a roller coaster?"

"Oh, not since I was a kid."

"Do you still like scary movies?"

"I haven't watched one for a long time, since . . ." I had to think about it. *The accident that killed my parents.* "I think . . . when I found out how scary real life could be. Being afraid wasn't fun anymore."

Sam understood. "I felt that way after I left the farm. I was excited about starting a new life, free to do what I wanted, things my parents would never allow. I thought about all the fun I would have, the people I would meet. It was good for a while, but after a few nights of sleeping under bridges and being hungry, and dealing with people who weren't friendly, it wasn't so exciting. I knew I could protect myself physically, but . . . being alone in the world was scary in a way I never imagined. I didn't feel safe for a long time."

"I didn't know things were that bad for you." I often assumed life was easy for Sam. "How did you learn to feel safe again?"

"Um . . . it wasn't something I learned. It just happened."

"When?"

There was a long pause, and he swallowed hard. "Yesterday, when you gave me the key to the house. And you didn't freak out when I told you about my job."

It took my breath away. I leaned in and put my hand on his wrist, gently petting the back of his hand with my thumb. He had tears in his eyes, so I didn't linger in the moment. I withdrew my hand, and we went back to our food.

We discussed the best way for Sam to leave his job at the Harbor View. He would offer two weeks' notice and see how the manager responded. He wanted to take responsibility for all the meals he ate at the restaurant and let the chef off the hook. "I'm embarrassed to admit it, but I knew Chef had a thing for me. I told myself he liked to see people enjoying his food, but there was more to it than that. I can't let him get fired."

I watched him put butter on his second baked potato. "For what it's worth, watching you eat is pretty sexy."

"Stop it. You can't say everything I do is sexy."

"Yes, I can. Your appetite is very manly. I like it. I don't know where you put all that food."

He flexed his biceps and pointed to it. "It's in there. That's made of doughnuts."

I laughed. Sam was funny, on top of everything else. "It still pisses me off."

"When you were twenty, you probably ate as much as I do."

"I ate more than I do now, but not that much. And I sure as hell didn't grow muscles like you have. I never lifted weights."

"You didn't grow up on a farm either. We were always lifting stuff. But you remember what I looked like when I first came here? I was twenty pounds lighter, and I didn't start working out seriously until later, when you told me to put on more muscle."

"I did?"

"Remember? You said I should be an example for people at the health club, and gay people are fussy, so if I wanted to find Mr. Right I should be more muscular. I took your advice because you were the guy I wanted, and I figured that's what you liked."

"Sam, I never should have said that. You were already hotter than hell."

"But you like the way I look now, don't you?"

I wanted to say the right thing for a change. "Do *you* like the way you look?"

"Yes . . . as long as you like it."

"It's your body, Sam. It shouldn't matter what I like."

"It does matter. I know it's my body, but . . . I want you to enjoy it as much as possible. Those things you said this afternoon . . . about what it's like to look at me? I've never been so turned on in my life. Seriously, if I can do that for you, and for me . . . of course I'll do it."

I wondered if this was an elaborate dream I was having. *Deep breath.* "Yes, I definitely like the way you look now." I couldn't sustain eye contact. "Aren't you attracted to more athletic guys? They'd be a better match for you."

"No. Why would they be a better match? Adam, some of the things you feel insecure about are things that turn me on. Like your age. I've always been attracted to guys who are a little older than me. And your body? I know you're self-conscious about it, but . . . you've got something that really gets me going." His gaze made me feel naked. "I'll leave it at that before I get too cranked up." He put the last piece of steak in his mouth.

I couldn't sit still anymore. "Are you ready for dessert?" I gathered the dishes.

He pretended to be ambivalent. "I suppose." He followed me into the kitchen with the remaining items. "Are we having ice cream?"

"Whatever you like and as much as you want."

"Will you have some?"

"Sure."

"Awesome!" He pumped his fist and opened the freezer to choose a pint. "Grab a couple of spoons."

"Do I need my own spoon tonight?"

"I can feed it to you again if you liked it."

"It caught me off guard, but I did like it. It was kind of seductive."

"Oh? That never occurred to me." He stepped backwards into the dining room with a mischievous expression.

* * *

The ice cream was gone in no time, the dishes were washed, and it was still too early to call it a night. "Do you want to sit in the living room for a while? Wait, you don't like the furniture." I walked into the room, turned on the lamps, and sat on the Victorian sofa to see how it felt. I rarely sat in that room.

"It's not comfortable to sit on for very long." Sam joined me on the sofa. "Do you think it's comfortable?"

"It's stiff. The Victorians were stiff. They didn't lounge around in the parlor. It was a formal room for polite visits."

"Is that what you use it for?" He smiled.

"No, I don't have . . . oh, shut up!" I realized he was teasing me. "One of these days I'll have guests and prove you wrong."

"I look forward to that." He sat back and rested his hands in his lap.

"I suppose I could move this furniture into the bay window and get more comfortable furniture in here."

"That would work." He looked around the room. "I'm surprised you don't have any house plants. It would add a little life to the place."

"You're right. Maybe a few ferns."

"It's a beautiful room. Your parents must have put a lot of work into this."

"Yeah, they loved it. My mom hung all the wallpaper and the drapes. Dad repaired things. They were a good team."

"Do you miss them?"

"Yes, of course."

"Were you close?"

"Um . . . I don't know. We got along. They were good to me, but I don't think they knew me. I didn't make it easy for them."

After a long pause, he asked, "Did they love each other?"

"I'm sure they did, but they wouldn't show it much. You had to look for it. They could sit in this room for hours and read their books without talking. Sometimes I would catch them looking at each other, and I knew it meant something."

The sun had gone down. Outside, a bird repeated a plaintive call.

"I want to kiss you, Adam. Would that be okay?"

I stared at the oriental rug. "I don't think I would be good at that."

"Why not?"

"I've read that people are either good kissers or they're bad at it. I should do more research before I try it."

"Research?"

"Yeah, the internet has instructions for everything. There's probably something on eHow or YouTube. I could look it up now." I started to go, but Sam caught my hand.

"Stay here, Adam. I won't make you do anything you don't want to do."

I sat down on the edge of the seat. "It's not that I don't want to . . . I don't want to ruin things."

"You won't. I might be bad at it, too."

"I doubt it."

"I've only kissed a few people. I'm not an expert. We could learn together."

"On the internet?"

"No . . . right here. Sit back. Try to relax."

"Okay, but we have to go to work tomorrow."

"I'm not staying all night. I just want to kiss you."

I eased myself back onto the sofa and decided it was not a comfortable piece of furniture. I started shopping in my head.

Sam touched his lips to the back of my hand. His kiss made the tiniest little sound. He paused to look at me. "How was that?"

"Fine." I searched his eyes. "Is that all?"

He smiled. "Whoa, slow down, tiger. We have to go to work tomorrow."

I grinned and looked at the rug again.

Sam put one finger on my wrist and traced the vein leading to the crook of my elbow. My blood seemed to rise at his touch. He leaned down and used the tip of his nose to draw a little circle on the inside of my forearm, then kissed it, leaving a glistening spot on my skin. He pursed his lips and gently blew on it until it disappeared. The back of my neck tingled. He sat up, shifted his body closer to mine, and waited.

I liked Sam's forearms, so I touched the one closest to me. I stroked the dark hair and the smooth underside where his veins stood out more than mine. Sam quietly watched. I felt the weight of the big, masculine hand that made Edward O'Neill apologize. I pressed my lips against it, held them there, and pulled away. My heart beat faster. One side of my mouth curled into a half-smile.

"That was nice, Adam."

"I've been wanting to touch your arm for months."

His eyes traveled over me. "Are you okay so far? Do you want to continue?"

"Yeah, I'm okay." I wasn't convinced.

"Can we get a little closer so I don't have to lean in?"

"Sure." I awkwardly rearranged myself.

"It would be more comfortable if I put my arm around you. Otherwise it gets in the way."

"Okay." I felt the warm weight of it across my shoulders.

"How's that? Are you comfortable?"

"Uh huh."

"I'm a little nervous, Adam. I've been thinking about this for a long time."

I looked at his face and almost melted. I studied all the elements that came together to form such a satisfying whole. His eyes were green jewels framed by dark lashes and brows. His young skin was so smooth and clear it was surprising to see stubble on his jaw. I noticed the bow shape of his upper lip and the gentle curve of the one below it. I was glad he kept me from doing research on the internet. I knew what I wanted to do with those lips.

"I'll kiss your neck first, okay?"

"Okay." He could kiss anything he wanted to at this point. I was his.

He nuzzled the side of my neck and softly kissed it in a few places. I closed my eyes. He nudged my chin so he could nibble at my Adam's apple, then returned to a spot below my ear for a firmer, longer kiss that gently pulled my skin as he drew back. He paused. "Do you like it?"

"Oh yeah. I knew you would be good at this."

"I'm doing what appeals to me. Don't overthink it."

I raised my eyebrows slightly. "I don't overthink things."

He smiled and offered me his neck.

I moved in slowly, barely touching his skin with my nose. He smelled clean, but there was something subtle underneath that, something I wanted to taste. I licked the side of his neck. I thought it might be salty, but it wasn't. I licked it again, slowly. Sam's eyes were closed. I took his earlobe between my lips and tugged on it like a puppy with an old sock until he laughed.

"That was unexpected."

"You taste good."

"I do, huh? Um . . . is it too early in our relationship to ask if you're a cannibal?"

"Yes."

"You are a cannibal?"

"It's too early to tell you." I playfully bumped the tip of my nose against his.

His eyes sparkled. "This is going pretty well, isn't it?" I nodded. He turned his body a few degrees toward me. "Remember, it doesn't have to be perfect. We can practice as much as we want."

"Every day?"

"Yes."

"For how many hours?"

"Every free moment."

"I'll want lots of practice."

He kissed me on the mouth, softly grasping my lip between his lips and pulling away, repeating it slowly. I did the same to him until it became a dance with no one leading. I lost count of the kisses. We developed a rhythm that ebbed and flowed like a lovely piece of music, pausing here and there, and launching into the main theme again. I kissed his sandpaper cheek and liked the way it scratched my lips and nose. We lapped at each other with the tips of our tongues and tasted each other's mouths. We made juicy noises that sent tingling sensations all over my body. I saw colors in his eyes that I didn't know existed. It was gloriously and inexplicably perfect.

When we paused to breathe, his chest rose and fell while he stared at my mouth and searched the rest of my face. He looked disoriented. "I didn't think it could be that good, Adam. I've never felt anything like that before. Did you feel it?"

"Yes."

"What was it?"

I searched my mind. "I don't know, but I want more of it."

We danced to the same music, but with more confidence this time. Our kisses were longer and deeper. I grabbed his hair while he cradled my head in one hand. When he tried to twist his hips toward me, an ominous cracking noise stopped us cold.

We froze, and he carefully stood up. I slid forward and turned to examine the sofa. There was no visible damage. I tested the seat with my hands, then knelt on it and pulled the back forward. It moved. "A joint probably came unglued. Nothing major."

"I'm sorry. I shouldn't be allowed on the good furniture."

"Don't worry about it. It was both of us."

"No, it was me. Sometimes I forget my strength and break things."

"Um, that's kind of hot. Come here." I stood on my toes to kiss him. He accepted it tentatively, paused, and leaned in for another one. We continued until our necks hurt.

"I should go," he said. "I have to get up early tomorrow."

"Okay." Reluctantly, I led him into the kitchen. "What time do you have to leave in the morning?"

"I want to get there early so I can talk to the manager and see what he wants to do with me."

"Will you be here for dinner?"

"Yeah. I'm not scheduled to work in the restaurant, so I'll be done by four." He trapped me against the kitchen counter and pressed his nose and forehead to mine. "This is for those steaks." His kiss was slow and wet and made my knees wobble. He pulled back and looked in my eyes. "Thank you."

He was about to push himself away when I grabbed the front of his shirt and pulled him back in. "I didn't thank you for breakfast." I kissed his lower lip in three places, his stubbly chin, and the smooth skin of his throat. "I like the variety of textures." I scanned his face for more options.

Sam locked his eyes on mine and made a low growling noise. "I need to get out of here before I commit a crime."

"All right. I would hate to be responsible for your downfall." He smiled and stepped away. *Dammit.*

I followed him to the porch where he turned back to look at me for a long moment. "It was perfect, Adam. Wasn't it?"

"It was. It was perfect. Good night, Sam."

"Good night. See you tomorrow." I closed the door and watched him through the glass. Halfway across the driveway he crouched down, pumped his fist and exclaimed, "Yes!" Then he bounded up the stairs to his apartment.

I turned my back to the door, listened to my heartbeat . . . and felt happy.

10

I slept like a rock and woke up with enough energy to go for a run before breakfast, like I used to do every day. It was time to get into better shape for things I would soon be doing with Sam. Like swimming.

As I arrived at work, I smiled and greeted the people I passed on the way to my office. Some of them looked at me strangely, so I stopped in the restroom to make sure I didn't have something stuck to my face. I didn't. As I settled in at my desk, my colleague Donna burst through the door without knocking.

"Someone told me you were cheerful. What's wrong?"

Did I mention she's sarcastic? "Please come in. And I'm always cheerful."

"Oh, honey, you actually believe that, don't you? That's tragic."

I sighed. "How was your weekend?"

"It was fun. We went to . . . wait a minute . . . you never ask about me." She wasn't being sarcastic anymore. She narrowed her eyes. "You look different. Were you out in the sun?"

"Yeah, I was gardening."

"Is that all? Did you go somewhere this weekend?"

"No, I hung out at home, grilled some steaks. What about your weekend? Where did you go?"

"Did you say 'steaks,' plural? Who was with you?"

"Uff! What the . . . I'm . . . my tenant . . . doesn't know anyone in town . . . so I . . . we grilled some steaks together. Okay?"

"Huh. Aren't you afraid she'll get the wrong idea about that?"

"He. Him."

"Oh." There was a long pause while she waited for me to offer more information. She closed the door. My office became very quiet. There may have been a cricket in there with us.

I couldn't stand it anymore. "Um . . . can I ask you something, Donna? I don't want to put you on the spot or anything, but I was wondering . . ."

"What?" Her expression was completely blank.

"Um . . . someone asked me the other day whether I had any friends at work. I said I had one. Was that . . . accurate?"

Her eyes softened. "Yes, I am your friend, Adam. We are friends."

"Okay. I thought so, but I didn't want to assume." I paused and nodded. "And . . . again, I don't want to put you on the spot, but, if I were . . . oh, let's say if I were . . . gay . . . would it make a difference?" My heart thumped.

"Yes." Her chin quivered. "I would like you more."

"Oh . . . that's too bad, because I love your tits."

Her laugh was so loud it scared a flock of birds off the roof of the neighboring building. Her sense of humor was so dry I rarely heard her laugh. Especially not like that. The secretaries in the outer office stood up from their desks to see what was going on. Donna glanced back at them. "Let's put on a show." She put her hand on one side of my head and planted a big kiss on the opposite cheek. "They'll talk about us for weeks." She turned to go. "I'm taking you out to lunch today. I'll be back at 12:30."

"Don't I have a say in that?"

"No." And she was gone. She was my kind of woman.

* * *

Accounting isn't the most exciting work in the world, but it requires enough focus to distract me from all the other thoughts swirling around in my head. It also makes me feel like I'm bringing order to chaos. This was especially important to me now that the other part of my life was less orderly and predictable. Work had been my refuge for years.

I was deeply immersed in a financial statement when I realized, too late, that I hadn't closed my door after Donna left. A tapping noise made me look up. *Shit.* It was the cute guy from the tax department. *What's his name?*

"Hey, Adam. I hope I'm not disturbing you."

But you are. "No, not at all. What's up?"

"Um . . ." He squinted at me. "Do you know you have lipstick on your face?" He pointed to his own cheek.

"Oh, crap! How long has that been there?" I grabbed a tissue and scrubbed my cheek.

"How many times have you been kissed today?" He smiled, and I swear his teeth sparkled like they do in those chewing gum commercials.

"Donna was in here earlier. She did it."

"Oh, are you and Donna . . . " He knit his handsome blond brows.

It took me a minute to catch his drift. "No! God no, she's a married woman, and I'm not . . . interested." *Awkward!* "So, what can I do for you?"

"I was wondering if you'd like to grab lunch later."

"I'm having lunch with Donna today. But thanks."

"Too bad. That's another great tie, by the way. Where do you buy those?"

I looked down at my bland, striped tie. "I don't know . . . Sears?"

He laughed. "You're funny!"

Did I make a joke? I noticed the way his shirt followed the contours of his body.

"I was hoping to see you at Millie's house over the weekend. Most of the people from the office were there."

Someone named Millie works here? "Yeah, I'm not very sociable. I'm surprised people still invite me."

"They probably want to get to know you. Like I do."

"Mrowr, fofay." *Dammit! Not the gibberish again!*

He raised an arm to scratch the back of his head, accidentally flexing his respectable biceps. "We could have lunch another day."

Absolutely not! "Yeah, definitely. Let's do that." *What the fuck?!*

"Cool." He showed me his teeth again. "All right, see you later." As he left, three pairs of secretaries' eyes followed his butt down the hall, then turned back to shoot daggers at me. I closed my door tightly.

* * *

I'd had lunch with Donna many times before, but this was different. Now that she knew I was gay, I felt more relaxed with her. I didn't like to think my sexual orientation was that significant, but apparently it was. She suspected for a long time, but knowing how private I was, she didn't say anything.

She told me about her weekend with her husband, Kevin, an electrical contractor, and their three kids. It was nice to hear about an ordinary family doing ordinary things. I could tell she was a good mother from the way she talked about each of her children, what she worried about, and what she hoped for. She surprised me by saying how much my parents' death affected her parenting. Realizing she could suddenly be taken away from her children, she spent more time with them and made a point of showing her affection in a way that didn't come naturally to her.

"I worried about you after the funeral, Adam. We both have a hard shell we wear out here in the world, but you crawled so far into yours, I wasn't sure if you would ever come out. Lately, you've been more like your old self again. So . . . what changed?"

"In January this new tenant moved into the apartment above my garage."

"Yeah."

"I like him."

"Does he know that?"

"Now he does. And he's gay."

"That makes it easier. Does he like you?"

"Yes, he says . . . I believe he does."

"So . . . is there a problem?"

"I'm afraid it won't last."

"Why not?"

"He's a lot younger."

"How young? Is he legal?"

"Of course! I'm not an idiot. He's twenty."

"And you're what . . . twenty-eight?"

"Thirty-two."

"Oh, you look younger. Um . . . is he mature? Is he smart?"

"Yes, both."

"How do you feel when you're with him?"

"Half the time I'm scared out of my mind, and the other half, I'm so happy I could wet myself."

"Wow."

"I'm afraid I'll get hurt."

"Well . . . yes, you will. If you do it right, you're guaranteed to get hurt. It's part of the package."

"I don't understand."

She thought for a minute. "You know how they show Cupid firing arrows into people to symbolize falling in love? I didn't understand that until I fell in love with Kevin. It was wonderful, but I felt like I was wounded. It hurt to be away from him. After the honeymoon phase wore off, it hurt to be with him sometimes. The littlest things can sting like hell. It's not all sunshine and roses."

"Great."

"It's the same with my kids. I remember the first time my oldest son said he hated me because I wouldn't let him do something. You know how kids say, "You're the worst mother in the world!" I thought I would die. But I knew what was best for him. If you love them, that's what you do."

"That sounds exhausting. Is it worth it? Because I don't mind being alone."

"It's worth it, but it's hard. And vulnerability works both ways, Adam." She paused. "I want you to remember this. It is a terrible thing to find out how much you can hurt someone who loves you. I've done it. Early in our marriage, I hurt Kevin badly. And he forgave me." Her smile was tempered by sadness. "I didn't think anyone could love me that much. I had to learn the hard way."

"So you're saying I should go ahead and get hurt."

"I'm not talking about abuse, but . . . yeah . . . take the risk, be vulnerable. Love hurts, but I recommend it. My advice won't make any difference, though. I think the arrow is already in you."

I sighed. "I'm glad you're paying for this lunch because it's pretty depressing."

"Don't be such a baby. You can handle it. I can't believe you're thirty-two."

"I should have had lunch with . . . what's the name of the new guy in the tax department?"

"Henry? The guy I told you about?"

"I thought his name was Chad, but yeah. He invited me to lunch today, too."

"I knew he was after you. Did you tell him you're in a relationship?"

"Uhhh . . ."

"Do you want me to scare him away from you?"

"Why do you have to be involved?"

"Let's see . . . we've worked together for eight years and you just figured out we're friends. I think you might need some help with relationships."

"Why can't I have a friendly lunch with him, like this? Not everything is about sex, you know."

"You mean you're not putting out after I paid for lunch?"

"Bleh! That's gross!"

"Don't play with fire, Adam. Stay away from Henry."

"I know how to handle myself. Don't worry about it."

"You're going to be like one of my kids, aren't you? Except they have more sense than you."

"Come on. We need to get back to work."

* * *

After a more productive afternoon with fewer interruptions, I drove home in my pretty blue truck and saw the old washing machine and radiator from the basement sitting on one side of the driveway. Sam was putting a second coat of paint on the garden shed. He greeted me as I climbed out of the truck. "Hey boss, how does it look?"

"Great. How did you get so much done?"

"It turns out I didn't have to work today. I gave my two weeks' notice and the manager wanted me to leave immediately. He said he wouldn't accuse me of theft if I went away quietly."

"What theft?"

"All the meals I ate in the restaurant. He said they were worth a lot of money. I suppose he's right."

"I suppose he's a dick! What about the chef? Is he in trouble?"

"We negotiated about that. He won't get fired."

"How can you be sure?"

He hesitated. "I can be persuasive when I need to be."

Hmmm. Do I want to know what that means? I didn't ask. "It was nice of you to protect him."

"Yeah. So I won't get any more paychecks and my health insurance will be cut off at the end of the month. I'll go to the clinic tomorrow to get tested. I can start working for Dave this week."

"I'm glad things turned out okay."

"Where did you get that tie?"

"I don't remember. Do you like it?"

"No. How old is that?"

"Maybe it was my father's. Should I get rid of it?"

"Yes. In fact, I'll take it off you so I can throw it in the trash." I raised my chin as he reached forward to gently loosen the knot. It was kind of sexy. He drew the narrow tail through the knot and extracted it from my shirt.

"Someone complimented this tie today."

"Did this person have a white cane?" He unbuttoned my collar.

"You're not afraid to express your opinions, are you?"

He undid one more button on my shirt and twirled his fingertip in the tuft of hair on my collar bone. "If I were wearing something ugly, I would want you to tell me."

"You'd look good in anything." He rolled his eyes. "I see you brought the radiator up from the basement."

"Yeah, and I moved my weights down there."

"I wish I'd been here to watch that."

Sam grinned. "Don't start. I can't work with a boner. What time is dinner?"

"Does that mean you're hungry?"

"I could eat the asshole out of a skunk."

"Oh! I did not need that image in my head. I'm broiling salmon fillets. They won't take long." I walked toward the house. "Are you going to finish that coat of paint?"

"Yeah, after I burn this tie. I'll come in when I'm done."

* * *

Dinner was nearly ready when Sam came in the back door, freshly showered. He was wearing a snug black t-shirt that made me do a double take.

"I saw that!"

"Damn, you should warn me before you walk in here all sexed up."

"What? This old t-shirt?"

I laughed. "Don't pretend you didn't know what you were doing when you put that on."

He put his hands on my shoulders and kissed the back of my neck a few times. "I didn't greet you properly when you came home."

"I'll ruin your dinner if you keep that up."

"Ugh!" He pulled away. "You made salmon?"

"Yes, with jasmine rice and broccoli."

"Is that all?"

"Are you kidding?"

"Yes, I'm kidding." He planted another quick kiss on my neck. "I'll set the table."

"It's already done."

"Oh . . . then I'll have to kiss you until it's time to eat. There are no other options." I turned to look at him. He smiled and shrugged.

"What got into you?"

"I don't know. I'm glad to be done with the Harbor View."

"You can put the rice and broccoli in those bowls while I make the sauce."

"Okay. It smells great."

When everything was done I brought a bowl of wasabi cream sauce to the dining room where Sam was already piling food on his plate. "This might be too spicy for you. I should get a pitcher of ice water."

"Why? Do I look like I can't take it?" He puffed out his chest.

"Have you ever had wasabi?"

"Wasa-what?" I liked this goofy mood he was in. "Stop fussing over me. I can handle your spicy food." He ladled a generous portion of sauce over the salmon on his plate.

"You might want to try a little bit before you dig in."

"Shush! I'm hungry." He took a big saucy bite. I watched him quietly. "Mmmm!" He swallowed, doing his best to hide his reaction, but I could see it. His smile became a grimace before he jumped up and rushed into the kitchen.

I shook my head. *Donna's right. I'm already in love with him.*

After a brief absence, Sam came back to the table with a pitcher of ice water and a box of tissues. "I must be coming down with a cold. My sinuses are draining, and I feel dehydrated."

I played along with his false excuse. "I'm sorry to hear that."

Bravely, he continued eating the salmon.

"Are you going to ask me about my day at the office?"

"I'm sorry, how was your day?"

"Interesting. I did something that will make you proud of me. I came out to my friend Donna."

His face lit up. "Really? I am proud of you! I'll reward you for that later." He winked.

"I'll remind you. She took me out to lunch and we talked about relationship stuff."

"Did you tell her about me?" He filled his plate again.

"Yes, I did."

"You did? What did you tell her?" He picked up the bowl of sauce.

"You don't have to eat the sauce if you don't . . ."

"I like it!" he snapped. "Continue your story. What did you say about me?"

"I told her you were a buck-toothed yokel who showed up on my doorstep, and I took you in because I felt sorry for you."

"It's best to be honest. Did you mention my doughnut addiction?"

"No, I didn't want to turn her against you right away."

"Thank you. What's her story? Is she married?"

"Yeah. Husband, three kids. She has an interesting view of love and how difficult it can be. She says it's painful, but worth it."

Sam nodded. "That sounds right."

"It does? Why?"

"Most things worth having require work and sacrifice."

"What about pain? I don't like the sound of that."

"That's the risk you take. When you love someone, they can hurt you more than they could if you didn't care about them."

"That's pretty much what Donna said." I took another piece of salmon before he made it all disappear. "How do you know these things at your age?"

He pointed his fork at me. "First of all, I'm almost twenty-one, so I'm not a spring chicken."

"I stand corrected."

"Secondly, you're talking as if you never heard about love being painful, but you have."

"Where have I heard it?"

"In the book . . . *Tess.* She suffers more with the man she loves than she did with the guy she didn't love."

I thought about it, and he was right. *Does he have to be smarter than me on top of everything else?* "How much more did you read?"

"I picked it up before I went to bed last night and I couldn't put it down. I can't believe Angel ran off to fucking Brazil when he found out Tess wasn't a virgin. What an asshole! But Tess still loves him, even though she's working herself to death since he abandoned her. And she refuses help from that other jerk, Alec, when he shows up again and offers to take care of her. She's better off starving."

"Is that as far as you got?" He nodded. "I should have given you a different book."

"Why? I love it."

"It's very dark."

"It's real. People have relationships like that. Most aren't that bad, I hope. You told me *Tess* was one of your favorite books. Why do you like it so much?"

I should have seen that coming. I had to think about it.

Sam moved the last salmon fillet to his plate. "Well? I'm waiting."

"I'm thinking!" I had to admit, I liked the darkness of the story, and I had many similar books. But why? *Does it reflect my experience?* I didn't have any experience. *Do I expect relationships to be like that?* Probably. *Then why am I trying to talk Sam out of thinking that way?* Good question.

Sam was trying to distract me by performing fellatio on a stalk of broccoli. Even as a child, I was never as playful as he was. He was awakening my belief in the sweet romance and happy endings I had been rolling my eyes at for so many years. I didn't want him to become as cynical as me.

I was ready to answer his question. "I can't believe you're getting me to admit this, but I like the novel because it reinforces my pessimistic view of relationships. I don't want you to be as pessimistic as I am."

"It's only a book, Adam. I don't expect our relationship to be like theirs. And let me assure you . . . no one could be as pessimistic as you. That's a competition I wouldn't bother to enter."

"Thanks a lot."

"You're welcome."

"So you won't run off to Brazil?"

He looked surprised. "Wait . . . you're comparing me to Angel?" He let it sink in. "That would mean you're Tess. No way! I'm the young and innocent character in this story."

"No, *you* seduced *me!*"

"Then I'm Alec? I guess that could work."

"So you admit you seduced me!"

His eyes grew bigger. "I . . . no!" He pushed his chair away from the table.

"You seduced me with the ice cream!" I rose from my chair.

He couldn't help smiling. "That was completely innocent! I wanted you to taste it!"

"And that tight shirt . . ." I approached his chair.

"A lot of my shirts are tight now! What am I supposed to wear?"

I mocked him in a high-pitched voice. "I'm taking off my shirt in the yard, Adam."

"Oh, come on!" His protests softened while I kissed him. "I'm an innocent farm boy at the mercy of an evil accountant. I wouldn't know how to seduce anyone." He put his hands behind his head and flexed his biceps, stretching the sleeves of his black t-shirt. My hands moved in that direction, but before I could get there he lowered his arms. "Ah, ah, ah . . . no touching. Shouldn't I get dessert before you take advantage of me?"

I exhaled like a deflating balloon. "You're definitely the evil character. I suppose you need ice cream to cool down your mouth after that wasabi." I kissed his lower lip.

"I didn't have a problem with your wabaseebee. I can handle whatever you dish out."

"That sounds like a challenge." I turned to see what was left on the table. "You ate everything. What a stud."

"It feels great in here." He drummed his fingers on his abdomen. I know I keep saying this, but he was so damned sexy. I reminded myself to make an appointment for STD testing.

We took the dishes into the kitchen where Sam selected a pint of ice cream. He ate it standing up while I filled the sink. "Adam . . . where can we make out without breaking furniture?"

"Huh. That's a question I never thought I would be asked."

"I'm planning ahead." He wandered around the kitchen, looking closely at pictures and knickknacks.

"Um . . . I don't know. Can't we let things develop and see where we end up?"

"Okay, Mr. Spontaneous. I can't believe you said that without having any wine."

"Oh, yeah? I'd like to go all spontaneous on your ass right now, but I'm not sure you could handle it."

He grunted dismissively, too focused on an old photograph on the wall to see me creeping up behind him. I carefully slipped my arms around his waist and planted my hands on his stomach. He jumped and squirmed. "Hey, I almost dropped my ice cream!"

"Was that too spontaneous?" He twisted himself around to face me, leaning against the wall. I slipped my hands under his t-shirt and felt his solid, warm flesh. He didn't object, so I lifted the hem of his shirt to see what I was touching. "Wow!" He arched his lower back, offering himself to me while he finished his ice cream.

I explored his narrow waist, marveling at the lean muscularity of it. I ruffled the trail of hair below his navel with my thumb. He crushed the empty ice cream carton in one hand, threw it on the table, and carefully tossed his spoon toward the sink where it plopped into the dishwater. "Show off." I patted his belly.

He raised the hem of his shirt. "You like my tummy?"

"I love your tummy. I can't believe how flat it is." He flexed his abs, bunching them into stony lumps. "Oh man, I never thought I would see this up close, let alone touch it." I noticed a bulge in his shorts and thought he would ask me to back off. While I had the chance, I leaned forward and kissed one of his abdominal muscles.

"Okay, slow down, Adam." He covered himself with his t-shirt.

I wiped the drool off my mouth. "Thanks for dessert."

He grinned. "I didn't think you had that in you."

"I surprised myself, but it was totally worth it. I'll be replaying that in my head tonight."

He growled quietly. "We'd better get the dishes done. I'll wash."

I took a clean towel out of the drawer and stood next to him at the sink. "I need to get a dishwasher."

"Why? I like washing dishes with you. It's one of our things. When I'm washing dishes in my apartment I think, 'I wish Adam were here.' That's not the only time I think that."

How lucky am I? "Now that you mention it, I looked forward to doing the dishes when we first started eating together. We had some of our best conversations at the sink."

"I know. And it was the only time I could get near you." He bumped his hip against mine.

"So, you'll start working with Dave tomorrow? Do you know what you'll be doing?"

"I need to learn about the stock so I can help people find things, and I'll move on from there."

"Do you know what your hours will be?"

"We have to work it out, but he wants me there on weekends and most evenings because that's when it's busy."

"Oh." This was not good news. "We won't be spending as much time together."

"I know, I'm not happy about it, but I need the money. Could we eat dinner later? Maybe around eight?"

"Yeah, I suppose. I'll have more time to cook after work."

"And I'll be here every night. No more dinner shifts at the restaurant."

"That's true. But the weekends . . . when will we have lunch with Flora? We were going to use the pool."

"Maybe we could do a Sunday dinner. Can you take any time off during the week?"

"I don't know. I've never taken time off."

"We'll work it out. Other people do it."

"I know, you're right. I don't know why I'm so disappointed. I never expected to have someone like you in my life anyway. I should be happy with whatever time we have together."

"We'll make the most of it." We continued doing the dishes in silence. "It'll be fine, Adam." He drained the sink and rinsed it out, and we were finished. "Come here and kiss me."

After a nice kiss on the lips, he drew me into a tight hug. I wanted to get back to the playful mood we had going before we talked about his work schedule. "You promised me a reward for telling Donna I'm gay."

"That's right, I did. What would you like?"

I quietly asked, "Will you flex your arm for me again?"

His eyebrows went up. "You liked that, huh? Okay." He raised his arm and flexed, looking at his biceps. He relaxed and flexed again, as if he didn't get it right the first time.

"That's beautiful. Can I touch it?"

"Yeah. I'll have to get used to this." He blushed.

I put one hand under his arm and the other over the ball of muscle. "It's so hard. For as long as I can remember, I've wanted to do this with a guy built like you."

"I've seen bigger arms at the gym. I'm not huge or anything."

"I'm impressed. You should be proud."

"I don't know. It seems . . . arrogant. But it feels good, and I like the way it looks."

"It looks great, especially when you wear a shirt like that." He looked uncomfortable. I glanced down to see a tent in his shorts, bigger than my own, so I let go of his arm. "Thanks, I enjoyed that."

He grimaced and pressed on his erection. "This thing is starting to get on my nerves."

"I know, mine too." I adjusted myself carefully. "Sam, I want you to understand, I love your body, but I wouldn't be doing any of this if you weren't such a wonderful guy. You've been so patient and sweet." I laid my hand over his heart. "This is the best part of you." *I can say it.* "I love you, Sam."

He held his breath and searched my face.

"I love you. I do. You're the best thing that ever happened to me."

Tears came to his eyes. Or were those mine? I'm not sure. He scooped me into his arms and I wrapped my limbs around him, trying with all my strength to merge our bodies into one entity. We kissed the way we did the night before, hot and urgent, coming up for air, slowing down and starting again, over and over until we were exhausted.

Did he say it? Yes, more than once. I already knew, because he showed it day after day. Still, it was good to hear it. When we said good night and he went back to his apartment, it was difficult for him. But he knew I wasn't ready yet. I would be, soon, but not yet. That night, for the first time, as I lay in my bed and waited for sleep, I imagined him sleeping next to me.

11

Once Sam started working at the nursery with Dave, our interactions during the week were more regular. He came home after seven, we ate dinner, and we had a couple of hours to enjoy each other's company before it was time to sleep. We continued to learn more about each other through our conversations and during the gradual development of our physical intimacy. Predictably, there were bumps in the road.

I spent a lot of time thinking about Sam's body and what I would like to do with it. But a lifetime of pleasuring myself with two-dimensional images and vaporous fantasies didn't prepare me for a real-life sexual relationship. Pictures on the internet didn't talk or have feelings or want anything, but Sam did. He wanted me.

On a warm night in June, after eating meatloaf with mashed potatoes and gravy, Sam rose from the dining room table and lured me into the living room by pulling off his shirt. With a disarming kiss, he effortlessly wrestled me to the floor in the middle of the oriental rug. He sprawled on his back and purred contentedly. "That's my favorite meal. I wouldn't complain if you made meatloaf three times a week."

I reclined next to him and rubbed his chest, feeling the thickness of his pectoral muscles. "You look hunkier. Are you doing something different?"

"More bench presses with more weight. Does it please you?"

I grinned. "It pleases me very much." I lightly tickled one of his nipples and watched it rise and harden.

He rolled onto his side, pushed me onto my back, and kissed me, first on my forehead, then down the side of my face and neck to my collarbone. "Take off your shirt so I can kiss more of you."

"Oh, you don't want to do that." I tried to distract him by tickling his other nipple.

"Um . . . I'm pretty sure I do. I've been wanting to do that for a long time now."

"We should do the dishes." I tried to sit up, but he put his hand in the middle of my chest and gently pushed me back down.

"Adam . . ." He looked me in the eye. "What are you worried about?"

"I'm not worried." I was worried. "I think it's best to get the dishes done before we get too comfortable." I tried to sit up again. "Unf!" He kept me pinned to the floor without even pressing on my chest. I found this both frustrating and arousing. "You like doing the dishes with me!"

"This isn't about the dishes. What is it?"

"Wha . . . you always think there's some . . . hidden . . . reason . . . okay, fine! I'm not comfortable with my body. I would rather get comfortable with your body before we work on the other thing."

"What other thing?"

"The . . . the . . . my part. My thing. You know . . . me."

"Is it this part?" He put the tip of his finger at the top of my chest and played with a tuft of hair.

"That part's okay, but . . ."

"You feel warm. Let me open this one button to give you a little more air." He pushed my collar back and nuzzled my chest. "Mmm, you smell good."

"I probably dribbled gravy on myself."

"Let me check." He licked my breast bone with his wide, wet tongue.

"Oh . . . there's no need for that." But it felt so good.

"I don't taste gravy, but there's something . . . there . . ."

"What?"

"I can't quite see it." He undid another button and slid his hand under my shirt.

"Ah! I know what you're doing!"

"I'm looking for something." He rubbed my chest and probed me with his fingertips until he found a nipple.

"Ow!" He pinched it. "Don't do that!"

"What is that?"

"You know perfectly well what it . . . Ow! I told you not to . . ."

"Is it a growth? Like a tumor?"

"Very funny! That's a good thing to joke about."

"I'm concerned about your health. I think there's another one over here."

"Ow! Hey! You're making my penis hurt!" I sounded like a twelve-year-old.

“Are these the knobs that control your boner?"

I wanted to smack him, or kiss him, but his hand was still on my chest, so I grabbed one of his nipples and twisted it. "There! How do you like it?!" He winced and sucked air through his teeth, so I let go.

"That felt good. Do the other one."

"No. I refuse." He was turning my crank, but I wasn't ready to cooperate. Fortunately, Sam had figured out my 'I'm saying one thing, but I want something else' brand of fuckedupness. Is that a word?

"Okay, back to you, then." He knelt over me, straddling my body. I tried to sit up again. "No, you stay there."

"Sam!"

"Sam, what?" He put his hands on his hips. "I'm working my ass off to look good for you, and I let you touch me all the time, but you won't even take off your shirt for me?"

"I know, you're right, but . . . I need more time. I mean . . . look at you! I can't live up to that."

"You don't have to. I like your body." He sighed. "Maybe it's a mistake to keep working out if you can't feel comfortable with me. I could go on a diet and get back to the way I looked when . . ."

"Okay, okay! No more crazy-talk. What do you want from me?"

He placed his hands on the floor so he was looking straight down at me. "This is the new rule: I get to touch the same parts of your body that you touch on my body."

"But . . ."

"Adam . . ."

I took a deep breath and conceded. "All right."

"That's a good boy." He dipped his head down and kissed me on the mouth - a nice slow one, with tongue.

"You want to do this now? We couldn't wait until next week?"

"No." He sat up and opened two more buttons on my shirt. "I don't know why you're being so shy. I've seen you with your shirt off."

"I look better from a distance."

"I disagree." He ran his hands over my chest and ribs. "Let's get this shirt off." He undid the last two buttons. "Sit up."

I did as I was told. "You're bossy today." I liked him that way, but I didn't want to tell him yet.

"Well, you're acting like a cranky child . . . sometimes I can't believe you're twelve years older than me."

"Oh, great . . . remind me of the age difference. That's what I needed."

"Quit whining and get your arm out of that sleeve." After tossing my shirt aside, he silenced me with another kiss while easing me back onto the carpet. He lay on his side next to me with one of his legs across mine to prevent my escape.

"Now what?"

"Now I get to look at my hot boyfriend and grope his hot body."

"Yeah? When is he getting here?"

He shook his head. "I could have had other guys, Adam. I wanted you."

I held my tongue. It was unusual for him to acknowledge his options.

He moved his hand slowly up and down, back and forth, feeling my skin, my flesh, my bones. I wanted him to stay away from certain parts, but there was no point in saying it. How could I explain the uneasy feeling rising within me? This was particularly true around my belly, where I felt soft and vulnerable. He was very gentle, and spoke quietly. "I love your chest. I like where the hair is, and where it's not."

"I should do more pushups."

"Whatever. I'm not attracted to those guys who spend half their lives in the gym. You look like the men I admired when I was growing up." He kissed random spots on my torso while he talked. "They'd work all day on their farms, doing hard physical labor. They never looked like the guys at the health club, but their bodies were strong and masculine."

"My dad looked like that, even though he worked in an office most of his life."

"If he looked like you, I bet he was a DILF."

I snickered quietly. The thought of someone wanting to fuck my dad was . . . *eew*.

"And those farmers didn't eat egg white omelets and tuna . . . they ate the food they produced and burned it off with real work." He traced my ribs with his fingertip. "They never talked about exercise or working out . . . it was just plain work."

"Didn't they get fat eventually?" I would think of that.

"Some did, especially after they got married, and they weren't ashamed of it. People would say things like, 'Hank, it looks like marriage agrees with you,' and Hank would rub his belly and say, 'Yeah, she takes good care of me.' He wasn't only talking about her cooking." He smiled. "Farmers are hot . . . but now I like accountants."

"Is that a step up, or down?"

"Up . . . definitely up." He kissed my shoulder and upper arm. I tried to relax and let him do his thing. He straddled my legs, then carefully laid his hands on the flesh around my waist. "I like this."

I didn't like it. It triggered something in me . . . a deep vulnerability no one had ever seen. "I know I have a spare tire, but I've been running every day, and I lost a few pounds . . ."

"Adam . . ."

"I need to lay off ice cream, and wine, and . . .'

"Adam, did you hear me?"

My heart was beating too fast. "What?"

"I like your little tummy."

"You shouldn't. It's bad. It's bad for my health."

"It's normal. It's not a spare tire and you're not overweight. I can see your ribs." He leaned on his elbows to kiss a spot above my belly button.

He wasn't doing anything I hadn't done to him, but there was a reason I put him off for so long. A swarm of confusing emotions and irrational fears came buzzing out of their hive. His lips traveled across my abdomen leaving wet tracks and goosebumps. I laced my fingers into his hair. "Please don't do that. Why are you doing that?"

"Because you're beautiful, and I love you, and I want you."

I felt like crying but didn't know why. "I'm not. I'm not beautiful. Can't you see that?"

"My eyesight is fine, thank you." He kissed the soft bulge at the side of my waist.

I pulled his hair. "Don't! That's disgusting!"

"I think it's sexy."

"Well . . . you're wrong! You're fucked up!"

Sam hesitated for a moment, confused by my tone. "Maybe I am, but this is what I like." He ran his fingertip around my navel.

I grabbed my hair with both hands. A wave of guilt washed over me. I wanted to keep it inside, but I spit it out in a low, bitter voice. "You could have done so much better than me. What the hell is wrong with you?"

He sighed and rested his forehead on my chest. "I got exactly what I wanted, Adam. I wanted you."

I knew I was ruining everything. "I'm sorry, I shouldn't have said that. I'm so stupid!"

Realizing something was off, Sam looked up. His expression changed immediately. "What's wrong, Adam?"

"I don't know! I should be happy, but I'm ruining it!"

"Shh, shh, shh, it's okay, you're not ruining anything. Was I going too fast?"

I didn't want to say what was coming. It was irrational and desperate, but I couldn't stop it. "Please don't leave me, Sam. Please!"

"What are you talking about? I'm not leaving you. I just got here. I love you."

"I know!" I grabbed my hair again. "I know you do, but why? It doesn't make any sense!" I didn't want to say that either.

He was confused. "It doesn't have to make sense. I love you, and that's all there is to it."

"But you know what I'm like. Sooner or later . . ."

"No."

"I'll hurt you, I know I will."

"I'll take my chances."

"I'll disappoint you."

"No, you won't."

"You don't know that."

"Yes, I do."

"I'll disappoint you, and you'll leave me."

"I won't leave you!" He refused to give in.

The pain was terrible - I've never felt anything like it. If he had been weaker, if he were more easily frustrated, if he could have given up on me, I wouldn't have had to say it. But I did. It came out of me in a tortured voice I had never heard before: "Everyone leaves me!"

And there it was: the irrational foundation for my fear and loneliness. I knew who I was talking about, but Sam was one step behind.

"Who left you?"

"They did! My parents!"

"They didn't leave you . . . it was an accident . . . they died."

"I know, but . . . people kept saying, 'God has a plan' and . . . 'Everything happens for a reason.'"

"No . . . not everything."

"What if they were right?"

"You don't believe that. It was an accident."

"They could have been happier. I could have been . . ."

"It had nothing to do with you."

"If I had been normal, they could have had grandchildren."

"Oh, God, don't do this, Adam."

"They had to be disappointed . . . I was so fucking weird . . . I didn't even have friends."

"Stop, please." There were tears in his eyes.

I struggled to contain the next thing that entered my head, but it hurt too much to keep it in. "Are you my friend?" My pathetic insecurity made me cringe. I thought he would realize he had to get away from me. *He should go. I'm too needy. I'll drag him down.*

But he cradled my head and put his lips close to my ear. "Yes, I'm your friend, and I won't leave you. I promise I won't leave you. I won't leave you. I won't leave you. I won't leave you." He whispered it again and again until I stopped crying and was breathing normally. Sam gently stroked my arm.

"I'm sorry I ruined it."

He kissed my temple. "You didn't ruin anything. I got to second base."

I was quiet for a minute. "I'm fucked up, Sam."

"No, you're not. You miss them."

"I think it's more than that."

"Hmm. Maybe." His finger traced circles on my chest. "I'm sorry I pinched your nipples."

"It's okay, I liked it."

"That's not what you said."

"Half the things I say to you are lies."

"I don't think of them as lies. You have a . . . creative way of expressing yourself."

I shook my head. "You are so full of shit."

He smiled and kissed my chin. "Are you seeing your doctor tomorrow to get tested?"

"Yeah, during my lunch hour."

"Could you do me a favor?" He kissed my neck.

"What?"

"Could you ask him about your weight?" He kissed my shoulder and wrapped his arm around me. "Ask him if he wants you to lose more weight."

I hesitated, but knew there was only one correct answer. "Okay."

"Thanks."

I waited for him to say more, but he didn't. "It's getting late. We should do the dishes."

"No, I'll do the dishes tonight. You go to bed." He stood up and walked to the dining room.

"Why?"

"Because you're tired, and you did all the cooking, and I'm very grateful." He put on his shirt and smoothed it over his torso.

"I can help with dishes. I'm not that tired." I reached for my shirt.

"You look tired, but . . . I tell you what . . . I'll allow you to help with the dishes if you let me stay with you tonight."

"You'll *allow* me to help? Wait, what was that other part?"

He looked at me with big eyes. "I need to stay with you . . . I don't want to be alone tonight."

His reason wasn't convincing, but I went along. "Well, if you need it."

"I'll sleep on the floor next to the bed."

"You're not sleeping on the floor."

"We'll figure it out later."

After the dishes were dried and put away and the lights were turned off, Sam followed me up the stairs. He watched me brush my teeth, then borrowed my toothbrush to do the same while I changed into a t-shirt and boxer shorts. When I turned down the bed covers, he hesitantly entered the room and waited for me to get settled. The bed was large, but I took my usual position closest to the door. He was standing on the other side of the bed. "Are you sleeping in your clothes?"

"No, in my underwear. I'm waiting for you to turn off the light."

I rolled on my side and switched off the bedside lamp. I heard him take off his clothes and set them on a chair before lying down, leaving plenty of distance between us. I still felt the warmth from his body. For a few minutes, I listened to the sounds the house made as it settled down for the night.

"Sam?"

"Yeah?"

"Could you put your arm around me like you did before?"

"Sure." We moved toward the middle of the bed where he draped his arm over my side and spread his hand on my chest. "How's that?" The tip of his nose touched the back of my neck.

"That's good. Thank you."

I fell asleep listening to him breathe.

***

I woke to the sound of my alarm clock and immediately felt something was missing. Sam was gone. On the bed where he had slept, there was a plate holding a big powdery doughnut and a small note. "Eat this. I love you."

I couldn't remember the last time I ate a doughnut. This was a heavy bismarck with something like chocolate frosting sticking out of one end. I propped myself against the headboard and bit into it, sprinkling powdered sugar down the front of my t-shirt. The filling was so sweet it should have had a warning label, but I liked it. I automatically felt guilty and put my hand on my stomach. Remembering the night before, I pulled up my shirt to look at myself. *I can't believe Sam likes this.* When I took another bite of the doughnut, a blob of chocolate cream dropped onto my belly. I smiled. *If he were here, he'd be all over that.*

It was difficult to concentrate at work that morning while I was rehearsing the conversation I would have with my doctor. I not only had to talk to him about gay sex and STDs, but he would probably scold me about my weight. I hadn't done what he recommended last year. I tried to stay calm. *He's a nice guy. How bad could it be?*

The dreaded time for the appointment arrived. As I left my office, someone called my name. "Hey, Adam! Are you heading out for lunch?"

I turned around to see Henry trotting toward me, as sleek as a greyhound. *Crap!* "Hey, uh . . . no, I have a doctor's appointment."

"Is everything okay? You look great."

"Fruff." *Dammit!* "I'm fine. It's my annual check-up."

He stood a little too close to me. "I was hoping we could grab the lunch we talked about."

"Oh yeah . . . sorry, today's not good." I took a step away from him.

He took a step forward and smiled. His tanned complexion made his teeth look whiter than ever. "I'm starting to think you're avoiding me."

"No! Why would I do that? I'll definitely get back to you, but I have to go now."

"Are you available Friday?"

"Uh . . . yeah, sure. Why not?" *Shit!*

"Great! It's a date, then."

"Um . . ."

"I'll just skip lunch today and do cardio at the gym."

"Well . . . enjoy that. I'll see you later."

"See you Friday."

Fuck!

The nurse at Dr. Rubin's office took my vital signs and weighed me before ushering me into the exam room. I had lost six pounds since my last visit, more than I thought. When Rubin came in he was pleasant, as always, making small talk before getting down to business.

"So, the last time we met you told me you weren't sexually active, but I understand you'd like to be tested for sexually transmitted diseases. Have you been sexually active?"

"No, but I'm planning to be."

"Okay, but you can't catch anything from thinking about it."

"I know, but the guy I'm seeing thought we should get tested before we . . . um . . . have . . ."

"Have sexual intercourse? That's a smart precaution. I wish more of my patients were that careful. Has he been tested recently?"

"Yes. He's fine."

"Good. Was he tested for HIV, herpes, syphilis, gonorrhea . . ."

"Yes, everything."

"Did he show you the results?"

"Yes, I saw them. He's clean. He takes a lot of showers." I was joking.

"That doesn't prevent STDs."

"I know. I was . . . never mind. But he smells good." *Shut up!*

"Good to know. I assume you want all the same tests."

"Yes."

"Okay. Let's have you strip down to your underwear and hop up on the table so I can examine you."

I hate this part.

"Have you been under any unusual stress lately?"

"Um . . . I don't know . . . I don't think so. Well . . . I guess it depends."

"You're uncertain. Lie down, please. Have you been seeing the psychologist I recommended?"

"Uh, I . . . I think I lost his card."

"Does this hurt?"

"No."

"Sit up, please. You could have called the office to get his name again."

"I've been meaning to, but I was busy."

"For an entire year you've been too busy to make a phone call? Take a deep breath for me, please. Again . . . again . . . again . . . okay."

"I'd like to get his name again, and I promise I'll . . . "

"I see you've lost six pounds. Do you remember what I told you last time?"

"Yes."

"Stand up, please, and pull down your shorts. What did I say last time?"

"That I should gain a few pounds."

"Five pounds. I'm going to examine your genitals. I asked you to gain five pounds. Do you know how many of my patients would love to hear me say that?"

"Yes."

"Turn your head and cough, please." *Cough!* "Again, please." *Cough!* "Okay, keep your shorts off but lie down again. Are you vomiting after meals?"

"No, I don't do that."

"What have you eaten so far today?"

"A doughnut. A big one."

"Anything else?"

"Coffee?"

"Coffee. How many per day?"

"Like . . . how many pots?"

"Never mind. Are you planning to have lunch today?"

"This is my lunch hour, so I won't be . . . "

"No lunch and lots of coffee. Okay, I'll do a urethral swab as part of the STD testing. Try to relax."

"Wait, you're not putting that in my . . ."

"Hold still."

"AH! Ah, ah!"

"There, that wasn't so bad, was it?"

"I didn't like it."

"You can get dressed."

"Jeez! You'd think they would come up with a more comfortable way to do that."

"We usually don't do that unless you have symptoms."

"I don't have symptoms"

"I do it that way for guys who don't follow my recommendations."

"What? That's . . . can you do that?"

"I just did. Have a seat." He scribbled notes in my chart. "I'll have the lab take blood and urine samples before you go, and I want to make sure your electrolytes aren't out of whack . . . liver, kidney and thyroid functioning . . . are you having trouble sleeping?"

"No."

"Okay." He wheeled his stool to where I was sitting. "Look at me."

Reluctantly, I looked him in the eye.

"Are you okay?"

"I don't know. In some ways, I'm better. I mean, this guy I'm with . . . he's great and he's been good for me. But it's bringing up some . . . weird stuff. I should have seen that psychologist. I know I need to see someone."

"They'll give you his card at the desk. He's good, I've seen him myself. Do you want me to prescribe something for depression?"

"No, I don't want to gain . . . weight." I should have stopped myself.

Dr. Rubin looked at me for a very long minute. "You have to promise me you'll see this guy."

"I promise."

"Cut down on coffee, and I want you to gain ten pounds. Does your boyfriend have trouble eating?"

"Uh, no, he does not."

"Good. You'll get a copy of your test results in about a week, but I want you back here in three months. Not a year . . . three months. Is that clear?"

"Yes."

"I know where you live."

"Um . . . are you allowed to . . ."

"Don't test me, Adam! Schedule before you leave here, and get something for lunch on your way back to the office. Any other questions?"

"No. That's it."

"Always good to see you. Don't forget to stop in the lab."

"Thank you."

"Enjoy your lunch." He closed the door.

Huh. That wasn't as bad as I expected.

* * *

That evening, I greeted Sam with a hug when he came in the back door. "Nice!" he said. "What did I do to deserve this?"

"Just being yourself." I tilted my head up to kiss him. "There's an appetizer in case you're hungry." I pointed to a plate of crackers with squiggles of cheese on them.

"Is that spray cheese? I love spray cheese."

"I had a feeling you would."

"This is so nice. Are you having some?" He sat down at the kitchen table.

"I already did. Those are yours."

"Have another one. Come on."

"I already had some. I can't eat as much as you do."

"Well, I'm not very hungry either. I think I'll pass."

I knew why he was doing this. "Fine, I'll have another one." I shoved a whole cracker in my mouth.

"It's good, isn't it?"

"I wrow! I wready hadsum!" My mouth was full.

"Then why are you eating mine? You're so rude." He popped one in his mouth and smiled. He had a gift for being adorably annoying. It made my groin tingle. "How was your day at the office?"

"Fine. How are things at Dave's?" I continued to prepare dinner.

"Busy, but I like it. Dave asked why you haven't been there lately."

"I don't need anything."

"You don't have to buy anything. Come for a visit."

"One of these days. By the way, thanks for the doughnut. It was delicious. I never had one of those before."

"Those are my favorite. How did it go with your doctor today? Did you get your tests done?"

"Yeah. Hey, when you had yours done, did they stick a swab in your penis?"

"No, they took blood and urine. Did your doctor do that?"

"Yeah." *I guess Rubin wasn't kidding.* "He's very thorough."

Sam had eaten all the crackers and was looking in the refrigerator. "Do you like him?"

"I do. He cares, and he knows how to motivate me."

Sam found the can of cheese, stuck the nozzle in his mouth and sprayed.

"We have more crackers."

"I wrike id dis wray." He savored the fatty, salty goo until it oozed down his throat. "Did you ask him about your weight?"

"He brought it up."

"And?"

I muttered.

"What was that?"

"He wants me to gain ten pounds."

"Oh my God, that's awesome!" He wrapped his arms around me from behind. "I can feed you ice cream every night, and we can eat more pizza." He kissed me behind one ear.

"You knew he would say that, didn't you?"

"You'll be so sexy, I won't let you wear clothes in the house anymore."

"You knew, right?"

"When will you get your test results?"

"In about a week. You're not answering my question."

"What question? What are you making? It smells wonderful. Or is that you?"

"You're . . . annoying, do you know that?"

"Yes, I do. What's for dinner?"

12

On Friday, I woke up feeling like something bad was about to happen. Then I remembered my lunch "date" with Henry. *Why do I do this to myself?* I thought about calling in sick, but he would ask me again the next week. *I should be more optimistic.* He seemed nice enough. *Maybe he's looking for a friend, or a mentor. Yeah . . . he probably wants my advice.* I put on a French blue shirt and my most expensive tie. I'm . . . not sure why I did that.

At the appointed time, Henry came to my office and placed one hand on each side of the door frame, stretching his perfect white shirt across his chest. He had nipples. He was a good-looking guy, as I've said. His pants were so tight, I thought I could see his . . . is this too much detail?

Henry smiled. "Hey buddy. Wow, look at you! I'm flattered."

"You're . . . this? You look . . . that's a nice . . . so where are we going?" *Articulate as usual.*

"You have an interesting way of talking. Is Sylvia's okay?"

Very trendy. "Sure. Sounds good. Uh, shall we? You lead the way."

"Hey guys!" *Shit!* It was Donna. "Where are you going?" Her eyes accused me of something.

"Lunch."

"Oh, can I join you?" Henry made a face and my palms felt sweaty.

"No, it's just for dudes. No girls allowed." I knew I would pay for that later.

"Oh, okay, *dude.* I'll see you later, *dude.* There's an account I need to discuss with you as soon as you return. The very minute you return. Got it?"

"Got it." I caught up with Henry.

"Is she your boss?"

"No, no. A friend."

"She didn't sound friendly."

"Maybe she has a sore throat."

"I'm glad we're finally doing this. I was afraid she would ruin it."

"Ruin what? Wait, you mean lunch, but . . . Sylvia's, huh? Have you been there?"

"Yes, I used to date one of the waiters."

It was a beautiful, sunny day, so we walked to the restaurant where we were greeted by an attractive young man who was a little too excited.

"Henry! Hi! We have your table ready. I was afraid we wouldn't see you here anymore since you and Ken had your little . . . drama. I'm so glad he's not working here anymore. That was soooo awkward." He led us to a table on the outdoor deck with a view of the water. "I made sure you got the very best table. Who's your handsome friend?"

"This is Adam, we work together. Thanks for the great table."

"Oh, no problem at all. *Any* time at all. Welcome, Adam. Melissa will be your server today." He lowered his voice. "Henry, if you ever want to talk, you can call me any time, day or night." He handed Henry a small piece of paper.

"Thanks, I appreciate that." As soon as his admirer went away, Henry crushed the piece of paper and dropped it over the side of the deck.

"I guess you won't be calling him."

"If I wanted him, I would have had him already. You've never been here before?"

"No, I don't get out much." I looked at the menu. "Does that happen to you a lot? Guys giving you their numbers?"

"Yeah, pretty much. You, too, I suppose."

"Uff! No. Well, once . . . a pizza delivery guy."

"Did you call him?"

"No! No, I would never . . ."

"Why not?"

"Well, I'm with . . . I'm in a . . . relationship, so . . ."

"I didn't know that. And you're monogamous?"

"Um, yeah. I . . . assume we are."

"You can't assume anything. Is this a new relationship?"

"Yeah, pretty new."

"So, you know how it goes. Once you've had all the sex you want, and you finally get to know each other, that's when you discover all the other shit he's been doing."

"I know, that's . . . so true." *And the lying begins!* "I think this guy is different."

He snickered. "That's funny. It's so stupid, but we all think that, don't we?"

We do? "Yeah, we're all so stupid!"

"Men can't be monogamous. It's a scientific fact."

"Scientific?"

"Yeah, we're biologically programmed to reproduce as much as possible, so it doesn't make any sense to have sex with only one partner."

"But gay sex doesn't produce . . ."

"It's the same principle. We need to spread our seed around, like plants."

"Oh . . . you're right. Plants do that. Huh." The waitress arrived, and I ordered lobster macaroni and cheese. When Henry ordered a tofu salad with no dressing, I felt a twinge of guilt.

"How can you eat things like mac and cheese and stay so slim?"

"I try not to think about it, but my doctor told me I need to gain weight."

"What? That's crazy! Sounds like you need a new doctor. I made the mistake of gaining three pounds during grad school and I've been fighting to keep them off ever since."

"It looks like you're winning."

"Thanks. You look great today, too. Blue is definitely your color."

"I've been told that before. How do you find shirts that fit you like that? There's no extra fabric anywhere."

"It's custom tailored. I have all my shirts made for me. They look great and it gives me extra motivation to stay fit. Feel this fabric." He stretched his arm across the table. I hesitated. "Go ahead, I don't bite. At least not in public." He dazzled me with his smile.

I felt his sleeve. The fabric was silky smooth. His arm was warm and firm.

"Nice, huh?"

"Very nice."

"Adam, I wanted to ask your advice about something."

I knew it! This is all perfectly innocent and friendly.

"I've only been at the firm for a few months, and we're the only two gay people there, right?"

"As far as I know." *He's asking the wrong person.*

"I know you keep a pretty low profile, but are you out at work?"

"No, I'm very private about . . . well, about everything, so I . . . no, I'm not."

"How well do you know Zipinski?" Mr. Zipinski was our boss, the owner of the firm.

"I don't know him well personally, but I know about him."

"Is he gay friendly?"

"I doubt it. He belonged to my parents' church. I got this job because they knew him. He used to criticize the parish priest for not being in line with Catholic teaching, so I'm pretty sure he's not gay friendly."

"Too bad."

Our food arrived. The mac and cheese was delicious, but I felt self-conscious eating it while Henry grazed on raw vegetables and tofu. "Why do you want to know about Mr. Zipinski?"

"I'd like to get promoted. I'm looking for something to leverage."

"When I was promoted, it was because I worked hard and never made mistakes. That's probably what he's looking for."

"That's the long road. I'd like something quicker."

"It might be a little too soon for you."

"With my qualifications? I don't think so. I have a degree from one of the best schools in the country. If the economy hadn't tanked, I would've had much better offers. The faster I can improve my title, the sooner I can get out of this shit hole."

"Okay. I'm curious . . . what would you do if Mr. Zipinski were gay friendly?"

"That depends, but anything can be useful. I'd suck his shriveled old dick if I thought it would help."

I'm sure I blushed. "You're kidding, right?"

He swallowed a small cube of tofu and looked me in the eye. "Of course I'm kidding. I'd make him suck my dick."

I could only sustain the eye contact for a few seconds before I lowered my head. I smiled and looked out at the water. "You're something else. I wish I had your confidence."

"I don't know why you don't. You're smart and handsome. Everyone wants to get to know you better."

"They're only curious because I don't talk about myself. People love a mystery."

He leaned forward. "I think there's more to it than that."

"It's nice to talk openly. I never had a gay friend at work."

"Well, now you do, and so do I." The corners of his eyes crinkled attractively when he smiled, but that's not relevant. He wanted my friendship, and I felt honored. The few friends I had when I was younger were all shy and awkward, like me. I wouldn't dream of having a friend with Henry's confidence, talent, social skills and . . . other stuff. I wanted to know him better.

"What happened between you and the waiter who worked here?"

He sat back and crossed his arms. Apparently, he was finished eating. "That's a dull story. I met him here, he's hot, so we fucked for a while. I guess he thought we were exclusive. When I came here for dinner with another guy, he made a scene and got fired. No big deal. Obviously, he had issues."

"How embarrassing."

"I don't let things like that bother me. Life is too short."

The waitress brought our bill and took Henry's plate. I picked up the check. "I'll get this."

"Thanks." He didn't argue.

"We should do this again so I can hear more about your game plan to get a promotion. I could learn a few things."

"Definitely. I'm sure you'll be useful to me, too. Your advice, I mean."

"I'm happy to help."

As we left the restaurant, the maître d' smiled and waved at Henry. He returned a tight smile. "Goodbye, whatever your name is."

* * *

Back in my office, I thought about checking in with Donna, but I didn't want to be scolded. I sat down at my computer and . . .

"Hey, *dude.*" There she was at my door.

"How did you know I was back?"

"I have eyes everywhere."

I believed her. "I was about to come to your office."

"Liar." She closed the door and sat down in front of my desk.

"Please come in and have a seat so we can talk."

"How was lunch with your second boyfriend?"

"Just stop! It was nothing like that. Henry is a nice guy who wants a friend and some advice. That's all."

"Uh huh. Advice about what?"

"Stuff about being gay in the workplace, being accepted, things you couldn't relate to."

"Yeah, what would a *girl* know about discrimination at an accounting firm? Since when are you being gay in the workplace? Zipinski would never guess his favorite worker bee is batting for the other team."

"Funny you should mention him, because that's who Henry wanted to know about."

"He thinks Zipinski is gay?"

"No! He wanted to know if he's gay friendly. I told him he's not."

"No kidding. He's not friendly to anything."

"He's not that bad."

"What? Where have you been working all these years? He's horrible!"

"He's a little stiff, but he's nice enough."

"Something on him is stiff, but that's another story. Let's get back to your boyfriend."

"Sam?"

"Who's Sam?"

"My tenant . . . I mean, my boyfriend. I don't like that term. We're not boys."

"And I'm not a *girl*, Adam!" She instantly softened her tone. "His name is Sam? You never told me."

"I thought I did. What about him?"

"Not him, your other boyfriend, Henry." The angry tone was back.

"He's not my boyfriend!"

"I don't trust him."

"Why? Have you ever talked to him? What's your reason?"

She hesitated. "I think he's a Cylon."

"Oh, nice." This was a *Battlestar Galactica* reference. Donna and I became friends because of BSG. We talked about the series every week, speculating about which characters were the humanoid robots trying to destroy the human race. "He would make a good Cylon. He's so perfect."

"See, I knew you were into him!"

"I'm not into him, but he is . . . impressive. He's confident and smooth."

"You touched him?"

"No! Well, I touched his shirt. It was very smooth."

Her tone changed again. "He does wear nice shirts, I'll give him that. The way they hug his body . . . and his pants? But, never mind that, where was I?"

"He's a Cylon . . ."

"Yes! I think he's out to destroy us."

"And your evidence is . . ."

"Women's intuition."

"That's a myth."

"Oh . . . screw you! I've met a lot of guys like him. Believe me, he doesn't give a shit about anyone but himself. Do not trust him!"

"Give me some credit . . ."

"No!"

". . . for being a good judge of character."

"No!"

"I chose *you* as a friend!"

"No, I chose *you!*"

I narrowed my eyes. She did pursue my friendship until I gave it to her. I had no regrets. To acknowledge my affection for her, I said, "I don't like you anymore!"

"I hate your fucking guts!"

"Mr. Zipinski!"

"What about him?"

I whispered, "He's at the door."

"Shit!"

He knocked.

"Come in!"

He entered and spoke in his usual unctuous way. "Good afternoon. I wanted to speak with both of you regarding a . . . delicate matter. May I join you?" He closed the door.

"Yes, of course Mr. Zipinski, please have a seat. How can we help you?"

He folded himself onto the other chair in front of my desk. "I'll get right to the point. I regret to say there have been rumors around the office concerning the two of you and the . . . how shall I say it . . . the relationship that has developed."

"Relationship?"

"Yes." His expression suggested constipation. "The interaction I overheard is enough cause for concern, but I was shocked to hear reports of . . . kissing . . . in full view of the support staff. I must say, I'm surprised at both of you, but especially you, Adam."

Donna gave him a look that could roast an elephant.

"As you know, I try to maintain an atmosphere that encourages the ethical and, dare I say, moral development of my employees, without imposing my own religious beliefs on others. This conduct diminishes that atmosphere and sets a poor example for the younger, more impressionable staff who look to us as models of integrity and family values. For a married woman with children to carry on in such a way is, I'm sorry to say, shameful."

I jumped in before Donna could erupt. "Mr. Zipinski, I assure you, no such relationship has developed between the two of us. We're friends and nothing more. You've been given the wrong impression."

Donna interrupted me. "Adam, it's okay. Mr. Zipinski, I take full responsibility for my actions. I did kiss Adam, and although it was a kiss of friendship, it was inappropriate for the workplace. It won't happen again, and Adam did nothing to encourage my behavior." She stood up. "Now, if you'll excuse me, I'll go back to my office where I would be happy to continue this discussion if you wish."

He looked at her with an expression halfway between pity and contempt. "Thank you for acknowledging your error. I have nothing further to say to you on this subject, but someone from our human resources department will be contacting you to discuss documentation of this incident and the appropriate disciplinary action. You and your family will be in my prayers."

My mouth hung open as Donna left the office and closed the door. I was stunned. "Mr. Zipinski, she hasn't done anything wrong. She's my friend, that's all."

"Adam, we have been taught that Satan comes to us in many forms. You must not be taken in by women who represent themselves as friends. Her friendship belongs to her husband, and not to any other man."

"But . . . she loves her husband, and she's been very kind to me."

"You have a generous heart. Because your parents raised you in the one true church, I know you have a good moral foundation. Unfortunately, they were taken from you when you still needed guidance. That woman is not your friend. You should be starting a family of your own, free from the influence of people like that."

My mind was full of things I wanted to say to him, but I couldn't jeopardize my position at the firm. I remembered what Henry said about making use of things. I decided to take advantage of the situation.

"Mr. Zipinski, I appreciate your guidance, and I've been meaning to ask you about something. I've met someone I care about very much, but the difference in our work schedules has made it difficult for us to develop our relationship. Would it be possible to adjust my schedule to have time off during the week, and work on Saturdays instead? I don't want to take advantage of your kindness, but . . ."

"On the contrary, Adam, I'm pleased you asked. I'm happy to encourage the development of families." He formed a creepy smile. "I trust you to meet your responsibilities on a modified schedule. Submit your proposed hours and I will sign off on them for human resources. I'm very glad to hear this."

"Thank you, Mr. Zipinski. I feel fortunate to be working here."

We stood and shook hands. "You're most welcome, Adam. You're a fine young man. Your parents would be proud." He opened the door, then turned back. "You haven't been attending employee gatherings lately. I hope to meet your young lady at the next social event."

I smiled. "I can't wait."

* * *

I called Donna as soon as Zipinski left my office. "What the fuck was that? Are you in trouble?"

"I told you he's horrible. This has nothing to do with you and me. He's using this against me because I know things that could get him in a ton of trouble."

"Like what?"

"I can't talk about it now. Can we meet for a drink after work? I need a big one."

"Sure, but we probably shouldn't leave together."

"We'll meet at our usual place." She hung up.

It was difficult to focus on my work. I kept reviewing my conversations with Henry and Donna and Mr. Zipinski. I wanted to ask Henry for advice about how to handle the situation, but I decided to talk with Donna first. *Life was so much easier when I didn't talk to anyone.*

We met at the bar in a Chinese restaurant near our office, a place we liked because of their sweet but potent tropical drinks. I ordered my usual Zombie with no umbrella, and Donna chose a Suffering Bastard. The things she told me about Mr. Zipinski forever altered my impression of him as an old fashioned but highly principled man. He had been sexually harassing and abusing female employees for years. Donna was never a target - he was smarter than that - but she knew who the victims were and had encouraged them to file a joint complaint about his behavior. Zipinski discovered this and was looking for something to use against her. Unfortunately, she gave him ammunition when she kissed me in my office.

She was worried, so I was worried. "Who told Zipinski about that kiss? You know all the women who work outside my office, don't you?"

"Yeah. I wouldn't have done it if I thought one of them would report me. Did you talk to any of them afterward?"

"Uh . . . I don't talk to them much, except to say good morning, or if I need something."

"Honestly, would it kill you to chat with people occasionally?"

"I don't think they like me. They always glare at me like I've done something wrong."

"That's not glaring, you idiot! They think you're hot."

"Oh, come on!"

"Do you want me to repeat some of the things they say about you?"

"No! Never mind. What will you do about Zipinski?"

"I'll keep my head down and my mouth shut for a while. I'd like to find a different job, but where? There aren't many opportunities with the economy the way it is. I have my kids to think about."

"It'll blow over. I'll do what I can to help."

"What did Zipinski say after I left?"

"It was weird. He thinks you're an agent of Satan, but I already knew that."

"Thanks, you're helping a lot."

"He said I should be starting a family of my own instead of hanging around with a married woman. So I asked him if I could rearrange my schedule to spend more time with Sam."

"You told him about your boyfriend?"

"Well . . . not exactly. I told him there was someone I care about very much."

"And he didn't catch on it's a guy?"

"Uh . . . he said he'd like to meet my young lady."

"And you corrected him."

"Come on, you don't seriously expect . . ."

"You lied about who you are."

"I don't think so. I didn't correct him. I have to protect my job, too."

"He can't fire you for being gay."

"He would find another reason, like he's doing to you."

"I suppose, but will Sam be okay with you pretending to have a girlfriend?"

"I'm not pretending . . . and . . . he doesn't need to know what I said to Zipinski."

"You'll lie to him, too?"

"You have a different definition of lying. It's not lying if it leads to something good."

"Then tell him you lied to Zipinski, and I'm sure he'll be fine with it."

"Uh . . . okay . . . I will consider that."

"Right after you tell him about your lunch with Henry?"

"Wha . . . uh . . . why wouldn't I tell him? I can have lunch with a friend, like I'm having a drink with you."

"Please don't put me in the same category as that snake. If there's an agent of Satan around here, it's probably Henry."

"You're wrong about him. He's the one who inspired me to ask Zipinski for time off during the week."

"That proves my point, doesn't it?"

"No, it's a good thing. He told me anything can be useful, so I used this situation to get something I wanted."

"Oh . . . great! I'm glad I could be useful to you. This day keeps getting worse. I'm going home to my family." She stood up and pulled her wallet out of her purse.

"Why? What did I do?"

"You ignore my advice, but you're letting Henry teach you how to be more devious and dishonest. That's what you're doing." She laid money on the bar.

"Donna, come on, it's not like that. I listen to your advice."

"Just forget it, Adam. I'm in a bad mood. I'll see you next week."

"Okay." As she walked out I added, "Everything will be fine!"

I felt uneasy, but I was sure she was wrong about Henry. *He was nice. He said we're friends.*

* * *

When Sam came home that evening, I was at my computer researching discrimination and sexual harassment in the workplace. He must have been surprised I wasn't in the kitchen. "Adam? Where are you?"

"I'm in here."

He came to my little office. "Hey. Are you mad at me?"

"No, why would I be mad at you?"

"You're not cooking. Is something wrong?"

"No, I ordered Chinese food. It should be here any minute." I stood up and put my arms around him, burying my nose in his chest. He was wearing a dark green polo shirt with 'Dave's Nursery' embroidered on it. It looked good with his khaki shorts and the summer tan he got from being outside most of the day. "Mmm, you smell good. Were you handling boxwood?"

"Yes, you have a good nose. Dave asked me to help him plant a lot of boxwoods for a lady who's putting in a formal garden. I wish you could see it."

"I love the smell of boxwood."

"I think it smells like cat piss, but I'm glad you like it."

The doorbell rang. "There's our food."

We went to the front door and took the bags from the delivery man. Sam unpacked them on the dining room table. "What made you think of Chinese food?"

"It's from a place near my office. I stopped there after work to have a drink with Donna."

"That's nice. How is she?"

"Not too great today. We were scolded by our boss, and she's being written up.

"For what?"

"For kissing me in front of the staff. I'll get the plates and stuff."

"Uh . . . wait a minute, what did you say?"

"I'll be right back."

He followed me. "Did you say she kissed you?"

"Yeah, when I told her I'm gay . . . she kissed me on the cheek in front of the office staff, and Mr. Zipinski heard about it. He's our boss." We gathered what we needed and went back to the dining room.

"Why would he care if it was an innocent kiss?" He scooped sweet and sour pork over a large mound of rice. "Do you want any of this?"

"No, you can have it." I tasted the Hunan beef. It was spicy and delicious. "He's using it against her because she tried to get him in trouble for sexual harassment."

"He harassed her?"

"No, other women in the office. She encouraged them to file a complaint, so he might threaten to fire her."

"That sucks. Will it affect you?"

"I don't want Donna to get fired, but things turned out pretty well for me today. Mr. Zipinski is letting me take time off during the week and I'll work on Saturdays instead. You and I can spend more time together."

"No way! What day?"

"If you can take Wednesdays off, that would work for me."

"Yeah, I asked Dave. As long as I work on Saturdays, I can have Sundays off and another day during the week. I told you we would work it out."

"You did say that. I guess it pays to be optimistic. Like this morning, I decided to be optimistic about my lunch with Henry, and it went well."

"Lunch with who?"

"Henry, at work. We went out to lunch today."

"I don't remember hearing about Henry."

"I'm sure I mentioned him. He works in the tax department."

"The hot guy who was interested in you?" He stopped eating.

"Did I say he was hot?"

"Yeah, a couple of times, remember? First at the paint store, and then you offered to introduce me to him."

"I didn't say he was hot."

"It was a few weeks ago. You sat right there and said you weren't interested in him, but I should meet him because he's so . . ."

"Forget that. Everything is different now. He wanted advice and it's nice to have a gay friend at work."

"You're friends now? When did this . . . back up a minute."

"To what? Why did you stop eating?"

"Whose idea was it to go out to lunch?" He took a mouthful of food.

"He invited me a couple of times, and I was putting him off, but I finally gave in and . . ."

"Why were you putting him off?"

"I was afraid he was . . . I don't know, really, but it turned out okay, so . . ."

"He was persistent."

"I'm the only other gay person there, and he wanted to know if it's safe to be out at the office."

"How did he know you're gay? I thought Donna was the only one who knew."

"Um . . . that's a good question, I'm not sure. He kept complimenting my ties."

"He's the one who complimented that ugly tie?"

"Was it that ugly?"

"Yes. And you don't think he's interested in you?"

"Well . . . look, Donna said the same thing, but even if he was interested, I told him I'm in a relationship. So there."

"And what did he say to that?"

"He asked if . . . um . . . we talked about . . . it was interesting. He has interesting views."

"About what?"

"Could we change the subject for a minute? There's something I wanted to ask you." I opened a carton of shrimp with pea pods, scooped some onto my plate, and handed it to Sam.

"Okay, but I'm not done with your new friend."

"I don't know what you're worried about. I'm not interested in him."

"I didn't say you were, but if he's up to something . . . I'm just saying."

"He's not like that, but it's sweet that you're jealous."

"I'm not . . . okay . . . fine, I'm a little jealous. I don't want to be one of those guys, but things have been going so well between us, I wouldn't want anything to mess it up." He stabbed a shrimp. "What did you want to ask me?"

"Um . . . okay, we never discussed this, but I thought we should. In our relationship, are we . . . I mean, should I assume we're . . . monogamous?"

He stopped eating again. "Why would you ask me that now? Did he ask you that?"

"You know, it sounds bad in retrospect, but he brought up a good point."

"Did he?" He looked angry.

"I said, I assume we're monogamous, and he said I shouldn't assume anything unless we've discussed it. That's good advice, isn't it? So I thought I would ask. Uh . . . you're bending your fork, Sam."

"Sorry." He loosened his grip and carefully bent the fork back to the way it was. "Okay . . ." He was trying to stay calm. "Yes, I want a monogamous relationship. Is that what you want?"

"Of course, I assumed it was."

"Good. We've discussed it, and it's settled." He took a breath. "Now . . . if you think he brought that up to be helpful, then . . . I'm sorry, but you're wrong. He wants to have sex with you."

"No, really, he doesn't. He has plenty of people to have sex with."

"I'm sure he does. But he's after you, too."

"It doesn't matter because I'm not interested. He couldn't hold a candle to you, Sam."

"That's good to know, but believe me . . . it's tempting when an attractive guy is interested in you. It happened to me at the Harbor View all the time. You might be surprised by what you do."

"You trust me, don't you?"

"I do. I know you love me, but . . . based on my experience, you get flustered when a guy flatters you. Henry could take advantage of that."

I thought about it. "I see what you mean. I should be careful around him."

"That's all I'm asking. I won't say who you can spend time with or anything like that." He looked at the remaining food. "But it makes me a little bit crazy to think he's after you."

"I've never seen this side of you before."

"Neither have I. Did you have enough to eat?"

"Yeah, I ate more than usual today."

"Good. Keep it up." He picked up the Hunan beef.

"Be careful, that's very spicy." Sam rolled his eyes and emptied the carton onto his plate. He ate one of the chili peppers, turned red, and gulped down a glass of water to cool his burning mouth. I rested my head on my hand. "Why would I waste my time with any other man when I can come home to a magnificent stud like you." He almost choked on his water.

I let my eyes wander all over him while he finished eating. He noticed and pushed his chair back from the table. "I see where this is headed."

"Where?" I sat up.

"I need to step up my game to compete with Henry."

"You're not competing with Henry. There's no contest."

He stood up and gestured for me to do the same. "Is Henry as tall as I am?"

"No, not even close."

He pulled off his shirt and tossed it aside. "Is Henry built like me?"

"Definitely not." I rubbed his chest. "Nothing like this."

He pulled me in for a hug. "Do you mind if I take off your shirt?"

"No." I raised my arms, allowing him to pull off my shirt.

"Can I put my hands on your waist?"

"Yeah, let me show you." I guided his hands to a comfortable position.

Sam bent down and offered his lips. I accepted, kissing them slowly. He pulled back. "Let me know if anything bothers you, okay?"

"I will."

I felt the pressure of his hands on my hips. He whispered in my ear, "Hold on." Before I understood his meaning, he lifted me, effortlessly, and held me so we were eye to eye and my feet dangled. I grabbed his shoulders. He smiled. "Can Henry do this?"

I was speechless. An erection was my response.

He looked down. "You like it." I nodded emphatically and felt the hard muscles on his shoulders and arms as he raised and lowered my body a few times. I had a feeling he could do it all day, but I wrapped my legs and arms around him in a tight embrace. We kissed for a few minutes, then he sank to his knees and laid me on the rug. He lay next to me, on his back.

"That was hot, Sam. You must have known I would love that."

He bent his elbows and laced his fingers under the back of his head. "If you got turned on watching me lift that radiator, I figured you would like it. I have all kinds of ideas about things I want to do with you. When I'm waiting to fall asleep at night, I picture something in my head and think, 'I'll do that to Adam one of these days, and if he likes it, I'll do it over and over.'" He glanced at me and grinned. "I'm thinking of a few things right now."

"Oh, me too . . . believe me."

"I'm young and horny and I have a lot of energy. I'm warning you, I'll be taking up most of your free time."

I laughed. "I'd better stock up on ibuprofen."

He rolled onto his side and gazed into my eyes. "Henry couldn't lift you like that."

"Henry who?"

13

I had a list of things to get done on Saturday while Sam was at work, but my nearly empty drawers and closet reminded me I had been neglecting my laundry. There was a large pile of dirty clothes at the bottom of the laundry chute in the basement.

When I went down there, I saw the changes Sam had made during the last few weeks. The basement was clean. The layer of dust on everything was gone. My father's tools were neatly organized and there was space on the work bench where Sam had been working on a project.

The area I called the junkyard had been cleared out to make space for Sam's weightlifting equipment. There were rubber mats on the floor, the bench in the middle, and an impressive array of weights on bars and racks. It reminded me of the weight room at my high school. I never used it myself, but I passed it whenever possible to look at the guys who were there all the time. The memory of it revived my adolescent fantasies. The number of plates Sam had on the bars was intimidating, but I was less interested in lifting weights than in watching him use them.

Above my head I saw one of his projects. Sam had assembled a pull-up bar by attaching an old pipe to the joists. I hadn't done a pull-up in years, but I was good at them in high school. I reached for the bar and had to jump to grab the pipe. I strained to pull myself up until my eyes were even with the bar, then let myself down and dropped to the floor. It bothered me that it was so difficult, but it made me want to improve. I jumped up and grabbed the bar with my palms facing me. I pulled my chin above the bar three times before I had to stop. The burning sensation in my muscles reminded me I liked that feeling as much as I liked running.

I decided to do a few pushups while I was at it. I got down on the mat and did twenty, but I wasn't sure about my form. *I'll ask Sam to help me with that.* I continued with sit-ups, rested after twenty, then did ten more. *That sucks.* I remembered doing fifty, easily, when I was in better shape. *No wonder my belly is soft.* I vowed to start doing calisthenics every day. If I had to gain weight, I would do it right. I would never be big and muscular, but I knew I could feel better about my body. After sorting my clothes and loading the washer, I went upstairs to eat a large, healthy breakfast.

The garden needed work. The warm June weather had everything growing like crazy and most of the flowering plants were covered with blooms. I strapped on my iPod, stuck the buds in my ears and queued the Indigo Girls, because they're awesome. I trimmed plants, clipped off faded flowers, and did the kind of maintenance that is constantly required during the summer.

While I was dead-heading columbines and appreciating the lyrics of '*Love Will Come to You*', I was startled to see someone standing next to me. I jumped up and pulled out an ear bud. "Don't sneak up on me like that!"

The woman stepped back, "I tried to get your attention, but you couldn't hear me!" I had never seen her before. She had a stiff hairdo and smelled like money.

"I'm sorry, can I help you?"

She smiled too sweetly. "I'm Helen Van Wootten, president of the Eden Place Neighborhood Association. I wanted to invite you to our next meeting."

I pulled out the other ear bud because I wasn't sure I heard her correctly. *What neighborhood association?*

"I've been wondering who lives in this lovely house. The flowers are spectacular! Your wife must have a green thumb."

"What organization did you say you're with?"

"The Eden Place Neighborhood Association." She handed me a flyer. "We're working to make the neighborhood a safer place to raise our children. Is your wife at home?"

"No." I was irritated. "I've never heard of this neighborhood association. When did this start?"

"We are a young organization. When my husband and I moved to Eden Place last fall and discovered there was no neighborhood association, I told him I had my work cut out for me! I was president of the association we had in Denver, so I thought, 'Who is better suited to this task than you are, Helen?" She smiled as if she'd said something amusing.

I don't like her. "This is already a safe neighborhood and I'm not a group person, so . . ."

"We can never be too careful when it comes to our children. Do you and your wife have any . . ."

"No, I don't have a wife, so why don't you . . ."

"Who do you hire to plant these flower beds?"

I hate her. "I did it. They're mine. *I'm* the gardener!"

"Oh. A man who enjoys flower gardening? I can't say I've ever . . . that's very modern."

What century are you from, you pinch-faced weasel-woman?! I tried to make her head explode with my thoughts.

"I saw a young man mowing the lawn here the other day and thought he must be your hired help. We could use a good handyman if he's . . ."

"No, that's Sam. He lives here and he's not available." *Can't she see I hate her?!* "I'd like to get back to . . ."

"I'm sorry, did you say that young man lives with you?"

My face twitched. "He's my tenant. He rents the apartment above the garage. Not that it's any of your business."

"Well! I'm sorry if you're offended, but one of the reasons we need a neighborhood association is to identify potential threats to our children. It terrifies me to think of all the . . . alternative lifestyles . . ."

I'm done with this bitch! "No one here is a threat to your children! I don't even like children." I pointed at her with my pruning shears. "I'm not interested in your organization and I'd like you to leave now!"

"Oh, dear!" She backed away. "Please don't hurt me!"

"What? I'm not . . ." I realized what I was doing with my shears and hid them behind my back. "Just . . . leave me alone, okay? I'm not interested."

"I'm going, I'm going!" She hurried toward Flora's house next door. I watched her run up the steps and ring the doorbell with a fearful look. I put my ear buds back in as Flora's housekeeper stuck her head out to look at me and invited the horrible woman into the house.

Well . . . I think I handled that effectively. I returned to my chores.

As I trimmed a clump of bergenias, I was startled, again, by something poking me in the ribs. It was the tip of Flora's cane. I looked up, smiled, and removed the ear buds. "Mrs. O' . . . I mean, Flora. Hello."

Her expression was stern. "Adam, what did you say to that woman?"

"What? Nothing. I told her I wasn't interested."

"Stand up, young man!" I obeyed. "Did you threaten her?"

"Uff! No! I . . . may have pointed my pruning shears at her, but I didn't threaten her."

"And did you tell her you don't like children?"

"She caught me off guard . . . it wasn't the best choice of words, but . . ."

"Adam! Do you realize you made an enemy of someone who could turn half the neighborhood against you?"

"I . . . all I did was . . . she implied that I'm a . . . a . . . threat to children!"

"Have you no sense of social politics? How do you manage to conduct business in the world?"

"I'm not a . . . I've never been good at . . ." I sighed heavily, conceding defeat. "How bad is it?"

"It's not good, but you are fortunate she fled to my house." Flora looked around. "Why are there no chairs in your garden? It is customary to invite guests to sit down. For pity's sake, Adam . . ."

"I'm sorry, I'll get chairs." I ran to the back porch and brought the only two chairs I had outside the house.

Flora sat down and muttered, "Even cemeteries have benches here and there."

"You're right, Sam said the same thing. We need to go shopping. So . . . what did the Weasel Woman say about me?"

Flora's eyes brightened at the nickname. She couldn't help smiling. "It's true, her eyes were very small. And she needs a new hairdresser."

"I know! Do you think that was a whole can of hairspray?"

She chuckled quietly. "You're trying to win me over with catty remarks, but I'm very cross with you!"

"I can tell. I don't like it when you're cross."

"Then you should behave!" She shook her finger at me. "I dislike that woman as much as you do. However, unlike you, I know how to charm horrible people and prevent them from giving me trouble. I won't even repeat the manipulative things I said to put you in a sympathetic light."

"Yeah, I'd rather not know. Will she give me trouble?"

"She is a small-minded bigot. Of course she'll make trouble."

"But I haven't done anything wrong. What can she do to me?"

"Never underestimate the fear people have of things they don't understand. All she needs to do is raise suspicion. Your sexual orientation will be her weapon."

"But no one knows! We're not having sex on the front porch. We haven't even done it yet."

"Adam . . . you are two handsome young men living in a Victorian house surrounded by magnificent flower gardens. Where is the camouflage?"

"Come on, you make it sound so obvious . . . like a stereotypical . . . uh . . . huh . . . this is so gay, isn't it?"

"You have everything but the flag, my dear. Your flowers have been drawing attention for years, but your stunning young man has been the favorite topic of conversation among the ladies on this street for two months now."

"Dammit! I shouldn't let him mow the lawn with his shirt off."

She laughed. "On the contrary, he should wear shorter shorts."

"Flora!" I was genuinely shocked.

"Trust me, honey. You could have learned so much from Mr. O'Neill. He was the most charming man who ever lived. All the ladies loved him, and none of them were fooled by the thin veneer of our marriage. No matter how much he flirted, they knew he posed no threat to them or their children. You could be somewhat charming if you were less . . . abrasive."

"I . . . I don't . . ." I was speechless.

"Don't misunderstand me, dear. You're a lovely person, but you have been such a curmudgeon lately."

"I know, I'm sorry. I used to be better with people, but now . . . I'm out of practice."

"All is not lost. I will take charge of your rehabilitation, but you will eventually need to meet more of our neighbors."

"Okay." *Crap.* "Not all at once, I hope."

"Let's move on, shall we? When will I meet this extraordinary young man of yours?"

I agreed to bring Sam to lunch on Wednesday. As I walked her back to her house, she advised me . . . no, she ordered me . . . to smile and wave at neighbors who walked by whenever I was in the front yard. This would be the first step in my social rehabilitation. *Sigh. I guess it won't kill me.*

* * *

As I finished my work in the garden, I took a long look at the frustrating, flowerless peony, wondering what I could do to make it bloom the next year. I clipped off the underdeveloped buds that had turned black. I would normally ask Dave for advice, but I hadn't been to his nursery since the day I picked up my plants. I was still angry that he warned Sam to be careful with me. *Why would he say that?* It hadn't kept Sam from trusting me. *Maybe I should let it go.* Flora encouraged me to have a more positive attitude towards people. *Maybe that's what I need.*

I decided to visit Dave's Nursery before going to the grocery store. I could say hello to Dave and see Sam at his new job. I put another load of laundry in the washer, made a sandwich, and grabbed a banana. Pretty soon I was in my big pickup truck, tearing hunks out of my sandwich as I drove, and feeling butch. *I'm like a trucker, eating on the road to save time.* My stereo system blasted Pink's Greatest Hits. *Like a gay accountant trucker. Eating turkey and Gruyère with mango chutney on millet bread. In his big-ass truck!*

I pulled into the far end of the parking lot and saw Sam at the other end loading shrubs onto one of Dave's trucks. Keeping my distance, I watched him interact with the customer, a well-dressed middle-aged woman. The way she looked at him made me think she appreciated his help in more ways than one. After the plants were loaded, the woman went to her car and Sam followed her out of the parking lot in the truck. Apparently, it was a home delivery.

I went into the main building to have a look at the exotic annuals. Before long, as always, Dave saw me and came over. "Adam! I was starting to think you gave up gardening! How the hell are you?" I reached out for a handshake, but Dave surprised me with a manly, back-slapping hug. This never happened before. "Were you mad at me? Why did you stop coming around?"

Time to start lying. "I don't know . . . I was busy, and I didn't want Sam to think I was checking up on him."

"Are you joking? He'd love to see you here. Adam, the kid never shuts up about you. It would drive me nuts if I didn't know you."

"Um . . . I . . ." *Does Dave know about us?*

"Best employee I ever had! Most of these damn kids are too busy with their cell phones to get any work done. But Sam comes in and puts them all to shame. Now they all try to keep up with him! The customers love him." He nudged me and winked. "Especially the ladies. It's great for business."

"I saw him loading a truck for a woman who looked like she might pounce on him."

"I know who you mean. She's a cougar. One of my best customers. That broad shits money, and I'm picking up as much as I can. She used to come in and ask for me, but the kid stole my mojo. Now he gets the big tips."

I didn't like the sound of that. "What does he have to do for tips?"

"Oh, it's not what you're thinking. Hell no! Even if he wanted to, I wouldn't allow it. The first rule I tell my employees is, 'Don't fuck the customers.' But . . . if he takes off his shirt while he plants those shrubs, he'll probably get a hundred-dollar tip. With the shirt on, he'll get fifty. A guy like Sam gets ten bucks for smiling. He knows how it works. I taught him."

I didn't know whether to feel proud of Sam, or appalled by the whole conversation. "You encourage that?"

"Adam, it'll happen whether I encourage it or not. Thirty years ago, when I started landscaping, good looking, well-built guys got more jobs. The harder I hit the gym, the more money I made. It gave me an edge over the competition. That's how I built this business. I was a fuckin' stud back in the day."

I remembered being drawn to Dave when I first visited his nursery as a teenager. He sold great plants, but he had something extra that made me want to talk to him, as shy as I was. He treated me like I was his favorite customer. *Doesn't he treat everyone that way?* I joked, "I bet you're still the favorite with the older ladies."

He snorted. "Yeah, but they pinch pennies when they're on social security. My old ass is lucky to draw a five-dollar tip these days. Good thing I own the place. But you, kiddo . . . you would've done well if you had worked for me. You could've paid for college with those tips. I was disappointed when you turned me down."

His compliments made me uncomfortable, of course. I was surprised he thought I was tip-worthy. "I'm sorry, Dave. I appreciated the offer, but I was too shy for customer service. I hope I made up for it by introducing Sam."

"He's great, and he wants to learn the business. He was lucky to snag you. I didn't think you'd go for a younger guy, but it seems to agree with you. I know he's happy."

I can't believe he knows about us! How embarrassing! "I didn't . . . I wasn't sure if you knew. I'm not used to talking about this."

"I know. Don't worry about it."

"But . . . so . . . you're okay with this? You don't think it's wrong?"

"Wrong? Hell, no, I think it's beautiful. I'm happy for you. I was worried about you after your parents . . ." He paused and looked down, then cleared his throat. "I'm real happy for you, Adam." He pounded me on the back as if I were the one getting choked up. Maybe I was, a little. "I'd better get back to work before everything falls apart on me. These damn kids need to be watched. It was great to see you. Don't be such a stranger."

"I won't be. Tell Sam I was here, okay?"

"You bet. Look at those New Guinea impatiens. They're the best in town, and the price is good!" Always a salesman.

I bought a few hanging baskets of impatiens for the front porch, and a couple of potted ferns for the living room, as Sam had suggested. By the time I got home from the grocery store and put everything away, it was late afternoon. I continued doing laundry, vacuuming and dusting. I cleaned the bathrooms and mopped the kitchen floor. It wasn't easy to maintain a large house by myself. I had more time for it when I wasn't cooking every day and making out with Sam every night. But I wouldn't give that up, no matter how dirty the house would get. Looking forward to Sam's return every evening made my day pass more quickly.

I finished cleaning and started dinner. I planned to take a shower before he got home, but time slipped away. The next thing I knew, Sam walked through the door and kissed me on the back of the neck. I turned around to smile at him. "I love it when you do that. You look tired."

"I'm hungry and dirty." He filled a glass with water and drank. "I should take a shower before we eat."

"I was going to shower, too, but I ran out of time."

"Maybe we should do it together." He wiggled his eyebrows and drained the water from his glass.

I knew he was kidding, but it sounded good to me. "We could." I attempted puppy dog eyes, not knowing whether I had them or not. *I probably look deranged.*

As it dawned on him that I might be serious, one side of his mouth turned up. "Isn't it too soon for that?"

"I'm not talking about sex, but we could be naked together, couldn't we? I'd love to see you naked and wet."

He put his hand over the front of his shorts. "I want to see you, too, but . . . I would need to . . . finish."

I shrugged. "Me too. Wouldn't that be okay in the shower?"

"Yeah, but . . . are you sure you're ready?"

"As ready as I'll ever be. I can't keep letting my anxiety hold me back. Do you feel ready?"

"I think so. I'm a little nervous about being naked with you."

"Are you kidding? If I looked like you, I would never wear clothes."

Sam's expression changed. "Adam . . . you know, sometimes . . ." He stopped and shook his head.

"What? Tell me."

He hesitated. "Sometimes you . . . dismiss my feelings . . . like nothing should be difficult for me. Maybe you don't know this, but I worry about what you think of me. You know you can hurt my feelings, right?"

"I'm sorry. Did I?"

"No, I'm just saying . . . you could. I try to be careful with you because you're insecure about certain things. I want you to do the same for me." It must have been difficult for him to confront me. He couldn't look at me.

"You're right, Sam, I'm sorry. The truth is, I'm so impressed by everything about you, I forget you're an ordinary person. I know that sounds bad, but in my head, it seems very, very good."

"That's a lot to live up to, Adam. I'm a long way from perfect."

"I know. I haven't seen any evidence yet, but I believe you. I don't want to be insensitive. Always tell me when I'm being a dick, okay?"

"Okay. Dick." He looked up and smiled. "I guess I am tired. And hungry. Big surprise, huh?"

"Why don't we eat? Dinner is almost ready. "

"Don't I smell bad? I was sweating a lot today."

"Let me check." I wrapped my arms around him and buried my face in his shirt. "You smell good to me, and I'm not one of those guys who's into body odor." I went back to preparing dinner. "I wonder if you smell that good to other people."

"I'm not taking a poll." He opened the refrigerator and grabbed a can of spray cheese. "Dave said you stopped by. You made his day." He sprayed a blob of cheese onto his tongue.

"Yeah, I'm glad we had a chance to talk. He caught me off guard, though. I didn't realize you told him about our relationship."

"I didn't tell him. He knew."

"What do you mean?"

"He knew right away, the day you introduced me to him. That's why he came over to talk to me."

"When he warned you about me? I still don't understand that."

"Oh my God, Adam! Are you still thinking about that?"

"Well . . . yeah."

"He didn't warn me about you. He warned me to be careful with you. He threatened me."

"What?"

"He said, 'I'm glad you and Adam are friends, but be careful with him.'" He impersonated Dave's way of talking. "'Because if you hurt him, I'll come after you! I don't care how big you are, I'll take you down! Do you understand me?'"

I was shocked. "Why didn't you tell me that part? All this time I've been thinking . . ."

"I tried to tell you! You weren't listening! You were so angry and defensive right away."

Oh yeah, I was. "Okay, okay . . . you're right. That was before I realized we were . . . wait a minute . . . Dave knew we were in a relationship before I knew?"

"Yep."

"God dammit!" _#!%&+@^$*<!!!!!_ I cursed like a sailor in my head.

Sam came up behind me, put an arm around my chest, and rested his chin on top of my head. "What difference does it make now? Isn't it good to know Dave has your back? Believe me, I didn't take it lightly, and I haven't forgotten it."

"Why would he be so protective of me? I've known him for a long time, but it's not like we're close friends or anything."

Sam leaned against the counter and crossed his arms. "I don't know. I wondered about that, too. Sometimes when he talks about you, it . . . no, I probably shouldn't say that."

"What?"

"No, never mind. You'll think I'm . . . never mind."

'I hate it when people do that! Tell me!"

"All right! But I don't want you to think I'm all . . ."

"Spit it out!"

"It makes me jealous, okay? The way he talks about you makes me think, 'You can't talk about Adam that way. He's mine.' I don't know why, but . . . it's like when you were telling me about Henry."

"Oh, for God's sake! Let me get this stuff out of the oven so we can eat."

"What can I do? Is the table set?"

"No, you can do that." I pulled out a pork tenderloin with roasted red potatoes, baby carrots and pea pods. We settled down to eat and were so focused on the food, we didn't talk for a while.

"This is great, Adam. I'm lucky you're a good cook. I didn't eat much for lunch."

"I saw you today at the nursery. You were loading shrubs for someone."

"Yeah, I had to plant all of those for her. That lady gets on my nerves."

"Why?"

"It's hard to explain."

"Did you take off your shirt while you were planting the shrubs?"

He looked like a kid who was caught with his hand in the cookie jar. "How did you know about that?"

"Dave told me about her and how you get the biggest tips." His face turned so red I felt sorry for him. "It's okay, I didn't mean to embarrass you."

"Oh. Okay." He continued eating.

I let it go for a while, but it didn't feel right. "Sam, you don't have to do that if it makes you uncomfortable. You can keep your shirt on."

"I don't mind that. It's more comfortable to work with it off, and it keeps the shirt from getting ruined. But I don't want you to think I'm, like . . . a hustler. It feels wrong when they give me such big tips." He paused to chew a forkful of meat. "You're probably the wrong person to ask, but . . . really, why? She gave me a two-hundred-dollar tip today."

Holy fuck! "Wow! That is a big tip. But, you are . . . something special. I mean, you're very good looking. More than that. I don't know how far you want me to go here. You're scorching hot. Like a walking wet dream."

"All right! Okay. Enough." He shifted in his chair. "You know I get a boner when you talk like that. I love that you're hot for me, but . . . doesn't it bother you when other people look at me like that?"

"Mmm, no. If they're only looking. And if they're women. You're not taking your shirt off for any guys, are you?"

He shrugged his wide shoulders with an ambiguous expression.

My heart skipped a beat. "Seriously . . . you're not, are you?"

"Who's jealous now?" He raised his eyebrows. "I'm messing with you. Dave assigns us to the home deliveries and landscaping jobs. He sends one of the other guys out with the gay customers, like my buddy, Greg. He's hot, but he's straight. His tips are pretty good. Not as good as mine, though. I don't always tell the others how much I get. They tease me enough as it is. Greg calls me the 'stud muffin.'" Sam seemed to like that.

"Huh. I'll have to meet Greg."

"Why?"

"Just . . . no reason . . . so I know who you're talking about. That's all."

"And when will I meet Donna?" His eyes twinkled. "I could visit your office."

Nope! "Um . . . I'll think about that. Here . . . finish these potatoes."

"Or your friend, Henry. I'd love to meet him." His eyes did not twinkle.

I ignored him. "Hey, I forgot to tell you . . . I scheduled lunch with Flora this coming Wednesday. She's dying to meet you."

"Sounds good."

"Do you have a swimming suit? She wants us to use the pool."

"I have one but I'm not sure it still fits."

"Since you became a stud muffin?"

He laughed. "Yeah . . . that. I think my ass is getting fat."

"That isn't fat."

"It sticks out pretty far."

"I'm getting hot. Can we take a shower now?"

"I'm just talking about my swimming trunks!"

"And your ass. It needs to be evaluated for fat content."

"All right, let me finish dinner before we get naked." Sam usually took the lead when we made out, but I was feeling frisky after all that talk about hot, shirtless landscapers. I slowly unbuttoned my shirt in the most provocative way a self-conscious nerd could manage. He swallowed a mouthful of food. "Are you in a hurry? I'm eating as fast as I can."

"Take your time. I wonder what I have to do around here to get a decent tip."

He smiled and shoved his hand into the pocket of his shorts. He laid four fifty-dollar bills on the table next to his plate. "Show me what you've got."

Dammit! I asked for it. "Um . . . okay." I finished taking off my shirt and looked down at my torso. "Let's see . . . what can I say? I have these nipples. Only two of them, I'm afraid. Some people have an extra one."

"I like the symmetry."

"That's why I stopped at two. No need to overdo it. My chest . . . well . . . my ribs show, don't they?"

"Don't worry, we'll fix that." He pushed his empty dinner plate aside. "Come over here so I can get a better look at the merchandise."

"Merchandise?" I stood up. "If I'm the merchandise, I should be marked down for final clearance."

He stuck two fingers in the front of my shorts and pulled me between his splayed legs. "I love a good bargain, but you're not much of a salesman."

"I'm not much of a product." He unbuttoned my shorts and tugged on the zipper. "Uh . . . what are you doing?"

"I need to check under the hood to make sure you're running properly."

"I might be running a little hot right now."

"That's okay." He drew my shorts down and helped me step out of them. I stood before him in a pair of blue briefs and a full-body blush of embarrassment. He looked at my bulge. "Is that a six or eight-cylinder engine?"

I adjusted my boner. "I don't know, I'm not a car guy."

"It looks pretty powerful to me."

I felt bashful. "Thanks. You're sweet, but . . ."

"Shhh, I need to listen to something." He pressed his ear against my chest while my heartbeat quickened. "Hmm . . . very nice." He pulled back and ran his hands over my torso, front and back, and up and down my arms. He caressed the back of my thighs and kissed the center of my chest. "I can't find anything wrong with you. I might have to pay full price for the first time in my life."

"I'm not . . . you shouldn't . . ."

Sam looked up. "You haven't kissed me yet today. Don't you like to kiss me anymore?" I leaned in to give him what he wanted. It was such a pleasure to feel his lips against mine, I had to wonder why I hadn't done it as soon as he walked in the door. *Note to self . . .*

We kissed for several minutes while he reached for the fifty-dollar bills and tucked them, one by one, into my underwear. I reluctantly withdrew from his mouth. "I'm getting too excited."

He glanced down. "Do you want to take a break and clear the table? Should we get the dishes done?"

I stroked his stubbled cheek. "You're so damned cute I can't stand it."

His eyes sparkled. "We're supposed to do our chores before we play."

"You want me to wash dishes in my underwear?"

"You can do everything in your underwear as far as I'm concerned." He squeezed my butt.

"Why don't you take off your clothes, too?"

"And let you treat me like a sex object? No way!" He grinned and started clearing the table.

"You could at least take off your shirt."

"Hey, I'm not a piece of meat! Now get your hot ass in the kitchen where it belongs." He snickered.

It was weirdly sexy to be in my underwear while Sam was still dressed. I collected some of the dishes and headed for the sink. When we finished, he patted me on the butt. "Nice work, sweet cheeks." I had to laugh. I never imagined I would have such a hot boyfriend, and certainly not one who would talk to me that way.

"Will you take off your shirt now?"

"Why don't you try to get it off me?" He raised his arms above his head, stretching toward the ceiling.

I rubbed my hands up and down his abs. "You're too tall for me to reach."

"Oh, am I?" He knelt on the floor in front of me. "How's this?"

"Much better." I lifted the hem of his shirt to his arm pits. "Put your arms up." He obeyed, but in a purposely lazy way that made it difficult for me to accomplish my task. While I struggled, he tried to kiss me. "Knock it off!" He didn't stop. After a lot of tugging, I managed to get the polo over his head and off his arms. I tossed it on the kitchen table. Sam's hair was attractively tousled. I kissed him once, then moved away from him, pulling his tip money out of my underwear. "If you want this back, you'll have to earn it."

He stood up and came after me. As we walked through the dining room, he kicked off his sandals and left them there. I smiled and waved the fifty-dollar bills. "How would you get a two-hundred-dollar tip from a stingy old man like me?" He slowly pursued me through the dimly lit living room. I hoped my neighbors couldn't see me running around in my underwear. *I won't masturbate on the first floor, but now I'm doing this!* I backed into the entrance hall and turned on the light over the staircase. "I've never given more than a twenty-dollar tip in my life."

"Well . . ." Sam paused in the shadows of the living room to unbutton his khaki shorts. "You never experienced my level of service." The shorts fell to the floor. He kicked them aside and stepped into the light, placing his hands on either side of the wide doorway. He looked like a hunkier version of the Vitruvian Man in black compression shorts. I had to lean against the front door for a moment.

The proportions of Sam's body were as good or better than any I had seen in photographs. He wasn't as muscular as a body builder, and there were plenty of fitness models who had been waxed and groomed to a prettier finish, but all my fantasies were satisfied by his height, the breadth of his shoulders, his narrow waist and powerful legs. And, even though he was trying to be sexy, Sam had a limited grasp of how sexy he was. That made him hundreds of degrees hotter.

"Do you like my underwear?" He asked as if that was the most attractive thing about him.

"Sure, but that's not what I'm looking at."

He approached and leaned against the door with his hands above my head. "So . . . what are you looking at?" I scanned his body while he tensed and relaxed various muscles. "Hey, my eyes are up here, mister."

I looked up to see his sly smile. My head felt light. "Upstairs," was all I could say. I ducked under his arm and walked backwards to the foot of the staircase. He paused to flex his chest, looking down to see if his pectorals were bunching up adequately. I stumbled and landed roughly on one of the stairs. Using my elbows, I pulled myself up to the next step.

"Are you okay?" He planted one foot next to me and leaned forward, looming over me. "Remember . . . that ass is mine and I don't want it bruised."

Fuck! I had to clamp my hand over my crotch. Meanwhile, his big lumpy package was practically in my face. I wanted to peel him and eat him immediately.

Sam stroked his thigh. "Do you want to touch anything?"

"Yes. I mean, no thank you. Not yet. Can we just . . ."

His nose nearly touched mine. "Can we just what?"

"Take a shower?"

"Yeah, that's where we're going." He dragged his fingertip down the center of my body to my navel. "But I need to perform a service to earn my tip." I thought of at least a dozen services I would be thrilled to receive. While I was distracted by the pornography in my head, Sam slipped one hand behind my back and another under my knees. He stood up with me draped over his thick arms. "I meant transportation service, of course."

My reaction was predictably articulate. "Oh, fuckety fuck!"

His smirk was adorable as he climbed the stairs. "The best thing about being this strong is seeing what it does to you."

"I fucking love it!"

"Does that mean I'm getting a big tip?"

"Yes, all of it! I'd stick it in your shorts, but I don't think there's any more room in there."

He grinned. "Just drop it on the stairs. I'll get it later."

When I opened my hand to let go of the money, one of the bills stuck to my damp palm. I shook it free. "I wonder if people ever think about where their money has been."

Sam kissed my forehead. "I like that money better knowing it was in your basket." I giggled. "Maybe I'll keep all my money in your underwear from now on. Then I'll have an excuse to shove my hand in your pants at the store."

I laughed louder than I had in a long time. "Oh my God, you say the goofiest, sexiest things."

"Um . . . thank you?"

"Oh, yes . . . it's definitely a compliment. I'm so lucky you can make me hard and make me laugh at the same time."

"Okay, but please don't laugh when I take my shorts off. That wouldn't be cool."

"I won't. I might scream like a game show contestant."

He rolled his eyes. "Whatever."

When we reached the bathroom, Sam set me down. We didn't waste any time shedding our underwear. Believe me . . . Sam, naked, was nothing to laugh about. I was especially impressed by his magnificent ass, despite his crazy idea that it was fat. He let me focus on it for a minute. "Damn! This looks like it was sculpted by Michelangelo."

"Doesn't it stick out too far?"

"No, that's one of the best things about it. It's all muscle, but it's soft and warm and a little bit fuzzy. I want to squish it!"

"You make it sound like a stuffed animal."

"Oh, man, I would love to have a stuffed version of this! I could give it a name!"

"What? That's weird. Can we move on?" He twisted around to face me.

"No! Don't take away Mr. Buns!"

Shaking his head in disbelief, he pulled me into a tight, naked embrace. "I swear, I'll hug the stuffing out of you."

We spent a ridiculous amount of time exploring each other's bodies in the shower. His enthusiastic attention made me feel more comfortable with myself than I thought I could be. For the first time in my life, I ejaculated in the presence of another person. Sam invited me to play with his incredibly stiff prick until he erupted with a loud cry. By the end of the shower, I felt relaxed and liberated and excited about our future together. I couldn't get enough of him.

While we toweled each other dry, I suggested, "You should get a tan on your thighs to match your legs."

"Okay. Should I sit out in the front yard so the neighbors can see me on their way to church?"

"Yeah, while I rub oil on your body. I'm sure the Weasel Woman would love that."

"Weasel Woman? I'm afraid to ask."

"I forgot to tell you about that." I told the story of my encounter with Mrs. Van Wooten and Flora's intervention.

"Wow. You certainly have a way with people, Adam."

"Well, what would you have done?"

"I don't know, but I wouldn't have pointed a scissors at her and told her I hate children." He cracked up before he finished the sentence.

"I didn't do either of those things, so shut up! Her interpretation was the problem!" I jabbed him in the ribs and tried to tickle him. He squirmed away and made me chase him into the bedroom. "Flora thinks I could be charming if I tried."

"You wouldn't be Adam if you were charming. Being charming is my job." He paused to wiggle his butt.

"Yes, I see that, but I could learn."

"We'll see. I hope Flora doesn't ruin you. I like you the way you are."

"Aww! You are totally fucking charming."

"See? It comes naturally." Sam stretched out on the bed in all his naked glory. I joined him and turned off the light. He pulled me against his body and spooned me, just the way I liked. I settled into his warmth. "I like this naked stuff. How about you?"

"I'd be willing to try it again."

"So, what should we do first tomorrow?"

"I wouldn't complain if you gave me another hand job."

"That's fine, but I was talking about chores and errands and stuff."

"Oh. I should cut the grass. The weather is supposed to be nice, so I could get some sun on my thighs. I want to make a good impression in my swimming suit when we go to Flora's."

"First impressions are all about the thighs."

"Hey, it was your idea."

"I know, I approve. Let's shop for garden furniture in the morning, then we can catch the afternoon sun in the back yard. I want to even out my tan, too." My eyelids were getting heavy and his breathing was slowing down.

"I should buy a new swimming suit."

"I definitely want to be there for that."

"I think I'll get board shorts so my ass has room to grow."

"No, I was picturing a red speedo."

"Yeah, right. I'll wear one if you wear one."

"Agreed. We'll buy them tomorrow."

Sam was quiet for a minute before saying, "You're kidding, right?"

I didn't respond.

"Adam? I hope you're kidding."

I smiled and pretended to be asleep.

14

I crawled out of bed in the morning and looked for the clothes I was wearing the previous day. I remembered they were downstairs. Sam yawned and stretched his long body in a very attractive way. "I need coffee."

"Me too. Let's go."

Both naked, we left the bedroom and followed the trail of discarded clothing and fifty-dollar bills. Sam stopped in the entrance hall to put on his shorts. "What happened here last night? Did you take advantage of me?"

"Yes, I did. You might be pregnant."

"Oh, no. My mother warned me about men like you."

"Yeah . . . I'm sure." I found my clothes and put them on.

We spent the morning as planned, bringing home a large umbrella table and chairs for the garden, a pair of sturdy Adirondack chairs, and a set of wicker furniture for the front of the house. After putting the settee and two chairs on the porch, Sam helped me hang the baskets of impatiens I bought the day before. He could reach the hooks without a ladder. While I was handing him one of the baskets, he asked, "Who is that woman taking pictures of the house?"

I looked at the street and saw a stiff-haired woman with a camera standing next to a BMW convertible. "Shit. That's the Weasel Woman I told you about. She's taking pictures of us."

He put his hand on my shoulder. "You know what? I'll go introduce myself." He went down the stairs.

"That's a bad idea, Sam."

He trotted toward her, raised his hand in a wave and called out a cheerful "Good morning!" She let out a high-pitched shriek, like a terrified Chihuahua encountering a Great Dane. "Beautiful day, isn't it?" She jumped into her car and started the engine. "Wait a minute, I want to . . ." Her tires screeched as she sped away. Sam returned to the porch with a disbelieving look. "What the hell?"

"I told you."

"I was being friendly."

"I know, but she resisted your charm. She must be a witch, or a demon."

"I didn't threaten her with a weapon or say I like to hurt children."

"I did not threaten her! Just . . . stop!"

He snickered and gave me a quick kiss on the side of the neck. "She's obviously messed up."

"Oh, *now* you believe it's her problem and not mine, because *you* couldn't win her over!"

He smiled. "I didn't say that."

"You were thinking it. I can be friendly, you know. It's not rocket science."

"Do you want me to water these plants right away?"

"Don't change the subject."

"I'm going to sit in the sun. Are you coming?"

"Don't try to distract me."

"I might need help with the tanning oil."

"All right, I'm coming. Dammit."

I sat in one of the new Adirondack chairs while Sam sprawled on the grass reading the final chapters of *Tess of the d'Urbervilles.* The sun felt so good, I almost stopped worrying about skin cancer. I hardly ever relaxed in the beautiful private garden I spent so much time developing. I enjoyed the sights and sounds, all the flowers, the birds and the buzzing insects. I also admired Sam's body as he reclined in various positions in his skimpiest pair of shorts. When he caught me looking, I didn't bother to look away as I would have in the past. He went back to reading as if everything was as it should be.

Eventually he closed the book and lay flat on his back with his hands over his face. I gave him a few minutes before asking, "Are you crying?"

"No."

"Are you sure?"

He didn't answer right away. He took his hands away from his face. "I didn't think they would execute her!"

"She murdered Alec. What did you think they would do?"

"I don't know. I thought they would escape and . . ."

"What? Live happily ever after?"

He sighed. "I guess not. It wouldn't have worked." He sat up and crossed his legs. "Tess and Angel loved each other in the end. No matter how messed up their relationship was, at least they had that."

"Yeah, and Alec got what he deserved." He sat there, looking like he had lost a friend. "Are you sorry you chose that book?"

"No, not at all. It was sad, but it was worth it. I understand why it's one of your favorites."

"Yeah, I love a good tragedy." He looked up at me with a subtle smile. "We should go inside before we get a sunburn. It's past time for lunch. I'm surprised you haven't complained."

"Didn't you hear my stomach growling?" He followed me up the back steps and into the kitchen where he set the book on the table and opened his arms for a hug. I accepted and gently stroked his back. He kissed my shoulder. "I'll never leave you, Adam. You know that, right?"

"Yeah, you told me. I love you, Sam. I love that a book can make you cry."

"I love you, too." He gave me a final squeeze and released me, then turned away to rub his eyes with the back of his hand. "Can I get another book from your library?"

"Sure. Do you want me to recommend something?"

"No, thank you." He picked up *Tess* and headed to the front of the house.

I was afraid of what he would choose. "Are you sure?"

"Yes, I'm sure." He went up the stairs.

While I made sandwiches, I tried to telepathically direct Sam to something by Jane Austin or Daniel Defoe. Anything by Dickens would be more hopeful than Thomas Hardy's novels. *I need a happier library.* Lunch was ready by the time he came down with his choice. "What did you find?"

"*Wuthering Heights* by Emily Bronte."

No fucking way! "Not that one." I lunged toward him to take it away. He held it high in the air so I couldn't reach it.

"Why not? It's famous. Isn't it good?"

"It's brilliant, but it's horribly depressing and twisted."

"That sounds even better. I can't wait."

I made a futile attempt to knock the book out of his hand. "Give it to me!"

"Stop trying to shelter me! I can handle it. I'll take this to my apartment. I'll be right back."

I growled and muttered under my breath while my handsome young lover, eager to read one of my favorite books, ran up the steps to the coach house in his tight little shorts.

Why can't things ever go my way?

***

After lunch, we cleaned up, got dressed, and headed to the mall on the outskirts of town so I could look for living room furniture at the department store. Sam wanted to look for a swimming suit, but he didn't want me to come with him. "Why not?"

"Because you'll embarrass me."

"No, I won't." *Yes, I would.* "I'll behave." *I wouldn't.*

"No, you won't, and you know it." I'd swear he could read my thoughts. "Go look at furniture. I'll find you there when I'm done."

I took the escalator up to the 'Fine Furnishings' department and strolled through the different room settings looking for something to match the style of the living room. *Too modern . . . too feminine . . . too bright . . . too ugly . . .*

"Adam?"

I froze in my tracks. *Shit! Who could possibly know me?* It was Donna. "Dammit, you scared me! I hate being seen in public."

"Well, you're not quite invisible yet, so keep working on that. What are you doing here?"

"Looking for new living room furniture. How about you?"

"The same. The stuff I have is shot."

"What style are you looking for?"

"I have kids, Adam. I'm looking for something I can clean with a garden hose."

I was reminded of how much I liked her. "I'm sorry about the other day. I was a jerk."

"I know, but I still like you. It was a rough day."

"Are you worried about your job?"

"Maybe I should be, but the more I thought about it, and after talking to Kevin, I decided not to let Zipinski control my life. I'll be more careful, I'll try to keep my mouth shut, but if he wants to get rid of me, he will. I'll figure something out. I'm good at what I do. He can't take away my family. That's what really matters."

"That's a good attitude. I wish I could be more like that."

"Yeah, you're a worrier. That's why I'm surprised you aren't being more cautious with Henry. You should be worried about what his agenda might be."

"He wants to move forward in his career. He's ambitious and talented . . ."

"And good looking. Admit it, if he were ugly, or if he had a vagina, you would see him for what he is."

"But his looks have nothing to do with . . ."

"Hey, speaking of good looking, don't turn around, but there's a guy coming this way who is . . . wow . . . there should be a law against looking that good. I want a divorce."

Crap! I'm not ready for this.

Sam approached us. "Hello."

Donna smiled and fluttered her eyelashes. "Honey, I would love to help you with something, but we don't work here."

Sam looked at me, then at her. "Adam?"

Donna looked at me. "Do you know each other?"

"Yes." They both looked at me.

Sam held out his hand. "Hi, I'm Sam."

Donna shook his hand. "I'm Donna. I work with Adam. We're friends."

"Oh, it's nice to meet you! Adam told me about you, but I wasn't sure if you were an imaginary friend or a real one. I'm glad you're real."

Donna glared at me. "Adam is this . . . *that* Sam . . . your . . ."

I looked back and forth between them.

"Yeah, I'm his . . . Adam? Would you like to say what I am?"

"Yes . . . of course. Donna . . . Sam is my . . . ten- . . ."

Before I could finish, Donna snapped. "Don't you fucking *dare* say "tenant" or I will beat you to death right here in this store!"

Sam's eyes grew as big as saucers.

Donna took it down a notch. "Sorry. I overstate things sometimes. He's your boyfriend, Adam. Don't tell me he's your tenant."

Sam gushed, "Wow! Adam didn't tell me how awesome you are!"

"Likewise! You're a freakin' hottie! How old are you?"

"Twenty. Almost twenty-one."

"Adam, why would you even look at Henry when you have this?"

Fuck! I sank into an overstuffed chair and covered my face with my hands. "I am not interested in Henry!"

Sam asked Donna, "What's your view on Henry? Tell me everything."

"He's a manipulative, cold-blooded, self-centered ladder-climber who will use and destroy anyone who stands in the way of his ambition. I'd like to cut off his dick and feed it to the fish."

"Do you know him pretty well?"

"No, but I'm sure I'm right."

"I trust you."

I was flabbergasted. "You just met her!"

Sam continued. "Is he good looking?"

"Well . . . yes. He's very . . ." She gestured. "Sleek, I guess. His clothes fit him like a glove, and his ass is so . . ." She moved her hands in a very undignified way.

"I get the picture."

"He's nowhere near your league. I could eat you with a spoon!"

"Oh, please, don't embarrass me. You're as bad as he is." He pointed at me.

"Don't be embarrassed! You're a beautiful young man. Be proud! Will you come and live with me? My husband can move out. Do you like kids?"

"I already have a place, but thanks."

"Adam's a great guy, even though I want to wring his neck every other day."

I looked up. "I can hear you! I'm right here!"

"I know what you mean. He says he hates people, but under that shell . . . well, he still hates people, but he's been good to me. I don't know what I would have done without him. Great cook, too. I can't believe he didn't get snatched up before I came along." He glanced at me and lowered his voice to a whisper. "And he has *no idea* how good looking he is. It's incredible."

Donna whispered too. "I *know!* You should hear what the women at work say about him. He doesn't have a clue. It's so adorable, I want to squeeze him to death."

My face burned. *How long do I have to put up with these compliments?*

Sam looked at me. "How are you doing over there?"

I sulked. "I want to buy a fucking sofa!"

He turned back to Donna. "See what I mean? How could I not fall in love with him? I told him earlier, I'll never leave him. And if Henry crosses the line, I want you to call me right away. I'll come over, we'll torture him and kill him, and we'll make the body disappear. Okay?"

Donna's chin quivered, and she threw her arms around him. "No one ever wants to murder anyone with me! You really love him, don't you?"

Sam hugged her, but he looked at me. "I do. I really do."

Despite my intense discomfort with their absurd display of affection for me, I had a tear in my eye. I was, reluctantly, feeling . . . fortunate. I wiped my eye. "Are you finished? I didn't come here for feelings. I came here to shop."

They ended their embrace. I stood up and pretended to brush something off the front of my shirt to cover my awkwardness. Donna snuck up and caught me in a hug, pinning my arms against my body. Sam grinned at her violation of my comfort zone. She rocked me back and forth. "I'm so thrilled, you stupid jerk." *Finally, something negative!* She grabbed my head and kissed me on the cheek while I squirmed like a schoolboy being infected with girl germs.

"Augh! Get your lips off me! Jeez! That's what got you in trouble at work."

She released me from her torture chamber and hit my arm. "You need to be nice to Sam, do you hear me?"

"OW! Stop hitting me! I *am* nice to him!"

"He is nice to me, it's true. You can stop hitting him . . . for now."

She took a deep breath and expelled it. "Okay then." She smoothed her clothing and pushed her hair back from her face. "What room are you trying to furnish?"

"It's a living room. My parents had a Victorian parlor suite in there, but Sam broke the sofa because he was making out with me too hard." *It's my turn to embarrass him! Yay!*

Donna raised one eyebrow at Sam. "Oh?"

He blushed. "It's not broken. It came unglued."

"I want something more comfortable, but sturdy. Maybe more masculine looking."

"That's right, because you're a dude." She rolled her eyes and scanned the showroom floor. "Found it. Come with me." She marched us to another section and stopped in front of a tufted leather sofa with large rolled arms and brass nail head trim. It was perfect. Sam sat down on one end of the sofa and stretched his long arm across the back. The sofa looked even better. I sat at the other end and found it to be very comfortable. She looked at us and shook her head. "What a gorgeous couple. Seriously. I'll fantasize about the two of you tonight while I'm with Kevin."

"Eeew! Stop it!"

Sam covered his eyes with his hand.

Donna kept going. "By the way, leather is easy to wipe off in case Sam gets . . . fluids . . . on it. These young guys can be messy."

Sam was mortified. "Come on, that's private stuff!"

"Sam, honey . . . I was talking about beverages. What were you thinking?"

He covered his eyes again and whispered, "Dammit."

Donna winked at me. I grinned. "I have to run, guys. I need to pick up the kids. Sam . . . no, don't get up . . . it was great to meet you." She pulled out a business card and handed it to him. "Call me so we can have lunch and talk about Adam."

"Absolutely not!" I said. They ignored me.

"Adam, I'll see you tomorrow. Buy the sofa and the matching chair. Bye!" And she left.

We sat on the sofa and watched her walk away. When she was out of sight, Sam looked at me. "I like her. And she scares me."

"Yes. Exactly. She certainly likes you."

"I hope I didn't embarrass you too much."

"Were you trying to embarrass me? I didn't notice." He knew I was lying. I moved toward his side of the sofa.

"I know we talk that way at home, but I wasn't sure if . . . I don't know if you're comfortable letting people know about us."

I moved very close to him so his arm was behind me. "Sam, if I only did things I'm comfortable with, I'd still be miserable and lonely. I'm not embarrassed to be seen with you."

"Maybe we should have a signal of some kind, so if I cross a line you can . . ."

"No, let's not. I'd use it all the time if you let me get away with that. Keep doing what you're doing. You're good at this." I leaned into him and rested my head on his shoulder. A young woman wearing a store badge came toward us with a big smile on her face.

"Someone is coming, Adam."

"I see her." I didn't move.

"You look very comfortable. Can I help you, gentlemen?"

"Yes, I'd like to buy this sofa and the matching chair."

"Okay. Are you aware there's a matching love seat, as well?"

"Oh, I like the sound of that." I pictured my living room and the available space. "Yes, I'll take that, too."

"And do you want the ottoman to go with the chair?"

"What the hell, let's do it."

She laughed. "I'll get an order form. You stay there and relax." She started to walk away, then turned back and spoke hesitantly. "Can I say . . . the two of you look so sweet together. It's great to see you feeling comfortable in public. My younger brother is . . . well, never mind. I'll get the paperwork. I'll be right back."

We were quiet for a minute. "That was nice." I heard Sam sniffle. He put his fingers on the bridge of his nose. "Are you crying?"

"No."

I paused. "Are you sure?"

He sniffled again.

15

I didn't like to miss dinner with Sam, but on Monday night I had my first appointment with the psychologist Dr. Rubin recommended. Sam had to fend for himself. When I finally got home, the house was dark but the lights were on in the coach house. I took my mail from the box on my porch and went straight up to his apartment, pounding loudly on the door. "Open up! It's your landlord!"

A few seconds later Sam threw open the door. "You scared me! Get in here!" He wrapped his hand around the back of my neck and kissed me rather aggressively, penetrating my mouth with his tongue and taking as much of me as he wanted. He ended the kiss with a smirk. "Are you here to collect the rent?"

"No, but I feel like I got paid." I wiped my mouth with the back of my hand. "You set a new standard for after work greetings."

He smiled proudly, looking as cute as ever in a tight grey t-shirt and white boxer shorts covered with yellow smiley-faces. He closed the door and padded across the floor in his bare feet. "How was your day?"

"Long." I sat down at his kitchen table and peered into a paper bucket that held the bones of at least one chicken.

He gathered empty containers from mashed potatoes, gravy, coleslaw, and who knows what else. "Are you hungry? Do you want anything?"

"Is there anything left?"

"Uh . . . no."

"That's okay, I had a burger before my appointment."

"Yeah, how did that go?"

"It was interesting. Difficult. Good."

"Do you want to talk about it? You don't have to if you don't want to."

"I don't mind. He asked me a million questions, I told him how fucked up I am, he made some observations, and we talked about how to proceed."

Sam wiped the table with a wet cloth. "Did you like him?"

"I felt comfortable with him. It's not easy to talk about personal stuff with a stranger, but he made it easier. He said something at the end that I have to think about."

"What did he say?"

"I told him I wanted to feel more in control, and he said, 'Haven't you had enough of that?' He asked me to come up with a better goal."

"Huh." Sam rubbed his chest with a thoughtful look.

I shuffled through my mail. "I got something from Dr. Rubin's office. Probably my test results." I opened the envelope, unfolded the papers and scanned their contents while Sam looked over my shoulder. "Looks like I don't have cooties. Everything is negative. Here you go." I handed the papers to him and stood up to get a drink of water.

He read the results, folded them up and stuffed them back in the envelope. "I'm not surprised, but that's good news."

I finished drinking my water and turned around to find him standing right there. He grabbed the front of my trousers and unzipped my fly. Before I could react, he had me backed up against the refrigerator with his hand inside my pants.

"Whoa! Slow down, I need to get out of my work clothes and . . . oh! Aaaaah."

He maintained eye contact while massaging my genitals. "I'll take your clothes off when I'm ready. I like you in your work clothes."

"Okay, that feels good, but I'll go back to the house and . . ."

"You're not going anywhere." He had the slightest smile on his lips.

"That's . . . sexy, but we'll be more comfortable over there."

"You could *try* to leave." He stroked my silk necktie with his free hand.

I realized he was playing with me. I tried to push myself away from the refrigerator, but he pressed me back with the tips of his fingers on my chest. I liked it. When I tried to move sideways, he carefully enclosed my balls in his hand. "Aaah, ah . . . okay." I stopped trying to move.

He kissed me gently on the mouth. "Do we have an understanding?"

"I get it. You're in control."

"That's right. In my house, we play by my rules."

"Technically, I'm the owner." I smiled as if I had won a point.

This seemed to amuse him. He pinned me against the refrigerator with his forearm across the top of my chest, removed his hand from my pants and unbuckled my belt. "Okay, Mr. Owner Man . . ." He finished unfastening my trousers and let them fall to my ankles. "Oops. Your pants fell down."

I tried to kiss him, but he pulled back, teasing me. He licked his lips and left them slightly parted. I struggled to reach them. "Please?"

"No."

"Come on!"

"Why do you want to kiss me?"

"Unf! Because I love you, I love your face, I love your stubble. I want it."

He waited. "Is that all?"

"Mmph! Your lips! I want them!"

"Whose house is this?"

"Yours!"

He kissed me aggressively, like he did at the door, thumping the back of my head against the refrigerator, lips, tongue and stubble. My erection stretched my underwear. Sam took control of it, unwrapped it, and held it. He withdrew his tongue and slowly pulled his lower lip away from me. I stretched my neck forward, like a hungry baby bird. "More!"

"Don't be greedy. It's rude."

"When you're at my house, I feed you as much as you want."

A smile flashed across his lips. After a moment's hesitation, he kissed me again, hard and deep. He moved his hands to my waist and picked me up. I heard a ripping sound and grabbed his shoulders. He walked me across the floor and plopped my butt onto the kitchen table.

"What was that sound?"

He lifted his arm to reveal a gap where the seam of his shirt separated. "I knew that would happen. This thing is too tight." He removed my shoes without untying them, threw my trousers onto a chair, and pulled off my socks.

"Why am I on the table? This is unsanitary."

"It's my table."

"What are you doing?"

"You don't need to know."

"I don't? But I'm involved."

Exasperated, he clamped his hands on my thighs. "Is your dick hard?"

"Yes."

"Then shut up and enjoy it!" He pushed at my chest, forcing me to prop myself on my hands, and grabbed my briefs, roughly tugging them toward my knees.

"Don't tear them."

Sam stopped and glared at me. Without breaking eye contact, he clenched his fists and jerked his hands apart once, then again. He lifted my torn briefs and held them for a moment between his thumb and forefinger before dropping them on the floor. "I guess I don't know my own strength."

My boner throbbed with approval. As if that wasn't enough, he grabbed the collar of his t-shirt and effortlessly snapped it in half, tore the shirt down the middle, and ripped the remaining pieces off his body.

"Oh my God, that's hot! I've seen that in videos, but I never thought I would see it in . . ."

Sam lunged forward and swallowed the full length of my erection.

“Oh! Fucking hell!" He applied suction. "Jesus H. Christ! Mother of God, mother fucker!" My Catholicism was coming out with profane updates. I lowered my back to the table and gave in to my very first blow job.

Five minutes later, as I lay on his kitchen table trying to catch my breath, Sam looked rather satisfied with himself. "I waited a long time for that. How was it?"

"Hoooo! That was amazing! Thank you."

He came around the table and gave me a kiss. "My pleasure. Of all the sex stuff I've tried, sucking dick is one of my favorites. You know me, I'll eat anything." He loosened my tie and took it off.

"Well . . . anytime you want a snack, let me know."

He started to unbutton my shirt. "It sounded like you were praying, except for the swearing."

"I don't know what that was." I realized he was undressing me. "Wait, I might as well keep my shirt on to go back to the house."

"You're not going back to the house."

I sat up. "What? I've got things to do."

"Like what?"

"Um . . . I haven't checked my e-mail."

"Who do you get e-mail from?"

"Best Bargains . . . Office Mart . . . a place in Canada that sells Viagra."

"They can wait."

"But they might have a sale."

His brow crinkled. "Is this for real, or are you teasing me?"

"Uh . . ." *Am I, or not?*

"You're staying here. Lift up your arm or I'll tear your shirt."

I obeyed. "But I have my routines. They help me feel more . . ." I stopped.

He removed my shirt and hung it on the back of a chair. "More what?"

"Never mind."

He faced me again with his hands on my knees. "More in control? Is that what you were about to say?"

I looked at the ceiling. "Maybe."

"I want you in my bed." He picked me up and threw me over his shoulder.

I tried to grab his smiley-face boxers, but I couldn't reach. "My bed is bigger."

He smacked me on the butt.

"Ow! That hurt!"

"Do we have to go over this again? Who's in control?"

I sighed. "I don't know . . . is it you?"

He smacked me again, harder.

"OW!! You're in control! Sir!"

"Oh, I like the sound of that." He dumped me onto his bed. "I'm not done with you yet."

"What now?"

He rolled his eyes. "You're not clear on the concept, are you?"

He was right. I knew my life was too controlled, but I didn't know how to overcome my habits. Sam was challenging me. Despite the powerful incentive of his sexy ways, it was not easy for me to surrender. I settled into the bed and tried to be less difficult. "I like your boxers."

"Yeah? They're happy to see you." He waited for his dumb joke to affect me. "Get it? They're smiling?" I couldn't keep a straight face. He was so fucking cute and I loved his goofy grin. "I was waiting for you to say something about them." He took them off.

I could not get the smile off my face as he straddled me. "Oh, now I get to do you!"

"Did I say that?"

"Well, no, but . . . okay. I'll be quiet."

"Good, you're catching on." He kissed my nose and proceeded to teach me, in detail, how to give him as much pleasure as I had experienced a few minutes earlier. His instruction helped me overcome worries about my inexperience, and I enjoyed it as much as I thought I would. By the time we finished, his body glistened with perspiration and he looked very, very satisfied. He thanked me with a tender kiss and stretched out next to me with his head resting on one hand. "So . . . how did you like it?"

"I loved it. You're very sweet."

"Aww."

"You're sweet, too, but I meant your jizz. It tastes like ice cream and doughnuts."

He laughed and laid his arm across my chest, kissing the side of my face and my ear. "I'm so crazy about you, Adam, do you know that? You drive me absolutely crazy in so many ways."

"I believe that." I believed it in so many ways.

"Let me turn off the lights so we can cuddle up for the night." He crawled over me, rubbing himself against me more than he needed to. I watched his beautiful body move through the apartment. He came back to the bed and rubbed himself across me again.

I thought about how to get comfortable. "Um, I sleep on the right side in my bed."

"You're not in your bed, are you? You'll sleep on the left in my bed."

"Hmm." I looked around. "Where's your alarm clock?"

"I don't use one."

"I need to get up for work."

"So do I. I'll wake you up."

"What if you oversleep?"

"I won't." He waited to see if I would say anything else. "You'll have to trust me."

"Okay. I like to get up at six-thirty so I have time to exercise and eat breakfast."

"I don't have any clocks."

"What? That's insane!"

"I'm kidding! Jeez! I'll wake you up at 6:30, I'll put you through a military calisthenics routine, I'll make French toast for breakfast, and then you can go over to the house and get ready for work. Satisfied? Can we cuddle now, or are you too busy?"

"All right." I tried to settle down, but I had issues, officially confirmed by a mental health professional. "Maybe I'll wait until you fall asleep and go back to the house."

"Ugh! You were doing so well, but you couldn't let it go. Now I'll have to sleep on top of you so you can't go anywhere." He crawled on top of me, face down, with his limbs spread across the bed.

"Mmmrph!" I couldn't breathe. He was very heavy, and I felt as flat as a chalk outline at a murder scene. "Mmmmph!" I managed to pinch him.

He took some weight off. "Is something wrong?"

"Get off me! I can't breathe!"

"I don't know . . . do you promise to stay?"

"Yes!"

"Who's in control here?"

"You are!"

"Okay." He rolled off me and I filled my lungs. I wanted to hit him, but I knew he was helping me. He pulled me against his body, spread his hand on my chest and nuzzled my neck.

Yes, I had a lot of issues, but I would get better . . . or Sam would suffocate me. It was a good arrangement. I felt safe. "Sam?"

"What?"

"Can we do this every Monday?"

"I'll allow that. Go to sleep now."

"Thank you . . . sir."

"Mmmm. That makes me want to fill you with my seed."

"God, that's sexy."

"It was supposed to be funny."

"Still . . . very sexy."

***

At the end of the day on Tuesday, I left the office feeling cheerful and optimistic. As I was about to get in my truck, I heard someone call my name. *Dammit! Now what? Probably some horrible disaster I'll have to deal with.* I turned around to see Henry trotting across the parking lot. *Oh, I haven't seen him for a while.*

"Hey, Adam! How are you? Nice truck, dude. It looks brand new. Your boyfriend takes good care of you."

"It is . . . he doesn't, I mean he's not . . . I bought it. Myself." I leaned against my shiny blue pickup.

"It matches your eyes."

My eyelashes fluttered. "How are you?"

"I'm fine. How do I look?" He peered at his reflection in the window glass above my shoulder.

"You look good, as usual . . . I mean . . ."

He smiled. "Thanks, I'm meeting a guy for drinks. He's been begging for a date for weeks."

"That's nice."

"You look hot."

"Uff!" I rolled my eyes.

"You should unbutton your collar in this weather."

"Oh."

He loosened my tie and opened my top collar button. *That's very thoughtful.* While he did that, he asked, "Have you heard anything about personnel changes in the office."

"Changes? Who? What? I haven't heard anything."

"You haven't? Oh, well . . . never mind. They were probably rumors."

"What rumors? What did you hear?"

"No, I shouldn't repeat rumors. If you haven't heard about it, they're probably not true."

"I'm not in the loop."

"But this was about a friend of yours, so it can't be true."

"Donna is my only friend. Did you hear something about her?"

"Hey! What about me? I'm your friend."

"I'm sorry, of course you're my friend. I was thinking of Donna because she's having problems with Mr. Zipinski."

"She is? What's that about?"

"He might try to get rid of her because she has information about him . . . wait, I shouldn't be talking about this . . . she'll kill me."

"Why? I'd like to help, if I can."

"Um . . . I guess it would be good for you to know about this. Apparently Zipinski has been doing some nasty stuff to a bunch of female staffers and Donna wanted them to file a formal complaint."

"That's great! I mean, it's terrible. That old mummy has a functioning dick?"

"I can't confirm that."

"I'm friends with a lot of the ladies in the office because . . . well, you know why they like me. I could probably find out who those women are and talk them into filing a complaint. Maybe if they hear it from a man, it'll be more persuasive."

"I never thought of that." *I knew he was a good guy!* I'm glad I told you, Donna will be . . ."

"Don't tell Donna. She needs to stay clear of this."

"Oh yeah, right. She'll shut up about it for a while. I won't tell her we spoke. That'll be easier for me, too."

"Hey, do you want to grab a drink with me right now? We could go to the bar across the street. I fucked the bartender, so he'll probably discount us."

"I thought you had a date."

"I can blow him off. He'll call me again anyway."

"I'd like to, but I have to go home and make dinner. I can't let my man go hungry."

"He's a lucky guy, whoever he is. I'd like to meet him some time."

"That wouldn't go well."

"Why do you say that?"

"Uh . . . he's a little jealous. In a good way."

"Is there a good way to be jealous? I wouldn't put up with that."

"Oh, it's not like that. He doesn't control me. Well, most of the time. But that's different. It's complicated."

"Adam . . . you're running home to cook dinner for him . . . he doesn't want you to have friends. It's not exactly paradise, is it?"

"No, he's great. Really, I don't deserve him. But thanks for your concern. It's fine."

"I hope so. If you ever need help with him, let me know."

"That's sweet, Henry, but you have no idea what you'd be up against. And there's no need. He's fine. I'm fine. Everyone is fine, okay?"

"I'll take your word for it, but I worry about you, buddy! You'd better go, or he'll be angry."

"That's not true." I looked at my watch. "Oh, shit! I need to get a roast in the oven. I'll see you on Thursday."

"Thursday? What about tomorrow?"

"I'm not working on Wednesdays anymore. Zipinski is letting me work on Saturdays instead so I can spend more time with my boyfriend." I climbed into my truck.

"Zipinski knows about your boyfriend?"

"No, no! I let him think I have a girlfriend. He'll never find out. Have fun with your date. Don't do anything I wouldn't do."

"No, of course not. See you Thursday."

As I drove away, I was glad I accepted Henry's offer of friendship. *If Donna and Sam knew him the way I do, they wouldn't be so suspicious of him. It feels good to trust people. My life has been so much better since I started trusting people. I don't know what I was afraid of all those years.*

I flipped on the radio. Chris Isaak was singing "*Baby Did a Bad Bad Thing.*"

I cranked it up and sang along.

16

On Wednesday morning, I woke up with Sam's arm draped over me. Usually he was up first, so this was a pleasant change. I tried to roll over, but shifting his arm was no easy task. As soon as I moved, he pulled me closer as if I were a stuffed bear.

He muttered, "Where do you think you're going?"

"I wasn't going anywhere. I wanted to roll over and look at you."

"Oh. Okay." He lifted his arm and I turned to face him, lying on my side. Without opening his eyes, he brought his hand back down, found my ass and gave it a squeeze. "Nice butt. What's your name again?"

"Phyllis." He smiled, and I kissed the tip of his nose. "It's nice to wake up with you here."

"You wore me out last night. I can barely move."

"If you weren't such a weakling, you could keep up with me." I squeezed his thick upper arm. "I'm getting up to exercise. Do you want me to make breakfast for you?"

He rolled onto his back and rubbed the sleep from his eyes. "No, I'll go to the doughnut shop and get my usual. Do you want anything?"

"Doughnuts again? You'll get too fat for your new swimming suit. What will Flora think?"

He propped himself up on his elbows, flexing his clearly defined abdominals. "You're right, I am getting flabby." He looked at me with a straight face.

I waited about five seconds before pouncing on him. I surprised him with a playful, buzzing kiss on a ticklish spot at the side of his waist. He laughed, flipped me onto my back, and kissed my stomach. I still felt uneasy about being touched in that area, but I was getting used to it because he did it with such obvious enjoyment. He moved up my chest to my neck, and my cheek, and then kissed me slowly on the mouth. I looked at his eyes and his tousled hair, and the shadow of a beard on his jaw. "If we don't get out of bed right now we'll be here all day."

"You're right. I'm so tempted." He rolled off the bed and stood up to stretch. I watched his morning stretch whenever I could. I hopped off the other side of the bed and stretched in my own way. He scratched his chest and waited for me to finish. "What time are we supposed to be at Flora's?"

"Noon."

He put on his shorts and t-shirt. "I need to pump some serious iron this morning so I can live up to my role as your trophy boyfriend."

"Stop it. You're not a trophy."

“Yeah? How would you describe me to other people?”

“Just . . . an average, ordinary guy. Likes to read.”

“Uh huh.” He crossed his arms and stood in front of me.

“Tall. Good dental hygiene.”

He cracked a smile. "Thanks." He reached down and patted my naked ass. “You’re the trophy. I'll see you later."

***

When it was time to go to Flora's house, Sam was more nervous than I had ever seen him. He wore navy blue chino shorts and a bright yellow polo shirt that complemented his tanned skin, dark hair and green eyes. "Do I look okay?"

“You’re gorgeous. Is your new swimsuit under there?"

"Yes."

"Do you want to show me before we go?"

"No."

"Why are you being so mysterious about it?"

He shrugged. "Just to bug you. You look handsome, as always. Not that you would ever ask.”

“Okay, whatever. I mean, thanks. Shall we go?" I had a box of pecan pralines from a high-end candy maker downtown. Flora had Southern manners, and I wouldn't show up without a hostess gift. We went out the back door, and I was about to cut through the gap in the hedge.

"Adam . . . shouldn't we go to the front door? We're not burglars."

"Oh . . . yeah, I guess you're right." We walked around to the front of her house and rang the doorbell.

Sam bounced on the balls of his feet. "I feel like we're on our first date." We never had that experience. This was the first time we were socializing as a couple.

We were greeted by Flora's long-term housekeeper, Agnes. "Mr. Adam, please come in." She always addressed me formally, even when I was a boy visiting with my parents. Agnes had a stern face, a warm heart, and a hint of Scotland in her voice.

"Agnes, it's good to see you again. This is my friend, Sam."

"Mr. Sam, welcome."

"I'm pleased to meet you, ma'am."

"Ye'll call me Agnes, dearie, I'm not the Queen of England."

"All right . . . Agnes. Please call me Sam."

"I certainly will not. We have standards in this house." A flash in her eyes suggested she was all bark and no bite. I don't think I had ever seen her smile, but I knew she had a sense of humor. Flora couldn't abide humorless people. "I'll take ye to Mrs. O'Neill."

We passed through the house filled with antique furniture and other beautiful objects that were probably in Flora's family for generations. The large kitchen smelled wonderful. I knew Agnes was an excellent cook. At the back of the house, we walked onto the terrace where Flora stood in the shade of a large umbrella, inspecting the place settings on the patio table. "Your guests are here, ma'am."

Flora turned and smiled, stepping toward me with her arms open. "Adam, it's lovely to see you." I kissed her cheek, as expected, and felt her soft hand on my face. She looked up at Sam.

"Flora, this is Sam, the one I've been telling you about."

"Mrs. O'Neill, I'm so pleased to meet you, finally." Sam took her hand and bent down to kiss it, and I fell in love with him all over again.

"How charming! Welcome, Sam. I've been looking forward to this as well. Is it Samuel? My father's name was Samuel."

"My full name is Samson, but I prefer Sam."

"Oh, but that's a splendid name! Samson . . . it suits you." Her eyes took his measurements. "Agnes, this is the young man who nearly broke Edward's hand. Isn't he magnificent?"

"Aye, ma'am. I like him already." Her expression didn't change.

Sam blushed. "I'm so sorry about your son, Mrs. O'Neill. I shouldn't have . . ."

"There's no need to apologize, honey, I'm sure he deserved it. When Clarence told us the story, we must have laughed for ten minutes. Didn't we, Agnes?"

"Aye, ma'am. It was a good day."

"Just look at these two! When was the last time we had such fine young men in this house?"

"Too long, ma'am. I do miss it."

Flora put her arm around my waist. "Hasn't Adam grown into a handsome gentleman? Can you believe this is the same boy who came here with his parents?" Now I blushed.

"Quietest boy I ever saw. Like a rabbit. I used to think he was up to something, but he wasn't." If I'm not mistaken, that was high praise coming from Agnes. "Looks like his father, now, doesn't he ma'am?"

"Indeed, he does. But he has his mother's eyes." I would have cried if they hadn't stopped.

Agnes lifted her chin in Sam's direction. "This one's built like a plow horse we had when I was a wee girl."

Sam took it in stride. "You grew up on a farm? So did I."

Flora apologized. "You'll have to forgive us. Since Mr. O'Neill passed away, we've hosted too many card parties for old women. We're excited to have testosterone in the air."

I held out my gift. "I brought pecan pralines. I hope you like them."

"Oh, you know I love sugar! Thank you, dear, that's very thoughtful. Agnes, will you take these into the house, please?"

"Aye, ma'am. Shall I begin serving?"

"Yes, please. I'll leave it in your capable hands. Samson, dear, why don't you sit across from me, and Adam can sit between us. Agnes has outdone herself today by preparing a five-course luncheon, so I hope you're hungry." Sam's eyes lit up. "Honestly, I tried to talk her out of it, but she thinks young men still eat like farm hands. I know how weight-conscious some of you boys are."

"We'll manage, won't we Sam?"

"Yes, I'm hungry."

We heard a pop from the kitchen. "I thought we'd have champagne to celebrate. Do you drink?"

"I certainly do." I looked at Sam.

"I haven't tried it. I'm not twenty-one yet."

"My stars, I had no idea you were so young. It's been so long since I corrupted a young man. Will you do me the honor of letting me corrupt you with champagne? I won't insist." Agnes approached with the bottle.

I nodded at Sam. "Okay, I'll try it." He smiled shyly. "If I'm going to be corrupted, I suppose it should be done by an expert."

Flora and I laughed. Agnes' mouth twitched as she filled our champagne flutes. "He knows ye already, ma'am."

As we sipped the champagne, Agnes served salmon bisque garnished with watercress. Flora questioned Sam. "Where is your parents' farm, dear?"

"Up north, in Sorek County. It's isolated, there's not much to see."

"Do you still have family there?"

"My parents are there. No one else."

"And how often do you visit them?"

"I haven't had any contact with them for almost a year. They don't approve of choices I've made. That's what they would say. They're very religious, so . . ."

"They condemned you for being a homosexual." Flora liked to get things out on the table. "I'm so sorry to hear that, honey."

Sam squirmed. "Thanks." He focused on his soup.

I would have dropped the conversation there, but Flora continued. "Do you miss them?"

"Yes. I miss them very much." He turned his champagne glass between his fingers, then picked it up and drank what was left.

"Oh, dear. I'm sure they miss you terribly. You're their only child."

I drained my glass as well. *Why do people have to talk about feelings? It's so awkward.* Agnes moved quietly around the table, refilling our glasses. When she came to Sam, she laid her hand on his shoulder very briefly. He looked up. "Thank you. The soup was delicious, Agnes."

"Thank you, Mr. Sam. Would ye like more?"

"No, thank you. I want to save room for everything else." He was being very polite.

She assessed him. "You've got room. There's a wee bit left here. It'll just go down the drain."

He glanced at Flora, at me, and back to Agnes' blank expression. "Well, it's too good to waste." She ladled the last of the soup into his plate, dropping a sprig of watercress in the center before returning it to him.

Flora smiled at their interaction. "Agnes, you could have offered some to Adam."

"I'm sorry, Mr. Adam. Did ye want more?"

"No, I'm fine. It was delicious."

Agnes picked up the soup tureen. "Rabbits don't eat as much as horses, ma'am." She returned to the kitchen.

Flora and I chuckled. Sam blushed again. "I'm sorry, Mrs. O'Neill, I have a big appetite. Adam knows better than anyone."

"Honey, it's perfectly fine, don't think twice about it. And please, call me Flora." She beamed at us. "I like a man who eats well. It's a very masculine quality, don't you agree?"

"I do agree. His appetite is one of my favorite things about him. But that's a long list."

She placed her hand over mine on the table. It reminded me of something my mother used to do when she wanted to say something important. "I'm so happy for you, Adam. I've been hoping to see you with a suitable man for a long time now. Your dear mother and I shared that wish many times before she passed."

This was news to me, to put it mildly. "My mother knew?"

Flora was taken aback. "Why, of course she knew, Adam. Your father as well. You were their greatest treasure and they loved you very much."

I wasn't expecting this at all. It brought tears to my eyes. *Too many feelings!* I picked up my glass and drank the champagne in two gulps. Sam rubbed my arm. Following my example, he drained his glass, too.

Agnes arrived with another tray and removed our soup plates. "What did I miss, ma'am?"

"Oh, dear! I told Adam his parents knew about his homosexuality. You know how clumsy I can be about these things. I had no idea he was unaware."

"You're a bull in a china shop, ma'am." Agnes patted me on the shoulder. "We all knew, dearie. It's just who ye are." She presented me with a golden-brown cloud. "Eat my cheese soufflé. You'll feel better." She served Flora and Sam, then refilled my champagne flute. Only mine.

Sam tasted the soufflé and moaned, "Oh my God! Agnes, will you marry me?" She scoffed and removed his empty glass, taking it and the soup plates into the house. "Uh oh. I think I've been cut off." There was a hint of silliness in his voice. "I like champagne!"

I asked Flora, "If my parents knew I was gay, why didn't they ever talk to me about it?"

'I don't know, sweetie. Your parents were lovely people, but . . . they lived more internally than externally, if you understand my meaning. They were intellectuals, they loved books, and they could converse on many interesting topics, but it took a long time to get to know them. They didn't talk about themselves easily."

Sam scraped the bottom of his soufflé dish. "I know exactly what you mean because he's the same way." He pointed at me with his spoon. "There's always something going on in there, and you have to drag it out of him. You're like a puzzle, aren't you, babe?"

Babe? He never called me that. *The champagne must have gone straight to his head.*

Flora smiled warmly. "You are like your father - the emotional world was unfamiliar to him as well. He was steady and loyal, and very proud of you. Your mother felt things deeply, but rarely showed it. I wondered how she managed it, living in that house with her quiet men. That's what drew us together. We felt left out by the men we loved. My life with Mr. O'Neill was a grand compromise. I enjoyed the men in his social circle, but I was never a part of their world." She paused for a sip of champagne. "Samson, honey, I don't know if Adam told you, but my husband was a homosexual."

"You're kidding! Why did you marry him?"

"I loved him. I have no other excuse. And the world was very different then."

Without a moment's hesitation, he asked, "Did you have sex?"

"Sam!" I scolded him, but Flora laughed.

He realized his error. "I'm sorry, that was rude. What's wrong with me?"

Agnes returned and put a glass of iced tea next to Sam, then collected the soufflé dishes.

Flora obviously wasn't bothered. "I believe you are experiencing the effects of champagne, my dear. It loosens the tongue. And to answer your question, yes, we did have sexual relations early in our marriage. He was eager to please me, and we wanted a child, so we had Edward."

"Huh." Sam found this interesting. "I bet you were pretty hot when you were younger, but . . ." I glared at him. He shrugged. "What? She's pretty. Don't you think she's pretty?" He still held his spoon even though his soufflé was gone. He made a face and pointed at me to suggest I was crazy. "Anyway . . . I don't know if I could have sex with a woman, could you, Adam?" He pointed his spoon at the sky.

I shook my head. "I don't want to discuss that."

He rolled his eyes dramatically. Agnes deftly slipped the spoon out of his fingers. He brought his hand in front of his face, then searched the table and the ground to see where he had dropped it. He looked at Agnes who showed him the spoon with her usual blank expression. He grinned. "You tricked me! I like you!" She marched back to the kitchen, and he asked, "What were we talking about?"

I lied. "We were talking about your job."

"We were?" He looked at Flora. "What did you want to know?"

"Tell me everything, honey. I'm very interested."

"Okay. I work at Dave's Nursery, and I'm learning all about plants and shrubs and trees and gardening and landscaping. And business. And Dave is cranky until you get to know him, like Adam, so I like working for him because I'm used to that, and he's teaching me all about how he runs the business and manages employees and stuff. He says I'm a good worker, and he reminds me of my dad." Suddenly, he was about to cry. I put my hand on his arm and gave it a squeeze. He pulled himself together. "I'm sorry. So . . . I like the people I work with. They call me 'Muffin.' We joke around a lot and it makes the days go faster. And when I take my shirt off I make more money. I like it."

"That's wonderful, dear. What did you say they call you?"

"'Muffin.' Short for 'Stud muffin,' because of all this." He waved his hand up and down to indicate his body.

I grinned and squeezed his arm again. Flora looked like she was about to burst. "Why, that's the best nickname I've ever heard! And well-deserved, Samson. You are the most charming person I've met in many years. I'd like us all to be great friends from now on. How does that sound?"

"Great! I can use another friend." He spoke to me in a hushed voice. "I'm so relieved. I thought I would embarrass myself."

"No, I knew she would like you as much as I do."

"Hey, what about Agnes? Is she included?"

"Yes, sweetie, Agnes is included."

"Awesome!" He whispered, "Are you finishing your champagne?"

"Yes."

He paused. "Are you sure?"

"Yes." I pointed at the glass of iced tea.

"Hey! Where did that come from?" He picked it up and drank.

Agnes arrived with the main course, medallions of beef and mushrooms in red wine sauce, accompanied by rosettes of oven-browned mashed potatoes and asparagus spears. Everything was plated as it would be in a fine restaurant. Sam's plate contained larger portions of everything. "I got more than you! Thank you, Agnes." He beamed at her. "You know, I used to be a waiter."

"And why would that interest me?"

"I'm just saying. I know you like me. I can tell."

One of her eyebrows moved up by a fraction of an inch. "Mr. Adam, would ye like anything else to drink?"

"I'll have iced tea, please."

"Ma'am?"

"I'll have lemon water, dear. This meal is outstanding, Agnes. I can't thank you enough for all you do."

"My pleasure ma'am."

The beef practically melted in my mouth, and the sauce was perfect. This was shaping up to be one of the best meals I ever had. Agnes was a hidden treasure, and she found the quick way to Sam's heart.

Flora raised the next topic of conversation. "So, gentlemen . . . what shall we do about Helen Van Wootten and her little crusade?"

Sam asked, "Is this the weasel lady?" I nodded. "You know, I tried to say hello to her the other day, and she ran away from me like I was an ax murderer."

Flora asked, "Did you point anything sharp at her, dear?" I looked sideways at her.

"No, but Adam did." I looked sideways at him.

"Again? Adam, really!"

"No! Not again. I didn't do anything this time. Or the first time! I told you, I didn't threaten her."

Sam explained. "She was taking pictures of us in front of the house, so I went down there to introduce myself, and she jumped in her car and drove away! She even screeched her tires! Adam stayed on the porch, because he's a chicken." I made a face. "Well . . . you are."

"She was taking photographs? What were you doing?"

I shrugged. "Hanging flower baskets."

Flora speculated. "In her narrow mind, any suggestion of a romantic relationship between the two of you would constitute a threat to the neighborhood."

Sam snorted. "It's a good thing she didn't see us last night."

I don't know why that triggered my anger, but I lashed out. "Sam, would you shut up and eat? We're trying to have an adult conversation here!"

He looked wounded. I regretted my words immediately, but, of course, he was the one who apologized. "I'm sorry . . . I was just . . . I'll be quiet." He looked at his plate and moved something with his fork. Suddenly the world seemed terribly silent. I drank the last of my champagne. As soon as I set the glass down, Agnes was there to snatch it off the table.

Flora put her hand on mine. "Adam, honey . . . he's feeling silly from the champagne. You remember what it was like the first time, don't you?"

I was flooded with self-loathing. I couldn't look at either of them. "Yes, I know. I'm sorry, Sam, I shouldn't have said that."

"No, you were right. I was talking too much, and I shouldn't joke about private things."

That only made me feel worse. *Why does he have to be so much better than me? Why can't he be an asshole, so I don't look so bad?* "You didn't do anything wrong, Sam. I was wrong. Please . . . accept my apology."

"I accept. I forgive you." He put his hand on my knee. "I love you, babe."

Someone else might have been comforted or relieved . . . perhaps amused. Anyone else would have felt fortunate. But I wasn't anyone else. His forgiveness cut me to the bone, exposing my weakness and inadequacy. Perspiration surfaced on my burning face. I felt this way with him once before . . . I wanted to warn him, to scare him away before I could hurt him again, because I *would* hurt him . . . I *knew* I would. I was about to cry and didn't know how to escape the humiliation. Fortunately, Flora knew how to help.

"Maybe you'd like to freshen up, Adam. You remember where the powder room is."

"Yes, thank you, I would like that." I stood up. "I'll be back in a minute."

As I walked toward the house, I heard Flora say to Sam, "No, dear, you stay here with me. He'll be all right. Finish eating, or Agnes will think you don't like her food."

I found the small lavatory and shut myself inside. I breathed. I splashed water on my face. I assured myself I would be okay and thought about my next therapy appointment. Eventually, I calmed down. When I felt more in control . . . *there's that word again* . . . I opened the door and put on a brave face. Agnes was in the kitchen as I passed through.

"Mr. Adam?"

"Yes, Agnes." I expected her to scold me.

"I'm not much of a talker, but I see things. It's not easy to be loved. It hurts sometimes. We think we don't deserve it." All her feelings were in her eyes, and her eyes were deep. "But ye are loved. Get used to it, because it won't stop."

I looked into her eyes for a long moment and felt that she knew me. "Thank you, Agnes."

"Will ye help me carry this tray, please?" I knew she didn't need help with it, but it would ease my transition back to the table.

"You're very thoughtful, Agnes." I picked up the tray of salad plates and followed her back to the terrace where she set one at each place.

Sam's tongue was still loose. "Agnes, the salad should come at the beginning of the meal. When I was a waiter, we . . ."

She reached for his plate. "Would ye like me to take that away, Mr. Sam?"

"No! I want it!"

"Are ye too full? Will there be no dessert for ye, then?"

"I want dessert. Dessert is my favorite part. I'm eating my salad."

I sat down. "This looks delicious. What is it?"

"Baby beet greens with avocado and grapefruit." She touched my shoulder briefly.

Flora observed our interactions. "Agnes, you continue to impress me after all these years. I'm so lucky to have you."

"Aye, ma'am." She returned to the kitchen.

I put my hand on Sam's knee, sliding my fingers under the hem of his shorts to squeeze his leg. He searched my face. I did my best to show him my anger was gone.

Flora picked up the conversation where we left off. "Now . . . we need a plan to deal with Helen Van Weasel, or Van Wootten. Honestly, Adam, that nickname you gave her will come out of my mouth at the worst possible time. You're a terrible influence on me."

Sam shook his head as he ate. "I don't understand. What will she do to us?"

"I wish we knew, dear. I believe she will try to convince other neighbors that the two of you are a threat to the children in the neighborhood. If enough of the neighbors agree with her, it could become very uncomfortable for you to continue living here."

"I'm not going anywhere," I said. "I don't care if they hate me. I don't need to talk to any of them." Flora gave me a look of pity and irritation in equal parts.

Predictably, Sam's attitude was very different from mine. "Why don't you invite all the neighbors over for a barbecue? They'd probably like to see your garden, and if they like us, there won't be a problem."

The thought of inviting strangers into my private garden was revolting. "The last thing I need is more people invading my privacy. If I'm nice to them, they'll probably visit all the time. That would be awful. I'd rather have people hate me."

I caught Flora rolling her eyes. "It is possible to be friendly while maintaining appropriate boundaries. I know you value your privacy, but how will you cope if your private life becomes the subject of public discussion?"

"If people want to talk about me, there's nothing I can do to stop them. I'm not doing anything wrong and I don't bother any of them. My house is well-kept, so they can't complain about that."

"Adam, honey, there are people on Eden Place who would benefit from your knowledge of gardening and the advice you could give. Perhaps it would improve the appearance of their houses and the neighborhood in general."

"I'd give them a piece of my mind about their overgrown shrubbery."

"That's a start, dear. You have opinions to share. Offering a piece of your mind might not be the best approach, but . . . we'll work on that. Oh, here comes Agnes with her famous dessert! I'm sure you'll enjoy this." Agnes approached with a tray of elegant dessert glasses containing layers of white cream and red berries.

Sam sat up like a puppy expecting a treat. "I ate my salad and I liked it. I never had one like that before."

"Aye, well done." Agnes removed our salad plates and set one of the desserts in front of each of us. "I hope ye like my Cranachan."

Sam grinned. "I love your cramikin, but what's in this dish?" Agnes almost smiled while Flora and I laughed. Sam was at his best - relaxed enough to be childlike, and demonstrating the quick wit I enjoyed during our dinners together.

Agnes tried to look stern again. "Don't be fresh with me, dearie, or you'll get no seconds on that!" Sam enjoyed his moment of triumph.

"Tell us about this . . . what did you call it?"

"It's Cranachan, an old Scottish dessert. It's nothing but raspberries and cream with a bit of honey and toasted oats. And a drop of whiskey."

"More than a drop," Flora said. "I ask her to make this all the time. Adam, this was one of your father's favorites, wasn't it, Agnes?"

"Aye, ma'am. It made him more talkative." She glanced at Sam and retreated to the kitchen.

Sam put down his spoon. I reassured him. "Go ahead and eat it. I like it when you're silly, so don't worry about my crabby ass."

He smiled. "Wow . . . champagne and whiskey in the same day."

"I'll take you to rehab this evening." I tasted the Cranachan and discovered a wonderful mixture of flavors and textures. It wasn't too sweet or too heavy after a substantial meal. The 'drop of whiskey' felt warm in my throat.

Flora watched us. "Isn't it marvelous?" I nodded. Sam ate quietly. "Adam, dear . . . I've invited a few ladies from the neighborhood to have lunch with me. Would you mind if I brought them over to meet you and to see your garden?"

"Sure, that sounds nice." *Wait a minute . . . who said that?* I took another spoonful of Cranachan.

"They'll be so happy to hear that. Thank you, honey."

"My pleasure." *Was that my voice?* I was tempted to lick the dessert glass. Sam scraped the bottom of his dish.

Agnes appeared at the table holding another dish of Cranachan. "I have one left. Will you have it, Mr. Adam?"

"Yes, thank you." I surprised myself and Sam. I looked at the dessert, then at him. "I suppose I could share it with you."

"No, I think I had enough. It's warm today, isn't it?" He pulled at the front of his polo shirt.

"Aye, you've had enough." Agnes set the dessert in front of me.

"This was the best meal I've had in years. You're wonderful."

She shook her head. "Just like his father, ma'am. The very image."

Flora chuckled. "He is, indeed, Agnes."

Sam pushed his chair away from the table and stood up a little too quickly. He wobbled, then straightened up and steadied himself. "I'd like to use the pool, now. Is that okay?"

"Of course, dear. I was about to suggest it. Did you bring your bathing suit?"

"Uh huh. I'll show you." He abruptly pulled his shirt over his head, revealing his muscular torso.

Flora gasped. "Oh my!" I turned my chair to enjoy the show. Agnes was in no hurry to get back to the kitchen.

Sam removed his sandals and unbuttoned his shorts. "I bought a new one because I knew we would go in the pool today." With no sign of self-consciousness, he unzipped his shorts and stepped out of them. He wore a yellow square-cut spandex swimsuit with a black panel in the front. He adjusted the waistband. "Do you like it?"

Agnes whispered, "Mercy!" My jaw went slack. The swimsuit complemented his physique beautifully.

"Adam told me to get a tan on my thighs so they match my legs."

Flora pressed her hands together with glee. "It's very flattering. I love that color on you, Samson. He's a well-made young man, isn't he, Agnes?"

"Aye, ma'am. I'll go inside and have a sit down." She tottered off to the kitchen.

"Adam, what do you think?" He turned to give me a side view, wanting my approval most of all.

"That's perfect for you. You have great taste in clothes, Sam."

He leaned down to kiss me on the mouth. "Thanks, babe. Are you coming in the pool with me?"

"You bet. Let me finish my dessert and I'll join you."

"Okay." He kissed me again. "I feel so happy right now!"

"Me too." It was strange to kiss him in front of Flora, but I felt more relaxed than usual. Sam turned around and jogged toward the pool. The yellow spandex showed off his perfect ass. He did a cannonball jump into the middle of the water with a huge splash and a joyful noise. I turned back to the table with a big smile on my face.

"Adam, he's wonderful!"

"I know. Almost too good to be true."

"I realize this is an indelicate question, but . . . is he . . . expensive?"

I swallowed a mouthful of my second dessert while the meaning of her question slowly dawned on me. "Oh . . . it's not like that. Did you think . . . do you think I pay him to be with me?"

"Oh, honey, I hoped it wasn't true, but I had to ask. There are many arrangements of that type. I meant no offense."

"Sam pays full rent for the apartment, and he's making payments on my old pickup. I pay for our food, but he helps me with the yard work. Our relationship is . . . it's not a business transaction." I felt hurt, but I didn't know how to be angry at Flora.

"I have offended you. Please accept my apology, dear. I see how much you care about him, and the way he looks at you. I wanted to warn you about financial complications that might harm you in the long run. Mr. O'Neill kept several young men during our marriage. It often ended badly and cost a great deal of money."

Her explanation made sense, and her apology seemed genuine. But forgiveness didn't come as easily to me as it did to Sam. I struggled to get the words out. "I understand." *Does she think he would only be with me if I paid him? Is he that far out of my league?* "He's too good for me, I know, and it probably won't last, but . . ."

"Nonsense, Adam! He's perfect for you, and he obviously adores you."

"What if he only feels that way because I'm helping him?" I shoveled Cranachan into my mouth.

"I'm so sorry, I shouldn't have said anything. You are handsome and lovable, regardless of the crusty shell you wear."

I grunted dismissively. "Yeah, my good old crusty shell everyone keeps mentioning. You know, it's hard to feel good about this relationship when everyone immediately falls in love with Sam and then tells me how difficult I am."

She was quiet for a few minutes, and I felt guilty about the tension between us. Eventually, she put her hand on mine. I wanted to pull away, but I didn't. "You are right to scold me, Adam. I have been too harsh with you." Her voice cracked. "When I look at you, I see the man I wish my son had become. It's easy for me to forget that, inside, you're still the shy boy who could barely look me in the eye. Sam is very attractive and likable, but he's lucky to be with you, nonetheless. I knew you and loved you long before I met him. Nothing will ever change that. Please forgive me for being insensitive."

I found the words I needed and croaked them out. "Thank you, Flora. I forgive you. I wish I could see myself the way you see me."

"Oh, honey . . . I wish you could see yourself the way *he* sees you."

She looked toward the pool and my eyes followed hers. Sam had climbed out of the water and was coming back to the table, his wet body glistening in the bright sunshine. I automatically looked at my hand, expecting to see a remote control that would switch the action to slow motion.

"Hey, I'm waiting for you, Adam." He crouched down next to my chair. "What are you talking about?"

"Flora was telling me how lucky I was to find you."

"You didn't find me. I came after you, remember? I'm the lucky one. Besides, she doesn't know how annoying I can be."

I could have argued with him about which one of us was lucky, but I decided to accept his view of things. Or we could both be lucky. "Do you want to finish this dessert? I'm full."

"I could squeeze it in." He took the dish and the spoon. "You're not trying to get me drunk, are you?"

"No, but Flora is."

Agnes returned to clear the table. In a false whisper, Sam said, "I think Agnes wants me drunk." He scooped the last of the Cranachan into his mouth.

"Give me that dish before I take a wooden spoon to your backside."

Sam's mischievous eyes grew larger. "Adam! She's flirting with me!"

Flora laughed. I intervened. "I think we'd better get in the pool before this gets ugly."

"Okay. Can I undress you?"

"No! For heaven's sake, there are other people here!" I stood up and moved away from the table.

"They might enjoy it, too." He stood with his hands on his hips, watching me.

I took off my shirt and kicked off my deck shoes. "You're making me self-conscious."

"No, you came that way. I think you're hot."

I unzipped my shorts. "I'll never let you drink again."

"You think you can stop me?"

I dropped my pants. I was wearing the red Speedo briefs I had since high school.

"Wow!"

"Last one in is a rotten egg!" I ran to the pool and dived in rather gracefully. Sam tried to do the same, but landed with an awkward belly flop. I was glad I got out of the way before he hit the water. As soon as he surfaced I started a water fight, but I should have known better. His powerful arms threw so much water at me, I cried uncle and begged for mercy. I felt like a kid again, laughing and playing.

When I think about that afternoon at Flora's house, I realize what a roller coaster of emotion it was. I felt like a complete mess and wanted to get myself under control. Now I know my life was expanding in ways I couldn't see at the time. My prolonged period of mourning had ended and I was building a new family. Sometimes I squalled like a baby . . . vulnerable, needy, and angry as hell. When I could calm down and breathe, I was happy. As with all roller coasters, there would be many twists, loops and terrifying plunges.

I challenged Sam to a swimming race, knowing he couldn't resist a competition. Had I told him I was a competitive swimmer in high school? I can't recall. We started swimming laps, counting them off as we went. It wasn't long before I knew I would beat him easily, but he was focused and determined.

Halfway through the competition, I heard a commotion on the terrace. I slowed down, trying to see what was happening. There was a man, a conflict. I stopped swimming and went to the edge of the pool. It was Flora's son, Edward. *Shit!* I kept my head down and listened.

I heard Flora say, "Edward, you are not welcome here today! Please leave, or I will be forced to call the police."

"You care more about those faggots than your own son?" He sounded drunk. "Go ahead! Call the police. I donate equipment to their department every year. Let's see who they listen to."

Agnes held a broom and seemed ready to take a swing at him. "Shall I call them, ma'am? I think I should."

"You don't scare me, you old hag. Hop on that broom and fly back to hell."

The next thing I knew, Sam launched himself out of the pool. *Uh oh!* I pushed myself up and went after him. "Sam, wait!"

He yelled, "Hey asshole! Remember me? How's your hand?"

I managed to get in front of him. Leaning into his chest, I pushed as hard as I could against his twitching, slippery body. It slowed him down, but not much.

Ed baited him. "Come on, faggot! Let's do this so I can get you arrested!"

"Edward!" Flora yelled. "You will not insult my guests without consequences! Leave here this instant!" She stood up and steadied herself with her cane.

Sam tried to pick me up and set me aside, but I wrapped my legs around him. "Get off me! I can take care of this!"

"I know! That's what I'm worried about!" He tried to peel me off, but I kept wrapping my limbs around him.

Ed stepped forward. "Jesus Christ! They're having sex right in front of us, like fucking animals!" Agnes swung the bristled end of her broom and hit him on the side of the head. Enraged, he grabbed the broom and pulled it out of her hands. She lost her balance and fell on her well-cushioned behind.

Sam couldn’t be delayed any longer, so I let go of him. Flora stepped forward and cracked her son on the kneecap with the silver handle of her cane. The sound of the impact proved she didn't hold back.

Ed buckled. "You fucking bitch! I'll kill you!"

Sam rushed in, ramming Big Ed with his shoulder and picking him up in the same movement. Without slowing down, he slammed him against the brick wall of the house with a resounding thud. The wind must have been knocked out of him. Ed was called 'Big' for a reason, but his weight didn't keep Sam from picking him up again and pressing him against the bricks with his feet dangling above the ground. "I will crush your fucking chest if you disrespect these ladies again." I rushed over to prevent Sam from going too far.

Ed snarled in my direction. "You mean this little faggot lady?"

Sam pressed his thumb into Ed's bloated torso until I heard the dull snap of a rib. Ed flinched from the pain.

"Sam, that's enough." My heart was pounding.

Flora approached. "Edward, this shameful behavior is a new low point for you. If the police come, the publicity won't help your campaign for City Council any more than I will."

Ed had a hateful expression on his sweaty red face, but he had to concede defeat. He curled his lip and sneered, "Yes, Mother dear."

"I promised your father I would let you run the car dealership, but I'll break that promise without hesitation if you cause any more trouble for me or my friends."

He snarled again. "Yes, Mother."

It was difficult to imagine what Flora was feeling. Maybe she saw something other than anger and hatred in the eyes of her only child. "All right, Samson. I believe Edward will leave now."

"Not yet." Sam wasn't done with him. "He needs to apologize."

Ed looked at him defiantly. An evil smile distorted his lips.

I worried about how this would end. I didn't care about Ed, but Sam could ruin his own life if he made the wrong choice. "Sam, his apology won't mean anything."

"It'll mean something to me. Apologize, you fat turd!"

Flora cautioned him. "Don't sink to his level, Samson. Let him go."

"Aye, dearie. You've done enough."

Sam let Ed's feet touch the ground. Then Ed drew a breath and spat in Sam's face. Sam slammed him against the wall again. The two ladies shouted, "No!"

I threw my arms around Sam. "Please, don't let him win!" His chest expanded and contracted. I could feel his heart thumping. I begged him, "Please don't leave me, Sam."

After a few deep breaths, Sam growled, "I'll take him to his car."

"Is that all?"

"Yes," he hissed.

Cautiously, I withdrew my arms and stepped back. Sam dropped Ed, then roughly grabbed the back of his shirt. He marched him around the side of the house while I followed. Sam hoisted the big man by his belt until his toes were skimming the ground. He would have fallen flat on his face if Sam let go of him. "Be careful, Sam."

At the front of the house, Sam glanced up and down the street to make sure there was no one in sight. He dragged Ed to the driveway and dropped him, face down, onto the hood of his luxury sedan. Ed tried to turn over and rolled off the front of the car. Sam issued a final warning. "Next time I won't be so gentle."

Sam turned, walking quickly while I scurried after him. I noticed a woman standing in the window of the house next door and remembered I was only wearing a Speedo. Not knowing what else to do, I waved. She gave me a thumbs-up, either for my Speedo or for Sam's treatment of Big Ed. "Sam, wait!"

"Not now, Adam. I need to cool down. Leave me alone, okay?"

"Okay. Do what you need to do." I slowed down. "I'm proud of you." He made a beeline for the pool and jumped in. I rejoined the ladies at the table on the terrace.

"Is Edward still in one piece, dear?"

"Yeah, we took him to his car."

"I'm sorry you boys got tangled up in this mess. Edward has a habit of showing up at the worst possible times."

"What did he want?"

"Money, as usual. He wants to run for the vacant seat on the City Council and wanted me to finance his campaign. When I told him I wouldn't even vote for him, he was not happy with my decision. That's when our hero came to the rescue. Is Samson all right? Is there anything we can do for him?"

"He needs to cool down."

"He's a fine lad, Mr. Adam. You've done well."

"He's unusually strong, isn't he, dear? Edward is not a small man."

"I know, but Sam doesn't like to talk about his strength. It embarrasses him, believe it or not."

"We will avoid the topic if it makes him uncomfortable. He must spend a great deal of time in the gym to maintain that physique."

"He lifts weights in the basement. Guys his age build muscle quickly."

"I imagine he's quite an athlete in the bedroom."

"Flora!"

"Oh, honey, one can't look at a man like that and not think about it. Don't you agree, Agnes?"

"Aye, ma'am. I'm thinking about it now."

I covered my eyes and shook my head. "Anyway . . . is this what it's like to have a social life? I had no idea."

Flora laughed. "Not quite, dear. Most of our luncheons are rather dull. This is the most excitement we've had in years."

"We should do this more often, ma'am."

"Yes, but without Edward, I think."

I rose from my chair. "I think I'll check on Sam. You wouldn't happen to have any ice cream, would you? He loves ice cream."

Agnes hopped up. "Indeed, we have. Would ye like some as well, Mr. Adam?"

"No, thank you. Iced tea would be nice."

"Ma'am?"

"I'll also have iced tea, but you must come and sit with us, Agnes."

"If you insist, ma'am."

I walked to the edge of the pool and sat down with my legs in the water. Sam was trying to float on his back, but he wasn't very buoyant. "How are you doing?" He swam over and rested his arms on the side of the pool. I slipped into the water next to him. "Are you okay?"

"I'm embarrassed."

"Why should you be embarrassed?"

"Are you kidding? If you hadn't stopped me, I would have seriously hurt him. Cracking his rib was just the beginning."

"I know, but . . ."

"Please don't tell me it turned you on."

"Okay. I was about to say . . . it doesn't matter what you could have done. The fact is, you didn't do it. The way you handled him was awesome, though."

"If you hadn't been there . . . you saved me, Adam. I thought I would protect you, but you protected me."

"You protected all of us. You did an excellent job of that. You're even stronger than I thought you were."

"I know." Sam was quiet for a few moments. "What do Flora and Agnes think? Are they afraid of me, now?"

"Afraid of you? No, they think you're the sexiest man alive. They're jealous of me."

"Oh, come on."

"I'm not kidding. Agnes is preparing a treat for you. We should join them, but I wanted a few minutes with you first. Let me in there." I slipped between his arms and kissed him.

"I wish you didn't see me get that angry."

"Why? I snapped at you earlier. I wish you never saw that."

"It's okay, Adam."

"No, it's not. I feel terrible about it."

"I already forgave you."

"I know, but . . ."

He pressed his mouth against mine for a slow, tender kiss. "I shouldn't keep Agnes waiting. She's pretty strict."

"I have a feeling she'll relax those rules. You're her hero."

"I'm not anyone's hero. I'm just a guy." We pulled ourselves out of the pool.

"Okay, then. You're an ordinary, boring guy."

"I'm not boring. I can hold a conversation."

"Meh."

He wrapped his arm around my neck and kissed me on the forehead as we walked toward the table. Flora opened her arms as we approached. "Samson . . . come here and give me some sugar."

"I don't want you to get wet."

"I don't care . . . come here." He bent down to exchange kisses. "Like your namesake, you have slain the lion. We are grateful for your intervention." Agnes showed up with her tray.

"I want to apologize if I did anything I . . ."

"You have no reason to apologize, dear. I'm sorry you were caught up in my family problems, but your conduct was admirable. You showed great restraint. Agnes and I were the ones who struck him, and I have no regrets."

Agnes placed an ice cream sundae in front of Sam. "What's this? We already had dessert."

Agnes' explanation was brief. "Ye earned it. Eat it."

He smiled. "I wouldn't want to disobey an order." He viewed the sundae from several angles and picked up his spoon. "Are you okay, Agnes? Did you get hurt when you fell?" He loaded his mouth with ice cream.

Agnes answered with a perfectly straight face. "My cramikin might be bruised, but I'll live."

Sam had to swallow before he could laugh. He choked a bit, and grinned. "You did that on purpose, didn't you?"

"Aye." She poured our iced tea and sat next to Flora to eat the dish of Cranachan she saved for herself.

We continued talking and laughing and enjoying each other's company. By the time Sam and I returned to the house, it was late afternoon. I asked him what he wanted to do for the rest of the day. "You decide. Whatever you want."

"Okay." He stroked his chin. "Anything? Are you sure?"

"Yeah, I don't always need to be in control." I winked.

"Well, we should take a shower to get the chlorine off."

"Okay. Then what?"

"Um . . . don't laugh, okay?"

"I won't."

"Could we cuddle and take a nap together?

"Why would I laugh at that? That's nice. Anything else?"

"Let's order pizza later and watch a movie."

"That sounds great."

"Can I sleep here again tonight?"

"I assumed you would."

"Okay. That's the plan."

I put my arms around him, pressing my face against his chest. "Sometimes I worry I'll wake up and realize this was a dream, like people have in TV shows. It's seems too good to be real."

"If this was a good dream, I don't think Big Ed would be in it. Or the Weasel Woman. Or Henry."

"All right, don't get started on Henry. Let's get in the shower. I want a closer look at your new swimsuit."

"You like it that much?"

"Oh, yeah. Mr. Buns never looked better."

"Don't get started on Mr. Buns."

"Shhh! You'll hurt his feelings."

"Whatever." We walked up the stairs. "Have you talked to your psychologist about Mr. Buns?"

"No, he doesn't do couples therapy. Besides, Mr. Buns and I get along very well."

"Uh huh. That's not what I meant, but . . . at least you're getting professional help."

"I need it, don't I?"

"Yes, you do."

17

The Fourth of July was on a Monday that year, so we both had two days off. When I heard people in the office talking about their plans for the holiday weekend, I realized we didn't have anything planned. We could enjoy each other's company at home, but I wondered if we should go out more often. Flora and Agnes were going away for the weekend with a friend. I thought it might be Clarence from the car dealership, but I didn't ask.

Every Friday, to bug me, Donna asked if I had plans for the weekend. She knew I never had plans. "What are you doing for the Fourth? Are you and Sam going anywhere? Are you having a party?"

"Nothing, no, and certainly not."

"How exciting. Gays have the most fun. I envy you."

"Why don't you come over? We'll have a cookout." *That'll shut her up.*

It did shut her up. Briefly. She pressed her hand to my forehead. "How long have you been feeling ill?"

"I'm not ill. Stop touching me."

"You never invite me to your house. You never even accepted an invitation to my house."

"I'm growing and changing. And I was at your house once. I met Kevin."

"You came to drop off a client file. You were there for five minutes."

"Doesn't that count?"

"No. And we have plans for the weekend with Kevin's sister, so let's do it another weekend."

"Uh . . . it doesn't work that way. The invitation was for this weekend. I'm sorry you can't make it."

"You only invited me because you knew I would have plans already! You're so full of shit. How about July 17th? We're free that day."

"I don't have my calendar with me. We might have plans."

"No, you don't! Now you're pissing me off. I'll call Sam and arrange this." She searched through her phone.

"You don't have his number."

"Yes, I do."

"He can't invite people to my house."

"He can invite us to his apartment. Maybe you won't be invited." She started dialing.

"Okay, fine! July 17th, then. What do the two of you eat?"

She put away her phone. "Don't forget about my kids."

"Oh . . . would they be coming?"

"Why wouldn't they be coming?"

"Will they touch my stuff?"

"What stuff?"

"You know . . . all my stuff. Will they ruin my flower beds?"

"Adam, they're not feral pigs, they're my children. This is the worst invitation ever."

"All right, but they'd better not break anything."

"I raised them right. They won't break anything." She paused. "If they break something, I'll pay for it."

I shook my head. "I regret this already."

"You're not backing out of it now. I don't care if the apocalypse comes, we'll be at your house on the 17th."

"I hate having a social life. This is exhausting."

"Being your friend is pretty exhausting, too, but I like a challenge. I need to get back to my office before Zipinski sees us together."

"At least you didn't molest me this time."

She whispered, "In my mind, I was licking you in private places."

"Eeew! Go away!"

She was about to leave when she turned back. "By the way . . . have you heard any rumors about anything around here?"

"No. Why? What did you hear?"

"Nothing, but . . . some of the women are acting weird around me, like they're hiding something. I might be imagining things, but . . ."

"Maybe they're planning a party for you."

"If they're planning a surprise party and you don't tell me about it, I will kill you. You know that, right?"

"Yes. It's already on the list of death threats I report to the police every week."

"Are they all from me?"

"Yes."

"Good. I'll see you next week."

"Hey, Donna?"

"What?"

I took a deep breath. "I appreciate your friendship."

Her chin quivered. "God dammit." She walked away.

My therapist had asked me to start expressing my feelings.

***

On Saturday, after a productive day of working alone at the office, I changed into a t-shirt and shorts and began to prepare dinner. I was looking forward to spending two whole days with Sam. When he got home from the nursery, he gave me a hug, but I could tell something was wrong. "Are you okay?"

"I'm fine, but . . ." He pulled a piece of paper out of his back pocket and unfolded it. "I saw this tacked to a light pole down the street."

It was a flyer with a photograph of us standing on the front porch. I was holding a basket of flowers, and Sam had his hand on my shoulder. The bold text read, "IS THIS WHAT YOU WANT ON EDEN PLACE? PROTECT OUR CHILDREN!!!"

"That fucking Weasel bitch! She can't do this!"

"That's what I was thinking, but . . ."

"I'm calling the police. There has to be a law against this."

"What could the police do?"

"Arrest her? Give her a ticket? At least they could talk to her!"

"But we don't have any proof she did it. I know she did, but we can't prove it."

"She can't get away with this."

"I don't know. It doesn't say anything specific."

"It implies we're child molesters, Sam! What the fuck?! Aren't you angry?"

"Yeah, I'm angry! But we shouldn't fly off the handle and make things worse. Besides, I'm too hungry to think straight."

"How can you be hungry after seeing this?"

"I'm always hungry. Come on, let's eat first and figure out the best way to handle this. I want to change my clothes. How long before dinner is ready?"

I sighed. "Twenty minutes." It made sense to calm down before taking any action against the Weasel Woman. Sam went to his apartment while I finished preparing dinner. He returned in a snug blue t-shirt and cotton gym shorts. His hair was damp from a shower.

We ate without much conversation. I didn't want to discuss the flyer because it would make my blood boil, but I had an idea. "I should talk to a lawyer and find out what we can do about this."

Sam nodded. "Good idea. Do you know a lawyer?"

"No, but I'm sure Flora does. We can't do anything until after the holiday anyway."

"I don't want this to ruin our time off. I was looking forward to this."

"Me too." I watched him lift a pitcher to refill his glass. His biceps bunched and rolled, stretching his tight sleeve. "Is there a reason you're dressed like that?"

"Like what?" He had a trace of a smile.

"You know what I mean."

"I like the way you look at me when I wear a tight shirt."

"How do I look at you?"

"Like a starving man would look at a turkey dinner. It makes me feel good."

"It makes me feel good, too."

“That fish was tasty. I was way too hungry. I usually go to the Sub Stop with Greg and get a foot-long sandwich, but he didn’t work today."

"I’m surprised you don’t get the three-foot sub."

“Very funny. Greg razzes me enough about the foot-long. He gets a six-inch sub because he’s worried about getting fat.”

“Is he overweight?”

“No, he’s in great shape. He was a wrestler in high school. They always worry about their weight. Have you been following your doctor’s orders?”

“I gained a few pounds.”

“Yeah, you look healthier. Keep it up.”

I should have thanked him, but compliments still made me squirm. “Let’s get these dishes done."

He smiled knowingly. “Okay.”

At the sink, as I washed and he dried, Sam playfully pressed himself against me. I liked it. "Do you remember the first time you did that to me? I freaked out."

"Was that the night I told you I was gay?"

"Yeah, I guess it was." The memory was bitter-sweet.

"That's when you made the five-alarm chili. It was snowing, and you invited me in for the first time. It was a big night for me."

"For me, too. I cried after you left. I sat on the floor and bawled like a baby.”

"Oh. Why?"

"I was afraid I hurt your feelings, so I felt guilty. I wanted to say more than I did, but I didn’t have the words. I wished I was someone else, someone with more confidence. I wished I could have an honest conversation with a handsome young guy without choking."

Sam waited for a while before responding. "Did your wish come true?"

"Well . . . I'm having an honest conversation with you now. I'm not a different person, but things turned out better than I could have hoped."

"I'm glad you're not a different person."

It was a very nice compliment. "Thanks."

"I felt bad that night, too. I was so intimidated by you. I didn't think I would ever be good enough."

"What? How could you be intimidated by a fucked-up mess like me?"

"I didn't see you that way at all. You were this hot older guy with a good education, a profession, and a great house. Why would you want a penniless farm-boy waiter with a high school diploma? It's a good thing you thought I was handsome or I wouldn't be here now. Things turned out a lot better than I expected, too."

"It boggles my mind that you didn't think you were good enough for me while I thought you were way out of my league. I still wish you had more faults so I didn't think you were too perfect for me."

"Be careful what you wish for."

"Why? Will you start leaving your dirty socks on the floor?"

"Yes! Why didn't I think of that? I'll start right away."

"Great. You seem more human already." I gently butted him with my shoulder. "One thing I know you'll never do is leave dirty dishes in the sink. You're a dishwashing freak."

"See . . . there's another weakness. They're adding up now."

I rinsed the last pan and handed it to him. "You know, I don't care what the Weasel Woman does. Nothing she can do would ever make me give this up. She can put up a million flyers. I don't care if people believe what she says. I'll still want to wash dishes with you. And other stuff."

"That's what I was thinking, too. I'm not letting someone like that tell me how to live, and I'm not running away."

"By the way, you're not here because you're handsome. It got my attention at first, but it's not what keeps this going."

"Thanks, Adam." He kissed me on the forehead and wiped the countertop before hanging up the towel. "So, if my looks don't matter, I suppose you wouldn't be interested in watching me work out for a little while."

"Well . . . I don't have anything else to do." Of course, I was interested. "Can you do that after eating?"

He shrugged. "It works for me." He led me down the stairs to the basement. "Did you see the pull-up bar I made?"

"Yeah, I've been using it. I'm getting stronger. I'll be able to beat the crap out of you pretty soon."

"That sounds like fun." He gestured toward the bar. "Let's see what you can do."

I wasn't expecting to be tested. "Okay, if you say so." I stretched my shoulders and stood under the bar. "I usually start with pull-ups and switch to chin-ups."

"Good thinking. Do you want me to boost you up there?"

"As long as you're offering."

He lifted me effortlessly until I had a grip on the bar. I pulled myself up as many times as I could with good form. When I waivered, Sam supported my butt with his hand. "Try a couple more with me assisting." I pulled myself up three more times before I was exhausted. He grabbed my waist and supported my full weight. "Switch your grip." I turned my hands and completed more chin-ups than usual with his assistance. My muscles were burning when he set me on the floor. He put his hands under my arms and felt my lats, squeezing them gently. "Do you feel the pump in your muscles?"

"Yeah, I do." I liked the way he was touching me.

"I can tell you've been exercising. You're more toned."

"I'd exercise even more if I had a hunky trainer groping me between sets."

Sam reached up and grabbed the bar. Unlike me, he had to bend his knees to hang from it. He cranked out perfect wide-grip pull-ups with smooth, controlled movement. After thirty of those, he did hanging leg lifts, slowly and with perfect form. He showed no signs of fatigue, but stopped again after thirty. He briefly put his feet on the floor to change to an underhand grip and completed thirty chin-ups. He let go of the bar, shook out his arms and briefly flexed.

"Let me feel those while you're pumped up." He raised his arms and let me appreciate his work. I was aroused, of course. "I know you're not done with your workout, but there's something I need to show you upstairs."

"Where upstairs?"

"In the bedroom."

"The bedroom? What could that be?"

"It's a surprise. And it's urgent."

"Oh, let me guess. Did you get new sheets?"

"Mmm, no, but keep guessing while we walk. Come on."

"Is it a lamp?"

"It's not a lamp."

***

Sam woke me from a sound sleep.

"What?" I rubbed my face and looked at my clock. Three-thirty-six.

"I heard something outside." He pulled on his shorts and grabbed his t-shirt.

"What did you hear?" I sat up and switched on a light.

"I'm not sure, but I'm going down there." I heard a rip when he put on his shirt. "Fuck." I got out of bed and followed him into the adjacent room. "Adam, call 911! There's a fire!" He ran out of the room as I realized the light from the window was not the rising sun. It was too early.

I hurried into the bedroom and grabbed my phone, dialing with trembling hands while I looked for something to wear. When the operator picked up, I yelled my address and "Fire!" I set down the phone and kept repeating my address while I pulled on a pair of jeans. I heard her say help was on the way. I picked up a shirt and the phone and looked out the back window again. The garden shed that Sam had carefully restored was engulfed in flames.

I ran down the stairs while putting on the shirt. The phone slipped out of my hand, bounced down the stairs, and made a sickening sound when it hit the tile floor. The glass was shattered, but I heard the operator asking if I was okay. I raced through the house to the kitchen and found the back door ajar. The knob was missing, the jamb was splintered, and the window was cracked. Sam, in his haste, must have damaged it.

I saw him move across the driveway in the firelight. I knew the shed would be destroyed, but I was afraid the fire would spread to the house or the trees. "Get the garden hose!"

"Someone cut it! It's useless!" We stood there, helpless, wanting to do something but unable to stop the fire. Then there were sirens and flashing lights as a firetruck pulled up on the street next to the house. The firemen quickly had a hose aimed at the burning shed, but the cupola with the angel weathervane fell through the roof before the flames were extinguished. A cloud of sparks blew high into the air. The tree closest to the shed was burning, but the fire was put out before it could spread. The house was safe, my garden was mostly intact, and Sam had his arm around my shoulders.

***

Representatives from the fire department and the police department were there until the sun came up, asking questions and writing reports. They knew it was arson, but they had to wait for an official ruling. After looking at the back door, the police assumed someone broke into the house. Sam said he had done it, but it made them more suspicious. While we sat at the kitchen table, the older of the two officers said, "Are you telling me you broke out of the house, not in? I don't get it. If you live above the garage, what were you doing in the house?"

I tried to brush that aside. "Look, he didn't break in or out. He rushed outside to do something about the fire. He's a strong guy, there was a lot of adrenaline, and he broke the door. It's not an issue." Sam glared at the officer.

"What was he doing in your house in the middle of the night?" The muscles in Sam's arms twitched.

I took a deep breath and tried to remain calm. "He was staying with me. What else do you need to know?"

The younger officer spoke up. "Mansky, could we stick to what's relevant?"

"Of course you wouldn't be suspicious of him. I saw that coming."

The young guy, Hanson, continued. "You mentioned a recent problem with a neighbor. Could you tell us more?"

I retrieved the flyer Sam brought home and showed it to them. Mansky's lip curled. "I don't get it. What does this mean?"

"What do you think it means if someone is distributing this in the neighborhood?"

"It looks like they don't want you here. Are you a registered sex offender?"

My jaw clenched. "No, but you already know that. I'm sure you looked me up already."

Mansky tipped his head toward Sam. "I was asking him."

Sam said, "No." Nothing else.

Hanson asked, "Do you know who's distributing these flyers?"

"Yes, her name is Helen Van Wootten. I'm not sure which house she lives in."

He wrote it down. "Can I keep this flyer?" I nodded. "Can you think of anyone else who might have a grudge against you? Have you had any other conflicts recently?"

"Yes." It dawned on me. "Edward O'Neill."

Hanson and Mansky exchanged glances. "Big Ed? What was that about?"

I thought about how to tell the story. "His mother lives in the house next door. We're friends. She invited us for lunch last Wednesday, and while we were there, he showed up uninvited. He argued with his mother, she asked him to leave, but he refused. She asked Sam to show him out. Ed resisted, but Sam took him to his car." Unfortunately, as I was telling the story, Sam chose to crack his knuckles. I gave him a stern look.

Hanson asked Sam, "Is that what happened?"

Sam answered him in a softer tone. "Yeah. He didn't want to leave, so . . . I made him leave. It could have been worse."

"What do you mean?"

Sam looked Mansky in the eye. "He's not in the hospital." There was a long silence.

"That'll be all for now. If we have any other questions, we'll contact you." Mansky moved toward the door but turned to look at Sam again. "If you don't mind a little advice . . . you might want to keep your private life more private. Your neighbors don't want to think about what you people do to each other."

Sam stood up from the table and squared his shoulders. He looked like a bad-ass in his torn t-shirt, smeared with black soot. I hurried around the table and stood in front of him. "Thank you, officer. Goodbye." Mansky left, satisfied that he had penetrated Sam's skin.

I turned around to face Sam. "You should go upstairs to clean up." He avoided my eyes and took a couple of deep breaths. He glanced up at Officer Hanson, turned around and left the room.

Hanson handed me one of his cards. "I'm sorry about Mansky, he's an asshole. That shit was aimed more at me than at your . . . friend. He doesn't like being partnered with a gay guy, but the chief didn't give him a choice."

What's that? Hanson is gay? I wouldn't have guessed. He was clean cut, well-built, masculine. Hot, to be honest. "That must be awful for you."

"It's not easy, but you know how it is. There's always some asshole who wants to give us shit.' He smiled. "I've never seen you at any of the bars. Are you new here?"

"No, I've lived here since I was a kid. I don't get out much."

"That's too bad. How long have you two been . . .?"

I felt awkward, but I didn't want to brush off a handsome, friendly guy. "A few months. It's good. We're good." I looked at my blackened bare feet.

"This always happens to me. I meet a great guy, and he's already taken."

"Sorry." I couldn't even look up.

"I didn't mean to make you uncomfortable. But why pass up a chance to meet someone new?"

"It's . . . I'm . . . flattered. But . . ."

"I get it. I hope things work out for you, but if they don't . . ." He tapped his finger on the card in my hand. "Keep me in mind. That's all I'm saying."

"Okay, thanks. Thank you very much." I managed to make eye contact for a fraction of a second.

Mansky yelled from outside, "Hanson! Come on!"

"I'll let you know if we come up with any leads, okay? And call us if you think of anything else that might be relevant."

"Okay. Thanks again." I shook his hand. It was rough and warm.

"Carl. It's Carl, by the way."

"Oh. Okay." I nodded. "Bye now."

"Bye."

Jesus, what next? I tacked his card on the refrigerator and headed upstairs. Sam was in the bathroom, shirtless, leaning against one of the sinks. "Hey," I said.

"Hey." He didn't look up. "What did he say about me?"

"What did who say?"

"Carl. Did he tell you about us?"

"Carl? About . . . us? Who?"

"We met before. Did he tell you he knew me?"

"No, he didn't. You knew him? From where?"

"He was a member at the Health Club. We . . . messed around once."

"Oh." *Oh!* "I see."

"Just once. It didn't mean anything. It was before you and I were . . . you know."

"You didn't have to tell me. What happened before us is your business."

"But if it came out later, it would look like I was hiding something. I was planning to tell you as soon as he left."

"Okay. That makes sense." I leaned against the sink next to him. "He seems like a nice guy. How come you didn't . . . mess around more?"

"He is nice, but he's not my type. He's not like you. He wasn't into me either. It was just sex."

"It's hard for me to imagine anyone not being into you."

Sam nudged me with his shoulder. "You only see the best in me. Not everyone sees me that way."

I nodded a little. "I was afraid you would deck the other cop."

"I wanted to. You handled yourself very well, I was impressed."

"I surprised myself. He was such an asshole. Hanson apologized after you left."

"What else did you talk about?"

"Just how they plan to follow up. He gave me his card in case we think of anything else."

"I'm sorry about the door."

"It's okay. How did it happen?"

"I was moving too fast and I didn't turn the knob before I pulled. I'll fix it."

"I'll miss that shed. You did such a wonderful job on it."

"I know, I'm so pissed! It was the one thing I could give you, and now it's gone."

It took a moment for his words to sink in. "Sam . . . you've given me a lot more than that. The shed was great, but . . . you've done so much more." I stroked his forearm. "Let's go back to bed for a few hours. We're both tired."

"I need to do something about the door. Anyone could walk in."

"It can wait. I'm not worried with you here."

"No, I won't be able to sleep. I'll put something heavy in front of it." He left and went downstairs.

I turned to look in the mirror. I looked terrible. *How could Hanson be attracted to this?* I used a damp cloth to wipe the black streaks off my face. *Should I have told Sam that Hanson hit on me?* I didn't want him to feel jealous about another guy. I went into my dressing room, stripped, and dropped my clothes down the laundry chute. I crawled into bed and waited for Sam.

A few minutes later, he came into the bedroom. "I propped a loaded barbell against the door. I'll fix it this afternoon."

"Don't worry about it. Come to bed." He took off his shorts and joined me. I laid my head on his chest. His rapid heartbeat told me it would take him a while to settle down. "Try to relax. We're okay."

"Who do you think it was?"

"I don't know. It could have been someone we've never met."

"That's true. People we don't even know can hate us. Great."

"Let's sleep late, then I'll make a big breakfast. How does that sound?"

"I need to fix the door."

"The door will get fixed. You're doing everything you can to keep us safe."

"Do you think it'll happen again?"

"I don't know, Sam. You know what would help me? It's easier to fall asleep when I listen to you breathe. It's very soothing."

"Okay, do you want me to hold you?" He wanted to do something for me. Maybe he needed it.

"That would be great." I rolled over and let him pull me against his body.

"How's that? Are you comfortable?"

"Perfect. It feels so good to have your arm around me at night. I could fall asleep anywhere as long as I have that." I listened to his breathing. "That's right. Breathe, nice and slow. That's nice."

It did feel good. I felt comfortable and safe. I loved having Sam's arm around me. But on that morning, I waited for him to fall asleep. Then I could sleep.

18

The days after the fire were full of new experiences. My house and garden had always been a refuge from the world, but things were changing rapidly. The Weasel Woman's flyer had been left at the door of every house in the neighborhood, except mine. I didn't know what to expect from my neighbors. Any one of them could have set the fire.

Sunday was spent cleaning up the mess in the garden while Sam repaired the back door. The remains of the shed were surrounded by yellow barricade tape and the grass was a trampled swamp of mud and ashes. One of my perennial borders was badly damaged by water from the fire hose. I wanted to salvage as many plants as possible. Despite the warm, sunny weather, there was no way to do the work without being covered in mud.

Shortly after we started working, I heard a little voice. "Hello? Excuse me." I turned around and saw a woman who looked vaguely familiar standing in the driveway. "I'm sorry to bother you, I know you're very busy, but . . ." I cautiously approached her as Sam came up from the basement and stepped onto the porch. I could see she wasn't a threat. She looked like the women I used to see in church when I went with my parents. She was holding a pie.

"Hello," I said. "Can I help you?"

She smiled at me, then noticed Sam standing at the back door. "Oh! Hello, you don't know me, I'm Joan Miller. I live down the street here, and . . . I'm so sorry about what happened last night, I feel sick about it. I wanted to do something, but I didn't know what to do except to bake you a pie. I know it doesn't make any sense, but it's the only thing I'm good at. No matter what happens, I start baking. I always make cherry pie for the Fourth of July, so I made an extra one for you boys. Is that okay?"

"Sure . . . I . . . we . . ."

Sam said, "Thank you."

"Yes! Thank you. That's very nice of you. I'm covered with mud, so . . ."

"I'll get it." Sam stepped down from the porch and accepted the pie. "It's nice to meet you, Joan. I'm Sam, and this is Adam. He's not usually this muddy."

"Oh, I know that." She waved her hand at him. "I see you boys out here all the time. You do such a wonderful job with your flowers and everything is so well-kept. It's a shame to see this mess back here, but I'm sure you'll have it looking beautiful again in no time. I don't have your green thumb, so I'll stick to baking."

It was difficult to dislike her, even for an expert like me. "Well, thank you. I'm sure we'll enjoy the pie. Can I ask you something, Joan?"

"Yes, what is it, dear?"

"Did you find a flyer in your door? One with a picture of us?"

Her expression changed. "Yes, I did, and it was very confusing for me. It asked, "Is this what you want on Eden Place?" I thought, yes, this is what I want! I wish all the houses looked this nice. But I didn't understand the part about the children. So, I showed it to my husband, and he explained what he thought it meant. He was in the army, so he knows more about the world than I do. I can read a recipe and that's about it." She paused and pulled a handkerchief out of her sleeve. "But I'll tell you what . . ." She held the handkerchief and shook her fist at me, raising her voice. "People who love the Lord don't say things like that! They don't put flyers in your door telling people to hate each other!" She clamped the handkerchief over her mouth.

My throat felt tight. It was the last thing I expected her to say.

"I'm sorry." She sniffed. "I don't like to get angry, but sometimes people make me mad. I need to pray about this a lot. I'll let you get back to your work, I know you're busy. I wasn't planning to make a scene." She put the handkerchief over her mouth again and turned to leave.

I called after her, "Thank you, Joan!" She waved her hand without turning around. "Come and visit us any time."

Sam made a crazy face. "Come and visit us any time?"

"I know. It came out of me, like . . . there's a friendly person inside of me."

"I'm taking this pie in the house. I'll be back in ten minutes."

"I want some of that!"

"Are you sure? It might be poisoned. Maybe she burned the shed."

"She did not. You'd better leave some for me."

He grinned. "I'll save you a piece."

I went back to work, lifting the plants out of the flower bed with a spading fork, setting them aside, and figuring out how to rearrange them. Sam reappeared on the porch, making a big show of rubbing his stomach and licking his lips. "Yum!" I just smiled and shook my head.

A short while later, I heard another voice. "Hi there! Wow, what a mess! This is terrible!"

Sam said, "Hello." I turned around, scraping mud off my hands, to see a woman and a man. She was tall and narrow, he was short and round and held a casserole dish. She did all the talking.

"How awful! What a crime! Who would do something like this? I don't understand. I'm Jackie, this is my husband, Jack. I know what you're thinking, Jack and Jackie, right? Easy to remember. We planned it that way, didn't we,

Jack? No, we didn't. Those were our names, and then we got married. It worked out pretty well."

Sam and I exchanged a look, but we didn't have time to get a word in.

"You guys are gay, right? We don't care, not a problem, and we have kids. We're not worried. Do what you want, live your lives, you won't hear a peep from us, will they, Jack? No, you won't. Jack is shy, but he said to me this morning, he said, 'Jackie, I should make them that casserole you like so much. They can have it for dinner. Their house is probably a mess, and they won't want to cook.' He's quite a talker at home. So, I said, 'That's a great idea, Jack! You're such a sweet man! That's why I married you.' And he's a good cook. I don't cook. I don't have time with all my projects. I'm always busy. Thank God he cooks, or the kids and I would starve."

I wanted to say, "Thank you," but by the time I took a breath, it was too late.

"This casserole is like scalloped potatoes with chunks of sausage and cheese and there's beer in there and peas and it's so goddamn good I could eat the whole thing myself. You don't mind if I swear, do you? I hope not, because I can't help myself. When he makes this casserole I'm so happy, I run around the room like a poodle on crack. Don't I, Jack? And that's not like me. I'm usually tired from my projects." Jack cleared his throat. "What? Am I talking too much? He thinks I talk too much. Hey, I don't know your names! What's your name?"

"I'm Adam, and that's Sam. Thank you for thinking of us, that's very nice."

"Pleased to meet you. I love your house. And this garden! It's gorgeous! And so are you guys! Seriously! That mud is working for you! I'm teasing, of course. Give the casserole to this guy, Jack. Sam, right? He looks hungry, so give it to him."

Jack handed the casserole to Sam. "Three hundred fifty degrees for one hour."

"Thanks. It looks good."

Jackie had enough of being quiet. "We'd better let you go, I can see you've got your hands full. I've got projects to do. If there's anything you need, anything at all, you come and get us. We're at 3363 Eden Place. Got it? Easy to remember because it rhymes. Jack and Jackie, 3363. You can bring the dish back any time. You'll love that fucking casserole. I'm jealous of you. Let's go, Jack. These people are busy. It was great to meet you. I'm sorry about the fire. Did you say goodbye, Jack? Remember your social skills."

Jack said, "Bye." As they walked down the driveway, he put his hand on Jackie's butt and kept it there.

"Bye. Thanks again." When they were far enough away, I said, "Holy shit, she's bonkers!"

Sam laughed. "Why didn't you invite them to visit us?'"

"Maybe when she's medicated. But that was nice. I'm starting to wonder whether I should continue to hate people. I think I will, but . . . I'm having a crisis of faith."

Sam looked at me. "Sometimes I can't tell if you're kidding or not. I'll put this in the house."

"It needs to be cooked before you eat it."

"I know, I'll save it for dinner, but I don't know what you'll eat."

Throughout the afternoon, various neighbors stopped by to express their sympathy, their support, or their concerns. One man said he didn't want this trouble in the neighborhood and suggested we might be more comfortable in another part of town. I told him I wouldn't move and suggested rooting out the criminal rather than the victim. He admitted I had a point, shook our hands, and wished us well. A few people stood on the sidewalk to look but didn't speak to us. Everyone who came into the garden had the pleasure of seeing me covered with mud, while Sam, wearing my father's tool belt, looked like one of those ridiculously hunky carpenters on a home improvement show.

By late afternoon we had a pan of lasagna, a fruit basket, two cakes, zucchini bread, several dozen cookies, and a child's drawing of a fire truck rescuing two stick figures with tears pouring out of their faces. Every time Sam came out of the house he was brushing crumbs off his mouth. He needed a few things to finish fixing the door, so he went to the hardware store to get what he needed plus a new garden hose.

Not long after he left, an SUV pulled into the driveway with a handsome man at the wheel. It took me a minute to recognize Officer Hanson out of uniform, in shorts and a t-shirt. "Hey, Adam, how's it going?"

"All right. I'm trying to salvage these plants. I'd shake your hand, but . . ."

"I see you're not afraid to get dirty. Good to know."

"Why?"

"Never mind. Dumb joke."

"What can I do for you, officer?"

"Carl. Call me Carl, I'm off duty. Sorry to drop in like this, but I have information for you."

"Okay, Carl." Maybe it was because I was so dirty, but he looked very clean. He reminded me of a character from one of those Dick and Jane books we used in elementary school, except this character was all grown up and worked out a lot. And he was gay.

"Listen . . . you're not hearing this from me, and you can't repeat it to anyone else, but my partner and I found out Ed O'Neill was stopped for a traffic violation early this morning. It was around the time of the fire and he wasn't far from here.

He was ticketed for speeding, but the cop who stopped him said he was intoxicated."

"Was he arrested?"

"No, just the speeding ticket."

"Why? He was driving drunk."

"Here's the thing . . . Big Ed and the Chief of Police are close friends. O'Neill donates equipment to the police department, and the Chief makes some of O'Neill's problems go away. This isn't the first time O'Neill has been caught drunk driving. A lot of us on the department don't like it, but that's the way things work."

"He gets away with this shit?"

"So far, yes. But that's not what I came here to tell you. Again, you're not hearing this from me, but the cop who ticketed him said O'Neill had an empty gas can in his car."

"So he set the fire?"

"He *may* have set the fire. Or he may have been putting gas in his lawn tractor. It's circumstantial evidence."

I started to dislike him, despite his dimpled chin. "Then you won't do anything about it?"

"Hang on a minute, I'm not done. My partner, Mansky, won't let it go."

"That asshole? As if he'll do anything for us!"

Carl put up his hand to suggest I should simmer down. "You're right, he doesn't care about you. But Mansky is an asshole to everyone equally. He's a pretty good cop, believe it or not. He's got a grudge against the Chief for partnering him with me, and he hates O'Neill for selling him a shitty car a few years back. I've never seen him so motivated to bust someone."

"Oh." I hate it when assholes turn out to have good qualities. Of all the feelings I dislike, mixed feelings are my least favorite. "What will he do about it?"

"I don't know yet. It might take him a while, but he won't let it go."

"What am I supposed to do with this information, other than being pissed off?"

"Nothing, I hope. But I wanted you to know it probably wasn't a neighbor who set the fire."

I took a deep breath. "The neighbors have been pretty nice to us. A lot of them stopped by to bring food and stuff."

"That's nice. This seems like one of those neighborhoods where everyone knows each other."

"I hadn't met any of them until today."

“I thought you lived here since you were a kid."

"Yeah."

He looked confused but didn't ask. "Where's your . . . Sam?"

"He ran out to pick up some hardware. He'll be back soon."

"Okay, I should get going."

"He told me you knew him from the health club, and you had . . . whatever."

"Oh, I thought he wouldn't say anything."

"Why? He didn't want to hide it from me."

"That's good, but I hope you don't think I'm the kind of guy who does that a lot. I don't want things to be awkward between us."

"I'm awkward anyway, so it won't change anything."

He smiled. "Sam's a lucky guy."

Now things are more awkward. "I'm lucky, too." I looked at my feet.

"Yeah, Sam is . . . a good guy . . . as long as you don't piss him off. I'd prefer it if you didn't tell him this stuff about Big Ed. I'm afraid he might take things into his own hands, if you know what I mean."

I knew exactly what he meant, and I knew he was right. "Okay, I won't tell him, but . . . does Sam have a reputation?"

"Oh, man . . . you're putting me on the spot here. You know . . . gay gossip is the worst, and Sam is one of those guys everyone claims they've been with. I don't know how much of it was true."

"Uh, that's not what I was . . . I thought it was something about his temper."

"Oh, shit, I'm sorry! Yeah, his temper. Well . . . there was an incident with the manager of the Harbor View when Sam got fired . . . you knew he was fired, right?"

"Yeah, and I know why he was fired."

"Okay, I'm not sure what happened, exactly. He didn't hurt anyone or do any damage, but . . . the manager was worried after he fired him. He knew I'm a cop, so he said if anything happens to him, I should keep Sam in mind. Nothing ever happened, and I forgot about it until I saw the way Sam looked at Mansky last night. He was pretty intense."

"Yeah, but he calmed down. He'll be home soon, so maybe you should . . ."

"Yeah, I should go. Um . . . good to see you. You have my card. I'll keep you posted, okay?" He moved rather quickly toward his vehicle.

"Thanks for stopping by, Carl. I appreciate the information."

"You're welcome." He waved and backed out of the driveway. Again, rather quickly.

Before I could return to my work, Sam pulled in. As soon as he was out of his truck, he asked, "Who was that guy who just left?"

"Officer Hanson. He came by to give us an update."

"What did he say?"

"They have a promising lead."

"On what?"

"A suspect."

"Who?"

"He wasn't at liberty to say. He wanted us to know they're working on it."

"That's it? He came over for that?"

"Yeah. It was nice of him."

"Why wasn't he in a squad car?"

"He's off duty."

"And he made time to come and tell you practically nothing while I happened to be at the store."

"What are you suggesting?"

"Did he flirt with you?"

"What? No! He doesn't seem like the flirting type. Besides, why would he be flirting with me?"

"He knows how to flirt! I remember. And why wouldn't he flirt with you?"

"Because he knows we're in a relationship."

He rolled his eyes. "Yeah, and everyone respects that!"

"Come on! You need to get a grip on your jealousy. Do you trust me, or not?"

"I trust you, but I don't trust other guys around you."

"Do you think I'll surrender myself to any guy who flirts with me?"

He studied my face. "Why do I feel like there's something you're not telling me? I trust you, Adam, but I'm keeping my eye on Carl."

"Maybe you want to get together with him again."

"Hey, that's not fair!"

"Are you fucking kidding me? I get interrogated about every guy who so much as looks at me, and I can't make a comment about a guy you actually messed around with?" I felt my blood pressure going up.

Sam looked away. "I bought your garden hose."

"DON'T CHANGE THE SUBJECT!"

"Okay! Okay! I'm sorry. You're right. I need to work on my jealousy. But you're so adorable . . ."

"I AM NOT!" I gritted my teeth. "I'm an average guy with a truckload of issues. I can barely look people in the eye!"

"You're not average."

"Just stop worrying some guy is going to steal me away!" I took a deep breath and let it all out.

"All right. I'm sorry. I didn't mean to upset you." He sheepishly went back to fixing the door.

The absurdity of our argument stayed with me for the rest of the day. *As if I'm the one who would get stolen from this relationship!* I tried not to ruminate, but it was difficult. I wished Carl hadn't told me about Sam's reputation.

After dividing some of the perennials, I reassembled the flower bed by late afternoon. Sam fixed the door so it could be locked again, and all it needed was paint. Things were awkward between us, but when he joined me in the shower and gently washed me, the tension went down the drain with the mud. He apologized again, and I forgave him. I felt guilty that I hadn't been honest with him about Carl. He was flirting with me.

***

On Monday, the Fourth of July, the weather was hot and humid. We finished a few outdoor chores in the morning and spent the rest of the day relaxing. We sat in the living room in our shorts, with a fan aimed at us, reading and napping, with very little conversation.

"I think I'll take the day off tomorrow. I need to call my insurance company and get someone out here to assess the damage. Do you think Dave would let you have the day off?"

"No, we're starting a landscaping project tomorrow. There's no way. Besides, aren't you tired of me after two days?"

"No. Are you tired of me?"

"No. I was just thinking how much I like being with you and not talking. It's comfortable."

"Yeah, it is."

I was grateful I didn't have to cook because of all the food from the neighbors. I ate cookies and cake all afternoon, like Sam. We had Jack and Jackie's potato casserole for a late dinner, and the last of Joan's delicious cherry pie. After the dishes were washed, Sam had a suggestion. "Do you want to go for a swim in Flora's pool? We could cool down before bed."

He didn't need to talk me into it. "I'll go put on my swimming suit."

He grabbed my hand and held me back. "Let's swim naked. It's already dark and there's no one around."

"Um . . . I guess we could. I've never done anything like that before."

"Come on. It'll be fun."

We entered her yard through the gap in the hedge, though it was easier for me than for him. I reminded myself to enlarge the opening to accommodate his size. The pool had dim lights built into the perimeter to make it visible in the dark. I looked carefully at the neighbor's houses. As far as I could tell, no one would see us. Sam removed his shorts and stood naked in the shimmering light. Cautiously, I undressed and stood next to him. "Let's keep it quiet. We don't want to draw any more attention in the neighborhood."

As soon as we slipped into the water, Sam kissed me. His hands were everywhere. His erection pressed against my belly. It was exhilarating to be the object of such an intense craving, something I never thought I would experience. It occurred to me his attraction to my body could equal my lust for his, despite my low opinion of myself. Why should I question his taste in men? He wanted me when he could have had others. Maybe I wasn't so bad after all.

We alternated between swimming and sliding our bodies against each other until we saw fireworks rising above the trees in a public park not far away. Hanging on the edge of the pool, we watched the gigantic blooms of light fade into the black sky. Sam was close behind me, quietly oohing and aahing in my ear. When the last fiery bouquet fell behind the trees, I twisted around and spread my arms along the pool's edge. I quietly studied his face, then touched my forehead to his.

"I love you, Sam. I'm sorry I don't say it enough."

"It's good to hear it sometimes, but you show it, too. You make me feel important . . . like I matter to someone. Even when we're apart, I know you're thinking about me. I'll always love you for that."

We kissed again and again. The water shimmered in the dim light. From the corner of my eye, I saw the dark silhouette of a person standing at the side of the pool.

"Agnes?"

"Good evening, Mr. Adam, Mr. Sam."

Sam quietly said, "Hello."

"I thought you were out of town with Flora."

"I don't like to be the third wheel. I was visiting an old friend in the country. I've just returned."

"How long have you been standing there?"

"Long enough. I didn't want to interrupt. Will ye have a night cap or ice cream?"

"Uh . . . sure."

"Yes, definitely."

"All right, I'll serve ye in the kitchen." She stood there.

Sam looked at me, then at her. "I'm sorry, but we're not wearing our swimsuits."

She waited. "I suppose you'll want some privacy, then. I'll leave ye to cover up whatever it is you're embarrassed about. Ye know where the kitchen is." She paused to peer into the water and returned to the house.

I raised an eyebrow. "She wants Mr. Buns."

"I knew you would say something like that!"

"She's not getting him. He's mine."

"Stop it! You're making this more awkward. We'll visit for a little while, then I'm taking you to my bed. It's Monday, so I'm in charge."

"Oh, good! I forgot about that."

Sam made sure Agnes was out of sight before he climbed out of the pool and quickly put on his shorts.

***

When I woke up in Sam's bed, he was getting dressed for work. He saw me move and jumped onto the bed, straddling me on his hands and knees. "Good morning! How do you feel?" He was awfully cheerful.

"Stiff."

He gave me a quick kiss on the lips. "You're beautiful, but I have to go or I'll be late. Dave doesn't like that. You should call your boss and tell him you're not coming in."

"Yeah." *How could he possibly have so much energy?*

"You'll be by yourself today. Will you miss me?"

"After I have coffee I'll miss you. Not right now."

"Oh, I should have made coffee! Do you want me to do it before I go?"

"No, you'll be late."

He kissed me again. "You were awesome last night. I feel fantastic."

"I can hardly tell. Have a good day."

"I'll see you at dinner. Bye!" He jumped off the bed and bounded out the door.

I lay there on my back, feeling like I had taken an advanced yoga class the night before. It was the most invigorating, fun and satisfying sex we had up to that point. *I certainly won't need to exercise today.* I forced myself to get up, stripped the sheets off his bed, and took a shower in his bathroom. I locked the door on my way out and went back to the house to call my office and my insurance company.

Later, while I was sitting in the garden making a list of things that were in the shed, Flora walked up the driveway with Clarence. She held out her arms, inviting me into an embrace. "Oh, Adam! Agnes told us all about the fire. I'm so sorry! You remember Clarence, don't you? He helped you purchase your truck."

"Of course, hello." I shook his hand. We all turned to look at the ruins of the shed. After a few minutes of head shaking and sympathetic exclamations, I invited them to sit down at the table I now had in the garden.

Clarence asked, "Do the police have any idea who might have done it?"

I hesitated and looked at Flora. She reassured me, "You may speak freely in front of Clarence. He knows everything." We discussed the possibility that a neighbor reacted to the Weasel Woman's flyer. Then I told them what Officer Hanson said about Big Ed being pulled over by the police. It brought Flora to tears. "I can't apologize enough, Adam. After all the work Samson put into your shed, I may never forgive myself for allowing things to get to this point. I promise I will make it right. The Chief of Police is an old acquaintance of mine. I had no idea he was brushing Edward's offenses under the rug."

To lighten the mood, I told her about all the friendly neighbors who visited. She was very pleased. While we talked, Officers Mansky and Hanson walked up the driveway. "Good morning, officers."

"Are you Mrs. Flora O'Neill, ma'am?"

"Yes, officer. How may I assist you?"

I stood on the driveway with Carl while Mansky spoke to Flora and Clarence. "What's going on?"

"Just following up. We went next door and the housekeeper sent us here. He's asking her about the fight between Sam and Big Ed." We heard Flora getting stern with Mansky. "He'll be an asshole, but he'll get the job done."

"You won't like this, but I told her about her son's relationship with your chief. She might say something to Mansky."

He closed his eyes and shook his head. "Great! I'll catch hell for that."

I grimaced. "Sorry, but I think she'll help him nail her son. She's fed up with him."

"All right, I understand. You didn't tell Sam, did you?"

"No, but he knows you stopped by yesterday because he saw you leaving."

"Will I have to worry about him?"

I knit my eyebrows. "I don't think so. Do you think so?"

"We'll see. I guess I won't be coming by anymore."

"Um . . . why would you need to?"

He looked at the ground, then at the horizon, and changed the subject. "Hey, we stopped to talk to the woman who made the flyer before we came here. Helen Van Whatever?"

"Van Wootten. I call her the Weasel Woman."

He smiled. "I like that, it fits. She denied any knowledge of the flyer. That didn't play well with Mansky. He scared the shit out of her."

"Good. I wish I could have seen it."

"Yeah, it's one of the few good things about working with that asshole. Sometimes people deserve to be treated badly."

Mansky finished with Flora and came toward us with a scowl. "Hanson! We're done here, and we need to have a chat." He stomped down the driveway toward their squad car.

Carl sighed heavily. "Okay, maybe I'll see you again, Adam. I hope. Do you still have my card?"

"Yeah. I'm sorry about your partner. Thanks again." I watched him go, thinking he would be a good friend to have if it didn't bother Sam.

I returned to Flora and Clarence. "What an unpleasant man! Nevertheless, I believe he will pursue this matter with Edward. I told him I would speak to the Chief of Police."

"When you do, could you please say something nice about Officer Hanson? He did us a favor and I'm afraid he might be paying for it right now."

"I'll put in a good word. Clarence told the officer Edward has been fuming about his encounter with Samson ever since you purchased your truck."

I stood up to thank them, and Flora noticed I was stiff. "Did you injure yourself, dear?"

"No, Sam showed me a new exercise program yesterday. I think I overdid it."

She smiled knowingly. "Yes, of course. Clarence had me exercising this weekend as well. You might notice I'm leaning more heavily on my cane today." Clarence turned as red as a beet and pulled her away before she could elaborate. She called out, "Give my greetings to Samson!"

"I will. Maybe we'll use the pool tomorrow."

She turned around. "Oh, yes! Agnes told me about your visit last night, in detail! It was the highlight of her weekend." She laughed and continued down the driveway while I tried to rub the embarrassment from my face.

***

An investigator from my insurance company arrived after noon to take photographs and ask a lot of questions. Fortunately, I had taken photos of the shed after Sam restored it so he could see how nice it was. As he was leaving, a middle-aged man I didn't recognize walked around the corner of the house. "I'm sorry, if you're busy I'll come back another time."

"That's okay, we're finished." The investigator got in his car and backed down the driveway. This man's posture was . . . unusual. He looked crooked, literally. "How can I help you?"

"I'm one of your neighbors. Name's Joe."

"I'm Adam. Pleased to meet you." We shook hands.

"Sorry about the fire. It's a terrible thing. Your house is beautiful. It's a shame to lose any part of these older homes."

"I know. They don't build them like this anymore."

"My house is a few years older than yours. My great-grandfather built it. Been in the family all this time, but it's just me and my daughter now. We're the end of the line. Anyway, I came over because I have a garden shed, too. It's in terrible shape, but it's around the same age as the one you had."

"You should fix it up. This one looked great before it burned."

"No, no, I won't fix it up. I'd like to give it to you."

"What?"

"I'd like you to take it off my hands to replace your shed. It's rotting away in my back yard. This is a better place for it."

"I . . . I don't know what to say. That's very generous."

"You haven't seen it yet. It needs a lot of work, but I can show it to you. Do you have time now?"

"Uh, sure. Why not? Let me lock my house and I'll be right back."

We walked the short distance to his house, but he walked slowly. He explained that he broke his back years ago on a construction site where he worked. Joe had been disabled ever since. He had a surprisingly good attitude about it. "It worked out pretty well, so I can be at home for my daughter. My wife is gone." As we approached his place, I realized it was one of my favorite houses in the neighborhood, a fantastic Gothic Revival mansion with a wraparound porch. It had seen better days, and was badly in need of a paint job, but it was a great house.

"I've always liked this house, Joe. I wondered who lived here."

"Well, now you know. Let's walk around the back." We went to the back yard which was much smaller than mine. In one corner, surrounded by overgrown brush and weeds, was the weather-beaten shed. I loved it immediately. It was built to match the house, with frilly gingerbread trim and pointed arch windows. It would need a lot of work, but I wanted it. "What do you think? Would it work for you?"

"It's beautiful. I can imagine what it would look like when it's restored."

"It's yours, then. You and Sam can figure out how to get it to your place."

Sam? "Have you met Sam?"

"Well, sure. I thought you knew."

"No. How do you know him?"

"He shoveled snow for me this past winter. He saw my daughter and me out there one day, doing the best we could, and he took over. Had it done in no time. I tried to offer him money, but he wouldn't take it. Every time it snowed, he showed up and took care of it. When spring came, he started cutting the grass and trimming weeds. Never lets me pay him. Half the time I don't see him come and go, but it always gets done."

I had to clear my throat. *Damned emotions!* "That sounds like Sam, but I didn't know about it."

"He's a good man. When I saw the flyer the other day, I realized where he lived. If that nasty woman is ever found dead, I'd be a prime suspect."

"You know the woman who made the flyer?"

"I wouldn't say I know her, but I sure do hate her. She complained to the city that my house needs to be painted. She had the building inspector out here three times, and he finally gave me a citation. He didn't want to do it, but she wouldn't stop calling if he didn't. She's a mean-spirited creature disguised as a Christian. I can't stand people like her."

"I call her the Weasel Woman."

Joe had a long laugh. "Perfect! I'll call her that, too. It was good to meet you, Adam. I don't mean to kick you out, but my daughter will be getting home any minute and she usually wants a lot of attention."

"No problem, I'll get out of your way." We walked back to the street as a white van pulled up.

"Here she is. You can meet her before you go." A young girl, maybe in her teens, with Down Syndrome, climbed out of the van with a pink backpack. "Hey, Susie-Q!"

"Hi Dad."

"I want you to meet one of our neighbors. This is Adam. Adam, this is my girl, Susie."

"It's Susan, Dad! Only you can call me Susie."

"I'm sorry, honey. I forgot."

"Hello, Susan." I didn't know whether to shake her hand. *How are you supposed to greet children?*

"Hello, Adam. Where do you live?"

"Not far from here." I pointed in the direction of my house.

"Adam lives in the flower house, honey. You know the one. And you know who else lives there? Sam, the guy who helps us out."

"Oh."

"Yeah," I said. "I suppose you like him."

She shook her head. "No."

"You don't? I thought everyone liked Sam."

"He's too big." She made a face.

Joe shrugged. "She doesn't like big people. I don't know why."

"He's just too big, Dad! Can we go in the house, now? I have things to show you."

"Okay, Susie, but you know Sam is a nice guy, right?"

"I know. He's not coming over, is he?"

"No, he's not." Joe chuckled. "Go in the house, I'll be right there."

"Bye, Adam."

Joe smiled. "She's a character."

"She says what she thinks. I like it. I'll talk to Sam about the shed. We'll be home tomorrow, so maybe we can have another look at it. Thanks again, it's very kind of you to offer it."

"Say no more, I'm happy to do it. If I'm not here when you come over, go in the back and do whatever you want."

I walked home, thinking about all the people who had been friendly to us since the fire. And I thought about Sam . . . my big, kind, generous, amazing Sam. I walked down the street, smiling like a happy person.

19

By the middle of July, Edward O'Neill, Big Ed, the King of Cars and erstwhile candidate for the city council, was arrested and charged with driving while intoxicated, arson, and bribery of a public official. After the fire, Flora contacted the Chief of Police who assumed she was seeking special treatment for her son. He admitted he had helped Ed many times in exchange for 'donations' to the department. She reported their conversation to the District Attorney. The subsequent investigation uncovered a history of graft and political corruption that eventually led to the chief's downfall. The mayor gave a special commendation to Officer Doug Mansky. Officer Carl Hanson's assistance was also noted. Everyone expected Big Ed to hire a fancy lawyer and post bail, but the King of Cars had no money. He gambled away everything he inherited from his father and owed money all over town. Flora terminated him as the general manager of O'Neill's Automotive and refused to give him financial assistance.

It was a great relief to know Big Ed was locked up, but I wasn't prepared for phone calls from the local media wanting to know why he would burn down my garden shed. Officer Hanson's police report referred vaguely to a dispute that led to retaliation. On a Wednesday morning, Sam and I sat with Flora on her terrace and discussed how to tell the story. I wondered what, if anything, we would say about how Sam and I were related. When I brought this up, Flora was surprised, and Sam looked wounded, but I didn't think it would be good for either of us if our relationship was made known to the whole town. I tried to support my position.

"I'm a private person. Six months ago, I hadn't told anyone I was gay. Now the whole neighborhood is making assumptions because of those flyers. Do you expect me to tell the local media I'm gay, and my boyfriend is a twenty-year-old shirtless landscaper?"

Sam's face fell. "Is that how you think of me?"

Oh, shit. "No, no . . . it's not . . . it's . . . other people might see you that way, and I am older, so . . ."

"Why would other people see me that way? Do you think I wouldn't wear a shirt if a reporter came over? I may not have your education, but I'm not stupid, Adam!"

"I know you're not stupid. I'm sorry, I didn't mean it the way it sounded."

He wouldn't look at me. "I guess I should cover myself up from now on."

I pressed my hands against my face and whispered, "Oh, God, I'm such an idiot!"

Flora intervened, lightly touching his arm. "Samson, honey . . . you know Adam thinks the world of you, but he has a point. People might make assumptions."

"Like what? I'm not ashamed of being gay. I'm not embarrassed to say I love Adam. I don't get it."

Flora struggled to come up with a way to explain it without hurting his feelings. "Well, dear . . . you're a very handsome younger man. Adam is . . . more established financially. People who don't know you might think he provides . . . support in exchange for . . . your companionship."

"People might think he's paying me for sex? Is that what you thought when you met me?"

I held my breath. *This is getting worse.*

Flora blushed. "I'm sorry to say, before we met . . . I thought there might be a financial arrangement. Now I know it's not like that."

Sam stared at her, his face as red as hers.

"Sam . . . do you realize I could lose my job if my boss knew I'm gay? I can't take that risk if it's not necessary. Our relationship has nothing to do with the fire."

"Why would you . . . wait, your boss doesn't know you're gay? But . . . he let you change your work schedule so you could spend more time with me."

Fuck! "Sam . . . he's very conservative and Catholic. I told him I met someone I cared about very much . . . which is true . . ."

"Oh my God! You let him think you have a girlfriend!"

I said nothing. I had nothing to say.

He didn't look angry, though he was. His expression revealed something far worse: he was disappointed. I hadn't seen that before. He thought less of me now. "I'll let the two of you discuss this." He stood up. "Just give me the script I'm supposed to follow." He looked at Flora. "I'll say whatever I'm paid to say." He walked down the lawn toward the hedge.

Flora had tears in her eyes. "Samson, please! I'm so sorry!"

I stood up. "I'm going after him."

"Yes, of course! How awful!"

I caught up with Sam as he was squeezing through the opening in the hedge. His t-shirt snagged on a branch. Angry and impatient, he forced himself through the opening, tearing the shirt. He twisted around to unhook the fabric and saw me on the other side. "Leave me alone! I need time to think." He hastily tore the shirt off his body.

"Can't we talk this out?" I passed through the hedge and saw a woman standing in the driveway a few paces behind Sam.

"Excuse me." She looked at Sam. Shirtless Sam. "Are you Adam Evans?"

He awkwardly covered his chest with the scraps of his shirt. "Me? No." He pointed at me. "He is."

"Oh, I'm a reporter from the Daily Herald. I wonder if I could ask you a few questions about the fire. I tried to call you, but . . ."

We froze for a minute before I collected my wits. "Uh, sure . . . um . . . you caught us off guard. We were . . . what were we doing?"

In a businesslike voice, Sam said, "I'll go up to my apartment, Mr. Evans. We can discuss those other issues later." He backed away from the woman, keeping his nipples covered.

"Okay, thanks." He turned and ran up the stairs, then slammed his apartment door.

The reporter grimaced at me. "I'm sorry. I don't like to surprise people like this, but my editor insisted I speak to you today. Do you mind?"

She seemed nice. I went out on a limb and invited her to follow me back to Flora's terrace. As we walked across the lawn I asked, "If we answer your questions, and if we don't speak to any other reporters, would that be good for you?"

"An exclusive? Yeah, my editor would be pleased."

"Could you do me a favor in return?"

"I'd have to hear what it is first."

I told her about my relationship with Sam and asked if it needed to be included. She didn't see why it would be relevant but wanted to hear the whole story first. I introduced her to Flora, and we sat down. It didn't take long for the reporter to realize Flora was a more interesting subject for an article about the conflict between a mother and son, and her decision to do the right thing even though it would harm him. Sam and I were only the neighbors who helped during their final, dramatic conflict. Because I owned the property that was burned, Sam's name wouldn't even be mentioned. Our argument had been completely unnecessary.

After the reporter left, I went back to the coach house to talk to Sam. My anxiety reminded me of the day I came to his apartment for dinner. Back then, I was afraid Sam would discover I was attracted to him. Now I was afraid he was finished with me. *I knew it wouldn't last.*

He came to the door wearing a long-sleeved black sweatshirt despite the warm weather. "Mr. Evans . . . what can I do for you?" Apparently, he was still angry.

"Come on, Sam. Don't do that."

"I'm being careful. We don't want anyone to think we're friends. Is the reporter still here?"

"No, she left."

"What did you tell her?"

"That we're together, in a relationship, whatever you want to call it."

"And she'll put it in the paper?"

"Well . . . no. She didn't think it was relevant to the story."

"Did you ask her to leave it out?"

I hesitated. "Yes, I did, but she agreed it wasn't relevant."

His gaze hardened again. "Uh huh. That worked out well for you . . . your reputation is safe. And mine too. The whole city won't think I'm your full-time whore. Thanks for protecting me, Adam."

"Just let me in so we can talk about this."

"No."

"What?"

"No, you can't come in. I don't want to listen to your excuses for keeping our relationship a secret."

"It's not a secret, but I don't need to tell the whole city!"

"You could at least tell your boss!"

"No, I can't! I need my job!"

"I don't want to talk about this anymore. Go away and leave me alone."

"But it's our day off. We're supposed to spend it together."

"Too bad. Go away."

"Are you breaking up with me?"

"No! You're not getting out of this that easy!"

"I don't want to get out of it!"

"Then you have to put up with me being angry!"

"But . . . can't we make up and get it over with?"

"Aaaaugh!" He slammed the door so hard it cracked the glass in the window. "God dammit! Now I have to fix that!"

I turned to leave but I remembered something. I knocked on the door again.

"WHAT?"

"Do you want lunch?"

"I'm not hungry!"

"What?" I heard him, but I didn't believe it.

"I'm . . . not . . . HUNGRY!"

"Okay. What about dinner?" He didn't answer. "I'll make meatloaf." Still nothing. "Mashed potatoes and peas. Ice cream?"

"Fine! Go away!"

I listened for a minute. "You can't sit in that hot apartment all day. You should sit in the garden."

I heard him stomp across the floor. He pulled the door open to make a point. "I suppose you want to see me half naked! Am I being paid for that?" He slammed the door again. I heard something fall off the wall and break. "God dammit!"

"I'm not paying you for anything! Sit in there and roast! I don't care." I clomped down the stairs.

He called out, "I *know* you don't!"

I let him have the last word. I marched across the driveway, up the porch stairs, and through the back door. I stood there, breathing heavily, my thoughts racing. *We never had an argument like that before. Am I wrong? I must be wrong. He's usually right. What have I done? Did I fuck everything up? Will he forgive me? Should I forgive him? Wait . . . what did he do wrong? I'm usually wrong. What did I do wrong?*

My thoughts went on like that for hours, but none of those questions were answered. I did what any normal person would do after an argument. I dusted everything in the house. I mopped the floors. I used a manicure scissors to remove every brown leaf from every frond of the ferns in the living room, then worried that I had killed them. I cried for five minutes. I took everything out of the freezer and put it all back in a more pleasing arrangement. I checked the attic for rat droppings and squirrel damage but found none. I went on the internet to read an article about carpenter ants. I prepared the meatloaf and put it in the refrigerator. Then I polished the light bulbs in all the lamps and chandeliers. It was a productive afternoon. I was perfectly fine.

While I peeled potatoes, I saw Sam sitting in one of the Adirondack chairs facing a back corner of the garden. He wore a t-shirt instead of the sweatshirt he had on earlier, and he held my copy of *Wuthering Heights*. I watched him, not because I cared what he was doing, but because I happened to be near the window. He seemed to be reading, then got up and stared at something in the grass. He sat down to look at the book again, then picked a pebble out of the sole of his sandal. He didn't stay in the chair for more than two minutes at a time. I saw him trying to do a handstand, reading, staring at the sky, reading, creeping up on a squirrel, and reading. Once, he got up and walked around the chair a couple of times before sitting down again. I muttered, "Someone has issues." When he glanced at the house, I ducked.

I was preparing the cooked potatoes when Sam quietly came through the back door. I felt awkward and said nothing. He stood near me, looking uncomfortable. "Need any help?"

I didn't look up. "Do you know how to mash potatoes?"

"I can smash things."

I stepped aside and handed him the potato masher. He crushed the potatoes in the pan. "Let me throw some butter in there." I cut a chunk and dropped it in.

He worked the butter into the potatoes. "They don't look right."

"They're not done yet." I added milk. "Now they need to be whipped." I plugged in the electric mixer. "Do you want to do it, or should I?"

"You do it, I'll watch." I started beating the mixture while Sam stood behind me. When I shut off the mixer, I could feel him very close to me, breathing. He touched my shoulder. I turned and put my arms around his chest, hugging him tightly. He reciprocated. We both apologized at the same time, took all the blame, said we were stupid, and kissed. I didn't want to let go of him, but dinner was ready.

We ate in the dining room to get away from the heat of the kitchen. It took a while for a conversation to start. I asked him, "So . . . what did you do all afternoon?"

"A lot of reading. What did you do?"

"A little cleaning."

There was a long pause before he said, "I don't like being angry at you."

"Good. I don't like it when you're angry at me either."

"Weren't you angry at me?"

"I wanted to be, but I couldn't figure out what you did wrong."

He thought for a minute. "It wasn't fair to expect you to tell your boss about us. I know about discrimination, and I don't want you to lose your job. I just wish you told me from the beginning."

"I was afraid you would be disappointed in me. I'm still afraid."

"That's what I'm always worried about, too . . . that you'll think I'm too young, or uneducated. I try to make up for those things by looking as good as possible, and that works against me, too."

I felt guilty. "It doesn't work against you, and you don't have to make up for anything. I'm sorry I called you a shirtless landscaper, I didn't . . ."

"A twenty-year-old shirtless landscaper."

"Yes, I know . . . I said that, but . . . it has more to do with what other people might think rather than what I think. I don't have any problem with your age or your education, but other people might not understand our relationship. And I don't love you because of the way you look. It doesn't matter . . ."

"Oh, come on, Adam! Don't pretend it doesn't matter what I look like. It matters to me what you look like."

"It does?"

"Well, yeah! How many times have I told you how handsome and sexy you are? I'm not just saying that. If I didn't think you were hot when I met you, I probably wouldn't be here. And if you didn't think I was good looking, I wouldn't be here. So don't say it doesn't matter."

He was right, but it felt so shallow. "But it's not what keeps our relationship going. If I were a complete asshole instead of an occasional asshole, you wouldn't still be here, would you?"

"I suppose not."

"And, yeah, I love the way you look, but there's so much more I love about you. Like, the way you help Joe by shoveling snow and cutting his grass, and you didn't even mention it. That stuff makes me melt inside. You're one of the nicest people I've ever met."

"It's not such a big deal."

"Yes, it is! No one else was doing it for him. I'm glad you're proud of your body, but you should be proud of your mind and your heart, too. You're a wonderful man, and people like you for that. Believe me, it would be easy to hate you for being so damned hot."

He didn't have an immediate response. After a few minutes, he asked, "Doesn't it bother you that Flora thought I was your paid companion?"

"It was as much of an insult to me as it was to you. But I can't blame her for thinking what I thought when we were getting to know each other. I couldn't believe you were attracted to me. The hunkier you got, the more unbelievable it seemed. But you convinced me, mostly."

"You also used to think you were too old to start a relationship."

"I did, and it wasn't that long ago. I'm glad you proved me wrong."

"Me too. I like proving you wrong." He smiled and put more meatloaf on his plate.

***

The next day I received a lot of attention at work because of the newspaper article about Flora and Big Ed and my garden shed. I hated it. I wanted to get my work done, but I was subjected to words of sympathy and concern. There was a picture of my house with the story, so I had to endure compliments about how beautiful it was. It was terrible. *Why do people care?*

Donna stopped in my office to say how much her family were looking forward to dinner with us on Sunday. She made small talk and asked what I would be serving for dinner and whether she could bring anything. She didn't say a word about the article. It irritated me. "You know, my garden is a crime scene."

"Yeah, the kids will love it."

"Are you sure you want to expose them to that?"

"Yeah."

"Won't they have nightmares?"

"No."

"We could reschedule for another weekend."

"Nope."

She was working my last nerve. "You could at least show some concern!"

"Oh? Do you like that kind of attention?"

I grumbled, "No."

She stood up to leave. "Okay, see you later!"

Dammit, she's good!

Once things settled down, I closed my door to get some work done. I wondered why Henry hadn't made an appearance. When I heard a knock on my door, my heart did a little somersault. I'm not sure why. "Come in!"

Mr. Zipinski entered. *Crap.* "Adam, my good man, I see you're working diligently. Very impressive, considering all the excitement you've been through." He closed the door behind him.

"Yes, well . . . my job comes first," I lied.

"I appreciate that. May I sit and speak with you?"

"Yes, of course. You're the boss." *That was lame.* I made a fake smile.

"It's true, I am the boss, but I hope our relationship is not as formal as that."

But it is, isn't it?

"After all, your parents were friends of mine." He showed his yellow teeth.

Friends? They went to the same church.

"There are two reasons for my visit, Adam. Firstly, I would like to express my concern for you, again. I learned from the article in today's newspaper that you have a social relationship with Flora O'Neill. I would like to caution you . . . she has a rather disturbing reputation in the community."

"Oh? I didn't know." I had a pretty good idea what he was talking about.

"I will not go into details because I am not one to spread gossip. Her unfortunate son, Edward, has been a friendly acquaintance, but I prefer not to be associated with him at this time. Perhaps, if he is cleared of these charges . . ."

"Cleared?" I blurted. "I don't think he'll be cleared. He burned my shed."

"Let's allow the courts to decide. I merely want you to consider those with whom you associate. Far be it from me to tell people how to live their lives, but you can't trust a woman with a scarlet reputation." He raised his bony hands in the air. "Now I've said too much. Satan is having his way with me."

I smiled weakly. *Satan is so far up your ass his tail is coming out your ear!*

"The second reason I'm here is to thank you for your loyalty to me, personally, and to this firm."

"Um, you're welcome. I appreciate your trust in me."

"I will be depending on your friendship in the days to come. I'm afraid there is . . . turmoil ahead."

"Turmoil?"

"Scurrilous accusations are being made against me, and I must face them bravely. The Lord has seen fit to test me. This struggle may interfere with my leadership of this firm for a while. You may be asked to take on more responsibility. There will be financial rewards, of course . . . because of your loyalty." His eyes sent a chill down my spine.

I tried to sound vaguely supportive. "I will be happy to do what I can for the good of the firm. I can handle more responsibility." *And I wouldn't mind a financial reward.*

"I have no doubt. I'm glad we have an understanding. I trust you won't share this information with certain female associates." *Meaning Donna.* "Women are so histrionic."

"Yes, why can't they be more like us?" *God, I hate myself right now.*

"Indeed. If you need to discuss matters of importance with a trustworthy person, there is someone here at the firm who has impressed me with his intelligence and ambition. He has become a trusted adviser and a supportive friend at this challenging time."

"Who do you mean?"

"Henry Verdorven. I believe the two of you are acquainted. He speaks highly of you."

My mouth fell open. "Henry . . . yes . . . we are friends. He's your trusted adviser? He hasn't been here very long."

"He is new to the firm, but I see it as an asset. He hasn't been corrupted by some of the . . . bad influences who have spread their roots here. He attended a very fine school, as I'm sure you know, and he descended from an old Dutch family who settled the colony of New York."

"Huh. I didn't know that."

"He's an all-around good chap. He reminds me of some of my fraternity brothers, although he is young enough to be my son." *More like your grandson!* "I encourage you to spend more time with him. You could be the leaders of this firm someday."

"I'm . . . nearly speechless. Thank you so much."

"I've taken enough of your time. Back to the grindstone, as they say." When he stood up, I thought I heard his knees creak. "May I ask, how are things progressing with your sweetheart?"

"Very well, thank you. My new schedule has helped."

"I'm glad to hear it. I hope you keep that in mind during the days ahead." He opened the door.

"I certainly will. Thanks for stopping by."

"Good day, Adam."

"Good day, sir."

***

On Friday, we all received a memo announcing that Henry Verdorven would be leaving the tax department to become the first vice president at the firm, with the additional title of personnel manager, overseeing human resources. The director of human resources had submitted her resignation rather suddenly and was already gone.

The women in the office were generally thrilled with Henry's promotion. Donna did not share their enthusiasm. She blew into my office like a thunderstorm. "What the fuck is going on, Adam?"

"I don't know. I'm as surprised as you are. Close the door."

She closed the door but didn't sit down. "How could he get into a position like that after being here for less than a year?"

"Zipinski is very impressed with him. He told me himself."

"When did you talk to Zipinski?"

"He was in here yesterday after you left."

"Why didn't you tell me?"

"I haven't had time! It all happened so fast."

"Tell me everything."

"I think Zipinski is in trouble."

"What kind of trouble?"

"The trouble you told me about."

"But I dropped it! I haven't talked to any of those women since Zipinski threatened me."

"I know, but I think they must have done something without involving you."

"So that's what they've been hiding from me! And they're saying things will change for the better with Henry in that position? What the fuck? How does he figure into all of this?"

"He's very charming with the ladies."

She gave me a look. "And with some of the men."

"Shut up. Henry may have encouraged them to file a formal complaint."

"But, how would he know about . . ." She glared at me. "Adam . . . what did you do?"

Now I was afraid. "I may have let something slip about it."

Her eyes bored into my skull. "You may have?"

"I did. I said something. It was an accident!"

"ADAM!"

"I was trying to help you! It did help! Zipinski is in trouble!"

"And Henry is the fucking VICE PRESIDENT!"

"Shhhh! Keep your voice down! Jesus!"

She sat down and narrowed her eyes. "You know all those times I threatened to kill you? I'm not kidding anymore."

"Stop saying things like that! As a recent crime victim, I'm very sensitive."

"I'll do it right now."

"No, you won't! You're coming to dinner on Sunday. You said nothing would interfere with that."

"Dammit!"

"Besides . . . who do you think is the best friend of the new vice president?"

"God DAMN it!"

"Henry spoke very highly of me to Zipinski, and Zipinski encouraged me to spend more time with Henry. He said he's 'an all-around good chap,' and the two of us might be the leaders of this firm someday." I was very satisfied with myself.

"He actually said that?"

"Yes."

"And you believed him?"

"Well, yes. Why wouldn't I?"

She stared at me. "Because he's a lying, hypocritical son of a bitch."

Oh yeah. "But . . . it could happen."

"And you could start farting marshmallows!"

"Oh, Sam would love that."

She smiled despite her anger and frustration. "Adam . . . I love you, but you are one of the most infuriating people I have ever dealt with."

"I know, I feel the same way about myself. I'm sorry."

"If this blows up in your face, I will be the first in line to say I told you so."

"Well, duh! I knew that."

"If I lose my job, I will kill you. Then Kevin will kill you a second time."

"Stop making death threats. They're not effective anymore." She made a sudden move forward and I nearly jumped out of my chair. "AAH! Don't do that!"

"Not effective anymore, huh?" She stood up.

I cowered in my chair, guarding my head. "Don't damage my face. I'm starting to like it."

"What time are we supposed to be there on Sunday?"

"I don't know. Five?"

"We'll be there at four."

"Okay. I can't wait."

"Me neither. I need to talk to Sam."

I didn't like the sound of that.

***

I enjoyed working alone on Saturdays. I could dress casually, there were no interruptions from co-workers, and I got a lot done. Some people would see it as an opportunity to screw around all day and get paid, but I liked being productive and had deadlines to meet. Also, I could talk to myself out loud. Some of my best conversations were with myself, despite our frequent arguments.

I was fully absorbed in my work when I was startled by unfamiliar clunks and clicks. A door opened and closed. Someone else was in the building. I looked around for something to use as a weapon and grabbed a three-hole punch. I held it up, and little paper dots fell all over the place. I cursed out loud. "Fuck me!"

"What did you say?" I jumped. It was Henry.

"God, you scared me!"

"Sorry. And you don't need to call me 'God.' Henry is fine."

"What? I didn't . . . I meant . . . okay, I get it now . . . a joke. What are you doing here?"

"I was cycling and saw your truck in the parking lot, so I thought I'd pay a visit." He smiled his sparkly white smile. He wore a skin-tight green cycling jersey and shorts that revealed more about his body than I wanted to know. "I haven't seen you for a while, my friend! How are you?" He grasped the top of the door frame and stretched himself in the opening.

"I'm okay. Fine. Everything's fine. How are you?" He looked fit as a fiddle.

"Things are going well for me. I assume you heard the news." He entered my office.

"Yes, congratulations. I was stunned . . . and happy . . . for you, I mean . . . vice president . . . wow."

"Thanks. I wish I could have been here yesterday to tell you myself, but I had to meet with Zipinski and his lawyer for most of the day." He looked at the floor. "Were you throwing confetti to celebrate?"

"No, I made a mess." I brushed the paper dots off my clothing.

His eyes scanned me like an airport security booth. "Look at you in your shorts and t-shirt. Casual looks good on you. Nice legs, dude! Have you been working out?"

"Huh, what? My . . . I . . . I run . . . I do exercise . . . stuff." I sat down awkwardly in my desk chair.

"Well it's paying off, Adam. You're seriously hot now."

"Upfff! Not . . . no . . . I don't . . ."

"No, seriously." He sat down on the corner of my desk, too close for comfort, with his knees far apart. I didn't know where to look. "I can see the difference. You look younger."

"Awf! I mean, I feel . . . I'm . . . thank you, I appreciate it. Tell me about your promotion. How did you manage that?"

"I owe it all to you, buddy, and it won't be forgotten." As he talked, he stretched his triceps behind his head. "The info you gave me about Zipinski's bad behavior was exactly what I needed. I knew it would make him vulnerable, so I gave him a heads-up and I was there when he needed a friend and adviser. I've never charmed anyone as repulsive as Zipinski before. I'm at the top of my game." He placed his hands on his thighs and stroked them casually. "And if those women get a settlement out of him for sexual harassment, that's good, too."

"It's great that you encouraged them to file complaints."

"Yeah, sure. Do you have anything to eat in here? All I had for breakfast was a spoonful of chia seeds."

"No, sorry. I already ate my sandwich."

"I'll be right back." He went into the area outside my office where various staff members worked. I rested my hand on the desk and felt a damp warmth. It was the spot where he had been sitting. I pulled my arm back and saw the shape of my hand in the middle of an imprint of his ass. He returned holding an apple and sat on my handprint. I wiped his perspiration on the front of my t-shirt.

"Where'd you get the apple?"

"Off someone's desk." He polished the apple against his well-formed chest. "Do you want a taste?"

"No, thanks. I don't eat other people's food."

He took a bite and smiled while he chewed. His arms and legs were hairless, so his tanned skin had the same smooth sheen as his spandex outfit. "You're one of those guys, aren't you?"

"One of what guys?"

"A good guy. A person of moral character." His smile was disconcerting.

"I try to be. I don't think I'm that good."

"Then why keep trying? Live a little." He took another bite and slurped apple juice off the heel of his hand.

"I am living. I don't think I'm missing anything."

"Are you sure?" His gaze never wavered. He shifted his hips and spread his knees a little wider. I noticed a bulge.

I squirmed and cleared my throat. "My life is better than ever. I'm happy."

"You can always be happier. I'd like to help. You could learn a lot from me, Adam." He was about to take another bite, then stopped and extended his hand. "Are you sure you don't want a bite of this? It's very juicy."

Jeez! "All right . . . I'll try it." *To shut him up.* I took the apple from his hand and looked at it. *I don't want to eat the part he slobbered on, but if I avoid it, he might be offended. Oh, what the hell.* I bit off a chunk and chewed. "Wow, this is good." *Better than I expected.* "I wonder what kind of apple this is."

"See . . . you were missing something." He smirked.

I returned a crooked smile. "Okay. You were right." I offered him the apple.

"Finish it. I'm full." He leaned back and put his palms flat on the desktop. Veins sprouted from his wrists and branched up to his biceps.

I took another bite and allowed my eyes to travel over his sinuous body. He noticed. "There isn't an ounce of fat on you, is there? You must work out constantly."

"If sex counts, the answer is yes."

I looked at the lengthening bulge in his crotch, then met his eyes. "So . . . what would I have to do to get a promotion around here?"

His expression showed a hint of surprise. "That depends. How much can you handle?"

"Oh, I can handle a lot. And I work very hard. But I have one condition." I ate more of the apple.

"A condition? Like, what?"

"My friend, Donna . . . her job has to be secure." Again, there was a flicker in his eyes.

"You don't need to worry about her. All the women in the office are safe. If any of them were fired now, it would look like retaliation."

"Good to know." I nibbled the apple down to the core. "When will I get more responsibility and more money?"

He leaned forward. I was messing with his seduction. "Well, it could happen, depending on what happens to Zipinski. He talked to you, didn't he?"

"Yeah. He said I should spend more time with you. I told him we were already friends."

He smiled and leaned back again, flexing his hips. "Okay. That's what I wanted to hear." His erection had grown longer, but it was rather thin. *Pencil dick.*

I threw the apple core into my waste basket. "I'm looking forward to a good working relationship with you, Henry." I gently squeezed his knee. "You should go, now. I need to finish this work."

"What?" He sat straight up. "You want me to leave?" His expression was priceless.

"Yeah, I'm here to work. This is your day off. You should go home."

"But . . . don't you want to . . ."

"What?"

"Don't you want to fuck?"

"With you? No! Is that what you expected? Oh, my goodness! My boyfriend keeps telling me how naive I am . . . I guess he's right. I'm sorry! But, no . . . that's out of the question. You know I'm in a committed relationship. What were you thinking?"

"I thought we would finally fuck!"

"But that's a terrible idea, especially because you have authority over me now. With these harassment complaints . . . do you realize how this might look to other people? Oh, my goodness!" I laid it on thick.

"No one would have to know."

"But, what about the security cameras?" I waved my finger around.

"Are there cameras in here?!" He put a hand over his crotch.

"Don't all these buildings have them?" There were no cameras.

"Fuck!" He jumped off the desk.

"There's no need to panic, Henry. I won't tell anyone you tried to seduce me. I'm flattered, by the way. I can't wait to brag to my boyfriend."

"No! You can't!"

"Oh, right! What was I thinking? Gosh, all these secrets! It's a good thing we're friends or my conscience would bother me."

He paced back and forth. He had a great ass, but there were paper dots stuck to it. "Listen, Adam, I'm sorry for the misunderstanding. I was joking about the fucking, okay?"

"Oh, what a relief! I wouldn't mind plugging your fine ass, but . . ."

"Stop it! That's not funny!" He raked his fingers through his hair. "I shouldn't have come in here."

"Well, you're free to leave. Congratulations, again. I look forward to working with you. We should do lunch again one of these days. Your turn to pay."

"Yeah, sure. I'm counting on you, Adam. I can't blow this opportunity. The vice president title will give me a better chance of getting out of this shit hole. You help me, and I'll help you. That's the way things work in business."

"Is it? Wow, I'm learning already. You pat my ass, and I'll pat yours. Is that how the expression goes?"

"I have to go." He rushed out of my office. A door closed.

I spun around in my chair. *That was fun! So, Henry was trying to seduce me all along. I was naive. Sam and Donna were right. Do I have to tell them? No, they'll want to kill him.* I knew they would want me to stay away from Henry, but I was sure it would be better to have him as a friend rather than an enemy. And now that I had something to use against him, I didn't need to trust him.

I licked my lips. *I need to find out what kind of apple that was.*

***

When I got home I was surprised to see Sam's truck in the driveway. I found him in the kitchen with his mouth full of spray cheese and crackers. He made a noise like a greeting.

"You're home early."

He finished chewing and swallowing. "Yeah, it wasn't too busy, so Dave sent me home. He says 'Hi' and wants to know why you never come to see him anymore. I told him you get all your stuff at Garden Mart now."

"Don't say that, he'll have a stroke."

"You should have seen his face, even though he knew I was kidding." He pulled me into a hug and gave me a cheesy kiss. Then he made a face.

"What?"

"What's that smell?" He sniffed my t-shirt. "You smell different. What were you doing?"

"Just working. Why? Do I smell bad?" *Is it Henry?*

"My buddy Greg would say, 'You smell like ass.'"

"Oh. He sounds like quite a wit."

"He's cool. He's my *bro!*" It was my turn to make a face. "But seriously . . . you don't smell like yourself."

"Maybe I brushed against something."

"Or someone?" He squinted to show he was kidding. "What's for dinner?"

"Do you want to go out?"

"To eat? Together? In public?"

"Yes, together. We've gone out before."

"Not to a restaurant."

"What are we waiting for? I'll go change my shirt and get this smell off me."

"Good, then I can mark you with my scent." He bit his lower lip and rubbed his crotch against my hip. "I need to change, too. I'll meet you in the driveway."

I walked toward the front of the house. "How about Mexican food?"

"Hell yes! I love it!"

On the stairs, I pulled my shirt up to my nose. I couldn't smell anything. *I should tell him about Henry's visit. I have nothing to hide. Nah . . . it's better to wait for the right time.*

20

I admit it. I was nervous about having Donna and her family over for dinner. I never invited anyone other than Sam into the house. And there would be children. *Will I have to talk to them or play with them?* Her husband, Kevin, was a nice guy. I talked to him for five minutes once. I don't usually last that long.

They showed up around four, as Donna promised. Their oldest son, Colin, was a gangly sixteen-year-old with bangs over his eyes. It looked like he was hiding behind them. I understood the appeal of it. The girl, Sarah, was confident and talkative like her mother. Their youngest, Mike, arrived with a soccer ball and enough energy to light up a small village. I was terrified.

After greeting them on the front porch, I pulled Donna aside. "What will he do with the soccer ball?"

"He can kick it around your living room if he gets bored. And he's always bored." Typical Donna. I narrowed my eyes until she gave me a better answer. "He has a lot of energy, so I thought he could kick the ball around your yard until he wears himself out. Is that okay?"

"Will he stay out of the flower beds?"

"I'll tell him, but I can't guarantee it. I could ask Colin to watch him."

"What are you two plotting over there?" That was Kevin.

"Nothing, dear! Hey, Mike . . . Adam says you can kick the ball around if you stay away from the flowers, okay? Colin, could you play with him for a while?"

"Why do I always have to watch him? I don't want to kick a stupid ball."

Mike shot back, "I don't care! You're bad at it anyway!"

I sighed. *And the fun begins.*

Sam stepped in. "I'll kick the ball with you, but you'll have to teach me. I never played soccer."

Kevin said, "You must've played football in school."

Sam shook his head. "No."

"Basketball?"

"No."

"Baseball?"

"A little, but I didn't like it. I was in the chess club, and I was on the debate team for a while."

Kevin looked baffled. It was understandable to think Sam was an athlete. No one would look at him and think *chess club.* I loved that.

Mike had to get moving. "Come on, Sam, I'll show you! I'm really good!" Sam followed him onto the front lawn.

Donna thanked Sam. "Keep him running around until he collapses." She turned back to me. "So . . . can we have a tour of this beautiful house?"

I took the rest of them through the house, explaining how my parents restored it. They were impressed, especially by the entrance hall and staircase. Sarah asked twenty questions, but Colin was quiet until we got to the library. "Awesome! How many books do you have?"

"I don't know. I never thought of counting them."

"Have you read all of them?"

"Most. Some of my parents' books didn't interest me."

He skimmed the shelves. "We don't have any books at our house."

Kevin said, "That's not true. Your mother has books."

Colin scoffed. "Crappy romance novels. The *Twilight* books."

I looked at Donna with disgust. "*Twilight*? Seriously?"

"Shut up. Sarah wanted them."

Sarah didn't cooperate. "You read them first, Mom."

Donna changed the subject. "Colin wants to be a writer."

"Oh yeah? What do you write?"

He tilted his head so his bangs covered his eyes. "Personal stuff."

"Okay." I tried again. "What sort of books do you like?"

"Good ones."

I didn't think he was being sarcastic or intentionally difficult, but . . . I looked at his parents.

"Welcome to our world, " said Kevin.

Sarah offered, "I like Jane Austen."

"Typical girl," said Colin. He looked at me through his bangs. "Who's your favorite writer?"

"Oh . . . it's hard to say. I like Jane Austen, too, but I guess I'd have to say Thomas Hardy is my favorite."

He thought for a moment. "*The Mayor of Casterbridge*?"

"Yeah, have you read it?"

"Uh huh."

"What about *Tess of the D'Urbervilles*? Sam just finished reading that."

"Not that one. It's on my list. I read *Jude The Obscure.*"

I was impressed, but also a little worried. "That's dark and depressing stuff for someone your age."

"I don't think so. It's realistic."

He sounded like me, which was not so good. *Time to change the subject.* "Do you want to see my garden?" I led them to the stairs, and the kids went down first.

Donna whispered, "That was more words than I've heard from Colin in two years."

"Hmm. I like him already."

"How bad are those books he mentioned?"

"Why don't you read them and find out? They're not about sparkly vampires."

"Fuck you. Are you enjoying this?"

"Oh, yes! I didn't realize how much I would learn about you."

Kevin cleared his throat. "Would you two quit whispering? You're making me uncomfortable."

"Sorry, Kevin. Donna started it."

"Did not."

"Did too!"

Kevin rolled his eyes.

I took them through the kitchen and out the back door. The air was filled with the sweet scent of lilies at their peak. Colin and Sarah made a beeline for the pile of burnt lumber that once was my garden shed. The crime scene tape had been removed, but Sam put a rope barrier around it to protect the kids. We discussed the fire and the latest developments in the story of 'Big Ed' O'Neill and the disgraced Chief of Police.

Soon the kids settled into the Adirondack chairs to play with their cell phones. Kevin, an electrical contractor, talked to me about installing security cameras. Donna went to the front of the house to check on Mike and Sam. A few minutes later, Kevin stopped talking in the middle of a sentence. "I hear my wife yelling at someone." We listened. I heard an argument.

As we jogged around the house to the front yard, there was a screech of car tires. Sam stood on the grass with his hands over Mike's ears and Donna was in the middle of the street, yelling at a car down the block. Mike broke away from Sam and ran up to Kevin. "Dad! You missed it! Mom yelled a bunch of swears at the lady in that car!"

"She did? Don't repeat any of those, okay? Those are only for adults."

Sam looked shaken. "I'm not even old enough to hear some of the things she said."

I took a wild guess. "Was it the Weasel Woman?" Sam nodded.

Mike was fascinated. "What's a Weasel Woman?"

"Um . . . it's a woman who looks and acts like a weasel."

"Cool! Dad, what's a weasel?"

"We'll look it up when we get home." Donna stomped up the lawn. "Honey . . . what happened?"

"That fffff . . . woman . . . was taking photographs of our son playing with Sam! I saw her when I came around the house, so I went right down there to ask her what the fffff . . . heck she was doing. She was spouting crap about . . . stuff I can't repeat, so I gave her a piece of my mind!"

Kevin looked worried. "Was it the really angry piece of your mind?"

She took a deep breath and let it out. "Yes, that piece."

"Oh, God. Did you hit her?"

"No! I was very calm!"

"Yeah, I could hear how calm you were from the back yard."

"Kevin . . . if you had met this ffff . . . woman . . . "

I jumped in. "It's true. The Weasel has a gift for making you lose your shh . . . temper. Right Sam?"

"She's not very friendly." I stared at him. *Is that all?* He shrugged.

Donna poked her phone. "I took a picture of the fff . . . here! Look at her!" She shoved the phone at Kevin.

"Oh! Those eyes!" He made a face. "Why would she take pictures of Mike? And why is she called the Weasel Woman?" I glanced at Mike, and Kevin understood. "Hey Mike, go in the back yard and tell Sarah and Colin what happened."

"Oh, yeah! They're gonna be jealous!" Mike grabbed his soccer ball and ran.

Kevin added, "Don't repeat the words she said!"

Sam followed Mike. "I'll keep him away from the shed."

Donna called out, "Thanks, Sam! You're a sweetheart!"

We sat on the front porch and discussed the history of the Weasel Woman and her flyer. Donna caught her taking photographs and got close enough to confront the Weasel before she knew what hit her. "She asked me why I would let my son play with a 'sexual deviant.' I wanted to scalp her with my bare hands." Donna was still visibly angry.

Kevin rubbed her shoulders. "I'm so proud of you, honey. You stayed out of jail this time."

I crinkled my forehead. *This time?* There was a lot I didn't know about Donna. "You were smart to take pictures. Those might come in handy. Did you get a picture of her car and license plate?"

"You're damn right I did! That's when she claimed I was violating her rights. Can you believe that fucking bitch?"

"Oh, I believe it. Do you think the pictures she took will look bad?"

"Mike was trying to tackle Sam, so he was wrapped around his leg. They were playing, but anything can look bad to someone with a fucked-up head."

"She definitely has a fucked-up head. She's been harassing a disabled man down the street about the peeling paint on his house."

"Are you kidding?"

"No. She got the building inspector to give him a citation. Hey, what did you think of her hairdo?"

"You mean her helmet? Do you know how much hairspray that takes? I wish I had a lighter with me . . . she would be so flammable."

Kevin tried to settle her down. "Don't start fantasizing, Donna. You know where that leads."

Where does it lead, dammit? I want to know! Kevin had a calming influence on Donna, but I could tell he loved her explosive side. I stood up. "I'm sorry you had to meet the Weasel, but we shouldn't let this spoil our time together. I'll get started on dinner before Sam and the kids get too hungry."

Kevin smiled. "You talk like he's one of them. How old is he anyway?"

"Twenty . . . almost twenty-one, as he would say."

"Oh, he looks older. Hey, was he kidding about the chess club?"

"No, he was serious."

We walked back to the garden where Sam was kicking the soccer ball with all three of the kids. Kevin and Donna were amazed he could get them all to cooperate on anything. Sarah and Colin wanted to know more about Donna versus the Weasel Woman. Apparently, Mike had built the story into an epic battle worthy of a comic book series. The kids seemed to admire Donna's ferocious temper, but I wondered if they ever got a taste of it when they misbehaved. If they did, it didn't hurt their relationship with her. I was glad she was my friend and not my enemy, and I was a little jealous of her family.

I invited everyone to get beverages from a cooler on the back porch - soft drinks for the kids, and beer for Kevin. Sam picked up a bottle of beer and glanced at me for a sign of approval. I shrugged, not wanting to be parental. Donna joined me in the kitchen where I pulled a big box of White Zinfandel from the refrigerator. We had the same taste in alcoholic beverages - cheap, sweet and available in large containers. She sat down at the table with her glass while I prepared dinner. "Do you want any help?"

"No, I have my own way of doing things."

"I thought you might. What are you making?"

"Hot dogs and Italian sausages, macaroni and cheese, fruit salad and raw vegetables. I made lemon meringue pies for dessert. Will that satisfy everyone?"

"Sounds great. Colin doesn't eat meat. I'm surprised you didn't make something weird and fancy."

I furrowed my brow. "Why? Because that's how gay men cook?"

"Yeah, pretty much."

"Well, the mac and cheese is made with smoked Gouda."

"See what I mean? You couldn't use Velveeta."

Sarah joined us. "Can I hang out in here, or are you having a private conversation?"

We welcomed her, but I had second thoughts when she started asking questions.

"Adam . . . what's it like to be gay? Do you like it?"

"Um . . ." I looked at Donna, hoping to be rescued, but all I got was a blank stare. "Well . . . no one ever asked me that. I don't know what it's like to not be gay. It was hard while I was growing up, but I think every kid has something to struggle with. I'm getting used to it." I paused to think. "It's a lot better than it used to be. I like it now." Donna smiled.

Sarah had more questions. "How long have you known Sam?"

"Since December, so . . . six or seven months."

"Did you have another boyfriend before?"

"No, he's my first."

"You didn't date any other boys?"

"No, I didn't."

"How come?"

Should I be honest? Why not? "Because I was too afraid."

"You were? I'm afraid to have a boyfriend, too."

"Oh? Why?"

She took her time. "Because it's . . . I don't know . . . it makes me feel weird, like I won't know what to do and I'll make a mistake, and everyone will make fun of me and I won't have friends anymore."

"Yeah, that's pretty close to the way I felt."

"So how did you get over it?"

"I didn't. I felt weird, and I didn't know what to do, and I was embarrassed. But Sam wouldn't give up. He kept trying until I wasn't so afraid. I don't think it was easy for him either, but he had more courage. I was lucky. I think everyone is afraid at first, right, Donna?"

"Uh huh."

Sarah stood next to me at the counter. "Sam is super cute."

I grinned. "Yes, he is."

"Is that why you liked him?"

"At first, but I found out he's smart and funny, too. I don't talk much with most people, but I liked talking with him. I still do."

"My friend Andrea says gay guys have sex all the time with as many people as possible. Is that true?"

"Um . . . Donna, did you want to jump into this conversation?"

"No."

"Okay . . . well . . . I don't think we have sex more than straight people do. And some straight people have sex with as many people as possible, so why would your friend say that?"

"I don't know. She thinks she knows everything. I can't wait to tell her she's wrong."

"I'm glad I could help." That was the last of her questions, but she had one thing to add.

"Sam loves you."

"How do you know?"

"I asked him."

I laughed. "Of course you did. You ask a lot of questions."

"I know! Everyone tells me that. Sam said my other questions were too personal, so he only answered the first one."

Why didn't I think of that? "Do you see why I love him?"

She smiled. "Yeah."

Just then, Sam walked in. Sarah sat down with her mother and they giggled. "What's going on in here?"

"We were talking about you."

"Yeah? What were you saying?"

"Sarah thinks you're super cute."

"Adam! You weren't supposed to tell him!" She put her head on the table and covered it with her arms.

"Sorry."

Sam smiled. "Huh. She said the same thing about you a little while ago."

Sarah groaned. "Oh my God! I'm so embarrassed!"

Donna stroked her hair. "You don't need to be embarrassed, honey. I think they're super cute, too."

"Mom! You're married! I'm telling Dad." She got up and headed for the door.

"Go ahead. He knows what I'm like." She shrugged and drank more wine.

Sam looked over my shoulder. "Do you want me to start the grill?"

"Yeah, I'll get the meat ready."

When we were alone again, Donna said, "You're a sweet man, do you know that?"

"Shut up!" I knew she wasn't kidding, but I wanted to pretend she was.

She waited a minute. "Sam was lucky to find you."

"Shut up!" *God! Why do people have to get all mushy?*

***

By the time the hot dogs and sausages were on the grill, the sky was cloudy and a summer rainstorm was about to break. We would have to eat in the dining room, so I asked Donna to help me set the table with china and glassware.

"Why don't you use the paper plates and plastic cups you have in the kitchen?"

I looked at her like she was crazy. "Those are for outdoor eating. I'm not putting those on my dining room table."

"Okay, whatever. I knew you would find a way to make it fancy. We'll have hot dogs on fine china."

"Do you want your kids to experience Gay World, or not?"

"I bet Sam would use the paper plates."

I repeated her words in a high pitched, mocking voice, like a mature adult. "Have your kids ever eaten off china?"

"I have china. It was a wedding present."

"That's not what I asked."

"Sam would have used the paper plates."

As soon as raindrops hit the windows, the kids came through the back door. Mike yelled, "It's raining!" and ran into the dining room. When he saw the table set with china, he stopped in his tracks. "Whoa! Do I have to sit at a separate table, Mom?"

Donna smiled sweetly. "No, Adam wants us all at this table! Isn't it fancy?"

"It's like the restaurant you took us to where I broke that thing."

Donna watched my face for a reaction, but I refused to show any sign of disturbance. "Try to be more careful this time, okay, Mike?"

"I will. Can I sit at the end?"

"Adam? Do you have place cards for us?" Her tone was a little sarcastic.

"No. He can sit at the end. Maybe you or Kevin can sit next to him."

Colin immediately sat at the opposite end of the table. Sarah took a photograph with her phone. "Andrea will be so jealous." She and Donna took the chairs closest to Mike's end of the table.

I went to the kitchen to take the mac and cheese out of the oven as Kevin came in with water spots on his shirt. "Sam's getting wet out there. Do you want me to carry anything?" I sent him into the dining room with the fruit salad and vegetable tray.

A minute later, Colin came into the kitchen. "My dad said I should offer to help you. Do you want help?"

"Sure. Get the cooler from the porch and give people whatever they want."

"Can I have a beer?"

"Do you want your mother to kill us?"

"Never mind." He went out and came back with a platter full of grilled sausages. "What should I do with these pig guts stuffed with ground pig scraps?"

I couldn't help but smile. I liked the kid. "Take them in the dining room. But the hot dogs are made from ground cattle scraps."

Sam finally came in carrying the cooler. His hair and shirt were soaking wet. "It's pouring out there." The light blue t-shirt stuck to him like a second skin.

"Do you have any clean shirts in the laundry room?"

"No, I took them to my apartment this morning."

“Use the towel in the bathroom to dry off. I'll get the rest of the food on the table.”

I sat across from Donna and Kevin and served the macaroni and cheese. When Sam took the chair to my left, Donna’s eyes showed how much she appreciated his wet t-shirt. Sam was pleased to see the china. "I was hoping we would use the good dishes."

Hah! "Donna thought you would prefer the paper plates, but I insisted on china."

"No way. Paper plates are for picnics. Can you pass the buns over here?"

Donna tried to get the evil grin off my face. "Sam, you'll be sorry later when Adam makes you wash all these dishes."

Sam smiled. "He won't have to ask. I like to wash dishes." I wish I could have photographed Donna's curled lip so I could keep it as a trophy.

Kevin muttered, "Thanks a lot, Sam. Did you have to raise the bar one more notch?"

"Sorry."

Donna rubbed her husband's arm. "Don't worry, honey. No one could be as perfect as Sam, but you're still well ahead of Adam."

Sarah defended me. "Mom! That's not very nice."

I chimed in like a spiteful brat. "Yeah, Donna . . . that's not very nice."

Kevin asked Sam, "What is it with these two? Are they friends or enemies? They act like they’re eight years old."

Sam said, "They like each other so much it scares them, so they pretend they don’t like each other." Donna and I made faces. He was spoiling our fun.

Kevin sat back in his chair. "That's exactly what she's like. He's the same way?" Sam nodded and shoved a hot dog in his mouth. "Sam, we should go out for beers one night. We’d have a lot to talk about."

Donna said, "That's not happening!" at the same time I said, "Absolutely not!" Our better halves grinned.

"Does everyone have enough mac and cheese? Don't be shy. Mike? Do you like it?"

"It's not like my mom makes. It smells like feet." He giggled.

"Mike, that's rude. Eat your hot dog."

Colin said, "It's made with real cheese instead of radioactive orange powder. I'll have more."

Sam noticed he didn’t have any meat. "Is there something wrong with the sausages? Did I cook them long enough?"

Kevin said, "They're good. Colin doesn't eat meat."

"Why not?"

"I won't eat anything with a face. Do you know what’s in sausage?"

"Yeah, I grew up on a farm. We made sausage all the time. The animal's face is in there, along with a lot of other parts." He launched into a description of sausage making that amused Colin and Mike, for distinct reasons. Mike liked gross things, and Colin enjoyed the looks on our faces while we listened.

When he was finished, I held up the platter of sausages. "Would you like more? Anyone?"

Mike raised his hand. "I wanna eat a pig's face!"

Colin was pleased. "I bet you're all sorry you ate those sausages."

"I'm not." Sam speared another Italian. "They won't go to waste while I'm around. Do you want to know how cheese is made?"

Kevin said, "No! If you ruin cheese for me, we won't be friends."

I was glad the visit was going so well. Then Kevin brought up another topic.

"Donna tells me you've got a new vice president at your office. What's his name? Henry something?"

Sam's fork stopped halfway to his mouth. *Shit!* I looked at Donna who saw Sam's reaction. Kevin looked at Sam, then at me, and then at Donna.

Sam lowered his fork. "Henry was promoted?"

"Yeah, didn't I tell you? It was announced on Friday."

"And you didn't think to mention it?"

"It just happened. I thought I said something about it."

"No, I would have remembered."

The kids were paying close attention and Kevin looked confused. "I'm sorry, did I stick my foot in something?"

Donna tried to explain. "Adam thinks Henry is his friend. Sam and I disagree."

I put my hand up. "I've changed my mind. I think you were right about a few things."

Sam couldn't decide whether to continue eating. "How did he become vice president?"

"You know the sexual harassment thing I told you about? Well, Henry used that situation to become Mr. Zipinski's confidant, and Zipinski decided Henry could be trusted to manage certain aspects of the business, like the human resources department."

Sam asked Donna, "How did Henry know about the sexual harassment?"

"This is where it gets interesting. Henry's good friend told him about it." She looked at me.

I felt heat coming off Sam's body. "Adam, why would you do that?"

"Henry wanted to help. I know it sounds like a mistake, but it turned out pretty well."

"You think it's good that Henry got promoted?"

"No, but the women in the office finally made a complaint about Zipinski."

Donna scoffed. "Yeah, now Henry can get rid of us!"

"No, he said that would look like retaliation. He told me your job is secure."

She narrowed her eyes. "What? When did you talk to him about me?"

"Um . . ." *Fuck! Fuckety, fuck! Things were going so well.*

"Henry wasn't there on Friday, so when did you see him?"

Sam spread his hands flat on the table and sat back. Kevin read the room and decided to evacuate. "It looks like the rain stopped. Why don't I take the kids outside so you can talk about this?"

Donna approved. "Kids, go with your father. We'll have dessert later."

I objected. "No, they should stay! We can talk about this some other time."

She shook her head. "No. Go on kids." Kevin stood up and waved his hand at the kids.

Colin said, "Dad, this was getting interesting."

Mike agreed. "I wanna see Mom get mad again!"

Sarah disagreed. "I don't like this. Good luck, Adam." She was the first to leave, followed by the reluctant boys and their father.

So, there we were. Suddenly it was very quiet in the room except for the sound of Sam taking deep breaths. *I hope he's going to his happy place.* Donna was thousands of miles from her happy place. I decided to take the lead. "Look . . . Henry stopped at the office yesterday while I was there, but . . ."

Sam banged his fist on the table, causing all the dishes to shift. "Dammit, Adam! Why don't you tell me about things when they happen so I don't get blindsided?" He raised his fist but stopped before pounding on the table again. He stood up and started pacing like a restless tiger.

"I was waiting for the right time!"

"Oh! This was a perfect time! While we have guests!"

"I didn't bring it up! Kevin did!"

"At least someone tells me what's going on in your life!"

"That's not fair, I . . ."

Donna intervened. "Stop it! The two of you can argue about this later. I want to know what happened with Henry."

"Yeah, Adam, tell us what you did while you were alone with Henry!" Sam was doing laps around the table.

"He was out riding his bicycle and he saw my truck in the parking lot, so he came into the office. I didn't want him there, but what could I do?"

Donna suggested, "You could have kicked him in the nuts! Did you do that?"

"Yeah, right! I should kick the new vice president in the nuts! Good plan!"

"What did he want?"

"He was just visiting . . ."

Sam didn't let me finish. "Adam, don't be so fucking naïve!"

“I'm not! I know you were right about him, but let me tell you . . .”

“What did he do to you?”

'Sam, if you don't settle down, I'm not telling you anything! You're scaring me!”

He stopped pacing and took a huge breath. Donna stood up. “Come on, Sam, sit here.” She pushed him into a chair. “We need to calm down and let Adam tell us what happened.” She massaged the base of his neck. “These muscles feel like rocks. Breathe deeply and relax your shoulders while Adam tells his story. We won't interrupt him, okay?”

“All right, I'll try.” He closed his eyes. “That feels good. I wish Adam would do that for me.”

I fluttered my eyelids to avoid rolling my eyes. “I know . . . I'm a shitty boyfriend. But you might change your mind when I'm finished.”

Donna snapped, “Just tell us!”

"First, let me say you were right about him. He tried to seduce me."

Sam leaned forward to speak, but Donna grabbed his chin and pulled him back, holding his mouth shut. He closed his eyes tightly and inhaled.

"He tried, but he didn't succeed. I played along with him . . ." Sam made a noise. ". . . to get what I wanted. I gave him one condition: that your job would be secure, Donna. He told me none of the women in the office would be fired because it would look like retaliation for the harassment complaints. He met with Zipinski and his lawyer on Friday." I paused to see if either of them would say anything. Donna let go of Sam's jaw, but he kept quiet.

"He kept trying to seduce me. He was so obvious about it . . ."

Sam tensed up again. Donna rubbed his shoulders, and her hands roamed a bit lower onto his arms and chest. "You could skip over some of the details. Sam doesn't need to hear this."

"Oh, yes I do."

"Yeah, I agree. I don't want to be accused of hiding anything. Henry was wearing a cycling outfit that showed everything, including his erection. I was not impressed." I held up my pinkie finger. Donna smiled. "He was so sure he was winning me over, but I wasn't tempted at all. You should have seen the look on his face when I told him to go home. It was priceless." Sam's expression softened. "Then I turned the tables on him and said it might look like sexual harassment, especially now that he has authority over me. I suggested there were security cameras in the offices that would have recorded what he was doing, and he believed it! He said he was kidding, that he was counting on me, and he practically ran out of there."

They stared at me. They weren't expecting my story to end like that.

Donna asked the first question. "You're telling us everything? You're not leaving anything out?"

"I don't think so. Wait! We ate an apple he stole off someone's desk. He ate part of it, and I finished it."

Sam had calmed down. "Maybe you should get tested for STDs again."

"I hope you're kidding."

"You didn't touch him at all?"

"I touched his knee. That was it."

Donna asked, "If you had to blow him to make him promise my job was safe, would you have done it?"

"No. No way. I told him I'm in a committed relationship and nothing will ever happen between us."

"That's the correct answer. I appreciate your effort to protect my job."

"Besides, I could probably floss my teeth with his dick, it was so thin. I'm used to something more substantial."

Sam smiled a little and turned red. "So you won't hang around with him anymore?"

"Sam . . . I have to work with him. I know he can't be trusted, but I'm better off having a friendly relationship with him. At least I'll know more about what he's doing. Wouldn't you agree, Donna?" *Please, please, please, please, please agree with me!*

"Well . . . I like the way you turned the sexual harassment thing against him. You handled him better than I thought you would."

Will she actually say she was wrong about me?

"I'm tempted to say I underestimated you . . . but . . . I don't think so. You've changed. You're stronger than you used to be."

I had to think about that. *Am I stronger? Huh . . . I think she's right. I don't want to say it, but . . .* "You're right. A few months ago, I wouldn't have handled this the way I did. I understand why you didn't trust me around Henry. But I feel more confident now, and you both had a lot to do with it. You've helped me feel better about myself. So, thank you."

A smile crept across Sam's face. Donna's chin quivered. "God dammit."

I gave her a moment to get her emotions back in their box. "Are we okay now? Can we call your family back in here for dessert?"

"In a minute." Sam stood up and walked around the table. "First I get to hug the crap out of you."

I was relieved he wasn't angry anymore, so I rose from my chair. "All right, I suppose I owe you that."

He wrapped his arms around me a little too tightly. It was not quite painful. He put his lips to my ear and whispered, "If Henry touches you or hurts you in any way, I will break a lot of his bones. A lot." He let me go with a kiss to the forehead. I felt dizzy.

Donna jumped up. "Okay, it's my turn."

"Oh, God, haven't I suffered enough? Make it quick, and don't get any lipstick on me."

"Sam, go get Kevin and the kids. They're probably dying to know what happened." She hugged me warmly and pressed her cheek against mine. She also whispered in my ear. "I didn't want Sam to hear this, but if Henry ever comes between the two of you, I will kill him. Do you understand? That's not an empty threat." She pulled away with an enigmatic smile.

What the fuck? Can't I get a normal, non-violent hug anymore?

The kids came through the back door with Mike in the lead. "What happened? Who won the fight?"

"It wasn't a fight, we had a friendly discussion."

Colin said, "Sure, Mom. Who won the friendly discussion?"

Sam conceded first. "Adam won. Didn't he, Donna?"

Because Sam asked, she gave in. "All right . . . Adam won." I felt like I had won an Oscar.

Kevin was impressed. "I thought you were a goner. I wouldn't have gone up against either one of these two, but both, together?" He held his hand in the air with his palm facing me. I looked at it curiously until he explained, "Uh . . . high five?"

"Oh, sorry." I awkwardly slapped his hand and felt a little tingle in my groin, signaling my initiation into realmanhood. I wondered if I would start chewing tobacco.

Naturally, Sarah had questions. "Who's Henry and what's wrong with him? Why don't you like him, Mom? Sam, are you still mad at Adam? Why don't you like Henry?"

Sam smiled. "You know what my dad used to say when I asked too many questions? He'd say, 'Why is the sky blue? Why is the grass green?' That meant I should stop asking questions." To reassure her and anyone else who might be worried, Sam put his arm around my neck and playfully pulled me against his chest. "Besides, how could I stay angry at this guy? Look at him!" He gave me a noogie.

I elbowed him in the gut and pulled away with a grin. On any other day, that would have been foreplay. I couldn't slip my hand inside his shirt or bite his nipple, but I was thinking about it. "Who wants lemon meringue pie?"

While we ate dessert, I asked Donna's family for embarrassing stories about her. The kids enthusiastically told stories about confrontations with strangers and things she did in front of their friends, while Donna tried to defend her behavior.

Kevin talked about how rude she was the first time he asked her out, but it was clear he loved her from the beginning. She rewarded his story with a kiss. Colin said, "Gross!"

Donna wanted a little revenge. "Sam, tell us about the first time you met Adam."

Sam looked at me for approval. I shrugged and nodded. He told the story of coming to look at the apartment for rent, and how I tried to discourage him at the same time I was giving him coffee and cookies while he filled out the application. For the first time, I was treated to his amusing impersonation of me. He finished the story by saying, "So I decided I would get to know him, whether he let me have the apartment or not."

Everyone was quiet until Sarah said, "Awww, Mom."

Donna was blotting tears with a napkin. "Gosh darn it!" Kevin rubbed her shoulder.

***

After we said our goodbyes and exchanged promises to get together again, we closed the front door and stood in the entrance hall. Sam looked at me to assess my mood. "Are we okay?"

"I don't know. Are we?" I put my hand on his chest and felt his heartbeat. "I've been wanting to touch you for hours."

"You can make up for lost time." He stood still and let me touch him. "I was afraid you were angry at me."

"For what?" I slipped my hand under his shirt. His skin was warm and smooth.

"For losing my temper again. For not trusting you."

"You had your reasons." I put my other hand inside his shirt. "I have a bad habit of withholding information."

He kept his arms at his sides, letting me feel him. It was unusual, but very sexy. He watched me enjoy his body. "Are you having fun in there?"

"Yes, thank you. It was nice to have people in the house, wasn't it? You were great with the kids."

"Thanks. You handled them well, too. I wonder what the Weasel Woman will do with her photos of me and Mike."

"I imagine Donna gave her a good scare. I don't want to think about the Weasel right now."

"Neither do I."

I pulled my arms out of his shirt. "Why don't you try to seduce me? Let's see if I can resist you now."

"You've been groping me for five minutes. It's not much of a challenge."

"Try me. Donna says I'm stronger than I used to be."

"All right, let's see." He palmed my ass with one hand and dragged me up the front of his body until the tips of our noses touched.

My lips brushed against the stubble around his mouth. "You win. Take me upstairs."

***

A couple of days later, as I pulled out of the driveway to leave for work, I saw a piece of paper stuck in my front door. I stopped the truck to find out what it was. I looked at the houses across the street and saw the same thing on most of the doors. *Fucking Weasel Woman!* I expected the worst.

I grabbed the piece of paper and unrolled it. There were two photographs side by side. The first showed Helen Van Wootten with an unflattering expression on her face. The second was a picture of a weasel. Under both, in large block letters, was the caption, "SEPARATED AT BIRTH?"

I stared at it. I read it again. I compared the photos and I smiled. It was going to be a good day.

21

Donna pretended she knew nothing about the 'separated at birth' flyer when I asked her about it, but five minutes later she admitted she distributed it. She was too proud of her handiwork to keep it to herself. Kevin wasn't happy when he found out Colin was her accomplice. "Kevin is the responsible parent and I'm the bad example, but he was glad Colin took an interest in something."

My neighbors assumed I made the flyer. Flora laughed when she saw it but didn't think we should sink to the Weasel's level. Joe thought it was the best way to deal with a bully. He kept his copy of the flyer on display in his house so he could laugh at it every day. We visited Joe to discuss moving his shed to my property. I decided it was best to hire a professional crew. The insurance money I received after the fire would cover the expense.

Sam did an excellent job of clearing away the remains of the burned shed. I half-heartedly offered to help, but he wouldn't let me. I found things to do in the garden so I could watch him, shirtless and shiny with perspiration, lifting the blackened lumber and loading it onto the bed of his truck. He knew exactly what I was doing and didn't mind. He was used to being watched by his landscaping customers, but none of them could look forward to soaping him up in the shower afterward.

While sifting through the rubble, Sam was pleased to find the iron weathervane from the cupola. I reminded him of the day he first showed it to me in the spring. "I pretended to look at the weathervane, but I was checking out your muscles."

"I'm glad to hear that. I did a lot of push-ups behind the house before I came out there."

"Are you kidding?"

"Do you know how hard I was trying to get your attention?"

"Do you know how hard I was trying to hide my interest?"

"You were such a doofus. But I was checking you out, too."

"That's right, I remember you peeking around the shrub while I was planting flowers."

"You saw me?"

"Yeah, but I pretended I didn't."

"And you still didn't think I was interested in you?"

"I don't know . . . I thought you were weird and shy and didn't want to interrupt me."

"Yeah . . . I was the weird, shy one."

"Shut up." I studied the charred weathervane. The paint had been burned off, and it was bent. "How will you fix this part?"

He took it in his hands and casually bent it straight again. "Like that."

"Unf. You're so smug and sexy, I could punch you."

"Go ahead, I dare you." He spread his arms and grinned. "Do it."

I playfully punched him in the chest. It was like punching a tree. I shook the pain out of my hand.

"I barely felt that. Hit me again." He bumped me with his chest. "Come on."

I laughed. Sam never ran out of ways to turn me on.

One morning when we both had the day off, I came out of the shower and found him reading in bed, with streaks of sunlight playing across his naked body. He was so absorbed in *Wuthering Heights* he didn't see me standing there. I quietly crawled onto the bed and lay on my side to look at him. Eventually he raised his eyes from the book. "I'm sorry, do you want to have sex again? I'm good to go if you are."

"Tell me about the book."

"What?"

"Tell me what you think of the book."

"Um . . . what can I say that you don't already know?"

"I want to hear your reactions. What do you think of it?"

"Uh . . . okay." He ran his fingers through his shaggy hair. He was due for a haircut. "This is the weirdest love story I've ever read, but there's something about it . . . Heathcliff is . . . I don't know . . . he's terrible, but I can't help but feel bad for him. Cathy didn't deserve him, if you ask me. She's horrible, too. How could she choose Edgar over Heathcliff?"

Once he started, he was on a roll. I felt myself getting aroused as I listened to him.

"I hate to think people could do such awful things even though they love each other, but it seems so real. I want to defend Heathcliff, even when he's being mean. It's like . . . his love for her justifies anything, because their love is the only thing that matters. It makes me shiver to say that out loud." He bunched his shoulders and raked his fingers through his wild hair again. I could picture Sam as young Heathcliff. "I'm probably reading it all wrong. I suppose most people hate Heathcliff, but he sounds hot to me. He's so intense." He rubbed his chest.

By the time he finished talking, my erection was throbbing. Sam noticed. "Hey, what's going on there? Were you even listening to me?"

I moved closer to him. "I heard every word."

"Did that make any sense? Did I get it wrong?"

"I agree with everything you said." I took the book and set it on the nightstand. "Heathcliff is so hot." I crawled on top of him and kissed his throat and jaw.

"Why are you so horny? Did I miss something?"

"I love it when you talk about books. You're so smart, it makes me hard."

"Oh." He stretched his arms across the bed and smiled while I kissed him. "You think I'm smart?" His eyes sparkled with little tears.

One evening at dinner, I brought up something I had been thinking about. "Sam . . . when you started shoveling snow for Joe, why did you do it for free? Didn't he offer to pay you?"

"Yeah, but he's disabled, and his daughter is disabled. I figured they could use the help. I would never let him pay me. Why would you want me to?"

"I don't. I wanted to know what motivated you."

"It feels good to help someone who needs it."

"Exactly. So, wouldn't other people in the neighborhood like to help him, too?"

"Are you saying I should stop helping him so other people can have a chance? That's crazy! What's wrong with you?"

"I'm not saying that! I'm saying, why don't we paint his house for him?"

"What? That's a big job! First, you tell me to stop helping him, and now you want me to paint his house? I don't have time for that!"

"I didn't . . . I'm not . . . Are you doing that to drive me nuts?"

"Doing what?"

"Making it sound like I'm saying things I'm not saying."

"I'm not doing that."

"Wouldn't it be nice if people in the neighborhood got together to paint his house? It would help him out, people would feel good about it, and it would improve the neighborhood. Everyone benefits."

"Well, that's a better idea than expecting me to do all the work."

"I did NOT expect you to . . ."

"Who would organize this? The neighborhood association?"

"NO! Not the fucking neighborhood association! I don't want anything to do with that Weasel bitch. She's the one who had the city inspector give Joe a citation! Besides, there isn't a fucking neighborhood association. They haven't even had a meeting yet."

"Then who'll paint his house? Is it all on me again?"

"NO! I'M NOT ASKING YOU TO . . . ugh! You're doing this to piss me off."

"Doing what? What are you talking about?"

"I'm talking about a group of people from the neighborhood who volunteer to do something to benefit the neighborhood! Am I not being clear?"

"No, I thought you didn't want anything to do with the neighborhood association."

I glared at him. "I know you're fucking with me. Why are you fucking with me?"

"I'd love to fuck with you, but I want to finish my dinner first. Why are you so impatient?" Finally, there was a trace of a smile on his face.

"You ASSHOLE! Why do you get me all worked up?"

He shrugged. "Because it's fun?"

"Were you paying attention to what I was saying?"

"You want to get a group of people from the neighborhood to volunteer to paint Joe's house. I think it's a great idea. It shows how much you've changed."

"What do you mean?"

"A few months ago, you didn't even want to talk to the neighbors."

"Oh. Yeah, I guess you're right. Well . . . change is good."

"Wow! Who are you?"

"You make it sound like I was so rigid. I was flexible enough to let you rent the apartment."

"Oh, here we go! I thought it was because I was hot."

"So? I still bent my rules. If I wasn't so friendly and welcoming, you wouldn't be annoying the hell out of me right now."

"Friendly and welcoming? Please! Are you finishing your pork chop?"

"No, I'll throw it away."

"No, you won't! Give it to me."

"Don't tell me what to do with my pork chop! I'm throwing it in the garbage." I stood up to take my plate into the kitchen.

"Adam! Don't make me come after you!"

"You'll be sorry if you do! I have a lot of knives in here!"

"Give me that pork chop!" He got up to follow me.

Ten minutes later we were on the kitchen floor, sweaty and mostly naked, recovering from a rather intense sexual experience. He reached up to retrieve the half-eaten pork chop from my plate. "We don't throw away food." He bit into it.

"I know, I was fucking with you." I took a deep breath and relaxed. "So, who do you think would help us paint Joe's house? We should make a list."

"You could bring it up at the neighborhood association meeting."

"I'm not going to any goddamn neighborhood association meeting with that fucking Weasel bitch! How many times do I have to say it?"

He smiled and nibbled at the pork chop bone. "You know why I like to get on your nerves?"

"Why?"

He put the bone back on my plate. "Sometimes I miss your old irritable self now that you're more mellow and friendly. I'm glad you're happier, but . . . when you're cranky . . . I want to hug you to death."

"You're so weird."

He threw his leg over mine, pressing himself against my hip. "Make your angry face again."

I couldn't do it. I had to smile.

"No! You're ruining it!"

"I can't be cranky because you want me to be! It has to come naturally."

"At your age, it should be easy."

"Shut up!" I socked him in the shoulder.

"That's it! More of that!"

I laughed.

"Adam! Come on!"

***

Donna was in my office again, discussing the latest developments at the accounting firm. "So, Zipinski won't be back as long as the EEOC is investigating the complaints. I'm glad I don't have to look at his creepy face. And I have to admit . . . if you repeat this to anyone, I'll deny it . . . the morale among the staff is a lot better under Henry's supervision. They like him, and he doesn't micromanage me, so . . ."

"Ooooh! Donna has a crush on Henry!"

"Shut up! You're the one who drools over him."

"I do not, but there's no point in pretending he's ugly."

"I'm telling Sam!"

"Oh yeah? Are you sure you want to see him angry again?"

"I don't mind, especially if I get to massage those broad shoulders. He is one beautiful slab of manhood."

"I didn't appreciate you groping him. That's my job."

"It must be a very big job. I'd like to help."

"You're disgusting." There was a quiet knock at the door. "Come in!"

It was Henry. "Oh, sorry! I don't want to interrupt anything. I'll come back."

"That's all right, Donna's leaving."

She gave me a nasty look. "Yes, I am."

"Donna was complimenting your management style, Henry. She said the morale among the staff has improved." Her eyeballs turned to ice as I spoke.

"I appreciate that, Donna. And thank you for all the work you do."

Her fake smile made me shiver. "You have no idea how much that means to me, Henry. Let me give the two of you some privacy. I'll talk to you later, Adam."
Yes, she certainly will.

Henry sat down. "I never know how to read her. Was she being sarcastic?"

"No, she said the staff like you."

"Okay. I'm surprised because she doesn't respond to me the way most people do."

"What do you mean?"

"It's like she's not attracted to me. I know she's married, but is she a dyke?"

"I'm pretty sure she's not. Do you assume everyone is attracted to you?"

He smoothed the front of his perfect ivory shirt. "Why wouldn't they be?"

I shook my head. "You're good looking, but that doesn't mean everyone will fall all over you."

"You certainly haven't. I'm still disappointed about our last encounter."

"That can't be the first time you've been turned down."

"It's extremely rare. By the way, I found out there are no security cameras in these offices."

"Oh, that's a relief."

"You knew that, didn't you?"

"No, I assumed there were cameras." *I still know how to lie.* "And we should behave as if there were cameras."

"Like people of good moral character? I appreciate the advice. It's good for me to have a friend who thinks so differently."

"How can I help you today, Henry?"

"Alvin suggested splitting my supervisory duties with you."

"Alvin?"

"That's Mr. Zipinski to you." He handed me a document. "I've made a list of the departments and accounts you'll keep track of. They're all pretty self-sufficient, but you should check with them regularly to make sure everything is getting done in a timely manner."

"How will I be compensated for these additional responsibilities?"

Henry smiled. "Don't worry, I took care of you. Your salary will be increased by thirty percent, effective immediately."

Holy shit! I contained my excitement behind a placid expression. "That's acceptable. And will I be a vice president too?"

His smile broadened. "It pleases me that you're asking for more than you deserve. You're following my example. Alvin suggested the title of managing director."

"That'll do for now."

"Good." He stood up and looked down at me. "I told you I would help you. I trust you'll find some way to show your appreciation."

"You mean, like . . . a box of chocolates?"

He stretched his arms above his head. "Do I look like I eat chocolates?"

"How about a bunch of kale?"

He smirked. "You'll think of something. You can start by taking me out to lunch again." He opened the door.

"All right, one of these days. Thank you, Henry."

"My pleasure, Adam. I look forward to our mutually beneficial collaboration." As he left, he smiled and waved at the female staff outside my office. They all blushed and smiled back.

I felt dirty, like I needed a shower. But first, I wanted to call Donna and tell her I was her new supervisor.

***

That evening during dinner, I told Sam about my conversation with Henry and didn't leave anything out. I had learned from my mistakes. My new title and increased salary overshadowed Henry's thinly veiled sexual advances. When I told Sam what my annual salary would be, he was shocked.

"You get paid that much? I mean . . . I knew you made a good living, but I didn't think you made *that* much."

"Accountants are well paid, and a thirty percent increase is a lot.

"I can't believe you make . . . four times as much as I do."

"I don't think . . . are you counting your tips? Well, it doesn't matter. You work hard, you like what you do, that's what's important. I was only working part-time when I was your age."

"You were in school."

"Yeah, and going into debt. I'm still paying for it."

"You are?"

"Yeah, student loans. I have a couple more years of payments."

"Whenever I think about going to college, that's what stops me. I couldn't afford it and I wouldn't want to be in debt."

"You shouldn't let that stop you. There are ways to do it without borrowing too much. You'd probably get grants. I could help you figure it out."

"I don't need a college degree. When would I have the time? And I don't know if I'm smart enough."

"Yes, you are smart enough! You would blow them away."

Sam continued eating without looking up for a while.

"What's wrong?"

He had tears in his eyes. "You really believe in me, don't you?"

"Sam . . . of course I believe in you. You have so many talents."

"One of these days you'll realize I'm not as good as you think I am and . . ."

"No, no, no! That's my line. You can't have it."

"Adam . . ."

"No. I'm not arguing with you about this."

It looked like he wanted to say something else, but he gave up. "Okay. You're right."

"Yeah, I'm always right." I joked to hide my emotions.

After a long pause, he asked, "Will you go out to lunch with Henry again?"

"It would make it easier to work with him. I know you don't like it, but I'll be careful."

"It's okay, Adam. Do what you need to do. I trust you."

I wasn't expecting that. I think he wanted to give me something, and his trust was something he could give. It touched my heart. "Thank you."

He nodded and looked at my food. "Are you finishing your chicken?"

I pushed my plate in his direction.

***

After work one day, I stopped at Dave's Nursery to pick up some of the supplies I lost in the fire. I hadn't seen Dave for a while, and if Sam happened to be there, why not visit? When I walked into the building and looked around, one of the guys who worked there greeted me. "Can I help you find something, sir?"

Sir? I hate that. "Is Dave around?"

"No, he's out on a landscaping job. He should be back soon, but I can help you." He was a good-looking kid, the type I envied when I was younger. Obviously an athlete, he had dark hair, olive skin, muscular arms and legs. "Sir? Is there something I can help you with?"

"Oh, sorry! I spaced out for a second. I'll browse through the fertilizers and stuff, but if Dave comes back, could you tell him Adam is here?"

"Adam? Okay." He paused. "Are you Muffin's boyfriend?"

"You mean Sam?"

"Yeah, sorry, I'm so used to calling him Muffin, I forgot his real name." His smile was charming. "I'm Greg. Muffin's my bro. I'm the one who named him Muffin."

We shook hands. "Yeah, he mentioned you a few times."

"He did? What did he say?"

"Not much. He said you're his . . . 'bro' . . . and you eat lunch together, and . . . that's about it."

"Did he tell you I got more tips than he did last month?" He was grinning from ear to ear.

"No, he didn't mention that. I'm surprised."

"He's such a sore loser. Of course, he didn't tell you."

"He must be hard to beat."

"Tell me about it! I've been working out like a maniac to keep up with him." He rubbed his broad chest.

"Sam won the genetic lottery. It pisses me off, sometimes."

"Too bad he's so ugly, though. He talks about you a lot."

"Yeah? What does he say?"

"Oh, dude, I can't repeat that stuff. It's too embarrassing. It's like watching a chick-flick with my girlfriend." He made a squinty face. "Good for you, though."

"Thanks?" I'm sure I blushed.

"Hey, I need to go help this lady. She's a big tipper. Dave and Muff . . . I mean Sam, should be back soon. I'll tell them you're here."

"Thanks. Nice to meet you."

Greg squared his shoulders and puffed out his chest as he approached a fortyish woman wearing twentyish clothes. "Mrs. Cameron, you look lovely today! How can I help you?"

"Oh, Greg, you're so sweet! I always look for you when I come in."

"And I look for you, Mrs. C." He was good. He looked good from behind, too. *I'd let him load a few shrubs on my truck.*

"Adam!" I nearly jumped out of my skin. It was Sam.

"You scared me! Greg told me you were out."

"You met Greg? Cool! What did he say about me?"

"He said he got more tips than you did last month."

Sam lowered his voice. "I let him think he got more."

"He could give you a run for your money. He's easy on the eyes."

"What? Why were you looking at him? Are you shopping for a younger man?"

"Well, you're almost twenty-one. I need to think about it."

He glanced around. "There's something I want to show you in the storage room."

"What about my cart?"

"Leave it there. Come on." We walked to a corner of the building, through a door marked 'private,' and into a room full of boxes and supplies. As I hoped, he put his hands on the wall above my head and kissed me. We never made out away from home. He was pulling out all the stops and getting me fired up when, out of the corner of my eye, I saw someone enter the room.

"DUDE! Oh, fuck! I didn't know you were in here! What the fuck, bro?"

I wanted to crawl under something. Sam pulled away from me and looked at Greg like he was making a big deal out of nothing. "What's your problem, dude? You never saw real kissing before? You want us to teach you?"

Greg pressed the heels of his hands against his eyes. "The fuck, Muff! I'll have to scrub my eyeballs now!"

"Oh, yeah? Maybe I should slap you into next week to take your mind off it."

Greg uncovered his eyes and smiled. "Bro! I've been traumatized here!" Obviously, he didn't feel threatened by his larger friend.

“How many times have I seen you kiss your girlfriend? You think I like watching that?”

“Hey! She's beautiful, I'm beautiful . . . what's not to like?”

Sam grabbed a handful of Greg's shirt. “Are you saying Adam's not beautiful?”

I wanted to be left out of it, but it was sexy to see him dominate a guy I would have been afraid of in college.

“No, brah, Adam's a hot dude.” Greg pulled Sam's hand off his shirt. “But you're so fuckin' ugly, bro! That was nasty!” He backed away from Sam and ran for the door.

“That's it, bro! I'm throwing you in the mulch bin!” Sam took off after him, leaving me alone in the storage room.

Well . . . this is something new. I wiped my mouth with the back of my hand and followed the sound of their voices to one of the large storage bins at the edge of the parking lot. After a brief struggle, Sam easily picked up Greg and tossed him into the mulch. Greg landed on his back, laughing and cursing under his breath. Sam returned to me with a big grin on his face.

“Sorry, but I had to remind him who's boss.”

“He didn't stand a chance.”

“He knows that, but he still likes to challenge me. So, where were we?”

“Uh, you were showing me something in the storage room.”

“Oh, yeah. Wait . . . here comes Dave.”

“Adam! How the hell are you?"

"Hey, Dave. I'm good, how are you?"

"Wait a minute . . . what is that idiot doing in the mulch bin? I'll be back in a minute." He stalked off to confront Greg.

"Why didn’t you say something? Will Greg get in trouble?"

"If he does, I'll say something, but he usually talks himself out of these things. It's nice to see you here. You should visit more often."

"I will if I can watch you do things like that! I'm so turned on right now, I can't wait for you to come home."

"That turned you on?"

"The way you handled him? Hell, yes! He looks pretty strong, but compared to you, he's a weakling."

"Do you want me to bring him home and throw him around the yard for a while?"

I laughed. "No, but I wouldn't mind if you threw me around the bedroom."

"What? I don't want to hurt you."

"You wouldn’t. We would be playing. You know how much your strength gets me going."

“Okay, I'll think about it.”

"I can't wait. I'd better get out of here before I do something indecent."

"Stay and talk to Dave. You know he likes to visit with you. I have other things to do, so I'll see you at home." He gave me a discreet pat on the ass before he walked away. I watched him go, and watched the way other people watched him. *What is it like to have so many eyes on you all the time?*

Dave returned from the mulch bin. "I don't know why Sam likes that kid. I think he's a fuckin' idiot. He's popular with the customers, though."

"I can see why. It's good to see Sam with a friend closer to his age."

"What do you mean? How old is he?"

I assumed Dave knew Sam's age. "He's almost twenty-one."

"You're kidding! I thought he was twenty-five or twenty-six."

"I know, he's mature for his age."

"It's been great to have him here. People like him, and he understands the business side of things. He works harder than two of these other guys. I should pay him more. I was thinking about giving him a little more responsibility, maybe a title. I'll make something up."

"He'd be proud to hear that, Dave. He likes working with you. He says you remind him of his father."

"Am I that old already?" Dave shook his head. "Guys like him used to want to go out with me."

I blinked a few times. "Go out with you?"

"Yeah. And fuck."

I couldn't stop blinking. "You're . . . gay?"

"Well, yeah. You knew that."

"I didn't . . . you don't seem like . . . how would I . . . I'm . . . I'm fucking clueless."

"You must be. I knew you were gay the first time I saw you. What were you, sixteen or seventeen when you started coming here?"

"Something like that. But I never saw you with any guys. You never had a partner."

"I kept my private life away from the business. But outside of here was another story. I scored a lot of ass, and I mean a lot. I had a reputation around town. That was back when we had more bars, and the bathhouse on Third Street. They're all gone now." He smiled wistfully. "I'm lucky I survived. A lot of my friends didn't. Now, things are different. You guys don't know how good you have it."

I stared at him. You know what it's like when you have an idea of someone in your head, and you find out they're not who you thought they were? That's what I was feeling. Dave, the irritable, profane nurseryman, used to be a bathhouse slut. My mind was thoroughly blown.

"Don't look so shocked! You know I have a dick, don't you?"

"I never thought about your . . . I mean, why would I . . . I came here because you had good plants, and you were nice to me."

"I have the best plants! And yeah, I was nice to you. You'd come in here with all your serious questions about perennials and how to improve the soil. I got such a kick out of it, I didn't want anyone else to talk to you. And you were so goddamn beautiful. Compared to all those sarcastic queens I drank with, and the rent boys, truckers, addicts and God knows what else I fucked, you were . . . like an angel. I was always happy to see you. Still am. You know I am."

I was truly speechless. This was too much information to absorb.

"I'm glad no one else got to you before that big goofball came along. Sam is the only guy who comes close to deserving you, kiddo. And that body . . . you hit the jackpot, Adam. But I warned him to be careful with you, because . . . I swear to God, if he ever hurts you . . ." He pushed his fist into the palm of his other hand.

I was touched, and disoriented. I felt like I had been living in a parallel universe all these years.

"This was a good talk!" He startled me out of my trance. "You should come around more often. I have stories about the old days that would give you nightmares. Hey, don't tell Sam about the promotion I'm planning for him. I want to give him a hard time before I surprise him. I love doing that."

"Okay."

"Come here and give an old man a hug. It's the only action I'm getting these days." He put his arms around me and slapped my back with both hands. "I've got a million things to do. Come back on the weekend and I'll have half-price perennials for you. I know you like a bargain."

I walked to my truck in a daze. I was halfway home before I realized I didn't buy any of the things I went there to purchase.

Later that evening I asked Sam, "Did you know Dave is gay?"

"Well, yeah . . . didn't you?"

"No, not until today."

"You've known him for years, haven't you?"

"Yeah, but it never crossed my mind. You know how I can be."

"Dense?" He smiled.

"Yes, thank you very much. He told me he was promiscuous when he was younger."

"Yeah, I've heard some stories. I've learned a lot."

"Like what? Does he give you sex advice?"

Sam hesitated. "How else would I know how to do things? It's not like my dad taught me anything about gay sex."

"Mine didn't either. That's what the internet is for."

“My parents didn’t have the internet. I could only use it at school, and I wasn’t looking up gay sex in the library.”

“Huh. I thought you were coming up with stuff on your own."

"Some of it. I have a pretty good imagination." His smile made me think he was coming up with something new on the spot. "How have I been doing? Are you satisfied most of the time?"

My eyes must have bugged out of my head. "Satisfied? Are you kidding? I mean . . . wow! Every time."

"That’s a 'yes'?"

"Yes!" I nodded vigorously.

"Okay, I wanted to make sure."

"And if there's anything more you want me to do, please ask."

"It can wait until after dinner . . . but thanks." He grinned.

"Maybe I'll find out what you learned today in man-whore class."

His eyebrows went up. "You'll see."

22

Sam came bounding up the back stairs one evening in August. “Adam!” He burst through the door with a big smile on his face. “Ask me what happened at work today!”

“What?” He pulled his green polo shirt over his head. “Why are you taking off your shirt?”

“It's, like, ninety-five degrees out there. I'm hot. Are you going to ask me?”

Distracted by his bronzed, sweaty torso, I forgot the first part of the conversation. “Ask you what?”

“What happened at work today.” He kicked off his sandals.

“Not much. It was boring.”

“Not *your* work . . . my work! Ask what happened to *me* at work today.”

"Oh, sorry." He unzipped his khaki shorts. "Are you getting naked?"

"I might." He dropped his shorts and stepped out of them. "Quit stalling and ask me."

"You need to get new underwear. That's not doing its job anymore."

"Whatever. Ask me!" He tore a few paper towels from the roll on the counter and blotted his skin.

"What is . . . I'm sorry, I forgot again."

"Are you getting senile?"

"No, I'm distracted!"

"By what? What happened today? Are you okay?" He tugged at his underwear.

"Nothing. No. I mean, yes. You . . . you're . . ."

"Maybe you're overheated. Let's get your shirt off."

"Okay."

"Dave gave me a promotion today." He pulled my shirt over my head.

"That's great!" My arms were straight up in the air, and when my shirt came off, Sam’s damp pectorals were inches from my face. I opened my mouth and leaned forward, but he moved away before I got there. "A promotion?"

"Staff Manager is what he's calling me. I think he made it up."

"No, I've heard that title. Let me guess . . . will you be managing the staff?"

"Yes, I will, smart ass." He shoved two fingers into the waistband of my shorts and pulled me closer. "Why haven't you kissed me yet?" Before I could answer, he pressed his lips against mine, grabbed my ass and lifted me off the floor. After a minute of rather aggressive smooching, he set me down and continued the conversation as if nothing had interrupted it. "And he gave me a nice raise. Guess how much?"

"I'm a little dizzy right now."

"Thirty percent! Same as you got for your promotion. Can you believe it?"

"Yeah, you deserve it. He says you're the best employee he's ever had."

"He wants me to think about becoming his business partner someday."

"Wow, that's fantastic! Congratulations!"

He knelt in front of me and kissed my stomach. "What's for dinner?"

"Me, apparently."

"You'll make a good appetizer. What else?" He unbuttoned my shorts.

"I made shrimp and cucumber . . . Oh! Ah . . . that shrimp and cucumber salad you like, and . . . fuck . . . focaccia . . . bread . . . whatever . . . oh . . . give me . . . some warning . . . before you . . ."

He came up for air. "Will it keep in the refrigerator?"

"Yeah."

"Good." He picked me up as he rose to his feet. "Let's go upstairs." He carried me through the house.

"Why are you so horny today?"

"What makes you think I'm horny?"

"What? The minute you came in . . . you're like . . ."

"Can't a guy offer a simple greeting when he gets home without being called names?"

"If that was a simple greeting . . ."

He carried me up the stairs. "Why don't you ever initiate sex? Aren't you attracted to me anymore?"

"Uff!! You don't give me a chance! When would I?"

"I'm waiting for you to suggest something." He threw me onto my bed and pulled off my underwear, then his own.

"What the . . . I would suggest things if you'd give me a chance to speak before you . . ."

"Why do you talk so much when I'm trying to make love to you?" He crawled over me. "Could you be quiet?"

Dammit, why do I always fall for this? I glared at him. "I will beat the living shit out of you."

He smiled. "That's what I want to hear!" He scooped me up and wrapped his arms and legs around me, surrounding me with hot, sweaty muscle. "Beat me, Adam! Beat the shit out of me!" He puckered his lips like a fish and made goofy kissing noises.

Sigh. So . . . fucking . . . sexy.

***

I scheduled a crew to move Joe's garden shed from his house to mine. I decided to use one of the many vacation days I accumulated over the years. I never took any time off, except for my parents' funeral. Unfortunately, I had to get Henry's approval.

"Another day off in the middle of the week? You already have Wednesdays off. Why couldn't this be done on a Wednesday?" He rubbed a tiny scuff mark off his four-hundred-dollar Italian shoes.

"The crew wasn't available on a Wednesday, Henry. What's the big deal? I have a right to use a vacation day every five or ten years, don't I?"

"We have an office to run."

"But you could go to New York last week."

"I had to get out of this shit hole and spend time in a real city. It was medically necessary."

"Why are you giving me a hard time about this? It's one day. All of my work is on schedule."

"I don't want to be accused of favoritism because you're my best friend."

Best friend? I felt queasy. "It's one vacation day!"

"I can't be too careful with all the accusations being made around here."

"Will you approve it, or not?"

"All right, but if anyone asks, tell them I gave you a hard time about it."

"No one will ask."

"I need to maintain my reputation."

"For what? Being an ass-wipe?" *Shit! I said that out loud!*

Henry smiled. "You continue to surprise me, Adam. Just for that, you'll have to take me out to lunch."

"I can't this week. I have to get ahead on my accounts before I take a day off." I backed away. "But we'll do lunch one of these days."

"Yes. 'One of these days.' You always say that. Close the door on your way out. I need a power nap."

"Yes, Mr. Vice President." I quietly pulled the door shut and turned to find Donna standing six inches away from me. "Oh, Christ! How do you do that?"

"What were you doing in there?"

"Having sex. Why do you ask?"

She narrowed her eyes at me.

"I asked him to approve a vacation day."

"Why do you need a vacation day?"

"I'm having . . . wait a minute . . . I'm your supervisor now. Who are you to question me?"

"I'm the person who will squeeze your balls until you answer."

I answered, faster than I'd like to admit, "I'm having my neighbor's old garden shed moved to my garden."

"Okay. I'll allow it."

"You'll . . . what?"

She patted my cheek. "You can go back to your office now."

"I can go wherever I damned well please!" I stepped around her.

"Where are you going?"

"My office!"

"Good boy."

I wheeled around. "I hate you!"

She wagged her finger and sang, "Hostile work environment!"

***

On the day of the move, Sam offered to stay home but there was no reason for both of us to miss work. The contractors would do everything anyway. In the morning, I sat with Joe on his back porch, watching the crew jack up the shed and shift it onto rollers so they could move it to the street. A couple of the workers were young and well-built. I took the opportunity to ask Joe about his house.

"Painting this place will be a big job. Have you been getting bids?"

"Yeah, I talked to a few guys, but they're all too expensive. I don't know where I'm supposed to come up with the money. I spent the last of my savings having the roof replaced a couple years ago."

"These old houses can be expensive to maintain. Can you get a home improvement loan?"

"Already tried that. Since the housing market tanked, the value on this place is lower than you would think, especially the way it looks now. On my disability income, the banks don't want to take the risk."

Stroking my chin, I pretended I was coming up with a new idea. "Maybe we could get a bunch of volunteers from the neighborhood to help paint your house."

"Oh, no. I don't think so. Why would people want to do that?"

"Because it would improve the neighborhood. This is one of the houses that makes this area unique. If we don't preserve these places, it'll affect the value of all our houses."

"Guess I never thought of it that way. Are you trying to make me feel guilty?"

"I'm throwing out ideas."

"You know . . . one of the contractors I talked to is a young guy here in the neighborhood who's starting his own painting business. He wanted the job and he was willing to cut his price. I wonder if I could work out a deal with him."

"Do you have his name and number? I need to have some work done."

"Doesn't Sam do all that stuff for you?"

"He's getting busier with his job. I can't expect him to do everything."

"I think I have the guy's card." He stood up with some difficulty. "Let me look for it." He hobbled into the house.

I was pleased with myself for putting my plan in motion. I watched the two handsome young crew members exerting themselves. Unfortunately, the flabby older guy was showing the most skin.

"Adam?"

I jumped. "What? Oh . . . Officer Hanson." *Where did he come from?*

"It's Carl. Remember?"

"Of course I remember you."

"No, I mean . . . remember to call me Carl. Please."

"Yeah . . . Carl." *Was he that handsome a few weeks ago?* "What are you doing here?"

"I was patrolling the area and I saw a truck backed onto the sidewalk."

"Oh, they're here for me. Well, not for me, really, I can walk. They're here for the shed. I'm taking this shed over to my garden to replace the one that was . . . well, you know what happened to the other one. It burned. As you know." *Am I babbling?*

"Is the homeowner here?"

"Joe? Yeah, he's inside. He knows about this. I wouldn't steal someone's shed, he's giving it to me. Doesn't use it. Very nice of him."

"Okay. Can I speak with him?"

Does he really think I'm stealing this shed? "I'm sure he'll be right out . . . ah, here he is."

Joe stepped onto the porch. "Can I help you, officer?"

"Yes, I was checking to see why there's a truck parked on the sidewalk."

"There is? Hey, what are they doing to my shed?"

Carl looked at me.

"He's kidding! He knows about this. Tell him, Joe."

"Do I know you?"

I looked back and forth between them. "I'm . . . he's . . ."

They laughed. Joe put his hand on my shoulder. "We had you going, didn't we? How are you, Carl?"

Dammit! Why does everyone want to fuck with me?

"I'm fine, Joe. How are you and Susan?"

"We were fine until this guy came along and tried to steal my shed."

"Do you want me to cuff him?"

"Maybe you should. He's involved in all the trouble in this neighborhood."

"That's what I've been hearing. How are you, Adam?"

"I'm okay. How do you two know each other?"

“Carl was a volunteer coach at Susie's school. He tried to teach her how to play volleyball.”

“I did my best.”

“You did an excellent job. Susie still talks about it.”

“Yeah? I miss those kids. The ones I work with now are a different ball of wax.”

My curiosity was piqued. “You do volunteer work with kids?”

“Why do you sound surprised?”

“I'm not, I'm . . . impressed, I guess. What kids are you working with now?”

“It's a rehabilitation program for juvenile offenders. We help them do community service to meet their sentencing agreements, and we run sports programs.”

"Wow. You're . . . nice."

"Again, sounding surprised." He folded his arms across his chest. They were quite thick, with prominent veins under the tanned skin. But that's irrelevant.

I changed the subject. "Did you find that card, Joe?"

"Yeah, here you go. Nice fella, seems eager to work."

Carl asked, "What's this about?"

"Adam wanted the name of a painter who gave me a bid on the house."

"You're looking for someone to paint your house? Why didn't you ask me, Joe?"

I interrupted. "Don't tell me you paint houses when you're not fighting crime and helping kids." It sounded more sarcastic than I intended.

"No, but this would be a good project for some of the older kids in our program. We could teach them skills and provide free labor."

"I was thinking of getting volunteers from the neighborhood, but . . . more is better. What do you think, Joe?"

"I don't know. People will think I'm a charity case."

"It wouldn't be like that," Carl said. "These kids need more opportunities for community service, and you'd still have to pay the contractor. He won’t work for free. Let me and Adam talk to him to see if we can work something out."

Uh . . . when did we become a team?

"I guess it wouldn't hurt. I've got to figure out a way to paint this place before the Weasel comes after me again."

"The Weasel Woman?" Carl remembered her. "Is she bothering you, too?"

Joe nodded. "She's a piece of work. Carl, come inside for a minute. You should see the flyer Adam made. It's hilarious."

"I didn't make that flyer!"

My moving crew started rolling the shed across the yard. A short while later they had it loaded and secured on their truck. Carl stayed to deal with traffic while the truck traveled the few blocks to my house.

Joe stayed at his house to rest before his daughter came home. "Thanks again, Joe. I'll get back to you about this painting project." Carl walked with me to the street. "Where's Officer Mansky?"

"He's not my partner anymore. That was part of his reward for locking up Big Ed. I have a rookie in the car."

"What's that like?"

"It's fine when he puts down his damned cell phone. He's so young, it makes me feel old."

"I know that feeling."

"How are things going between you and Sam?"

"Great. Better than ever."

"Good." His tone conveyed something other than 'good.'

Later, we stood in my garden watching the crew move the shed onto the new concrete slab. Carl remarked, "Those two younger guys are hot, aren't they?"

"I don't know. I hadn't noticed."

He raised an eyebrow. "I suppose you only have eyes for Sam?"

"Well . . . I still notice other men."

"But you didn't notice those two?"

"I . . . okay, I was watching them at Joe's house."

"Why did you say you didn't notice them?"

I shrugged. "Habit, I guess. I'm not used to being open about these things."

"Hey, is that Sam? Shit!" One of Dave's trucks pulled into the driveway.

"Yeah, that's him. Don't worry about it." Sam got out of the truck. "Hi, Sam! Are you on your lunch break?" I was a little too cheerful.

His expression was hard to read. "I was doing a delivery and thought I would stop to see how it's going." He nodded at Carl. "Carl."

Carl nodded. "Sam."

Sam draped his arm across my shoulders and gave me a longer, deeper kiss than I would have preferred with so many witnesses. I nearly choked on his tongue. When he finished, he looked directly at Carl. "Did someone commit a crime?"

"No." I wiped my mouth with the back of my hand. "Carl helped with traffic while the shed was being moved."

"Traffic? On this street?"

Carl cleared his throat. "I'd better get going, Adam."

Before I could respond, Sam said, "Okay. Bye." His tone was unpleasant, to say the least.

"Sam, don't be like that. Carl was helpful."

"Uh huh. But now I'm here, and he can go help someone else."

"You know, it would be nice if we could be friends." Carl extended his hand, but I grabbed it before Sam could get his grip on it.

"Thanks, Carl. We'll have to work on that." I stepped in front of Sam to prevent them from shaking hands.

Carl walked toward the squad car where his young partner was fiddling with his phone. He turned and pointed at me, "Let me know if you talk to the painter, okay?"

"I will. Thanks for your help."

"What painter? What did he mean?"

"Sam, you were rude to him."

"How was I rude?"

"What was that kiss about?"

"I greeted you. What's wrong with that?"

"Don't play dumb! You were being an asshole, and you know it. I won't let you mistreat guests at my house."

His face turned red. "That's right, it's your house and I'm the hired help. I'm sorry, boss! Please don't fire me!"

The workers were watching, so I stepped closer to him and lowered my voice. "That's not what I meant! You treat me like I'm your property, and you have the nerve to get angry when I call you on your shit? Go back to work! Maybe Dave can talk some sense into you."

"Fine! I'm sure Carl will be back as soon as I pull out of the driveway."

"Oh, fuck you!"

"Not tonight you won't!"

When he turned to leave, we were startled by Agnes, who was standing behind him on the driveway, as stone-faced and motionless as a wax figure. We froze in our tracks like children who had been caught misbehaving. "Mr. Adam. Mr. Sam."

"Agnes! I didn't see you there."

"Aye. I gathered as much."

Sam was embarrassed. "I . . . I'm . . ." He looked at the ground.

"Are you done bickering?" Her expression remained flat.

"Did you come to see my new shed? Isn't it great?"

"It's a fine, fancy shed. Worthy of a queen."

I'm sure she wasn't referring to me. *Was she?*

"Mrs. O'Neill sent me to invite ye to lunch next Wednesday to celebrate Mr. Sam's birthday."

Sam looked up. "How did she know my birthday was coming up?"

"We know everything."

"Okay. I'd like that. Is it okay with you, Adam?"

"Sure. Sounds great."

"Mrs. O'Neill also wanted me to ask if Mr. Sam had any favorite dishes I could prepare. I don't know why she can't trust me to come up with a menu."

I smiled. Sam knew how to reply. "I like everything, especially anything you make, Agnes. I'd rather be surprised."

"Excellent choice, Mr. Sam. Ye won't be disappointed."

"I have a request, though. Do you think on that day you could call me Sam? Like a friend?"

There was a change in her eyes. "I'll have to ask Mrs. O'Neill."

"I understand. I'll look forward to Wednesday, but I need to get back to work. Dave is probably wondering where I am."

"Aye, but not before ye patch things up with Mr. Adam. I'll leave ye to it." Agnes had a gift for combining deference with quiet authority. She turned to go.

"Thank you, Agnes." I waited for her to get halfway down the driveway before turning to Sam.

He leaned against his truck and folded his arms over his chest. It took him a minute to look up at me. "I'm sorry. I don't know what's wrong with me."

"Apology accepted. I'm sorry I swore at you, but Carl has been nothing but a gentleman. He doesn't deserve to be treated like an enemy."

"I know. I'll apologize to him if I ever see him again."

"Uh . . . you will see him again, but I'll tell you more about that later. It's nothing you need to worry about."

"Okay." He sounded skeptical. "I'd better get going." He opened the door and climbed into the truck. I felt like we should have hugged, but the workmen had already seen enough.

The shed was securely installed with only minor damage from the move. I paid the crew and spent the rest of the afternoon cleaning up the yard and deadheading perennials. They were blooming like crazy in the hot August sun. It was nice to have the garden to myself for a few hours, just me and my flowers and my many thoughts.

Every now and then I looked up from my work, thinking I would see Sam puttering with one of his own projects. He had become so much a part of my life, it was hard to believe we met only eight months ago, started eating together only four months ago, and first kissed each other only ten weeks ago. I counted the weeks in my head and thought about other milestones. *Was our first argument the day before our first kiss? How many arguments have we had now? Is that a bad sign? How much longer can this last?* I always came back to that question. I wondered if I would ever stop thinking that way.

At dinner, I told Sam about Carl's friendship with Joe and Susan, his volunteer work, and the ideas we had about getting Joe's house painted. He showed great restraint, didn't ask too many questions, and assured me, once again, that he trusted me. "But you're including me in this project, aren't you?"

"Of course. That's why it would be nice if you could be friendlier with Carl. I don't want all this tension between the two of you. He's a good guy."

"I know. Remember, I knew him before you did. I wouldn't have had sex with him if I thought he was a jerk. Although I made that mistake with other jerks."

"Yeah? How many guys have you had sex with?"

"I don't know. I'm looking forward to lunch next Wednesday. It was nice of Flora to think about my birthday."

"That reminds me . . . what should I get you for your birthday? Any ideas?"

"You don't need to get me a present. You do too much for me as it is."

"Yes, I'm getting you something. It's your twenty-first birthday. Do you want a case of liquor?"

"Phfft! Yeah, right! You'd regret that."

"You don't have a computer. Do you want a laptop?"

"No! That's too expensive! Jeez!"

"Well, you'd better give me some ideas, or I'll get something extravagant."

"All right." He thought about it while he chewed. "I could use clothes. Some of my shirts are too tight."

"That's a good idea. How about underwear?"

"That's what my mom would buy me."

"I wouldn't buy the same kind she would."

"Nothing weird, I hope."

"Weird? Why would I buy something weird? Do you like leather?"

"Now you're scaring me. Will we have our own celebration for my birthday, just the two of us?"

"Sure. What would you like to do?"

"Um . . . eat . . . have sex."

"We do that most nights."

"Okay. Eat more? Have more sex?" He grinned.

“What if we went somewhere for the weekend, like a cabin on a lake?"

"That would be awesome, but too expensive."

"Why are you worrying about money? I can afford it after the big raise I got. Do you know how long it's been since I went anywhere? I went to the Grand Canyon with my parents when I was sixteen. That's sad."

"Well . . . if you want to, I won't object."

"I’ll see if I can find a place. Do you think Dave will give you the Saturday off?"

"I schedule the staff now, so I can give myself the day off. Dave won't mind if it's for my birthday."

"Great. Sounds like a plan. And I need to go to the kinky underwear store. Oh! I shouldn't have said that out loud."

He pointed his fork at me. "Remember, your birthday is next month, so it'll be payback time."

"That will be interesting." He continued eating while I watched him. "Can we make a promise to each other, Sam?"

"What promise?"

"Whenever we have an argument like we did today, let's promise to work it out. I don't want us to waste time being angry at each other."

"I know. I'm glad Agnes told me to apologize before I left, or I would've been angry for the rest of the day. So, I promise to work things out with you as soon as possible after an argument."

"Okay. I promise not to hang onto my anger, or hold grudges, or give you the silent treatment. Even when I know I'm right." I smiled.

"Did you have to add the last part?" His eyes twinkled. "If you want an argument right now, I'll give you one." He curled his hand around mine.

"Do you want to watch a movie tonight?"

"Sure. What movie?"

"Well, there's a documentary I've been wanting to see about dolphins being slaughtered in Japan. '*The Cove*,' I think it's called. It's supposed to be disturbing."

"Sounds good. Do we have ice cream?"

"I just bought some."

"Okay." He was still holding my hand.

How many guys would have watched that movie with me? Curled up together on the couch, sharing a carton of ice cream, we watched, we cringed, and we talked about the film. Later, as I fell asleep listening to his funny little snoring sounds, I wondered if I deserved him. Maybe I didn't, but he was with me for the moment, and that's all that mattered.

23

There were only a few days each year when I wished my house was air conditioned, and this was one of them. It was one of the hottest days of the summer, with the temperature expected to exceed a hundred degrees. Flora called the night before to say we would celebrate Sam's birthday in the cool comfort of her dining room instead of roasting on the terrace. She also invited us to have a swim in the pool before lunch. That sounded good to us.

I woke up grumpy. Even with a ceiling fan over my bed, I didn't sleep well because of the sticky heat. Sam slept like a log, as usual. I kept my distance from him because his body generated even more heat. I would appreciate that in the winter, but right now, not so much.

He woke up and saw me on my side of the bed. "Do I smell bad?"

"No, you're too hot."

"Thank you. You look good too."

"You know what I mean."

"Yeah . . . you mean I'm a handsome stud. Stop complimenting me so much." I grunted and gave up. He stretched his arm across the bed, caught me around the waist, and dragged me over to him while I made a whining noise. "Are you cranky?"

"I didn't sleep well."

"Awww. You can stay in bed while I go to the doughnut shop. I'll get you something special."

"All right."

"Don't sound so excited."

"I'm tired! Get me one of those chocolate cream doughnuts."

"Jeez. Whose birthday is this?"

"Your birthday is on Saturday, not today."

"Okay, then." He rolled out of bed. "It's a good thing I fell in love with you when you were cranky."

"Yeah, it is." My eyelids felt heavy. "Wake me up when my doughnut gets here."

***

When we arrived at Flora's house, Agnes opened the door. "Good morning. Come in Mr. Adam." She hesitated, then said, "Sam," as if she were passing a small kidney stone.

"You didn't call me 'mister!' Thank you, Agnes!" Sam raised his arms. "Do I get a hug?"

"Certainly not!" I knew that would never happen. I imagine Agnes hugged her mother briefly when she left Scotland, and it was the last time her arms wrapped around anything other than a bundle of laundry. I respected that.

Flora showed up with enough affection for everyone. "My beautiful boys! Welcome! Samson, come here and give me some sugar." He kissed her cheek and embraced her gently. "Happy birthday, dear. My stars! If you get any more handsome we'll have to shield our eyes." He blushed. "Adam, honey, are those for me?"

"Yes, from my garden." I brought a bouquet of spectacular dahlias.

"Good heavens, they're beautiful! You have such a gift. Aren't they lovely, Agnes?"

"Aye, ma'am, I've never seen the like." She took the flowers.

Flora hugged me and pressed her cheek against mine, a gesture that reminded me of my mother. "Adam, it warms my heart to see you so fit and happy." She stepped back to look at me. "Samson's youth must be rubbing off. You've never looked better. Aren't younger men wonderful?"

It was my turn to blush. Sam and I exchanged an understanding glance. We learned to accept her lavish compliments without objecting.

Flora continued as we walked into the house. "Thank goodness Mr. O'Neill had the foresight to install an air conditioning system in this old barn." The 'barn' she referred to was her elegant neoclassical mansion. "It cost a fortune at the time, but it has been a godsend. You boys go and enjoy the pool while we finish our preparations. We'll have plenty of time to visit during the wonderful luncheon Agnes has in store."

Sam sniffed the air. "What did you make, Agnes? It smells good."

"Never mind . . . Sam . . . ye wanted to be surprised." Flora smiled at Agnes' struggle with informality. "There are towels on the terrace, Mr. Adam."

"You could call me Adam, if you'd like."

"It's not your birthday, is it? I'll put these flowers in a vase." She turned and headed into the kitchen.

Flora whispered, "Samson, I don't know what spell you cast on her, but you're the first guest she has addressed informally in all the years she's been with me. Whatever you're doing, keep it up!"

He shrugged. "All I did was ask her. But when I tried to get a hug, she nearly bit my head off."

"Oh, my word, you didn't!" Flora was delighted. "How extraordinary! I wish I'd been there."

Just then, Agnes reappeared. "Ma'am. We have a schedule to keep."

"I'm sorry, dear. I'll be right there." Flora turned back to us and made a face. "Enjoy your swim, but don't stay too long in the sun. We'll call you in when we're ready to start."

We stepped onto the terrace and the heat made me a bit dizzy. I should have had more than a doughnut for breakfast, but I wanted to save my appetite for lunch. I was not as energetic as I would have liked.

Sam was wearing a neatly pressed white guayabera he'd found in a thrift shop. Normally I would refer to it as a 'fat man's shirt,' but on Sam it was a completely different garment – snug around his shoulders and chest, and loose at the waist. The white cotton contrasted beautifully with his tan skin. He noticed me watching him undo his buttons. "Why aren't you getting undressed?"

"I'm busy."

The corner of his mouth curled into a dimple. "Let me help you." He stepped forward to unbutton my preppy gingham check shirt. "Do you think they're watching us?"

"I would if I were them. We're smokin' hot."

He laughed. "I'm glad you included yourself for a change. Flora was right – you've never looked better."

"Shush!"

"It's true." He ran his hands over my chest and down both sides of my body. "You're beautiful." The desire in his eyes was so genuine, it brought tears to my eyes. "Are you getting emotional?"

I nodded. "You don't know what it's like to have someone who looks like you tell me I'm beautiful."

"Let's get in the water before we get overheated." I finished taking off my shirt while he removed his and laid it neatly on the poolside bench. As he stripped down to his swimsuit, he caught me staring again. "What are you looking at?"

"I can't help myself. I'm addicted."

He unbuttoned and unzipped my khaki shorts. "I suppose I shouldn't say this, but I hope you never recover." He discreetly pulled the top of my red Speedo away from my skin to look at my equipment. "You did some trimming this morning. Very nice."

"Yeah, I was getting a little bushy." I stepped out of my shorts and threw them on the bench. "Let's get wet."

The water was refreshing, and swimming laps made me feel like I hadn't aged much since I was in school. Sam didn't bother trying to keep up with me. He knew I was a better swimmer. He enjoyed the pool the way a child does, splashing and making noise and wrestling with me in the water. I'm not sure I would have learned to be playful if Sam hadn't taught me.

Before long, Flora waved at us to return to the house, so we climbed out and used the towels Agnes provided. I was tempted to sit and stare at Sam again. Nothing I had ever seen on the internet surpassed the erotic beauty of my wet lover toweling off in the sun. We dressed and raked each other's hair with our fingers, then went in for lunch. The cool air was a relief, and the smell of food reminded me how hungry I was. The ladies greeted us with glasses of cold champagne.

"Samson, this is my last chance to corrupt you before you reach the legal drinking age. I couldn't pass it up."

"Well . . . if you insist. I know Agnes will cut me off if I get drunk."

"It's a special occasion. Ye can have a wee lie down in a spare bedroom if needs be." I had a feeling Agnes would like to see him passed out in one of the bedrooms.

"Ah, yes," Flora said wistfully. "When Mr. O'Neill entertained guests, Agnes and I opened the spare rooms to many young men who overindulged. We've seen a lot, haven't we Agnes?" She chuckled quietly. "Unspeakable things."

"Aye, ma'am. Beautiful things."

Sam and I exchanged a glance. "Happy birthday, Sam." We raised our glasses and drank. Agnes never drank with us before. It felt right to have her with us.

Flora led us into the dining room and Sam's eyes grew as big as saucers. They had pulled out all the stops. The mahogany table was set with elegant china, crystal goblets, gleaming silver, and a large vase filled with my dahlias as a centerpiece. It could have been a photo spread in a high-end magazine. On the near end of the table there was box wrapped in silver paper with a blue bow. I knew Sam was overwhelmed, so I squeezed his hand. "Well, ain't this fancy!"

That seemed to help him. "I can't believe you did this for me. It's too much."

Flora downplayed the extravagance. "Oh, honey, this is nothing special. We eat like this every night, don't we, Agnes?"

"Aye, ma'am. I live only to polish the silver."

"I hope that's not a gift for me. You shouldn't. I can't . . ." I squeezed his hand again.

"Please indulge me, Samson. I'm an old woman with no one to buy gifts for except Agnes, and she already has everything she needs."

"I'll give you a new list, ma'am."

"But I didn't spend a dime on this. Open it. Just lift the lid, no need to tear the paper."

He let go of my hand and stepped forward tentatively, setting down his glass of champagne. He lifted the lid. Inside, nestled in blue tissue paper, was a chess board made of inlaid wood with carved chessmen lined up on either side. The set was old, well made and well used. Sam's hand trembled as he picked up the black king and examined the fine carving. "It's beautiful."

"When we met, I knew you had a keen intellect. Adam wouldn't be with you if you didn't. I believe you have the mind of a chess player. Do you play?"

"My father taught me. We used to . . ." He trailed off.

"Oh, that's wonderful! I'm so pleased I've chosen well." It was a perfect gift on so many levels. "Mr. O'Neill was an avid chess player, always looking for worthy opponents. He would have enjoyed playing chess with you, Samson. This set belonged to him, but I want you to have it."

"Thank you. It's . . ." He set the king back on the board and sniffled. He raised his hand to his eyes.

Flora put her hand on his back. "Oh, sweetheart! You don't need to say anything else. I understand perfectly. Now let's get some food into you. Agnes, are we ready to start?"

"Aye, ma'am." She tipped her champagne glass against her lips and drained it. "Take your seats."

Flora sat at the head of the table, with Sam on her left and me on her right. There was a partial place setting next to me, presumably for Agnes when she could join us. "I don't want you boys to be intimidated by all of this silverware. I'll tell you what to do with everything. The setting may be formal, but we'll relax and have fun. There's a good chance I'll use profanity before the meal is over. Isn't that right, Agnes?"

"Every day of the week, ma'am."

The meal was another multiple course feast consisting of dishes so expertly prepared, well-coordinated and beautifully presented, that it could be described as a 'dining experience.' It started with a caviar appetizer followed by fresh, lightly seasoned gazpacho. When Agnes refilled my champagne glass, I noticed Sam hadn't finished his yet. I knew he wouldn't want to overdo it, especially after getting emotional earlier.

"Adam, honey, I've been wondering what you plan to do about the neighborhood association."

"I don't want anything to do with it. I keep telling Sam, I'd rather stick pins in my eyeballs than be in the same room with that fff . . . Weasel. I almost said a swear."

"Feel free, dear. So, you won't attend the meeting?"

"I'm not going to any damn meetings! She hasn't even scheduled anything. Maybe she gave up on it after Donna went after her. Donna is scary. She threatened to squeeze my balls the other day. Did I tell you that, Sam?" He blinked at me. "I love her."

"A meeting has been scheduled, Adam. Did you not get the latest flyer?"

"The last flyer was the one Donna made." Agnes came in and set small lobster tails in front of Flora and me, then presented a larger one to Sam. "Look at that! Do you know how much those things cost?" He gave me one of his looks.

Flora patted my hand. "Let's not worry about that, dear. You should eat before we continue our discussion."

"No, I can do both. Can I have more champagne, Agnes? I ran out already."

"Perhaps some iced tea, Mr. Adam."

"No, I prefer champagne. I don't get it very often. Which fork should I use on this thing?" Agnes pointed at a fork, refilled my glass, and went around the table to refill Sam's glass. I glanced at him. "Are you feeling okay, hon?"

"I feel fine. Are you okay?"

"I feel great! I'm glad we went swimming." I used my fork to stir the little bowl of melted butter next to the lobster. "Butter is so pretty."

Flora whispered, "Enjoy the show, dear. No harm will come of it."

I looked up. "What? What show?"

"This marvelous meal Agnes prepared for Samson."

"I know! She must like you, Sam. She's not usually this . . ." As I turned my head, I realized she was standing behind my left shoulder. "Sorry, I thought you were in the kitchen."

"Would ye care to finish your thought, Mr. Adam?"

My face felt hot. "No, thank you. I forgot what I was about to say." I turned back to my plate and hoped she would go away.

Flora covered my awkward moment. "Samson, I believe Saturday is the actual day of your birthday, is it not? Do you have plans for the day?"

"Adam wanted to rent a cottage somewhere on a lake, but I guess there weren't any available."

"Is that so, Adam? When did you start looking?"

"Twodayzhago." My mouth was full. I swallowed. "I guess a lotta people rent these places in the summer."

She chuckled. "Yes, dear, that's what they're for. I suppose your parents never did that."

"No, but we can have fun here at home, right Sam?" I tried to wink, but my face didn't cooperate.

He smiled. "It doesn't matter where we are."

"You're welcome to use my lake house. It's a lovely spot."

I straightened up and raised my eyebrows. "You have a lake house?"

"Yes, we bought it ages ago. Edward used it more than I have for the past several years, but Clarence and I went there recently. It's very comfortable and private."

"What's the bed like?"

"The bed?"

"Yeah. Is it big? Is it sturdy?"

Sam cringed. "Adam!"

Flora laughed. "Oh, my word! It's such a joy having the two of you here! Yes, dear, the bed is large and sturdy. There are two bedrooms, but the master bedroom has the largest bed."

My mouth was full again, so Sam responded. "That sounds great, Flora. Are you sure it would be okay?"

"Certainly. We won't be using it. I'll give you the directions and the keys and let you enjoy yourselves."

Agnes returned to collect plates, but I wasn't finished yet. "I'm sorry, I was talking too much." She made a noise of disapproval. "This is soooo good!" I tried to dig the last chunk of lobster out of the shell, but I lost control of it. It skittered across the table and clanked against Sam's water glass. "Oops." He picked it up and handed it to Agnes. "I guess I'm done. I'll keep my butter, though."

She glared at me. "What for?"

"Ummmmm." I had no idea. "Okay, you can have it back." She took my plate and left the room. Sam pointed to my face and made a circle with his finger, suggesting I had something on my lips. I used my napkin, leaving a large buttery imprint on the cloth. He gave me a thumbs-up. *He's so cute!* My champagne glass was covered with greasy fingerprints, so I drained it and used my napkin to wipe the outside of the glass. When I looked up, Flora and Sam were smiling. "What?"

"It's nothing, dear. As I was saying earlier, there was a flyer announcing the date of the first neighborhood association meeting."

"No there wasn't."

"Yes, there was, dear. We received it . . ."

"No there wasn't."

Sam covered half his face with his hand.

"Tsk. Agnes, dear . . . do we have the flyer about the neighborhood association meeting?"

"Aye, ma'am. I have it here."

"Could you bring it in, please?"

"I've got nothing else to do, ma'am."

"Shall I come and get it?" Flora rose from her chair, but Agnes bustled in.

"Keep your seat, ma'am. Here it is."

She handed me a pink sheet. The letters looked blurry. "Shitty printer." I read the text: "'Helen Van Wootten, Founding President, invites you to the first meeting of the Eden Place Neighborhood Association,' blah blah blah. What the fuck? 'Agenda items include derelict properties, safety issues, sexual predators and police harassment.' Fuckety-fuck, mother fucker, fuckin' Weasel!" I looked at Flora. "Why didn't I get one of these?"

"I assumed you did, dear. I've spoken to other neighbors who received it."

"She didn't invite us, Sam! Can you fuckin' believe this shit?"

He held up his hand. "Adam, could you settle down?"

"I am selted down!"

"You weren't planning to go anyway."

"Oh, I'm going! You bet your ass I'm going! She can't shut me out of this! This was my neighborhood first!"

"Fine, we'll go to the meeting, but . . . you're getting loud."

"Am I?" I looked at Flora. She nodded. "I'm sorry, I'm sorry. I get so . . . the Weasel makes me crazy. I could use a little more champagne."

"Adam . . ."

I twisted in my chair. "Agnes! We need more champagne!"

"Git yer own bloody champagne! I'm BUSY!"

We all looked at each other, shocked. Flora laughed. I felt guilty. "I'm sorry, Agnes! Never mind!" I made a face. "Should I go and help her?"

"No, I think it's best if you stay here. Agnes is very capable."

I looked across the table at Sam. "Are you enjoying yourself?"

"Yes, I am. It's more fun than I expected."

"You probably had enough champagne." I pointed to his glass. "Do you want me to finish that for you?"

He pinched his eyebrows together. "No!"

I threw up my hands. "All right! Don't blame me if you get silly." I lowered my voice. "You'd think a guy that big would have more toloberance." *Is that the right word?*

Agnes arrived with dinner plates for Sam and Flora. "I'm sorry for my outburst, ma'am."

"Please don't apologize, Agnes. You had every right. Now, fix a plate for yourself and eat with us. We're all friends here."

Sam chimed in. "Yeah, it's my birthday, I want to eat with you. Right, Adam?"

I looked up at Agnes and burst into tears. "Are you mad at me? I love you!"

"Och, ye numpty! Pull yourself together! I've put up with worse than you." She shoved my greasy napkin into my hand. "Put this in your lap. And sit up straight, like a gentleman. I'll get your dinner."

I wiped my eyes on my forearm. Flora leaned over and whispered, "That means she loves you too, dear." I sniffled and smiled.

Agnes sat next to me at the table while we ate boneless duck breast with roasted plums and julienne vegetables. Everything was delicious. Flora kept the conversation flowing and was never content with small talk. "Samson, you mentioned your father earlier. Have you had any recent communication with your parents?"

"No, I haven't."

"Do you plan to contact them?"

"I don't know. What good would it do?"

"They should know you're healthy and happy. They must worry about you."

Sam looked skeptical. "Maybe they're worried about my soul."

"I'm sure there's more to it than that. No matter what a child has done, most parents still want to know if they're alive or dead, happy or unhappy. I speak from experience, as you know. I condemn Edward's behavior and I won't pretend to like him, but I still love my son and care about what happens to him. There are bonds that can't be broken, dear."

I felt like crying again, thinking of my own parents. Sam was getting teary as well. One thing seemed very clear to me: *Sam can't handle champagne!* I maneuvered a piece of duck toward my mouth but dropped it in my lap. Agnes clicked her tongue.

Flora continued. "It must have been difficult to be with your parents before you left. Were they terribly harsh?"

"It wasn't as bad as you might think. They believed I was turning away from God, but I knew they loved me, especially my dad. My mom was always more . . . distant, but I don't think a day went by without my dad hugging me, including the day I left." He cleared his throat. "But they have beliefs I can't accept. Love doesn't fix everything."

"Oh, honey." She patted his hand. "I used to think that way. I hope one day you'll be surprised, as I was, to discover the extraordinary things love can accomplish."

Agnes quietly offered her own brand of advice. "It wouldn't kill you to send a letter, dearie."

I wanted to be supportive, but I had mixed feelings. I liked having Sam all to myself. I had no family and I wanted to pretend he had no family. I never asked about his parents. It was easier to say nothing.

We all complimented the meal as Agnes collected our dinner plates. While waiting for the next course, I tried to deal with an irritating itch. I slipped my hand into my shorts, assuming my napkin would conceal it. It did not. Flora was incredibly tolerant, but my behavior had crossed a line. "Adam, please . . . you need to use the powder room."

Sam stretched to see over the table. "Oh, for God's sake, Adam!"

"I'm scratching!" I pulled my hand out. "I trimmed my pubic hair and now it itches. But you're right, I'll go to the powder room." I leaned on a chair to stand up.

Sam watched me closely. "Do you want me to help you?"

"Sam! You can get in my pants later. I'll take care of this."

"That's not what I meant!"

"Yeah, right! You're terrible . . . but I like it. I'll be right back." I made my way into the hall and accidentally went to the kitchen.

Agnes looked at me. "Now what?"

"It's my pubic hair. Where's the powder room again?" She silently pointed me in the right direction. Once inside, I pulled down my shorts and Speedo and scratched with both hands, moaning with relief. I sat down on the toilet to pee, and I may have dozed off for a minute.

Sam knocked on the door. "Adam . . . are you okay?"

I sat up. "I'm fine! I'll be right out." I decided to take off my damp swimsuit. I put my shorts back on, stuffed the Speedo in my pocket, and washed my hands thoroughly. When I returned to the dining room, everyone stared at me. "What'd I miss?"

"Nothing, dear. Are you feeling all right?"

"Why does everyone keep asking me that? I feel great." There was a small salad and a big glass of iced tea waiting for me. I picked up my fork and looked around. "Why am I the only one with a salad?"

"We finished ours," said Sam. "You were in the bathroom for twenty minutes."

"I was not! You eat too fast. You know they called him 'Hoover' when he worked at the restaurant? I love that." I took a mouthful of salad and pointed my fork at him. "I love you, Babe!"

He smiled. "I love you, too."

I looked at my iced tea. "Is the champagne gone?"

Agnes said, "I drank the last of it myself."

I leaned over and nudged her with my elbow. "Good for you. Maybe you'll loosen up a little."

She grunted. "Anything is possible, now that I've seen this."

I felt talkative again. "So, Agnes, where were you when you turned twenty-one? Still in Scotland?"

She was probably surprised that I would ask about her personal life, but she answered. "I came to America at the age of nineteen. By the time I was twenty-one, I was working for another family here in the city. Horrible people. Mrs. O'Neill rescued me and brought me here, and I'm forever grateful for it."

"I'm so grateful that you accepted, Agnes. It was entirely selfish on my part."

"'Twas more than that, ma'am, and you know it."

"They were horrible people, it's true. My husband and I moved here from Georgia, and we were still getting established in this house. Mr. O'Neill had made the acquaintance of several prominent families in the area, so we were invited to parties at some of the finest homes in town. At one of those parties, I tasted Agnes's cooking for the first time. I simply had to meet her. The rest, as they say, is history."

"You're leaving out the meat of the story, ma'am."

"It's not my story to tell, dear."

"It deserves to be told. When she met me, my face was bruised from a beating I'd taken from the master of the house. He'd been using me for his own pleasure, and the missus was happy to allow it so she was free from the burden. Mrs. O'Neill sized things up and talked Mr. O'Neill into hiring me."

"I didn't need to convince him. He gave me whatever I asked for without question. But when he heard about Agnes's situation he arranged things very quickly, despite the trouble it caused with her former employers."

"Aye, Mr. O'Neill was a saint in my book. 'Twas a relief to work for a master who was only interested in my cooking."

"Don't forget my favorite part of the story, Agnes."

"I like it when you tell it, ma'am. Go on, then."

"Gladly, dear. Once Agnes knew she had a position here, she packed her suitcase and prepared one last meal before she left. The man and his wife spent more than a week in the hospital, but no one could prove what made them ill." She clapped her hands together and laughed. "Isn't that marvelous?"

Sam and I exchanged wide-eyed looks across the table. Agnes looked proud. "I learned the old ways from my grandmother. Some folk thought she was a witch."

Flora was still laughing. "Those horrible people would never attend a gathering at this house, and their reputation declined. Agnes and I have been thick as thieves ever since. Haven't we, dear?"

"Aye, ma'am. We've had our adventures." She stood up. "I hope you're still hungry, there's more coming." She took my salad plate to the kitchen.

I whispered, "I wouldn't want her to be mad at me."

"Don't worry, you're one of Agnes's favorite people. Both of you are. Now . . . I know it's the middle of the day, but we have a very nice Port I was hoping we could enjoy . . . only if you feel up to it, Adam. I don't want you under the table." She went to the sideboard to retrieve a bottle and crystal glasses.

"I can handle it. I don't know if Sam should have any more."

"Adam, I'm not drunk. You're the one who should slow down." It seemed like he wasn't kidding.

"Whataya mean? I used to drink a whole box of wine every weekend before you came along." I felt tearful again. "Just because I'm a little emotional doesn't mean . . . *sniff* . . . My shrink says emotions are good!"

"Look, Adam, you can have more if you want. I like it when you're not so in control."

"I'm in control!"

"Okay, whatever! I'll make sure you get home all right."

"Awww, you're so sweet." More tears. "Wait . . . we live next door."

"Samson, have you ever tasted Port?"

"No, but I'll try anything."

"That's the spirit." She set glasses in front of us. "Agnes will be bringing cheese in a moment. Hardly anyone serves a cheese course anymore, but we like it." As if on cue, Agnes came in with plates for each of us. There were small pieces of cheese arranged in a pattern, drizzled with a golden liquid. "This is something I first tasted when Mr. O'Neill and I traveled in Italy. Pecorino Toscano served with truffle honey."

"Pecker what?" I wasn't sure I heard her right.

"Pecorino Toscano, dear. It's a cheese made from ewe's milk, from Tuscany, and the honey is infused with truffles. It's a delicious combination." Agnes sat next to me with her own plate and glass of Port.

Sam tasted his. "Wow, that's good. I never would've thought of cheese with honey."

I tried mine. "Mmm, mmm, mmmmmmmmm. Mmm! That honey is . . . mmmmmm . . . like, pepper, but . . . mmm." Not my most articulate review. I tried the Port. "MmmmMMMmmmm!" I took another swallow.

"You might want to sip it, Adam, it's quite strong. Do you like the Port, Samson?"

"Yeah, it's sweet and it feels warm going down. I like it a lot."

I finished my cheese a little too quickly and stared at the honey left on the plate. Flora wasn't looking at me, so I looked sideways at Agnes. "I know what you're thinking, dearie." I picked up my plate and licked the honey. I couldn't get enough of it. The taste was so familiar, and yet so different from any honey I'd ever had.

Sam looked to Flora for permission. She smiled and shrugged. "Shall we?" She picked up her plate and stuck out her tongue. Sam grinned and did the same.

Agnes held out. "I'll take mine to the kitchen." Sam looked at her with puppy dog eyes. She shifted nervously in her chair and looked at Flora who held up her clean plate. I offered to lick it for her.

"You will not!" She snatched up the plate as if I would steal it from her, then turned away and licked it. She showed us it was clean, and Flora led a round of applause and laughter. Agnes took a long sip of Port. "We must never speak of this."

After a few moments of contented silence, I took a breath and let out a long, satisfied sigh. "I'm happy! I like being happy. Hey, Flora, did you see the garden shed I got from Joe?"

"I have. It's a lovely little building. It was very kind of him to give it to you, and I can't wait to see it restored. Will you be doing the work, Samson?"

"Yeah. It might take a while because of all the fancy trim, but I'll use the same paint colors I used on the other one."

"Speaking of painting," I said, "I'm planning to get volunteers together to paint Joe's house. Do you know the house he lives in?"

"Yes, I believe it was one of the first houses on Eden Place. It has seen better days. Wouldn't that be quite a large project for a group of volunteers, dear? I think a professional painter would be required."

"Well, there's a painter in the neighborhood who would do it for a lower price, but I don't think Joe can afford it. Fortunably, I have a lot of good ideas." I tapped my finger against the side of my head. "My friend, Carl, the police ossifer, does volunteer work with kids who could help and get credit for something or other . . . I forget . . . service . . . some kinda service . . . community service! That's it."

"Do you mean Officer Hanson, the handsome younger policeman who helped put Edward in jail?" Sam rolled his eyes.

"Yep, that's the one. Turns out he's friends with Joe and he was there when we moved the shed, so we talked about painting the house and stuff and he wants to help and he does voluntary work and sports with kids and . . . did I tell you this already? Anyway, he'll go with me to talk to the painter. About stuff." Sam crossed his arms over his chest. "Sam doesn't trust him."

"I didn't say anything."

"You looked . . ." I made a face, ". . . like that."

Agnes collected our cheese plates. "I'll prepare the dessert, ma'am."

"Thank you, Agnes. Now boys, what's this about?"

"Nothing."

"He thinks Carl will steal me away like I'm some kind of prize. I mean, he's a nice guy and he's handsome and all, but . . ."

"He's not that handsome."

"Yeah, he is! Come on!"

"Well, he has a small dick."

"Boys . . ."

"Maybe smaller than your big . . ."

"Smaller than average!"

"Boys! Please! Stop for a moment!"

"Sam has a large . . ."

"Adam! That's none of her business!"

"Oh, but Carl's dick is her business?"

Flora finally raised her voice. "STOP! Both of you!"

Agnes shouted from the kitchen, "I'll beat ye both with a ladle in a minute!"

Everyone was quiet. Sam swallowed the rest of his Port.

"What on God's green earth has gotten into the two of you? Is Officer Hanson a homosexual?"

"He's gay. We say 'gay' now."

"All right then. Has he made advances toward you, Adam?"

"Mmmm, he let me know he'd be interested if things don't work out with Sam. But I told him things were going great between us, so he dropped it."

"I see. Samson, how are you familiar with Officer Hanson's . . . attributes?"

"Yeah, Sam! Tell her!" Agnes appeared beside me with a large steel ladle. "I'm sorry! I'll be quiet!" I sank into my chair.

Sam lowered his head and quietly admitted, "I had sex with him . . . before Adam and I were . . . whatever."

"Oh, this is rather complicated. Did things end badly with the officer?"

"No, we just weren't into each other."

"Do you have reason to distrust Officer Hanson?"

He hesitated. "I guess not, but . . ."

"But what, dear?"

"Well . . . I know what I would do. If Carl wants Adam as much as I wanted Adam . . . he won't give up, unless he's an idiot." He looked me in the eye. "And he's not an idiot."

Flora turned to me. "If Officer Hanson pursued you aggressively, could you be worn down? Would you betray Samson?"

"No."

"Forgive me for asking, but . . . how can you be so certain, dear?"

Her question surprised me, so I had to think about it. *Could it happen?* "It feels good to know a guy like Carl is interested. I suppose I can't be a hundred percent sure, but . . . Sam is perfect."

"I'm not perfect, Adam."

"You're perfect for me. Why would I give you up for someone who's . . . not you? It doesn't make any sense."

"Okay."

The room was silent again. Agnes lowered her ladle and quietly returned to the kitchen.

Flora grasped Sam's hand. "May I share something I learned during more than forty years of marriage?"

"Yes . . . please. I need all the help I can get."

"During our marriage, Mr. O'Neill had more sexual partners than I could count, and it was very difficult for me to accept. How could I trust a man who would do that to me? I hoped, if I loved him enough, he would change his ways and devote all his attention to me and be with me as a husband should be with his wife. I watched the young men come and go. He was quite fond of some of them. I accepted them and grew fond of them as well. But they never stopped coming and going. As the years went by, I realized I was his only constant companion . . . the one he loved more than all the others. I learned to trust his love, even under those circumstances, no matter how many men captured his attention."

Sam shook his head. "I could never do what you did."

"I understand, dear, but your circumstances are different. You and Adam are sexually compatible. The point of my story is that there will always be temptations. If you try to avoid them, it will only impoverish your lives. Officer Hanson seems like a nice young man who could be a friend, if he's willing. Why turn him away simply because he's attracted to the man you love? You're both very handsome, and there will be many other men who will tempt you. Learn to trust the love you have for each other."

"I need to work on that. I don't like myself when I'm jealous. It makes me think I don't deserve him, and I wouldn't blame him for looking for someone new. That makes me worry even more. It makes me crazy."

"Yes, jealousy can do that. It's not easy, but the best way to learn to trust each other is in the presence of temptation. If there were no temptations, we wouldn't need trust, would we, dear?"

I watched Sam's face change as he absorbed the truth of what she said. "You're right, I never thought of it that way. Thank you, Flora."

I sniffled. "I think I might be a little drunk." The room seemed to move as if we were on a ship.

"That's okay, sweetie. Would you like more Port to go with your dessert?"

"Can I, Sam? Do you mind?"

"No, go ahead. Good things have happened when you were a little drunk." He winked.

Flora poured more wine for us. Agnes called out from the kitchen, "Are we ready ma'am?"

"Yes, Agnes, your timing is perfect."

I turned in my chair to see a great spectacle coming through the door – a tall chocolate cake with twenty-one burning candles. The three of us sang 'Happy Birthday.' Sam's face glowed in the flickering light as Agnes set the cake in front of him. When our disharmonious racket ceased, he blew out the candles and we applauded.

"Did you make a wish?" I asked.

"No. Was I supposed to? I never had a birthday cake before."

"Didn't your parents celebrate your birthday?"

"Not like this. My mom would make rice pudding or apple pie. She thought candles were a waste of money unless the power went out."

Agnes removed the candles from the cake. "Were your mother's people Scots?"

"No, they were German. This looks so good, Agnes. I love chocolate cake."

"I'm pleased to hear it. You'll take home whatever is left so Mrs. O'Neill doesn't make herself sick on it."

Flora scoffed. "Oh, for heaven's sake, you exaggerate, Agnes."

Agnes gave her a look. "Do I, ma'am?" Flora didn't argue.

The cake was delicious. She added cinnamon to the chocolate and the thick frosting must have had a pound of butter in it. As full as I was from the meal, I asked for a second piece before I finished the first. "If I don't get it now, Sam will eat it all."

Flora revived our conversation. "Adam, if you organize a group of volunteers to paint Joe's house, I would like to offer a financial sponsorship in the name of O'Neill's Automotive. We could use positive publicity following Edward's disgraceful behavior. Do you think Joe would be comfortable with that?"

"Mmm, mmmhmm!" I licked frosting off my fingers. "Sure! Why not?" I had to lick the handle of my fork, too.

"I'm so pleased you're reaching out to the neighbors. It will help counteract whatever trouble Mrs. Van Wootten might cause."

"Mrrmm, weaselbitch." I pushed more cake into my face.

Sam was keeping an eye on me. "I bet Dave would offer to plant new shrubs for Joe after the painting is done. The ones he has should be replaced. We could lay new sod, too."

"Mmm!" I bobbed my head. "Thazgreat!" I took a sip of wine, leaving a smear of chocolate on the glass. Sam gestured for me to wipe my face again, so I reached for my napkin and rubbed the cloth across my mouth. When I held it out to see what I had removed, the cloth was bright red. "Uh oh. Am I bleeding?" I wasn't. I had pulled my Speedo out of my pocket.

Sam and Flora cracked up. Agnes clicked her tongue. "Och, yer moagered! Be still, I'll grab a cloot." I had no idea what that meant, but she went to the kitchen and brought back a damp cloth. She grabbed me by the hair and roughly wiped my face while I squinted and giggled. Sam reached across the table and took the Speedo away from me. Agnes wiped my hands clean as if I were a messy baby, then took my wine glass back to the kitchen. The rest of us couldn't stop giggling.

She returned to the table and finished her cake while shaking her head at our silliness.

I can't recall any more conversation, but I laughed until I was out of breath and my belly hurt. I remember Sam grinning and saying something about getting home so I could 'sleep it off.' I made it out of the dining room on my own feet. Then I was in Sam's arms with my head on his shoulder. He slapped my hand when I tried to unbutton his shirt. I thought I saw Agnes smile. Flora rubbed my back.

***

I woke up on the leather sofa in my parlor. The setting sun threw gold and orange streaks across the ceiling. An electric fan hummed. When I lifted my head, it felt like my brain was too big for my skull. Sam was in the adjacent armchair with a book in his hand and his legs stretched across the ottoman. He looked up. "How do you feel?"

"My head hurts. A lot."

"Do you want some aspirin?"

"No. Let me die quietly." I put my hand over my eyes.

"Okay."

"I didn't ruin your day, did I?"

"No, I had a fun time. That was the best meal I've ever eaten, and you were the life of the party."

"In a good way, I hope."

"Yeah, in a good way."

"So, no one is angry?"

"Nope."

"Unbelievable. Where's my shirt?"

"I took it off and put detergent on it to get the stains out. Your Speedo, too."

"What stains?"

"You dropped food on your shirt and you had chocolate frosting on your Speedo."

"Oh yeah, I remember." I thought about why my Speedo was in my pocket. "Did I have my hand in my pants at the table?"

"Yes, you did, but only for a few minutes."

"Well . . . as long as it was only for a few minutes." I groaned. "I'll never drink again."

"Uh huh."

"What time is it?"

"About seven-thirty." He set down his book and stood up. "I'm getting something to drink, do you want anything?"

"Is there any cake left?"

"No."

"I knew it."

"She made it for me. It's my birthday."

"It's not your birthday! Saturday is your birthday."

"Are you starting that again?"

"I'm just saying."

"You're always just saying." He unbuttoned his shirt, took it off and laid it neatly over the back of the chair. "Do you want water?"

"Yes, please. Aspirin, too."

He casually stretched and scratched his chest and abs. "It's still hot, isn't it?"

I smiled. "Yeah. Very hot."

24

Because Sam and I planned to spend the weekend at Flora's lake house, I needed another vacation day to cover that Saturday. I had to ask Henry's permission again. *What a pain in the ass.* My head was still tender from overindulging the day before, so I didn't want to argue with him. *Maybe he won't be so difficult this time.*

No such luck. "Another day off? Adam, this doesn't look good. What will people think?" He inspected an expensive silk tie from the selection a local haberdasher sent over at his request.

"It's a Saturday, Henry. No one will know I'm not working."

"That's part of the problem, isn't it? You're not here on Wednesdays so it looks like you only work four days a week. I hardly see you anymore."

"Is that what this is about? You want me to spend more time with you?"

"I hoped we would work together as partners, but it seems like you're avoiding me." He held a shimmering red tie against his gray shirt.

"Tell you what . . . let me have the weekend off, and I'll take you to lunch next week. We can talk about working together more often."

The corners of his mouth turned up. "Thank you, Adam. I knew you would come around eventually. You can have your weekend with . . . what's his name?"

"Sam."

"Yes. When will I meet this person?"

"Why would you want to meet him?"

"To make sure he's real. After all, we allow you to have a special work schedule for this relationship."

"He's real, Henry."

"He must be pretty special to make you want to be monogamous. What does he look like?"

I shrugged. "The usual . . . he's tall, muscular, and looks like a movie star."

He raised an eyebrow. "Fine . . . you don't have to tell me the truth. I'll look forward to our lunch next week. Before you go, tell me which tie looks good on me."

"They all look good on you, Henry." I wasn't lying.

"You see, we do think alike. I'll buy them all. If I don't see you tomorrow, have a good weekend, my friend."

I believe he thought of us as friends, but it made my skin crawl when he called me that. I left his office feeling a little bit sorry for him. Then I got over it.

***

After work, I stopped at Dave's Nursery to ask Sam what food he wanted for his birthday weekend. I greeted Dave at the front of the store and let him know how happy Sam was about the promotion and raise he got. When a customer asked for his assistance, he pointed me toward the back lot where Sam and Greg were stacking bags of peat and manure. As I approached, I could hear their 'bro' banter.

Greg was taunting Sam. "Come on, dude! Yafraid ya got competition, now? Zat it? Let's see 'em! Come on!"

"Jesus, dude, do you ever shut up? No wonder your girlfriend is getting tired of you. You talk more than she does, and that's a lot, man." Sam looked up and saw me. "Adam! Thank God, someone normal I can talk to."

"DUDE!" Greg dropped a bag on the ground and ran up to me, grabbing my shoulders in a way that startled me. I usually kept my distance from straight guys, especially the hot ones. "Bro, ya gotta do me a favor! You're perfect for this!"

Sam interrupted, "Just say, 'no,' Adam."

"Let me hear it first." I liked seeing Greg up close.

"Okay. I'm hittin' the gym like crazy, dude, and I'm jacked as shit." There was ample evidence to support his boast. "So I said to the Muffin, 'Let's compare arms, bro, I want to see if I'm catchin' up to ya,' but he won't do it!" He looked over his shoulder at Sam. "Chicken-shit muffin-fucker is on the RUN!" He turned back to me. "You can be the judge, okay? Make him do it."

"Huh?" I was distracted by the way his dark eyebrows moved with his lips.

Sam shook his head back and forth.

"He'll do it for you, dude. We'll flex, and you be the judge. You ready?"

My head was spinning. *Come on! This stuff doesn't happen in real life.* I looked around for the hidden camera. *How often will I get a chance like this?* "Okay, let's do it."

"YES!" Greg hopped around Sam like a boxer warming up for a fight. Sam looked at me with a tight smile.

"What are you worried about? It's a friendly competition. Roll up your sleeves."

Greg stood in front of Sam, pulled up the sleeve of his green polo shirt, and flexed his biceps without being asked. He grinned at me.

"Impressive! You must have put a lot of work into that."

"Damn right! Watch this." He twisted his wrist and pumped his arm. Sam stood behind him, refusing to participate.

"It looks like a softball. Can I feel it?" Sam's smile disappeared.

"Sure, dude. Be my guest."

I grabbed his biceps the way I thought a dude would do it – roughly, with both hands, gripping it like I imagined I would hold a football if I ever touched one. "It's like a rock, dude!" *That was so not me.*

Sam had seen enough. "Okay, let's get this over with." He pulled up the sleeve of his oversized shirt. Greg flexed as hard as he could. Sam put in just enough effort prove there was no contest. "Are you happy now?"

Greg turned and looked up. "Fffuuuck! Muff, dude, that's sick! Where've you been hidin' that?" Sam put his arm down while Greg flexed again. "How close am I to Muffzilla?" Greg liked himself so much, he wasn't bothered that his friend was so much bigger. As far as he was concerned, it was still a close race.

"Sam is built bigger than you, but you're definitely catching up. Not just your arms, either." I ran my eyes up and down his body. "I'm a little jealous of your girlfriend." It was a risky thing to say, but what the hell.

His face exploded into a grin. "WO-HOA, DUDE! That's like, the best compliment I ever had!" He practically knocked me over with a dude hug, with fists clenched, and appropriately brief so there would be no misunderstanding. I caught Sam's eye with a wicked smile. "You're a cool dude, bro!" He pointed his thumb at Sam. "Why are you settling for this ugly mo-fo? I know a few gay dudes. I could hook you up."

Sam clamped a hand on Greg's shoulder. "All right, dumbass, quit hitting on my boyfriend or I'll tell Jennifer. You know how that'll go."

"Dude, I can handle her. I'm not whipped."

"Oh yeah? She wasn't happy with you the last time she was here."

"That was nothin'. She got over it."

I thought Greg would be a catch for any girl, so I was curious. "She must be thrilled with your progress in the gym."

"That's what I thought! Who wouldn't want a ride on this?" He thrust his hips a couple of times. "But, no! She thinks I'm gettin' too big! Chicks, man! Can anyone figure 'em out?"

I shook my head. "Not me, bro." *Am I pulling off the bro-speak? Probably not.*

"She blames the Muffin. Says I'm spendin' too much time with this meathead."

Sam looked surprised. "You didn't tell me that."

"Yeah, I did, brah! You don't listen."

"Well, you talk so much . . ."

"Quiet! I'm talkin' here! I told you, she wants me to find a different job."

"Not that part! Did she call me a meathead? I'm not a meathead."

"Dude! You're fuckin' huge! You don't exactly look like a straight 'A' student."

"But I *was* a straight 'A' student. Does she think I'm dumb?"

"Bro, why do you care what my girlfriend thinks? You're not bangin' her. I'm sure Adam's hot for your brain and all. It can't be for that face."

I jumped in. "I am hot for his brain." Greg blinked at me a few times. "I mean . . . the package is nice, too. By 'package' I don't mean . . . you know . . . his *package*, I mean . . . the *whole* package of . . . well, you know what I mean. He's hot in every way."

"Dude, please stop. I listen to him talk about you that way all the fuckin' time. I can't take any more."

"Oh. Sorry."

Sam grinned and grabbed his friend from behind in a rough hug. "You see, bro! That's what I'm talking about! That's what love sounds like."

"Shit, man! Leggo o' me before I barf!" He tried to wrestle himself out of Sam's arms.

Sam pulled up the front of Greg's shirt and slapped his hairy belly a few times. "You feelin' sick, dude? Maybe you eat too much. You need to lose some of this puppy fat." He smacked Greg's perfectly respectable abs again. This could have been the opening scene of a gay porn video. A really good one.

Greg managed to slip out of Sam's grip, but with his shirt turned inside out over his head. I was getting an eyeful of Greg. *I should visit Sam at work more often!* He pulled his shirt down and immediately resumed bobbing and weaving around Sam with his fists up. "You think you can take me, bro? I can kick your ass any day, but I don't want to embarrass you in front of your boyfriend." Sam playfully swatted at him.

Greg was amusing. I wouldn't want to spend too much time with him, but I understood why Sam enjoyed his company. "Please don't damage Sam's face. I like it the way it is."

Greg stopped jumping. "Dude! That's unbelievable." Sam smiled. He knew how handsome he was.

"Could I talk to Sam alone for a few minutes?"

"Sure, bro. You want some privacy to kiss and stuff. I'll stay here and do all the work, as usual."

"Yeah, right!" Sam followed me.

"That was fun."

"Do you know you have a huge boner?"

I looked down. "Shit! Do you think he saw it?"

"How could he miss it? It has its own shadow."

"Dammit! Why didn't you tell me?"

"Like, how? Why are you popping wood anyway?"

"Are you kidding? After all that flexing, and wrestling, and . . . whatever."

He didn't get it. "We were horsing around. We do that all the time. I could help you with that problem down there."

"I didn't come here for that . . . now I can't even think straight." After a few deep breaths, my head cleared. "I'm buying groceries for the weekend and I came to ask what you want."

"I don't want you cooking all weekend. We're supposed to have fun together."

"We will have fun. I'll buy things that don't need to be cooked." I pulled out a scrap of paper and a pen to make a list. "Meat and cheese for sandwiches, and bread."

"Roast beef, and that crusty bread. I'd like pie on my birthday."

"What kind do you like?"

"Um . . . all of them. Let's say cherry. Or maybe blueberry."

"I'll get both. I know you'll eat them."

"Could you get the stuff to make pancakes on Sunday? And bacon."

"Do you want eggs?"

"Oh, yeah. And cereal for Saturday morning since I won't have doughnuts. Don't forget milk. Chips. Cookies."

"I still can't believe you eat all this junk."

"Hey, it's my birthday. What about dinner Saturday? Do you think they have take-out food up there?"

"I wouldn't count on it. I'd like to take you to a nice restaurant, but I don't know what's in the area."

"I won't want to get dressed up anyway. I'd like to be naked most of the time." He wiggled his eyebrows.

"Would you please let this boner go down! I could make spaghetti for Saturday. That's easy."

"Ooh! With meatballs? And lots of sauce."

"I'll get frozen meatballs. Anything else?"

"Do you think we'll have enough snacks?"

"Um, chips, cookies, two pies . . ."

"There must be a grocery store there in case we run out of anything."

I looked him in the eye. "Is this one of those jokes where you're pretending to be serious and you're waiting for me to figure out you're kidding?"

"Which part?"

"Any part."

"Uh . . . I'm not . . ."

"Forget it. It's fine. Are you sure you don't have any other favorite things you'd like?"

"Spray cheese! And crackers. Oh, I forgot ice cream! We need ice cream."

"Okay, so that should . . ."

"I know this is stupid, but have you ever had those gummy worms?"

"No, but I'll find them. What about beverages?"

"Root beer. Regular."

"You don't want sugar free?" I was being sarcastic.

"Are you getting a box of wine?"

"Would that be for me or for you?"

"For you. I assume you have a separate list of food you want."

"Do you mean . . . are you thinking I won't be eating any of the food on *this* list?"

He kept a straight face for . . . one, two, three, four beats . . . then he smiled. "I'm pulling your leg."

I released a breath I didn't realize I was holding. "God dammit! Starting from where?"

"Right after the wine."

"Oh."

"You made a joke about the sugar free root beer, so I thought . . ."

"Yeah, I get it."

"I'll bring a big bottle of lube so you don't have to pack yours."

"Great. That's a load off my mind."

"You're not mad at me, are you?"

"No, but I need to go home and jack off before I go to the store, thank you very much."

"No, you don't." Sam looked in all directions. There weren't many customers around, and Dave was busy inside the store. "Hey, Greg! Cover for me!"

Greg yelled back, "Gotcha, dude! Have fun!"

"Come on. Come with me."

"Oh, no! We're not . . . no way . . . I'm leaving!"

"No, you're not." He wrapped his arm around me and all but carried me toward the storage room where Greg caught us kissing.

"Hey! You can't just pick me up and do whatever you want."

"You told me I could."

"Dammit!" I wasn't resisting, but I didn't want to get caught in an embarrassing position, especially by Dave.

Sam closed the door of the storage room and locked it.

Seven minutes later I felt as relaxed as a boiled noodle. He tucked in my shirt, made sure I was presentable, and patted my ass as he sent me off to the grocery store.

I waved goodbye to Greg who shouted, "Lookin' good, bro! It's like you're glowing or . . . ack!"

Sam wrapped his arm around Greg's neck and gave him a noogie.

***

I left work a little early on Friday so I could pack up the food we were taking to the lake house. I had my clothes and toiletries in an overnight bag, and a few wrapped birthday gifts. Sam also left work earlier than usual and got home as I was filling the cooler. He went up to his apartment to get his things and came back to the house. "Holy mother of God! Why are you dressed like that?" He wore an old t-shirt and gray fleece shorts that were tight enough to risk a charge of public indecency.

He smiled and stroked his chest. "I was getting rid of these, but I thought you might like the way I look in them."

"Oh, I like the way you look, but . . . I guess we'll be in the truck. No one else will see you. Did you pack a bag with your other stuff?" He held up a small plastic grocery bag. "What's in there?"

"My swimsuit, my toothbrush and my bottle of lube."

"That's it?"

"What else do I need?"

"Um . . . more clothes, maybe? What if you tear those? What would you wear on the way home?"

"I'll wear my birthday suit." He tried to keep a straight face, but he cracked into a grin. He loved his dumb jokes.

"I walked right into that, didn't I?"

"Yeah, you did. My bag is on the porch."

"But you're still wearing that outfit?"

"Do you want me to change?"

"No, but if I run off the road because I'm distracted, it'll be your fault."

"I can live with that. Are we eating before we leave? I'm hungry."

"What a surprise. Let's stop at a drive-through and get burgers to eat in the car."

"Sounds good. I'll take this stuff out to the truck."

It took about an hour and a half to get to the lake. Sam happily chattered away about all kinds of things while eating two large burgers, fries, and a chocolate malt. I grew tired of listening to most people after about fifteen minutes, but not Sam. His conversation never wore me out, but my truck seemed too small to contain his energy, and the longer he was confined in it, the more energy he seemed to have. When we arrived at the lake house, he jumped out like a spring-loaded snake in a trick can of nuts.

"Wow, this is beautiful! Come and look." It was a handsome Arts and Crafts style house with a full-length open porch facing the lake. The property was surrounded by woods and it was far enough from the access road to provide complete privacy. I followed Sam down to the shore where we stood on the pier and looked across the water. The sun was about to set, so the sky was streaked with shades of pink and orange. He stood behind me with his hands on my shoulders and his chin on the crown of my head. "Thank you for bringing me here, Adam."

"You should thank Flora. It's her house."

"No, I'm thanking you." He put his arms around my waist. "Every time I think I'm as happy as I could possibly be, you make me a little happier."

"Well, it's nothing compared to what you've . . ."

"Adam . . ."

"What?"

"Just say, 'You're welcome.'"

"Oh. Okay." I let my brain settle down. "You're welcome, Sam." I stroked the hair on his forearm while we watched more colors crowd into the sky.

We unloaded the truck and explored the house, checking out the master bedroom and the shower, and then talked about what we should do. "We could build a fire in the pit outside and make s'mores and talk. Maybe a little kissing and a little cuddling. We could do more if you want, but . . ."

"Sounds perfect, I'd love that. What's a samoor?"

"A s'more? You've never had a s'more?"

"No, is it food?"

"Yeah. I can't believe I get to introduce you to s'mores. You'll like them so much, you'll want s'more. Get it? Some more? S'mores?"

"Oh, that sounds like one of my jokes. Do you want me to start the fire?"

"Sure, I'll get the stuff we need."

There was an ample supply of dry firewood stacked on one side of the house. Soon we were sitting at the fire pit, watching the flames. Sam had never toasted a marshmallow. I loved to show him new things, but it also made me more curious about his childhood. "What did you do for fun when you were a kid?"

"Fun? Um . . . let me think. There was so much work to do on the farm. When I was little I liked to chase the chickens around, but my mother made me stop. My dad took me fishing a couple of times, and he taught me how to play chess. Uh . . . I liked to make things out of sticks and scraps of wood."

"How about with other kids? Did you play any games?"

"There weren't any other kids near us. The only place I ever saw them was at church. We couldn't do much there, especially in our good clothes."

The marshmallows I was toasting reached a perfect shade of golden brown. "What about at school?"

"I didn't go to school until I was fourteen. My parents taught me at home, then my dad wanted me to go to the high school in town. My mom was against it, but my dad got his way."

I carefully deposited a hot marshmallow onto a graham cracker with a square of chocolate, topped it with another cracker, and handed it to Sam. "That's a s'more. It'll be messy, but it's worth it."

He bit into it, catching the pieces of cracker that broke off. I watched his expression. By the time he swallowed the first bite, I knew he would be eating a lot of them. "Oh, that's good! Is this a well-known thing?"

"Yeah, a lot of people eat them in the summer, especially when there's a fire like this. I was surprised you never heard of them. But I guess you wouldn't if you didn't . . . you never had a . . ." I wanted to say he didn't have a "normal" childhood, but it sounded rude. I shoved a s'more in my face. "Mmm, I haven't had one of these for years." I chewed and swallowed. "It must have been hard for you to go to school for the first time at fourteen. That's such a difficult age for most kids."

He nodded while eating and licking his fingers. "Yeah, it was hard. I didn't know any of the other kids. I never used a computer or a cell phone, and everyone had those things. I never watched television or saw a movie. I felt like I was visiting from the stone age. And my clothes were embarrassing. That's why I'm fussy about what I wear now. A lot of the kids lived on farms, but at least they had decent jeans and athletic shoes. I had bib overalls and white t-shirts and work boots. And flannel shirts for the winter."

I felt bad for him. "I bet you wished your father didn't make you go to that school."

"At first I did, but later I appreciated it. He knew I needed to learn about things beyond the farm, and people who weren't in our church, and everything else. He also wanted me to be prepared for my purpose in the world."

"Your purpose? What purpose?"

"He wanted me to enlist in the military. This was right after the September 11th attacks, so he thought it was my destiny to fight terrorists. Muslim terrorists, specifically. The enemies of Christianity. It all started with my weird strength. Everything after that was my parents trying to make sense of it."

I handed him a stick with two marshmallows on the end. "Try toasting these. Don't get too close or they'll catch on fire." He followed my example. "So, when did you realize you were so strong? That must have been pretty amazing."

"Amazing? Not really. My dad noticed it when I was helping him with chores. I wouldn't have known there was anything strange about it. I copied what he did, and I was lifting things that should have been too heavy for a kid my age. He didn't say anything at first, but I knew something was off. My mother . . . well, she was never very affectionate . . . but she looked at me like I was a stranger. There was a lot of whispering between them. I knew it was about me, but I couldn't figure out what I did wrong."

"They didn't talk to you about it?"

"No, not for a long time. Your parents knew you were gay, but they never talked to you about it. Maybe all parents are like that." I noticed his marshmallows were getting black, but before I could say anything, they burst into flame. "Oh, shit!"

"That happens all the time." He blew on them until the marshmallows were merely smoking. I volunteered to eat them. "I like the burnt ones."

"No, I'll eat them."

"Let them cool off first."

"They're cool enough." I held up my hand to stop him, but he closed his mouth over the blackened blob. Predictably, his eyes bugged out. He jumped up and ran into the house. I don't know why I still bothered to warn Sam about anything he put in his mouth. He never listened.

He returned a few minutes later with a cold bottle of root beer and a glass of wine. "I brought you a beverage."

"Oh, is that why you went in the house?"

"Do you want it or not?" I took it with a smile and he sat closer to me than before. "Why didn't you warn me how hot those were?"

"I'm mean."

"I know you are." He reached for the bag of marshmallows.

"Do you want me to toast them for you?"

"No, I can do it. If I can toast bread, I can toast these."

"Your toaster toasts your bread."

"Just let me! I've got it!"

"Okay," I said doubtfully. Then my marshmallows burst into flame. "Dammit!" We laughed at ourselves and were quiet for a while.

"You never asked about my childhood before."

"I know. I should have. I can be . . . self-centered." He didn't disagree. "When did your parents finally talk to you about your strength?"

"I started to misbehave. I argued with them, didn't do what I was told. I lost my temper a few times and . . . damaged things . . ." He trailed off.

"What kind of damage?"

He cleared his throat. "The kind of damage normal people can't do. It was bad. Expensive."

I put my hand on his arm. "You were a confused kid."

"I know. I mean, I understand it now, but I was a mess then. It felt like they shut me out. They were my entire world, and they shut me out and didn't tell me why."

"But eventually they talked to you about it."

"Yeah. They told me I wasn't like other kids, that I should keep it hidden and be careful. That's when they changed my name to Samson, which was even more confusing."

"It wasn't your original name? I thought it seemed like too much of a coincidence."

"I was called Micah when I was baptized. They had our pastor change my name to Samson in the church record. And they went to the county courthouse to make it official. That's what they called me from then on."

"So they were trying to make sense of why their kid had this gift?"

"Well, it was either a gift or a bad omen. It could have gone either way. That's why my mom was so distant. I think she was afraid of me."

"This is my bias against religion, but it seems like anything different from the norm is automatically bad."

"Yeah, unless it's a special gift from God. If you believe the Bible has all the answers, and you look in the Bible for something about supernatural strength, what do you find?"

"Oh . . . Samson. I see."

Sam had mastered the art of toasting marshmallows and ate s'mores as fast as he could make them. I reached my limit after three. I thought about how his parents had handled things. "Maybe they were trying to protect you by naming you Samson."

"How would it protect me?"

"Well . . . if anyone found out about your strength, or if you got into trouble because of it, you would automatically be associated with a biblical hero who was super strong. That's a lot better than what people might think on their own."

"Huh." He stared into the fire. "That's interesting. It fits with some of the things my dad told me before I went to high school. He said people wouldn't understand it if they knew, and it was better to keep it hidden. He didn't want me to get involved in sports. Not that I wanted to, but it would have been a way for me to fit in a little better."

"You mean the chess club wasn't your ticket to the cool kid's lunch table?"

"No. I had a couple of friends, though. It turned out okay. I had a lot to learn in a few years."

"I bet you were like a sponge, soaking it all up."

"I read everything I could get my hands on. I learned to imitate the way the other kids talked, and I faked my way through things. My grades were good. I was at the top of my class when I graduated."

"I'm not surprised. Then your parents wanted you to enlist in the military."

"Yes, because Samson was a warrior. He supposedly killed a thousand men using only the jawbone of a donkey."

"I remember that. The Philistines, right? And he pulled down their temple and killed everyone in it."

"Yep, that's Samson. He kills, and he kills, and he kills. That wasn't me at all. I didn't like seeing our animals slaughtered, so the idea of killing other people, even in self-defense . . . I wasn't interested."

"What did you want to do?"

"I could have been happy as a farmer. I never thought about anything else. I wouldn't get married and have kids like everyone would have expected. There was a boy I liked. He liked me, too, but . . ." He shook his head.

"It didn't work out."

"That would be an understatement. Someone from our church saw us together in the corn field. We weren't having sex, but we were headed in that direction. When we were called out, my friend claimed I forced him into it. I didn't deny my feelings for him, so . . . after carefully hiding my strength for all those years, that wasn't what made me an outcast. It was because I had a crush on a boy. My parents were devastated."

"I bet they were. Parents feel guilty when their kids don't turn out the way they expect. They wonder if they did something wrong, if they should try to change you, or accept you . . ."

"My parents were definitely on the side of changing me. We argued about it for a year. The longer it went on, the more I knew I couldn't stay there. So I left, and I ended up here." He carefully squeezed a hot marshmallow between two crackers and watched it change shape.

"That's quite a story, Sam. I should have asked you sooner."

He shrugged. "I'm not sure I would have told it until now. I never told anyone before. You're the only one."

It took a minute for that to sink in. *He trusts me.* I felt something physical in my chest . . . not a bad feeling, but not entirely pleasant. It was a responsibility, like he had given me something very important to hold on to. *He trusts you. Don't fuck this up.*

The fire had disappeared into glowing embers. "What do you think about your strength now? Why do you think you have it?"

"Hell if I know. Do you have any theories?"

I shrugged. "I don't know. I suppose it's as pointless as asking why my parents died when they did."

"Exactly. We look for meaning in things that are probably random. Maybe we don't have any purpose in life. Shit happens, and we need to roll with it."

"Unless you're here to . . ." I stopped myself. "No, I shouldn't say that. It's not right." I looked at the ground, embarrassed I even had the thought.

"What? I want to hear it. I don't care if it's not right."

Reluctantly, I said, "Maybe your purpose in life is to save me. Maybe you're my hero." I looked up. "I mean you are. You are my hero." I waited for him to make a joke, but he didn't.

He moved closer, put his arm around my waist and pressed his lips against my neck for a long moment. "It's the best theory I've heard so far. I'd be happy to live for that purpose." He rested his chin on my head.

My throat felt tight. "You wouldn't have anything better to do?"

"Not that I can think of. Besides, I need someone to save me, too. You already saved me. Everything I have now came through you, so . . . you're my hero, too."

I sniffled. "I'm no hero. I don't have any superpowers."

"What about controlling things? Or maybe your powers will pop up later, when they're needed."

"I suppose it could happen. Maybe I'll develop the power to keep you from putting hot things in your mouth."

He sat up. "*That* would be your superpower? Are you kidding?"

"Well . . . I wouldn't want anything flashy. And there's a need for it."

"Of all the possible superpowers . . ."

I raised my head. "I don't have time to save the world. I have enough chores to do. I wouldn't look good in spandex anyway."

He reached for the last two marshmallows and put one in his mouth, untoasted. "I think you would look great in spandex."

"Not as good as you. I would be your sidekick." I slid my hand over his thigh. "That reminds me, I wanted to give you one of your birthday presents tonight."

"I get more than one? Adam, I didn't want you to spend that much."

"I didn't spend much." *I spent more than I planned.* "Stop worrying about it. Should we go inside?"

"Might as well, we're out of marshmallows." He popped the last one in his mouth. "I'll get water from the lake to put out the fire." He stood up and walked into the darkness toward the water.

I looked at the sky, marveling at the number of stars visible outside the city. The crickets chirped loudly, and a bird repeated a lonesome call. *I hope I can sleep with all this racket.* The woods looked different at night. I wondered if anything was watching me. I scanned the darkness for sets of eyes. I was about to call Sam's name until I saw him returning.

He drizzled water from his root beer bottle over the fire pit until all the glowing embers were extinguished. "It's pretty out here at night, isn't it?"

"Uh huh." *Sort of.*

"Do you hear the whippoorwill?"

"Is that what it is?" *The bird that won't shut up.*

"Yeah, I used to fall asleep to that sound every night. I love it."

"Oh, that's nice." *Sounds like an alarm clock to me.* "Do you think there are any animals in these woods?"

"Of course. Lots of them."

"Let's get to your birthday present." I walked a little too briskly toward the house.

"Adam . . . you're not afraid out here, are you?"

"No! Pffft! Are you kidding?" *Yes, I'm afraid.* "I'm excited to give you your gift." As soon as we were inside, I locked the door.

Sam gave me a funny look. "You know animals can't turn doorknobs, right?"

"Who said anything about animals? I thought . . . you know . . . in case some serial killer escapes from prison."

"I hate it when that happens." He wrapped his arms around me in a tight hug. "I'll protect you."

"I know." I pretended it didn't mean as much to me as it did. I retrieved his smallest present from its hiding place. "Let's go upstairs and open this in the bedroom."

"Is it *that* kind of present?" He followed me up the stairs.

I smiled. "I don't know what you mean." We sat on the end of the bed and I handed him the gift bag.

"What is it?"

"You're supposed to open it to find out."

He removed the tissue paper, then reached into the bag and pulled out six brightly colored boxer briefs with the name of a popular designer printed on the waistband. "Underwear. *Fancy* underwear! Wow! I never had colored underwear before. They're so bright." Each one was a different vibrant color. "Won't I look silly in these?"

"Silly?! No! You'll look gorgeous in these, like you do in your swimsuit. Try one on. I want to see how they fit." He stood up and wriggled out of his tight shorts and well-worn white briefs. "Take off your t-shirt, too."

He grabbed the hem and stretched it over his elbows. The seam on one side split before he got it off. "It's time to get rid of this."

I took the shirt from him and pressed it against my face, inhaling his scent. "I'll hang onto it. For a dust rag." Sam rolled his eyes. I smelled it again.

"Which color do you want me to try on? How about this pink one?"

"It's magenta. Yeah, try that one."

"Magenta. Okay. This isn't the kind of underwear my mom bought for me." He stepped into the briefs and pulled them up his long, tanned legs. The fabric spread over the twin globes of his ass like a coat of bright paint. He adjusted himself in the front pouch, filling all the available space. He turned toward me. "How do they look?"

"Amazing. Better than I imagined, and believe me, I spent a lot of time imagining. Let me see the back."

He twisted his torso to look over his shoulder. "Does this color make my ass look even fatter?"

"It's not fat. How many times do we have to go over this? You have a perfect, muscular butt." I touched it gently and felt how firm it was. He tightened his glutes. "You even have dimples here on the sides." I pressed my finger into the indent.

"It sticks out more than it used to. I feel like I'm being followed."

"You probably are being followed . . . by people looking at your ass. Come over to the mirror. That color looks great on you."

He stood in front of the mirror, turning slightly from side to side. "I like these. Thank you, Adam."

"You're like . . . the best underwear model ever."

"This isn't the way I picture myself in my head."

"How do you picture yourself?"

"Smaller, thinner. It feels wrong to look at myself like this."

"Wrong? Why?"

"It's prideful. That's why I didn't want to compare myself to Greg yesterday."

"He's certainly not humble. Why shouldn't you be proud? You have an amazing body."

"It's okay for you to say that." He briefly rubbed his thighs, then turned to the side and curled one of his arms to flex the biceps briefly. "I have to admit, I like the way people look at me."

"Don't get too full of yourself. One of the sexiest things about you is that you don't believe you're this sexy."

"I could say the same about you. Let me undress you." He pulled my t-shirt over my head and tossed it onto the bed. He ran his hands over my chest and down my sides. I passively watched his face while he felt me up. "You used to freak out when I touched you like this."

"I did, didn't I? Now I love it."

He unbuttoned my shorts and helped me step out of them. He stroked my legs and squeezed my butt. Without asking, he took me in his arms, carried me the short distance to the bed, and laid me on the side I preferred. He slowly stripped off his new briefs, turned off the light, and lay beside me with his hands behind his head.

It was a warm night, so we left a window open. The crickets chirped, and the whippoorwill called. I imagined a younger version of Sam, on the farm, lying alone in his room at night. I remembered lying alone in my room when I was young.

I turned to look at him. "Have you thought about going home to see your parents? You must think about it sometimes."

"Going home?" He stared up at the ceiling. "I don't know." He was quiet for a few moments. "Home." He took a slow, deep breath and let out a long sigh.

I searched his face. "What are you thinking?"

He turned his head. "I never thought about it until you asked me." He rolled onto his side and gently caressed my body. His eyes glistened. "You're my home now."

My chest rose and fell. I felt the weight of his hand over my heart.

25

The next morning, I woke up before Sam, so I spent a few minutes looking at him. After months of sleeping together, I still found it hard to believe a guy who looked like *that* was in bed with *me*. But there he was. I started to kiss him awake . . . very, very slowly . . . everywhere and everything, at least once. Long before he stirred or opened his eyes I saw the smile on his lips. I continued my work, adding a few gentle bites. Eventually he laughed and pinned me to the bed with his leg across my thighs. His floppy cock climbed up my hip. "What time is it?"

"I don't know. Morning."

"Okay." He ran his fingers through his hair. "Would you like to have sex with a twenty-one-year old?"

"That would be a nice change from the twenty-year-old I've been sleeping with. I was getting bored with him."

"Bored, huh? Maybe someone a little more mature can keep you entertained."

"I bet you're right. Happy birthday."

"Thank you." He looked down at his full erection. "Shall we begin?"

***

After the morning's entertainment, we showered together, and Sam decided to shave before breakfast. He was worried he would rub my skin raw by the end of the day if he didn't remove his stubble. I got dressed and went to the kitchen to make coffee and put out the breakfast cereal Sam wanted. He came down the stairs wearing only his new magenta briefs. "Do you mind if I keep my clothing to a minimum today? I like the way these fit."

"I bought them so I could see you in them. They were a gift for me." I winked.

"Mmm, Crunch Berries!" He sat down at the table and poured himself a big bowl of the sugary cereal, added milk, and studied the box while he ate. "Who is this crunch captain, and how can he be in the navy *and* the cereal business?"

"Those are excellent questions. You're right to be suspicious of him."

He shoveled a spoonful of the breakfast junk food into his mouth and chewed in the noisy, open-mouthed way that was inexplicably sexy. "Why are you wearing a shirt? Are you cold?"

"No. I always put on a shirt in the morning."

"It's my birthday. Take it off."

I liked it when Sam pretended to be bossy. "As you wish, your highness." I took off my shirt. "Anything else?"

"Yeah, the shorts, too." He nodded and chewed.

"Are you sure?" I unbuttoned my shorts and waited. "I'm not wearing undies."

"Really? That's not like you. But . . . too bad. Take 'em off."

I slowly unzipped the fly, revealing my red Speedo, and dropped the shorts.

"Ah ha! A trick!" He grinned. "You know what I like."

"I thought we would go in the lake today."

"Definitely, but do we need our swimsuits? This place is very private."

"Aren't there fish in the lake?"

"Yeah. So?"

"Is it safe to be . . . dangling in the water?"

He paused. "You think a fish will chomp on your wiener?" He covered his mouth with the back of his hand.

"Well . . . wouldn't it look like a fat juicy worm?" Sam laughed. "It makes sense to me!" He shook his head. "Shut up! Not everyone grew up on a farm, you know!"

"We didn't have a lake on the farm!" He laughed harder. "You're too funny, I can't stand it." I thought he would fall off his chair, but he recovered. "You are the expert when it comes to worrying about things. Sit down and have some cereal."

"I don't know if I can eat that stuff. It's nothing but sugar."

"That's not true." He grabbed the box and looked at the ingredients. "Corn flour, sugar, oat flour, brown sugar . . ." He stopped there. "See . . . it's good for you. Try it."

I set my coffee on the table and got a cereal bowl from the cabinet. He filled it and added milk. I ate the Crunch Berries, and they were good. I knew it wasn't health food, but so what? With Sam's help, I had gained the weight Dr. Rubin ordered me to gain, and I was in the best shape I had been in for a long time. The added stamina and flexibility would come in handy as the day went on. Sam's appetite for sex matched his appetite for food. When we weren't doing it, I knew he was thinking about it. It felt good to be wanted as much as I wanted him.

When he was finished with breakfast, I asked him to go back to the bedroom so I could give him the rest of his birthday presents. I brought him another gift bag and a wrapped box. The bag contained three polo shirts in different colors, one of which was a shade of green that drew attention to his pretty eyes. At the bottom of the bag was a pair of dark denim jeans. I congratulated myself on getting a pair that fit him so well. The soft denim hugged his thighs and butt without being too loose at the waist. He looked so good, I had an argument in my head about whether he looked better naked or clothed.

I wasn't sure if he would like the clothes in the box. I bought him a pair of gray wool-blend dress slacks, a high-quality ivory dress shirt, and a classic silk tie, extra-long, with blue, green and yellow stripes. He opened the box. "We can return these if you don't like them. They would need to be tailored to fit you better anyway." He put on the shirt while I babbled. "They probably won't look good on you now but try them on and we can take them back to the store next weekend."

He put on the pants. "We're not taking them back. They're beautiful."

"You like them? I was afraid maybe you wouldn't want . . . here, let me pull this back." I gathered the excess fabric around his waist and tucked it into the back of the slacks. "The tailor will remove some of this so it fits your body better."

"I don't know how to put on a tie. Can you show me?"

"Sure, or I can do it for you and teach you later. It takes a while to get the hang of it." He stood still while I put the tie around his neck and concentrated on making the knot in reverse. He sniffled, and I knew what was coming.

"You're too good to me, Adam. I don't deserve all these . . ."

"Shh, shh, don't start . . ."

"No, it's true, but I'll work harder to make more money . . ."

"You already work hard, and I don't care how much money you make. You don't have to earn anything from me."

"But . . ."

I put my fingers over his mouth. "No buts. You're everything I want you to be and more. Okay?" There were tears in his eyes, but he nodded and kept quiet. I finished tying the tie and pushed the knot up to his throat. "Okay, go look in the mirror if you can stand it. You're so fucking handsome." I thought about what it would be like to go out in public with him dressed up like that. I would be proud to be seen with him, but I wondered if I could handle the attention he would get. If I were wearing nothing but my speedo, as I was then, I might get a few looks as well.

He stood in front of the mirror, gently adjusting his tie and smoothing the shirt with his hands. "I never thought I would have clothes as nice as these. Where would I wear this?"

"To a nice restaurant, or if we went to a concert or a play. Or you can wear it for me at home, and I'll sit and stare at you." He turned around and smiled. He was truly breathtaking. "I can't wait until Donna sees this."

"Why?"

"Because she'll be speechless, for once."

He opened his arms and pulled me into a tight hug. It felt wonderful and reminded me of the first time he did that, months ago, when it still made me uncomfortable. This time he held me so long, it seemed like he wouldn't let me go.

"Adam, I know you want to go swimming, but . . . could we . . ."

"Yes, please." I removed his tie while he carefully unbuttoned his new shirt. I took it from him and laid it on a chair. He did the same with his new pants, then scooped me up and took me back to bed.

What we did together wasn't sex, technically, but it was sexy. We held each other and kissed. He wrapped his arms and legs around me repeatedly, holding me motionless for long minutes, as if trying to join my body with his. We communicated without speaking, foreheads together, eye to eye. We were indescribably vulnerable to each other. I can't explain it, but I know it was real. It was the most intimate connection I ever felt with him.

We lay in each other's arms for a long while until we agreed to get some fresh air. For a few more minutes, I played with the fine, straight hair on his chest. "You're getting furrier."

"I know. Do you want me to shave?"

"No, I like it."

"Okay, it stays."

He was so eager to please me, it worried me sometimes. "Could you start wearing shirts with the top three buttons open, and a gold medallion around your neck?"

"No, that won't happen."

"Good. That was a test."

"I thought so." He rubbed the sparse hair on my chest. "You, on the other hand, would rock that gold medallion."

"We should get out of bed now."

"Already?"

"What's the point of being at a lake house if we don't use the lake?"

"I know. You're right."

"Of course I'm right."

"Here we go. Come on."

Sam put away his new clothes and put on his sexy yellow swimsuit. It was such a warm, sunny day I felt guilty for spending so much time in the bedroom. We walked to the shore and gazed across the water. There were other houses on the opposite shore and a distant sailboat. White birds swooped down and skimmed along the water. It was a beautiful place, very quiet, and very relaxing. Sam turned to me. "I'm taking off my swimsuit."

"Are you sure?"

"Yeah, I'm sure." He pulled the front waistband away from his body and looked inside. "I suppose the fish will go crazy for this."

"Don't say that!"

He shook his head and laughed. "You are one of a kind, Adam." He stuck his thumbs into the sides of his swimsuit and slid them down. My eyes were glued to his beautiful, pale rump. There's something about an untanned area of skin that makes it extra sexy, as if his ass needed any help with that. He threw his swimsuit onto the grass. "Are you taking yours off?"

"No way. It's . . . indecent."

"You think this is indecent?" He turned and wiggled his butt at me.

"Let me get a closer look." I lunged toward him, but he ran into the water until it was deep enough for him to swim. I was close behind and, being a better swimmer, I caught up with him easily and tried to grab his ass. We wrestled in the water, laughing and splashing until he suddenly looked serious and plunged his hands below the surface. "What? What's wrong?"

"Oh my God! I think a fish bit off my dick!"

"All right, that's it!" I jumped on him and pushed him under the water. He retaliated by launching me into the air with one hand. I hung there for a split second before splashing down like a cannonball. When I surfaced, I coughed and spit until I found his grinning face. "You fucker!"

"Yeah, I'm pretty strong, huh?"

"Can you do that again?"

"Sure, easily. Get your butt over here." I grabbed his head and kissed him on the lips, hard. He was pleased with himself. "Do you want to go higher this time? You want to go to the moon?" He tossed me in the air until I was worn out. He wasn't. He had tons of energy. I paddled around aimlessly while he swam so far out into the lake it worried me. He turned and swam back to find me sitting on the wooden pier, enjoying the sun.

Sam climbed onto the pier and turned to look at the lake. He stretched his body with his arms over his head, then spread them wide as if he would embrace the entire world. In the sunlight, with the warm breeze coming off the lake, my naked lover stood with his arms extended, looking like a young god. The image is burned into my memory as one of the peak experiences of that miraculous summer.

We lay in the sun on the pier for a while, then slipped back into the lake for another swim. Half the time I was in his arms, kissing him, with my legs wrapped around his waist. A cool breeze drew our attention to a dark cloud passing overhead and we decided to go back inside. By the time Sam grabbed his swimsuit, big drops of rain started to fall. He raised his face to the sky.

I was startled by a loud crack of lightning. "Come on, let's go!"

"Why? We're already wet." With a long rumble of thunder, heavy rain began to fall. He grabbed my hand and led me away from the shore. "Let's do it on the grass."

"Do what?"

"Sex. Let's have sex in the rain."

"You can't be serious. We could get struck by lightning out here!" I had to speak louder to be heard above the pelting rain.

He shrugged. "The danger makes it better. Come on! Please?"

I still don't know why I gave in so easily, but I let him take me. Astounded by my own behavior, I stretched my arms over the grass and watched him focus all his energy on me, biting his lower lip, his dark hair dripping over his brow. It didn't take him long to finish, as excited as he was. Running his hands up and down my thighs, he slowly withdrew himself from my body and fell onto the grass next to me. The downpour was reduced to a steady rain. With a contented smile, I placed my hands behind my head and opened my mouth to catch raindrops.

Sam moved closer and put his hand around my erection. "Did you like that?"

"Yeah, it was exciting. How about you?"

"It was awesome. I didn't hurt you, did I?"

"No, I'm fine." I knew I would be sore as hell the next day, but I didn't care.

"Do you want me to finish you off?"

"I don't think you'll get anything out of me after this morning, but thanks for offering."

"Adam, you're the best birthday present I'll ever get." He threw one leg over me and kissed my neck and jaw.

I chose to accept his praise. "Well, I am the master when it comes to sex. All those years of study on the internet weren't a waste of time."

"I bet you never thought you would have sex outside during a thunderstorm."

"When you're as adventurous as I am, you take these things in stride. Good thing this place is so private."

"Yeah, but I was thinking . . . wouldn't it be cool if someone across the lake had a telescope?"

Why didn't I think of that? "Um . . . cool?"

"Yeah, to have someone watching us and getting off on it." He smiled, knowing the effect this would have on me.

"Maybe we should go inside now." I tried to push him back.

"Why? The rain feels good, doesn't it?" He kept his arm around me.

"Aren't you ready for dinner? Spaghetti and meatballs, remember?" I glanced at the lake and hoped the rain would obscure the view through a telescope.

"Not yet. I'm not finished with you."

"Will you ever get enough?"

"Never." He groped me like a sex-starved teenager. I squirmed and pretended I was trying to escape. We ended up wrestling in the grass, tumbling like a couple of frisky puppies until the rain stopped and sunlight broke through the clouds. The birds chirped loudly, as if they appreciated the show.

I looked across the shimmering water again, wondering whether someone could be watching us. An unfamiliar feeling came over me. *Go ahead and look! I've got nothing to hide.*

***

Sam allowed me to put on my clothes while I made dinner. He hung around me in his underwear being his playful, annoying self, eating candy and crackers with spray cheese. "I can't believe you forgot to feed me lunch." He had a gummy worm dangling from the corner of his mouth.

I watched the worm get shorter. "We were busy indulging your other appetite, remember?"

"I know, but I'm starving to death." He flexed his abs to show how lean he was. He entertained himself by trying to get me aroused. It usually worked. He would stretch, or flex, or stroke himself seductively, waiting for my reaction. He never got tired of it. Neither did I.

I was hungry enough from our active afternoon to eat a substantial portion of spaghetti with meatballs while he polished off the rest in the same amount of time. By the time he was done and patting his taut belly, I was fired up for the next round of sex. Predictably, he insisted on washing the dishes first.

He kept rubbing up against me or flexing his arms in my face. When I tried to touch him, he pulled away. "Oh my God! Have some patience, Adam! What is wrong with you?" Then, with a sly smile, he resumed his seductive activities. I wanted to kill him for being so fucking adorable. I drummed my fingertips on the countertop as he was drying the last of the dishes as slowly as he could. He looked at me with his big, innocent eyes. "Do you want to play cards, or watch a documentary?"

"You know I want sex."

"You do? How many times have we done it today?"

I had to think. "It depends on what counts as sex."

"Haven't you had enough? Maybe we should stop for a couple of days and let you recharge."

I shook my head. "What do you plan to do with that?" I pointed at his obvious erection.

"Um . . ."

I moved toward him as he put the last plate in the cupboard. "I want you. Now."

He took a step back. "But it's my birthday. Shouldn't I get to choose? I wish I'd brought my chess board."

I kept moving toward him as he continued to back away, covering his crotch with both hands. "You can't hide it. I know you want it, too."

"I have a headache."

"No, you don't."

"I'm not in the mood."

"You're always in the mood."

"I'm feeling fragile. Could you just hold me?" The expression on his face was so perfectly silly I laughed out loud. Then I lunged at him. "Ah! Help!" He ran up the stairs, taking two at a time. I didn't bother to rush. I knew where he would be.

When I got to the bedroom, he was lying on the bed with one arm across his forehead, trying to look like a helpless, submissive victim. Without a word, I walked straight into the connected bathroom and closed the door. About a minute later he called out, "Hey! I'm waiting to be attacked here!"

"I need to pee!" It was true, I was peeing.

"Well, hurry up before I escape."

"Okay." As much as I wanted to pounce on him, I was a little nervous about what I wanted to suggest. I finished peeing, washed my hands, brushed my teeth, and opened the door. He was sitting cross-legged in the middle of the bed. "Hey, Sam, I've been thinking . . . I know you're a top, and that's fine, but . . ."

"I'm a what?"

"A top. You know . . . I'm the bottom, you're the top. Because you fuck me."

"I never said that."

"But you are. I mean, that's the way it is."

"It doesn't have to be that way. You didn't want my butt, and I love yours, so, here we are."

“I wasn't ready for it when you offered it, but that doesn't mean I don't want it.”

"Are you saying . . . you want to do that now?" He rolled to the edge of the bed and stood up, obviously excited.

"You wouldn't mind?"

"Mind? Hell no! How do you want to do this?"

"Just get yourself nice and clean. I left a rubber syringe on the counter in the bathroom."

"Do you want me to use bleach?"

"Wouldn't that burn?"

"I was joking."

"Oh. Just water then. And keep rinsing until . . ."

"Don't worry. I've watched you clean the kitchen. I know what your standards are."

"Am I that fussy?"

"Trust me . . . I'll be clean." He hurried into the bathroom and closed the door.

I prepared the bed and settled down, listening to him cheerfully singing what might have been a song if it wasn't so far out of tune. I twiddled my thumbs and tried not to think about what he was doing in there. I pictured his sexy butt, focusing on why I wanted to do this. By the time he came out of the bathroom I was semi-erect. Seeing him in all his naked glory took me the rest of the way.

He rubbed his hands together. "I've never felt so fresh and clean!" He clambered onto the bed, face down, propped on his elbows. He looked over his shoulder at his perfect ass and smiled. "Do you want me to sprinkle powdered sugar on it?"

I laughed. "Shut up!"

"I'm ready for inspection. What position do you prefer?"

"You can stay there for now." I straddled his legs and put my hands on his butt. It was warm and slightly fuzzy, so I wrapped my arms around it and hugged it, rubbing my cheek against the soft skin.

"Uh . . . that's not what I was expecting."

"Just let me do my thing. I'll love your ass in my own way."

"Okay, fine. You can even call it Mr. Buns if you want to."

"I thought you didn't like that."

"Well . . . I kind of missed it after you stopped, so . . ."

I hugged him tighter. "Mr. Buns! Where have you been? I thought I would never see you again." I kissed his fuzzy 'face.' Sam groaned. "You look so healthy! Have you been working out?"

"I didn't say you could have a whole conversation with him . . . it."

I whispered. "Don't listen to him. He thinks you're fat. I'm the only one who loves you as you are." I kissed him all over.

"Now we're getting somewhere, but you're still a lunatic."

"See, Mr. Buns?" I whispered, "He's mean to me, too. We'll have to run away together, just the two of us."

Sam whispered, "Please don't tell me I washed out my ass for this."

"All right, all right." I went back to my normal voice. "I don't know why I waited so long to do this. I love your ass every bit as much as you love mine."

"Actions speak louder than words. Come on, now." He flexed his glutes.

"Ooh! Impressive. Promise me you won't crush my dick."

He giggled. "Adam, will you please shut up and get started."

"Okay." I reached for the bottle of lube. "Ready or not, here I come."

I could say I fucked Sam, but crude sexual language doesn't fit the experience. Once we moved past the playfulness, I gave him everything I had with firm, urgent movements. Rocking, pushing, flesh on flesh . . . it left us feeling warm, tired, and emotional. We tangled and rolled until we settled into a unified shape, embracing and kissing, expressing the feelings we had been sharing throughout the day: we were in love, we were happy, and we weren't alone anymore.

***

Chirping birds and the smell of bacon eased me awake. I moved cautiously, knowing my body would ache from all the pleasure I endured the day before. There was a glass of water and my bottle of ibuprofen on the bedside table. *He's so thoughtful.* I swallowed two tablets and carefully stood up, feeling like a creaky hinge. After a quick shower, I could walk down the stairs with relatively fluid movement. Sam was standing at the stove in purple boxer briefs, flipping pancakes. He greeted me with, "Morning, Sunshine!" No one had ever called me that.

"Good morning. You're up bright and early." I stood next to him and rested one hand on his purple rump while he leaned down to give me a kiss.

"How do you feel? Did I wear you out yesterday?"

"I'm a little sore, but it was totally worth it. I suppose you're no worse for wear."

"I wouldn't say that." He hooked a thumb under the waistband of his briefs and exposed an area on his butt with a clear set of teeth marks. He covered himself and raised an eyebrow.

"That's terrible. Did something attack you last night?"

"Yeah. A male cougar." He leaned down to give me another kiss, then returned his attention to the pancakes. "I think I made enough. I hope you're hungry." I was very hungry. We sat down to eat and I stuffed myself. Sam knew how to cook breakfast.

While we washed the dishes, Sam thanked me again for everything I had done for his birthday, including my sexual performance. I secretly hoped he would brag about me to Greg. Maybe even to Dave. I liked the thought of them knowing I could satisfy a big young stud like Sam.

We had another swim in the lake before sprawling on the grass, side by side, letting the sun shine on every part of our naked bodies. I don't think I had ever felt so relaxed and comfortable with myself.

By early afternoon we started packing our things. I made sandwiches to eat in the car, and we locked up and headed home. As we drove, he talked about restoring the garden shed and I discussed the plan to get Joe's house painted. Carl and I would meet with the painting contractor that week. Flora's offer of financial assistance would make things much easier. We easily slipped into talking about simple day-to-day realities, the coordination of schedules, the chores that needed to be done around the house, our friends, our jobs, and our lives together.

During a lull in the conversation, as Sam bit into a sandwich, I blurted out what I was thinking. "I want you to move into the house, Sam. I'd like you to live with me, for real, so it would be our house."

He turned to me and swallowed. "Are you sure? I mean . . . so soon?"

"It's not that soon. How long has it been? You moved into the coach house in January, so we've been together for eight months."

"But we've only been *together* together for . . . what? Three months? I know it seems longer, but . . ."

"What difference does it make? I know it's what I want. I've never been so sure about anything in my life. I trust you, I love you . . . what else do I need to know?"

"But we're still getting to know each other."

"We know each other. There's always more to learn, but . . ."

"What if it doesn't work out? Where would I go?"

"Well . . . why would you have to go anywhere? Why wouldn't it . . . we're together almost every night."

"Almost, but not *every* night. And sometimes you stay at my place. I like having my own apartment. This is the first place I ever had that was mine."

I was irritated. "Technically, it's mine." It was a bitchy thing to say, and Sam shot me an angry look. The tone of the conversation had changed. He took a deep breath and kept quiet. I knew I was wrong, so my face felt hot. "I'm sorry, I shouldn't have said that." No response. "I know what you mean. I remember living in the apartment when I was your age. Even though my parents were right across the driveway, it was different. I felt more independent, like an adult."

"Exactly." He looked down at his hands.

We were quiet for what seemed like a long time before I spoke again. "I thought you would want to move in with me. I thought you felt the same way."

"I love you, Adam. But we're still getting to know each other."

Why does he keep saying that? Does he think I'm hiding something? What am I doing wrong? I asked for clarification. "Do you think . . . sometime in the future . . . you might want to live with me?"

"Yes, definitely. But not now, not yet. I like the way things are going. Why don't we wait until my lease ends and we'll see where we're at?"

"I can't find a new tenant in January. It's the worst time of year."

"Then we'll wait until spring, or whenever."

"You want to put it off until spring? Wow."

"Adam . . . come on. I'm not going anywhere. Are you hearing me? I'm not leaving. But I'm not ready to give up my own place."

I took a deep breath and tried to resist all the negative thoughts crowding into my head. *He doesn't feel the same way. He has other plans. He met someone else. I'm too old for him. He's out of my league. It was nice while it lasted, but . . .*

"Adam . . . what are you thinking?"

"Nothing." My eyes were getting wet. "I was thinking you're right. We shouldn't rush into anything. I shouldn't pressure you to do something you don't want."

"I *do* want it, Adam. I think about it all the time. But I'm twenty-one years old, and I'm still figuring things out. Give me time, okay?"

I sniffled. "Okay, I get it. I'm sorry."

"The offer means a lot to me. Really. I mean it."

I nodded. "I know."

I didn't know what else to say. Eventually, I reached out. He took my hand and held it while I kept my eyes on the road ahead of us.

26

After our weekend at the lake house, I launched myself back into work and spent more time on household chores. My garden was overgrown. Weeds were gaining ground in the flower beds. It wouldn't be noticed by the neighbors who walked by, but it wasn't up to my usual standards. The garden was accustomed to getting all my free time. It seemed I was being punished for shifting my priorities. Like a jealous mistress, she would not be ignored.

At work on Monday, while reviewing the accounts I supervised and making sure everything was still on schedule, I happened to be near Donna's office and thought it would be polite to stop in. She was in the middle of a phone call, so I used gestures and facial expressions to say I would come back later. Before I could leave, she told the caller she needed to deal with a crisis and would have to call back later. When she hung up, I closed her door. "You didn't have to do that. I only wanted to say hello." I sat down.

"You rarely come to my office. I figured something was up."

"No, I was stopping in to be polite." I chewed on my index finger.

"Uh huh. How was your weekend? Did you and Sam go somewhere?"

"Yeah, Flora O'Neill let us use her lake house. It was great. Beautiful place, very private. We had a lot of fun."

"You mean non-stop sex?"

"Tsk." I gave her a look. "Yeah, pretty much. Not that it's any of your business."

"Uh huh. So, free use of a private lake house, non-stop sex with your gorgeous young boyfriend . . . your life is awful, isn't it?"

"I'm not complaining. I came in here to visit. How's Kevin? How are the kids?"

"Kevin is working sixty hours a week and the kids are at home all day getting into fights and destroying the house. Things are great. Now will you tell me what's wrong?"

"Nothing is wrong! Jeez!"

"Why are you biting your nails?"

"I'm not biting my nails. I'm only biting this one." I held up my well-chewed finger. "Why are you so suspicious? You should get help for that."

"Uh huh. Do you and Sam want to come over to our place for a cookout this weekend?"

"I'm busy."

"All right then."

"I asked Sam to move in with me. Into the house."

"Oh, that's great! Congratulations."

"He said, 'No.'"

"Ah, that's why you're here."

"No it's not."

"Why did he say, 'No'?"

I looked down at the floor. "He likes having his own place. It's his first apartment. He says we're still getting to know each other and we should wait and see how things go."

"Well, that makes sense. I suppose he's never been on his own before, and it is a little too soon to . . ."

"Fine, take his side. I figured you would."

"I'm not taking sides! There are no sides. What the fuck, Adam?"

"He doesn't feel the same way I do. I knew it wouldn't last." My voice cracked. "I don't know why I let myself get suckered into this."

"Oh, boy. Here we go."

"He doesn't want to live with me. I probably drive him crazy."

"Is that what he said?"

"No. He says he loves me and wants to be with me, but he's not ready to give up his apartment."

"Obviously he's lying."

Tears came to my eyes. "Do you think so?"

"No! But that's what you're thinking!" She pulled a couple of tissues out of the box on her desk and threw them at me. "Sam loves you so much it makes me jealous of you. Can't you see that?"

"What am I doing wrong?"

"Nothing! Everything is going well. Don't try to rush things."

"But I'm almost thirty-three! I should be settled down by now."

"Oh, please don't make me slap you. Besides, he's a lot younger. He might think it's too soon to settle down."

"There's too much of an age difference."

"Stop it! Give him time to figure things out."

"That's what he wanted."

"See? Listen to him. Pay attention to the way he looks at you, and the way he treats you when you're together."

I thought about it. "I feel so good when I'm with him. I never felt like that before. What if he leaves me?"

"He won't leave you."

"You don't know that."

She was quiet for a minute. "I told you, Adam. When you first got involved with him, I told you. Love is like an arrow through the heart. It hurts like hell. But, trust me . . . it'll be worth it."

I dabbed at my eyes and wiped my nose. "I don't know why you do this to me. I come in here to say hello and you start prying into my private life . . ."

"I know, I'm sorry. Will you be okay?"

"Yeah, I'll be okay. I can take care of myself!"

"I know you can." She looked worried.

"Do you have any office gossip for me?"

"No. Henry's behavior has been suspicious, but that's nothing new."

"I have to take him out to lunch this week."

"Why?"

"I promised, to make things easier when I asked to take another vacation day. I guess he needs attention."

She rolled her eyes. "Whatever. See what you can find out about the complaints against Zipinski. I haven't heard anything lately. No one will talk to me about it."

"I'll ask him. Is that all you needed?"

"I didn't need anything."

"Then why did you keep me here all this time? I have a lot to do."

"You're such a jerk. Get out of my office."

I stood up and opened the door. "I'm going, and I'm not coming back."

"Good."

"Thanks."

"You're welcome."

***

On Tuesday after work, Carl Hanson and I met with the painting contractor at Joe's house to discuss what I was now referring to as 'our community project.' The painter, Ledell, was an eager young guy who lived in the neighborhood and was getting started in business. He wanted a project that would attract attention, so restoring one of the oldest houses on Eden Place as part of a neighborhood initiative involving skills training for at-risk youth, with sponsorship from a local business, was more than he could have hoped for. For his part, Joe was happy his financial difficulties wouldn't be the focus of attention. Carl explained that he would take full responsibility for the teenagers who would be earning community service hours. He was still in his police uniform and looked very handsome and authoritative, but that's irrelevant. Flora was putting up the money for all the paint and other materials, so we agreed Ledell would start erecting scaffolding before the end of the week. The project was getting off the ground.

As if I didn't have enough to deal with, the stupid neighborhood association meeting was scheduled for Saturday afternoon. I didn't want to go, but I wouldn't give the Weasel Woman the satisfaction of shutting me out of her evil plans. According to Flora, most of our neighbors were planning to attend, and many of them were opposed to the Weasel's agenda. Nevertheless, her fear-mongering might have won as many supporters for her attempts to cleanse the neighborhood of anything that didn't fit within her narrow world view. Besides, it would be an opportunity for me to gather volunteers for our project.

Because I would attend the meeting, I couldn't work on Saturday . . . again. Rather than deal with Henry's complaints, I decided to work on Wednesday, when Sam and I normally had our day off. He also had to make up the hours from last weekend, and he wanted to attend the meeting, so we wouldn't be spending much time together that week.

When I arrived at work on Wednesday, I was surprised to find my office occupied - by Henry and Mr. Zipinski. "Adam, I didn't expect to see you today." Henry was going through one of the drawers in my file cabinet while Zipinski sat in my desk chair.

"I decided to shift my hours around this week. Mr. Zipinski, it's good to see you. How have you been?"

"Quite well, Adam, thank you for asking. I'm only here for a brief visit. My time away from the office has been a blessing in disguise." He showed his teeth with his creepy smile. "When God closes a door, he opens a window."

Why don't you jump through that window? "Can I help you find something Henry?"

"We're looking for the Ellis file. I know you supervise the account, and some questions have come up."

"I'm not supervising Ellis. That was on your list when you divided the accounts between us." Ellis Industries was a large manufacturing firm and one of our biggest clients.

Henry's face seemed rosier than usual. "I think you're mistaken, Adam. I hope you don't mind me going through your files. I assume you have nothing to hide."

"Not at all. Go through anything you'd like, but you won't find any of the Ellis files in here." I sat down and opened my briefcase.

Zipinski looked at me rather intently. "You're looking very healthy, Adam. Has your young lady put you on a new health regimen? They do love to fuss over us, don't they?"

"I've been exercising more, and I've gained a little weight."

"From her home cooked meals, no doubt. You were probably living on canned goods before you met her, as I did when I was a bachelor."

"No, I'm a good cook. I make all my own meals."

"Good heavens! What on earth will your little missus do if she can't cook for you?"

Fortunately, Henry interrupted that awful conversation. "Ah! Here it is." He held up a file with 'Ellis' on the tab.

I was surprised, to say the least. I stood up to have a look at it as he opened it to view the contents. "I've never seen that file before. I don't know how it got into my file cabinet."

Henry made a doubtful noise. "You must have been working on it if it's in your office, Adam. There's no need to be embarrassed. I'm sure everything is in order."

"But I haven't worked on it. None of these pages have my mark on them."

"Your mark? What are you talking about?"

"I put a little mark in the corner of every document I review. One of my professors recommended it when I was in school. Here . . . let me show you." I pulled a random file out of the cabinet and showed them what I meant. On every piece of paper in the file I had the same mark - a version of my initials.

Henry seemed flustered. "I never noticed that."

Zipinski clucked his approval. "How clever of you, Adam. I knew there was a reason I hired you, apart from my friendship with your dear, departed parents."

Henry still needed to be convinced. "Even if you haven't worked on this particular file, it doesn't mean you aren't responsible for the account, Adam."

"Henry . . . I have the list of accounts I was asked to supervise."

"I know, Adam. Mr. Zipinski and I found it in your desk drawer before you arrived." He shoved a sheet of paper at me. Ellis Industries was at the top of the list.

"That's not the list you gave me. It doesn't have my mark on it."

Henry shook his head. "Adam . . . I want to believe you, but . . ."

"I kept the list in my briefcase. I have it here." I kept everything Henry sent to me since he was put in charge of the firm, and I never left any of the documents in the office. I pulled out the list and showed it to Mr. Zipinski first. The list was identical, except Ellis Industries wasn't among the accounts. Henry's initials were at the bottom, and my mark was in the corner.

Henry's ears turned red. Zipinski handed the list back to me. "This is turning into quite a detective story. I'm sure we'll get to the bottom of things. Shall we go, Henry? Adam has work to do."

Henry pointedly asked, "Why aren't you with your girlfriend today, Adam?"

"Work comes first, as you so often tell me." I put my arm across his shoulders in a collegial way. "It was the right decision to put this man in charge, Mr.

Zipinski. I've learned so much from him. Of course, no one could replace you, sir. But we've become great chums, haven't we Henry?"

He was caught off guard. "Uh, yes. Yes, we have. He's like the brother I never had."

Zipinski looked back and forth between us. "I'm happy to hear it. I knew the two of you had something in common."

I swept my arm toward the door to usher them out. "Let me know if you need any more help with that account. And don't forget about our lunch tomorrow, Henry. I'm looking forward to it."

"Great. Me too."

After they left, I closed the door, sat at my desk, and wondered what Henry was trying to get away with. I was about to call Donna when the phone rang. Donna's name was on the display. I picked up. "What?"

"Why are you here? And why is Zipinski here? Someone told me they were in your office."

"Which one of these women over here is your spy? I keep trying to figure out who . . ."

"Never mind! I want answers!"

I told her everything that had transpired between Henry, Zipinski and me. "Don't you work on the Ellis Industries accounts?"

"No, I was taken off that. I thought you knew. I was surprised because Ellis liked me. Anyway, Robert Bergdorf, our contact from Ellis, came in and met with Henry one day. Later I was told I wouldn't be working on their stuff anymore. And I wasn't the only one taken off the account."

"You should have let Robert see your boobs."

"I did, but . . ."

"You did not!"

"I didn't pull them out, but I usually show cleavage when I meet with male clients."

"What the hell is wrong with you?"

"Wake up, Adam! It's a man's world. It's not enough for a woman to be smart and competent. I use everything I've got."

"Oh . . . that's . . . "

"Shut up! I bet you hire people because of the way they look."

I thought about the hot plumber I called whenever my drains were clogged. And my auto mechanic. "Could we stick to the subject please? So Robert rejected your boobs."

"He's not into boobs. I think Henry is more his type. I assume that's why they wanted him to handle the account. I didn't mind, I have plenty of other work."

"Henry's up to something."

"Well, duh! In case you missed it, he tried to throw you under a bus."

"Yeah, I'll ask him about that at lunch tomorrow."

"What? You would still go to lunch with that fucking snake? When will you learn, Adam?"

"I have to work with him, Donna! I'm better off staying close to him. Besides, I think Zipinski is starting to see through Henry."

"Don't bet on it. They're two of a kind."

"Don't worry, I'll undo a few buttons on my shirt tomorrow and Henry will tell me everything."

"Yeah, right. Why aren't you at home with Sam today?"

"He had to work, and I can't work on Saturday. The Weasel Woman scheduled a neighborhood association meeting that day."

"Ooh, can I come? I have a few things to say to her."

"No, you'll get arrested."

"That's true, and I promised Kevin I would make it through the year without going to jail."

"That's the second time I've heard about you going to jail. What have you done that would get you . . ."

"Oops, I have a client on the other line. Gotta go." She hung up.

I stared at the phone. *Dammit!*

***

At dinner that night I told Sam what happened at the office, maintaining full disclosure about all things related to Henry. He was surprised by my attitude about it.

"You don't sound worried, Adam. Henry is trying to get you in trouble."

"But for what? I don't know if there's anything wrong with the Ellis account. Apparently questions were raised."

"Whatever it is, he tried to dump it on you."

"Yeah, I was there. But I had my ass covered, and Zipinski saw what Henry was doing, so he can't pin it on me. I'll ask Henry about it tomorrow when we go to lunch."

"And I suppose he'll confess everything." He stabbed a pork chop like he was practicing for something else. "Wait . . . you're going to lunch with him again?"

"Don't start with me. I told you, like I told Donna, I have to work with Henry. It's part of my job. I know he's not my friend."

"It's worse than that. He's your enemy. You can't believe anything he says."

"I know, I'm not an idiot. I don't know why you get so worked up about Henry. You never even met him."

Sam continued eating with a sullen expression.

"What's wrong with you? Did you have a rough day at work?"

"No, it was fine."

I didn't believe him. "How's Greg? Is his girlfriend still nagging him about finding a new job?"

"Yeah, I guess. He pretends he's looking, but he's not. He might go back to school in the fall."

"Was he in school last year?"

"Yeah, but he partied too much and didn't do well, so he'd have to go to the community college."

"What does he want to study?"

"He doesn't know what he wants to do."

I watched Sam for a couple of minutes, trying to figure out what was wrong. "Are you afraid he'll go away and you won't see him anymore?"

He looked up with a strange expression. "No. I don't care what he does. It's his life."

"But he's your friend. Wouldn't you miss him?"

"I don't know . . . maybe. He's pretty annoying sometimes. Why are you so interested in Greg?"

"I'm not. I'm wondering why you seem different today. Did the two of you get in an argument?"

"No!" He was exasperated. "Adam . . . look, I'm sorry, I'm in a bad mood. I didn't mean to be, but I am. Okay?"

"I've never seen you in a bad mood, except when you're mad at me."

He shrugged. "I have bad moods, like everyone else. And I'm not mad at you."

"That's good to know. Do you want ice cream for dessert?"

"Yeah, sure."

"I guess you're okay, then. If you didn't want dessert, I would worry about you." I stood up, but he stopped me.

"You don't have to wait on me, I can get it." He picked up some of the dishes. "Do you want anything?"

I sat down again. "I'll have some of your ice cream, if you don't mind sharing."

"Fine with me." He opened the freezer and called out, "Is Pistachio okay?"

"Yeah, that's great."

He came back to the table and tested the ice cream to see if it was soft enough. He scooped out a spoonful and fed it to me, then took a scoop for himself. "Adam, how did you decide what you wanted to study when you went to college? Did you know you would like accounting?"

"I didn't decide based on what I would like. If I had, I would have done what you're doing."

He made a face. "Working for Dave?"

"Maybe. Or starting my own place. Gardening was what I enjoyed the most."

"You wouldn't have made a very good living."

"Yeah, well . . . that's why I chose accounting. I knew I would be good at, and I could make a decent salary. I didn't follow my heart. I made a practical decision."

He fed me more ice cream. "Do you enjoy accounting, or do you hate it?"

"I don't hate it. I like to work on problems with clear solutions. If the numbers add up, I know it's right. It's usually black and white, there aren't many gray areas, so I feel like everything is in order and under control."

He nodded and swallowed another spoonful. "I wish I could feel like that."

I was surprised Sam felt out of control in any way. He seemed so calm and content most of the time. "Control is overrated. That's why I see a shrink, remember?"

"Is it?" He smiled. "I thought it was about Mr. Buns."

"No, but we'll get to that someday."

"Are you learning to follow your heart?"

I think he knew the answer, but he had to ask, and to hear me say it, even though it brought tears to my eyes. "Yeah. I'm learning to follow my heart."

When he looked up, I saw the emotion in his eyes as well. "Doesn't it scare you?"

"Yeah, it scares me."

"Then why are you doing it?"

"I can't help it, Sam . . . I love you. I can't change that now, it's too late. And I wouldn't change it if I could."

He scraped at the bottom of the ice cream carton and set it on the table, nodding slowly. "I'm scared, too."

"It's okay to be afraid. You probably have good reasons to be."

"You probably do, too." He avoided my eyes.

I took a deep breath to relieve some of the tension I felt. "It's still worth it, Sam. I don't have any regrets, so don't worry about me." I stood up from my chair and stacked a few dishes together. "Will you stay with me tonight, or do you want to go back to your place?"

"No, I'll stay with you if you don't mind."

"I don't mind at all." I touched his hair, pushing it away from his eyes. "Let's do these dishes."

He stood up and helped me gather them.

***

The next day, Thursday, I was surprisingly productive in the morning despite some anxiety about my lunch with Henry. I decided to be very direct with him, but not hostile. There was no point in engaging in a war that could damage our careers and do untold damage to others who worked at the firm. At the appointed time, I went to his office to find him. In the past, he would have come to me.

"Oh, are we still doing lunch?" Henry wore a snow-white shirt with a shimmering ice-blue tie.

"Yes, why wouldn't we? I thought you wanted us to interact more."

"I thought, after yesterday, you might not want to spend time with me."

"It'll give us a chance to talk about that. Shall we go? I made a reservation at Sylvia's, where we had lunch the first time we went out together. Is that okay?"

He made a face. "It'll do." After the short walk to the restaurant, we were greeted by the same young man who had fawned over Henry a couple of months ago. He was notably less enthusiastic about seeing Henry.

"Good afternoon gentlemen. Henry. Do you have a reservation for lunch?"

"Yes, for Adam Evans?"

"Ah yes. Right this way please." He showed us to a perfectly acceptable table near the entrance to the outdoor seating area.

Henry was disappointed. "Could we have a table on the deck please? I'd like a view of the water."

"I'm sorry, those tables are reserved for other guests who requested them." His tone seemed spiteful. Henry silently surrendered and sat down.

As the young man walked away, I whispered, "That's what you get for turning him down when he was after you."

"I gave him a pity fuck about a month ago."

"A 'pity fuck?'"

"Are you not familiar with the term?"

"No, but I understand the meaning. I can't imagine why he wouldn't appreciate such a condescending gesture."

"He's lucky he got that much."

Or maybe you're not as good as you think you are. We looked at our menus in silence.

The waitress was polite but seemed less than cheerful when she came to the table. I ordered a salad niçoise with seared tuna, and Henry ordered a roasted vegetable salad, with a warning. "Tell the chef if there's too much olive oil on it I will not be happy."

"Yes, sir, I remember the last time you were here. I'll let the chef know it's for you." In her hurry to leave the table, she forgot to ask us about beverages.

I raised an eyebrow. "You have a reputation. Maybe we shouldn't have come here."

"It doesn't matter. All the restaurants in this town have dreadful service. I can't wait to get back to New York."

"Are you planning to leave any time soon?"

"As much as I would like to, I promised Zipinski I would stay at least until the harassment complaints have been resolved."

"Yeah, how is that going? I was surprised he came into the office yesterday."

"He seems confident a conclusion will be reached within the next two months. Perhaps sooner."

"And then what?"

He gave me a knowing look but raised his hands to indicate he knew nothing. "It depends on how things are resolved."

I wouldn't be getting any more information on that subject. "So, about yesterday . . . I can't help but think you were trying to shift blame or responsibility onto me for something to do with the Ellis account."

He played with a silver cufflink set with a sparkling sapphire. "I know that's how it appeared, but honestly . . ." He looked straight into my eyes. "It was a big misunderstanding, and I apologize for suggesting you dropped the ball on something."

He caught me off guard with his seemingly heartfelt apology. His eyes never wavered. I hadn't realized how blue they were. "I appreciate your apology. What was the misunderstanding? Why did you think I was handling Ellis Industries?"

"After we spoke, I remembered I originally planned to let you supervise the Ellis account until Robert asked me to be the point man on it."

"Robert?"

"I'm sorry, Robert Bergdorf, the representative from Ellis. We met and he insisted I personally supervise all the work we do for them. That's when I revised the lists of accounts you and I would handle. Somehow a copy of my original list must have been sent to you before I gave you the revised list. That's why there was a discrepancy."

The waitress brought our salads. Her hand trembled as she set the plate in front of Henry. "The chef asked me to make sure your salads are satisfactory before I leave the table."

I approved my salad and asked for iced tea. Henry used his fork to examine some of his vegetables. "It's acceptable this time. I'll have water with lemon, but I want the lemon on the side, freshly cut into wedges, not slices."

I dug into my meal, hungrier than I thought, and continued my inquiry. "I'd like to know how an Ellis file got into my office. And that list was not in my desk drawer where you found it."

"I promise to investigate. Are there any employees at the firm who might have a grudge against you?"

"Not that I can think of." *Other than you.* "What's wrong with the Ellis account anyway? Why are there questions about it?"

"I'm sure it's nothing. Mr. Ellis called Zipinski to make sure his company's accounts were being handled properly while Zipinski is out of the office. He had some concerns. It's probably something on their end." Henry picked at his food, eating a few vegetables. "How's your salad?"

"Dewicious." My mouth was full. I didn't bother to ask about his salad. "I still don't understand, Henry . . . if you were supervising the Ellis account in response to a personal request from Robert Bergdorf, how did you forget you were handling it instead of me?"

There was a flash of irritation in his eyes. "I delegated much of the work, as anyone in my position would do. I am very busy, Adam. I spent less time on it than you might imagine." Before I could ask another question, he changed the subject. "I'm still amazed you can eat like that and look healthier than ever. Which gym do you use?"

I blushed at his compliment and realized I was eating too quickly. "I don't go to a gym. I run in my neighborhood and do calisthenics at home."

"People still do that? But you're missing out on the eye candy at the health clubs. And they're missing out on you."

"Pfffft. I think they'll survive. Where do you work out?"

"I've been all over the place. I think I've used the free trial period at every place in town. Lately I've been going to the new club a few streets over. It's as classy as this town gets, and they have a steam room. I've had a lot of fun in the steam room." His eyebrows suggested something wicked.

"Seriously? Are you going there to work out or to hook up?"

"Why not both? I've hooked up with very hot guys at these gyms, especially some of the trainers. They're perfect because they work out all day and they're so eager to please." He smiled, apparently enjoying his memories. "I'm working with this big Latino guy now . . . he's so polite, and he's trying to be professional, but all I have to do is stand a little too close to him and he pops wood. I love it. By the time I'm finished teasing him, he'll be begging me to fuck him."

I shook my head. "That's awful. Do you ever stop to think about how it might affect him?"

He shrugged. "He'll have the best sex of his life, and he'll thank me for it. What else is there to think about?" He put one more roasted vegetable in his mouth. "One of my favorites was this young kid who worked at another place. Beautiful guy . . . tall and dark. He wasn't huge, but I was impressed by the amount of weight he was lifting for a guy his size."

This sounded uncomfortably familiar. "Which gym was he at?"

"It was a dumpy place down by the harbor. It's in that hotel."

"The Harbor View?"

"Yeah, that's it. Have you been there?"

A chill went up my spine. "Just to the restaurant."

"Oh yeah, this guy was a waiter there, too. He was a shitty trainer, but no one seemed to care. He was this big, dumb kid who didn't realize how hot he was. All I had to do was pay him a few compliments and he was ready to go home with me."

"I don't I want to hear any more of your stories, Henry."

"No, you'll enjoy this, it was so fucking hot. I took him back to my apartment and he was all over me, like he was starved for affection. He kept trying to kiss me, but I don't do that. I told him I would fuck him, and he went along with it. He was so stupid, he let me do it bareback."

Henry laughed while I thought about removing one of his eyes with my fork. I couldn't speak.

"When I fuck guys, especially these young jocks who think they're alphas, I say all kinds of shit to them while I dominate their asses. I was insulting him and calling him filthy names and basically humiliating him, and suddenly he went nuts and threw me off his back. He yelled and told me not to talk to him that way. I just laughed. I couldn't help it."

I found my voice, but it was low and quiet. "Stop . . . right now . . . I don't want to hear . . ."

"Wait, this is the best part. He got so angry, he punched my bedroom door and his fist went through the door and into the wall behind it! This kid was so strong I thought he would kill me. He grabbed his clothes and was about to leave . . . and I wasn't stopping him . . . but he dropped everything and came at me. He threw me onto the bed and fucked the hell out of me. I mean, he was rough! It felt like he would break me in half."

My anger was about to boil over. "Why did you tell me that? The way you treat people is disgusting!"

"No, really, it was one of the hottest experiences I ever had."

"Do you care about anyone other than yourself? Do you have any idea what you did to him?"

"He must have liked it. He fucked me two more times after that. The last time was in the alley behind the hotel, next to a dumpster. Can you imagine *me* being fucked against a dumpster? I rarely let someone dominate me, but it was hot as hell. A week later, he disappeared. I heard he got fired. I hate to think a big, dumb stud like that is going to waste."

"Why do you say he was dumb? Did you even talk to him?" I pushed my plate aside and threw my napkin on the table.

"Talk to him? He was just a trainer. He probably went to a community college. You can't have a conversation with someone like that."

I stood up abruptly, accidentally toppling my chair. Everyone in the restaurant looked at me. "You're a vile human being, Henry. There is absolutely nothing about you I like or respect. Just in case it's not clear to you yet . . . we aren't friends. I hate your fucking guts!"

"Why are you so upset? It was a great story!"

"I'm leaving, and you can pay for lunch for a change." I saw the waitress near the door, keeping her distance. I reached for my wallet and pulled out a couple of twenties, handing them to her as I left. "This is for putting up with that asshole. I'm sorry I made a scene."

"It's not a problem. Thank you, sir. Come back any time." The maître d' smiled and nodded at me.

Out on the street, the heat of the midday sun hit me like a fist. I rushed to the nearest trash can and vomited my lunch. I wiped my mouth on the back of my hand and staggered back to the office, hoping Henry wouldn't follow me.

I slipped into the restroom to splash water on my face, then hurried into my office and closed the door and the blinds. My mind reeled. I sat at my desk and tried to worry about whether I would lose my job. It was much better than thinking about Henry and Sam . . . together . . . fucking. The phone rang – of course it was Donna – so I picked it up.

"What's wrong?"

"Nothing."

"Why are your blinds closed?"

"I need privacy."

"How was your lunch with Henry?"

"Fine."

"Fine?"

"It was fine, thanks for asking. Talk to you later." I hung up while she was still speaking. She would be at my door in a few minutes. I couldn't tell her what Henry said about Sam, so I gathered my things, walked out of my office, and told the staff, "I'll be out for the rest of the day."

I exited through the stairwell, went to my truck, and I drove. I just drove.

27

After my lunch with Henry, I couldn't stay at the office where Donna would ask questions I didn't want to answer. I couldn't go home because I wasn't ready to confront Sam about what Henry had told me. I kept driving. I needed to think, but every time I tried to sort out my thoughts I was overwhelmed by emotion. I headed north, beyond the suburbs, through farmland and forests, until I realized I was driving to Flora's lake house. It made sense. I could be alone there. *We were happy there.*

I parked the truck on the grass. I didn't have the keys to the house, so I took a chair from the porch and carried it down to the pier where I could sit and look at the water. It was so peaceful, so unlike the chaos that had erupted in my head and my chest when I realized Sam had been with Henry. The lake was as beautiful as I remembered it. *At least I didn't imagine that.*

Pieces of the puzzle fell into place – Sam's repeated warnings about Henry, his jealousy, his reminder that we were still getting to know each other. *All this time he must have known who Henry was. Why would he lie to me?* I alternated between sitting and pacing. Henry's description of their sexual encounters was at odds with my image of Sam. *Could he be that aggressive? Would he hurt someone when he's angry? Is that who he is?* I argued with myself, I cried, and I fumed.

When the sun began to set, I thought about Sam coming home from the nursery, expecting to find me in the kitchen preparing dinner. I wondered what he would think when he found the house locked and dark. I carried the chair back to the porch and took a last look at the lake and the house and the grass where Sam and I made love in the rain.

Once I was back in the truck and on the road, I realized I was very hungry. I stopped at a burger joint to get a quick meal and sat in the restaurant watching people while I ate. There were kids with irritable parents, teenagers laughing and talking too loudly, and a young couple whose public display of affection tested the limits of propriety. At one table, a middle-aged man and woman sat with blank expressions, not talking and never looking at each other. An elderly woman sat in a booth next to a window, alone, with a small beverage cup between her hands. She smiled at people who walked past, trying to catch their eyes, to say a few words, to connect with someone for a minute or more. When she glanced in my direction I turned away, stared at my food, and decided I'd had enough.

It was dark by the time I got home, and as soon as I hit the remote control to open the garage door, Sam came out of his apartment. Before I was out of the truck he asked, "Where have you been? I've been trying to call you for hours.

Don't you have your phone with you?" I did, but I ignored the messages from him and from Donna. "I was worried about you."

"I'm sorry, I must have turned it off. Did you have dinner? Do you want me to make something?"

"Adam . . . where were you? What happened?"

"Nothing . . . I went for a drive and I lost track of time."

"Donna said you left work early."

"She called you?"

"Yeah, she was worried, too. Where did you go?"

"I drove up to the lake house."

"The lake house? Why? Who were you with?"

His question surprised me. "I was alone. Who did you think I was with?"

He opened his mouth, but nothing came out at first. He stammered, "I . . . I don't know. I just . . ."

"Did you think I was with Henry?"

Again, he opened his mouth and made a sound, but no words. He looked down at the driveway and shoved his hands in his pockets.

"We should talk. Let's go inside." Sam followed me into the house without speaking and stood near the door until I invited him to sit at the kitchen table. "Do you want anything? Did you eat?"

"I picked up some chicken." He looked miserable, like a kid sitting outside the principal's office.

I suppose I was torturing him a bit. "Anything to drink?"

"No, thank you."

I sat down on the other side of the table. "You know Henry, don't you?"

"Yes." He was barely audible.

"How long have you known he was my co-worker?"

He shrugged a bit. "Almost from the beginning. But I swear, Adam, it was over before our relationship started. That's why I wanted us to get tested before we did anything."

"Why didn't you tell me?"

His face was very red. "I didn't want you to talk to him about it. I thought . . . maybe it would be better if you didn't know . . . and you wouldn't find out. That's why I didn't want you to get too friendly with him."

"Yeah, I thought so. How many times were you with him?"

"Three times. Once at his place . . . once in a room at the Harbor View . . . and the last time in another place."

"In the alley, next to a dumpster?"

The look on his face said it was true. "He told you that?"

"Yes, he did."

"What else did he tell you?"

"Everything, probably. A lot more than I wanted to know. Did you punch a hole in a door?"

He closed his eyes and nodded slowly. "And the wall. I lost control." He hung his head and stared at the table.

"Why did you go back? Why didn't you leave?"

"I wish I had." He paused, then confessed something I didn't know. "I wanted to hurt him. I was so angry . . . I knew I could do whatever I wanted, and he couldn't stop me . . . so I went back and did it to him . . . what he did to me, but worse. I thought I would give him a taste of his own medicine and he would leave me alone. But he liked it. The rougher I got with him, the more he liked it. I didn't expect that. I didn't know there were people who liked that." He looked disgusted and had tears in his eyes. "But the part that really makes me feel sick is . . . I liked it, too. I liked having power over him. There's a dark place in my head, Adam. I don't like to think about it."

"Why did you leave the Harbor View? Did you tell me the truth about that?"

He took a deep breath, preparing for the next round. "I didn't tell you everything. It was partly about the meals the chef gave me, but the main thing . . . the big issue my manager brought up was . . . I had a reputation."

I remembered Carl said something about Sam's reputation. "A reputation for what?"

He knit his fingers together, turning his knuckles white. He forced the words out. "I had sex with a lot of guys. A lot."

I felt a dull pain in my chest, but it didn't last long. "How many is a lot?"

He shook his head. "Thirty? Forty? Probably more. I didn't want to count. It wasn't only at the gym, I went to the bars, too. There were guys everywhere, and so many offers. I had no idea it could be so easy to have sex. Back home, there was nothing, and the one time I tried it . . ." I knew how that ended. "There were men who offered me money." Another pain in my chest. "Sometimes I took it. I had nothing, and I needed money, so I took it. Most of them were nice to me. It felt good to be wanted. My parents didn't want me, but someone did."

"I wanted you." I couldn't look at him without losing it. "I know I didn't show it, and I should have. Maybe you wouldn't have done some of those things if I had been more . . ."

"No, you didn't have anything to do with it. I knew you wanted me, but it was different with you. You were my friend . . ." His voice cracked. "You liked me, you talked to me, you treated me like a person. Most of those guys . . . it wasn't like that. And Henry . . . he was the worst. I knew I had to make a change. And you helped me."

I stared at the table and nodded. "It's a good thing you came here when you did. Who knows what might have happened to you?"

"You didn't want anything from me."

"Yes, I did." I kept nodding. "I did. I'm not so different from the rest of them."

"You are, Adam. You're completely different."

"Am I?" I finally looked up. His eyes were swollen and bloodshot. For once he didn't look good. I probably didn't either. I pushed my chair back and stood up, not sure where I was going. "So, what do you want to do?"

He put his head down and sniffled. "I don't know. I'll have to find another apartment. It might take me a while, but I think I can manage on what I'm making now. If you'll give me time . . . I know I don't deserve it."

He was so lost in his shame and fear, he couldn't see past it. I knew what that felt like. I lived like that for years. "No, Sam . . . I meant . . . I'm not asking you to . . ." I took a deep breath and started over. "I was wondering if you wanted to watch a movie."

He raised his head. "What?"

"I don't want you to leave."

"But . . . I lied to you."

"I know. You're a better liar than I thought you were, I'll give you that."

He looked confused. "Aren't you angry? Why aren't you yelling at me?"

"What for? I'm not angry." I thought for a moment. "It seems like I should be, but I'm not. I got it out of my system while I was at the lake. I had time to think. I'm glad I drove up there."

"I don't understand. I was afraid to tell you about Henry and all the others because I thought you would kick me out. I wanted to tell you. I knew it would be worse if you heard it from him first."

I shook my head. "I think it was better this way. To hear him describe it . . . it was disgusting. Of course, he doesn't know about us. He was telling me about guys he met in different gyms, the ones he had sex with, and when he described you . . ."

"What did he say about me?"

"That you were beautiful, and tall, and very strong . . . I knew it was you. I left out Henry's comment about Sam's intelligence because it wasn't true. "I know it was just sex for him, and there was no relationship. He didn't even know you. He used you. I was so disgusted I made a scene in the restaurant. I told him I hate his fucking guts and I stormed out. I'm sure I'll pay for that somehow."

"Shit! This is all my fault."

"No, it's not. He deserved it, even if he hadn't been talking about you. I finally saw him for what he is." I heard my phone vibrating in my briefcase, so I went to get it.

"I thought your phone was turned off."

"I lied about that. It's Donna, I'd better answer." I tapped the screen. "Hello. Yeah, I'm at home . . . I'm fine. He's here with me. I'm sorry . . . yeah, I know . . . I know . . . I went for a long drive . . . I know I should have . . . you know I'm not a good communicator . . . all right . . . I know." Sam stood up and moved toward the door. He seemed to be wondering whether he should stay or leave. "I'll tell you about it tomorrow . . . no, I'm tired and I want to go to bed. I'm fine, I promise. He's okay, do you want to talk to him? Okay." I handed the phone to Sam. "She doesn't believe me."

"Hello? Yeah, he's okay. Well, you know how he is . . . I know . . . you're right . . . Donna . . . it's okay, really." Sam covered his eyes and turned his back. His voice wavered. "Because I love him, that's why . . . no . . . I think I'm getting a cold . . . no he's not, you're just angry . . . I'm fine . . . I'm sure he'll tell you about it tomorrow . . . okay . . . I know, I remember . . . okay . . . thank you . . . good night." He tapped the screen and gave me the phone. "She didn't believe me either." He sniffled and wiped his eyes with the back of his hand.

"We should go to bed."

He stepped into the back hall. "Okay, I know you're tired . . ."

"Wait . . . where are you going? I thought you would stay here."

He looked at me like I was crazy. "Adam . . . don't you understand what I've done? Why are you being so nice to me?"

I looked at him for a long minute. "Because I love you, that's why."

His eyes filled with tears again. "You're making a mistake."

"No, I'm not. I'm not, Sam. When I was at the lake, I thought of all the reasons why I should put an end to this, to protect myself so I won't get hurt anymore. But I thought about last weekend and the way we were together . . . the way you are when you're with me. You can lie about some things, but not that. All those other guys . . . it doesn't matter . . . that's not who you are. You're here now, and you're good to me. That's what matters."

"I do love you, Adam. I'm not lying about that."

"I know. That's why I want you to stay with me. Or let me stay with you at your place."

He gestured toward the coach house. "I left my lights on, and the door isn't locked."

"Then I'll come over there. It'll be easier."

Hesitantly, he agreed to let me join him in his apartment. I locked the house and followed him up the stairs to his place. I remembered something while we undressed. "Sam . . . when I asked you about being more aggressive with me during sex . . . did that remind you of what happened with Henry?"

"Yeah." He didn't look at me. "I don't want to treat you that way, even if it's pretending."

I crawled into his bed. "I'm sorry I asked you to do that."

"That's okay, you didn't know." He switched off the lamp on the bedside table and settled on his back, covering himself with the sheet as if he didn't want me to see him naked. He seemed stiff.

I waited a few minutes to see if he would do anything. He didn't. "Can I cuddle with you?"

"Sure. Do what you want." He lifted his arm to let me move next to him but continued to lie there like a corpse.

I rubbed his chest. "Relax. Everything is okay."

"I think I would feel better if you yelled at me. I deserve it."

"I'm sorry, but I won't yell at you." I pressed my ear against his chest and listened. "I love to listen to your heartbeat at night."

He tried to speak. "I . . . I wish I could . . ."

I continued to stroke him gently. "I'm sorry Henry hurt you. You didn't deserve that."

He drew a sharp breath and covered his face with one hand. He tried not to cry, but he needed to. A moment later, he let it go, and he cried for a long time.

***

On Friday I lied to my friend. I told Donna I argued with Henry about the Ellis account and his attempt to make me look bad. I said I went for a drive because I didn't want to face her, knowing she and Sam were right about Henry all along. "I don't know why it's so hard to admit I'm wrong. I need to talk to my shrink about that."

It caught her off guard. "Well . . . you don't need to beat yourself up. We all have . . . issues. Maybe I've been too . . . harsh . . . with you at times." Her chin quivered. "I want you to be able to talk to me about anything."

"Thank you for calling Sam."

"He was very worried. He's so protective of you, Adam, but you need to protect him, too. He's an innocent kid underneath . . . you know . . . the way he looks."

"I need to keep that in mind."

"I told him he should get angry at you sometimes. He's a little too forgiving, don't you think?"

"He is, I agree. I'm sorry I made you worry about me."

"Oh. I wasn't that worried. Did I sound worried? Is that a new shirt? It's a good color for you."

"It's white."

"It looks good with your skin. I should get some work done." She stood up.

"Okay, I'll let you go. Let me know if you hear anything about the Ellis thing, or the harassment stuff."

"You bet. And . . . don't run off again."

"Okay."

She left my office. I had never seen her so worried about me.

***

Later, a staff member delivered an envelope containing a brief, formal memo from Henry, who had been in his office all day with the door closed. The memo read:

"It has been decided that we can no longer accommodate your request for an altered work schedule. Effective immediately, you will be expected to work Monday through Friday along with all the other employees of this firm. Also, all vacation days must be requested at least two weeks in advance."

This was the price of my anger at Henry. I would be spending less time with Sam.

28

The Eden Place Neighborhood Association meeting was on Saturday, and I was not looking forward to it. I hadn't seen or heard from the Weasel Woman since Donna chased her down the street in front of my house, but based on the flyer she had distributed to every house but mine, Sam and I were still targets of her campaign of intolerance. I knew we had to attend to represent ourselves. Flora and Joe had been stirring up support among the neighbors they knew, so we didn't expect the meeting to be a cakewalk for Helen Van Wooten.

The meeting was being held in the basement of an Evangelical Lutheran church in the neighborhood – not the best venue in my opinion. Carl and I agreed to show up early so we could talk to people about volunteering for our painting project. Although he didn't live in the neighborhood, Carl had been asked to attend the meeting as the police department liaison. Sam would come over from the nursery in time for the meeting. When I arrived at the church, Carl was already out front, in uniform, talking to a middle-aged woman. Carl introduced me, and she greeted me warmly.

"Ah, so you're Adam Evans. I'm Kate Fletcher, the pastor here at St. Paul's."

Kate? Not Pastor Fletcher or something like that? I shook her hand but maintained an awkward silence. My poor social skills were already showing.

"I hoped to see you before the meeting. I've heard about you from Mrs. Van Wooten."

"Great. I can imagine how that went."

Kate smiled and looked at the sky. "I wanted to meet you to get a more balanced view. I saw the flyer with your picture and the . . . unfortunate innuendo."

"You mean the one that implied we're child molesters?" I realized my tone was harsh when Carl gave me a look.

"Yes, but I also saw the flyer comparing Mrs. Van Wooten to a weasel."

"I didn't do that!"

She held up her hand. "Regardless of who distributed either flyer, I hope we've seen the last of it. We're here today to bring the neighborhood together, not to divide it."

I grumbled, "She started it." Carl gave me another look.

Kate moved on. "I've been admiring your house for years, and your gardens are spectacular. I wonder if you would give me advice about improving the plantings around St. Paul's. Maybe you and your partner could come for dinner some time and we could discuss it."

I was suspicious. "You're not trying to get me to come to church, are you?" Carl closed his eyes and shook his head ever so slightly.

Kate smiled. "No, not at all. I would appreciate your advice, and I like to have company occasionally. Think about it . . . no pressure. I'm sure I'll be seeing you anyway. I already told Officer Hanson I'll help with your project. I think it's a great idea."

"Oh." *Unexpected niceness.* "Okay."

"I'll go inside to make sure the Van Wootens have everything they need. I'll see you later."

As she walked away I said to Carl, "She's awfully friendly."

"You make it sound like a bad thing. You don't deal with people very often, do you?"

"Why do you say that?"

"Just an observation. Hey, have you ever seen Dr. Van Wooten?"

"The Weasel's husband is a doctor? No, I've never seen him."

"He's a dentist. I'll be interested to hear what you think of him."

"Why?"

"Wait until you see him, then we'll talk."

We stood outside the church and greeted people as they arrived for the meeting. I printed handouts about the project with a list of tasks people could volunteer for. Carl's amiable and somewhat official presence drew people in and made it easier for me to meet and talk to my neighbors. Some of them were people I met after the fire. Joan, the woman who brought us a pie, came with her husband. Jack and Jackie were there, too, but Jackie wasn't nearly as talkative as she was the first time we met. Flora and Agnes arrived in a big sedan driven by Clarence, Flora's . . . whatever you want to call him . . . who would return to pick them up after the meeting. Joe walked over with Ledell, the painting contractor who was building the scaffolding around his house. Joe's daughter, Susan, was in an art program at her school.

There were plenty of people I hadn't met before. Some of them kept their distance and seemed to glare at me in a hostile way. Or it may have been my imagination. Many others who introduced themselves were familiar with my house. I received a lot of compliments on my gardening. I was almost comfortable with it by the time the meeting was supposed to start. Sam hadn't arrived yet, so I took a seat near the back of the room and saved an empty chair next to me. Flora and Agnes were seated near the front, and Joe was with a group of people on the other side of the room. I was surprised at how many people were there and wondered whether it was a good or a bad sign.

The meeting was brought to order, not by the Weasel, but by her husband. "Hello, everyone! Thanks for coming today. I'm Dr. Leonard Van Wooten and I've been asked to introduce the person who made all of this possible." He had a surprisingly high-pitched, lilting voice. "My lovely wife, Helen, has many years of experience organizing and leading neighborhood associations in several cities throughout this great country of ours." He had big hair with blond highlights, the kind that requires a lot of work. "She's done such a fabulous job of putting this meeting together." *Fabulous?* His face was unnaturally smooth, with a tan that could only come from a bottle. "She cares so much about our children and all the great families who live in this neighborhood, I'm sure you'll love her to pieces, like I do!" He was the most stereotypically gay man I had seen in quite a while. *That's what Carl was talking about.* "Please welcome the light of my life, Helen Van Wooten."

There was a smattering of applause from some people in the crowd while the Weasel stood up and came to the lectern. Carl caught my eye from across the room. I wished Sam had been there to see and hear Dr. Van Wooten. The Weasel spelled out her agenda. "I know we are all concerned about safety in Eden Place, and we want to be especially vigilant about the presence of sexual predators. Later I will address the issue of properties that aren't being properly maintained." She didn't mention the issue of police harassment listed on her flyer. Perhaps because she was introducing Carl.

"I personally spoke to the Acting Chief of Police about our plans for Eden Place. He was kind enough to send a liaison, Officer Carl Hanson, who is here with us today." Carl smiled and held up his hand. "I requested a higher-ranking member of the department, but we appreciate Officer Hanson's willingness to attend." *Ouch!* Carl blinked a few times, but his smile never wavered. "Officer, perhaps you could give us an idea of the crimes we need to watch out for in our neighborhood." Carl approached the lectern, assuming the Weasel would yield it, but she did not. "No, honey, you can talk from there. This is my spot." There were a few mumbles and chuckles from the crowd. Carl started talking about crime statistics and garage burglaries.

I wondered where Sam was. Meanwhile, I scanned the faces in the room, trying to assess the level of support for the Weasel agenda. Everyone would be interested in preventing crime in the neighborhood. I was more concerned about what she would say about sexual predators. Carl came to the end of his presentation. "So, keep in mind, Eden Place is one of the safest neighborhoods in the city, but it pays to take precautions like increasing exterior lighting, strong deadbolts on your garage doors, and keeping an eye out for people you don't recognize, especially at night."

Mrs. Van Wooten had a follow-up question. "Could you tell us how to spot people who molest children or try to recruit them into alternative lifestyles? I'm sure many of the parents in the neighborhood are worried about that."

Just then, there was a clunking sound from the back of the room as Sam came through the door. Many heads turned to see what made the noise, and Sam was hard to miss. He saw me and moved as quietly as possible to sit down, but the metal folding chair creaked loudly under his weight. He grimaced and blushed. "Sorry, a delivery took longer than expected. How's it going?"

"Your timing is great. She just got to the part about child molesters."

The Weasel was waiting for an answer to her question. "Officer, what can you tell us about people like *that*." Her emphasis on '*that*' suggested she was referring to Sam.

Carl hesitated. "This is not my area of expertise, ma'am . . ."

"Doesn't the police department provide training on such a critical issue?"

A man in the audience stood up. "Excuse me! Can I say something?" The Weasel held up her hand to shut him down, but he continued. "We all saw the thing about the two gay guys and how we need to protect our children, right? That's the main reason I came to this meeting, so why don't we quit pussyfooting around?" I didn't like the sound of this. He looked like someone who would buy into the Weasel Woman's scare tactics. "I'm a typical guy. I don't know any gay people, I don't need to know any gay people. I figured they all lived in California and New York." A few people laughed. It made me more nervous. "When I saw that flyer, I didn't know what to think. This tall guy comes into my shop every morning . . . nicest guy you could ever meet . . . one of my best customers . . . all the girls who work for me are in love with him . . . and it turns out he's living with the little guy who grows all the flowers!"

Who is this? Wait a minute . . . I'm not little!

"So I asked the girls about him and they say, 'Of course he's gay! What are you, stupid?" I guess I am, because I never would have guessed."

Sam leaned over and whispered, "He owns the doughnut shop."

"Oh, okay. Why did he call me the little guy?"

"Shhh, I want to hear this."

The man continued. "My point is, I don't need to know what these guys do at home. It's none of my business. I don't want to know what you and Dr. Pompadour do at home either." Dr. Van Wooten looked indignant. "But if you think driving my customers out of this neighborhood will improve things, I'll fight you on that. Because I don't see *you* in my shop every morning, do I? So stop trying to make trouble!" With that, he sat down. Joe clapped loudly, and several people joined him.

The Weasel sputtered, "I'm trying to do what's best for our children!"

A woman stood up. "I have a question for Officer Hanson, please? Ever since I got the flyer I've been checking the sex offender registry on the internet, and I don't understand why those men aren't on the list. Aren't they required to register?"

A wave of murmurs swept through the crowd. Before I could say something offensive, Carl replied in his best police officer voice, "NO, ma'am! They are *NOT* required to register because they are *NOT* sex offenders! Whoever distributed those flyers is perpetuating an ignorant myth with *NO* basis in fact!" The Weasel's face hardened into a tight-lipped, beady-eyed mask. "Those men are law-abiding citizens who don't have as much as a parking ticket in their names. That's a matter of public record."

Flora was on her feet before Carl finished talking. When she held up her cane, everyone's eyes were drawn in her direction. "Helen, dear!" She used her sweetest southern drawl. "It would help if you explained to everyone why you decided to draw attention to these men. What made you believe they were dangerous?" I didn't like her sympathetic tone.

The Weasel hesitated at first, then exploded. "He threatened me with SCISSORS!"

The audience gasped. "You mean the big guy?"

"No, the little one! The gardener!"

Dammit, I'm not little! I rose from my chair to confront her. "I didn't threaten you with ANYTHING, you beady-eyed . . ." Before I could finish, Sam grabbed the back of my collar and yanked me down onto my chair.

He scolded me, "Don't call her names!" He let go of me and I popped back up.

"I'm sorry." I cleared my throat. "I didn't threaten her! She came up behind me while I was gardening and listening to music. She startled me, and I had pruning shears in my hand." The crowd made sympathetic noises.

The Weasel took another shot at me. "He said he doesn't like CHILDREN!!" There was a round of mumbles from the people.

Flora addressed me. "Is that true? Tell us the truth, Adam." She nodded slightly.

I scanned the crowd. "Yes, it's true." Murmur, murmur, murmur. "They get on my nerves. I'm not used to them. They're noisy and messy, and sometimes they pick my flowers without asking."

"I blame the parents," one woman said. There were more grumbles and a couple of, "Damned kids!" The Weasel was expecting people to be up in arms, but most of them seemed reasonable.

Flora continued, "So you are not trying to recruit children for any purpose?"

"No! That's so stupid! I don't want to deal with them at all if I can avoid it." The expressions on people's faces seemed to be softening.

A man jumped up and yelled, "Why do you people have to flaunt your sexuality in front of the whole neighborhood? Why can't you keep it to yourselves?" He sat down abruptly.

Sam quietly warned me not to overreact as my hands curled into fists. "Listen . . . I have lived in this neighborhood since I was twelve years old, and I bet most of you didn't know I existed." I pointed at the Weasel. "Until SHE put out that FLYER! I didn't ask for this attention! I want to be left alone! SHE flaunted my sexuality all over the neighborhood! So you can blame HER!"

A boozy older woman snarled, "You're setting a bad example for young people!"

I was reaching the limits of my self-control, but Flora rescued me from the hag. "Well, I declare, Margaret! You've been married and divorced *three times* since I've known you! What example are *you* setting for young people?" This got a big laugh. Apparently, Margaret was a known quantity. I took the opportunity to sit down.

The Weasel was desperate to regain control of the meeting, but she made the mistake of appealing to Flora for support. "Mrs. O'Neill . . . I took refuge at your house after that man threatened me! Your servant woman saw him with the scissors in his hand!"

Servant woman? Uh oh!

Agnes popped up next to Flora. "Mr. Adam did nothing to deserve what you've done to him. If the scissors had been in *my* hand, ye wouldnea be standin' here today, ye sour-faced cow!"

Sam whispered, "Holy crap!"

Mrs. Van Wooten clutched her pearls and exclaimed, "Leonard! Did you hear that?" She turned to her husband who was no match for a Scotswoman. He reluctantly rose from his chair. "Mrs. O'Neill, I believe your maid owes my wife an apology."

"Holy crap." Sam's eyes grew larger. "That's her *husband*?!"

Flora leveled her gaze at the Van Wootens. "My dear friend, Agnes, has lived in this neighborhood longer than most of the people in this room." All the sweetness was gone from her voice. "She has as much right to express her opinion as your sexually frustrated wife."

We said, "Holy crap!" in unison. Joe burst into a loud laugh. A man in front of us said to his wife, "This is the best meeting I've ever attended."

Pastor Fletcher rose from her seat to address the assembly. "Please! All of you! I'm afraid we're headed in the wrong direction. This is not what I expected when I agreed to host a neighborhood association meeting in our church. We need to work toward common goals and avoid these personal attacks. Could we please move on to something more productive?"

A guy I didn't recognize stood up. "I have a question about the painting project you're sponsoring. I think it's a great idea but I'm wondering about these young criminals who are being brought in to help with it. I don't want . . ."

Carl was about to address the man, but the Weasel beat him to it. "Sir, I'm sorry to interrupt you, but the Eden Park Neighborhood Association has nothing to do with that project, and I plan to have it shut down."

What? There were grumbles from the audience and the man looked surprised. "No, ma'am! I don't want it shut down! It's the best thing I've heard about today. I want to know . . ."

She interrupted him again. "I have the same concerns you have about these young thugs being brought into our neighborhood. Officer Hanson . . . I thought you were sworn to protect the public rather than exposing us to dangerous criminals. What do you have to say for yourself?"

Carl's amiable disposition was crumbling. From across the room I could see a vein popping out on his forehead. "These are not criminals! They're kids who got into trouble because they made dumb mistakes! This program helps them get back on the right track *before* they turn into criminals."

"Can you guarantee they won't rape our daughters?" The Weasel's voice was like fingernails on a chalkboard.

The voices of the crowd became louder, with some agreeing and others disagreeing. If I had been Carl, with a gun on my belt, I would have shot her right there. I wouldn't make a very good police officer. I wanted to say something to take the pressure off him, but I couldn't think of anything but vicious insults. While I was thinking, Sam stood up.

"Excuse me! Could I say something?" Everyone turned to look at the impressive figure at the back of the room. When they were quiet he continued. "The Pharisees asked Jesus' disciples, "Why does your teacher eat with tax collectors and sinners?" When Jesus heard that, he said, "Healthy people do not need a physician, but sick people do." Sam paused. "I did not come to call righteous people, but sinners."

My mouth hung open. You could have heard a pin drop.

"That's from the gospel of Matthew, chapter nine. I know not everyone here is a Christian, but many of you claim to be Christians." He looked directly at the Van Wootens. "You say you're worried about children and want to protect them, but when there's an opportunity to help some kids who really need it, you want to turn them away. Carl . . . Officer Hanson, is trying to help those kids. So . . . are you serious about protecting young people or not?" He looked around the room and added, "I'm just saying." He sat down.

Joan, the pie lady, broke the silence with an "Amen!" I reached over and squeezed Sam's arm. Helen Van Wooten had been put in her place for the moment.

The man who raised the question about the painting project stood up again. "I just wanted to know if my fifteen-year-old son could get involved. I don't want to take a job away from these other kids, but my boy is getting into trouble and I don't know what to do for him anymore. I'm sorry if I offended anyone."

Carl had calmed down. "Sir, I'd be happy to talk to you about your son after the meeting. I'm sure we can work something out."

The Van Wootens whispered to each other at the front of the room. I had a feeling he was trying to talk her into leaving, but she wouldn't budge.

While they were distracted, Jackie stood up to talk. "I'm Jackie and this is my husband Jack. Easy to remember, right? Some of you may know us and some may not . . ."

I assumed she would rattle on for a while without saying anything. I leaned over to have a quiet conversation with Sam. "You were amazing. I've never heard you talk like that before. You sounded like a preacher."

"I had twelve years of Bible study. Hypocrisy gets on my nerves."

"It was nice of you to defend Carl."

"Well, he defended us, and I still need to apologize for the way I treated him the last time." I heard the Weasel arguing with Jackie. Sam continued in a serious tone. "Carl is a nice guy, Adam. If you want to spend more time with him . . . just the two of you . . . you should do that. I won't stop you."

I wasn't sure what he meant. My name was mentioned, and someone asked, "Is that the big one or the little one?" I wanted to object to being called 'little,' but I responded to Sam.

"Yeah, Carl is a good guy, and he's our friend . . . but that's all. He's just a friend. I want to spend my free time with you."

I heard Joe say, "I'll second the motion!"

"I know," said Sam, "but . . . if you ever want to change that, I want you to know . . ."

"Adam? Mr. Evans?" Pastor Fletcher called my name. I stood up. "Do you accept the nomination?"

"The nomination for what?"

"For president of the neighborhood association."

What the hell? The Weasel was fuming. Everyone looked at me. "Me? Are you kidding? I didn't even want a neighborhood association. I hate meetings . . . I don't like people . . . and if it were up to me, we would help each other make the neighborhood look better and forget about all this other crap!"

The owner of the doughnut shop yelled, "He's perfect!" People laughed and clapped.

The pastor spoke again. "There's a consensus that we should vote for the leadership we want. You've been nominated along with Mrs. Van Wooten."

I was dumbfounded. "Come on! There must be someone else . . ." I looked around the room. "Flora?" She shook her head. Joe grinned at me and Ledell nodded. Jack and Jackie looked at me expectantly. I realized Jackie had nominated me. There were hard, hostile expressions as well. Carl stood there with a little smile, waiting to see what I would do. I looked at Sam.

"You should do it."

I took a deep breath and let out a heavy sigh. "Fine. Whatever. Yeah, I accept." There was more clapping as I sat down heavily and muttered every profanity I had ever heard. Sam squeezed my shoulder.

Pastor Fletcher continued. "Shall we take a simple vote and see how it goes?' The crowd voiced approval. "I'll abstain and count the votes." She walked to the front of the room and quietly asked the Weasel to surrender the lectern. Dr. Van Wooten had to drag her away from it. A strand of hair stuck out from her stiff hairdo.

"We'll use a show of hands. Please keep your hands up until I finish counting. All those in favor of Helen Van Wooten for president of the neighborhood association raise your hands." Hands went up all over the room. I didn't want to see who would vote for someone like her. The room was quiet while she counted. "Twenty-two votes for Helen Van Wooten. All those in favor of Adam Evans for president, raise your hands, please." Sam raised his hand. I slid down in my chair, trying to decide whether I would prefer to win or lose. I thought about slipping out the back door. The counting seemed to go on forever. "For Adam Evans . . . forty-three votes." A cheer went up with another round of applause.

Fuuuuck! My life is ruined. This is the worst thing that's ever happened to me. I should move to another city.

Sam grabbed my hand. "Adam, stand up. Try to smile." I did as I was told and waved to my subjects.

The Weasel finally came unhinged. "You'll regret this! All of you! The gay agenda is an insidious disease! It will infect everyone!" Her husband tried to silence her. "They're everywhere! Where you least suspect! You'll see!" Pastor Fletcher helped Dr. Van Wooten move his wife to an exit. People who voted for her were leaving, and those who voted for me approached with congratulations and handshakes.

Joe yelled out, "Speech! We want a speech!" I made a mental note to kill him and find a new home for his daughter.

As more people chanted, "Speech," Sam spoke into my ear, "I'm sorry, but I need to go back to work. I'll see you later." He pulled away before I could stop him.

"But . . . wait! I need you." He was already near the door, and then he was gone. Reluctantly, I walked to the front of the room and approached the lectern. The opening chords of "Don't Cry for Me Argentina" sounded in my head. I scolded myself for being so gay.

"Umm . . ." *A wonderful way to start a speech.* "What can I say? I'm not much of a speaker." I remembered something important. "I wanted to point out that I'm not little. People were calling me the little guy, but I'm five-ten. It's just when I'm standing next to . . . Sam, my . . . um . . . he's the big guy. We don't live together, by the way. He rents the apartment above my garage. He's very tall. Anyway . . . um . . . could we focus on the painting project for now? That's about all I can handle. I think it's good for the neighborhood, so . . . anyone who wants to help can call me or Carl . . . I mean Officer Hanson."

"Carl is fine," he said.

"Okay . . . Carl. We're working together on this, so . . . I have more of those flyers if you want one. Um . . . meeting adjourned?"

The doughnut shop guy shouted, "Yeah! That's what I'm talkin' about!" There was a final round of applause, and the group started to break up.

I stayed to talk to some of the people who supported me. Joan promised to bring me a pie. I told Joe I would kill him. Ledell shook my hand so vigorously my teeth rattled. I listened to people's ideas for other projects until my head was swimming. Flora stepped in to rescue me. "Adam, you must be exhausted. We should get you home so you can recover from all this social interaction. Did you walk here? Let us give you a ride."

Carl came over to shake my hand. "Congratulations, I suppose. I could have warned you Joe was plotting to get you elected, but he asked me not to. He thought you wouldn't show up if you knew."

"He was right. I'm planning to kill him, by the way. Do you handle homicides?"

"No. We're still painting his house, right?"

"Yeah, we can't back out now."

I thanked Kate Fletcher and accepted her invitation to dinner without committing to a date. I liked her. I was afraid I would start liking random people and my life would spin out of control. As if it hadn't already.

I sat in the back of Clarence's car with Agnes. "Thank you for your contribution to the meeting, Agnes."

"You're welcome, Mr. Adam." Steady as ever, no emotion.

Clarence looked at us in the rearview mirror. "What did she say?"

I knew Agnes wouldn't repeat her remark. "Do you mind if I tell him?" She shrugged. "Uh . . . she called the Weasel Woman a sour-faced cow." I started laughing before I finished saying it. Flora joined me.

"You did not!"

"I certainly did. It's what she is."

Clarence's laugh was a funny, wheezing sound. The more I thought about Agnes' insult and the expression on the Weasel's face, the funnier it was. Flora kept laughing as well. Clarence had to pull over until he recovered. Agnes looked out the window.

***

After taking a long nap, I drank a glass of wine while making a seafood pasta salad for dinner. When I heard Sam's truck pull into the driveway, I went onto the porch to greet him. He looked tired, but he smiled. "Mr. President, how are you?"

"Better, now that you're here."

"Why? What's wrong?" He gave me a quick kiss.

What is wrong? Good question. "Nothing. I wish you could have stayed at the meeting."

"I had to go back to Dave's. One of the guys didn't show up for work and we were busy."

"I understand. But I liked having you there with me." So much was left unsaid. *I never want to be away from you. I can't do this alone. Everything scares me. I would be lost without you.* I didn't want to sound needy. "Are you hungry?"

"Of course. Are you kidding?" I had a plate of crackers loaded with spray cheese on the table. He sat facing the counter where I stood. "What's this for?"

"Appetizers for you. Do you ever wonder why they're called appetizers? Are they supposed to make you hungrier? What do you want to drink?"

"Iced tea is fine." He put a cracker in his mouth. "What did I miss after I left?"

I told him about the last part of the meeting, my awkward speech, my plan to kill Joe, the people who talked to me afterward, the invitation from Kate Fletcher, and the ride home in the car with Agnes. Sam's eyes followed me as I moved around the kitchen preparing our dinner. He ate his crackers and listened while I talked.

I served the pasta salad at the kitchen table without any fuss. He told me about the stresses of his day. I wanted to ask why he said I could spend more time with Carl, but our ordinary conversation about everyday things was familiar and comforting, and he was tired. *We can talk about that another time.* The tension I had been feeling since he left me at the meeting gradually dissipated. *He's here now. We're okay. There's nothing to worry about.*

30

The weather was hotter than usual for September. I spent a lot of time watering the flower beds so they wouldn't dry out. The large blooms of hydrangeas dominated the garden, but my blanket flowers held their own with a riot of orange and yellow. Japanese anemones floated above sturdy red sedum. Fat, happy bees buzzed around, tolerating my interruption of their work. The new showpiece was the perennial hibiscus I got from Dave in the spring. The blossoms were large enough to be intimidating.

The community painting project took up a lot of my time as well. We began work the weekend after the neighborhood association meeting when Carl arrived with the kids who would be helping us and the social worker who was the director of the program. The kids weren't as rough-looking as I expected, but some of them would rather have been sleeping. There was a heavy-set girl with a lot of tattoos and piercings who scared me at first, until I discovered her dark sense of humor. We had a little competition to see which one of us could come up with the *worst* worst-case-scenarios in any given situation. I won more often than she did and earned a few worried looks from the social worker.

Sam and I had to adjust to having fewer days together. He was upset that Henry changed my schedule, but Sam's work schedule created the problem in the first place. The nursery did most of its business on weekends and that wouldn't change. While I spent weekends working on Joe's house, Sam covered more weekend shifts for some of his co-workers. At least we had our evenings together.

I was due for my follow-up appointment with Dr. Rubin, so I scheduled it during my lunch hour one day. He came into the exam room with my chart open in his hand. "Adam, good to see you. I'm a little concerned about something."

Oh, fuck! "What is it?"

"Well . . . I told you to come back and see me in three months . . . and you did what I asked." He pressed his hand against my forehead. "Are you feeling okay?"

I sighed with relief. "Are you this sarcastic with all of your patients?"

"No." He continued to look at my chart, shaking his head. "This is very strange."

"Now what?"

"I asked you to gain ten pounds and you've gained twelve. Take your shirt off and hop on the table, please?"

"I wasn't trying to gain more than ten. I suppose you'll want me to lose weight now."

"No." He poked and prodded me. "Your weight is at the low end of the normal range for your height and age. That's fine. Your muscle tone has improved. Are you exercising more?"

"Yes. Running and calisthenics."

"Hmm. I bet you haven't seen the psychologist I recommended."

"Yes, I have. I was going every week at first, but now it's every other week. He says I'm getting better."

"What do you think?"

"Yeah, I'm better. I'm happier. I feel more confident. I don't know if you'll think this is good or not, but a couple of weeks ago I stood up to someone who used to intimidate me. I told him I hated his guts. He's an asshole."

"Hmm. Who is he?"

"A coworker, and my temporary boss."

"Okay. Aren't you worried about that?"

"Not really. Whatever happens, happens. It was worth it. I'll be okay."

"Huh." He finished his exam. "I hate to say this, but you appear to be healthy and normal. You'll put me out of business if you keep this up. Do you have any other concerns?"

"Um, yeah, could you repeat those tests you did last time?"

"For sexually transmitted diseases? Are you still in a relationship? Are you having unprotected anal sex?"

"Yeah, we're still together, and yes, we . . . do that."

"Anal sex? Can you say anal sex?"

"Do I have to?"

"Yes."

"Fine. We have anal sex. Without condoms." My face felt hot.

"Why? It's not safe."

"It didn't feel right with condoms, and we got tested before we did it."

"Are you monogamous?"

"Yeah."

"Then why do you want to get tested again?"

I sighed. "He was . . . promiscuous . . . in the past. Not anymore. I don't want you to think he's a . . . whatever. Sam's a great guy. But he's young, and he was on the wrong path for a while. It's over now. Everything is great."

Dr. Rubin nodded. "Well, if he has anything to do with the improvement I'm seeing, he must be good for you. We can repeat the tests."

"Do you have to stick those things in my penis again?"

"No, you can pee in a cup this time. That's your reward for following my orders for a change. Or I could give you a sucker.

"Can I have both?"

He smiled. "Sure. I'll get you a sucker on your way out. You look good, Adam. Keep it up."

***

As soon as I returned to my office, the moment I sat down in my chair, my phone rang. Guess who it was? "Donna, seriously . . . who is telling you when I come and go? This is creepy."

"Never mind that. Zipinski was here again."

"Was he looking for me? Was he in my office?"

"No, he was in Henry's office. Voices were raised. Henry didn't look happy when it was over."

"What were they talking about?"

"I don't know, I don't have spies everywhere. Where were you, anyway?"

"I'm surprised you don't already know. I had a doctor's appointment."

"What's wrong with you?"

"Nothing. I'm healthy. He wanted me to gain weight and I did."

"Are you kidding me? I wish my doctor would say that. How are things with you and Sam? Is he still pretending it was okay for you to run off that day?"

Here we go. "Uh, no . . . he yelled at me recently." I invented things to satisfy her expectations. "It was like a delayed reaction. He wouldn't have sex with me for three days. I certainly learned my lesson."

"Good! I'm glad he doesn't put up with your bad behavior. It must be awful to have a man like Sam around and not have sex with him. That body . . . his smooth young skin . . ."

"I'm hanging up now. Hey, weren't we planning to get together again this summer?"

"No, I'm too busy."

"Busy with what?"

"Stuff. My weekends are full. I have a call coming in. Bye." She hung up on me.

I stared at the phone. *How rude! Who responds to an invitation that way?* I chewed the remains of my sucker and returned to my work.

***

On a Sunday after we started painting Joe's house, Sam had the day off and agreed to come and work with me. Carl and his young crew were already busy scraping the old paint off a section of the wooden siding and trim under Ledell's supervision. Carl's well-built upper body was on display in a gray ribbed tank top. When he climbed down from the scaffolding to greet us, his arms were shiny with perspiration. But that's irrelevant. I wasn't looking at him.

When Sam reached out to shake Carl's hand my heart thumped with anxiety, but I didn't intervene. It was a friendly handshake, firm and manly, but no bones were broken. I breathed a sigh of relief. "I'm glad you came, Sam. Thanks for your support at the neighborhood meeting. You must know the Bible well if you can quote it like that. I was impressed."

Sam shrugged. "My parents drilled it into me. Listen, Carl, I owe you an apology for the day the shed was moved. I was rude, and you didn't deserve it. I'm sorry."

Carl looked surprised. "Okay. Apology accepted. You made up for it at the meeting. And I'm pretty sure you gave Dr. Van Wooten a woody."

Sam blushed, I snickered. "What's up with him? Do you think the Weasel doesn't see what's right under her nose? He couldn't be more obvious!"

Carl laughed. "I know, but even *he* might not know he's gay. He wouldn't be the first guy who was so far in the closet he couldn't see the door."

Sam shifted the focus back to Carl. "You look like you've been hitting the weights pretty hard. Your arms and shoulders are jacked."

"Thanks." Carl flexed a little, but I barely noticed. "I've been lifting heavier. I want to look like I can handle myself out on the street, you know? Besides, I need to look my best to attract someone like Adam."

Uh oh. This might take an ugly turn . . .

Sam paused. "There's no one else like Adam."

Carl realized he may have said the wrong thing. "I know, I didn't mean . . ."

"But I'll sell him to you for a hundred bucks."

Hey! I glared at Sam.

Carl didn't know what to say. "Uh . . . he's worth more than that, isn't he?"

Sam grinned and wrapped his arm around me. "Yeah, he is." He kissed my head. "I don't deserve him."

"You two look good together. You complement each other."

A lump of emotion got stuck in my throat. *Damned emotions!*

Sam let go of me. "It looks like you have enough volunteers here, Adam. I should go back home and work on the garden shed today. I need to get it done before summer is over."

"What? But . . . "

"You'll be done around dinner time, so I'll order pizzas and we can eat in the garden. How about that?"

Carl looked back and forth between us. "There's plenty of work here, Sam. You could work with Adam."

"No, you can keep each other company. That shed has a lot of fancy trim, so it'll take me a while to do it right." He backed away from us.

I was glad Sam didn't mind me working with Carl, but . . . I didn't like this. I approached him so we could speak privately. "Sam, I wanted to spend the day with you."

"I'll be a couple blocks away. You can call me during breaks and we'll spend the whole evening together. I'll think up some hot stuff for us to do tonight." He kissed my forehead. "I'll see you later." He turned and walked down the street. I came back to Carl with tears in my eyes, but I pretended they weren't there.

"Is everything okay? Are the two of you . . ."

"Yeah, we're fine. Everything's fine."

"You don't have to stay here if you don't want to."

"I want to be here. This whole thing was my idea. Sam has his projects and I've got mine. We can't spend all our time together. We'd get sick of each other, right?"

"There's nothing wrong with wanting to be together. You have a good thing going with him. I wasn't sure it would work at first, but I see it now. Sam seems more mature."

"Does he? He's . . . he's good for me. It works for both of us."

"He's different with you, Adam. He's not like he was before."

"Thanks, Carl. I'm sorry I'm all . . . emotional. Let's get to work. I didn't come here for conversation." I grabbed a paint scraper. I threw myself into the work and distracted myself by talking to the other volunteers. I only called Sam once during a break. I didn't want to be too needy. Everything was fine.

After we were done for the day, I said my goodbyes, thanked Carl again, and I walked home. The closer I got, the more anxious I felt. I was afraid Sam wouldn't be there. I picked up my pace. When I saw him standing near the garden shed, shirtless and covered in paint chips, I ran at him. He saw me coming and opened his arms. He must have been tired, because he lost his balance and fell onto the grass with me on top of him.

He laughed. "What the hell, Adam? You never did that before."

I kissed every part of his face. "I missed you. I was afraid you wouldn't be here."

"Why wouldn't I be here? I'm not going anywhere." He wrapped his strong arms around me. "I promised you, remember? I won't leave you."

I kissed his sweaty chest. "Yeah, I remember. But you know how I am."

"Yeah . . . I know how you are." He hugged me tightly.

"Uh . . . dudes? Is this a bad time?"

Startled, I rolled off Sam and looked up. It was the pizza guy – the cute scruffy one who gave me his phone number.

"Did you order pizzas?"

"Yes, we did." I stayed on the ground. "How are you this evening?"

"All is well. Do you want me to put these somewhere?"

"On the table is fine." I sat up and felt the back of my shorts for my wallet. Sam stayed on the grass with his hands behind his head. *Is he showing off his biceps?*

The guy set down the pizzas and looked at us with a goofy expression. "I could join you dudes down there if you're cool with that."

I grinned. "Mmm-no." I pointed at Sam. "If he weren't here, I might take you up on that, but . . . he gets kinda jealous." Sam flexed his biceps and grunted.

Pizza Guy held up his hands. "Dude, I'm just bein' friendly. Everything's copacetic."

I stood up to pay him. "Can I ask you something? When you leave your phone number with guys . . . does it usually work for you?"

He nodded and smiled. "I do all right."

I looked him straight in the eyes. "I bet you do. Thanks for the offer. Have a good evening." I handed him enough money to cover the pizzas and a big tip.

He gave a mock salute. "Dude . . . Big Dude . . . it's been a pleasure. Enjoy yourselves." He walked away with his fist full of cash. He had a nice butt, too.

Sam reached up and pulled me on top of him again. "If I didn't know better, I'd say you were flirting with him."

"Yeah? What if I was?"

He spoke softly with his face very close to mine. "Well . . . I might have to hurt him."

"Mmmm." I kissed him. "That's so hot."

29

My birthday was approaching, and Sam hadn't said anything about making plans. I hadn't celebrated my birthday for years, but . . . I made a fuss over his birthday. I dropped a few hints about it. He didn't pick up on them. One night during dinner I asked him directly, "Are we doing anything for my birthday? It's coming up pretty soon."

"Oh, yeah," he said blandly. "I thought I would take you to a nice restaurant. I could wear the new clothes you bought for me. Would you like that?"

"Sure, that sounds nice. I don't want you to spend too much, though. We could go out to lunch instead. It's cheaper. Or breakfast. I haven't gone out for breakfast for a long time."

"Okay, breakfast it is, then."

What?! "Um, really?"

“No.” He gave me one of his looks. "I already have a restaurant picked out. Dave says it's one of the best."

"What is it? What's it called?"

"Um, let me think . . . I know it has the word 'taco' in the name. Taco Hut? Taco Barn? Something like that."

"Uhhhh . . ."

"It's not a taco place, Adam. Let me make the plans and surprise you, okay?"

I wasn’t crazy about surprises. "You won’t spend too much, will you?"

He rolled his eyes. "Enough! I have extra cash from the tips I've been getting this summer. Don't worry about it or we'll talk about how much you spent on my birthday."

That shut me up. "I wonder if Flora will invite us over for my birthday. It's your turn to get drunk if she does."

"She hasn't mentioned anything yet? Does she know when your birthday is?"

"Yeah, I think so. It would be awkward if I brought it up."

"I'll ask her if I see her, or Agnes. If I think of it." He didn't sound motivated.

"Next Sunday would be the closest to my birthday. I'm just saying. "

"Okay. Why don't we plan to go out to dinner next Sunday, and if they invite us for that day, we can do our dinner the following weekend. Unless you already have other plans."

He must have been kidding. "What other plans would I have?"

There was a twinkle in his eye. "I don’t know. Now that you're the president of the neighborhood association you'll probably get lots of invitations."

"God, I hope not. That reminds me, I have to kill Joe." Sam looked up at me briefly. No reaction. He knew me too well. I tried to get on his nerves again, just for fun. "Are you going to ask what I want for a birthday gift?"

He sighed. "Okay. What would you like for your birthday?"

"Oh . . . I don't need anything." He stared at me. "Maybe a certificate for an oil change? That's a nice gift." I waited for him to react.

His face was blank. "Good idea. Anything else?"

Dammit! I thought I had him. "Um . . . I could use a new spatula. You know, the rubber kind?" *That should do it.*

His face twitched. "I should write these down." He knew what I was up to. "What else?"

I'd better go big this time. "Well . . . what I really want . . . I don't know if you'll be comfortable with this, but . . . you know how most people have a picture of their family on their desks at work?" His eyes softened. "I'd like to have a plaster cast of Mr. Buns."

His mouth curled into a smile. "You're getting too good at this. I need to improve my game." He shook his head.

I didn't smile. "I'm serious. I could use it as a pencil holder."

"Just stop. I almost believed the oil change, but that was it." He speared a piece of meat and stuck it in his mouth. "Now, what day is your birthday again? And how old will you be?" He was trying to get on my nerves.

***

The next day I received a phone call from Flora inviting us to an early dinner on Sunday. "I'm sorry to give you such short notice, dear. It slipped my mind. Thank goodness Samson reminded me. I hope you haven't made other plans."

"Nothing we can't postpone. Of course we'll be there. I suppose Agnes has something special planned?"

"I'm afraid we haven't discussed it yet, dear. I'm sure she'll come up with something. We know you don't like to be fussed over, so let's keep it simple, shall we?"

"Um, sure." *I could live with a little bit of a fuss.* "Simple is good. Just the way I like it." *Nice to know they're putting so much effort into this.*

"All right, dear, I'm sure you're busy, so I'll let you get back to work. We'll see you on Sunday."

"Okay. Thank you. Bye now." *Hmph!*

***

On Sunday morning, Sam followed me from my bed into the shower. After he finished rubbing me dry with a big fluffy towel, I sat on a stool, naked, and watched him shave at one of the big marble sinks in the bathroom. This was one of my favorite things to do on days when we woke up at the same time. He looked so good with a white towel around his narrow waist, his smooth, tanned skin glistening with moisture. Accustomed to my lustful gaze, he let me enjoy it.

"I wonder what Agnes is cooking for your birthday. Did you make any requests?"

"No. Flora said they would keep it simple, whatever that means."

"I told them you wouldn't want a big production. I didn't want you to feel embarrassed."

"Good. Thanks." *Thanks for asking ME what I wanted!*

"At least it's not so hot today. Maybe we'll eat on the terrace."

"Will you wear your swimming suit? We can use the pool."

"Uh, yeah. I guess so." He seemed hesitant. "Do you have anything other than your red Speedo, or is that what you always wear?"

"Why? I thought you liked my speedo."

"I do, it's just . . . sometimes I feel self-conscious wearing next to nothing with other people are around."

"You mean Agnes? She certainly likes to look at you, that's for sure. Who wouldn't?"

"Yeah, yeah. I'm not used to it, except with you." He rinsed the shaving cream off his face. The wet hair on his forearms settled into dark swirls.

"I'm glad you're comfortable with it, because I never get tired of staring at you."

He removed the towel from his hips and pressed it against his face. He inspected his smooth, sculptured jaw in the mirror. "I'm tempted to take you back to bed, but we should probably get dressed."

"Yeah, and I want to eat breakfast so the champagne doesn't go to my head this time." I stood next to him, rubbing his butt like a good luck charm.

"Do you remember saying you would never drink again?"

"No. You must be thinking of someone else." I puckered my lips like a fish.

He bent his knees to kiss me. "Yeah. Someone else."

Sam went back to his apartment to get dressed and returned a while later wearing the green polo shirt I bought for him - the one that matched his eyes - with crisp khaki shorts, and preppy tan deck shoes. He had a gift bag I used for one of his birthday gifts. "I figured you would approve of reusing this bag." He sat down at the kitchen table.

"This is for me? You shouldn't have!"

“Yeah, right.”

I reached into the bag and pulled out three cotton t-shirts in bright blue, fire engine red, and black. I didn’t expect clothing, but I was pleased. "Nice!" I saw the size on the labels. "These are mediums. I wear large shirts."

"I know, most of your clothes are too big. You should show off your body a little more."

"Me? What are you talking about? I'm not built like you."

"I don't want to hear about me. This is about you. There's something else in the bag." I looked and pulled out the last item - a pair of cream colored shorts made of soft cotton, one size smaller than I normally wore. I looked at Sam skeptically. I never would have bought those shorts. "Try those on with the blue shirt."

I paused for a minute to make sure he wasn't kidding, then started to undress. I stripped down to my Speedo and stepped into the shorts. As soon as I pulled them up I felt like they were too small even though they buttoned easily. It seemed like there wasn't enough fabric. He smiled with approval, so what could I do? I squirmed into the shirt. When I pulled it down, it barely covered the waistband of the shorts. Most of my shirts covered my crotch.

"Oh, yeah! That's more like it."

"But . . . if I raise my arms, my belly will show." I did it, and it did.

He nodded. "Uh huh, it sure does." He licked his lips. "We need a mirror. Let's go upstairs." He gently pushed me through the house and followed me up the stairs. "Your butt looks great in those shorts."

In my dressing room, I stepped in front of the full-length mirror while he stood to the side and watched me. I expected to look silly, but . . . I didn't. I turned from side to side, running my hands over my chest, my hips and my butt. "That's weird. I look thinner, even though I gained weight."

"I know, you look great." He gave my chest a little squeeze. "That's from all those push-ups you've been doing."

"My arms look better, too. And my shoulders."

"Yeah, they do." His fingertip traveled down my triceps. "It's hard to choose a favorite part, though. There's so much to like."

"Such as?" Yes, I was fishing for compliments. *I used to hate compliments.*

"Let me show you." He lifted the front of my t-shirt. "This patch of hair on your chest . . . I like that a lot." He traced it with his finger. "I like the way it smells at the end of the day."

My face lit up in the mirror. *I didn't know that.*

He pulled the shirt down and smoothed it over my body. "And I like the way your jaw is shaped." He touched it gently. "I remember how much I wanted to kiss it when I first met you." He leaned down and demonstrated. "Right there. That's the best spot."

I had to admit, I looked handsome with a smile. *Not bad. Not bad at all.*

He crouched next to me and slid his hand up my leg until it was on the inside of my thigh. "And this." He squeezed. "I love seeing the white skin above your tan line." He stroked the hair in that spot. He knew I was getting aroused. "Do you know how often I watch you? When you're in the kitchen, or in the garden, bending over a flower bed. You gained weight in all the right places."

Who wouldn't want to hear that? "Are you sure these shorts aren't too small?"

"Let me check." He stood up and slipped his hand down the front of the shorts until he cradled my genitals. He kissed the side of my neck. "If I can get my hand in your pants, they're big enough."

"Okay, you convinced me. How much time do we have before we need to be at Flora's?"

"I think we have enough time."

"We'll have to take another shower."

"I can live with that."

"Should I wear these clothes today?"

"Oh, yes. Definitely. But right now, I want them off. Hurry."

***

We arrived at Flora's later than expected, our hair still damp from the shower. Flora opened the door instead of Agnes, and I apologized. "I'm sorry we're late. I was doing yoga and I lost track of time. Then we needed to shower, so . . ."

Flora smiled knowingly. "Yes, dear, that's a very convincing story." She chuckled and Sam blushed. "You look very relaxed, Adam. Yoga does wonders for you. Have you lost weight?"

"No, I've gained weight. Sam bought these clothes for me and they fit better than my other stuff. I think I'll let him make all my decisions from now on."

Sam scoffed. "Yeah, like that'll happen."

Flora put her arm around Sam's waist. "Samson, your physique is extraordinary! I hope you're not using those chemicals that are so popular these days." She squeezed his thick forearm.

He blushed again. "No, I don't do steroids. Adam forces me to work out every day. He's very demanding."

I nodded. "It's his job to look pretty."

Flora laughed. "You're starting to sound like an old married couple, like my husband and I did." She turned and raised her voice. "Agnes, dear! Our guests have arrived! Where are you?"

Agnes could be heard before she was seen. "All right, keep your bloomers on! I was preparing the steaks." She bustled into the hallway wiping her hands on a towel and gave us quite a shock. Instead of her usual black uniform, she was wearing a dress with a subtle floral design in brown and beige. It was such a departure from her usual appearance I couldn't help but blurt out a comment.

"Oh my God! Look at you!"

She stopped in her tracks and glared at me. "And a good day to you, as well, Mr. Adam." Sarcasm. "Is there something you'd like to say?"

"No! I'm . . . you're . . ."

"Agnes, you look great!" That was Sam, of course. *Always makes me look bad.*

"And why do you sound surprised?" *Okay, maybe it backfired.*

Flora defended us. "Agnes, dear, you must learn how to take compliments. They're admiring your new dress."

Agnes looked uncomfortable. "Aye, ma'am, but if I'd known people would be leering at me I'd have stayed in the black. My apologies. We're pleased to have you here, as always."

"If it'll make you feel better, you could compliment us. We're not comfortable with it either."

"Adam bought this shirt for my birthday, and I bought him those clothes. What do you think?"

She inspected each of us with her usual blank expression. "Truth be told, I prefer ye both with your kit off."

Flora laughed. It took me a moment to understand what Agnes meant. Sam didn't get it. "Without clothes," I said. He winced and put a hand over his eyes.

"I'll serve champagne on the terrace." Agnes turned and went back to the kitchen.

Flora explained in a whisper, "I've been trying for years to get her out of her maid's uniform. After the Van Wooten's comments at the neighborhood association meeting, she agreed to buy a dress. She's terribly self-conscious about it. I only wish I could get her to stop talking like a servant."

Sam seemed distracted. "Let's go outside, Adam. I want champagne." He grabbed my hand and tugged on my arm.

"Jeez! What's the rush? Are you planning to get drunk again?"

"Hey, you can't lecture me after the last time we were here. It's okay to tell me if I've had enough, but I'll do the same for you. Agreed?"

"Okay, Dad. Whatever you say." He opened the sliding glass door. I stepped onto the terrace and a cry of "SURPRISE!" scared the shit out of me. I tried to run back into the house, but Sam had a firm grip on my arm.

Cries of "Happy birthday, Adam!" came from all around. It felt like there were a hundred people, but I realized it was only Donna and her family. And, most surprising, Dave stood to one side looking like he didn't know what to do.

"What the hell? Who invited you guys?" Yes, my social skills were improving.

Donna made a face. "I knew you would be thrilled. Just for that, I'll hug you." She got her arms around me before I could run away and planted a purposeful kiss on my cheek. I had a feeling she put on extra lipstick for me. When she finally let go, she stepped back and did a visual assessment. "You look sexy today. Who did this to you?"

"Sam. He says most of my clothes are too big."

She looked at Sam. "Thank you! Finally! Now I get to hug *you*." She pounced on him.

Kevin rolled his eyes and shook his head. "Good to see you again, Adam. Happy birthday."

We shook hands. "Thanks. I hoped we would get together again this summer, but your wife claimed she was too busy."

"She was trying to keep this a secret. Sam invited us a few weeks ago."

"He definitely surprised me." *He made a fuss after all!*

Dave approached sheepishly. He looked different in a plaid sport shirt instead of his green polo. "Adam, I hope you don't mind me being here. The kid pressured me to come, no matter how many times I turned him down."

"Why would I mind? You're one of our friends. Who's running the nursery while you're here?"

"I shut the place down for the day. We're getting into the slow season and I haven't taken a day off in ten years." He glanced around. "I can't remember the last time I went to a party."

"It'll be fine. You'll be glad you came when you taste whatever Agnes is making. She may be the best cook in town."

"That's what Sam says. Wouldn't shut up about it until I agreed to come."

"He's persistent. Have you met Kevin already?"

"Yeah, Mrs. O'Neill got us all acquainted. She's quite a lady. I hope they have more than champagne, though. I'm not that fancy."

"I'm sure they do. Let me say hello to the kids. I'm working on my manners." I left Dave with Kevin and approached Sarah, who was eavesdropping on Donna and Sam. "Hi, Sarah. How are you?"

"I'm fine, thank you. How are you?"

"Good. What are they talking about? Tell me everything."

She smiled. "I'm not sure, I can't hear all of it. Something about you."

"Good or bad?"

She laughed a little. "Um, mostly good. It's like . . . Mom is telling Sam you're a good person, and he says he already knows, and then she says the same thing again. She does that with me all the time. Did you have an argument with Sam?"

"Uh . . . sort of. I mean, I did something . . . I ran away from home for a day, and I didn't tell anyone where I was, and they were mad at me."

"Why did you run away?"

"I needed time to think about something."

"Did it help?"

"Yeah, it did. But I should have called to let them know I was okay. They were worried about me."

"My mom worries about me, too. I wish she would stop. I'm, like, almost fifteen already and she treats me like I'm a baby. It's so annoying."

"It's annoying, but . . . what if you were having a rough time and *no one* was worried about you? How would that feel?"

She was quiet for a minute. "I guess it wouldn't be very good." She laughed nervously and looked at the ground. "Do you worry about anyone?"

"Oh yeah, I'm good at that. I worry about myself a lot, and I worry about Sam, and your mom sometimes but she can take care of herself. I worry about a lot of stuff."

"You can worry about me if you want. If you have time, I mean. And I could worry about you."

She caught me off guard. A lump of emotion was stuck in my throat again. *Dammit!* I bobbed my head up and down while trying to get a word out. "'Kay." I kept nodding. "Okay."

"What are you two talking about?" It was Donna.

I shook my head back and forth. "Nothing. It's private." Sarah smiled.

"You're having a conversation with my daughter and you won't tell me what it's about?"

"You don't need to know everything. What were you and Sam talking about?"

"Nothing."

"Okay then. I'm getting champagne. Do you want any, Sarah? Wait, you're too young. Never mind." I started to walk away.

"What about me? I'm old enough."

"You certainly are. Do you know Mike is down by the pool? Are you watching him?"

"Are you questioning my parenting skills? I have eyes in the back of my head." We heard a splash. Donna didn't turn around. "Kevin?"

"I'll get him."

She smiled. "You see? I have everything under control."

"Fine, I'll get your champagne." I approached the table where Flora was helping Agnes. "I understand the two of you were planning this surprise party for weeks."

"It was Samson's idea, dear, but we were happy to be a part of it. Apparently, the secret was well-kept."

"Yes, it was. You all had me fooled. I don't like surprises, but . . ."

"We knew that, sweetie. Samson pointed out - and I believe he was correct - you never would have agreed to have your other friends celebrate with us. But here we are, and we'll all have a wonderful time." Agnes looked sympathetic.

I took two glasses of champagne and had to explain they weren't both for me. Apparently, I would never live down my drunkenness at Sam's birthday dinner. Donna had gone to the pool to help sort things out with Kevin and Mike while Dave stood near them. Sarah questioned Sam. Colin sat alone, playing with his phone, his pale, thin limbs sticking out from his black t-shirt and black shorts. I joined him. He looked up and held out his hand as though one of the glasses of champagne was for him. "Nope. That's for your mother. How are you?"

"Okay."

"What have you been up to?"

"Nothing."

"You're back in school, right? Are you a senior this year?"

"Junior."

"What classes are you taking?"

"Are you really interested?"

Hmm. "No. Read any good books lately?"

"Yeah." I thought he wouldn't elaborate, but he did. "I read *Tess of the D'Urbervilles*."

"Oh, what did you think?"

"I liked it. Near the end, I was afraid it would have a happy ending, but it didn't. It was good."

"You don't believe in happy endings?"

"No, they're stupid."

"I used to think the same, but now I'm not sure. Sam liked that book, too."

"He reads books?"

"He loves to read. He recently finished *Wuthering Heights*, and I don't know what he's reading now. Does that surprise you?"

"Yeah. He looks like . . . never mind." He went back to playing with his phone.

"He looks like a big, dumb jock."

Colin's face flushed. "I didn't want to say that, but . . . yeah."

"It's okay, but Sam was never a jock and he's very smart." I took a sip of champagne. "Are you going swimming?"

"No."

"Why not?"

He shrugged.

"Will you sit around and think gloomy thoughts?"

He smiled. "Maybe."

"Fine with me. Here comes your mother, we'd better stop talking about her."

Donna heard me. "What were you talking about?"

"Nothing." We snickered.

"Is that my champagne? Give it to me." She drank half the glass in one swallow. "I'm going in the pool. Are you coming, Colin? I brought your swimsuit."

"God! Stop nagging me!"

She sighed and turned to me. "Do you think Sam will join us?"

I squinted. "Why do you ask?"

"Just curious."

Colin said what I was thinking. "You're disgusting, Mom."

"Yeah!" I lowered my voice. "Sam gets self-conscious around people who stare at him. Seriously."

"He does?"

"Yes. Women don't like it when men leer at them, so . . . it's the same thing."

"Awww! He's so sweet. Okay, I'll behave myself. Are you coming, Colin?"

"All right! Jeez!"

"Sarah! Do you want to get your swimsuit on? We're going in the pool."

Sarah was still talking to Sam. "Okay, I'm coming."

That gave me a chance to talk to Sam. I gave him a hug. "Thank you for planning this, despite the surprise part."

"I knew you would hate that, but I thought it would be nice for all of us to be together."

"It is, you were right. I can't believe you got Dave to come."

"It wasn't easy. He kept saying no, but I had a feeling he would like it. He asks about you all the time."

"He's known me nearly as long as Flora and Agnes have, but I only ever saw him at the nursery. I should show him my garden."

"I invited Joe, but he thought Susan wouldn't do well with a lot of strangers. They might stop by later for a few minutes to see how it goes. I even invited Carl, but he wasn't comfortable with it, so . . . I wish I hadn't screwed that up."

"Oh, Sam . . ." I hugged him again.

"All right, break it up!" It was Dave. "You're makin' me jealous."

"Hey, did you get anything to drink yet? We should ask them what they have."

We approached Flora and Agnes who were fussing at each other about seating arrangements. "Adam, would you *please* tell Agnes she should sit with us for dinner? She's working on my last nerve!"

Agnes didn't give me a chance. "Och! Don't waste yer breath. I won't have a chance to sit while I'm serving the meal, and there's only enough room for the guests."

Sam offered to assist. "I was a waiter, Agnes, I can help serve."

"No, Mr. Sam, I won't have it. I've been serving dinner parties for over forty years and I'll do things my way, thank you very much."

Sam kept his mouth shut. I held up my hands in surrender.

Dave observed our interactions with a curious expression, then addressed Agnes. "Say there, Lassie . . . have you got anything else to drink besides champagne? I wouldn't mind some whiskey, but a beer would do."

Agnes straightened her spine. "We have beer and whiskey, but if you call me 'Lassie' again, I'll make soup out of your bollocks."

Dave wasn't fazed. He let out a loud "HAH!" Sam and I took a step back. "D'ya think I'm afraid of you, dearie? I've fought with women tougher than you! You might have these young fellas stepping to your tune, but not me." He pointed at her. "You're going to get some whiskey, and you and I will have a stiff drink. Then you'll sit next to me at dinner or I'll drag you out of the kitchen by your hair. And I'm not interested in anything under your dress, so don't get your hopes up."

My heart may have stopped beating. *Oh . . . my . . . GOD!* Sam and I took another step back. Flora fanned herself with her hand.

Agnes hadn't moved an inch. She measured Dave with her eyes and raised her chin a bit. "Do ye drink Macallan?"

Dave smiled. "It's better than what I usually drink. Let's go." He stepped forward and offered his elbow.

"Do I look like an invalid? Try to keep up with me." She marched toward the house. Dave winked at us and followed her.

Flora had to sit down. "How extraordinary! Like a scene from *The Taming of the Shrew.* I've never seen her so irritable."

I was amazed. "How did he do that?"

Sam replied, "He speaks his mind, but . . . wow! I can't believe he talked to Agnes that way. Do you think they'll both come out alive?"

Flora laughed. "They'll be fine. Your friend had the right idea. She'll settle down after she has a drink. I believe she's nervous about having so many guests, with children to top it off. Agnes doesn't like to admit she's not as spry as she once was. Now, could the two of you move that table over here so we can all sit together?" We carried the table from the other side of the terrace and rearranged the seating area so there was plenty of room for everyone.

Mike came running up from the pool, dripping wet. "Sam! Hey, Sam! Come in the pool! I've got some cool stuff to show you! I can do a somersault and I can do a back flip! Come on! Come on! Please? Come on!" He grabbed Sam's hand and pulled as if he could move him.

Sam shrugged. "I guess I need to go. Are you coming in, Adam?"

"I'll stay here with Flora for now. Have fun." He glanced back at me as though that was unlikely. I sat next to Flora and refilled our champagne glasses. "Poor Sam. He's too popular for his own good."

"He's such a sweetheart. He loves you very much." She put her hand on top of mine the way my mother would have done. "How are you dear? Is everything going well?"

"Yes, for the most part. A few bumps in the road, trouble at work, things like that."

"There are bumps in every road. They help keep us awake while we're driving. And how is Alvin Zipinski these days?"

"You know Mr. Zipinski?"

"We are acquainted, I'm sorry to say. I've been hearing rumors about some of his activities."

"Was it something about sexual harassment of female employees?"

"That's a nice way of putting it. It's not the first time he's been accused of such things. In the past, stronger words were used. Words like 'rape' and 'intimidation.'"

"Well, I think he'll get nailed this time. The EEOC is investigating."

She looked skeptical. "Keep in mind, Alvin has a lot of money. I assume his victims have very little. Once some of his money changes hands, you may be surprised at how little influence the authorities have. But I heard another rumor about your employer, something I hadn't heard before."

"Oh? Like what?"

"Are you familiar with Ellis Industries?"

"Yes, they're one of our biggest clients. What have you heard?"

"There's a story going around about money that's gone missing. Something the accountants should have seen. I won't repeat the unsavory details. Are you involved in any work for Mr. Ellis?"

"No, I'm not. In fact, Mr. Zipinski's new protégé, Henry Verdorven, has been handling Ellis Industries. He's a piece of work, too."

"Well, steer clear of it if you can, dear. It might get ugly. I would hate to see you caught up in dishonest business."

"Thank you, I'll be careful. Do you mind if I share this with Donna? She used to work on the Ellis account but she was taken off of it a while ago."

"Share it with whomever you trust. That's what rumors are for."

Kevin came up from the pool in wet swimming trunks and a damp t-shirt, blotting his hair with a towel. "Mind if I join you? Mike wore me out. That kid has more energy than I ever had at any age." He sat down. "I'm glad Sam took over for me, but when he stripped down to his swimsuit I had a sudden urge to put on a shirt."

I smiled sympathetically. "It's intimidating, isn't it? I felt the same way for a while, but now I know he's self-conscious about his body too."

"Come on! Guys who work out always want to show off. Some of my employees are like that. I don't think they own any shirts with sleeves."

"I'm telling you the truth, though. Sam isn't like those guys."

Flora was surprised as well. "For heaven's sake, when did men become so self-conscious? In my day, it was the women who tortured themselves over such things. The men could be as fat as they wanted to be."

"I blame the gays." Kevin winked. "They keep raising the bar for the rest of us. Now our wives expect us to shave and shower every day, and wear clothes that match, and make conversation at dinner. Donna even bought me this little machine for trimming my nose hair. Can you believe it? I should be able to sit around with my hand in my pants and drink beer and smell like a skunk if I want to. That's what makes us sexy! This is America!"

"My, oh my! I'm appreciating Mr. O'Neill more than ever. No wonder so many women don't want to have sexual intercourse with their husbands."

Kevin laughed. "That's what my friends say, but I have the opposite problem." Donna approached us wearing a bathing suit that revealed more of her than I wanted to see. "My wife wants it all the time."

I stuck my fingers in my ears and sang, "La la la la la . . ."

Donna asked, "What are you telling them about me?"

"Nothing." Kevin opened his arms to her. "Sit on my lap, gorgeous."

She dismissed the invitation with a wave of her hand. "That chair won't hold both of us. We're not in our twenties anymore." She sat down next to him.

He reached for her hand and held it. "I'm surprised you didn't stay in the pool with Sam. I know he's ugly compared to me, but you don't want to hurt his feelings."

"His skin is so perfect. I swear there's not an ounce of fat on him. It made me feel old, so I left him with the kids to punish him."

Kevin leaned over and kissed her on the cheek. "You're not old. You're still the girl I married."

"You're such a liar. That's what I like about you."

Flora and I glanced at each other. It was nice to see a married couple so obviously in love.

The rest of the afternoon was filled with enjoyable conversation, laughter, and great food. Dave, using a combination of whiskey and the dark arts, transformed Agnes from a threatening storm cloud into the stern, attentive hostess we had come to love. They also provided our entertainment. Watching the two of them argue about the best way to grill a steak was one of the funniest things I've ever seen. Agnes won, of course, but she seemed to enjoy the challenge. Flora found it all very amusing and was happy to sit back and let someone else bicker with Agnes for a change.

Unaccustomed to sitting still, Dave ended up serving half the meal under Agnes' direction. When Colin made a remark about the "dead cow," Agnes surprised him with two grilled Portobello mushrooms that filled his entire plate. "Eat those. You're too thin." Before Colin could respond, Dave added, "Do as you're told, kid." Colin started eating. Donna and Kevin smiled.

Dave refused to eat until Agnes agreed to join us, so she brought the last two plates and sat down. Sam immediately noticed the steak on Dave's plate was bigger than his. I watched him look back and forth between his plate and Dave's as if an error had been made. I leaned over and whispered, "Agnes has a new favorite. You've been dethroned." He let out a disappointed, "Aww."

Despite the casual presentation, the meal met Agnes' usual lofty standards. The steaks were served with crumbled blue cheese, and there was a green salad with cucumbers and fresh dill, warm corn muffins, and caramelized roasted cauliflower florets. Those of us who were drinking wine shared a couple of bottles of Merlot. Agnes passed the last of the cauliflower to Colin. "Eat!" He didn't complain.

Donna asked, "Is this how you usually celebrate your birthday, Adam? I wouldn't know because this is the first time I've heard about your birthday in the eight years I've known you. Maybe a few years from now I'll know your favorite color."

"There you go, trying to invade my privacy again." I addressed everyone else, "She has people spying on me at work. She knows every move I make." Donna twirled her finger around one ear to suggest I was crazy. "I can't remember the last time I celebrated my birthday. Sometime before my parents were . . . I suppose . . ."

Flora interjected, "You've had other birthdays with us, Adam. Do you remember, dear? It seems so long ago."

"Oh yeah . . ." I remembered. "Was I in high school? I must have been. I remember coming here and . . . I was afraid of you, Agnes."

Dave nudged Agnes with his elbow. "Things haven't changed much." She jabbed him more forcefully with her own elbow.

I continued, "Do you remember that cake you used to make? What was it?"

"I've cooked too many meals to recall the details. I remember you were very quiet." She looked sideways at Dave. "One of the finest qualities a man can have." Dave laughed.

"Well, whatever it was, I know it was my favorite. My mother wasn't much of a baker. I loved your desserts."

"I'd best get to it, then." Agnes stood up.

Colin offered to help. Donna and Kevin looked shocked. "What? You always tell me to help."

"Thank you, Mr. Colin. You could clear away these dishes. Perhaps Miss Sarah would assist you." Agnes poked Dave in the shoulder. "You stay seated. I've had enough of your help for one day."

After she bustled off to the kitchen, Flora complimented Dave on his rapport with Agnes. "You're a brave man. There aren't many people who can handle her with the colorful flourish you displayed. You must visit again."

Dave blushed. "Aww, come on! Anyone can see she's soft under the surface. She's not fooling anyone."

"Like Adam," said Donna.

"What? I'm not like that. Shut up!" Sam rolled his eyes. "I'm not!" I wanted to maintain my reputation.

A few minutes later, Agnes brought the dessert. Colin and Sarah followed with plates and a pot of coffee. Everyone sang, and I blew out the single candle in the center of the cake. As soon as she cut into it, I knew what it was – banana cake with lemon buttercream frosting. My old favorite. "Agnes, you remembered!" It brought a tear to my eye.

She dismissed it. "A fortunate coincidence, nothing more." Flora smiled and shook her head. We knew better, but we didn't press the issue. Agnes had a reputation to maintain.

***

After dessert, while everyone else continued chatting on the terrace, I took Dave next door to show him what I had done with all the plants he sold to me over the years. Though the garden was past its peak for the season, he was impressed. He commented on some of the plants and remembered things about my visits to his nursery when I was younger. He noticed the peony I bought on the day my parents died, now a leafy shrub. "Is that the one . . .?"

"Yeah. It had buds this year, but they didn't open. I'm thinking about digging it up."

"Don't do that. Give it another season. Some things take longer to get established, but they're worth it. You're a good gardener."

"Thanks."

"You have a nice family, too."

"Family? You mean my friends."

"Those people are more than friends, kiddo. You've got something special here. Hang onto it so you don't end up like me."

The word 'family' seemed . . . I'm not sure. It wasn't something I expected to have anymore, but I understood what he meant. "There aren't many people who remember what I was like before my parents died." I looked down at the grass, not sure if I could say what I wanted to say. "You're one of those people, Dave."

He turned away and looked at something in the distance. He pulled out his handkerchief, blew his nose, and cleared his throat. "Sorry. Must be my allergies." Eventually he faced me again. "You and Sam . . . is it good? Is it what you want?"

"Yeah, it's good. I was always afraid to admit what I wanted because I didn't think this would ever happen. I feel lucky."

"He's lucky. I tell him all the time."

"I probably shouldn't say this, but . . . I appreciate the . . . personal advice you give him. The benefits of your many experiences."

He looked confused. "What experiences?"

"You know . . . the tips . . . about sex."

"Sex? You think I talk to him about sex? No sir. I'm his boss. I wouldn't risk it. I don't need to have one of these guys accuse me of being a horny old pervert. Where are you getting this from?"

"I . . . I'm sorry. I think I must have misunderstood something. Never mind."

"Did he tell you that? I need to talk to him. What the hell is he thinking?"

"No, please don't talk to him about it! It was my mistake. He was talking about someone at work and I . . . I guess I assumed it was you. Don't mention it, okay? Please?"

"All right. If that's the way you want it." He looked concerned. "Is he lying to you? I warned him, if he ever does anything . . ."

"No, Dave, seriously, it's fine. Everything is fine. He's great, he treats me well, and things are better than ever, okay? Thanks for looking out for me, I appreciate it."

"Okay. If you say so." He looked at the garden shed. Sam had scraped off the old paint and was repairing the trim. "Is he working on this?"

"Yeah, he's doing an excellent job."

Dave looked it over. "He's got a long way to go."

Sam appeared through the opening in the hedge. "Hey, you guys . . ." He approached us. "Donna and Kevin are ready to go. You should come and say goodbye."

Dave pointed at the shed. "You need to get linseed oil on those window frames or they'll rot."

"I know, Dave, I'm working on it."

"Work harder. Winter is coming." Dave didn't wait for a reply. He walked across the garden and into Flora's yard.

Sam crinkled his brow. "What got into him? Did I do something wrong?"

"No, of course not. You know how he is. He had a good time. Let's go and say our goodbyes. I hope you didn't eat my cake."

***

It was dark by the time the guests left and we finished cleaning up. I hugged Sam on the driveway, wrapping my arms tightly around his waist. "That was a very nice party. Thank you for planning it."

"You're welcome." He rubbed the back of my head. "You give good hugs."

"I had a good teacher."

"I have another gift for you. Do you want it now, or do you want to wait until your birthday?"

"Is it a part of your body?"

"No, it's not a part of my . . . tsk . . . you really know how to ruin a nice moment."

I rubbed my face on his warm chest. "I'm sorry, but you have very nice parts."

"Do you want it now or later? The gift, I mean, not . . . sex."

"I'd like it now, please. Where is it?"

"In my apartment. Do you want to stay with me tonight? You haven't been coming over lately."

"I wanted to give you your space. But I'll stay there tonight. Let's go."

He followed me up the stairs, pulled me against his body and nuzzled my neck while unlocking the door with his free hand. He flipped on the lights without letting go of me. "Maybe I will give you sex. I can return the other thing."

"No, too late now. I know I'll get both."

"You're right. I want you to open your gift. I'm anxious to see what you think of it." He nudged me toward the kitchen table where there was a large oblong box covered in wrapping paper.

"I hope this is the spatula I asked for." I pulled at a corner of the paper and tore it, revealing a plain cardboard box. *What could this be?* I opened the flaps and pulled out balls of crushed newspaper to uncover something wrapped in white tissue paper. I lifted it out of the box.

"Careful, it's breakable." Sam removed the box from the table to give me more space.

When all the wrapping was finally removed, I held one of the most beautiful objects I've ever owned. It was a large antique Bristol glass vase, hand painted with pink Hydrangea blossoms, branches and leaves. The colors were muted, and the design reminded me of Japanese watercolors, with highlights of warm metallic gold.

"The woman at the antique shop said it was Victorian, from England. It looked like it belonged in your house. I thought it would be nice to bring more flowers indoors. I suppose you already have vases, but . . ."

"It's beautiful, Sam." It was a very thoughtful gift because it was related to the things I loved. "It's perfect."

"You like it? Good, I like it, too. I liked the colors as soon as I saw it. It's not too girly, you know. They had a lot of vases there. We should go there sometime and look around. I like antique shops . . ." He was babbling.

I moved the tissue paper aside and set the vase in the center of the table. I grasped his hand and pulled him toward the bedroom. He kept talking. He seemed happy enough but may have been nervous. He'd get like that sometimes and I would wonder what was going on inside. I didn't need to know everything.

I pushed him onto the bed and climbed on top of him, straddling his waist. He spread his arms and stopped talking when I leaned on his chest. He searched my eyes. I loved him so much. Too much, really. I knew I would get hurt. By that time, I knew it. He hid things from me, he made up stories, and I wasn't sure he was faithful to me anymore. Admitting that to myself . . . I was flooded with emotion.

"What's wrong, Adam?"

"Nothing is wrong. You're so . . ." I didn't want to tell him how beautiful he was again. *He must be getting tired of it.* "I love you an awful lot, Sam. You know that, right?"

"Of course. I know you do."

"I want to thank you, okay? I want you to remember this. Thank you for everything, for all of it. For everything we've done, and for everything that's coming."

"What are you talking about? You're scaring me."

"It's okay, don't be scared." I stroked his cheek. "But remember . . . you changed my life, Sam, and I'll always be grateful. Thank you for changing my life. Thank you for the party. And thank you for the beautiful vase. And for my new clothes that make me look thinner."

"Are you sure you're okay?"

"I'm fine. Now, what about the sex you mentioned. Is that still available?"

"Yeah, but we did it this morning." He gently stroked my arms.

"Did I wear you out? I thought you were stronger than me."

There was a glint in his eye. "Take off your shirt."

I pulled off my new t-shirt and tossed it aside. "Now it's your turn. Come on."

"Will you get off me?"

"Why don't you make me?"

He smiled and accepted my challenge.

31

A couple of days after my birthday party, I received a call from Henry's assistant. He wanted to meet with me in his office. We hadn't spoken since I stormed out of the restaurant, so I was dreading this conversation. I never knew what he was thinking and I was tired of trying to figure it out. I wanted to cut through the bullshit.

Henry had become more isolated in recent weeks, keeping his door closed and communicating with people through his assistant, a young woman who was fiercely loyal to him and seemed slightly unhinged. When I arrived at his office, she notified him by intercom and told me to go in. He was sitting at his desk looking out the window. There was a stack of file boxes marked 'Ellis Industries' next to the desk.

"Hello, Henry. Should I close the door?"

"Yes please. Have a seat, Adam." I sat in front of his desk, folded my hands in my lap, and waited. He continued to gaze out the window for a few minutes before turning to look at me. "How have you been?"

"Fine. And you?"

"I've been waiting for you to come and talk with me."

"About what, Henry? What's on your mind?"

He stared at me coolly. "An apology, perhaps? Is that too much to expect?"

I thought about it. "I suppose if I phrased it carefully, I could come up with something sincere. Would you like me to make the effort?"

One side of his mouth turned up a bit. "I would."

It took me a moment. "I'm sorry I made a scene at the restaurant."

He gently tapped the tips of his fingers together. "I forgive you, and I understand why you were so upset by my story. I understand completely."

"Do you?"

"Yes. I've seen that green-eyed monster before. Many people envy the way I indulge my sexual appetites. For someone like you, who is . . . let's be honest . . . past his sexual prime, and has stayed on the safest possible path in life, it must be painful to see what you've missed. I understand. I didn't mean to rub your nose in it, Adam. I know how happy you are in your monogamous relationship with your boyfriend." He put air quotes around "monogamous" and "boyfriend."

Henry had taken a few strands of my insecurity and twisted them into a sharp hook. I had to summon every bit of my willpower. "I forgive you, too." I didn't mean it. I wanted to press his face against a hot stove. The only satisfaction I could derive from this exchange was denying him the reaction he hoped for. "Was there anything else you wanted to discuss, Henry?"

The sparkle in his eye disappeared. "Yes. Mr. Zipinski will be returning next week. As a courtesy, I thought you should know before everyone else finds out."

"But what about the harassment complaints and the investigation?"

"All of that has been resolved. The employees who complained will quietly depart by the end of the week."

"What? He's guilty and you know it!"

"No, I don't know anything. There were ugly rumors being spread by . . . let me think . . . who was it who told me? Oh, it was you, wasn't it?"

"You offered to help those women!"

"I did help them, Adam. I encouraged them to file complaints, and they are better off financially because of my help. Zipinski needed help because of the accusations, and I was there for him. I'm a very helpful guy. I helped you get a big raise, didn't I? All I do is help people, and what do I get in return? You think I'm an asshole."

If I didn't know what he was like, his argument might have been convincing. "So Zipinski will get away with his disgusting behavior."

"Adam . . . there you go again, envying other people's sexual adventures. I'm feeling sad for you." He paused to frown. "By the way, you can't tell anyone those complaints were resolved with financial settlements because everyone signed non-disclosure agreements. We need to portray Zipinski in the best possible light. If word goes around that he paid off his victims, I'll know where it came from. I would hate to have our boss find out you've been spreading rumors about him again."

"Are you threatening me?"

"No! Of course not! We're friends, remember? Besides, I'll need your support when Zipinski gets back. He thinks I mismanaged the Ellis account and I'm depending on you, the squeaky-clean boy scout, to tell him how honest I am in my dealings with people, and what a great job I did in his absence, like you did when we were all in your office. That was perfect."

"You mean the day you tried to make it look like I was handling Ellis? What were you trying to pin on me, anyway? Embezzlement? How did you fuck up their accounts?"

"Embezzlement? Please! Have you been watching soap operas? Whatever is wrong with Ellis Industries is on their end. Maybe I overlooked a few irregularities as a favor for a friend, but who hasn't? That's how the world works. I talked Zipinski into giving you a substantial raise, now it's your turn to say nice things about me."

"We don't all live in your fucked-up world, Henry. Why would I protect your reputation?"

"Because I'll protect your reputation. That's what friends do for each other." He opened his desk drawer and pulled out a sheet of paper.

"We're not friends, you evil piece of . . ." He laid the paper in front of me. It was a copy of the Weasel Woman's flyer with the photo of me and Sam in front of my house, and the words, "Protect our children!" A chill went up my spine. "Where did you get that?"

"I have a few loyal pets here at the office, and you are not universally loved, Adam. Maybe you should have been friendlier to the staff." He smiled in a way that used to put butterflies in my stomach. Now it made me uneasy for a different reason. "Being handsome and fit goes a very long way with simple-minded young women . . . and men. Do you know my assistant? I think she would do anything for me. All I need to do is park my hot butt on the edge of her desk and smile. I asked her if she had heard anything negative about you, and a few days later she brought this to me."

I was so angry and nauseous I could have vomited on his desk. "What are you planning to do with this?"

"Nothing if you're nice to me. But it would come in handy if things don't go smoothly during the next few weeks. Can you imagine Zipinski's reaction if he saw this? It would distract him from whatever he thinks I've done wrong."

"So what! He can't fire me for being gay."

"Can't he? What would you do? File a complaint with the EEOC? I could help you with that." He winked.

I hated him more than I thought I could hate someone, but I had to consider the consequences. *How hard would it be to say vaguely positive things about him? I had no proof he did anything wrong. I wouldn't be lying.*

"Don't worry, Adam, you won't need to sing my praise for long. I'm actively seeking a new position far away from here. By the way, I'll need to use you as a reference."

I was disgusted with myself. "All right . . . anything to get rid of you." I crushed the flyer in my fist.

"That's a photocopy, of course. The original is in a safe place. By the way, your boyfriend, what's his name, looks even better than he did when he fucked me. I can't believe he ended up with *you*."

A new wave of sickness washed over me. I hadn't connected all the dots until then. "Did you see this flyer *before* we went out to lunch?"

He showed his teeth. "Yes, I did."

I rose from my chair. "You told me that story . . . *knowing* I was with him?"

"Yes. I did you a favor, Adam. You probably thought he was an innocent young thing. I assume he was dumb enough to confirm the details?"

Blinded by rage, I grabbed a marble paperweight from his desk and drew my arm back, ready to bury it in his skull. I stopped, remembering Sam's confrontation with Ed O'Neill on Flora's terrace. *Don't let him win.* I stood there, holding the heavy weight in the air, trembling.

Henry didn't move. He didn't look frightened. He looked satisfied. "You could do it, couldn't you, Adam? You hate me that much. Do you think you're better than me? Look at yourself. Whose fucked-up world do you live in now?" He glared and waited.

Slowly I lowered my arm and returned the paperweight to his desk. "Are we done here?"

"Do you understand what's expected of you?"

I curled my lip. "Yes. I'll spin things to make you look good, but I won't lie, and I won't cover up anything illegal."

He considered this for a minute. "We have a deal, but you need to control that hostile cunt you're always talking to. She has to keep her mouth shut." He turned to look out the window again. "Go and clean yourself up. You look terrible."

My face was covered with sweat. I turned and left Henry's office, passing his sycophantic assistant without looking at her, and walked straight to Donna's office. She was on the telephone. I entered without knocking and sat down.

"Oh, darn it!" she said into the phone. "I spilled coffee all over my desk. Can I call you back in a little while? Thanks." She hung up. "What the hell happened to you?"

"I had a meeting with Henry."

"I'm guessing it didn't go well. Are you in trouble?"

Was I? "No . . . not really."

"What did you discuss?"

I thought about it. "If I tell you, I will be in trouble."

"What can you tell me?"

"I came very close to bashing in his skull with a paperweight."

"Why? What did he say?"

"I can't tell you."

"Then why did you come in here?"

"To vent!"

"Nothing is coming out, Adam! That's not venting! What's going on with the Ellis account?"

"I don't know, he didn't tell me."

"What's going on with Zipinski and the harassment complaints?"

I didn't answer.

"Adam?"

"I can't!"

"I wish I had a paperweight. Why don't I have a paperweight?" She looked for a blunt instrument.

"Donna . . . have you ever thought about leaving here and starting your own business? Some people do that."

"Yeah, I looked into it after Zipinski had me written up. Our employment contracts have a non-compete agreement, so I'd have to move out of the area. Kevin's business is here and the kids are in school. But if Zipinski gets taken down by the complaints against him . . . who knows? Everything could be up for grabs."

"Henry is on his way out."

"How do you know?"

"He told me."

"Why didn't you tell me?"

"I just did!"

"Why didn't you tell me sooner? Is he in trouble?"

"No. Maybe. But he's looking for a new position far away from here. I'm guessing New York."

"Good! What can we do to push him out the door?"

"We need to say nice things about him for the next few weeks. Or at least keep quiet about him. And don't get mad at me if I compliment him. Can you do that for me? Please?"

"This is driving me crazy, Adam. What is going on? You're not leaving this office until you give me more information. I'll break your legs if I have to."

"You know, I'm feeling vulnerable right now, and it doesn't help to . . ."

"WHAT IS GOING ON?"

I jumped. "He's threatening to tell Zipinski about me and Sam. He has a copy of the Weasel Woman's flyer."

"Oh, for fuck's sake, Adam! If you hadn't lied about yourself in the first place you wouldn't have this problem!"

"No, I would've been fired months ago, and I wouldn't be sitting here now!"

"He can't fire you for being gay."

"What could I do about it?"

"You file a discrimination complaint, like . . ."

"Yeah, a fat lot of good that'll do!" *Crap! I shouldn't have said that.*

"Wait a minute . . . have the complaints been . . . is Zipinski coming back?"

"I didn't say that!"

"I need to talk to those women and find out what . . ."

"NO! Don't talk to anyone! Keep your goddamned mouth shut for a change! Remember, I'm your supervisor now. I'm *ordering* you not to discuss this with anyone!"

She stared at me with her mouth open.

"I'm sorry, but . . . you can't talk about any of this. You have no idea what Henry is capable of. Keep quiet and let the situation play itself out. If we're lucky, Henry will be out of here in a few weeks and things can go back to the way they were before he interfered in . . ."

"Before you paved the way for him to become vice-president?" There was a bitter edge to her voice.

I wasn't in the mood for any more of her criticism. "Yes, Donna, before I fucked everything up! Is that what you want to hear? Are you satisfied now? I can always count on you to tell me when I've fucked things up! I guess that's what friends do for each other." She didn't respond. I stood up to leave. "Do you understand what's expected of you?"

Her expression hardened. "Yes, I do. *Boss.* Are we done?"

"I think so." I opened the door, stepped out of Donna's office, and closed the door behind me. The women working nearby threw daggers with their eyes. I focused on the carpet and walked back to my office.

***

The rest of the day was not productive. Driving home, I was annoyed by the other cars on the road. Everyone was driving too slowly. No matter how aggressively I tailgated them, they wouldn't get out of my way. I didn't feel like cooking, but I had already taken meat out of the freezer. *Might as well cook it. Vegetables. Potatoes. Whatever. It'll be good enough.* I put the roast in the oven and went to my computer to check my e-mail. I began to look at Tumblr sites and alternated cooking with photos of naked guys and porn videos. I was standing at the stove when Sam came through the door.

"Hey, Adam. How are you?"

I didn't turn around. "Fine."

"Smells good." He came up behind me. "What are we having?"

"Pork roast." He seemed to be waiting for something. He slipped his arm around me and kissed the side of my neck. I twisted away from him. "Would you let me finish this before you start pawing me, please?"

"I'm sorry." He backed away. "Are you angry at me?"

"No, not everything is about you, you know."

"Okay."

I knew I was being a dick. "Could you set the table? Let's eat in the kitchen. It's easier."

"All right." He went to the cupboard to get plates and glasses. "The weather was so nice today. A little cool, but the sun was out. Comfortable for working."

"It doesn't matter if I'm in an office."

"Did you have a bad day?"

"Yes."

"What happ-"

"I don't want to talk about it."

He took utensils out of the drawer and set them on the table. "I think I'll have a beer tonight. Do you want wine?"

"No, just water." I thought about mashing the potatoes, but I dumped them into a bowl. I did the same with the vegetables. Sam filled my glass with water and got a beer from the refrigerator, pulled off the cap and sat down at the table. I started to slice the roast, then decided it was a waste of time. I put two pieces of meat on my plate and plopped the platter in front of Sam. "Here's the knife. Take what you want."

I grabbed the salt and pepper shakers from the counter and sat down. Sam awkwardly cut a piece off the roast. "That's not how you carve meat. Here, give me that."

"No, I'll do it."

"Give it to me."

"No!" His expression made it clear he wouldn't back down. He removed a chunk of meat and put it on his plate.

"Maybe I will have wine." I took a glass from the cupboard, filled it from the box in the refrigerator and took a big gulp. I topped it off with more wine. The absence of conversation was uncomfortable, to say the least. I knew I should apologize, tell the truth, or make small talk. But I didn't.

"This is tasty."

"It's just a pork roast." That earned me a few more minutes of silence.

"Is Donna taking you to lunch on Thursday for your birthday?"

"I doubt it."

"Why? Did you have an argument?"

"Yes."

"About what?"

"I don't want to talk about it!"

He stabbed his food more aggressively.

My stomach was in knots. I was punishing him for something that wasn't his fault. Sort of. *If he hadn't been such a slut . . . if he hadn't fucked Henry, maybe . . .*

"Am I still taking you out to dinner this weekend?"

That's right . . . part of his birthday gift for me. I'm such a jerk. I nodded. "Yeah, if you can put up with me."

"If you'll be like this, we'll postpone it."

"No, I'll be better. I'm sorry."

"Everyone has a rotten day occasionally. I get it. I had a rough day today, too. Not that you asked."

"You work at a garden center. How bad could it be?"

That was the last straw. Sam put his hands flat on the table. "All right, I'm giving you some space tonight." He stood up.

"I'm not asking for space. I'd rather . . ."

"I'm giving it to you anyway. I'll go lift weights for a while, then I'll sleep at my place. Leave the dishes in the sink and I'll do them tomorrow." He stepped into the back hall.

"Sam, I'm sorry. Can we . . . can I come downstairs while you work out?"

"No, you need to leave me alone. I'll see you tomorrow after work."

"But . . ." He clomped down the basement stairs, muttering to himself. I didn't dare follow him. I stood up to clear the table and heard something like a tree branch splintering, then wood landing on the concrete floor. It sounded like he was taking out his frustration on some scrap lumber. I collected the dishes and put them in the sink. I would have washed them, but he told me not to.

The noises from the basement continued: the clang of metal against metal, grunting, creaking and banging. I put away the leftovers. *When was the last time I had leftovers?* After everything was in the refrigerator, I paused to listen and recognized the steady huffing and puffing of Sam's breath as he lifted weights.

I filled my wine glass again and went to watch television. Nothing interested me, but I kept flipping through the channels. Then Sam stomped up the basement stairs and left the house. I turned off the TV and sat there feeling sorry and miserable and angry. Underneath it all, I was worried. Afraid. Scared shitless. It felt better to be angry.

I forced myself off the couch and into the kitchen. I left my glass in the sink, locked the back door and went down to the basement to look around. Sam's scent was in the air. I found a short piece of two-by-four lumber that had been snapped in half. Several pieces of scrap metal were mangled into tortured shapes. I had never seen Sam destroy anything. For the first time ever, I was grateful my father saved all that junk.

Sam's barbell was loaded with an improbable number of plates. I put my hand on the padded bench and felt what remained of his body heat. *I'm such an idiot. I knew I would drive him away. I'm surprised he lasted this long.*

I went back up the stairs and turned out lights as I moved through the house. I entered my dressing room in the dark and looked through the window. Sam's blinds were open. He was reading in his underwear, a pair of the brightly colored briefs I gave him for his birthday. *Why do I keep fucking things up?* One hand held the book propped against his thigh while the other played with the hair on his leg. He was too big for the old armchair he had in his living room, but he never complained. *I should buy him a bigger chair. Maybe it would keep him from leaving.* It was too early to go to bed, but I didn't feel like doing anything else, so I undressed. I stared at Sam for a few more minutes and went to bed alone.

***

At work the next day, I accomplished a lot because no one was talking to me. The numbers I dealt with were comforting. They were cold and dispassionate. They did what I wanted and expected nothing. I immersed myself in spreadsheets and reports. I made neat stacks of paper and stapled them at a perfect forty-five-degree angle. I cleaned my stapler with a disinfecting wipe. Then I did my telephone. And my keyboard. And the top of my desk. I wiped the doorknobs as I left.

On the way home I saw a large furniture store and impulsively turned into the parking lot. I wandered around until I saw a wide upholstered armchair big enough to hold two normal sized people. It was priced at twelve-hundred dollars. I stood and looked at it for . . . I don't know how long.

I was startled by the voice of a salesman. "Can I help you, sir? Do you have questions about that chair?"

"No, I'm just looking. It's a big chair."

"Oversized. That's what they call them. Did you sit in it?"

"No, it's not for me." *What am I doing here?* "I'd better go. I remembered I need to meet someone. Thank you." I walked out and drove home.

Sam's truck was in the driveway. He had been working on the garden shed, but he wasn't outside. I went up the stairs to his apartment and knocked. "Sam? It's me. Are you in there?" He came to the door and opened it. "Can I come in?"

"Yes."

"I'm such an asshole. I treated you like crap last night and you didn't deserve any of it." He moved closer. "I'm sorry. Just because I had a shitty day, that's no excuse for me to behave that way." He was inches away. "I don't know why you put up with me. You've never treated me like that. You can't let me get away with this crap! Seriously, Sam, I'll get worse! I know I will. You have to call me on this bullshit."

He wrapped his arms around me and squeezed until I couldn't talk anymore, holding me for a very long minute before releasing me.

My lungs filled with air. "Ouch."

"I forgive you." He loosened my tie and unbuttoned my collar.

"You can't forgive me that easily."

"Yes, I can, as long as you say you're sorry and you mean it." He crouched down to take off my shoes. He was wearing a pair of fleece drawstring shorts and one of his tighter t-shirts. He must have taken a shower because his hair was damp.

"I don't know, Sam. I don't think I'm a good person. I knew I was being an asshole, but I didn't stop. It's like there's something missing in me." He pulled my belt out of my pants. "Do you think there's something wrong with me?"

"I think you worry too much." He finished taking off my tie.

"No, I mean something more. Like, something fundamentally wrong. Why would I be so rude to you?"

"Because you're not perfect." He pulled the tails of my shirt out of my pants. "Do you want your pants on or off?"

"What are we doing?"

"We're taking a nap together."

"Oh. I guess I'll keep them on. No, wait, I'll take them off. But it's cool in here. Maybe I'll go and change my clothes and then we can . . ." Sam wrapped his arm around me and picked me up. "Or maybe I'll go with you." He laid me on his bed and settled down next to me. He started unbuttoning my shirt. "I thought we were taking a nap."

"We are." He slipped his hand under my t-shirt and spread his hand on my chest. "I need to feel your skin. Roll over." He spooned me, pulling my back against his warm body. It felt so good, like the safest place I could possibly be.

"My clothes will get wrinkled."

"I'll iron them for you." Sam liked to iron. He kissed my neck. "I'm glad you're back."

"I didn't go anywhere."

"Yeah, you kind of did." He held me a little tighter. My heart slowed down . . . my thoughts grew quieter . . . and I fell asleep.

***

I woke up a few hours later when Sam withdrew his arm from my shirt. I rolled onto my back to watch him stand up and stretch. It was always a pleasure to wake up to that. He lowered his arms, scratched an itch and saw me looking. "What?" he asked.

"What do you think? I like to look at you."

He crawled back onto the bed and lay next to me. "You still like my body?"

"Well, yeah. Why would you think otherwise?"

"You don't talk about it as much as you used to. Sometimes I wonder."

"I don't want you to think it's the only thing I love about you, but I'm turned on every time I look at you."

"Even last night?"

"That was bad, wasn't it? If I had pulled my head out of my ass and looked at you, I would have forgotten everything else."

"Will you tell me what happened at work yesterday?"

"I was called into Henry's office. He asked me to apologize for what I said at the restaurant. I did, but it wasn't sincere. He said some awful things that made me feel like shit . . ."

"Like what?"

"He said I was jealous of him because I didn't have all the sexual experiences he had, and because I settled for a monogamous relationship."

Sam looked down. "Is that true?"

I didn't want to give him the easy answer. "I have regrets about being so closeted when I was younger, in college . . . there were opportunities I missed. But I haven't settled for anything with you. You're more than I ever would have hoped for."

He smiled briefly, then looked down again. "Do you want to have other experiences?"

"No." I thought carefully before saying what I was thinking. "Do you?"

"I've had enough. None of it was like this. What I have with you is completely different. Everything else is just sex."

I wasn't sure that was the whole truth. "Sometimes I wonder what it would be like to be with someone else, but I'm not so adventurous. I love being with you and that's enough for me."

He shifted his position to rest his head on my shoulder but didn't say anything.

"Anyway . . . Henry told me Zipinski is coming back next week, and he wants me to say positive things about him to keep the boss off his back."

"Why would you do that?"

"Well . . . this is where it gets complicated. He's threatening to tell Zipinski I'm gay and I lied about having a girlfriend. He has a copy of the Weasel's flyer, the one with the picture of us standing on the porch."

"He does?" Sam propped himself on his elbow. "Did he recognize me? Does he know about us?"

"Yeah, and it gets worse. He knew about us before he told me he had sex with you. He did it to hurt me."

Sam sat up abruptly, resting his arms on his knees. "That fucking bastard!" He rubbed his face with both hands. "This is my fault. If I hadn't been such a whore . . ."

"Come on, Sam, you couldn't have known where this would lead. Give yourself a break."

"A break? You mean *another* break! How many breaks do I get? You shouldn't have to deal with him, I should deal with him." He jumped off the bed and started pacing.

"No! Absolutely not! Don't even think about it. Besides, he's looking for a new job out of state. He might be gone in a few weeks."

"What if you lose your job? I can't let him do that to you!"

"If Zipinski wants to fire me for being gay, then I don't want to work for him. He would find out sooner or later anyway. I can't keep hiding who I am."

"But I could get rid of Henry sooner, before he has a chance to hurt you. He could be gone tomorrow."

"What are you talking about? You wouldn't . . ."

"I don't mean I would kill him, but I could persuade him. I can be very persuasive, Adam. I would *love* to persuade Henry to leave."

"Sam, I don't like the sound of this. I don't want you to do anything to Henry. Let me handle this mess and, hopefully, we'll be done with him soon."

"What does Donna think?"

"Um . . . about what?"

"About how to handle Henry."

"I had to ask her not to say anything negative about Henry when Zipinski gets back. She didn't take it well. I suppose I could have phrased it better, but . . ."

"Is that what you argued about?"

"Yeah."

"But now that you're past that, what does she think?"

"We're not exactly past it. We haven't talked since then."

"Can't you apologize to her?"

"I did, and, you know . . . I'm tired of apologizing. She can be pretty harsh with me. She's still busting my balls for driving up to the lake house and not telling you where I was, as if I'm abusing you."

"Doesn't she know why you went up there? She knows what Henry said at the restaurant, right?"

"No, I . . . I didn't want her to know about you . . . and him. That's your business. She doesn't need to know your whole history."

"You've been protecting me."

"Well . . ."

"You would damage your friendship with Donna to protect me?"

"Is that wrong? I would do anything to protect you."

He looked like he might cry, so he rubbed his face again while he paced up and down. "I'm such a piece of shit."

"Sam, no."

"Do you want me to call her?"

"No! Let me handle it!"

"Why won't you let me help you with anything? I want to help!"

"I know, but . . . let me . . . can't you . . . dammit, I want to be in *control* of this! Can't I be in control of *anything* anymore? I know you want to help, but you help me in other ways."

He crawled onto the bed again. "If you want to be in control, then you're in control. But don't be afraid to ask for help, okay? You're not good at asking for help."

"I know." I gazed into his pretty eyes. "You know what I need right now? I need to eat. What time is it?"

He looked up at the window. "It's dark. It must be seven o'clock or later. Tell you what . . . let's go out for burgers. My treat. Will you let me do that for you?"

"Okay, but I'm very hungry. Bring all your money."

"That's fine, I've got it." He rolled off me. "I'll put on some pants and we'll go."

"Do you have to? I like those sexy shorts."

"Yeah, but they're for you, not for the public. I'll wear the t-shirt, though." He winked.

I climbed out of bed and tried to make myself presentable, tucking in my rumpled shirt. I went to the kitchen to get my belt and shoes while he pulled on a pair of jeans. I noticed a pizza box from our favorite place. "Did you order a pizza?"

"Uh, yeah. For lunch." He came into the kitchen buttoning his jeans.

"Was it our usual delivery guy?"

"No, another guy. A girl, I mean. Someone I've never seen before." He grabbed the box and crushed it until it fit easily into his small trash can.

"Oh." *Was it a girl or a guy?* "I love their pizza. I think it's the best . . ."

"This wasn't as good. We should try something new next time. Greg told me about a place he likes. Are we ready to go? Oh, wait, I need shoes. And my wallet."

I wished he wasn't so flustered, but he was. I tried not to dwell on it.

He pulled on his shoes. "Are you driving, or should I drive?"

"I can drive."

***

I woke up on my thirty-third birthday and my thoughts were . . . a little negative. *How did I get so old? Pretty soon I'll be thirty-five. That's close to forty. Forty is halfway to death. Unless I have a stroke. Sam is only twenty-one. Twenty-one! Why can't I be twenty-one? It's not fair.* I went into the bathroom and checked my head for gray hairs. I didn't find any. *They probably fell out. I'll be bald soon.* I went down to the kitchen to make coffee and found one of those obscenely rich doughnuts Sam liked. It had a birthday candle in it, a book of matches next to the plate, and a note: "Happy Birthday, Adam! You are not old, so knock it off." *Hmm. Lucky guess.* I lit the candle and hummed "Happy Birthday" to myself.

At work I avoided eye contact with everyone. I hoped no one knew it was my birthday. I wasn't expecting any acknowledgment from Donna. Sam wanted me to patch things up with her, but . . . *maybe it would be better to wait. Let her cool down for a while. There's no hurry.* I heard a gentle knock at my door and looked up. *Shit!* It was Donna. *Wait a minute . . . Donna never knocks.*

"Can I come in?"

"Uh, sure."

She closed the door behind her. "Do you mind if I close these blinds?"

"Um . . . I guess not." While she did that, I stood up. I felt too vulnerable sitting down.

She turned to face me. "Sam called me."

"Dammit! I told him to let me handle things."

"He told me why you ran away the day you had lunch with Henry."

I didn't respond. *Did he tell her about his past? About Henry?*

"I was wrong about you, Adam. I thought you were being selfish, but you weren't. And I thought he was an innocent kid, but . . ."

"He is, though . . . the stuff he did . . . he was confused. It didn't mean anything."

"You love him an awful lot, don't you?"

"Yeah, I do."

She shook her head slowly. "I underestimated you. I didn't think you could love someone that much."

"Thanks a lot."

"Well, not everyone can do it. It won't be easy."

"I know. You warned me."

"Adam . . . you know it's hard for me to . . ." Nothing else came out.

"Apologize?"

"Yes, and . . . neither of us is good at . . ." She put her hand on her chest.

"Expressing . . ."

"Yeah . . . we joke around a lot, but . . ."

"Underneath . . . I think we . . ." I pointed at her, then at myself, and at her again.

"Absolutely. I mean, I know . . ." She shook her head.

"I do, too." I nodded. "You are. Always."

"When it comes down to it. *And* you."

"You bet. No matter what."

"We'll still drive each other . . ."

"Oh, yeah! Which is fine." I nodded. She nodded. We stopped nodding.

After verbalizing so much, we paused for a long minute. I took a good look at the carpeting. Her eyes seemed to be following a bird over a distant building. Eventually she spoke.

"I was afraid I wouldn't be able to . . ."

"No, you did fine. I'm glad we could . . . because I told Sam I would."

"I know. He said. So . . ."

"Today's my birthday."

"Yeah." She grimaced. "How's that going?"

"Meh." I made a face. "Does my hair look thinner to you?"

"No."

"You would tell me if it was?"

"No."

"But I thought . . ."

"Not that. No way. Would you tell me if I'm getting fat?"

"Uh . . . before I forget, are you doing anything for lunch?"

"I'm meeting someone. Sorry."

"That's okay. Who are you meeting?"

"I can't say."

"Ah. Understood. Well, thanks. That's a load off."

"Yeah, me too."

'So . . . do we hug?"

"I don't think so. Not today."

"Good. I didn't want to. There's only so much . . ."

"Exactly. I'll see you later." She opened the door. "Hey, you'll like the restaurant Sam is taking you to this weekend."

"Oh, which one is it?"

"None of your business." She walked away.

"Dammit!" *Good talk, though.* I was exhausted.

***

When I pulled into the driveway that evening, Sam's pickup was already there. He wasn't usually home that early, so I wondered what he was up to. I checked his apartment to see if he was there. The lights were off and the door was locked. I entered the house, which was also dark. "Sam?" No response.

I turned on the kitchen light and saw a note on the table. *Now what?* "Adam – an old friend of yours is waiting upstairs to wish you a happy birthday." *An old friend? What friend?* My heart beat a little faster. I left my briefcase in the kitchen and headed for the stairs. *Why does everything have to be a surprise? Can't we plan things a week in advance, like normal people?* My inner voice was a few sessions behind me in therapy.

It was weird that there were no lights on upstairs. "Sam?" Still no answer. I flipped the bedroom light switch. The room was empty. *What the hell is going on?* Then I saw him lying on my pillow - my GI Joe, in all his shirtless glory. I picked him up and rubbed my thumb over his sculpted plastic torso. *So that's my old friend.* I heard the floorboards creak and turned around.

"Stay where you are, sir! I'm here to secure the area." I sucked in a deep breath. It was Sam, wearing camouflage pants and an olive-green army vest, with a matching bandana tied around his head. He was holding a plastic rifle. His muscular arms and chest were oiled and shiny. "Drop the doll, buster. There's a new soldier in town." I was so excited I couldn't speak.

He barked commands at me. "Put your hands against the wall and spread your legs! I need to frisk you." I did as I was told and he rubbed his hands over every inch of my body. "What's that in your pants, sir? Is that a weapon?" As hard as I was, it certainly felt like one. "Take off all your clothes, sir. Don't make any sudden moves or I'll shoot you." He watched me strip with his plastic gun pointed at me. His facial expression was stern, despite the glint in his eye.

Before I removed my briefs, he poked my erection with the barrel of his gun. It was sexier than I would have guessed. "Put your hands up so I can confiscate your weapon." He backed me against the wall, set down his toy gun, and slipped his hand into my underwear. "Is this thing loaded?"

"It certainly is."

"I'm afraid I'll have to empty it, sir."

"I thought you might. It won't be difficult."

He softened his voice. "I'm a highly trained expert, sir." It wouldn't be long before my ammunition was spent.

An hour later, GI Sam released me from his custody and spread himself across my bed, panting and glistening with perspiration. "Wow! That was quite a workout. Did you like it?"

I made a small squeaky noise. With considerable effort, I dragged myself closer and stroked his shiny chest. "Best . . . sex . . . ever."

"Do you like the costume? I went to a few thrift shops to find stuff."

Sam looked better than my adolescent fantasy man. "Hot. Very hot. Thank you."

"My pleasure. Sex with you is so much more fun than with other . . . hey, do you want more? I could go again."

"I don’t think I could take it."

"Was I too rough?"

"No, I liked that. You're so fucking strong."

"Yeah, that comes in handy."

I ran my hands over his shoulders and arms. "You're my favorite toy now. GI Joe means nothing to me. I can honestly say this is my best birthday ever."

"Aww! Come here, climb on top of me so I can squeeze the stuffing out of you."

He nearly cracked my ribs. I loved it.

***

On Sunday, Sam took me out to dinner as part of my week-long birthday celebration. He put on the dress clothes I bought for him and I showed him how to tie his necktie. "I have to ask again; do you know how handsome you are?"

He looked in the mirror and shrugged. "I like what I see. I like the way I look in these clothes. I look good."

"That's a lot more than good, Sam. You're stunning."

"So are you. I don't see the difference, except I'm bigger."

"Pfft!" *He doesn't get it.* I was nervous about being seen in public with him. We had gone out when he was casually dressed and scruffy. Now, clean shaven and dressed up, his good looks and impressive stature had their full impact. Also, because we were having dinner at a nice restaurant rather than a taqueria, I assumed people would guess we were a couple, rather than a couple of guys. Not that I was embarrassed to be seen with him. Quite the contrary.

I let Sam drive my truck because he refused to tell me where we were going. I would usually advise him about the best route to take, but I couldn't do that, so . . . *wait a minute.* "Hey, are you keeping this a secret so I can't tell you how to get there?"

"No. Of course not. Why would I do that?"

Do I detect sarcasm? "Will you tell me what neighborhood it's in?"

"Nope." He grinned.

"Because if it's downtown, you should have taken Sixth street all the way over to . . ."

"Adam, give me a break!"

Yep. I was right.

Eventually I realized he was taking me to the Como Villa, a romantic Italian restaurant on a wooded hill overlooking the water. While many other restaurants in the area had come and gone, Como Villa had been there forever. It was the scene of many marriage proposals, family celebrations, prom dates, and the boozy business lunches of the city's old guard. I understood why Dave recommended it and Donna endorsed it. It was practically a historic landmark. I was one of the few people in town who had never been there.

There were hints of autumn color along the road that wound up the hill. The restaurant was surrounded by birch trees decorated with tiny white lights. The landscaped areas had been filled with colorful chrysanthemums and ornamental cabbages. A handsome statue of Cupid preparing an arrow stood in the center of a gurgling fountain near the entrance. "This is beautiful, Sam. Whoever does their landscaping has a good eye for foliage. Look at the way they alternated the textures and shades of green. There must be six different varieties of ferns in there, and coral bells, and I don't know how many hostas."

"Eight kinds. I could name them if you want. I'll tell Dave you like his work."

"You guys did this? You're kidding?"

"He redesigned the whole layout a few years ago and he let me put in these fall annuals last week. In the summer it was all New Guinea impatiens and caladiums. You should have seen it."

I was very impressed. I wanted to say I was proud of him, but I was afraid it would sound patronizing. "Sam, this is amazing. I wish I had done this."

"Dave did most of it, but he's teaching me a lot. I'm proud of it."

"You should be. There's a real art to landscaping and not everyone has a talent for it." Without thinking I put my arm around his waist and gave him a half-hug. Then I remembered there were other people nearby and let go. It would take me a while to get comfortable with that.

The inside of the restaurant was also beautiful. The walls were covered with Italian landscape paintings, vintage photographs of famous landmarks, and signed pictures of local celebrities and more famous people who had eaten there. The atmosphere was comfortable and classy and undeniably romantic. Sam greeted the hostess, a conservatively dressed woman who could have been anywhere between fifty and seventy years old.

"Hi, Maria. Do you recognize me?"

"My goodness! Sammy, look at you! You're like a movie star, you're so handsome. Let me get Sal. He should see this." She stepped around the corner to the bar area. "Sal." She waited. "Sal!" Another pause. "Salvatore! Come here. Because I said so. Sammy is here with his friend. Just come! Put that down. Come. Come now!" Sam and I looked at each other. "Salvatore, I swear to God . . . then you should have come the first time I said so."

The handsome older man who was obviously her husband came around the corner. "Sammy! Maria, why didn't you tell me Sammy was here? Welcome, my friend." He grabbed Sam's hand in a firm handshake.

I envied Sam's natural social grace. He introduced me to Sal and Maria without a trace of awkwardness. They welcomed me to their restaurant, obviously aware of our relationship, and showed no sign of discomfort with it. Sam made small talk in a way that sounded intimate rather than superficial, and he drew me into the conversation so smoothly, I didn't have to wonder when I should speak or what I should say. Sal was a talker, and he might have continued for quite a while if Maria hadn't touched his arm. In the silent language of their long and apparently successful relationship, she was signaling him to wrap up the conversation. She spoke to me.

"Sammy tells us you take very good care of him, so we'll treat you like a king. Everything is planned. Let me get you seated and Sal will bring wine." As she led us through the restaurant, everyone who was already seated paused to look at us. I thought they would all focus on Sam, but people looked at me as well. A hush fell over the room. I never experienced anything quite like it. Maria took us to a cozy booth in a corner and gave us a handwritten menu of the courses they would be serving. "Salvatore and I will be taking care of you so anything you need or want, please ask, okay?" She left us.

I looked at the menu. "Did you plan all this, Sam?"

"No, I asked them to put together the best meal they could make. I figured it would all be good."

"It sounds great. How much will this cost? Are you sure . . ."

"Don't start with me, Adam. This is why I didn't want you to see the regular menu. It's already paid for, so relax."

I had to smile at my own predictability and the way he handled me. "Thank you."

"You're welcome."

"So . . . they call you Sammy."

"Yeah, I don't know why."

"People like to give you nicknames. Like Muffin." I watched him shrug and make a face. He was so damned cute. "I admire you, Sam."

"You what?"

"I admire you. You're so good with people. Everyone likes you. The way you introduced me to them and made it comfortable for me . . . it all looks so easy for you. I could never do that." He didn't say anything. "Would it bother you if I was proud of you?"

His eyes glistened. "No. I don't understand it, but it doesn't bother me."

"You don't understand it? Well . . . I know I'm not old enough to be your father, but if you were my son I would be so proud of the man you've become. You're a good man."

His eyes were wet. "Uh . . . you'll have to stop saying things like that or I'll start bawling."

"Okay, I'll stop." There were tears in my eyes as well. "But you should write to your parents. Tell them where you are and what you're doing. They should be proud of you."

Sam nodded and blinked, trying to keep his tears in check. "Are you done now?"

"Yes."

Sal came to the table with the wine and distracted us from our emotional moment. If he noticed anything, he didn't let on. The food started to arrive. There was a parade of antipasti on small plates, and an incredibly creamy risotto with pumpkin and sage. I tried to pace myself. The main course was rabbit cacciatore with polenta and grilled vegetables. I was stuffed before I could finish all of it. I sat back and watched Sam clean my plate while I admired the way he filled his tailored dress shirt. He set down his fork, put his hand on his abdomen and stared into my eyes. The wine made me feel bold. I slipped one foot out of my shoe and used it to caress his leg. The look on his face made me want to get him home as soon as possible.

Maria came to the table to take our plates. "You ate everything. You must still be hungry. I'll bring salad." The arugula with olive oil and lemon was refreshing. I drank more wine. Sam had stopped after one glass. During the long pause before dessert we barely spoke to each other. My foot confirmed what I suspected – Sam was as aroused as I was. I hadn't felt such sexual tension since we first started eating together. We cooled down a little while we ate homemade cannoli.

After more than two hours of sensual indulgence and sexual restraint, we were ready to go. We thanked our hosts profusely and promised to return. They insisted it had been their pleasure and said goodbye as though they were sending their own children across an ocean.

Before we left, we went to the restroom and stood at adjacent urinals. "This is another first for us, Sam. We never peed together before. Isn't it romantic?"

"You'd better not look at my wiener or I'll tell everyone you're gay."

"Keep your voice down, there might be someone in one of the stalls."

"If you weren't looking at my wiener, it wouldn't be a problem." He closed his eyes and emptied his bladder with a soft groan.

The door to the restroom opened and someone entered. After a couple of footsteps, he spoke. "Well, well . . . if it isn't the happy couple. I thought that was your truck in the parking lot."

We turned toward the voice.

Fuck!

It was Henry.

32

So much for our romantic evening.

Henry sneered at us while we stood with our dicks in our hands, literally. "Look at the two of you! Are you here for your engagement party? When's the wedding?"

I forced myself to stop urinating, hoping to tuck myself in and zip up before Sam could do the same, but I failed. As quick as a flash, Sam spun around and grabbed the knot of Henry's necktie, pulling him up with one hand until Henry's heels were off the floor.

"Sam! What are you doing?"

"Lock the door. Quick!"

"What are you doing?"

"I don't know! Just lock the fucking door!"

I locked the door and stood with my back against it. "Put him down!"

He glared at me. "No! I need to think."

Henry's face was turning red, but he smiled. "Fuck, you look good! I've missed you."

"Shut up!" Sam swung him around and thumped him against the tiled wall.

Henry's smile grew wider. "Does that turn you on? Your dick is getting hard, isn't it?"

I looked down and saw a bulge in Sam's pants. He glanced at me briefly, his face covered with shame. I started to panic. "Don't hurt him. Let him go."

"Then what?"

Henry answered. "Take us out back and fuck us until we bleed. That's what you want, isn't it?" His tight slacks revealed his own erection.

Sam looked like he might lose control. He lifted Henry higher and slammed him against the wall. With his free hand, he tore the tails off Henry's necktie and shoved them into his mouth. Henry tried to bite his fingers until Sam squeezed his jaw so hard I thought it would break. Sam poked the last of the silk into Henry's maw.

I approached Sam carefully and gently touched his arm. "We have to stop and think . . . how will this end? We all need to walk away from this, okay? It's gone far enough."

Sam nodded. "I know."

There was a sound at the door, then a knock. Henry moaned, so Sam pressed a thumb into his throat. I called out, "I need a few minutes. I'm sick and you wouldn't want to come in here right now." The man mumbled something and went away. "Can you knock him unconscious?"

Sam looked at me like I was crazy. "No! I don't know how to do that! I thought you didn't want me to hurt him."

"We need to keep him in here long enough for us to get away."

"I'll put him in one of the stalls." With one hand around Henry's throat, Sam dragged him to the stall at the end of the room and shoved him through the door. I was close behind, wondering what he would do. Sam could do things other people couldn't, and his solution to this problem wouldn't have occurred to me. He picked Henry up, folded him at the waist, and shoved his ass into the corner between the toilet and the wall. He tucked his arms behind his back and pushed him down until he was firmly wedged into the tight space. "It's a good thing you never eat, you scrawny fuck." He leaned close to Henry's face and warned him in a voice unlike anything I had ever heard from him. "If you *ever* do *anything* to hurt Adam, or make him lose his job, or *anything* I don't like, I will come after you. Do you understand me? I'll tear chunks of you off your skeleton, starting with your skinny little dick. I don't care if I go to jail, I don't care what happens to me. This is your final warning." I couldn't believe my ears.

But Henry smiled. Yes, he smiled. It was the creepiest smile I have ever seen.

I tugged on Sam's sleeve. "Let's get out of here."

He straightened up and followed me out of the stall. "Pretend you're sick, and head right for the door." I'm sure I looked sick anyway.

I unlocked the door and stepped into the corridor with Sam against my back. The man standing there looked familiar, but I couldn't remember where I had seen him. "I'm sorry, I was sick. I wouldn't go in there."

He looked confused. "Was anyone else in there? My boyfriend was going to the restroom."

"Nope, there's no one else in there. We need to go, he's very sick." Sam pushed me toward the exit. The cool autumn air was a welcome relief as we walked briskly toward the truck. Sam handed me the keys. "You need to drive. I can't." I tried not to spin the tires as I pulled out, but I drove faster than usual on the winding road down the hill. Sam told me to slow down. I ignored him. "Slow down, Adam! You'll get us killed!"

I hit the brakes and pulled over to the side of the road. As soon as I shifted into park, I jumped out, leaned against a tree and vomited. I coughed and wretched until my entire dinner was on the grass. Sam leaned over to offer me paper napkins from the glove compartment. I wiped my mouth and climbed back into the driver's seat.

"Are you okay?"

'I think so." I continued driving at a safer speed. We went quite a distance without speaking.

"I have a temper, Adam."

"NO SHIT!"

He hesitated. "Are you afraid of me now?"

"No." It hadn't occurred to me. "Should I be?"

"I don't know. Maybe. My mother was afraid of me."

I felt bad for him. "I'm not afraid of you."

"Why not?"

I thought about it. "Because you're on my side."

He sniffled. "I meant what I said to Henry. If he hurts you, I'll . . ."

"Don't! Don't say that again. I don't want you to do *anything* to him, no matter what he does to me. I'm asking you not to. I mean it." I wanted him to know I was serious. "Why did you grab him? What were you thinking?"

"I don't know. I wasn't thinking, and once it started . . . what could I do?" It was hard to imagine anything good coming out of that scenario. Henry was evil. No matter what either one of us did, something bad would have happened. "Do you think I'll be in trouble? Will the police look for me?"

"It depends on whether he reports it or not. You could be charged with assault. At least you didn't draw any blood. He'll probably have bruises."

"He didn't report the other times."

"Yeah, but . . . that was sex."

"There was sex involved, but it wasn't that different from this, except we didn't finish this time."

"I don't understand why you had an erection. Why would that turn you on?"

"I don't *know*, Adam! Do you think I have a choice? Do you think I want to be like this? I mean, how many ways can I be a freak?"

We were already at the house, so I pulled into the driveway and shut off the engine. "You're not a freak."

"Aren't you disgusted by what I told you?" I didn't respond. "And guess what? It's still hard!" He lifted his hand from his lap to reveal the outline of his erection. "This is what happens when I assault someone in a public toilet."

I briefly looked him in the eye, then turned away. "We're not discussing this in the car. Let's go inside." I opened my door and got out.

"Of course!" He got out and walked around the truck. "It's okay to get a boner from beating someone as long as we don't discuss it in the car. Is that one of your rules?"

"I didn't say that! Besides, you didn't beat him. Keep your voice down."

"Yeah, you wouldn't want anyone to know your boy-toy is a freak."

I unlocked the door. "Shut up and get in the house, NOW!" He followed me. I flipped on the lights and threw my keys on the table.

Sam barely set foot in the kitchen before he tried to leave. "There's no point in discussing this, Adam. I'll go to my apartment and jack off thinking about what I would have done to Henry. That's what my dick wants. Why fight it?"

I stuck my finger in his face. "You are *not* getting off on Henry! Never again! Do you hear me? I forgave you for lying to me about that shit. You *owe* me!"

"I owe you? What do I owe you? Is this about money?"

He was pushing my buttons. I slammed my hands into his chest, but he barely moved. "When have I *ever* complained about money? *Never!* But this . . ." I clapped my hand over his crotch. "This is mine! Henry doesn't get this." I rubbed him aggressively. Sam pushed my hand away and backed up. I grabbed him again and backed him into the wall.

He struggled with me briefly. "Stop it! Get your fucking hands off me! I'm not a piece of meat!"

"I know you're not! But if you want to act like a piece of meat, then you're *my* piece of meat!" I pounded my fist on his chest. "You want to be a whore? You're *my* whore!" He stopped struggling but his anger was rising with each word. "I gave you a place to live . . . and my truck . . . I helped you find a job . . . I put those clothes on your back . . . and I feed you every fucking day. If you want to get off on beating someone . . . it better be me!"

I had never seen such anger in Sam's eyes. He grabbed my tie and the front of my shirt. "You want to see what I can do to you?" He shook me like a rag doll. "I could throw you through that fucking window and halfway into the garden!"

"Do it then! If that's what gets you off, do it! I'm getting hard!"

"Don't fuck with me! I could do it!"

"I know! I've seen your strength. All that power, and you never get to use it. Give in to it, Samson. Show me who you are."

"Shut up! This isn't a joke!" His hot breath was in my face. I saw confusion in his eyes, as if he couldn't decide whether to kiss me or snap my neck.

I didn't back down. "Well? What are you waiting for?" I knew he wouldn't hurt me. I didn't believe he could do it. He had the strength to hurt me, but it wasn't his nature.

Sam released me with a slight shove and stepped back.

I softened my tone but made it clear I was in charge. "Get your angry ass up to my bedroom and take your clothes off." He narrowed his eyes, then turned and headed for the bedroom. I took a few deep breaths to calm down, turned off the lights, and followed him up the stairs. I brushed my teeth to remove the lingering taste of vomit, and went to find Sam.

He was naked, sitting on the corner of the bed with his elbows on his knees. He still had an erection. One of his knees started to bounce nervously.

"Are you thinking about Henry?"

"None of your fucking business!"

"STOP! Look at me!" I started to undress. "LOOK at me!" He raised his head and threw daggers at me with his eyes. "Henry is an evil creep. You're nothing like him. He didn't deserve to touch you and everything you did with him was a mistake." I threw my clothes on the floor as I took them off. "You belong with me. I *earned* this. *You* earned this. I will not let that fucking snake interfere with what we have. He has no power here unless we give it to him, and we're not giving it to him anymore. Do you hear me?"

His expression softened. I approached him and lowered my voice. "Lie down so I can take care of you."

"No." He shook his head but lacked conviction.

"Yes. Lie down." I knelt in front of him and stroked the hair on his shins. He leaned back. I pushed his knees apart and rubbed his thighs. He lowered himself onto the bed with a heavy sigh. "Remember the first time we did this? You were so patient and nice about it. I had an idea of what to do, but you made me feel so much more comfortable. That's who you are, Sam. You're kind and sensitive." I wet my lips and took him in my mouth.

He groaned. "Stop it, Adam. Stop trying to make this into something good. It's sick, it's not good."

I knew it wouldn't take long, so I continued with my hand. "Do you remember the first time we kissed, Sam?"

"Yeah."

"That was a good day, wasn't it? I remember when you left the house, you were walking across the driveway and you stopped and pumped your fist like you had won something."

"You saw that?"

"Yeah. I felt so lucky to have a hot young guy kissing me, and you acted like you were the lucky one."

"I was lucky. But I wasn't the person you thought I was." He covered his face with his hands.

"Yes, you were. You still are." I took him in my mouth again and squeezed the base of his shaft. His abdomen tightened as his body went rigid. When he was finished, I slowly cleaned him off, licking and kissing him until he was soft. Between kisses I told him, "You're not a piece of meat. You're not a whore. You're my sweetheart. You're my angel."

He was crying quietly. I crept onto the bed and touched his hair and kissed his tears. "You're a good man, Sam. You're thoughtful and generous. And you're gentle, even with all your strength. Don't let anyone make you feel sick or bad, because it isn't true." After a kiss on the lips, I rubbed his chest and climbed off the bed. I picked up my clothes to put them away. When I came back from the dressing room, Sam was putting on his pants. "Are you leaving?"

"I can't stay here tonight. I'm sorry." He sat down to put on his shoes.

"Why not?"

He shook his head. "I don't know if I can explain it."

I waited. "Could you try?"

He stopped what he was doing. "Adam . . . it's hard to live up to your image of me. I know this will sound wrong, but . . . you love me too much." His eyes filled with tears. "Sometimes it hurts." He stood up and gathered his things, pausing to wrap his arm around my head, cradling it to his chest and kissing my hair. Then he left.

I stood there naked and confused. *What did I do wrong? How could I love him less?* I didn't want to think about that, so I did what I always do. I moved on to something else. Something to do. Something concrete. If I kept moving, I wouldn't have to think about loving Sam less than I did.

I found my cell phone and looked up Carl's number. It was late to call someone, but this was important. I dialed and started pacing. He picked up on the second ring.

"Hello?"

"Hey, Carl, it's Adam."

"Yeah, I saw that, but I didn't believe it. It's late."

"I'm sorry, did I wake you up?"

"It doesn't matter. What's wrong?"

"I wonder if you could do me a big favor. Is there a way you could find out if any trouble was reported to the police at a certain place tonight?"

"Uh, maybe. Could you give me more details?"

"Do I have to?"

"Well, I need to know the place, Adam. Can you give me that?"

"Oh, sorry. The Como Villa. It's a restaurant."

"Yeah, I know the Villa. What's this about?"

"I'd rather not say."

He sighed. "How long ago?"

"Within the last couple of hours. Please."

"I know a guy who works second shift in that district. Let me call you back."

"Thanks, Carl." I hung up and got into bed, propping myself up on the pillows, waiting for him to call. I was tired and frustrated, so I started to masturbate. I felt like I deserved relief after an evening like that. I thought about Sam, then the phone rang. "Hey, Carl."

"Hey. I asked my guy if there was a call from the Como Villa tonight and there wasn't."

"Good. That's a relief."

"Is this about Sam?"

I paused. "Why would you think that?"

"Adam . . . you know I'm not stupid, right? Could you at least acknowledge that I'm not stupid?"

"I know you're not stupid. I'm sorry, Carl, I shouldn't have called you."

"No, I'm glad you called me."

"Why?"

"Because. I like to think you would call me if you needed me."

"Of course I would. You're one of the first people I would call."

"Really?" He was quiet for a moment. "Why were you at the Como Villa?"

"Sam took me out for a romantic dinner."

"Nice. It's a wonderful place. Are you alone now?"

"Yes. Why?"

"Just curious. If you had a romantic dinner, why are you alone?"

I took a deep breath and let it out. "It didn't end on a romantic note. We ran into . . . an acquaintance . . . after dinner, and it got ugly."

"Are you okay?"

"Yeah."

"Is Sam okay?"

"I hope so." Carl didn't say anything, but I could hear him breathing. "Are *you* okay, Carl?"

"Yeah, I guess. Alone, as usual. It's good to hear your voice." I was flattered. Carl had a very nice voice. Low and masculine. I hadn't noticed that before.

"Why are you alone, Carl? A guy like you shouldn't be alone. It's not right." I absentmindedly played with myself.

"What do you mean, a guy like me?"

"You know. You're a great guy. You're smart, and funny, and hot, and you're always helping people."

"You think I'm hot?"

"And smart, and funny, and nice . . ."

"And hot?"

I smiled. I knew he was fishing. "Yes, Carl, you're hot. You know that."

"Not really. Can you explain it to me? How am I hot?"

"Carl . . ."

"Come on, Adam. I did you a favor. Throw me a bone. So to speak."

"Tsk, you're bad. Okay, you're hot because . . . you're handsome." I closed my eyes to picture him. "Your face is . . . pleasing to the eye, especially when you smile. You have pretty eyes, that's important. And you're well-built. It's obvious you work out a lot. You look good in that gray tank top. Not that I've been looking, but it's hard to ignore when you're . . . anyway, the uniform works for you, too. It complements your physique. I've been wondering, do they come like that, or do you have them tailored? Those pants fit like . . . what am I saying? My point is, you look good in uniform. So, yes, you're hot. Does that answer your question?"

Carl breathed into the phone.

"Carl? Are you still there?" I knew he was there.

"Yeah, I'm here." There was a long pause. "Do you want to come over?"

My heart beat so hard I could hear it thump. "What did you say?"

"Do you want to come over?"

"Uh . . . pffffff . . . Carl! You're terrible! That's the last time you'll trick me into complimenting you. I'm sure you hear that stuff all the time. I appreciate your help. Really, you're a good friend."

He sighed. "Yeah, I'm everyone's good friend. Thanks for saying those things. Sorry if I made you uncomfortable."

"You didn't."

"Will you be working on Joe's house next weekend?"

"Sure, you bet. I'll see you Saturday. Thanks again."

"Okay, good night Adam. Thanks for calling."

"Good night Carl."

Now I had two things I didn't want to think about. But at least I knew Henry hadn't made a complaint to the police. I thought about the guy outside the restroom. *Henry doesn't have boyfriends. Who was that guy? I know I've seen him before.* I spent a minute thinking about it, then added it to the list of things I didn't want to think about. After turning off the lamp next to the bed, I slid under the covers and pictured Sam in his ribbed tank top. *Wait . . . he doesn't have one of those. I should buy him one.*

It took me a while to fall asleep.

***

In the middle of the night, I was awakened by a noise inside the house. I would have been alarmed, but somehow, I knew it was Sam. He crept into the room as quietly as he could and undressed.

I rolled over. "Hey."

"Hey," he whispered. "I couldn't sleep over there. Do you mind?"

"Come here." I lifted the covers and welcomed his naked body next to mine. He wrapped his arm around me, pulling me against his warm chest. I waited a minute. "That's a little too tight, Sam. I need to breathe."

"Sorry." He relaxed.

"It's okay." I stroked the hair on his forearm.

***

The following day, I drove to work with worst case scenarios spinning through my mind. I had no idea what Henry would do or say. *Will this be my last day? Will I be humiliated in front of everyone? Will I get paid for my unused vacation time?* I walked to my office pretending everything was normal, smiling and greeting people, forgetting that smiling wasn't normal for me. One of the women outside my office said, "Mr. Zipinski would like to see you when you're free."

"Oh, he's back. That's great! I can't wait to see him." I smiled again. She gave me a strange look. I got settled in my office, pretended to be busy, picked up the phone and pretended to listen to messages, then went to find Mr. Zipinski. He was in his office talking to a couple of other accountants, so I waited outside. I tried to make small talk with his middle-aged assistant. "How are you today?"

"Great." Her expression was completely flat. I liked her immediately.

Zipinski came out to greet me and ushered me into his office. His movements were stiff, like he was losing his battle against fossilization, but he maintained his cheerful facade. "It's good to be back in the office, Adam. You can't imagine how much I've missed it."

"No, I can't sir. Welcome back."

"You look healthy. I trust you're doing well."

"Quite well, thank you." *Please don't ask about my girlfriend. Please, please, please, please, please.*

"And how is your love life? Will there be wedding bells in your future?"

I forced a smile. "I'm sure there will be. I live near a church."

He didn't get it at first. Then his thin lips receded from his teeth and he shook his finger at me. "You're a clever young man, Adam. I'll have to share that with my wife at dinner this evening." His face shifted into business mode. "Tell me how things have been going here in my absence. Bring me up to date."

I gave him an overview of the work we had completed on the larger accounts I supervised, mentioning a few problems that still needed to be resolved. As far as I knew, the business had been running smoothly in his absence. Except for the part about a soul-eating incubus being left in charge.

"That's wonderful, Adam. You've stayed on top of things. I assume your friend, Henry, has been doing the same." He folded his hands on his desk and searching my face for clues.

"Have you had a chance to review the departments and accounts he supervised?"

"Not yet, because of his absence."

"His absence? Is he out of town?"

"I'm sorry, I assumed you knew. He took a tumble on his bicycle over the weekend. He'll be out for a few days while he recuperates."

"Oh, I hadn't heard. How bad is it?"

"Scrapes and bruises mostly. Nothing was broken, but it's difficult to walk."

"I'll give him a call to wish him well."

"Adam, I'd like to ask you something if I may. I know the two of you are pals, and I wouldn't want to put you in an awkward position, but business is business. I wonder if you could give me an objective opinion of Henry's leadership and his . . . moral character, if you will."

I took a deep breath. I was ready for this. "First, let me assure you, the best interests of this firm are my priority, regardless of any friendships I may have formed. Henry and I have a . . . cordial relationship, but we're not close friends. You may know him better than I do." I paused. "With regard to his leadership in your absence, I can only say that no one could fill your shoes, sir."

"I appreciate that, Adam, but . . . just between us . . . would you say he's honest? Is he an ethical man?"

I hoped his questions wouldn't be so direct, but I found a way to answer without lying. "I know how much you emphasize values here in the office. I believe Henry is as honest and as ethical as you are, sir."

If he hadn't been so self-righteous, Zipinski might have thought twice about that. But he took it as a compliment and an assurance of Henry's integrity. "That's good to hear. I must admit I've had doubts about whether I made the right choice in giving Henry so much responsibility. He will need to answer some questions when he returns to the office. I don't know how much he shared with you about our operating budget."

"We never discussed it. I had no reason to ask about it. Is there a problem?"

He hesitated. "We have cash flow issues due to . . . unexpected expenses. I'm afraid there won't be any bonuses this year."

I was in no position to complain after receiving such a generous raise a few months earlier. "We made it through the recession, Mr. Zipinski. I have confidence in you." I was getting queasy from all the ass-kissing.

"Thank you again, Adam. I'm touched by your remarks."

I saw an opportunity to ask, "Has everything been resolved with Ellis Industries?"

His expression changed. "Ah. The Ellis account. I meant to ask, have you met Robert Bergdorf, the accountant who works for Mr. Ellis?"

"Not that I recall."

"In your conversations with Henry, has he mentioned Mr. Bergdorf at all?"

"His name came up once. I think Bergdorf specifically asked Henry to handle the Ellis account."

"Is that so? Did he say why Mr. Bergdorf would make such a request?"

"No. No, he didn't."

"And yet . . . Henry claimed *you* were supervising the Ellis account. Isn't that odd?"

I could have highlighted Henry's suspicious behavior, but I stuck to our bargain, hoping to keep Zipinski from finding out about my relationship with Sam. "I never gave it much thought, sir. Maybe I'm naive, but . . . I tend to think the best of everyone." Of all the lies I ever told, that was the biggest.

The old man studied me for a moment. "Your innocence is refreshing, Adam, but it may get you in trouble one day. The Gospel of John tells us, "The whole world lies in wickedness." There is no shame in recognizing the power of the evil one."

I did not doubt his familiarity with evil. "Thank you, Mr. Zipinski. I'll keep that in mind. Were you going to say something about Robert Bergdorf?"

"No, I'm afraid I can't say anything more on that topic. I was only wondering if Henry and Mr. Bergdorf had developed a . . . *particular* friendship."

That's when it struck me. The man outside the restroom at the Como Villa – the one who was looking for Henry – was Robert Bergdorf. I must have seen him in the office in the past. That's why he looked familiar.

There was nothing else for me to discuss with Mr. Zipinski, so we parted with a handshake. I went back to my office to get on with my day, relieved to know Henry wouldn't be around for a while. It occurred to me that Henry and Robert might not have called the police because they didn't want to draw attention to their relationship. If the rumors Flora heard were true and money had been stolen, there was a good chance they were involved on some level. I was pleased to know Zipinski already suspected them.

I found myself wondering about Henry's injuries. I assumed he exaggerated them to justify his absence. *Sam didn't do that much damage. Unless something happened later.*

***

After work I had an appointment with my psychologist. There were many topics I could have discussed, but for some reason, for the first time, I mentioned that Sam might be having sex with other guys.

"Have you asked him?"

"No, I don't have any proof. It's a feeling."

"You don't need proof to ask him."

"I don't want to make waves. We have enough going on right now."

"Okay. If it's not important, there's no need to bring it up."

"I didn't say it wasn't important. I mean . . . he shouldn't be having sex with other guys. We agreed to be monogamous."

"You could remind him of that, to be clear."

"I did. Last night, in fact. I told him, whatever he's doing, he should be doing it with me."

"So you did discuss his sexual activity."

"I just told him not to do it with anyone else."

"And he agreed."

"Um . . . I think he . . . it's complicated because we were in the middle of something else."

"What would you do if you knew he was having sex with other guys?"

"What do you *think* I would do?"

"I'm asking you."

"I would . . . tell him to stop."

"And that's all it would take."

"I hope so."

"What if it wasn't?"

"I don't know, why are we talking about this?"

"You brought it up."

I sighed. "I wish I hadn't."

"It's difficult for you to think about, isn't it?"

"No, I think about it all the time." I was irritated. "I knew from the beginning this wouldn't last. I know he'll leave me, it's only a matter of time."

He rolled his eyes, having heard this so many times before. "You're waiting for *him* to leave *you*. Can you imagine any circumstance that would cause *you* to end the relationship?"

"Why would I end it? It's the best thing that ever happened to me."

"So you're leaving it up to Sam. You're expecting him to leave you, but he can stay as long as he wants, no matter what he does."

"I didn't say that."

"Not in so many words. Look, Adam . . . make your own choices. It's your life. But I'm wondering how much you would tolerate to maintain this relationship."

I knew what I wanted to say, but it wasn't the right answer. I tried to think of things I wouldn't put up with, but they were things I knew Sam wouldn't do. "It's a good relationship. I don't need to worry about stuff that hasn't happened yet. That would be trying to control the future. I can't control everything, remember?"

He smiled. "You're right, you got me. But keep in mind, pretending not to see things doesn't mean they aren't happening."

"Could we talk about my job now?"

He raised one eyebrow. "Sure. Let's talk about your job."

***

According to our established routine, when I got home I went directly to Sam's door. I wasn't sure what mood he would be in after everything that had happened, but he seemed okay and looked great, freshly showered and barefoot. "Hey, how are you?"

"Happy, now that you're here." He placed his hand on the back of my neck and rubbed my ear with his thumb. "I feel bad about the way our dinner ended last night. I want to make it up to you." He lowered his head and kissed me, slowly and deeply.

I was pleasantly surprised. "Okay, I suppose I should get undressed."

"No, not yet." He slid his knuckles down the length of my necktie. "I like it when you're dressed up and I'm not." Crossing his arms in front of his body, he grasped the hem of his t-shirt and peeled it off. He tossed the shirt aside and pushed his gray fleece shorts off his hips so he was completely naked.

I smiled at his seduction, if that's what it was. He didn't need to seduce me. I expected him to ask whether I saw Henry at work, or to be irritable, or distant. This was much better.

He took my hand and placed it on his chest. "What would you like to do with me tonight?"

"I get to choose?"

"Yeah. Anything you want. Use your imagination." He pulled me closer.

"Um, I don't know. You're better at this than I am. I like it when you take control."

He slid my hand down his body to his groin. "Touch me. Feel how hard I am for you."

It was true, he was already hard. I wrapped my hand around his erection. *Wasn't I going to talk to him about something from therapy? What was it?* I couldn't focus. *Whatever it was, it can wait.*

"That feels good." He kissed my jaw and whispered in my ear, "I want to fuck you with your shirt and tie on. That would be so hot."

I nodded. "Okay. Whatever you want." I nuzzled his chest and felt the muscles in his back. *He's so sexy . . . I'm so lucky.*

33

Autumn had reached its peak and the trees were full of color that year. I love the fall, but it's a sad season for a gardener. I spend most of my time cutting down the dead remnants of things that were beautiful a few months ago. But it's also a time to look forward to spring, to dig up and divide perennials that need to be replaced or moved, and to decide what to change the following year. There's always room for improvement in some part of the garden.

Several days after our encounter in the restroom of the Como Villa, Henry returned to work with fading bruises on his jaw and neck. He had a slight limp that quickly disappeared. He never mentioned what happened, but his creepy smile gave me the shivers. Stories circulated among the staff about meetings between Henry and Mr. Zipinski with raised voices. Auditors with somber expressions came and went. Rumors were flying and people took sides. I stayed out of it and Donna was on her best behavior. She didn't criticize Henry or Zipinski for several weeks, even when we were alone together. She seemed distant, but I could never pin down a reason for it. We were still friends, we made fun of each other and laughed together, but there was . . . something.

At home, our lives got back to normal a little too easily. We went to work each day, had our dinners together, and worked on our projects. Sam surprised me by paying off what he still owed for my old pickup instead of continuing his monthly payments. I was impressed by his financial discipline and he was doing well at the nursery. I took the cash and signed over the title to the vehicle. He was proud to finally own something substantial.

After a lot of thought, Sam wrote a brief letter to his parents. It would have been easy to simply say he was alive and well, but he chose to tell them about our relationship. It meant a great deal to me, and I admired his courage. He had to pace in front of a mailbox for a few minutes before he finally mailed it.

He spent more time with me in the house, reading in the living room or lounging in front of the television. We were often on the same couch, propped against each other. Sam read *Sense and Sensibility* while I burned through my mother's Agatha Christie novels, which I had previously dismissed as unworthy of my literary tastes.

We had sex less often, but when we did, we tried new positions and experimented with role playing and toys I bought online. I tied him to my bed and tickled him with feathers. I encouraged him to be more aggressive, and he spanked me hard enough to make me think of him every time I sat down the next day. I liked it more than I expected. The sex was hot, but it lost some of the tenderness of our earlier relationship.

One Saturday in October I took a break from working in the garden and went through the hedge to visit Flora and Agnes. The swimming pool had already been covered for the season to keep the falling leaves out of the water. Agnes heated some spiced apple cider and we brought each other up to date on our rather dull lives. Flora said she appreciated Sam's help when their pool maintenance person was covering the pool on a windy day. "It was a fortunate coincidence that he knew the young man. They should send two people for a job like that."

"Sam didn't tell me about that. He knew the guy?"

"I thought so. Perhaps I'm mistaken."

"They seemed quite familiar with each other, ma'am." Agnes looked away and took a sip from her cup.

Flora gave her a look. "You know Samson makes friends easily. He's very outgoing."

There was an awkward pause. "It's so typical of Sam to help other people and not say a word about it. Like when I found out he shoveled Joe's sidewalk and he never mentioned it."

'Yes, it's like that," said Flora. Agnes remained silent.

"Well, I'd better get back to work. My garden doesn't take care of itself. Thanks for the cider. This was nice."

"You're welcome, dear. We're always happy to see you."

For several days I meant to ask Sam about the pool maintenance guy, but it never came up.

***

Our neighborhood painting project was nearly finished. Joe's house looked great with its fresh coat of paint and repaired porch railings. The kids Carl worked with bonded as a group and enjoyed their experience, despite a few minor behavioral problems. The local newspaper ran a very nice article about Carl and declared the program a success. As president of the Eden Place Neighborhood Association, I contributed a quote praising Carl's connection to the neighborhood he served as a police officer. Ledell enjoyed good publicity for his painting business and lined up a few more jobs in the neighborhood and beyond.

When the reporter from the newspaper heard Joe had given me his garden shed after mine was torched, she wanted to do a separate story as a feel-good follow-up to Edward O'Neill's conviction for arson. Sam was nearly finished renovating the shed, but the more I thought about it, the less I wanted the attention it would bring to me, to my house and garden, and to my relationship with Sam. I told the reporter I was an intensely private person and she backed off.

While Carl and I helped Ledell take down the scaffolding around Joe's house, Carl shared some gossip involving his former squad partner, Doug 'Asshole' Mansky. "You remember his attitude toward gay people. Well, he's obsessed with guys who have sex in public parks. He's out there checking the bushes and watching for men who hang around alone. He convinced the new chief to let him set up this sting operation where one of the rookies was luring guys into the public toilet in the park downtown. Guess who they caught?"

For a moment I thought it was Sam, but I would have known about it. *And Sam wouldn't do that.* I tried to think of someone we both knew.

"Dr. Van Wooten. Mr. Weasel."

"No way!"

"Yes! The suspect was allegedly polishing his wood in front of the poor rookie Mansky roped into this operation. They arrested him for lewd and lascivious behavior." I loved it when Carl talked like a cop. "I'm surprised it hasn't been in the news yet. He wasn't the only one they trapped. I think they got about a dozen guys all together."

"That's so . . . I don't know. I would never have sex in a public place, but do they have to go out of their way to target guys who do?"

Carl shrugged. "It's against the law. I have mixed feelings about it. Believe it or not, Mansky had the balls to ask me if I wanted to help him with the sting. He thought I would enjoy it. I told him maybe he was enjoying it more than he wanted to admit. He almost punched me. After all the shit I took from him, it felt good to give some back."

"He was right about one thing."

"What's that?"

"You'd make good bait."

"Yeah, right."

"I'm serious. You could wear your gray tank top."

"You mean this one?" He unzipped his hoodie and shrugged it off. He was wearing the gray tank.

Shit. "Yeah, that one. You can put your jacket back on."

"Why? What's the problem?"

"Nothing. It's cold out here. Your nipples are getting hard."

He looked down. "Oh yeah." He poked one of them.

"All right. I'll go ask Ledell if he wants to break for lunch."

Carl grinned. "What's the matter? Am I too sexy?"

"Shut up!"

"You started it, bro."

"I did not!"

"I think you did."

I knew I did. That's what bothered me.

About a week after our conversation, the local media reported the sting operation and listed the names of the men who were arrested. A 'For Sale' sign went up in front of the Van Wooten residence.

***

Sam was trying to talk me into decorating the house for Halloween, something I had never done because it would attract children seeking handouts. *Why can't they buy their own candy? It's on sale right now.*

I agreed to a few tasteful decorations - pumpkins, corn stalks and bales of straw. At least I could use the straw for mulch in the garden. I stopped at Dave's Nursery to see what was available. Dave greeted me with his usual rough affection and pointed to a more extensive selection of Halloween decorations than I expected. "It's a bigger deal than it used to be, kiddo. I might as well make money on it. The kids who work here get pretty excited about it, so I let 'em dress up in costumes for one day. The customers like it."

"Sam wants me to decorate this year. I'm not sure."

"Sounds like a great idea as long as you buy all your stuff here. Look around. We have the best decorations in town. It's not like the shit at Garden Mart."

Despite our friendship, Dave never forgot I was a paying customer. "All right, I'll look. You never stop selling, do you, Dave?"

"Not until I'm dead. See that lady with the expensive purse? She's good for a couple hundred bucks. I need to get over there. Let me know if you need anything."

I looked at fake tombstones, inflatable ghosts, zombie pirate ships and motion activated witches. I hated them all. Then I saw a realistic life-sized vulture with glowing eyes. It spoke to me. Not literally . . . I mean it appealed to me. I stroked its wing. *Are you lonely?*

"Dude! The vulture is not a pet!" Startled, I hid my petting hand behind my back. It was Greg. "That thing will eat your face." He set down a carton of plastic skeletons.

"You know it's not real, don't you?"

"Yeah, brah, do you? You're the one gettin' cozy with it." He raised one of his handsome eyebrows.

"I wasn't . . . I didn't know you still worked here. I thought you went back to school."

"Nah, that didn't work out. Maybe in January." He squatted to open the box of merchandise, exposing a strip of skin above his butt that I didn't look at. "The Muffin's out back. You want me to go get him?"

"No, that's okay. I'm just looking at all this stuff. Sam wants me to decorate the house."

"Yeah, he's been talkin' about it. I can't believe he never had Halloween where he's from. I didn't know he was all religious and shit. I'm helpin' him with his costume." He cleared space on a shelf for the skeletons.

"What costume?"

"Dude, don't you guys talk anymore? Let me give you some advice, bro. There's more to a relationship than sex, even for gay dudes. I learned that the hard way."

"Hmm. Good to know." *Do I want to ask?* "How did you learn that?"

"My girlfriend broke up with me last month. I told her she was so beautiful I wanted to have sex with her every day, at least once. She thought that was too much, so I told her I would need two girlfriends. Man, she was *pissed!*"

"Did you tell her you were kidding?"

"Whataya mean?"

"About needing two girlfriends."

"No, I was serious. My point is, I should've talked to her more 'cause she liked to talk a lot, and if I gave her more of what she wanted, maybe she would've given me more of what I wanted."

"Uh huh." I couldn't decide if Greg was smarter than he sounded or dumber than he looked. "You think I don't talk to Sam enough? Did he say that?"

"No, Dude, I'm just sayin' if you don't know what he wants to be for Halloween, he's probably not bangin' you every day. See the connection?"

No, I don't. "Did you find a new girlfriend, or two?"

"No, bro, it's tough out there. I'm in the best shape of my life and it's goin' to waste. I'm horny as a motherfucker. That witch over there is startin' to look good to me." Indeed, he was in excellent shape, and the witch would have been lucky to snag him.

"Maybe if you went back to school you'd meet someone there. I'd like to get Sam into college, too."

"Dude! That would be awesome if we went to the same school! I could bang all the chicks and he could have all the gay dudes." Greg caught himself. "I mean . . . I'm sorry, he wouldn't do that 'cause . . . you know what I mean . . . I mean if he wanted to, he could . . ."

"I know what you meant. Don't worry about it."

Sam came around the corner. Greg said too loudly, "Here he comes! Get your hand off my ass!" I felt myself blush.

Sam looked serious as he approached. "Did you have your hand on Greg's ass?"

"No! He's joking!"

"He'd better be. Because his ass is mine." Sam palmed Greg's butt.

Greg jumped away from him. "Dude! Seriously! You know I have a headache!"

Ah, bromance! They were cute together.

Sam asked, "What do you think of the decorations? There's some cool stuff here."

"Which ones do you like?"

"The huge spider with the web. That would look good on the front porch. And some of these lighting effects would be creepy."

"Creepy? Is that what we're aiming for? Seems like we were just trying to convince people we *weren't* creepy."

"It's Halloween, Adam. It's different."

Greg leaned in to tell Sam, "Adam likes the vulture. I interrupted them in a private moment."

"All I did was touch its wing! It doesn't even have a penis." They looked at me like that was a weird thing to say. "Okay, I like the vulture. I want it."

"Fine with me. We could get a bunch of bats, and some of those rubber rats with blood on their mouths."

I shrugged and nodded. "I wish there was a stuffed weasel. That would be funny. What costume are you planning?"

"Frankenstein's monster." Sam stood in a stiff pose with a grim expression.

"Yeah, he won't need much makeup with that face," said Greg. "I'm gonna be Igor, the hunchback." He looked me up and down. "Dude! You could be Doctor Frankenstein! That would be perfect!"

"Oh, no! I'm not part of this. I don't do costumes."

"Come on, bro! Didn't you dress up for Halloween when you were a kid? Were you ever a kid?"

Sam thought that was funny.

"Yeah, as a *kid* I dressed up. My mom made my costumes for me."

"Like what?" asked Sam.

"I was a sack of potatoes when I was little, and then a hobo. King Arthur, Sherlock Holmes . . . those were my ideas."

Greg looked sideways at Sam, and back at me. "Uh, didn't you dress up as anything scary, dude? Like a monster?"

"Oh, yeah!" With a smile I remembered my best costume ever. "I was into biology one year, so I went out as an E. coli bacterium. I loved that costume." Greg's mouth dropped open. "It causes diarrhea."

Greg stepped forward and put his arms around me. "Dude, I feel so bad for you. I thought Muffin's story was sad, but yours is pathetic." He patted me on the back.

I liked the hug, but I didn't understand his reaction. *He obviously doesn't understand how scary a contaminated water supply can be.* I put my arms around him as well. *Why not?* He felt good.

When Greg let go, Sam moved in for a hug of his own. "I've never been more attracted to you than I am right now. I would love to see you in your bacteria suit. I hope you have a picture of it." I probably did, somewhere in the attic.

As much as I enjoyed the attention, I knew they should get back to work. "Listen, Sam, why don't you make a list of the decorations you want, or set them aside and I'll pick them up another day, okay? I need to get dinner started so it's ready when you get home. Good to see you, Greg. Thanks for your sympathy. And keep working out, you look great!"

As I walked away, I heard Greg say, "Dude, you are so lucky."

"Yeah, I know."

I smiled. Sam could have whatever Halloween decorations he wanted.

***

While I was working in my office on a Thursday afternoon, Mr. Zipinski interrupted me. "I wonder if you've talked to Henry recently."

"Um, a few days ago, maybe? A few words. We aren't working together on anything."

"I thought, perhaps socially, you may have seen each other."

"No, we haven't been socializing."

"Has he said anything about his plans?"

"Plans? I don't understand." I wouldn't mention Henry's plan to find another job, but I hoped it was happening. If he used me as a reference, I hadn't received any calls from prospective employers.

Zipinski paused for a long moment. "I don't want to alarm you, Adam. This may turn out to be a misunderstanding, but . . . Henry left the office early yesterday saying he had an appointment. He didn't come in today, he didn't call to say he was ill, and we haven't been able to reach him."

"That is strange. While you were gone . . . I don't mean this as a criticism of Henry . . . but his schedule wasn't regular. He came and went throughout the day. I assume he had meetings off site, so I never questioned it. Maybe he hasn't quite returned to his old routines."

Zipinski scowled and nodded. "Perhaps. As you know, I prefer a more disciplined approach to business." He looked down at the floor. "I'm sorry to say, I have been . . . disappointed in Henry. I wish I had asked you to take the helm in my absence." He did not look at me.

"Thank you, sir. I'm flattered, but I don't think I would have been a good fit. I don't have the right personality for leadership."

He raised his eyes and looked at me. "You sell yourself short." And that was that. He stood up and turned toward the door. "I will keep you updated on the situation. Thank you for your time."

"You're welcome, sir." I wondered where Henry might be. *Why wouldn't he call in sick, even if he was at a job interview? Maybe he got more than he bargained for from one of his sexual encounters.* I thought about Sam, then immediately tried to put him out of my mind.

Where was I on this spreadsheet? This very interesting spreadsheet . . .

Sam hadn't stayed with me the night before.

***

At dinner that evening, Sam was quiet. I had a feeling he wanted to say something, but it didn't come out. So I started an uncomfortable conversation.

"Sam . . . if I ask you something, will you promise not to get angry?"

"How can I promise when I don't know what you'll ask?"

"I know. That was dumb. I just don't want you to get angry."

He looked down. "Why? Are you afraid?"

"No, that's not what I meant. I want to enjoy our time together, but sometimes we need to talk about difficult things."

"Yeah. There's something I want to ask you, too. But you go first."

"No, you can go. That's okay."

"Adam, please. What do you want to ask me? I promise, I'll stay calm."

"Okay." I hesitated. "Have you seen Henry lately?" My chest felt tight.

His face dropped. "No. Why would you ask me that?"

I felt relieved, but also regretted asking him. "He didn't come to work today, and no one could reach him. He left work early yesterday."

"So, what were you thinking?"

Dammit, why did I bring this up? "I don't know . . . you didn't stay here last night. I was afraid, maybe . . . something happened."

"Did you think I hurt him? Or killed him?"

My heart felt like it would crack. "It crossed my mind, so I thought I would ask."

He closed his eyes and took a breath. "I can't blame you after what I did at the restaurant."

"I don't think you're a violent person, but with your temper, and some of your sexual interests . . ."

"I get it." He crossed his arms over his chest. "You don't need to spell it out for me. I swear to God, I haven't seen Henry since the restaurant. I don't want to see him. I don't like what he does to me."

"I believe you, Sam. I thought it was better to ask rather than wondering."

He nodded and pulled his arms into his chest. "I wish you didn't have to ask." His tone grew darker. "I wish I wasn't such a slut."

"Sam, come on. I don't see you that way. You know that."

"Yeah, but maybe you're blind or stupid." He grimaced. "I'm sorry, I didn't mean that. I'm sorry." He abruptly pushed his chair back and stood up, startling me. "Listen, I'm leaving. I shouldn't be around you when I'm like this. I'm sorry." He turned to go.

"Don't leave. Stay and talk to me."

"You shouldn't have to put up with this."

"But I want to."

"No." He turned his back on me.

"What were you going to ask me, Sam?"

He stopped but didn't turn around. "It doesn't matter now, forget it."

"I want to know. What did you want to ask?"

He stood with one hand on the door frame, facing the next room. "I wanted to ask . . ." He stopped and put his head down, then took a breath and continued. "I was going to ask if you still wanted me to move in with you."

I wasn't expecting that. It was the furthest thing from my mind. All I could say was, "Oh." It hung in the space between us as panic rose in my chest. *Say something, dammit! SAY something!*

He turned to look at me. "Bad timing, huh?" His eyes were wet. "I'll see you later, Adam."

Sam walked through the kitchen and left the house. I grabbed my fork and pushed the prongs into the top of my thigh until blood seeped into my faded jeans. *YOU FUCKING IDIOT! Why didn't you SAY something?!*

***

I set my alarm to wake me up before Sam left for work. I watched through the kitchen window until his door opened, then rushed out to meet him on the driveway. I grabbed his hand and placed his warm palm over my heart. I was so choked up I couldn't speak. I wanted to say something new, something he hadn't heard before, something that would make a difference.

Sam stroked my cheek with the backs of his fingers. We could see our breath in the cold autumn air. "You should have put on a jacket, Adam, it's cold out here." I sniffled and produced a few tears, but nothing else. "It's okay, Adam. Everything will be okay." He rested his forehead against mine. "I'll be home for dinner, I promise. We'll eat together . . . and we'll do the dishes." His voice cracked. "And we'll talk, okay? We'll be fine." He kissed my cheek and took a step back.

There was a smudge of powdered sugar on the corner of his mouth. Without thinking, I reached up and wiped it off with my finger. He stuck out his tongue and licked the spot, then smiled. "Thanks."

***

Henry didn't show up for work again that day. Everyone in the office talked about it in hushed tones. Some of the staff gave me dirty looks as I walked past their desks. *What did I do?* I talked about his absence with Donna. She shrugged, "Aren't you glad he's gone?"

"Yeah, but I'd like to know if he's gone for good, or what happened to him. I don't need any more surprises."

"I'm sure we'll find out sooner or later."

"You're awfully Zen lately. Are you on medication?"

"No. Do you think I need medication?"

"No comment." I paused, trying to verbalize what was different about her. "I feel like you're keeping something from me."

She hesitated. "You're right. I am. I wish I could talk about it, but I can't. It doesn't involve you."

"Oh. Okay, at least you're being honest. I won't pry."

She stared at me and waited. "Seriously? That's it? No more questions?"

"No, I'm respecting your boundaries."

She waited another long minute. "Are you trying to piss me off?"

"No! You can't talk about it, so I won't ask."

"You know, if you were keeping something from me, I'd badger you about it until you talked."

"I know. Do you want me to badger you?"

"No. It wouldn't work anyway."

"Okay then."

"Are you on medication?"

"No. Should I be?"

"Uh . . . how are things with Sam?"

I was about to say, "Fine," but I went with, "We've had our ups and downs. We're working on . . . stuff."

"Stuff." She nodded. "Do you want to ask my advice?"

"About what?"

"About the stuff."

"No. No, thank you."

"Are you sure you're not trying to piss me off?"

"Yes! I don't like it when you're angry." I was about to leave, but something had been on my mind. "I've been meaning to ask you . . . and your phone better not ring after I ask this . . . were you ever in jail?"

The corners of her mouth turned up ever so slightly. "Yes. Once."

My heart thumped. "What for?"

Her phone rang. She glanced at it. "That can wait." It rang a few more times and stopped. "Last summer, I took the kids to the County Fair. It was a Saturday, but Kevin was working, so it was me and the three kids. Mike and Sarah were having a good time running around, going on rides. But Colin, as usual, wasn't happy about being with us. I forced him to go, so he was punishing me by being sullen and playing games on his phone. He wouldn't even stand near me.

"While we were waiting for the other two kids to get through the line for one of the rides, some boys who knew Colin from school saw him and were harassing him. They were bigger than him . . . the usual teenage jerks who pick on kids who are different. They called him 'faggot' and 'toothpick' and things like that. He tried to ignore them. I didn't want to intervene if he could handle it himself, but this one asshole asked Colin why he hadn't killed himself yet. That's when I went over there."

"I grabbed the asshole's arm and twisted it behind his back. He struggled until he realized I was a mom, so I shoved him to the ground and knelt on his back. The things I said were harsh, even by my standards. The people around us were shocked, parents covered their kids' ears. The kid was begging for mercy when a sheriff's deputy pulled me off him. Big commotion, paramedics were called, the whole nine yards. I told the cops what the kid said to Colin. They handcuffed me. It was an interesting experience."

"An interesting experience? Are you kidding me? What happened?"

"The kid wanted to drop the whole thing, but he was sixteen, so they wouldn't let him. They called his parents and took him to a hospital to get checked out. Colin called Kevin. Mike and Sarah got off their ride and saw me in handcuffs. Sarah started crying, so the cops let me sit with the kids while we waited. When Kevin got there, the two younger ones ran to him. Colin played it cool, like it was just another shitty day in his world. But Kevin doesn't let him get away with that the way I do. He wrapped his arms around Colin and held him until he cried."

I grabbed the box of tissues from Donna's desk.

She continued. "I sat there and watched the way Kevin took care of the kids and I thought, "Why can't I be like that? Why can't I be the one who hugs them and tells them everything will be okay?" She wiped a tear from the corner of her eye with her fingertip. "But I'm not that kind of mom. I was booked and went to jail, and Kevin bailed me out that night. So that's my criminal past. You were probably expecting something more exciting."

I mopped tears and snot from my face. "That's the best story you've ever told me! Did you get in a lot of trouble?"

"The kid's parents were pretty reasonable. The judge let us resolve it through mediation and the charges were dismissed once I met all the requirements. We paid the hospital bill and I had to go to an anger management class." She rolled her eyes.

"Colin must have thought you were pretty awesome."

"Oh, no. Not at all. He was angry for a long time. He thought things would get worse for him at school. The story spread like wildfire and kids asked him about it. Sarah said all the girls thought I was the best mom in the world. They took an interest in Colin, but he was embarrassed about it and didn't know what to do with all the attention. The important thing, at least in my mind, is that none of those boys picked on him again because they knew what I would do to them."

"You would do it again?"

"Oh yeah. In a heartbeat. Nobody fucks with my kids."

"I think you're a great mom. I guess Colin is hard to please. I like him, but I don't know how you deal with that."

"Believe it or not, he's my favorite. I know parents aren't supposed to say that, but most of us have one. He was my first and he's always been a challenge. The other two kids are great but they're easy to love. I like a challenge. No matter what he thinks of me now, I believe we'll be good friends when he's older." She nodded and looked at me. "He likes you by the way. He asks about you."

"What? Why? What did I do?"

"I don't know. He's interested in a lot of weird things."

"Nice. Thanks. Well, I'd better get back to my office before Zipinski sees me with you. You're a bad influence."

"Hang on a minute. Why did you want to know whether I was in jail? Was this about Henry?"

I wanted to deny it, but I hesitated long enough for her to see through me. "Maybe."

"Are you wondering if I did something to him?"

"I remembered when you first met Sam. We were shopping for furniture. You talked about murdering Henry."

"And you think I'm capable of it?"

"It crossed my mind."

"Wow." Donna smiled. "Thank you! Thank you for believing I could kill someone. That's probably the nicest thing you've ever said to me." She was genuinely pleased.

***

By the time I got home, I felt better about my relationship with Sam. No matter how many barriers I had put between us, he never minded that I was difficult. Now that I was seeing what he told me all along - that he wasn't perfect

- it was my turn to be patient with him. He was worth it. I prepared dinner, and when he came through the back door I gave him my full attention.

"Hey, Adam." I watched him take off his coat and hang it up. He pulled off his work boots. I was reminded of the first time he ate with me in my kitchen, the day I offered him chili while he was shoveling snow. His cheeks were rosy, as they were that day. "How was your day?"

"It was okay. Interesting. Remind me to tell you a story about Donna. It's a good one." Sam leaned down to give me a peck on the lips. I responded with puppy dog eyes. "Come on, we can do better than that. Give me your best kiss."

"My best kiss?" His eyes twinkled. "Are you sure you can handle it?"

I grinned. "Are you sure you can handle mine?"

He stepped into me and grabbed my ass, then pulled me up the front of his body until our noses touched. He licked his lips, teasing me, warming my face with his breath. His lips grazed against mine, grasped them, and pushed them apart with his tongue. I wrapped my legs around his waist and my arms around his neck while our mouths imitated things our bodies had done. We stopped to breathe. "How was that?"

I scanned his face. "It was good, but when I look at the equipment you're working with, I think you could improve. We should keep trying."

One side of his mouth curled up and made a dimple. "I'm so hot for you right now. How do you do that?"

"I'm not doing anything."

"You started as soon as I walked in the door."

"I was looking forward to seeing you, that's all. You could put me down now."

"All right, but you're not going anywhere." He leaned against the counter with his arms on either side of me. He kissed me again. "Thank you for coming out to see me this morning. That meant a lot."

"I wish I could have said something. I was a mess."

"Yeah, I saw that. I think I'm a bigger mess than you are."

"Oh, I don't know."

"It's true. There's a lot of stuff I need to figure out. I hope you can be patient with me while I work on it."

"I can. Don't worry . . ."

"Listen, Adam, let me finish. I know you'll try. But if it gets to be too much for you . . . I want you to know it's okay to let me go. I'll understand. You've done enough for me already."

"I won't let you go. You were patient with me when we first started, so I can do the same for you. I'm stronger than I used to be."

"I know." He kissed me again, softly. "That's what worries me."

It was an odd thing to say. *I'll have to think about that later.* "I should get the meatloaf out of the oven."

"You made meatloaf? I love your meatloaf."

He took a step back and I went to the stove. "Should we eat in the kitchen?"

"Fine with me." He went to the cabinet to get dishes. "Was Henry at work today?"

I was surprised he brought that up. "No. No one knows where he is. I asked Donna if she did anything to him."

"You did? What did she say?"

"She took it as a compliment. She's something else."

"So she denied it."

"Well, yeah . . ." I paused. "Yeah, I think she did." I put the food on the table and we sat down to eat.

After a few minutes, Sam asked, "What was the story you wanted to tell me about Donna?"

"Oh yeah, thanks for reminding me." I told him how Donna had come to Colin's defense against the bullies and went to jail for it. I got a little choked up while retelling it. "Isn't that awesome? I can't believe Colin was angry at her. Who wouldn't want someone to defend them like that?"

Sam shrugged and pushed a few peas into his mashed potatoes. "I tried to defend you against Henry, but you didn't like it."

I sat back. "That's different. Colin is a scrawny kid. And your history with Henry . . . it's different."

He nodded slightly without looking up. "Okay. Well, if Colin needs any help, let me know. I remember what it felt like to be teased."

"That's right, you went through that, too. I keep forgetting you didn't always look like this."

"I know." He continued eating.

"But you could have . . . you were thinner, but you were strong, right?"

He nodded. "As strong as I am now."

"Why didn't you . . . I mean . . . you could have done something to stop them."

"Yeah, I could have. Were you ever bullied, Adam?"

"No, I was pretty good at blending in."

"Have you ever wanted revenge so badly you could have hurt someone?"

I thought about the day I grabbed the paperweight from Henry's desk. "Yes. Once."

"Imagine being an angry teenager, full of hormones, wanting revenge, and being as strong as I am. Do you think it would have been a good idea to fight back?"

A parade of possible consequences passed through my mind. "No, I guess not. That must have taken a lot of self-control."

"You have no idea." Sam looked down at the food left on his plate. I reached out to touch his arm, but he flinched and pulled away. I quickly withdrew my hand. "I'm sorry, you startled me. I didn't mean to do that." He extended his arm toward me. "Go ahead."

I reached out again and laid my hand on his forearm. I slowly stroked the hair while he watched.

He kept talking. "I kept a lid on everything when I was at school. I was like a robot. Sometimes my anger came out when I got back to the farm. That's why my mother was afraid of me."

I continued to pet his arm. "That must have been difficult. And lonely."

"Yeah, if it wasn't for my dad." He was quiet for a moment. "You know . . . the thing I wish you understood . . ." He paused.

"Tell me. I want to understand."

He hesitated. "It doesn't matter how strong you are, or how big, or smart, or how good-looking people think you are, because . . ." He raised his other hand and pointed at his chest. "In here . . . it might be different." His hand trembled.

My eyes filled with tears. I knew what he meant, but I thought I was the only one. "I'm sorry, Sam. I need to keep that in mind."

He nodded. "That would help. I mean, most of the time when I'm with you I feel great. But sometimes I feel so small and weak. It's not always you. It might be something that happened at work, or with someone else. Sometimes I wake up feeling that way. It can change from one minute to the next, like when you asked me for my best kiss . . . I felt big and strong and hot. Then you told the story about Colin . . . and I remembered who I am inside. Do you know what I mean?"

I sniffled. "Yeah, I do. I'm glad you're talking about this."

He looked down. "I don't want you to think I've got it all figured out. I used to have so much more control over my feelings, and now it's like . . . like a storm inside me. The books I've been reading have helped because I know other people feel the same way. Like Heathcliff in *Wuthering Heights*. He's so fucked up, but . . . I *get* it, you know? And in *Sense and Sensibility*, the one sister is so controlled and rational, and the other one is all feelings and romance and stuff, and I want to be like both of them, but not too much of either. It's weird how every book I pick up gives me a new way of looking at myself. Is it like that for you?"

I nodded. "Especially when I was younger. I felt like I wasn't alone." I had no idea Sam was struggling so much. I must have had my head up my ass for the last couple of months. I thought he was reading my books because they were good stories.

"And *Frankenstein* . . . have you read that lately? I thought it would be a horror story, and it turned out to be deep shit. I mean . . . this will sound weird, but . . . I feel like that book is about *me*, Adam. I feel like the monster, except he's not really a monster. On the outside he is, but . . . he's so angry and hurt . . . and he doesn't know how to make it better. If Victor would have talked to him more, maybe it wouldn't have ended so badly." He paused. "I'm sorry, I shouldn't be going on like this. I'm probably not making any sense."

He was making a lot of sense. I was reminded of my recent conversation with Greg - it had been too long since Sam and I talked like this. "Sam, everything you're saying makes sense. I'm sorry I haven't been listening to you. I don't know where I've been lately."

"It's not your fault. I don't know how to talk about this stuff half the time. I told you I'm a mess. It's easier to talk about characters in books." He took a deep breath and let it out. "Can we do the dishes now? I've been looking forward to it all day."

"Okay, let's." We stood up and cleared the table. "Why were you looking forward to it so much?"

He shrugged. "It reminds me of when we first started. That was when we talked the most. That's when I fell in love with you. Lately, I feel like we haven't been doing enough dishes."

"We'll have to work on that. Do you want to wash? I'll dry."

He filled the sink with hot soapy water. "Trick-or-Treat is on Sunday. Do we have enough candy?"

"I don't know; did you eat any of it?"

"Maybe. I'll buy more."

"I don't know how much we'll need. I've never done this before."

"I'll buy a ton of stuff. It won't go to waste because you'll eat what's left over."

"Yeah, I'm sure it'll be me."

"I'll wear my costume."

"Frankenstein?"

"The monster, not Victor. Are you sure you don't want to be the doctor?"

"It's too late to find a costume."

"I already have one for you. It's just a white lab coat, but people will get the idea. We can mess up your hair and make you look like a mad scientist."

Sigh. "Great. It's all planned." He smiled and handed me a plate to dry. I moved closer until my hip contacted his thigh. "I missed this, too, Sam. I don't know why we stopped."

"There was a lot going on."

"Yeah. No excuse."

"Do you mind if Greg hangs out with us during Trick-or-Treat? He likes Halloween and his parents don't do it anymore."

"That's fine. He knows what he's doing. Maybe I won't have to interact with any kids."

"Thanks. It'll be fun, you'll see. It would be nice if Donna and Kevin could stop over with the kids. They'll probably do something in their neighborhood, but if they want to swing by for a few minutes . . . what do you think?"

"I guess. If they're not busy. They're probably busy. I'll call Donna."

Sam had a sheepish look. "Um . . . I texted her this afternoon. They'll stop by."

"Uh huh." I stuck my tongue in my cheek to keep from grinning. "Is there anything else I should know about? Any other plans you've made?"

"No, I think that's it." He bumped against me with his shoulder. He was wearing his cute face. Sam had a lot of faces.

Out of nowhere I blurted, "You can move into the house whenever you want. I still want that." His expression changed, and I realized how awkward that was. "I'm sorry . . . that didn't fit there, did it? I meant to say it earlier. I wanted to say it last night, but I got all . . ." I pointed to my throat. "I didn't mean to . . . I didn't know you were still thinking about it, and you caught me off guard. I want you to live with me."

He continued to wash a pan. "Are you sure?"

"Yes."

"That's a relief. There's still hope for me. There's no hurry, though. It's probably too late in the year to get a new tenant."

"True."

"I'll think about it. It still feels risky. There are a few more things we should talk about before that happens. Some of the other stuff I'm figuring out."

"Okay. When you're ready." I felt better, despite the awkwardness. I felt lighter, and a little silly. "I feel like saying weird things that are in my head."

"Like what? Go for it."

"I've been thinking about this for a while. There's nothing you can do about it, and I don't want you to take it the wrong way, because I love everything about your body, okay?"

"Spit it out, Adam."

"Sometimes I wish you were smaller so I could hold you the way you hold me. I wish you could feel what I feel when you do that, but I can't get my arms around you." Sam stopped washing. "I'm sorry, does that hurt your feelings? I didn't mean to . . ."

"No. No, Adam, that's one of the best things you've ever said to me." His voice wavered. "I love that."

"Oh. Good." As bad as I was at expressing myself, once in a while I stumbled onto something effective. "Will you sleep with me tonight?"

"Yeah." He sniffled. "I'll show you how to hold me."

"Okay." I felt lighter again. "Sounds like a plan."

***

I was nervous about the whole Trick-or-Treat thing. So many things could go wrong. *Children everywhere! Chaos!* Greg came to the house early, obviously excited about the day.

"Nice house, Dude. Real spooky. Where's the Muffin?"

"He'll be right over. He's changing into his costume."

"He lives in a different building?"

"Yeah, above the coach house. The garage."

"You make him live in the garage? Seriously?"

"No, it's a nice apartment. He'll show you. Why don't you go over there now? Follow me." I took him to the back door and pointed at the coach house. "Go up those stairs and knock on the door."

"Thanks, Dude." He stepped outside and shouted, "Muff! Hey, Muff!"

I closed the door and rolled my eyes. *Time for a big glass of wine.*

They put on the costumes they had worn the day before at the nursery. Sam gelled his hair into a square flat-top and covered his face and hands with green makeup. Greg helped him add scars and sutures and glued rubber bolts to the sides of his neck. He was still handsome. It was impossible to make him look bad. Greg's hunchback costume was simpler - a brown hooded cloak over a foam rubber hump, gray makeup, and a set of protruding, ugly teeth.

By the time they came to work on me, I felt more relaxed with a second glass of wine in my hand. They frizzed up my hair and gave me a pair of fake eyeglasses with round black frames. I don't know where they found the white lab coat, but it made me feel important. I was ready to do surgery.

We went to the front porch and waited for children to appear. The decorations Sam put up the week before looked pretty good - nothing too elaborate or too scary. My vulture was perched on the railing glaring at anyone who approached. I sat behind it doing the same. Fortunately, the weather was warm enough to be comfortable.

Greg knew how to interact with the kids depending on their age and the way they reacted to Sam's towering presence. He hopped around and hammed it up, enjoying himself as much as any of the children. The kids' costumes were cute. People I met at the neighborhood association meeting showed up and chatted with me. Many talked about how good Joe's house looked now that it was finished. I had to admit, I was having a good time.

Halfway through the afternoon, Donna showed up with her kids. She wore a witch's hat. As soon as she saw me she pulled out her phone to take photos. "Please don't take my picture." She took several, then moved on to Sam who was happy to pose for her. Her son, Mike, was made up as a young zombie. Sarah dressed as Catwoman in a revealing, sexy costume that was a questionable choice for a girl her age. Colin wore black jeans, a black t-shirt, and a black jacket. He clomped up the stairs and sat down next to me. "Hi, Colin."

"Hi."

"Are you having fun?"

"No, are you?"

"Unexpectedly, yes."

"Are you drunk?"

"Do you smell alcohol?"

"No, I was kidding."

"Oh. Then I am not drunk." I took a sip of spiked apple cider from my thermos bottle.

Greg chased Mike around the front yard. Donna asked Sam, "Who is that guy?"

"That's my bro, Greg. We work together."

"How old is he?"

"Twenty, I think."

"Interesting."

Sarah said, "He's cute."

Donna spun around. "Stop looking at him! He is not cute!"

"Mom! I meant he's funny. Jeez!"

Mike ran up to Sam and hid behind his legs while Greg followed, panting through his horrible fake teeth. He took one look at Donna and stood up straight. "Hello, ma'am, I'm Greg." He stuck out his hand.

Donna just looked at it. "Ma'am? Seriously? Do I look that old?"

"No ma'am, I mean miss . . ." He gestured at Sarah. "Is this your sister?" Sam grinned and I snickered. Donna gave me a withering look.

Sarah held out her hand. "I'm Sarah." Greg bowed and reached for her hand as if he would kiss it, but Donna snatched it away from him.

"Don't touch my daughter! She's only fifteen!"

"I'm sorry . . . I was just . . . nice costume, Sarah."

"Don't look at her!" Donna took a step forward. "Look over there! Away from her!"

Greg backed up and raised his hands in surrender. "I'm sorry! I wasn't looking at her! Muff, could you back me up here, bro?"

"Sorry, dude. You're on your own."

"Dude!"

Donna gestured to Mike and Sarah. "Come on, let's go. We'll go around to the other houses in the neighborhood. Do you want to wait here, Colin?"

"Yeah."

Donna walked away with her two younger children. "I told you that costume was a mistake! Did you see the way he was looking at you?"

"He wasn't looking at me, Mom! Jeez!"

"So . . . that went well." I took another sip from my thermos.

Sam said, "Bro, you've lost your mojo. You're pathetic." *Very supportive.*

"Dude! It's the teeth, obviously! And thanks for the backup." Greg climbed onto the porch to get some candy. "Damn, she's a red-hot MILF!"

Colin and I said, "Eeew."

Greg looked at Colin. "Who are you?"

"Nobody."

"That's Colin, her son."

"No, I mean what are you dressed as, dude?"

Colin looked puzzled. "Nothing."

Greg scanned Colin's black clothing and nodded. "I get it. Like, nothingness. Negative space. I like it."

Once again, I had to wonder whether Greg was clever, or a dumbass. Colin seemed to be wondering the same.

Greg tossed a peanut butter cup into his lap. "Eat that."

While we had a break from the trick-or-treaters, Colin pulled a tattered paperback out of his pocket. He opened it to a page he had marked and passed it to me. "Can I ask you a question?"

"Sure." I looked at the front of the book: *Songs of Innocence and Experience* by William Blake.

"What do you think this poem means?"

"This one? *The Sick Rose?*" He nodded. I read it quietly while Colin ate his peanut butter cup.

O Rose thou art sick.
The invisible worm,
That flies in the night
In the howling storm:

Has found out thy bed
Of crimson joy:
And his dark secret love
Does thy life destroy.

"Um, okay. I remember this. Is this for school?"

"No."

I took off my fake glasses. "Well, it's more of an impression. I can only tell you what I think it's about."

Sam asked to see it. Colin nodded, so I handed the book to Sam. He stared at the page for a minute, then turned the page over, and back again. "That's it? Huh." He read it again with one finger on his green chin. "I like it. It's dark . . . well, maybe not. Wait a minute. No, that's not good. I didn't need to see that today." He gave the book back to me.

"So what's it about?"

I looked at Sam. He raised his eyebrows and shook his head. I turned back to Colin. "The important thing is what it means to you. It doesn't matter what we think."

"Uh, yeah it does. I have an idea, but I'm asking for your ideas."

"Is anyone gonna ask me to read it?" We all looked at Greg. He looked at each of us. "I know how to read, dudes." I gave him the book. He scanned the page with a serious expression. His lips moved until he reached the end. "The *fuck*?" He knit his eyebrows and tapped on his protruding teeth while he read it again. "Fuuuck!" He thrust the book at Colin. "Get that away from me!" Greg turned his back to us and crossed his arms over his chest. He sniffed.

We all looked at each other. Colin threw up his hands. "Will someone tell me what it's about?"

Greg bounced up and down on the balls of his feet. "It's about a girl who's about to get wrecked because the dude is cheating on her." He looked down at the ground and whispered, "*Fuck.*"

"It could be that." I glanced at Sam. "I think it's about how love inevitably fades as time passes. Time is the worm."

Sam shook his head. "No, it's sex. The desires of the flesh. Sexual immorality, or whatever you want to call it. Love is destroyed by lust."

Colin looked at the poem again. "Huh. So . . . let's say I gave this poem to a girl I know. What would she think?"

"Is this a girl you like?" I asked.

"Yeah."

"Don't do it."

"I already did."

Sam reacted strongly. "Seriously? Do you think she'll go out with you after reading that?" I signaled him to tone it down a bit.

Colin blushed and lowered his eyes. "She already has a boyfriend. He's popular but he's a jerk."

Greg turned around. "How does he treat her?"

"Bad. She doesn't know it, but he's cheating on her."

"Dude, it's perfect! Is that why you chose this poem?"

Colin looked up. "Yeah."

"Dude! That's genius!" Greg thrust his fist at Colin, causing him to flinch. "Sorry. It's a fist bump, dude. Make your hand like mine." Colin raised his fist. "Yeah, like that. Now bump." They bumped. "There you go." Colin smiled a little and looked down.

"Is she smart?" I asked.

"Yeah, she wants to be a scientist."

Greg threw another peanut butter cup at Colin. "Is she hot?"

"I think so. Probably too hot for me, but . . ."

"No, she's not," said Sam. "You're a good-looking guy. You have great eyes, but you need to look up more. And get that hair out of the way."

"Do you always wear black?"

"Mostly."

Greg looked at him. "That's not a costume?" Colin shook his head. "Dude . . . we have work to do. What color are your eyes? Let me see." Colin forced himself to look Greg in the eye. "Wow! The Muffin's right. Start wearing blue. Right, Adam?"

"Yeah, that would help. Blue T-shirts, polo shirts, whatever you want. People will notice your eyes more. You can keep the black pants and jackets and stuff if you want to maintain the depressed poet thing you've got going. Can you get your hands on a blue shirt?"

"I think so. My Mom always wants to buy clothes for me. I hate it."

"Tell her what you want. You won't even have to go with her. She'll bring the stuff to you and if there's anything you don't like she can return it. Tell her it was my idea. It'll be fine."

Colin stood up. "I have to go. They're back and she won't bring Sarah up here again. The hunchback might look at her."

Greg smiled with his ugly teeth. "You're all right, bro. I hope you get the girl." He held up his fist for another bump.

This time Colin knew what to do. Then he turned and offered his fist to me. I gave him a bump as if I did it all the time. He did the same to Sam as he walked past him. "Thanks." He walked across the grass to the street. Sarah waved at us while Donna told her to get in the car. Mike stuffed candy into his mouth.

I put on my fake glasses and swallowed the last of the cider in my thermos. Sam and Greg sat down on either side of me - a mad scientist, a monster, and a dentally-challenged hunchback - advisers to the lovelorn. We unwrapped candy and chewed for a while.

Greg spoke first. "Little dude's gonna be a lady killer if he plays his cards right."

Sam asked, "Am I the only one who thinks he's kind of hot?"

"No, he's good-looking. Smart and sensitive, brooding. It works for him. But that poem. Do girls like that stuff?"

"Depends on the girl," said Greg. "If she doesn't like it, she's the wrong girl for him." He paused and shuddered. "That poem messed with my head."

Sam agreed. "Yeah, I wish I hadn't read it."

I nodded slowly. "It's a great poem but . . . it made me think too much."

"Exactly, bro." Greg took another piece of candy. "That's why I don't like to read."

***

Later in the evening, after Greg went home and Sam removed his green makeup, we ate dinner, then we ate more candy. We were looking for something to watch on television when a teaser for the evening news came on:

"Tonight! A local accountant is found dead, and the cause of death has parents worried about the safety of their children! Details at ten."

34

When the news broke that Robert Bergdorf, an accountant at Ellis Industries, had been found dead in his condominium, the cause of death – autoerotic asphyxiation - became the primary focus of the story. According to an unnamed source, gay pornography was found at the scene. This led to a public discussion of what one radio talk show host referred to as the "plague of perversion" in the gay community. Within minutes, an angry mother called in to say, "How do I know one of them gay teachers won't show my son how to hang himself with his belt? And the liberals want to let those people get married? It's disgusting!"

The police announced they were seeking information about a white male who had recently been seen with the deceased, a man who often arrived by bicycle, according to Bergdorf's neighbors. Bergdorf had no family and no close friends and was described as a loner by everyone who was asked, making it difficult to obtain information about him.

Poor guy, I thought, *living alone, with no connection to anyone, stuck in a boring job. No wonder he got involved with someone like Henry.* At the time, it didn't occur to me that I had lived a very similar life before Sam came along.

Henry was still nowhere to be found. I spoke to Mr. Zipinski about Robert Bergdorf and I asked if he had reported Henry's disappearance to the police.

"I don't see any reason to waste their time with our personnel problems. I'm sure they have their hands full with burglars and drug dealers, Adam."

"But . . . it could be related to Bergdorf's death."

"Good heavens, what would lead you to such a rash conclusion?"

"Well . . . you asked me about Henry's relationship with Bergdorf, and the police are looking for a man who visited him on a bicycle. Henry was . . . I mean is, a bicyclist."

"Yes, but we heard the sordid details of Mr. Bergdorf's private life. It seems unlikely Henry would have socialized with him. However, it does shed light on Mr. Bergdorf's insistence that Henry handle the Ellis account. These depraved inverts can barely control themselves in the presence of attractive young men. It must have been difficult for Henry to work with him. No wonder he was lax about the audits."

I clenched my fists tightly. *Must . . . resist . . . violence.* "Mr. Zipinski . . . did it ever occur to you that Henry might have welcomed his advances?"

His expression was blank. "I don't understand. Henry was never passive or effeminate. Why would you suggest such a thing? The two of you were chums."

"I'm sorry, sir, but I thought you had suspicions about their friendship. Did I misunderstand you?"

"Nothing good can result from speculation. It would be best for our firm to put this unfortunate episode behind us, especially now that Henry is no longer employed here."

"He's not employed here anymore? Did he resign?"

"I had no choice but to terminate him for his unexcused absence. I sent out the letter this morning."

"Huh. May I ask if you resolved all the problems with the Ellis account?"

Zipinski bristled. "Did I say there were problems with the Ellis account? I'm afraid you have misconstrued things again. Perhaps I shouldn't speak so freely with my employees, but it is my nature to be open and honest in all my dealings. I hope I haven't misplaced my trust by discussing these matters with you."

"Not at all, sir. As always, my main concern is the well-being of this firm, and I hoped Mr. Ellis was satisfied with our work."

"Mr. Ellis is being difficult, but he is under a great deal of stress. Apparently, Mr. Bergdorf was diverting some of the company's funds. His suicide may have been precipitated by the fear that his crime had been discovered."

"Suicide? What makes you think it was suicide? I thought his death was accidental. It could have been murder for all we know. That's why I think the police should know Henry is missing."

I realized immediately that I had crossed a line. Zipinski's face hardened. "Let me be perfectly clear about this, Adam. I would not care to hear any further discussion of imaginary crimes, nor any suggestion of contacting the authorities about anyone associated with this firm. Is that understood?"

"Yes sir. I apologize for getting carried away."

"I hate to think of the consequences that might fall upon the employees of this firm if my good name is dragged through the mud again."

"I understand, sir. I hope you know . . ."

"Good day to you. You may go." He turned his chair toward the window and stared into the cold gray sky.

"Thank you for your time sir. Again, I apologize . . ." He raised his hand to dismiss me, so I turned and left his office. If I had a tail, it would have been between my legs.

***

I wasn't in my office for long before Donna came to see me. "We need to talk."

"I know. Zipinski just handed me my ass for asking too many questions about Bergdorf and Henry and the Ellis account."

"Not about that. About Colin. What did you do to him? I left him alone with you for twenty minutes and he comes back saying he wants to go shopping for clothes. I thought the gays weren't recruiting anymore."

"I'll ignore that because I know you're not stupid. We gave him a little advice."

"About what?"

"Guy stuff."

"Wearing shirts that match your eyes is not guy stuff. It's gay stuff."

"That's not true. Greg was the first one to suggest it."

"Oh, yeah, *that* guy. Why are you hanging around with a creepy hunchback who leers at fifteen-year-old girls?"

"Uh, he's not really a hunchback, Donna. And he wasn't looking at Sarah, he was looking at you."

"He's a . . . wait a minute . . . what did you say?"

"He was leering at you. I believe he called you a red-hot MILF. It made Colin gag. Me too."

"How old did you say he was?"

"I don't know. Twenty?" *Going on twelve.*

"What does he look like without the costume?"

"I can't imagine why it would matter, but he's hot."

"Do you know what hours he works at the nursery?"

"Donna! What is wrong with you? Kevin is, like, the perfect husband, and you're . . ."

"I won't do anything with him! But it's nice to be appreciated, and if there's a chance of getting a discount on merchandise, why not?"

"I think you have it backwards. You're supposed to tip them for being hot."

"You have a lot to learn. We should go shopping together. I could teach you."

"Yeah, maybe Sarah could come along in her Catwoman costume. She'd probably get stuff for free."

She nearly jumped across my desk. "Don't talk about my daughter that way! She's only fifteen!"

"Calm down! Jeez. What were you thinking, letting her wear that costume?"

"I thought she would be Catwoman from the old TV show, but she looked like a dominatrix in a telephone sex ad!"

"Well, you'd better wake up. She's old enough to get pregnant."

"ADAM!"

"Speaking of getting girls pregnant, weren't you asking me about Colin?"

Donna's eyes bugged out. "He didn't! I'll kill him!"

"No, he didn't get anyone pregnant! Where's your sense of humor?"

"It's not funny!"

"You worry too much. Why can't you be more relaxed, like me?"

"Aren't you the guy who was afraid of getting hit by a meteorite?"

"That was years ago. I was having a bad day."

"So what advice did Colin ask for?"

"It was about a poem. Something he gave to a girl."

"What poem? What girl? Tell me everything."

"No! If he wanted to talk to you about it, he would have. If I tell you what we talked about, he'll probably never talk to me again."

"What, are the two of you friends now?"

"Maybe. Can he come to my house for a sleepover?"

"Shut *up!*"

"I can't. I'm enjoying this too much."

"I'm leaving."

"Wait, what about Robert Bergdorf?"

"What about him? It sounds like he died happy."

"Donna! Don't be so cold. You know, Zipinski fired Henry."

"That's what happens when you don't show up for work."

"Don't you think Henry might have had something to do with Bergdorf's death?"

"Why? We don't even know if they were friends."

"Yes, we do. I mean I do. They were together at the Como Villa the night Sam and I were there. Bergdorf referred to Henry as his boyfriend."

"Why is this the first time I'm hearing about this?"

"Uh, I don't know. Because I didn't think you'd be interested?"

"Wrong answer! Are you planning to tell the police about this?"

"Zipinski told me not to. He was pretty angry."

"So what! If a crime was committed . . ."

"It could affect a lot of people, all of our jobs . . ."

"We'll be okay."

"How do you know?"

"I just know. I'm optimistic."

"Since when?"

"Since you got a boyfriend. Who saw that coming?"

"Fuck you!"

"You have to admit, it was pretty close to a miracle."

There were so many things I wanted to say to her, I didn't know where to start. "Okay . . . just go . . . get out."

"Fine. I was leaving anyway." She stood up and grabbed the doorknob. "By the way, Ellis Industries isn't the only place where money is missing. See ya." She opened the door and left.

"What? Wait a minute! Come back here!" The staff outside my office glared at me, but Donna was already gone. *God dammit!*

***

While I was preparing dinner, before Sam got home, I called Carl. Now that we weren't working together every weekend, I didn't talk to him unless we could think of reasons to call each other. I was surprised at how often we found reasons. For example, I called to report a car that was parked a little too close to a fire hydrant. He called to ask me about some gnats flying around one of his houseplants. This time I had a very good reason to call. He picked up after one ring.

"Hey stud, what's up?"

"No, it's me. Adam."

"I know. Caller ID, remember?

"Oh, I thought you said . . . never mind. How are you?"

"I'm okay. Always better when I hear your voice."

"Oh, you're so . . . whatever. Listen, I have a question for you. Do you know anything about this Robert Bergdorf thing?"

"Only what I've seen in the news, plus a few rumors from other cops. I'm glad they're taking this opportunity to talk about how gay people are so sick. I love that. It warms my heart."

"I know. Hey, do you know if the police are considering whether he was murdered?"

"Murdered? Why would they think that? The poor guy should have used a safer method, but as far as I know, there's no reason to suspect foul play."

"What about the guy on the bicycle they were looking for?"

"I think they dropped that. Why are you interested in this? Did you know him?"

"Not really, but I think I know who the guy on the bicycle was."

"Oh. Is it someone we both know?"

"I don't think so. Wait, do you mean Sam? No no no no! He has nothing to do with this. The guy on the bicycle was someone I work with, or used to work with. He's been missing for a few days now."

"This is getting interesting. Tell me more."

"Okay, you can't tell anyone where you heard this, but Ellis Industries is one of our clients. Robert Bergdorf was the contact person for Ellis, and this guy, Henry Verdorven, was handling the Ellis account. I also happen to know they were seeing each other outside of work. Apparently, Bergdorf embezzled money from his company and Henry helped him cover it up. Now Bergdorf is dead, and Henry is missing. Does any of this sound suspicious to you?"

"Yes. Who else knows about this?"

"The owner of our firm, Alvin Zipinski knows most of it, but he would never admit it. He told me not to talk to the police or there might be dire consequences."

"So why are you telling me?"

"I thought you could look into it, maybe do an investigation?"

"I'm a patrol officer, Adam, I'm not a detective. I can't launch my own investigation like the cops on TV."

"Oh, I didn't know how it worked. Do you know any detectives who could investigate it?"

Carl sighed heavily. "Yes, I know a guy who recently became a detective. Do you realize what you're asking me to do? This is not a small favor."

"A man died, Carl. Money was stolen. You're a police officer."

"Oh, great! A guilt trip! Thanks, Mom!"

"You have a mother?"

"Of course I have a mother! Don't get me started on her. How am I supposed to explain how I know these things about Bergdorf and this Henry guy and the embezzlement? Huh?"

"Well . . . couldn't you tell them you overheard it at a gay bar?"

There was a long silence before I heard him take a deep breath and exhale. "Adam . . . has anyone ever told you how aggravating you can be?"

"That sounds familiar. I didn't mean to upset you, Carl, but I don't know what else to do."

"You could go to the proper authorities and tell them what you know. How about that?"

"But . . . I could lose my job. And there would be a lot of questions that could lead to some other stuff that would be embarrassing for me and Sam."

"So Sam is connected to this in some way. I knew it!"

"Not directly. He had . . . encounters . . . with Henry before we were together. That's all. But it would be problematic if it came to light."

"Problematic? I don't even want to know what you're talking about."

"Wouldn't a detective appreciate having this information? I mean, if he uncovers the truth and makes an arrest, wouldn't it be good for him?"

"Yes, it would. Do you know who that newly promoted detective is? My former partner, Asshole Mansky! Now he's Detective Asshole because he arrested some gay guys for having sex in the park!"

"Oh, that's not right. But he'll make a good detective."

"THAT'S NOT THE POINT! The point is, I would be handing him a case that could make his career! He could become Chief of Police some day! Is that what you want?"

"Um . . . well, if he earns it . . ."

"Oh my GOD! Ugh!" Carl had never been angry at me before. I seemed to bring that out in people. "If I do this for you, it'll benefit everyone but me! And you probably won't even understand why I'm doing it."

Just then, Sam came in the back door. "Listen, I need to go but I appreciate your help. I promise I'll make it up to you some day."

"I can think of a few things you could do . . ."

"Gotta go. Talk to you later." I hung up. "Hey, Sam. How was your day?" I set my phone on the table.

"Not bad. How about yours?"

"Oh . . . stressful." I waited for him to remove his boots so I could greet him. We made a point of greeting each other properly every evening. Sometimes it went on for fifteen minutes. This time his kiss sent a chill up my spine because he slipped his cold hand down the back of my jeans to squeeze my butt.

"Who was that on the phone?"

"Nobody. Are you hungry?"

"You still ask me that after all this time?"

"It's a habit. I made baked ziti with sausage."

"Sounds good. I'll set the table in the dining room."

I opened the oven to check the ziti and the green beans I was roasting. When I turned around, Sam was looking at my phone. "What are you doing?"

"You were talking to Carl. Why didn't you say so?"

I felt my skin flush. "No reason. It wasn't important." I didn't like being questioned. "I can't believe you checked my phone. I would never do that to you."

"You can if you'd like." He pulled his phone out of his pocket and held it out to me.

I stared at it. *Should I? Do I want to see what's in there?* "No, I'm not like that. I trust you."

He looked me in the eye. "Do you?"

I couldn't hold his gaze for long. "Yes. I love you."

He put his phone away and went to the cabinet to get the dishes. "I don't have a problem with you talking to Carl. You don't need to hide it."

"Well, you used to be so jealous, I'm not over it yet."

"I haven't been that way for a while." He walked into the dining room with the dishes. When he came back, I was quiet. "Do you want wine tonight?"

"Yeah, maybe a little."

"I think I'll have some, too." He filled two glasses. I felt him standing close behind me. He wrapped one arm around me and palmed my crotch. "I want to make hot love to you tonight. How does that sound?" He licked the back of my ear.

"Would you say I'm . . . aggravating?"

He nibbled at my ear. "You can be. Like when I say something sexy and you seem to be on another planet."

"Do I do that?"

"You just did."

"Oh yeah, hot love tonight . . . that sounds nice. But is it difficult to be in a relationship with me?"

"I like you the way you are, but we both have things to work on."

"Do you think I'm working hard enough?"

"You've come a long way. A few months ago you could barely look at me."

It seemed like a long time ago, but it wasn't. And here he was, holding me, asking if I would have sex with him tonight . . . and I was worried about something Carl said. *What the hell is wrong with me?* I turned around. "I still don't look at you enough."

He stood tall, with his shoulders back, and gently pressed himself against me. "I'm right here . . . take a good look." He brought his arms up, leaned back, and stretched his beautiful young body, squinting and yawning before lowering his arms, rubbing his thick chest, and bending down to kiss me on the forehead. "I could literally eat you up right now. When will the food be ready?"

"In a few minutes." I placed my hand on the bulge in his jeans. "Are you sure you can wait?"

"For dinner, or for sex?"

"Maybe we could find a way to combine the two."

"Hmm . . . I like the sound of that. But how?"

I unfastened the button on his jeans. "Let's figure it out." I slowly opened his zipper.

***

A few days later, the local media reported that Robert Bergdorf had embezzled close to two million dollars from Ellis Industries in less than three months. The crime didn't fit the usual pattern for fraud. Diverting such a large amount of money over a brief period increased the risk of being caught, even if he had help covering it up. There was no evidence of a gambling problem, and Bergdorf continued to live a modest lifestyle apart from a brief trip to Europe during the summer.

Reporters speculated about an accomplice, and Bergdorf's death was now being investigated as a possible murder. Jasper Ellis, owner of the company bearing his name, publicly criticized the Chief of Police for assigning a rookie detective to be the lead investigator for such a serious and complex crime. The Chief, in response, assured the public he had "the utmost confidence in Detective Douglas Mansky, who uncovered key evidence in the case through his own initiative and dedication to uncovering the truth."

I woke up feeling funky, and when I got to the office, I felt worse. Several people were escorted off the premises after being fired by Mr. Zipinski. Based on what I overheard, all of them, including Henry's sycophantic assistant, had confessed to inappropriate activities with Henry while he gained access to company expense accounts, secure databases, and confidential information about clients and employees of the firm. A cute young guy who handled accounts payable was escorted to the door by a security guard when I was called to meet with Mr. Zipinski.

I think most people worry about getting called into the boss's office. I was already wondering how I would survive after losing my job. *If Sam sleeps with me every night, I could save a lot on heating bills. Maybe Dave will give me a job. Or Flora . . . I could wash customers' cars at the dealership.*

"Adam, please come in." I was surprised by Zipinski's cordial tone, but he was often friendly before he stuck a knife between your ribs. I sat down in front of his desk and waited for the unwelcome news. "These are challenging times for the firm, Adam. Henry's fraudulent activities left us in a very bad situation. Do you know we paid fifteen thousand dollars to a local tailor for custom made shirts and suits?" He shook his head and clicked his tongue. "It pains me to terminate employees, but they all helped him in various ways, in exchange for his . . . favors."

"I had no idea that was going on, sir."

"The things we found in Henry's files were enlightening, to say the least. Did you know he had a file on you? Zipinski lifted a folder from his desk and opened it.

"Other than my personnel file?"

"Yes, these files were retrieved from Henry's residence."

"Oh. Did the police search his place?"

He peered at me over his reading glasses. "The police were not involved. I have a resourceful private investigator who is indispensable at times like this. He acquired the files before the police began their investigation. It has spared me further embarrassment during this scandal."

"I see." I waited for him to confront me with the Weasel Woman's flyer. *What could I say?*

"Henry researched a number of employees for distinct reasons, but he took a particular interest in your financial situation. I had no idea you were a millionaire, Adam."

"Excuse me?"

Zipinski looked up. "Your assets. Your net worth exceeds one million dollars. One point four million according to Henry's calculations."

I shook my head and stammered, "I . . . but . . . that's not . . . my . . . no . . ."

He handed me documents from the file. "I don't know how he obtained this information about your accounts. He must have known someone at your bank. These retirement investments were originally in your parents' names and were transferred after their death. It appears they had a large life insurance policy with you as the sole beneficiary. This is a summary of your own retirement account. And your house was assessed last year at over three-hundred-thousand dollars."

"But . . . it would never sell for that much. The heating bills are terrible."

"Nevertheless, your parents left you very well situated, which is why Henry took an interest in you."

"I don't understand. I'm not rich."

"Adam, I have been forced to acknowledge that Henry was a professional swindler. I believe he was looking for a way to separate you from your assets. Like Robert Bergdorf, you were an ideal target because you have no living relatives. Fortunately, your tenant served as a barrier."

"My tenant?"

"This young man." He handed me a photograph of Sam cutting the grass, shirtless. "Does he live on your property?"

"Yes, in an apartment above the garage."

"He's a strapping young lad. Don't let your fiancé's eyes wander, or she'll end up like Lady Chatterley." He smiled and wagged his finger. "There are notes here about where the young man works, his hours . . . Henry was thorough. In the end, he decided you were of no use to him because, as he put it, you are too honest." Mr. Zipinski closed the folder and handed it to me. "Feel free to destroy this."

The Weasel's flyer was not in the file. Part of me was disappointed. I was tired of maintaining the charade of having a girlfriend. I opened the folder and glanced at Henry's notes: "Naive . . . sexually repressed . . . useless . . . too honest." I put the financial documents in the folder and closed it. "Thank you, sir."

"I would like to thank *you*, Adam, and to apologize for the way I spoke to you the last time we met. You were right about Henry. Because of your suspicions, I put my investigator on the job. Now that the police are investigating, it is important that we be portrayed as victims of Henry's crimes, not as facilitators."

"Have the police talked to you about Henry?"

"Not yet, but I believe Jasper Ellis will send them here. As you know, he insisted that your friend, Donna Gilson, supervise all our work for his company. I don't know why, but he trusts her."

"Donna is taking over the Ellis account? I didn't know that."

"Oh . . . you didn't? I hoped the two of you were still friends, though I discouraged it at one time."

"I didn't know about this, but we are still friends."

“Ah, I'm glad to hear it. Would you please impress upon her the importance of maintaining a unified front during challenging times?” He smiled enough to show his teeth, a clear sign of his discomfort. “I hope you understand my meaning.”

I understood he was afraid of what we might say to the police. “I do, Mr. Zipinski. You want us all to support one another.”

“Indeed. That's precisely what I meant.” He looked relieved.

“While we're on that subject, there's something I've been meaning to tell you, sir. I wish I had been honest with you from the beginning, but I was afraid you wouldn't be supportive.”

“Please, Adam, you have nothing to fear.”

“I don't have a fiancé, or a girlfriend. I never did. The young man in the photograph . . . he's my . . . we're together. We are a couple. He's my boyfriend. His name is Sam.”

Zipinski's face froze into a mask of insincerity. “I see. Well . . . thank you for trusting me with this information. I'm sorry you felt I wouldn't be supportive. We must all support one another. Mustn't we?”

“Yes, sir. I hoped you would see it that way. I feel better now. I'll talk to Donna about the importance of mutual support. Is there anything else you wanted to discuss?"

"No. That's quite enough for today, thank you." He seemed to retreat into his own little world, staring into space. "Everything will be fine if we all stick together."

I left his office with a mixture of relief and tension. I didn't feel safe after what I told him, but at least I was honest about myself. Except for the part about being a millionaire, a fact I adamantly refused to acknowledge since my parents' death. I walked down the hallway thinking, *I'm not rich, I'm not rich.* I stopped in the men's room to empty my bladder. Five minutes later, I returned to my office with beads of sweat on my forehead. *Fuck, fuck, fuck, fuck, fuck!* With the door and the blinds closed, I dialed my phone. "Yes, this is Adam Evans. Does Dr. Rubin have any openings this afternoon? It's urgent. Do I have to tell you? It's a personal problem."

***

I spent the next several hours trying to dehydrate myself so I would never have to urinate again. It was not a sound plan. At the doctor's office, his assistant gave me a huge cup of water and told me to start drinking. I sipped it reluctantly until Rubin entered the exam room. "Hello, Adam. You can forget about the water. We'll do this the other way." I whimpered when I saw the swabs.

Ten minutes later he gave me a paper towel to mop the sweat off my face. "So, do you have any questions about the importance of using condoms? No? I didn't think so. It's often something like this that gets people to take it seriously.

Because it's Friday, we won't get the lab results until next week. I'd like to tell you this is a urinary tract infection, but after swabbing your rectum, I think there's something else at work here. Probably chlamydia. I'll give you a prescription for a strong antibiotic, and you can't have sex for the next two weeks. Is that clear?"

I nodded.

"You've only had one sexual partner since the last time we tested you?" I nodded again. "And when was the last time he was tested?"

"As far as I know, a few months ago. At the beginning of summer."

"That means he's been with someone else since then." I nodded. "You need to talk to him about this. He needs to get treated, and he needs to stop spreading it around. Promise me you'll talk to him today."

"I promise."

"What's that puncture wound on your thigh? It looks like someone stabbed you with a fork."

"Um . . . yeah. I stabbed myself with a fork. I won't make a habit of it."

"I would hope not. I'll report that to your psychologist. I wish I could trust you to tell him yourself, but I can't."

"Are you allowed to do that?"

"I'll do it, and if you don't like it, you can sue me. How does that sound?"

"Reasonable." He knew me.

"Come back in two weeks for another test to make sure everything is clear. Make sure you have some pee for me or I'll swab you again."

"Don't worry, I've learned my lesson."

"We'll see about that."

***

I didn't cook that evening. After stopping at the pharmacy, I went home and sat in the living room, waiting. I ignored a phone call from Donna, then realized it was a mistake. After rehearsing a story, I called her back, told her everything was fine and distracted her by talking about my meeting with Zipinski. She congratulated me for telling him about my relationship with Sam. I congratulated her for being put in charge of the Ellis account. She promised to tell me about it on Monday, and we ended the call. *That wasn't so difficult.*

As soon as Sam came in the back door, he knew something was wrong. "Adam?"

I thought about going to greet him, but if I pretended everything was okay, I might want to keep that going, and the conversation would be put off again. I stayed where I was and called out, "I'm in here."

After hanging up his coat and taking off his shoes, he came through the dining room. "What's going on? Why are you in here?"

"I had to see my doctor today. He thinks I have chlamydia."

He stopped in his tracks, stuck his hands in his pockets and looked down at the floor.

I waited, but he didn't make a sound. "Are you going to ask me where I got it?"

Sam shook his head.

"Why don't you sit down." Slowly, he stepped in front of the sofa and perched on the edge of the seat. His right knee started to bounce. "Sam, I know you got it since the last time you were tested. Do you know who you got it from?" Still looking at the rug, he shrugged and slowly shook his head. I was afraid of that. "How many possibilities are there?"

He pressed on his bouncing knee with one hand but couldn't keep it still. Finally, he spoke quietly. "What difference does it make? One guy is too many."

"Clever answer, Sam. Did you rehearse that?"

He looked up briefly. "No, I didn't rehearse it. It's the truth. Do you think I feel good about this?"

I raised my voice. "Well, I *hope* not, because I feel pretty fuckin' bad about it!"

"I wanted to tell you. I've been trying to tell you, but I could never . . . it was never the right time. When things were good between us, I didn't want to ruin it, and when things were bad, I didn't want to make it worse. Honestly, I kept hoping you would ask me."

"Is that my job? 'Hi, Sam! How was your day? Did you fuck any other guys?' Is that what you expected?"

"No, but you knew, didn't you? Be honest! How long have you known?" He looked me in the eye.

"That's not the point! You should have told me! You put me at risk!"

"You *knew* you were at risk! But you didn't want to know, did you? There were plenty of things you could have asked me about, but you turned away from it *every time!*"

"Don't put this back on me, like it's my fault for not questioning you more! That's bullshit!" I stood up with the intention of storming out of the room because that's what people do when they don't want to deal with their problems. I turned and headed for the stairs.

"Oh, no you don't!" Sam came after me, caught me before I got to the foyer, and scooped me off the floor with one arm around my waist. "You're not running away again."

I flailed and yelled, "God dammit! Put me down!" My fists connected with his body in a few places. He tightened his grip. "GET your FUCKING hands OFF me, you FUCKER!" I twisted around and slapped the side of his head.

"OW! Not in the HEAD!"

"PUT ME DOWN!" I pounded on his arms and his back. "Put me DOWN!"

"NO! Not until you calm down! OW! Dammit! We need to talk about this, Adam!"

"Why? You'll just blame me for not keeping you from fucking half the guys in town!" I slammed my fist into his ribs.

"AHH! You little FUCKER! That HURT!" He pinned my arms against my body, so I kicked his shins. "You're RIGHT! Okay? You're RIGHT! That was bullshit. Stop kicking me so we can talk!" He tried to trap my feet between his legs, lost his balance, and fell backwards onto the floor with a boom that shook the house. I landed on top of him, wrapped tightly in his limbs, finally immobilized.

The front doorbell rang, so we stopped moving. "Mr. Adam! Open the door!" It was Agnes.

Sam whispered, "Did they hear us? You were yelling pretty loud." I grabbed his skin between my fingers and pinched him as hard as I could. "Ow! God DAMMIT!" He let me go.

I pushed myself off him and went to the foyer. He stayed put. I flipped the deadbolt and opened the door. "Hello, Agnes. How are you?"

"Donnae blow smoke up me arse! What was that racket? Is he hurting you?" She tried to see around me.

I opened the door wider and raked my fingers through my hair to make myself more presentable. "Does it look like he's hurting me?"

Sam sat on the floor, grimacing and clutching his ribs. Agnes stood in the foyer and had a look at him. Satisfied, she looked me up and down. "A'right, carry on, but be quiet about it or she'll send me back to deal with ye both." She left.

Sam called out as I closed the door, "What about me?"

"Did you fuck with their pool maintenance guy?" He closed his eyes and swore under his breath. "Yeah, I thought so! Agnes knows about you, too. I'm getting something to eat. Get off your ass if you want to talk to me."

I stomped into the kitchen and grabbed items from the refrigerator to make a sandwich. Eventually Sam followed and stood at a distance while I slammed things around. "Well? You wanted to talk, let's talk."

"You know, you hurt me, Adam! I'm not bulletproof!"

"Oh, please! I thought you liked it rough. Or was that only with Henry?"

"I knew you would bring that up! It didn't take long. Do you feel better now? What else have you got?"

I was making the messiest sandwich I had ever made. "Okay . . . did you fuck the pizza delivery guy?"

"No, we sucked each other off. You happy now? Is that what you wanted to hear?"

"That's disgusting." I took a bite out of my sandwich.

"What else? How many more stories do you want?"

I shook my head. "I've heard enough. I can't believe I was so blind."

"But you *weren't* blind, Adam! You saw enough to know what I was doing! You didn't say a fucking word about it! Why?"

I took another bite of my sandwich to delay my response. Then I ignored his question. "Why are you doing this to me? You can fuck me any way you want to, as often as you want, and that's not enough for you? How many times a day do you need it?"

"It's not like that, there's something about . . ."

"Is it because I'm too old? Am I bad at sex?"

"No! Adam, I love having sex with you! It doesn't have anything to do with you."

"So you're punishing me! Are you angry at me? You could tell me what I did wrong instead of doing shit like this."

"Adam, SHUT UP! Shut the FUCK up and LISTEN for a change!"

"Don't talk to me like that!"

Sam formed his fingers into a circle suggesting an urge to strangle me. Instead, pressed his hands against his temples and closed his eyes. "Adam . . . if I wanted to hurt you . . . this is when it would happen. At least give me credit for not choking you right now."

"Oh, sure! Do you want a little trophy?"

Sam took a very deep breath and let it out slowly. "Could I please get something to eat?"

"You want me to make your dinner? Unbelievable!"

"No! I'll make my own. Move out of the way so I can get at it." I rolled my eyes and took my sloppy sandwich to the table. Sam walked around the other side to make his own sandwich. He stood with his back to me. "I know you won't believe this, but when I have sex with other guys it doesn't have anything to do with you."

"It does when I get a nasty . . . "

"LISTEN! Please! I know it affects you, but I don't do it to punish you, or because I'm not happy with you, or don't like having sex with you, or anything like that. I mean . . . I've had sex with you a lot more than all the other guys combined, and I still enjoy it more with you. Even now I'd like to screw your brains out."

"I can't have sex for two weeks."

"I'm just *saying*! It's not what you think. It's not about you. It's . . . when I see a guy checking me out . . . it still surprises me. I think, "I could have *him?*" Then I want to prove it to myself. Like . . . it's not real unless I do it. I tell myself

I shouldn't. I think about you and how much it would hurt you." He leaned down and bit a large chunk off the crude sandwich he constructed. He chewed and swallowed. "I bargain with myself. I say it'll be the last time, and it won't hurt you if you don't know about it. I tell myself it doesn't mean anything. I even told myself you knew about it. One way or another, I end up doing it."

"Are you telling me you don't enjoy it?"

"No, I won't say that." He took another bite of his sandwich. "I like the way they react to my body, especially the first time they see me. It makes me feel good. I like being bigger than other guys. I think about the guys in high school who made fun of me in the locker room. I wonder what they would think if they saw me now." He continued eating with his back toward me.

I finished my sandwich and sat with my arms crossed, stewing. "Have you done it with the same guy more than once?"

Sam turned around and rested his butt against the counter. "No, after the first time, I lose interest. They usually want to see me again, but I make it clear I won't. If they're persistent, then . . ."

"Then *what?*"

"I say whatever it takes to get rid of them, and they think I'm an asshole. It's not like I'm making friends. I just feel worse about myself until the next guy comes along."

I shook my head. "Do you expect me to put up with this?"

"No, of course not. I need to stop. Maybe it'll be different now that you know. I can't believe I gave you a disease. Will you be okay? Did you get medicine?" He sat down at the other end of the table.

"He gave me an antibiotic that's supposed to take care of it, assuming it's chlamydia. He won't get the results until next week. You need to see a doctor, too."

"Yeah, I will. I'll see if I can get in tomorrow."

"Sam, you can't go around fucking every guy who flirts with you. How would you like it if I did that?"

"I wouldn't like it. But it's easier for you, isn't it? You're so oblivious, you wouldn't know if someone wanted you unless they shouted at you. It's not like that for me."

I blinked a few times. "So . . . it's easier for me to be faithful to you because I don't notice when guys are attracted to me, but you . . ."

"I was only saying . . ."

"Shut up and listen! But you have a tough time controlling yourself because you see guys who want you every day. Is that it?"

"Yeah . . . kind of. I have more opportunities, so . . . more temptation. And my sex drive is stronger because I'm younger."

"Okay, fuck you!" I stood up abruptly. "You should have stopped a few minutes ago." I went to the counter to put away the food. "Are you done with this or are you still eating?"

"I'm still hungry. Do we have any leftovers?"

"No, because you eat every damn thing I make!"

"I thought you liked that."

"Yeah, well . . . right now I don't." I looked in the refrigerator and found a container of curried chicken salad. "Here, eat this. I didn't like it anyway." I tossed the plastic tub at him. It would have hit him in the chest if he hadn't caught it.

"Adam, come on! Act like an adult!"

"Sorry! I can't control myself! I have more anger than you do!"

He went to the drawer to get a fork. "Look, I know I fucked up, but . . ."

I didn't listen. "Did it ever occur to you I would only need one opportunity to be unfaithful to you? I don't need to get a new offer every day. All I need is one person to tempt me until I break down. Do you think that would be easy to resist?"

"Are you talking about Carl?"

"I'm saying it's not easier for me."

"Has he been trying to . . . I thought the two of you were only . . ."

"Do you think I haven't thought about it? Do you think my dick shuts off when you're not around? You think you're God's gift, don't you?"

"No! Fine, you made your point, you get tempted, too!"

"Except I haven't done anything, and you have!"

"Let's agree you're a better person than me. Is that what you want?"

"It's a good start!" I was halfway through cleaning out the refrigerator without realizing it. "Use up this spray cheese. It's getting old." I banged it onto the table. "There's a box of crackers in the pantry, unless you ate those, too." I started checking the dates on things.

Sam threw away the container from the chicken salad and found the crackers. "Adam, I'm very sorry about what I've done. I know it's serious, and I'm the only one who's responsible for my behavior. I shouldn't make excuses."

I took a break from my frenzied activity. "That actually sounds like an apology. Now we're getting somewhere!" I stood up to get a damp cloth to wipe the refrigerator shelves and paused to look at him while he focused on putting a swirl of cheese on a cracker. Apart from his size and muscularity, he looked younger than his age. I went back to cleaning the refrigerator. "Is it really so hard for you to stop having sex with other guys?"

"Harder than I thought it would be, at least with certain types of guys. I don't do it with every guy who tries to get my attention. And it doesn't happen every day, or every week. I hope you don't think I'm *that* bad."

"I try not to think about it at all." I removed a single apple from the produce bin and set it on the table.

"Do you want me to eat that?"

"No, I'll eat it. Should we talk about an open relationship? Is that what you want?"

"No, I don't want that."

"I don't want it either, but if it's not realistic for you to stop . . ."

"No, Adam! Seriously. Maybe it works for other guys, but I don't see it . . . the thought of you with . . . no. No, I couldn't."

Everything was back in the refrigerator, neatly arranged. I closed the door, wiped off the counter, and rinsed the cloth in the sink. I sat down next to Sam and took a bite out of the apple. He set a cracker on the table in front of me. He had drawn a heart on it with spray cheese. It may sound dumb, but it brought tears to my eyes. I looked away from him because I wanted to stay angry. *I should be angry!* But it wasn't easy. "I don't want you to have sex with other guys anymore. It's not okay with me. Is that clear?"

"Yes. I can't promise, but I agree."

"What?"

"I'm being honest, Adam. I don't want to lie to you anymore." He set another cracker on the table in front of me.

I took another bite of the apple. "Did Dave give you advice on how to have sex?"

He looked down. "No, I made that up. I thought you would wonder how I knew so much. I tried to talk to Dave about sex once and he cut me off." He put a third cracker in front of me. Three hearts in a row.

I'd had enough of the apple, so I offered it to Sam. He accepted it and took a bite. I looked at the crackers while he waited to see what I would do. I picked one up and ate it. "I told Mr. Zipinski about you today. He knows we're a couple."

Sam was obviously surprised. "You did? You didn't have to do that for me."

"I didn't do it for you. I did it for myself. It was time."

"You won't lose your job, will you?"

"I don't think so. He can't afford to have me as an enemy right now. Or maybe he can't afford to have Donna as an enemy. Either way, he's up to his eyeballs in problems." I ate another cracker.

Sam nibbled the apple down to the core and hopped up to discard it. He paused and asked, "Can I touch you?"

I looked up. "Yeah. I suppose."

He leaned down and awkwardly placed his arms around me while I remained seated. He kissed me on the cheek, and on my temple. I closed my eyes tightly and leaned away from him as if I were being licked by a dog. He tightened his embrace.

"All right, that's enough."

He kissed me one more time, then sat down again. "I don't know how to thank you for putting up with me."

I grunted and ate the third cracker, trying to look annoyed. I didn't want to think about my life without him. I should have, but I wouldn't. He leaned on the table with his head on one hand, looking at me.

"What?"

"I'm glad you finally got angry at me."

"I've been angry at you before."

"Not like this. It seemed like you were holding back. I feel like I know you better now. And I'm glad you're not afraid of me. That means a lot."

"I don't understand."

"When you were pounding the crap out of me, you weren't afraid. Do you know what I could have done to you?"

"Yeah. I knew you wouldn't."

"That's what I mean. You weren't afraid. I love that, but you can't hit me anymore. Just because I'm stronger doesn't mean it's okay. I let you get away with it this time, but never again."

I blushed. "You're right. No hitting. Did I hurt you?"

"Yeah! I probably have bruises all over me."

"I'm sorry, but maybe you shouldn't have grabbed me when I was trying to walk away. Was that fair?"

"I suppose not. I didn't want you to avoid the argument again. As soon as things start to heat up, you run away."

"You could have followed me upstairs."

"Or you could stop running away. How about that?"

I sighed. "I guess I could work on that while you work on not fucking other guys."

"Fair enough." He bent down and pulled up his jeans on one leg. There were dark bruises on his shin. "Look at that."

I grimaced. "Oh, it does look bad."

"It's a good thing it's too cold for shorts." He exposed similar injuries on the other leg.

"Take off your shirt. I want to see what I did."

Sam stood and unbuttoned the long-sleeved green cotton shirt Dave's employees wore in colder weather. He wore a snug white t-shirt underneath. As always, he smelled good and he looked great. I didn't blame people for staring at him wherever he went. I never got tired of it.

"Sam, you know what you said earlier about the way guys look at you the first time they see you?"

"Yeah."

"It's like that for me every time we're together. I can't believe how beautiful you are. Every single time."

He smiled and lifted the hem of his t-shirt. "I know. I love the way you look at me."

I moved my hands over his abdomen. "Does this hurt?" He shook his head. I pressed on each muscle with my fingertips, then ran my hands over his abs again.

"I thought you were looking for bruises."

"I'm being thorough. Turn to the side." He turned and lifted his shirt higher. "Oh, that's what you're talking about." There was a large bruise on his lower ribs. I applied the slightest pressure. "Does that hurt?"

"Yes."

I took my hand away and gently kissed the bruise in several places. "How does it feel now?"

"Better."

I kissed it a few more times. "I'm sorry about this, Sam. I'll never hit you again, I promise." I slid my hand up the front of his t-shirt to rub his chest.

"Will you kiss all my bruises and make them better?"

"Yes, I'll do that upstairs."

"You still want me to sleep with you?"

"Yeah, I want to know where you are at night. And I want you to hear me scream every time I take a piss."

"I deserve that. How long do we have to go without sex?"

"Two weeks."

"Do you know how much I want you right now?" He wrapped his big arms around me.

"Too bad. Your diseased organ won't touch me again until we both get clean test results. And I'll make sure you know what you're missing every day until then."

He glanced at his arm. "Do you see that bruise there? What can you do about that?"

"Let me see." I kissed the bruise a few times. "Better?"

"A little."

***

The next day I received a plain white envelope in the mail with a postmark from Kennedy International Airport. Inside was a copy of the Weasel Woman's flyer. There was a brief handwritten note on the back:

"Au revoir! Thanks for all your help."

I knew it was from Henry.

35

My anger at Sam came in waves throughout the weekend. It was easier to feel it when he wasn't around, when I wasn't looking at him, wasn't remembering what it was like to be in bed with him, or thinking about how much better my life had been since he showed up in my driveway. When I had to pee, I wanted to kill him. It felt like hot acid flowing through my penis. Fortunately, the antibiotic Dr. Rubin gave me provided some relief. The pain of knowing Sam had deceived me was more difficult to treat. I could handle merely suspecting him of having sex with other guys. Now that he had confessed, I wished I didn't know.

I tried to distract myself by doing a lot of cleaning around the house. I took apart my vacuum cleaner and washed the parts. I cleaned the cabinet where I kept my cleaning supplies. I washed my dusting cloths, disinfected my sponges and mops, and rinsed the bristles of my broom with steaming hot water. I paused to call Carl, but he didn't answer. After leaving a message, I cleaned my phone with toothpicks, cotton swabs and rubbing alcohol. I called Carl again. He didn't answer again.

By the time Sam came home from work Saturday evening, I was in a foul mood and it showed. He didn't even try to get a hug or a kiss when he saw the way I looked at him. He quietly set the dining room table, then returned to the kitchen and sat down. He cleared his throat. "I went to the health clinic today to get tested. They can't give me a prescription until they get the lab results. And I don't have any symptoms."

"Aren't you lucky." I practiced my sarcastic tone all day and it was good. I turned around and held up a small plate. "I made an appetizer for you."

"You didn't have to do that." I set the plate in front of him. It held four crackers with little pictures drawn on them with spray cheese. "Are those . . . penises?"

"Yeah, I was feeling creative, and I know how much you like penises."

"Okay. Thanks?" He popped one of the crackers in his mouth.

"Did you fuck anyone at the health clinic today?"

Sam crinkled his brow as he chewed. He was about to respond when he was taken by surprise. "Shit!" He bolted for the sink, opened the faucet and slurped water from his cupped hands.

"Oh yeah, I spread wasabi paste on those crackers. Did I forget to mention that?"

He sputtered and coughed, then took a glass from the cabinet and filled it with water. "Dammit, that *burns!*"

"Does it? I wonder if it burns as much as my dick does when I have to piss." I took a sip from what was left of a large glass of wine.

Sam drained his glass and wiped his mouth on his sleeve while observing me through his squinting, watery eyes. "All right. I get it." He refilled the glass with water and returned to the table.

"Guess how many times I had to pee today."

He held up a cracker. "Was it four times?"

"Yep. Good guess." I turned around to finish preparing dinner while he ate the second cracker. "You didn't answer my question. Did you fuck anyone at the health clinic?"

"No, I did not." He sucked air through his teeth.

"Because if there's one time to use a condom, it's when you fuck someone at an STD clinic."

"I didn't fuck anyone today, but thanks for asking." He gulped some water. "And for the record, I haven't fucked anyone without a condom since before I was with you. Except you, of course."

I turned around. "How did you get chlamydia, or whatever this is?"

"Probably from sucking dicks. I asked them at the clinic. You can get it from anal or oral sex." He prepared himself to eat the third cracker. "Do you think anyone uses condoms for blowjobs? What would be the point?"

"Um . . . to not get a disease? Would that be the point?"

He sighed. "Fine. I'll wear a condom the next time you want to suck my dick." He put the third cracker in his mouth.

"If there *is* a next time." I watched Sam chew. The wasabi didn't burn as much now that he was used to it. I had to give Sam credit for playing along politely and taking his punishment without complaint. "Okay, I'll be honest . . . I didn't want to use condoms with you. I should take responsibility for that." I quickly turned around and busied myself at the counter. All I could do was rearrange things. Dinner was already prepared.

"I love that skin on skin contact, especially when I'm inside you. I feel closer to you. It's not the same with a rubber."

"I agree." I didn't turn around.

"I'm down to the last cracker. Do you want to watch?"

"All right." I turned to look at him. Sam licked the topping off the cracker and held out his tongue for a moment, displaying it for me. He chewed with his mouth open, drained his glass, and finished with an "Ahhhhh." He smiled. "Thanks, babe."

I crossed my arms. "You're welcome. And don't call me babe." I felt bad about deliberately burning his mouth. He had such a pretty mouth.

Sam took his plate and glass to the sink, then stood in front of me. He was so close I had to lean back to look at him. "Kiss me."

"No."

He searched my face and licked his lips. "Come on. Kiss me."

"No. You don't deserve it."

"I know I don't, but I'm asking anyway. Please kiss me."

I felt his warm breath and admired his stubbled jaw. He was asking for something he could easily take. I liked that. "What's in it for me if I kiss you?"

He shrugged. "You get to kiss me." He licked his lips again. It was a persuasive argument.

"Suppose I give in and I kiss you, and one kiss leads to another. Then what?"

He playfully tapped the tip of his nose against mine. "If one kiss leads to another . . . I'm all yours. You'll have me. You can do what you want with me."

I made a face. "I already have you."

"That's true, but what's the point of having me if you don't kiss me? I'm expensive to feed and my studliness is being wasted. You should get your money's worth and kiss me."

"Now you're making sense." I parted my lips and gently grasped his. I nibbled at them until he kissed me . . . gently . . . rhythmically. Kissing Sam was a pretty good substitute for sex. My anger dissipated.

We kissed until I was breathless, then he pulled away. "What are you feeding me next? Broken glass? Nails?"

"I wish I'd thought of that. I made a pork roast."

"Mmm. Is it poisoned?"

"You'll know within an hour."

"Let's get started."

"Okay." I waited for him to move. "I can't do anything with you looming over me."

"I want to make sure you're satisfied." He kissed me again. "Is there anything else I can do? Any other service I can perform? I'm at your disposal."

I tried to stay cool. "Could I trade you in for a dog?"

Sam turned on his puppy dog eyes. *Dammit, how does he do that?* "I can do what dogs do." He licked one side of my mouth and smiled. He licked my jaw, pushing my head back. Then he went for my neck.

"All right, all right!" He continued to lick me until I was grinning and giggling. I tried to push him off me, but he wouldn't go.

"Scratch me behind the ear and I'll let you go."

"Oh, come on!"

"Have it your way." He licked my cheek and moved toward my eye.

"Okay! I'll scratch your damned ear!"

He turned his head so I could scratch behind his ear. He wasn't satisfied. "Now the other one." I scratched his other ear and the hair on the back of his head. He closed his eyes and enjoyed it until I stopped scratching. His eyes opened. "Woof!" Sam was too adorable. I didn't stand a chance.

"Why couldn't you let me hate you for a few hours?"

"It was bad for my health. Try again tomorrow."

"I will."

"I know you will. I hurt you, and I'm sorry, but I still love you." He wrapped his arms around me and squeezed.

I surrendered. It felt so good to be in his strong arms. How could I possibly stay angry?

***

On Sunday, Sam put the finishing touches on the garden shed while I spread mulch over my perennials. The shed took longer than he expected, but he wasn't satisfied until every shingle and every bit of gingerbread trim was perfect. He installed the angel weathervane from the original shed on the cupola and stood back to assess his work. "Does that look level to you?"

"Yes. You did a beautiful job."

"Do you think the colors are right? Maybe I should have used the yellow paint on the big trim instead of the little trim."

"It's perfect, Sam."

"Are you sure?"

"I'm sure."

"Do you want to look at the inside?"

"I've seen it. It's great. I couldn't be happier."

"We could go in there anyway."

"And do what?"

"You could scratch me behind the ears again. Or wherever. I have a few itchy spots."

"I have work to do."

"Do you want me to fetch any sticks?"

"This is getting weird. Go lie down or something."

"Okay." He had a mischievous smile. "I'll be in the shed. You can visit me if you feel like it."

"Good to know. See you later." I walked back to the pile of bark mulch and shoveled some of it into my wheelbarrow. I looked at the shed. I rolled the wheelbarrow over to one of the flower beds and I looked at the shed again. I spread mulch around my Japanese anemones, then leaned on the shovel for a minute. *God dammit.* I dropped the shovel and went to the door of the shed. As soon as I touched the doorknob I heard a sound from inside - "Woof!"

***

When Detective Doug Mansky showed up at Zipinski and Associates accounting firm, everyone knew he was in the building. Despite the divisions that developed between the employees in recent weeks, most of them were united in their dislike for Detective Asshole. His noxious personality wafted through the office, leaving each member of the staff with a story to tell about his rude behavior. As much as I wanted to be a fly on the wall when Mansky met with Mr. Zipinski, I did my best to stay out of sight. I didn't want to show interest in the investigation.

Zipinski assumed, understandably, that Mansky would review everything related to Ellis Industries in his presence, but after talking to Zipinski briefly, Mansky asked to meet with Donna – alone. Ever since Mr. Ellis requested that Donna take over the Ellis accounts, she had been poring over a year's worth of records trying to piece together what happened. Every time I wanted to chat with her, she put me off because she was so busy.

While Donna was alone in her office with Doug Mansky, I was dying to know how they would interact. I kept calling one of the women who sat near Donna's office to find out if they were finished yet. After about six calls, she snapped and said she would call when they were done. She slammed the phone down before I could thank her. *Wow . . . some people need to work on their manners!*

I received the terse notification that Mansky was back in Zipinski's office, so I bolted out of my chair and scurried down the hall to talk to Donna. I thought she might try to put me off again, but she greeted me as though it was a normal day at the office. "Hey, what are you up to?"

"Tell me everything."

"About what?"

"About your meeting."

"What meeting? I have meetings all day."

"Don't play dumb! Your meeting with Detective Mansky."

"Oh, it was fine."

I stared at her. "Fine? It was fine? What did he want to know? What did you tell him?"

She shrugged. "Pretty much what you would expect. We went over the Ellis account."

"And?"

"And what? What are you looking for?"

"Did you figure out what Henry did? Did he take the money? Will they go after him?"

"I think we know what he did. What we can prove is another question. But there's more to it than that."

"More? Like what?"

"It's better if you don't know. Detective Mansky asked me not to talk about it."

"Yeah, right! That doesn't include me."

"Uh, yes it does. Why wouldn't it?"

"Because we're . . . you know . . . friends. We share everything with each other."

"Do we? You didn't tell me Henry and Robert Bergdorf were hanging out together."

"Wha . . . that was nothing. I had no reason to think . . ."

"Have you met Detective Mansky before?"

"Um . . . no. Where would I have met a . . ."

"He recognized your name."

"That's odd. Did he say when he . . ."

"He investigated the fire at your house, didn't he? He's the one who brought down Edward O'Neill."

"Uh . . . was that the guy? Let me think . . . there was a young cop and an older cop . . ."

"Why are you lying to me? Do you think I don't know when you're lying? You suck at it."

"That's not true! I've been lying all my life, and . . . dammit! Fine! I met him before. What's the big deal?"

"I don't know. What is the big deal, Adam? Why would you need to lie about that?"

"I don't want Zipinski to think I told the police about Henry."

"Did you?"

"Well . . . I told a friend who happens to be a police officer."

"Look, Adam . . . I'm not angry at you. I wanted you to tell the police what you knew, but you were afraid of Zipinski. I get it. But now is the time to come clean about everything."

"But if Zipinski finds out I brought the police here, I'm finished. Especially now that he knows I'm gay."

"Stop worrying about that."

"Stop worrying? Hello! Who do you think you're talking to? Worrying is my second job! I don't want to be unemployed, do you?"

"Trust me, we'll be fine. Zipinski should be afraid of us at this point."

"I don't know about that."

"I do. I've talked to everyone in this office who knew anything about Henry's work on the Ellis account, including the people Zipinski fired recently. Keep doing your work. We'll be fine."

I shook my head doubtfully. "How did Zipinski get pressured into putting you in charge of the Ellis account? He never would have chosen you on his own."

"Jasper and I have a history. He trusts me."

"Jasper?"

"Mr. Ellis."

"A history?"

"Yes. He doesn't trust Zipinski anymore, and he trusts me to find out what happened. So that's what I've been doing."

"Did you talk to Mr. Ellis about this?"

"Yeah, I went out to lunch with him a while back. It was on your birthday."

"Oh yeah, you didn't want to say who you were meeting. I remember. When you say 'history,' you mean . . ."

"I don't want to get into that. I've worked on the Ellis stuff off and on since I started here. I'm more familiar with it than anyone else in the office."

"But 'history' implies something more like . . ."

"Do you think Detective Mansky is attractive?"

"What?" I was stunned. "What?! Why would you ask me that? He's a fucking asshole!"

"Is he? I kept hearing that from everyone who met him, but he was very nice. Charming, in his own way. Everyone warned me he was such a jerk, then he turned out to be very professional and polite. It was a nice meeting. He's smart, too. I'm sure he'll get the job done."

"Detective Mansky. Douglas Mansky? You're sure you met with Mansky? Did he show you identification?"

"Yeah, it was Mansky. Zipinski brought him in here. Why are you freaking out?"

"He's an asshole! Attractive? Eeew! I don't even want to think about it. He's a good investigator, but there's nothing about him that's . . . eeew!"

"I'm not saying he's gorgeous, I just wondered what you thought of him."

"I think he's an asshole who happens to be a good cop. What did he say when you mentioned my name?"

"He asked if you had a fire at your house this year. I said yes, and that was it."

"Hmm. I hope I won't have to talk to him. I'd rather stay out of all this."

"I'm sure he'll interview you. You were Henry's right-hand man while Zipinski was gone."

"I wouldn't say I was his right-hand man. I hope you didn't tell him that."

"No, but Zipinski will."

"You're probably right. Crap! What will I tell him?"

"How about the truth? Do you remember what it's like to tell the truth?"

"You know, you make it sound simple, but the truth is very complex. Everyone has their own little piece of . . ."

"*Please* shut up! Answer his questions honestly. You don't have anything to hide, do you?"

"That's what I was trying to say about how complicated it is when you look at all the . . ."

"I have a lot of work to do, Adam, so I'll need you to shut up and get out of my office. I can't listen to this. Tell the truth. End of discussion."

"Are you sure I won't lose my job?"

"We'll be okay. Focus on your work and go home to Sam. I would think a hot young guy would be enough to keep your mind off all your worries."

"Of course. No worries there! You're right. Let's see if I can get back to my office without running into your new boyfriend."

"Whatever. Get out."

I opened the door and looked around. The coast was clear. I put my head down and walked quickly until I heard his voice.

"You! Hey, you!"

Dammit! Mansky came out of Zipinski's office. I looked around as if I didn't know where the voice was coming from.

"Evans! I need to talk to you!" His voice boomed across the office. Everyone stopped what they were doing to look at me. "Don't play dumb! You know who I am!" Mr. Zipinski stood behind him.

"I . . . yes, I remember but could you keep your voice down? You're making it sound like I'm a criminal."

"That's what I'm here to figure out. Do you have an office? Where's your office?"

I pointed. "It's on the other . . ."

"Let's go! I have a lot of questions for you."

"All right, follow me." Zipinski looked less than pleased as we walked away from him. Everyone we passed on the way to my office glared at me as if I were being led to the gallows and deserved it. *Very reassuring.*

Mansky sat down in front of my desk. I closed the door and sat down. He stood up to look out the window. "Pretty good view. Must be nice to work in a fancy office all day."

"You call this fancy?"

"It's an office. All I have is a desk."

"How can I help you, officer?"

"Detective."

"Oh, right. Congratulations on your promotion, detective. You have questions for me?"

"Yeah, I do. First question . . . why am I here?"

"Um, do you mean here on Earth, or in my office?"

"In your office, smart ass."

"Are you investigating something?"

"You tell me." He continued to stand at the window.

"I . . . um, I'm not sure what you're looking for. I think crimes have been committed, and you're here to investigate them."

"Exactly." He pointed his finger like a gun. "You . . . think . . . crimes . . . not one crime, but crimes . . . have been committed. That's why I'm here. I'm here because *you* wanted me here, because you *think* crimes have been committed. Here's my next question - Who the fuck *are* you?"

"I . . . uh, I'm . . . I don't know . . . no one, really. Just an accountant."

He shook his head. "No, you see . . . I don't believe that. You certainly *look* like a nobody but . . . here's why I don't think it's true. The first time you came to my attention, you suggested that one of the best-known businessmen in town burned down the little shed behind your house. It sounded crazy, but it turned out to be true. And where is Ed O'Neill now? He's doing time for arson. He's ruined, bankrupt, he'll never do business in this town again."

"And you're the one who put him away."

Mansky turned to look at me. "You're right, and I'm happy to take credit. But it also brought down the Chief of Police. He was a corrupt motherfucker, and I was glad to see him go, but still . . . two prominent people in town were ruined because one of them pissed you off. You!" He pointed at me again.

"Wait a minute, that's not true. I happened to be . . ."

He held up his hand. "I know what you'll say. I didn't think twice about it at the time, but hear me out. Humor me." He turned to look out the window again, placing his hand against the glass. My right eye twitched. *He's messing up my window!*

"Not too long ago, I rounded up some of your homosexual friends who were getting their rocks off in the public restroom down at the park. One of them was this faggoty dentist with a funny name – Dr. Van Wooten. I thought, where have I heard his name before? Oh yeah." He removed his hand from the window to point at the side of his head. There was a handprint on the glass. "The arson case . . . the loony woman who was harassing the homos. *Her* name was Van Wooten." It was a big greasy handprint.

Mansky crossed the room to sit down before continuing. "So . . . I talked to this dentist, and he *begged* me not to charge him. Told me this sad story about his poor wife who's over at the psychiatric hospital because of all the stress she's been through. Something about the neighborhood association. I remembered the flyer she made. I threw the guy in the slammer and I did a little search on the computer." He twiddled his fingers as if he were typing.

His story was interesting because it was about me, but there was a handprint on my window. I didn't like it.

"I found an article on the website of the local newspaper that mentioned the president of the Eden Park Neighborhood Association. Guess who it was? No, don't bother . . . I'll tell you. It was *you!* But I thought Mrs. Van Wooten was the president of the neighborhood association. So I went and asked the dentist about it and he tells me *you* stole the position from her and she hasn't been the same since. That's why she was out at the nut house. Now the dentist's reputation is ruined, and who knows what's happening to their kids. Maybe you can tell me . . . did you get to the kids, too, or did you let them off the hook?"

"Did I . . . did I get to their *kids?* Oh, come on! I didn't do *anything* to those people! She was nuts before I met her, and *you* arrested him, so don't blame that on me!" I opened the bottom drawer of my desk and pulled out a container of disinfecting wipes.

"I know, it sounds crazy, I admit it. But this lady pissed you off and now her family is ruined. Do you see a pattern here?"

I yanked a bleach wipe out of the plastic tub and stood up. "No, I don't see a pattern! This doesn't only *sound* crazy, it *is* crazy!" I went to the window to wipe away Mansky's handprint. "I thought you were here to talk about Robert Bergdorf and Henry Verdorven."

"Yeah, I'll get to that. I thought about this pattern for a while and I figured it was a coincidence. Lakeport is a small city, so it happens. By the way . . . do you know who else was in the article that mentioned you and the neighborhood association? You won't believe this! It was my former squad partner . . ."

"Carl Hanson. Yes, I know, I saw the article, I was quoted in it. It was *about* Carl. So *what?*" I wiped the window furiously, trying to get the streaks to disappear.

"I didn't know the two of you were friends. I thought it was interesting. Then I realized Carl's a gay, you're a gay, so you probably fucked each other at some point."

I whirled around. "I have *not* fucked Carl Hanson! You can get that out of your dirty little mind, you pig!"

"Hey! Watch yourself! Police don't like to be called pigs. It's offensive."

"*That's* offensive? *That?!* What about . . ." Mansky held up his finger as a warning. I stopped and took a deep breath. I should have known he would try to get under my skin. Fortunately, I was too smart to be tricked.

"Look, I don't care if the two of you are friends. Birds of a feather. You hang out with your kind, and the normal people hang out with everyone else. That's the way it should be."

I turned away so I wouldn't have to face him anymore. The window looked worse than it did when I started cleaning it. I gave up and sat down. "Detective, could we please discuss something relevant to your current investigation?"

"I was getting to that. Last week my old buddy, Carl, brought me this big fat tip you asked him to pass along."

"He *told* you he got it from me? I asked him to keep me out of it!"

"Nah, he didn't tell me that, but *you* just did!" The asshole smiled. "I suspected it when your pretty colleague told me you worked here. She got me thinking . . . I do a lot of thinking . . . what are the odds this same guy would be connected to a case like this? And yet, here I am, trying to figure out some serious shit that involves *you* again. Am I the only one who sees a pattern here?"

"It is NOT a PATTERN!"

"Come on! You're behind all of it! You're the puppet master!"

"The *what*?!"

"Save me some time and tell me who pissed you off. Who do you want to ruin now?" He took out his notebook and a pen.

"I'm not trying to ruin anyone!"

"Did you kill Robert Bergdorf?"

"No! This is *nuts!* I'm the one who got you in here!"

"I know, that's my point. You're the one pulling the strings." Mansky took a tissue out of the box on my desk and blew his nose into it.

"I am not pulling strings! I wanted someone to connect Henry to the stolen money and Bergdorf's death."

"So Verdorven pissed you off . . ." He started writing notes.

"Yes! He's a fucking snake! I never should have fallen for his . . . sparkling smile, and the tailored shirts, and the tight pants. When I look back on it, it's so obvious what he was doing."

"He seduced you."

"He did! I never had sex with him, but he tried, right here in this office! He sat on my desk with his boner in my face! Can you believe that?"

"Yeah, I believe it." He scribbled on his pad. "My pen crapped out. Can I borrow one of yours?" Mansky wiped his nose one last time with the tissue and dropped it on my desk. He rummaged through my pens with his snotty, germ infested fingers. "So he seduced you, but you didn't get what you wanted."

"I didn't want anything from him. I wanted to be left alone." I tried to think of a way to get that tissue off my desk without touching it. I reached for my disinfecting wipes. "But when I found out Zipinski made him the vice president, I was seriously ticked off."

"Ah, that's what did it!"

"Well, yeah! Can you see why? Henry had only been here for a brief time, and Zipinski trusted him with *everything!* He's such an idiot. Zipinski deserves whatever happens to him. He trusted Henry because he pretended to be sympathetic about the sexual harassment complaints against Zipinski. But Henry encouraged those women to file complaints after I told him about it." I covered the snotty tissue with one of my bleach wipes.

Mansky took a lot of notes. "Wait a minute, slow down . . . you tried to get Zipinski in trouble for sexually harassing employees because you were angry about . . . what? I lost track."

"The sexual harassment. Zipinski's a creep, and I wanted to stop him. Also, because he's such a fucking hypocrite. I had to pretend to have a girlfriend to get days off to spend with my boyfriend."

"You mean that big angry teenager you had at your house?"

"Sam. He's not a teenager, he's twenty-one." Shivering with disgust, I moved the snotty tissue to the edge of my desk and into the waste basket.

"Okay, you told Verdorven to get those women to file complaints against Zipinski."

"He volunteered to do it. I didn't have to ask him."

"And he cozied up to Zipinski and got a promotion . . ."

"To vice president, *and* personnel manager. He got me a big raise, which I asked for, and a promotion to managing director."

"Quid pro quo, right?"

"I guess you could say that. The title meant nothing, but I think I deserved the money. Then Henry messed with the Ellis accounts." I pulled out another disinfecting wipe.

"Did you tell him to do that? Do you have something against Ellis?"

"What? No! I didn't know what he was doing. But when Henry tried to make it look like I was responsible for the Ellis account, I knew he was up to something. He underestimated me, though. He shouldn't have fucked with me." I disinfected all the pens Mansky touched.

"I bet you wanted to kill him."

"I thought about it. I went out to lunch with him and he told me things . . . private things I won't get into because it's none of your business . . . but I made a big scene and told him I hated his fucking guts."

"Which restaurant?"

"Sylvia's. It's not far from here, you should check it out."

"I will." He made a note while I cleaned the last of the pens. "What happened next?"

"Let's see . . . I heard a rumor about money being stolen from Ellis Industries. Henry threatened to tell Zipinski that I'm gay, and I almost bashed in his head with a paperweight. Then I found out he was dating Robert Bergdorf. They were together at the Como Villa where we had . . . Henry was being nasty and . . . there was a conflict." Mansky was writing as fast as he could while I disinfected the top of my desk. "After that, Henry disappeared, and Bergdorf was found dead." Satisfied that my desk was germ free, I discarded the soiled wipe. "I feel better now."

"I'm sure you do. That's quite a story. Can you give me any details about Bergdorf's death?"

"Henry strangled him and made it look like an accident or a suicide. Either one works. It would be hard to prove it was murder."

"Verdorven killed Bergdorf?"

"Of course. Isn't it obvious?"

"What happened to Verdorven?"

"He ran away with the money. He could be in France or Switzerland. That would explain where the money went. Let me show you something." I reached down to my briefcase and pulled out the envelope Henry sent from New York. "Here . . . look at the postmark. He probably flew out of JFK that day."

Detective Mansky examined the envelope and opened it. "This fuckin' flyer again? See, all this stuff is connected. Why would he send this to you? And what's this note on the back? *"Au revoir. Thanks for all your help."*"

"Henry threatened to give the flyer to Zipinski. The note is his way of making me feel guilty about my role in his scheme. I do feel a *little* guilty."

"I don't get it. Are you saying he took advantage of you and committed all these crimes himself?"

"He did take advantage of me. I was so naïve I didn't see what he was up to."

"Do you think a jury will believe that?"

"I'm pretty dumb sometimes. I'm not proud of it, but I can sell it to a jury if I have to."

Mansky looked at me for a minute. "I underestimated you. You've got ice water in your veins."

I waved dismissively. "Please! Most people say I'm too nervous. You're not such a bad guy when you stop insulting people. I feel pretty comfortable with you now."

"It's a skill. I didn't become a detective for nothing. What do you plan to do with Zipinski? How will you ruin his life?"

I snorted. "Zipinski brought this on himself. Jasper Ellis will ruin him."

"Huh. You're counting on Ellis to take care of him." He made another note.

"Who knows . . . I might be running this place soon. Zipinski thinks I have leadership skills."

"That's impressive. You thought of everything."

"I've been reading a lot of Agatha Christie novels and it got me thinking . . . with my attention to detail, I could do what those people do."

"You got your ideas from murder mysteries?"

"Yeah, and I used to watch *Law and Order.* Do you like being a detective?"

"I haven't been doing it for long, but I like it so far. I didn't think it would be this easy."

"I'm glad I could help. Do I need to come down to the station to make a statement?"

He chuckled. "Most people aren't this cooperative. I need to step outside for a minute to make a call. Stay here."

"No problem, take your time. I'm glad I got all that off my chest."

"Most people feel better after they tell truth. I'll be right outside." He stepped out and closed the door.

Feeling cheerful, I grabbed the phone and dialed Donna's extension. She picked up. "Hey, I just finished talking to Mansky. You were right about him, he's not as bad as he seems. I told the truth. Yes, the whole truth. I may have given him more details than he wanted, but you know how I am once I get going. At first, he was acting like I was the mastermind of this whole criminal scheme to get revenge on people who pissed me off. Isn't that hilarious? Not the best tactic, in my opinion. Do you think I would make a good detective? Because Doug was impressed that I had it all figured out. Hey, I have to go, he's coming back in." I hung up.

Detective Mansky took a pair of handcuffs from his back pocket. "Adam Evans, you have the right to remain silent . . ."

"Wait, what?"

***

After many hours of grueling interrogation at police headquarters, I was released from custody. Donna followed us over there as soon as she heard I was being arrested. Eventually she called Sam, which was a mistake. He was agitated, and things got worse when he confronted Mansky. Donna took Sam outside to calm him down so he wouldn't be locked up. Sam called Flora and told her what was happening. Then he called Carl.

Carl arrived and had a very loud conversation with Mansky in another room. Whatever happened after that, I gleaned from different versions of events. Donna claimed she opened Mansky's mind with her soothing voice and a generous display of cleavage. Sam and Carl confirmed that Mansky was more willing to listen after talking to Donna, but they thought it was because she was calmer and more rational than they were. Donna rolled her eyes at that. Then Mansky received several phone calls that left him looking very, very angry.

Carl saw the look on Mansky's face and knew it was time to leave. He told Sam to leave as well, but it wasn't easy to talk him into it. Donna agreed to stay until I was released, and promised to bring me home. Reluctantly, Sam went back to the house to wait for me. Despite the late hour, Sam, Carl, Flora and Agnes were sitting in the parlor when we got there. I was glad I had cleaned the house that weekend. Flora reported that she reached out to the district attorney and the chief of police. Much later, I found out Donna contacted Jasper Ellis. Mansky must have been told not to charge me.

I was exhausted by the time I explained the huge misunderstanding to my friends. Sam gave me the benefit of the doubt at every opportunity, but words like 'naïve' and 'dense' were used. Carl understood the depth of Mansky's bias. Donna barely kept herself from exploding at me. She was the first to leave. Carl followed soon after, and Sam walked Flora and Agnes to their door.

When Sam came back, I was sitting on the stairs, half dazed. He asked, "Do you want something to eat?"

"No, I want to go to bed."

"Okay, I'll get the lights and check the doors. I'll be up in a minute."

I didn't move. "You know . . . I thought the one thing I had going for me was my intelligence. I figured I would be okay because I was smart."

"You're very smart, Adam. You know that."

"*Book* smart. That's what they call people like me. It's not a compliment."

"Well . . . you still have your looks. You'll feel better in the morning."

"I doubt it." I stood and went up the stairs. He turned off the lights, locked the doors, and joined me in the bedroom. "Normal people don't get themselves into these situations, Sam. There's something wrong with me."

"It does seem incredible but . . . it's part of what makes you interesting. And lovable." He gave me a quick kiss on the forehead. "You told me there's nothing wrong with being different." Sam yawned and stretched. "Let's get your clothes off." He started to unbutton my shirt.

"I can do it." I pushed his hands away and dealt with my own buttons. "I may be an idiot but I'm not a child." I was irritated, obviously.

"Sorry." He began to undress himself. "Are you sure you don't want anything to eat?"

"Do *you* want something to eat? Is that what you're getting at? Go and eat whatever the fuck you want! I'm not hungry!"

"I already ate, Adam. I'm fine."

"Shut up about it, then! You're so fucking annoying sometimes."

"I'm sorry."

I mocked him. "I'm sorry! I'm sorry! You sure are good at saying you're sorry." I left my clothes in a pile on the floor and climbed into bed in my t-shirt and briefs.

Sam stripped down to his boxer shorts, turned off the light, and crawled under the covers. I was on my side, facing away from him, as close to the edge of the bed as I could get. "Will you move over a little, or do I have to come and get you?"

"Don't!"

"Adam."

"Leave me alone."

Sam waited a few minutes. The silence seemed to increase the distance between us. Slowly, he moved closer until I could feel his warmth. His arm curled around me.

"Don't."

"I heard you the first time." Nevertheless, he dragged me to the center of the bed and spooned me.

My eyes filled with tears. "Do you have any idea how angry I am right now?"

"Yeah, I can feel it. Your skin is hot, and your heart is beating faster than usual. I don't mind."

"Fuck you."

"I wish. Not for ten more days."

"Whose fault is that?"

"Mine. I know." He squeezed me a little tighter and kissed my neck. I felt his heartbeat against my back, slower than my own. "I was so worried about you. When I saw you locked in that room, all I could think about was bringing you home and holding you like this. I was afraid I would have to bust you out of jail."

"Don't be stupid. You can't do things like that."

He paused. "Wanna bet?"

I didn't respond, but I couldn't keep myself from thinking about it, especially with Sam's powerful arm wrapped around me. Eventually, I said what I was thinking.

"That would've been hot."

***

The next day, I found myself sitting in front of Mr. Zipinski's desk, explaining myself again. "I don't know how he could have misunderstood me. He twisted my words. I didn't confess to anything."

Zipinski wouldn't look at me. "I was quite clear about how we should present ourselves to the police. I asked for a united front, did I not?"

"You did, sir. You were very clear, but he threw me off by bringing up all this other stuff. And he was messing up my office."

"How did Detective Mansky get the idea you were seeking revenge against me?"

"He was fishing for a motive. He had a lot of crazy ideas. In fact, I wouldn't be surprised if he's mentally ill. He called me 'the puppet master.' Does that sound sane to you?"

"Haven't I been generous with you, Adam? More than generous, I have been *tolerant.* Apart from my concerns for your immortal soul, I have given you a respectable place in society. This profession could help you rise above your objective disorder."

It was difficult to absorb such an insult, but I sat there and took it. "I appreciate everything you've done for me, Mr. Zipinski. I want the firm to get through this crisis, but we must acknowledge what Henry did. It's the only way to come out of this without looking like we were complicit."

"I had *no idea* what Henry was doing in my absence! I trusted *you* to keep an eye on him, and on all the work being done for our clients. Why else would I have made you the managing director?"

This was news to me. "I wasn't told about the responsibilities of my title. I thought Henry was in charge."

"That's simply not true, Adam. Your job description is very clear. It's right here in your personnel file." He opened the folder in front of him and handed me a sheet with the heading, "Managing Director - Zipinski and Associates."

I skimmed through the list of responsibilities. "I've never seen this before."

"But your identifying mark is in the corner of the page indicating that you reviewed it."

There was a mark, but I recognized it as a forgery. "I didn't make this mark, sir. Henry must have . . ."

"How many more lies are you willing to tell, Adam? This is what happens to those whose moral fiber has been weakened. Their integrity unravels until there is nothing left but a shabby rag of a man."

"Mr. Zipinski . . . Henry had control over the personnel files. It would have been easy to make it look like I had seen this. He knew I used this mark . . ."

"I had the deepest respect for your parents, and I have tried to be a surrogate father to you. But my tolerance has reached its limit. I cannot, in good conscience, sustain my commitment." He pressed a button on his telephone.

"Sir, you know Henry is behind this! You knew he was doing something deceptive with the Ellis account!"

The door to Zipinski's office opened and two security guards entered the room. "Your employment at this firm is now terminated. You will receive the severance I am contractually obligated to provide."

"Are you fucking kidding me? After all the shit I've been through?"

"Your profanity is unacceptable, Adam." He looked at the guards. "Take him away."

I stood up and leaned over his desk. "My profanity is unacceptable? You have some nerve, you fucking creep!" The two guards grabbed my arms. "How many employees have you sexually assaulted? Huh? How many had to be paid off? Do you think people don't know about you? It's all over town, you goddamned hypocrite!"

Zipinski's face turned red. The guards dragged me away from his desk, but I wouldn't go quietly.

"You knew what Henry was doing! You KNEW about it! Maybe you got some of the money! You're a fucking criminal! Do you hear me? A FUCKING CRIMINAL!" The guards had to lift me by my arms and carry me out of his office. "I want my stuff! You need to take me to my office to get my stuff!"

"Sir, your personal items have already been boxed up. We'll bring them to your car if you'll come along quietly."

"Why should I be quiet? I've been quiet for too long!" Many of the employees were standing at their desks watching the drama. "Where's Donna?" I didn't see her. "Hey Donna! DONNA, GET OUT HERE!" Her office door opened and she stepped out. "That old motherfucker *fired* me! Do something about this!"

The guards paused for a moment to see if Donna would respond. Her face was blank. She jerked her head to one side, telling them to get me out of there, so they dragged me toward the exit.

"Donna! What the fuck?! Do something!" She went back into her office. "GOD DAMMIT!"

The guards managed to get me into the stairwell. "Sir, would you please cooperate? We're trying to do our job. If we carry you down the stairs, we can't bring your box of personal items."

"FINE! I'll walk down the fucking stairs! I want my stuff!"

They handed me my coat and took me to the parking lot. "Will you be okay to drive, sir? You're pretty upset."

"Yeah I'm upset! I lost my fucking job! And stop calling me 'sir.'"

"Look, dude, we know this guy's an asshole. We hate this assignment, but we're trying to make a living, okay?"

"I know, it's not your fault." I opened my door and took the box from the other guard. "I can drive. I just need a few minutes to calm down."

"We have to wait here until you leave the parking lot." I nodded and took a few deep breaths. "You're the first one he fired who told him off. Way to go, man." He put up a fist. I bumped his fist and did the same to the other guy. "Peace, dude. Good luck."

"Thanks." I climbed into my truck and closed the door. I sat there for a while to clear my head while the security guards used the time to smoke cigarettes. As my anger receded, anxiety swept in. *What will I do? What will my life be like? What do I have left?* I needed to feel secure, to have something to hang onto. Or someone. I started the truck and pulled out of my parking space. The security guards waved as I drove away.

It took about fifteen minutes for me to get to Dave's Nursery. I parked near the door because there were very few cars in the lot. The gardening season was over, and it was too early to sell Christmas trees, wreaths and poinsettias. They were using the time to clean and repair the buildings and organize their storage space. A young woman in the shop recognized me and directed me to one of the greenhouses on the back lot.

My pace quickened as I walked along the dirt paths. I needed to see Sam and touch him. He knew what I needed when I was afraid. I felt safe with him. As I passed a storage shed, I heard a voice.

"Dude, I thought we agreed." It was Greg. I paused to listen, hoping to hear Sam's voice as well. I did.

"Come on, it works for both of us. Where else would you get it?"

"It's not right, Muff. You promised to stop. Oh, fuck!"

The door was ajar. I approached the shed and looked through a small window before entering.

"Oh, fuuuck! I wish you weren't so good at it. Ah, fuck, that feels good! Jesus, fuck!"

Greg leaned against a pallet of bags filled with potting soil. Sam was sucking his dick. I watched his hands move over Greg's torso, enjoying his friend's muscled body. And his dick. He was enjoying his dick.

I pushed on the door and the hinges creaked. Greg saw me. His face showed everything one would expect under the circumstances – shock, fear, guilt. It took him a moment to react. He clamped his hands onto Sam's head. "Muff! Stop!" Sam must have thought it was part of the game. He didn't stop.

I turned and walked back the way I came. Then I ran. Dave saw me passing through the main building and shouted, "Adam! What's wrong? Where are you going?" I couldn't say anything and didn't stop. I ran to my truck and jumped in. As I peeled out of the parking lot, I saw Sam in the rearview mirror, bolting through the door and chasing my bumper until he realized he wouldn't catch me.

***

I went home. Where else would I go? It was my house. If I lost everything else, I would still have the house, and my garden. There was always the garden. As soon as I was inside, my first instinct was to barricade the door. I knew he would come, but what could I do? He had a key and if he wanted to get in, he could get in no matter what I put in his way. I ran up the stairs. It didn't make any sense, but it felt safer, farther away from the door. I went into the library instead of the bedroom. He would expect me to be in the bedroom.

My thoughts raced as I paced up and down. *What will I do? What will I do? What will I do?* I started to cry but I didn't like the way it felt. *Too vulnerable. You can't be vulnerable.* I clamped down on my feelings as if I were squeezing them in a vice. I had done it many times before. It was a good skill to have. By the time Sam's truck pulled into the driveway, I was unnaturally calm. I stood still and waited.

The minute he came through the back door he called my name. "Adam!" I felt something in my chest, but I made it go away. "Adam, where are you?" His footsteps were heavy. He came up the stairs. "Adam?" He went in the bedroom. "Where the hell are you?" Finally, he came into the library. I stood in the bay window looking out. I didn't move when he came up behind me. "Adam . . ."

I spoke quietly. "I lost my job today. Zipinski fired me."

"Oh, God."

"I came to find you. I thought, "Sam will know what to do. I'll feel safe with Sam.""

"Yes, of course! I'm here for you."

I turned around. One side of his face was red and puffy. "What happened to you?"

"Dave punched me. Listen, Adam . . . what you saw . . . it doesn't mean anything. You know Greg is straight. I was helping him out, you know? This isn't a regular thing. He's between girlfriends."

"You need to give me your key."

"My key? What key?"

"The key to the house."

"What? Adam . . . no. We'll work this out, like everything else. It was a mistake. It doesn't mean anything."

"Yes, it does. It means something, Sam. Greg is not some stranger you hooked up with. He's your friend. Hell, I was starting to think he was *my* friend."

"He *is* your friend! He thinks you're great. We need to talk this out."

"We've talked enough. I'm tired. Give me the key."

"That key means a lot to me!"

"It means a lot to me, too. I trusted you. Now I don't."

"Look . . . get some rest. I'll go away and let you sleep for a while, and we can talk about this over dinner. I'll pick up some take-out."

"No, I want the key. Now. This has to stop."

The look on Sam's face would have been heartbreaking if my heart had still been working. But it wasn't. I was a dead thing . . . a shell of a human being. I had been that way before. It was familiar. I held out my hand. Sam reached into his pocket and pulled out his keys. There weren't many of them. He was young and didn't have a lot of doors to lock. Not like me. With trembling hands, he took hold of the house key and removed it from the ring. I waited for him to put it in my hand, but it took a while. "This is temporary, Adam. We'll work this out." He set the key on my palm and turned away.

"You should go. I'm tired." Without a word, he walked out of the room. I followed him down the stairs and through the house. As we passed the dining room table, I saw the beautiful vase he gave me for my birthday. Without a second thought, I picked it up. "Take this with you. I don't want it anymore."

"Adam." It was more of a whimper than a name.

"Take it, or I'll drop it on the floor."

He took the vase and looked at me with his wet eyes. He walked into the kitchen and out the back door. On the porch, he turned around. "Could we talk later? Maybe not tonight, but tomorrow. After work. We need to talk."

"You should look for another place to live. Your lease ends in January." I didn't wait for a response. I closed the door and locked it.

Sam stood on the porch and spoke through the window. "I won't leave you, Adam! Do you hear me?" He pointed at me. "I promised you! I won't leave you!"

I turned around so I wouldn't have to see him anymore. It wasn't easy to stay dead. It was harder than it used to be. I leaned against the door and waited for him to go away.

"We'll work this out! I love you! And you love me! I know you do!"

He had a point. *Well . . . when I was alive I loved him. Dead people can't love anyone.* That was the great advantage of being dead. It was the safest thing to be. *No one can hurt you when you're dead.* I knew from experience.

"Adam? Promise me we'll talk about this. I'll go away if you promise me."

I was so tired. It was lunchtime and I was tired. I decided to sit down, right there in the back hall. I sat down with my back against the door and closed my eyes.

"Adam? Are you okay? Say something, please."

I waited . . . and waited. I thought about what I would plant in the spring. *I should have planted more bulbs in October. What was I wasting my time on? A garden needs constant attention. That's what I did wrong. I neglected my garden. Never again. I learned my lesson.*

I heard his footsteps on the porch. He went down the steps. I listened carefully and heard him go up the steps to his apartment. It was quiet for a few minutes. Then he came down again. He got in his truck, started the engine, and drove away.

Finally, I'm alone. It's good to be alone. I heard my heart beating. *Why is that thing making noise? I thought I turned it off.* It kept beating. *Damned thing.* I felt a tremor, like an earthquake or at least what I imagine an earthquake would be like, except it wasn't coming from the earth. My whole body shook. It was very uncomfortable. I knew what it was. *Feelings. Those damned feelings. I'll show them who's in charge.*

I clamped down.

36

I woke up to the sound of the front doorbell. And pounding. There was a lot of pounding. It took me a while to get oriented.

What time is it? What day? Am I late for work?

I was not late for work. It was Saturday and I was unemployed. It was nearly eleven o'clock in the morning.

I never sleep this late. Did I get drunk last night? Were we at Flora's house?

We hadn't been at Flora's. There was no champagne, and there was no 'we.' I had taken Sam's key and kicked him out.

Who the fuck is at the door?

Whoever it was would not go away. I rolled out of bed and found my bathrobe. On my way down the stairs, I reconsidered my position on owning a handgun. It was not a good morning to be a liberal.

The voice outside the door was familiar. "Come on, Adam. I know you're in there, dude. I won't leave until you talk to me." It was Greg.

Great. Just what I need. Another buttload of excuses from an oversexed prick. I preferred not to open the door, so I yelled through it. "What do you want?"

"Oh, thank you! Adam, it's Greg. Will you open the door please?"

"No! What do you want?"

"I want to apologize, dude. Could you open the door? I want to apologize to your face, like a man."

I didn't trust him. "Say what you have to say. I don't need to see you."

"Please, Adam. Please. I feel so bad. This is the worst thing I ever did. I'm such a fuckup. I know you won't forgive me, but I want you to know how sorry I am. I knew it was wrong, I told him it was, but I did it anyway. I should have stopped him. It's my fault. He loves you. It's all my fault."

I couldn't take it anymore. I unlocked the door and opened it a few inches. Greg took a step back, afraid of what I might do. "Look . . . I appreciate the apology but you're wrong. What he did is not your fault. He needs to take responsibility for his own behavior. Don't you dare take that away from him."

"But, dude, if I didn't go along with it, you guys would still be together. You love each other, you belong together. I can't believe I wrecked that for a few blow jobs!" It was obvious he had been crying.

"Do you think you were the only one? He's been whoring around since we got together. He took advantage of you. Join the club!"

Greg shook his head. "He's fucked up, Adam. He's my bro and I love him, but I told him, there's something wrong."

"Then why did you let him blow you?"

"I don't know, I *don't know!*" He put hands on his head, raking his fingers through his hair. "He's like . . . he's my hero, dude! I wanted to be like him. He's the best guy I know . . . the only real friend I have. And he wanted me." His eyes filled with tears. "It doesn't make any sense, I'm not into dudes. I would never suck his dick. But he wanted *me.*" He wiped his nose on the back of his hand. "I don't know how else to explain it."

"Well, you'll have plenty of time to figure it out. He can suck your dick all day if you want him to."

"NO! That's over! Never again! I quit the job anyway, so I probably won't see him anymore."

I watched Greg try to wipe away his tears with the sleeve of his letter jacket. "Don't you have a handkerchief? Come in here." I waved him into the foyer. It was too cold to stand there with the door open anyway, especially wearing my bathrobe. I closed the door and led him through the TV room. "Go in the bathroom and do something about the mess on your face. It's gross."

He pulled off his jacket and left it on a chair. He came back with a handful of tissues. "Sorry. I don't usually cry this much."

"Why did you quit your job?"

"Dave would have fired me anyway, and if he fired me . . . he'd have to fire the Muffin. He can't fire him. He clocked him hard, though. Bam! I never thought I'd see that. I ran away before he could get to me. Dave is old as shit, but I wouldn't want to fight him. He never liked me. If Sam didn't stick up for me, he would have fired me a long time ago."

"Sit down for a minute. I want to ask you something and I expect you to be honest. You owe me that much. You spent a lot of time with Sam and I know he talked about me. What did I do wrong? Why did he get tired of me?"

"What? I don't . . . what are you talking about? He's not tired of you. You didn't do anything wrong."

"Why was he sucking your dick? I mean . . . I get it . . . you're younger and a hell of a lot hotter than I am, but . . . I let him do whatever he wanted with me, and he never complained about the sex."

"Dude . . . you aren't the problem. He's fucked up. I don't know why he's so fucked up, but he knows he's fucked up. We talked about it all the time. You should have seen the shit he used to do to me. Some lady would come into the store and check me out, and I'd be all helpful, smiling, making her feel pretty. He'd come up behind me and hang out in the background, pretending to do shit while he was showing off his muscles, trying to distract her, to see if she'd look at him instead of me, you know? A lot of times they would look, and then they'd ask him for help. Like . . . he stole them from me."

"He was fucking with you."

"I thought it was a joke, and that pissed me off enough, but when I called him a fuckin' douche nozzle and punched him in the arm, he didn't laugh about it like he does when he's fucking with me. He'd be all apologetic and get little tears in his eyes. He's such a girl sometimes. He'd swear he wouldn't do it again, and we'd hug it out, and a week later, maybe two weeks . . . same thing. It's so fuckin' weird. What is he trying to prove?"

"He couldn't even keep his promise to *you.*"

"Yeah . . . I guess. Because he's fucked up. That was my point. But he's still my best bro."

"Well, I hope you keep in touch with him because he'll need friends." I stood up to indicate our conversation was coming to an end. "Thanks for confirming I made the right decision."

Greg stayed in the chair. "You mean you won't give him another chance?"

"He already had a second chance. How many chances is he supposed to get?"

"I don't know." I could see Greg's eyes watering up again. "Does there have to be a limit?"

"Yeah, I think there does. You should go now. I'm not interested in hearing you defend him."

"Adam, I'm not defending him. Really, I'm not. He was wrong, and I was wrong. No doubt. But if there's one thing I know after listening to him talk about you for the last six months . . . he loves you, dude. He loves you a *lot.* Don't you love him anymore?"

He nearly got to me with that question, but I swallowed my emotion before it could weaken me. "That's irrelevant. Please leave." I took a few steps and waited for him to move. He looked at me sadly and got up to go. Without a word he put on his jacket and walked toward the door.

On the porch, Greg turned around. "Love is irrelevant? Really, dude?" He shook his head and walked away.

I closed and locked the door, walked up the stairs, and crawled back into bed.

***

I woke up occasionally and thought about eating but didn't want to decide what to eat. I used the toilet, I think. I must have. It was dark outside, so I didn't feel bad about sleeping longer. I needed the rest. I dreamt there were people in the house. I didn't care and I let them go about their business. Even in my dream I thought that was an unusual reaction, but it didn't matter. I slept a while longer. Then it was bright again. I didn't feel well, so I opened my eyes slowly.

I saw a handsome, shirtless, muscular man with flowing blond hair and a black eye patch. He was on the cover of a book called *The Blaggard's Heart.* Agnes sat next to my bed, reading. Startled, I twisted myself around and attempted to sit up.

I regretted it immediately. My head felt like it would split. I tried to speak, but all I could produce was a rasping sound.

"Good afternoon, Mr. Adam." Agnes set down her book. "Here's a bit o' water." She handed me a glass with a straw in it. I took a few sips while wondering how long she had been there. "You've had a nice long nap, haven't you?"

My alarm clock showed twelve minutes past one. I tested my voice again. "What are you doing here?"

"Keeping an eye on you. Mrs. O'Neill insisted."

"Did Sam let you in?"

"No, you took his key. Officer Hanson was kind enough to assist."

"What do you mean?"

"He assured us it was perfectly legal, but that didn't concern us. He was conscientious about his paperwork and the locksmith did the rest."

"I don't understand. Why didn't you ring the doorbell? I would have . . ."

"We tried that. Let's not worry about it now. I have a pot o' soup downstairs, I'll warm it up while you wash yourself. You smell like a goat."

I was so confused. "But . . . what day is this?"

"Monday."

Monday! "That's impossible, it was just Saturday."

"You slept all weekend. Whether you like it or not, it's Monday. Now get up and get to the shower. I want to be sure you can stand on your own." She held up my bathrobe to shield herself from my nakedness.

I slipped out of bed and quickly wrapped myself in the robe. I was surprisingly unsteady, so she stayed with me until I got into the bathroom. One look in the mirror confirmed I had several days' worth of stubble on my face. I swallowed two aspirin with another glass of water. Though it was difficult for me to imagine how I could have slept that long, I knew I would go back to bed if Agnes wasn't waiting for me.

After showering and shaving, I got dressed and went downstairs to find out what was going on. Flora and Agnes were talking quietly at my kitchen table. "Adam, honey, it's good to see you up and around. We were worried about you."

"I'm fine. I don't understand what this fuss is about. Why did you break into my house?"

"Sit down and eat something, you must be famished." The soup smelled good, but I didn't feel hungry. I sat down anyway, knowing I would have to eat whether I wanted it or not. "Do you often sleep for days at a time, dear?"

"No." I knew it was foolish to claim nothing was wrong, but I persisted. "I've been through a lot of stress. I needed the rest, so what's the big deal?"

"Oh, sweetheart! Do you think we don't know what you've been through? Samson told us all about it. I don't think he's slept a wink since Friday. I don't know how he's still functioning."

"Hmph."

Agnes put a bowl of soup in front of me. "It's beef barley, and don't tell me you're not hungry because I'll have none of that." She had a basket of rolls and butter on the table, and a block of cheese with a few slices already cut. She ladled a bowl of soup for herself and sat down, staring at me until I picked up my spoon and tasted the soup.

"It's good. Thank you."

Flora managed to stay quiet for a few minutes, but I knew she was dying to say more. When she couldn't bear it any longer, she spoke. "I understand you had a visitor on Saturday. Would you like to tell us about that?"

"No." I took a roll and tore it open, then busied myself with the butter.

"I see." There was an awkward moment of silence. "Well, what about your job? What happened there?"

"I was fired." I ripped a piece off the roll with my teeth and chewed it.

"I thought there might be more of a story attached to it, but . . . if you're not in the mood to talk . . ."

"I'd like to know why and how you broke into my house."

"Oh dear, you must be angry with us."

"No, I'm not angry. Just curious." It was something I would normally be angry about, but I didn't feel much of anything, honestly.

"Samson was very concerned about you Saturday evening. You wouldn't answer the door, so he came to us and explained what had happened. It was heartbreaking to see him so upset, wasn't it Agnes?"

"Aye, ma'am. Very sad."

"Naturally we were worried. Some people harm themselves under such circumstances. We called Officer Hanson to ask for his advice. He wants us to call him Carl. He's such a nice young man, and so helpful, wasn't he?"

"Indeed, ma'am. Very concerned."

"He was not sympathetic toward Samson, I'm afraid. But they set aside their differences. Officer . . . Carl explained he could do a safety check if there was sufficient reason to worry about your well-being. He called for a locksmith and had the lock drilled out. Carl and Agnes went upstairs to check on you and found that you were alive, thank heaven."

"Aye, dead to the world, but your heart was beating. Still is, I'm guessing."

"Sam didn't come in?" I don't know why I asked that.

"No, as worried as he was, he wouldn't cross the threshold. He thought you would be angry after . . . he was simply a mess, I must say." I gave Flora a look suggesting I wasn't interested in Sam's condition. She moved on. "Agnes has been at your bedside ever since. I offered to relieve her, but . . ."

"'Twas nothing, ma'am. The stairs are difficult for you." Another awkward silence followed.

I took a slice of cheese as my appetite seemed to return. "It sounds like you had an exciting evening." I realized it wasn't quite the right thing to say. "I appreciate your concern." I should have stopped there. "I suppose my door needs to be repaired."

Flora looked annoyed. "I took the liberty of having the lock replaced immediately at my own expense, so all is well. Your new keys are there on the counter."

"You didn't give one to Sam, did you?"

Flora didn't bother to hide her irritation this time. "No, I did not, young man, but I kept one for myself and I don't care what you think of it!" She looked at Agnes who focused on her soup. "I dare say, a little more gratitude would be the appropriate response, Adam! Do you have any idea how worried we all were? You could muster a little more sensitivity, despite what you've been through." She shifted in her chair, then tapped her index finger on the table to emphasize her displeasure. "You are not the only one who is affected by these events! Do you understand me?"

I said nothing. Flora had never been so upset with me. It didn't bother me as much as you might think. It seemed inevitable. She would give up on me soon enough.

"Would you like some soup, ma'am?" Food was Agnes' solution for most problems.

Flora snapped, "You can put that soup in your . . . never mind! It's not your fault, Agnes, I apologize. Adam . . . I'm sorry you've been hurt, I truly am! But . . . I'm fit to be tied. I hardly know what to say to you!"

I set my spoon down and crossed my arms over my chest. "Do you know what he did to me?"

"Yes! In fact, it is entirely possible we know more about what he's done than *you* do! Samson was so desperate to confess his sins, he told us much more than we wanted to hear. He *cried* . . . you don't know how much that boy cried! This has been difficult for all of us!"

"My goodness, you make it sound like he betrayed *you*."

Agnes quietly warned, "Tread carefully, young man."

Flora's eyes drilled into me. I would have been afraid if I still had feelings. Her voice was cold and steady. "Adam, I love you dearly but you can be as selfish and thoughtless as anyone I have ever met. I saw this side of you after your parents died. I thought I had seen the last of it. Samson did betray me. He betrayed all of us. No one understands that better than he does." She shook her head sadly. "We had such high hopes for the two of you. He brought you back to us, Adam. You might as well have been buried in that grave with your parents, but he brought you back to life before you knew it was happening. At the very least, he deserves credit for that, and for the perseverance it took to crack open your tomb."

I had to admit, she had a way with words. "That's a lovely image, Flora, and I don't disagree with it. I thanked him many times for that. This relationship was a valuable experience for me, but it's over now. He ruined it. I'm sorry for whatever collateral damage you suffered, but you should take it up with Sam. I'm over it already. I need to move on. I think we all do."

Agnes let out a long sigh. Flora pounded the floor with her cane, stood up and announced, "I'd better go before I say or do things I will regret. Agnes, keep me abreast of any developments."

"Aye, ma'am."

Flora moved toward the door. "Adam, I sincerely hope you will pull your head out of your ass. Good day." And she left.

I quietly ate another piece of cheese. Agnes got up and ladled more soup into my bowl. I had enough sense not to object. While she tidied up, I asked, "Does she expect me to forgive him again?"

"I'll not speak for Mrs. O'Neill. We don't see eye to eye on the subject."

I waited a minute. "Are you on my side?"

She was slow to reply. "There are no sides. Can't ye see that?" She stopped what she was doing. Barely looking over her shoulder she added, "But you can count on me."

I felt something when she said that. I couldn't allow it. "You don't need to stay here, Agnes. I can take care of myself. Flora needs you."

"I'll stay here until I'm satisfied you're safe to stay alone, and Mrs. O'Neill wouldn't have it any other way. I told you months ago . . . get used to being loved, whether you like it or not."

I wanted her to stop saying things like that. "You're not staying overnight again. I won't allow it."

She turned around with the soup ladle in her hand. "I'll look forward to your attempt to put me out." That was the end of that.

I finished my soup and insisted on doing the dishes. She let me win. She pointed to a card stuck to the side of the refrigerator. "Don't forget you have an appointment with your psychologist this evening."

Oh, yeah. "I'll call and cancel."

"And why would you do that?"

"I don't want to waste his time. I don't have anything to talk about."

"Nothing going on in your life, is there? Or would you like to be here when Mr. Sam returns from work? Perhaps you'd rather talk to him."

Hmm. "I guess you're right. I should go."

"The appointment is at six. Don't be late. I'll have dinner ready at 7:30."

"You know he's not eating here anymore, right?"

"I'm not daft. I'll take his food over there."

"You don't have to cook for him."

"I don't have to cook for you, either. I'm going in the other room to put my feet up and read my book. I'm getting to the good bits. Find something to keep yourself busy. And don't go back to bed or something terrible might happen to you."

I didn't want to find out what she meant. I resented her presence, but I felt safer with her there.

I sat at the kitchen table and checked my phone for messages. There were dozens of them. Donna, Donna, Sam, Donna, Carl, Donna, Donna, someone named Joanne, Donna, Sam, Sam, Donna, Carl . . . I decided to call Carl.

It rang once before he picked up. "Are you all right?"

"Yeah. Why?"

"FUCK you, Adam! I'm sick of your fucking games! Now answer the question for real!"

I was startled by his anger. "I'm fine, Carl. Calm down. Agnes is still here. She won't leave."

"Good! You need a babysitter!"

"I can take care of myself."

"Well you were doing a piss poor job of it this weekend! Do you have any idea how worried they were? What the hell is wrong with you?"

"I overslept and didn't hear the doorbell! I didn't do it on purpose. I can't believe she called you."

"She? *She* didn't call me, *he* did! And he had the balls to tell me what he did! He's lucky I didn't beat the living shit out of him."

"No! Don't ever try to do that Carl."

"Oh, you're *protecting* him now? Unbelievable! How much more of this will you put up with? I *told* you he had a reputation before you met him! I thought he grew up, but obviously he didn't."

"Carl, I'm not . . ."

"You know, guys like you deserve what you get! You'll put up with all kinds of shit because a guy is hot, and whine to your friends about how hard it is for you. Well, I'm telling you right now, I won't listen to it! If you want to make that choice . . ."

"Carl . . ."

". . . then shut up about it! It's not like you don't have options."

"CARL! I broke up with him! I took away his key! We're done! Didn't he tell you that?"

"Yeah, but . . . you're sticking to it?"

"Yes. He had a second chance and he blew it. It's over, I swear."

"Just like that . . . you're over it. It probably hasn't hit you yet."

"Yes, it has. Why do you think I slept all weekend? I won't mope around and feel bad about it anymore. I need to move on. I *am* moving on."

There was silence on the line for a minute. "Are you still seeing your shrink?"

"Yes, I'm seeing him tonight. What does that have to do with anything? I told you I'm fine. I'm not as fragile as everyone thinks."

"You don't get over something like this in a couple of days. You guys were . . . I mean, anyone could see how much you . . . are you sure you're okay? Can I talk to Agnes?"

"Why? No. Look, if you don't want to believe me, that's fine. But I was thinking maybe we could have dinner together."

"What for?"

"I don't know . . . as friends or . . . we could talk about . . . us."

Again, there was a long silence. "Are you fucking with me?"

"No. Why would I be . . ."

"If you're playing with me . . . that's shitty."

"I'm not playing. You told me, if things didn't work out with Sam . . . do you remember the night of the fire?"

"Yeah, I remember, but . . . don't you think it's too soon to be asking me on a date?"

"I didn't say anything about a date. Is dinner usually a date? I've never done this."

"I can tell. Look, Adam . . . I won't pretend I'm not interested, but this is too quick. It's not right. What will Sam think if we're already . . ."

"I don't give a shit what Sam thinks! He's been out doing what he wants to do. Why can't I?"

"Okay, I get it, you're angry. I don't blame you. But this isn't the way to get back at him."

"I'm not getting back at him. I'm moving on. Are you seeing someone else?"

"No, but still . . . I think you should wait a couple of weeks. Why don't you ask your shrink?"

"What for? He doesn't tell me what to do."

"Maybe he'll make an exception this time."

"I'm not getting any younger, Carl, and neither are you."

"I'm only thirty-one!"

"If you don't want to go out with me . . .

"I didn't say that! Fine, we can have dinner, but just dinner."

"That's all I asked for. You're the one who freaked out."

"I didn't freak out. I think you're moving too fast."

"No, I'm not. Are you free tomorrow night?"

"Tomorrow? Can't we wait until after Thanksgiving? What's the rush?"

"Why is everyone treating me like this?"

"Because something's not right. Shouldn't you talk things out with Sam before you move on? Not for him, but for yourself. He was pretty torn up the other night and you're acting like everything is fine. I have to say . . . despite everything he did, it seemed like the two of you were good for each other."

"That doesn't matter! It's over! Will you go out with me or not? Maybe I should sign up for Grindr."

"No! I promise I'll go out with you, Adam, but you have to wait until after Thanksgiving. I won't do it before then. I think you should be alone for a while."

"Fine! I hear you loud and clear!" I hung up on him. I was tired of people telling me what to do. I deleted the messages Carl left and thought about deleting him from my contacts. I heard a ringtone from another room and went to investigate.

Agnes was reading on the tufted leather chair in the living room with her feet propped up. Much to my surprise, she pulled a thin glassy cell phone out of a pocket in her dress. "Hello. Aye, he is. Oh, *did* he now? Yes. Aye, indeed. He can be . . . 'tis true. I know. Always was. Not to worry, I'll be here. I will. All right then, thank you kindly. Bye bye."

I walked into the room so Agnes could see me. She was not startled by my presence and didn't seem to care whether I overheard the conversation. "Who were you talking to?"

She looked me in the eye. "The butcher."

"Ugh! I'll be up in the library so you can talk about me all you want."

"Don't get into bed or I'll come up there with a bucket of cold water."

I didn't respond. I was reminded of arguments I had with my parents, but I didn't want to think about them. As I entered the library that had been my bedroom as a child, I remembered the countless hours I spent there, reading one book after another. *Those were the days.* I wanted my life to be simple again, so I could do whatever I wanted with no one to interfere. There was a time when I didn't have to cook every day or talk during dinner. No one came to my door and the phone never rang. No social obligations, no expectations, no bossy friends. Just me and the garden. *I'll have that life again.*

I was startled by the sound of my phone. Irritated, I pulled it out of my pocket. Donna was calling again. I decided to get this over with. "WHAT?"

"Hey, how are you?" Her voice was softer than usual.

"Fine. What do you want?"

"Did you get my messages?"

"I didn't listen to them."

"Look, I know you're angry at me, but you have to understand . . . there was nothing I could do once Zipinski decided to fire you."

"Do you imagine I sit around thinking about *you* all day?"

"No, of course not. But I want you to know I have a plan. We'll be fine when all of this is over."

"What are you talking about? It's already over."

"Zipinski won't win this time. He's going down, Adam. Did you hear from Joanne?"

"Who's Joanne?"

"Zipinski's secretary. She has something that would help you. Something about your job description."

"I don't know what you're talking about. Why is she interfering in my life?"

"I think she's trying to help you. You should find out what she's got. Mansky is still investigating the embezzlement and Bergdorf's death. You could still be accused of something if Zipinski wants to blame this on you."

"Who cares . . . let him. I don't have time to think about this. I'm tired and I have an appointment to go to. Stop calling me about this stuff."

"Adam . . . you need to think about this stuff! It's not optional."

"Stop telling me what to do! I'm SO fucking SICK of people telling me what to do!"

"What's wrong with you? Are you all right? Is Sam there?"

"No, he's not here!"

"I tried to call him over the weekend when you wouldn't answer the phone, but he didn't answer either. Is everything okay?"

"Yes! I keep telling you, everything is fine! Sam and I aren't together anymore, so if you want to know how he is, you'll have to call him. I'm sure he'll tell you all about it."

"What? Adam, what are you talking about? What do you mean you're not together anymore?"

"I broke up with him. It's no big deal, I knew it wouldn't last. I'm tired of talking about this. I'll see you around. Or not. Probably not. Anyway . . . I need to get to my appointment."

"Adam, what the hell is wrong with you?"

"I have to go. Bye." I hung up. Her questions made me uncomfortable. *She's so intrusive. I don't know why I spent so much time with her. I'm glad I won't have to deal with her anymore.*

I paced up and down between the bookshelves for a few minutes. You might think I was upset but I wasn't. I was fine. I felt restless and needed to move around. And I couldn't decide which book to read. *So many books and so much time.* My eye settled on *The Tin Drum* by Günter Grass, a book my father gave me when I was in college. I pulled it off the shelf and opened it to read the brief inscription: "Food for thought. Love, Dad." I hadn't read it since college, but I remembered admiring the determination of the protagonist, Oskar, to chart his unique course in life. *I could use some of that right now.* I took it into the bedroom and left it on my bedside table.

I told my psychologist how well I was doing despite a few recent bumps in the road. I went on about it for quite a while as he listened and nodded. It was nice to talk to someone who wasn't telling me what to do. He asked what I would do about employment, but I dismissed the question with a wave of my hand. "I don't need to think about that now. I'll come up with something. I'm fine. I'll be fine." *He's probably worried about my health insurance,* I thought. *You know how doctors are – they want to get paid.*

I told him how much I looked forward to a more solitary life that was a better fit for my personality. I mentioned the comment Carl made about needing to be alone for a while. I rolled my eyes. "I think he has problems with intimacy. But that's okay. I don't need another relationship. I'm fine without one. Sam took up too much of my time."

Then he said something odd, something that didn't seem to fit. "I'm sorry for your loss." I wish he hadn't said it, because it made me cry. It was the strangest thing. I cried so hard I could barely speak. It was difficult to recover my composure. I don't know where those guys learn how to do that, but I think they get a kick out of making people cry. I would rather have spent my time talking about how fine I was. Instead, the last part of the session was wasted on crying. It was very unproductive. I agreed to meet with him again later in the week so we could get some actual work done. I still liked him, though he was clearly off track in that session.

Driving home, I found myself wondering if Sam would try to talk to me. I don't want to say I was afraid of running into him. I had no feelings about him at all. But it would have been inconvenient. Also, there was nothing for us to talk about other than the termination of his lease. In my opinion, business should be conducted during business hours. Fortunately, he was nowhere in sight when I pulled into the driveway, though his truck was there. I calmly ran into the house, closed the door, and quickly locked it.

Agnes had prepared a simple but delicious meal of chicken, boiled potatoes and green beans. It was nice to have someone cooking for me, but I felt guilty because

I didn't need her help. While we ate together at the kitchen table, I asked if she had talked to Sam.

"I did."

I thought she might convey a little more information, but she didn't. Not that I cared. I was only making conversation.

"Your friend, Donna, stopped over while you were at your appointment. She said ye didn't sound like yourself on the phone. She was worried."

"I don't know what she's talking about."

"You certainly do. I told her you were out getting the help ye need."

I tried to give Agnes a withering look, but she wouldn't make eye contact. I complimented the food to demonstrate that I was perfectly normal.

She chose to share some news. "Mr. Sam received a letter from his father today."

"Oh." I was mildly interested in this. "Did he open it while you were there?"

"Aye. He didn't want to be alone when he read it, and he had no one else to ask."

"What did his father say?"

"I'm sure it was private." Agnes was devious. By being deliberately stingy with information, she forced me to show that I cared a little bit about the letter and about how it affected Sam. I did not appreciate this.

"How did Sam react to it?"

"There were tears."

"What kind of tears?"

"Whether they were tears of joy or sorrow, I cannot say. I had to come back here to serve your dinner. You could ask him about it."

"I can't."

"Why not?"

"I just can't." I moved a potato around on my plate. "I want to, but I can't."

"Ye could, but ye won't. It's as plain as day you're afraid of your feelings. I can't blame ye for that. Love is a fearsome thing."

"I can't love him anymore."

"Ye don't want to, but ye do."

"No . . . I don't want to. It hurts too much."

"That doesn't mean it's wrong."

"There has to be a limit. I have to stop."

"Do ye?"

"Shouldn't I? I don't know what to do. What should I do?"

Agnes thought for a while before answering. "Make us proud."

"What?" I didn't expect that. "I don't know how."

"I think ye do."

"No, I don't. I'll disappoint everyone, I know I will."

"No ye won't. You're a good man."

"I'm not."

"Ye are. Don't argue with me. Have ye had enough to eat?"

"Yes." She stood up and removed our plates from the table while I held my head in my hands. "I'm tired, Agnes. I'm so tired."

"I know. Some days it's a chore to stay alive. That's why I'm here."

"Do you mind if I go to bed early? I know I shouldn't but I'm exhausted."

"It's all right, but ye can't sleep all morning. Ye have to get up and face the day."

"I will, I promise." I stood up and shuffled away.

"And wear pajamas like a civilized person!"

"I don't like them." Agnes muttered as I left the room. I argued with myself about whether to brush my teeth before going to bed. Good hygiene won the battle, but I did a half-assed job of it.

I shuffled into my dressing room and saw Sam's apartment from the window. I didn't want to look, but it couldn't be avoided. I leaned against one side of the window frame, concealing myself. There were dishes on the table with uneaten food – chicken, potatoes, and green beans. A few pieces of mail and other things were scattered there as well. The apartment looked cluttered. His shoes were in a jumble near the door and his coat was thrown over a chair. Sam came into view. I was jolted by the sound of my phone. I fumbled to turn it off, but accidentally answered the call.

"Adam?" It was him. My hands shook so much I nearly dropped the phone. I saw him stop pacing and cover an ear with his hand. "Adam, are you there?" He looked terrible. One side of his face was bruised and he hadn't shaved for days. "Please." I disconnected the call and moved into the dark corner next to the window. My heart pounded out a message - *I can't. I can't. I can't.*

When I could breathe normally, I carefully peered around the edge of the window. A small, silent drama played itself out. Sam sat at the table with his head in his hands, reading what I assumed was the letter from his father. Agnes went up the steps to his door, knocked, and entered the apartment. Sam wiped his face on his sleeve while Agnes pointed to the uneaten food. He shook his head. She placed a fist on one of her hips and spoke with a stern expression. He shook his head again. Agnes gave up and cleared the table while Sam slumped a little lower in his chair. I would have liked this story if it had been about someone else.

Enough. I can't. Not my problem. I turned away from the window and pulled off my clothes. I dropped them on the floor without even thinking Agnes would pick them up later. I kept my underwear on as a concession to her comment about pajamas. I looked through one of my drawers for something I had hidden, found it, crawled into bed, and started reading *The Tin Drum*. When I couldn't keep my eyes open any more, I turned out the light, rolled over, and buried my nose in the stretched-out, torn t-shirt I saved from our weekend at the lake house.

***

For the next several days I didn't leave the house at all. Where would I have gone? Agnes tried to get me out, but I reminded her it was my house, and if anyone should leave, it ought to be her. She didn't go anywhere other than Sam's apartment. I inquired about Sam's appetite. "Ask him if ye want to know." At Flora's expense, she had fresh vegetables and other necessities delivered to supplement the food I had in the freezer and the pantry,

We did a lot of reading. I gave Agnes *Tess of the D'Urbervilles* and borrowed her romance novel, *The Blackguard's Heart.* It was terrible, but the sex was hot. I had no idea pirates could be such tender lovers. Agnes started swearing under her breath at Alec D'Urberville.

After I ducked too many phone calls from the usual people, they resorted to visiting me in person. I should have prevented that. Donna was the first to show up one day after work. When I saw her coming up the front walk, I asked Agnes to tell her I wasn't feeling well enough for a visit. She agreed and while I listened from the TV room, she opened the door. "Mr. Adam says he's not feeling well enough to visit, but we'll ignore that. Please come in."

Donna found me sitting on the couch with my arms crossed and a scowl on my face. She waved a DVD at me. "Hey. We're watching a movie together." Without asking, she turned on the television and put the disc in the player, then sat down on the other end of the couch. I was expecting an emotional conversation, or a pep talk but she barely spoke to me. The film was Wes Anderson's *Moonrise Kingdom*. "Have you seen this?" she asked.

"No." That was the extent of our conversation. I had never watched a film with Donna and I was relieved she wasn't one of those people who talks during movies. We watched quietly, like strangers sitting a few seats apart in a theater. The film was quirky, funny and sweet, unlike the heavy dramas I usually chose. The time passed quickly, and when it was over, I forgot I was supposed to be sullen. "That was good."

"Yeah, I liked it too." As if on cue, Agnes came in to say dinner was ready and invited Donna to eat with us. Donna looked at me for a sign of approval. I shrugged to indicate I was profoundly indifferent. I realized they might have planned this evening in advance. It wasn't the worst thing they could have done to me.

While we ate, Donna filled me in on the latest developments in Detective Mansky's investigation. I learned Henry was now suspected of murdering Robert Bergdorf. They found video confirmation of Henry at JFK Airport using Bergdorf's identity and his altered passport to fly to Geneva, Switzerland. Henry's current whereabouts were still unknown. Donna discovered several large transfers of funds from accounts at Ellis Industries to a personnel department expense account controlled by Henry. The same account had been used to pay settlements to each of the women who filed sexual harassment complaints against Mr. Zipinski. Jasper Ellis was furious. Dark clouds were gathering over the offices of Zipinski and Associates.

It did me a world of good to see Donna taking pleasure in the misfortunes of people she disliked. It was a quality we had in common and the cornerstone of our friendship. I had missed her. When the meal was over and the conversation slowed down, she gently touched the back of my hand. "I need to get going, but I want to visit Sam for a little while, okay?"

My eyes filled with tears. I don't know what the hell was wrong with me. "Okay." I nodded. She squeezed my hand. I stood up and let her hug me against my will. I hated it when she hugged me. I whispered in her ear, "He needs to eat."

She whispered back, "I'll see what I can do." I let her out the back door and watched through the window until the door to Sam's apartment opened. I stepped back into the shadows so he wouldn't see me.

Agnes quietly observed my behavior. "Ye could have gone with her."

I shook my head. "I can't."

"Ye won't. There's a difference." She was a stickler for honesty. Very annoying.

I filled the sink with soapy water. "How much longer will you stay here? I appreciate what you're doing, but I can take care of myself."

"All right, ye can cook dinner tomorrow, but I'm not leaving."

"You want *me* to cook for *you*?"

"And why not? Does it never occur to ye I might like to take a day off from cooking?"

"I suppose, but . . . what will you do?"

"Maybe I'll sit on my arse an' read books all day like your highness does!"

"Okay, I'll cook tomorrow." I thought about what I might make. "Do you think Flora would join us, or is she still angry at me?"

"She's coming the following night."

"I didn't know that."

"Ye don't need to know everything."

"It's my house!"

"So ye keep sayin'." She took a clean dish towel from the drawer and started drying dishes.

"I suppose I have to cook for him, too."

"Who's this now?"

"Sam. Do I have to cook for Sam?"

"Do as ye like; I have no authority here." I knew that was meant to get a reaction, so I bit my tongue.

"Do you like meatloaf?"

"I'm not particular when someone else is cooking."

"I'll make meatloaf with mashed potatoes and peas."

"Do ye want my recipe? It's a good one. Better than most."

"No thank you. My recipe is good."

"We'll see about that."

Against my will, I smiled.

***

Each day my routine changed a little bit. I slept less and got out of bed earlier. My relationship with Flora resumed, but we avoided talking about Sam. I left the house occasionally and answered my phone when Donna called. I even sent a brief apology text to Carl. He replied with, "Looking forward to dinner." I wasn't sure if I wanted that anymore.

One day I woke up early and came downstairs to find Agnes wrapped in a quilt on the sofa, snoring. I tiptoed past her and went to the kitchen to make coffee. As I was filling the carafe with water, I looked up and saw Sam standing on the stairs to his apartment, looking at me. He must have been leaving for work when he saw me through the window. I wanted to look away, but it was too late. The bruise on his face had faded and his stubble had grown into a thin beard. It made him look older. Even with his coat on I could see he lost weight. He looked tired and sad. Tentatively, he raised one hand to greet me. I wanted to return the gesture, but I couldn't. No . . . that's not true. I wouldn't. Sam lowered his hand slowly. I looked down and waited for him to go away. The door of his truck opened and closed, the engine started, and he pulled out of the driveway. I left the carafe of water on the counter and went back to bed until Agnes woke me up a few hours later.

I didn't say anything about seeing Sam, but Agnes wondered why I was so quiet. I said I was fine. Everything was fine.

"I think I'll sleep in my own bed tonight," she announced.

"It's about time. You don't need to worry about me. I'll be all right." I meant it. Sort of.

"I'll cook your dinner and I'll go. How does that sound?"

"Sounds good." I tried to make a joke. "Now that I'm being released from jail will you be my parole officer?"

She didn't laugh. Agnes was a tough audience. "I've never been called that before. I'm sure Mrs. O'Neill will find it amusing."

"You've been good to me, Agnes. Seriously, I appreciate . . ."

"There's no need for a fuss. Whether I cook here or there makes no difference to me. I finished that book of yours and put it back in the library." She meant *Tess of the D'Urbervilles.*

"What did you think of it?"

"A bit dreary for my taste, but the daft cow got what she deserved in the end."

I looked up to see if she was kidding. She was not. I put a hand over my mouth to stifle a laugh, but I couldn't hold it in. Her reaction was so funny, I descended into a fit of uncontrollable giggling.

"Are ye havin' a laugh at my expense?"

I shook my head. "No, it's just . . . I've never heard anyone say that about *Tess.* I can't wait to tell Sam!" I stopped laughing as quickly as I started. *Shit.* Then I was angry. *Fuck!*

"What's wrong?"

"Nothing. I realized . . . never mind. I'm fine." I focused on my coffee.

Agnes put away the milk and wiped the counter with the dish cloth. "Did your friend talk to you about Thanksgiving?"

"Donna? Yeah, she invited me to have dinner with them. I'll think about it. I'd rather stay here."

"Ye won't get away with that and ye know it."

"I'll figure it out before next week."

"Thanksgiving is on Thursday, *this* week. Today is Monday."

"Already?"

"Ye need to decide. I'll be cooking for Mrs. O'Neill and Clarence. You're welcome to join us. Perhaps your friend who runs the nursery could come if he's not busy."

"You mean Dave? I doubt it. What about Sam?"

Agnes looked at me curiously. "He left this morning."

"Left?"

"To the farm. He's gone to his parents. He left ye a note. Did ye not get his messages?"

My mind raced. "Uh . . . I haven't listened to all of them." I felt my pockets for my phone. "I left it upstairs." I stood up quickly, nearly toppling my chair. "I have messages . . . where would he leave a note?" The pitch of my voice had gone up.

"With the mail. Saturday, I think."

I couldn't remember if I checked for mail on Saturday. I hurried to the front of the house and opened the door to the mail chute. I saw nothing. I ran up the stairs and found my phone in the bedroom. I didn't want to tell Agnes I hadn't listened to any of Sam's messages since we broke up. There were more than twenty since the day I took his key, but I was saving them until I felt stronger. I listened to his most recent message. His voice was low and weary.

"Hey, Adam, it's me again. I wanted to see you but . . . I understand. Everyone says I should keep trying. I don't know anymore. I miss you so much. Anyway . . . I want you to see the letter, so I left it in your mailbox with a note. Keep it for me. If things had been different, maybe you'd be coming with me, but that's my fault. I wouldn't be going at all if it wasn't for you. I don't know what else to say. I love you."

His letter had to be somewhere. I went back to the mail chute and put my hand into the dark recess, searching the cold tin lining for paper. I found an envelope stuck against one side of the chute. Sam's handwriting was on it. I called out to Agnes, "I found it!"

"All right then."

I ran upstairs to open it in private, sitting inside the bay window of the library. Sam's brief note read:

Dear Adam,

There are three things I can't say too often – Thank you, I'm sorry, and I love you.

Forever,

Sam

The letter from his father was in its original envelope addressed to Samson Engel with careful penmanship.

Dear Son,

My heart is full of gratitude for your letter. I prayed we would receive a sign that you were alive and well. Your mother and I have struggled through many sleepless nights worrying and wondering where you have been. Now God has blessed me with a chance to let you know how truly sorry I am for being less of a father than you deserved.

Your mother did not want me to write to you. As you know, she is devout and strong in her beliefs. You have a matching strength, with different beliefs. Still, there is a place in her heart for you, though it may be difficult to see.

You say you found someone who loves you. I am not surprised. If he met the boy who sat on my knee, he would not be able to help himself. Though I may not understand the love you share with him, perhaps I will have the chance to congratulate him some day. Then I will pull him aside and warn him about the many ways you take after your father.

I am a weak creature, Samson. I love my wife, and I love my son. The preacher says I should love God above all others, but I cannot divide my love into pieces to be distributed according to a set of rules. I love you with all my heart. No matter how we may disagree, I will always love you. You are still my good boy.

May God bless you,

Papa

I can't fully describe the flood of emotion I felt as I read the letter. I felt happy for Sam. I regretted not being with him when he received it. I wished I had received that letter from my parents. And there was so much more . . . more than I could absorb. I carefully folded the letter and put it back in the envelope. I thought about going to bed, but I resisted. Because I couldn't decide what to do, I curled up in the chair and watched the light filter through the lace curtains.

***

Agnes was kind enough to leave me undisturbed for several hours. By the time she came up to the library, there were delicious smells coming from the kitchen. She reminded me I hadn't showered or shaved. I cleaned myself up, put on fresh clothes and went downstairs. For the first time since she commandeered my house, she set the dining room table rather than the kitchen table. Given her old-fashioned ways, I was pleased she felt comfortable enough to invite herself into the dining room. As it turned out, I was mistaken.

"That smells great, Agnes. What did you make?"

"Roast beef, Yorkshire pudding . . . everything's in the oven so you can serve yourselves."

"What? Who? What do you mean?"

"You and your guest."

"What guest?"

"Officer Hanson. And before you blame me, I had no part of it. I'm only the cook."

"Wha . . . but . . . who?"

"Mrs. O'Neill. I'll say no more."

"Dammit!"

"I will say he's been a good friend. He deserves a nice meal. What harm can come from it?"

"Are you staying?"

"No, I'm out the door now."

"Agnes!"

"He's a nice man."

"Yeah, but now it'll look like . . ."

"Yes, it will. That was my objection." The doorbell rang. "I'll get it."

"Dammit." I opened the oven door to look at the food. It was beautiful. I heard Carl's voice and went to greet him. "Hey, Carl, it's good to see you." He looked great, unfortunately.

"Yeah, you too. So . . . it'll be the two of us, huh?"

"I found out about this two minutes ago, so . . ."

"I hope Flora is okay. There's a nasty flu going around."

"Is she sick?" I looked at Agnes who made a bee line for the kitchen.

Carl watched her run away. "Yeah, apparently . . ." There was an awkward pause. "Wait a minute . . . did you know I was coming?"

"No, I didn't. But it's fine. I mean . . . it's fine." I felt nervous.

"Are you sure?"

"Yeah, it's just dinner. Do you want something to drink?"

"Do you have beer?"

"I don't know, let me look." We made it to the kitchen in time to see Agnes slip out the back door without saying goodbye. I opened the refrigerator to find a six pack of bottled beer sitting front and center. "Huh. It looks like we have Samuel Adams. Is that okay?"

"Perfect. That's what I usually drink."

"What a coincidence. I'll get a glass."

"No, the bottle is fine. Will you have one? I'm buying." He sounded nervous.

"No, I'll have wine." I pulled the box off the bottom shelf and set it on the counter. "I'll use a glass because you're here," I joked.

"No need to get fancy, it's only me." Carl understood my sense of humor.

I took a large wine glass from the cabinet and filled it halfway. "Listen, this whole thing is awkward but . . . just so you know, Sam is out of town. You don't have to worry about him being right over there." I sipped my wine.

"Yeah, I know. He called me."

I stared at Carl for a moment. "When?" Without a sound or a movement, I started shutting myself down.

"A couple of days ago. It was . . . I have to say, he was very cool about it. He wanted me to feel comfortable here, and he thanked me for being your friend." There was a catch in Carl's voice. "Sorry . . . I'm a little choked up here."

"Take your time." My voice was smooth and even. All my defenses were in place.

Carl took a sip of beer and cleared his throat. "He wants you to be happy." Carl shrugged. "I thought it was nice. Classy. Not many guys would do that."

"No, they wouldn't." I showed no trace of emotion. "Are you hungry? Agnes made a great meal for us."

37

I chose to have Thanksgiving dinner at Flora's house. When I called Donna to tell her I wouldn't be accepting her invitation, she didn't mind because I wouldn't be alone. "That means we get you for Christmas. Flora and I had an agreement."

"Your agreements don't affect me. I'll go where I want to go, or I'll stay home."

"Yeah, right. By the way, you never called Joanne."

"Who's Joanne?"

"Zipinski's secretary. I told you about this already."

"I can't listen to everything you say. It's too much."

"Well, it doesn't matter, because I asked her what she was planning to tell you. She wanted you to know the job description for your new title of Managing Director wasn't written until two days before you were fired. Do you understand what that means?"

"Do I have to think about this right now?"

"It means Zipinski wanted to make it look like you were responsible for whatever Henry did because it was your job to supervise him."

"That's bullshit."

"I know. Zipinski must have known what Henry was doing or he wouldn't be shifting the responsibility to you."

"Does any of this matter anymore?"

"Yeah, if Zipinski knew what was going on, then he was involved in the embezzlement from Ellis Industries. And he knew some of the money was used to pay off the women who filed complaints against him."

"Okay. Is that all you wanted to tell me? I have stuff to do."

"Like what?"

"Regular stuff."

"How was your dinner with Carl last night?"

"How did you know about that?"

"Someone told me."

"Who?"

"A bird."

I huffed into the phone. "I'm getting tired of everyone talking about my personal business behind my back!"

"Uh huh. So . . . how was it?"

"Fine. The food was good."

"That's not what I was asking about."

"We fucked each other all night. Is that what you want to hear?"

"Did you?"

"No, but I'll say anything to shut you up."

"He seems like a nice guy. I bet he looks good in uniform. I wouldn't mind if he arrested me."

"I'm sure it's only a matter of time."

"Very funny. Hey, we should go out together before Christmas. You can help me with my Christmas shopping."

"I would hate that."

"I'll buy you dinner."

"I don't care; I don't want to. There are too many people around this time of year."

"Okay, I'll call you about it over the weekend. There's a new Thai place near the mall that I want to try."

"I'm not going to a mall."

"I'll pick a day and let you know."

"I'm not going!"

"Talk to you later. Bye."

I shook the phone and growled at it. *God, she's infuriating! I'll never talk to her again!* I paced from the dining room to the parlor and back again. I made the trip a few times, then threw myself into a chair. I sulked and fumed until I realized I was getting hungry from thinking about Thai food. *I haven't had Pad Thai for a while. Thai food sounds good.*

***

Unexpectedly, Dave showed up at Flora's for Thanksgiving dinner. *I thought I told Agnes he wouldn't come. No one listens to me.* He greeted me awkwardly and as soon as we had drinks in our hands Flora made up a reason to take Clarence into another room so I would be alone with Dave. "I'm surprised they talked you into coming."

"I didn't fight it, kiddo. I wanted to talk to you about . . . you know who."

"You punched him."

"You bet I did. I warned him. I told him right after you introduced us, if he ever did anything . . ."

"Yeah, I remember"

"He's lucky I only punched him once. I wish I'd got my hands on that other idiot."

"You know, Greg's not so bad. I don't know why you don't like him."

"Are you joking? He's a bad influence. Sam acted like a stupid kid around him."

"He is a kid. It was good for him to have a friend his own age."

"I guess you're not mad at him anymore."

"I didn't say that. I'm only saying . . . about Greg . . . he apologized to me the next day. He didn't have to do that, and he really meant it. He's not a bad guy."

"I wanted to fire his ass, but he quit before I had the pleasure."

"Why didn't you fire Sam?"

Dave looked down at the rug. "I should have. Do you want me to fire him?"

"No, but I'm wondering why you didn't."

"I need him. I'm getting too old to run that business by myself. I'd like to think someone would take over when I'm gone. I thought maybe the two of you would run it together, but . . ."

"That wouldn't . . . it's not an option." There was a long silence. "Do you think he'll come back?"

"He'd better. I bought a second snowplow for him so we can take on more customers."

"What if he doesn't come back?"

"He'll come back."

"How do you know? His parent's might need him."

Dave looked me in the eye. "Trust me. There's something here he won't give up."

"No . . . he wants me to move on."

"Is that right?" Obviously, he didn't believe it. "How's that going?"

"I'm . . . there's someone else. Sam knows about it."

"The cop? Yeah, I heard about him."

"He's a nice guy."

"I suppose he is."

"I think I deserve someone who won't lie and cheat on me."

"You deserve a lot more than that."

"Like what? What are you suggesting?"

"I'm not suggesting anything. It's your life."

"Dave . . . I'd like your advice."

"Are you sure about that? You want advice from a guy who ended up with no place else to go on Thanksgiving?"

"Sure, why not?"

Dave swallowed some whiskey and stared into the glass. "He's the only guy you ever had sex with, isn't he?"

"Yes."

"Sex means something to you. But to a guy like me . . . I had sex with more men than I could count . . . it didn't mean much. I didn't know most of them, and I only cared about a few. It sure as hell didn't have anything to do with love. It was a lot of fun, though . . . and I wouldn't have given it up at Sam's age."

"You think he's too young to be in a relationship."

"No. He was doing well, wasn't he?"

"Yeah, except for the part about having sex with other guys."

"But you were happy with him, I could see it. And he was happy with you. I would've given my right arm to have what you two had."

"Are you saying I should've let him do what he wanted? I thought you were on my side."

"I am on your side. But I wish you wouldn't get so hung up on what he was doing with other guys. Maybe you should get laid more before you settle down."

"No, I'm not like that."

He raised an eyebrow. "Not like what? A dirty slut, like me?"

"Well . . . yeah, if you want my honest opinion. I don't think it's right to have meaningless sex with strangers."

Dave scoffed. "The only guys who say that are the ones who aren't hot enough to get any stranger they want."

"Excuse me?"

"Let's face it, kiddo . . . you have a handsome face and a great ass, but you waited too long to put yourself out there. When guys want to settle down, you're the type they look for, and you're a great catch in that category. But you don't have what I had years ago, and you'll never understand what it's like to be Sam. You couldn't handle that much attention. Do you know how lucky you were to land a guy like him for more than one night?"

"What the fff . . . I can't believe you would say . . ."

Agnes interrupted. "Dinner is served. Will ye join us?"

"You bet!" Dave stood up. "My stomach is growling like crazy. I haven't had a home cooked Thanksgiving dinner in years. Come on, Adam, we can continue this while we eat."

"I don't think so! I've heard enough of your advice." I wanted to walk out the front door and go home.

"You asked for it. You know I don't mince words."

I put my anger on the back burner and let it simmer. Agnes had a traditional turkey dinner laid out for the five of us. I didn't feel hungry, but Agnes kept putting food on my plate. I picked at it silently while Dave asked Clarence about the business of selling cars, comparing it to his own business, and putting in a plug for his snow removal services. Before long, Dave secured another customer for the winter. Clarence tried to talk Dave into a new car. I knew he wouldn't succeed.

Eventually, Flora noticed my silence and asked, "Have you thought about what you'd like to do next? Will you stay in accounting, or look at something else?"

"I don't know. Donna says she has a plan, but I'm not counting on it. I can't count on anyone. Did you know Dave thinks Sam was out of my league? He says I was lucky to get more than a one-night stand with him."

"Ah." Flora wasn't expecting the abrupt change of subject. "Tell me, dear, what do you think of the cornbread stuffing? I believe Agnes has perfected the recipe."

Dave jumped in. "Everything tastes great." He pointed at me. "For the record, I think Sam was lucky, too. But if you had more sexual experience, you'd know I'm right. And you might not be so quick to look down on people who like a little variety in their sex life."

"If he wanted variety, he should have said so! He's the one who wanted a monogamous relationship!"

"And you didn't?"

Flora tried to stop us. "Please, this is not the best time to . . ."

Dave wouldn't let me off the hook. "Didn't you want to hop in the sack with the cop? Or the guy at your office who stole all the money? Sam knew your eyes were wandering, so don't act so high and mighty! I bet you would've blown Greg if you had the courage to ask him." He paused to scan the table. "Would you pass the cranberry sauce, Agnes? I love that stuff."

I sat there with my mouth hanging open. Agnes passed the cranberry sauce.

"Gentlemen," Flora said, "if we must pursue this topic, I believe a distinction should be made between thoughts and actions. Samson was sexually active with other men. Adam may have had sexual thoughts about Carl, he hasn't acted on them yet, have you dear?"

"I don't think Clarence wants to hear about my sex life!"

"I don't mind. You should hear the salesmen at the dealership." He eyed the turkey platter. "Does anyone mind if I take that leg? It's calling my name."

Agnes put in her two cents' worth. "No one would blame ye for being distracted by Officer Hanson. He's a fine-looking man."

I deeply regretted bringing this conversation to the dinner table. "Yeah, Carl is attractive, but I didn't do anything with him."

"Did you think about it?" Dave seemed determined to make me look bad.

"Yeah, I thought about it! So what? It was nice to know he was interested. It felt good."

"You had a hot young stud coming home to you every night, and you were thinking about other guys? I thought you loved him."

"I do love him! I mean, I *did*." *Dammit!* "They were only thoughts. It's not the same as what Sam did."

"It bothered Sam that you were spending so much time with another guy. You knew that."

"Yeah, Sam was jealous. We argued about it a few times, but he got over it."

"Did he?"

"He told me it was okay to spend time with Carl."

"Did you give him a choice?"

"I wouldn't stop seeing Carl just because it bothered . . . I mean, Sam knew Carl was a good guy. He knew I liked . . . I wanted to work with him on our project. He encouraged it! I think he wanted me to have a friend."

No one was arguing with me and the room seemed much quieter. Dave scooped more stuffing onto his plate.

I looked at Flora. "He trusted me, didn't he?"

"Oh, honey . . . he trusted you, but he never believed he was good enough for you. He had you on such a pedestal."

"But . . . I told him, over and over . . . why would he think Carl would be better for me?"

"Carl could resist other temptations. Samson knew it was a matter of time before you found out about his . . . weakness, for lack of a better term."

"But . . ." I ran out of objections. I wanted to say it wouldn't have mattered if he had been honest about it, but I would have been lying. Sam knew me better than that. I was afraid he would find someone younger, or better looking, or . . . more normal. I expected it. To be completely honest, I planned on it. Carl was my backup. I could finally admit it.

Flora noticed I was staring into space. "Adam? Do you need to leave us for a few minutes?"

I snapped to attention. "No, no . . . I'm fine." I looked down at my plate and loaded my fork. "This is delicious, Agnes. What else is in the stuffing other than cornbread. Is that bacon?"

She looked surprised. "Aye, there's a bit o' bacon in there."

"Did my mother make Thanksgiving dinner? I can't remember, now." I smiled and made small talk for the rest of the meal as if nothing painful had ever been discussed. I was doing everyone a favor. It was best to move on. *Emotions are messy, and no one wants a mess at the dinner table, especially on a holiday.* If Dave would have stopped looking at me strangely, I might have forgotten there was any awkwardness. His manners left a lot to be desired. *Poor guy. He should get out more. He should get a life.*

***

While I was alone during the next few days, I listened to the messages Sam left on my phone. They started right after I kicked him out. He begged . . .

"Adam, please . . . talk to me. I know I was wrong. You can yell at me if you want to, but I need to hear your voice. Why won't you talk to me?"

He grew more desperate . . .

"Please, Adam. I can't do this. I feel sick. I haven't slept . . . I'm not eating . . . I swear, I'll do anything you ask me to do. I love you. I never wanted to hurt you."

The messages went on like that. Some were short and angry . . .

"You don't want to talk to me? Fuck you! You're such a fucking coward!"

Then there would be an apology . . .

"Forget my last message, Adam. I was angry. I didn't mean it. I wish . . . I'm sorry."

Some messages rambled until the time limit was reached . . .

"Adam, are you okay? Greg said he talked to you, but I haven't seen or heard from you since then. Let me know you're alive, that's all I'm asking. I talked to Flora and Agnes, and I told them everything. They know it was all my fault. They're worried about you, too."

Once he knew Agnes was in the house, Sam's voice changed. He became quieter. His tone was flat. There were long pauses when he was crying . . .

"I don't blame you . . . you deserve to be happy . . . that's all I want. Don't worry . . . I'll figure something out."

I had to take breaks from listening because it was too intense. I reviewed countless conversations in my head, wondering how much I had missed or ignored. Did he ask me for help? Did I blow him off? How could I have been so wrapped up in my own problems?

The tone of one of his messages made me nervous . . .

"Adam . . . I won't leave you. I promised I would never leave you, and I meant it. Even when you think I'm gone I'll still be here."

That night, I dreamt I heard noises in the house. I went downstairs to investigate. The sounds were coming from the basement. I crept down the stairs and saw Sam, shirtless and huge . . . taller than he really was. He stood with both arms raised, his hands pressed against a thick wooden beam the length of the ceiling. *"I warned you, Adam. I'll always be here. We'll always be together."*

"What do you mean? What are you doing?"

"We'll always be together." He pressed against the beam until it groaned and cracked. As the house caved in around us, I woke up in a panic, drenched in sweat.

It became more and more difficult to listen to Sam's messages . . .

"I'm sick, Adam. I'm so fucked up. How could I have sex with so many guys? How could I do those things with Henry? I think my parents were right. Maybe there is something evil inside me. Do you think there is such a thing? Do you think I'm mentally ill? I wish I could talk to you. You always made me feel better. I hate not talking to you when you're so close. I can't live like this."

There was one message - the worst one - that I played again and again as a punishment . . .

"Did you ever love me, Adam? Do you think anyone could love someone like me? I know I'd have to change a lot, but . . . do you think someone could?"

I cried a lot that weekend, more than I had before. I was afraid it would never stop. On Sunday morning I got out of bed, showered, ate, and decided I could make things better. My life might not be great, but it could be better. One of Sam's last messages helped:

"Agnes made you cook for her, huh? She's something else. Sometimes I wonder if you're forgetting about me, but you made my favorite meal, so . . . thanks. I ate all of it. She told you about the letter from my father. It was a great letter, Adam. I wish you were here when I opened it."

I went out to buy groceries. I turned on the radio in the truck, and Jose Feliciano was singing *Feliz Navidad*. I quickly changed the station and landed on a commercial about a "holiday sale spectacular featuring incredible door buster specials!" *Fuuuck! That shit already?* Obviously, I was getting back to my normal self. When I got home from the store it was snowing. The forecasters predicted one to three inches of heavy, wet snow overnight . . . or more if they were wrong. I wondered if my snow blower still worked after being idle through the previous winter. *If it doesn't, I'll use a shovel.* I tried to have a positive attitude. *No big deal. I have all the time in the world. I could use the exercise.*

***

I woke up to the familiar sound of a shovel scraping against pavement. I listened for a while, wondering which neighbor would be out so early in the morning. *Maybe some kid is doing Flora's sidewalk. They know she pays top dollar.* It sounded closer than that, like someone was shoveling my driveway. My heart beat a little faster. I raised my head. *Sam?*

I threw off my covers and jumped out of bed. There was snow on all the trees, sitting on the branches like a layer of cotton. I saw the truck. I saw someone scooping up snow and throwing it to one side of the driveway. I blinked a few times to make sure he was real, that it was Sam. *He's back. He came back.*

Despite my relief and a vague sense of happiness, my thoughts and feelings were far from clear. I had no idea what to do next. *Should I ignore him? Should I talk to him? Should I call him on the phone?* I utilized the most reliable method for dealing with confusion - I paced from one end of the room to the other. I realized he would finish shoveling and would leave for work before long. *Should I talk to him now? Should I wait? What should I say?* I threw on some clothes and went downstairs.

Without making a conscious decision, I found myself putting on my shoes and a coat. My hand was on the doorknob. *What am I doing?* The door opened, and I stepped onto the porch. Sam had cleared most of the driveway and was working his way to the front of the house with his back toward me. I thought he might hear my footsteps as I approached, or the pounding in my chest, but his ears were covered by his knit cap. I called his name too quietly. He didn't hear it. I said it louder.

Sam spun around and raised the shovel in the air, stopping before he hit me. "God dammit! Don't sneak up on me!"

I backed up. "I'm sorry! I'm sorry."

"What the fuck are you doing out here?"

"I was coming . . . I heard you, and I . . ."

"What do you want?" His beard was thicker, and his eyes were hard.

"Nothing, I was just . . . I was going to shovel, but . . ."

"It's *my* job! It's in the lease. Did you want an excuse to evict me? I'm not stupid, Adam!"

"I wasn't . . ." *Does he think I would do that to him?* I searched his face for something . . . something familiar and important. I didn't know what to say.

Abruptly, Sam turned away from me. He gripped the shovel with both hands and snapped it in half. "Fuck! Fucking idiot!" He shook the pieces in his fists.

"I'm going back in the house." I turned to walk up the driveway.

"Adam, wait. I'm sorry."

I kept walking. "No, I'm sorry. I shouldn't have come out here."

He followed. "I didn't expect to see you. You caught me off guard."

"I understand, but . . ." *But what? What next?* "Maybe later, or some other day. I'm not ready for this."

"When, Adam? How much longer?"

I climbed the porch steps. "Your lease ends in a month. We have time."

Sam stayed on the driveway looking up at me. "You would put me out in the middle of winter? Where will you find a tenant?"

"It doesn't matter, I don't need one. I can't deal with this right now." I ducked behind the door and shut him out again, deadbolt and all.

I heard his frustration. "God . . . ffffuck!" He threw the pieces of shovel to the ground.

Hopeless. Why did I even try? This is hopeless. I busied myself with coffee and cereal and thought about what I would have said if things hadn't gone so badly. *I would have apologized for shutting him out. I would have asked about his parents. I would have promised to be patient, to help him, to accept him as he is.* Sam's truck started, and he pulled away. *We would pretend that love can fix any problem. The sex would be exhausting. Our insecurities would get the better of us.*

I called Carl when I knew he would be awake. He sounded breathless. "Hi . . . am I interrupting something?"

"I was doing pushups. How are you?"

"I'm feeling better." I paused to listen to his breathing. "What are you wearing?"

"Hey, don't do that! I have to get to work in a little while."

"I'll just picture you naked."

"Stop it!" He laughed.

"Thanksgiving is over, so . . . will you do me the honor of having dinner with me this week? My treat."

"Yes, but only if you let me pay. You're unemployed."

"All I heard was 'Yes.' When are you free?"

"Tonight, tomorrow, the next day."

"Seriously?"

"Did you think I had a life?"

"Yeah, I did. Tonight would be good. What are you hungry for?"

"Meat. Any kind of meat."

"Okay, I'll find a steakhouse. What time can I pick you up?"

"Wow, you'll pick me up? This sounds like a real date. Um . . . I'll be ready at six. I hope that's not too early, but I get pretty hungry by the end of the day."

"That's good. I think a big appetite is sexy."

"Shit, you're giving me a boner. I have to go, I'll see you at six."

"Send me your address. And a picture of that boner."

"Knock it off!" He hung up.

Perfect. I need to move on.

***

When Carl had dinner at my house, we played it safe, interacted like friends, and discussed the things we usually discussed. The fact we had been set up made it a little awkward. As far as I was concerned, dating was inherently awkward. I got to know Sam by having dinner with him repeatedly, but it wasn't a problem because I never thought we were dating. Going out to dinner with Carl felt like a whole different thing, even though we already knew each other.

Carl lived in an old factory building converted into condominiums in an area being redeveloped for residential use. It was a neighborhood that was becoming trendy but was still edgy. He was waiting for me in the lobby and came right out to the truck. I protested, "I would have come to the door like a gentleman."

"I know, but I couldn't sit still, so I came down to wait for you." He sounded nervous. *That makes two of us.* He was wearing a little too much cologne, but it was a nice scent. *Sam didn't need cologne.* "Where are we going?"

"Nate's. Is that okay?"

"It's great. I love that place."

"Good, I've never been there."

"It's been around for a while."

"I don't get out much."

"Even with Sam?"

"No." *It didn't take long for his name to come up.*

"I'm sorry, does it bother you to talk about him?"

"No." I thought it would bother *him.*

"Do you know if he's coming back?"

"He is back. This morning."

"Oh. Have you talked to him?"

"Yeah." *Sort of.*

"How did that go?"

"Fine. Does this restaurant have a parking lot?"

"No, but they have valet parking."

"I'm not handing my truck over to a stranger. That's insane."

"People do it all the time."

"If everyone else jumped off a cliff, would you do it, too?"

Carl laughed. "Oh my God, I haven't heard that in years! That's funny."

It wasn't meant to be funny. I smiled and went along with the joke. "My Dad used to say it a lot." I didn't want Carl to think I was afraid of taking risks, even though I was. "I suppose I could try valet parking."

"It'll be fine. I'll talk you through it."

With Sam, I was the one with more knowledge of the world, apart from sexual experience. To Carl, I must have seemed sheltered. I didn't like being in that position, but I couldn't keep dating farm boys with strict religious parents. And Carl was nice about it.

The restaurant was dimly lit and elegant. We were seated in a booth that gave us some privacy. After we ordered our steaks, I felt like I was on an awkward date again, rather than having dinner with a friend. Carl wore a dark olive-green dress shirt that hugged his body and complimented his blond good looks. I had certain feelings about him . . . physical feelings . . . and I had no reason to deny them anymore.

"How was your Thanksgiving?"

"Okay." I told him who was there and how good the food was. I described it as "nice," and inquired about Thanksgiving with his family.

"Good and bad, as usual. It was good to see my brothers . . . well, one of my brothers. The other one I could do without, but I like his wife and their kids. My sister was in town with her kids, which was great. I can't believe how fast they're growing up. My mother . . . is a good cook." He made a face suggesting he was looking for more positive things to say but couldn't come up with anything. "Every holiday, she asks me if I've met any nice young women."

"She doesn't know you're gay?"

"Hell yes, she knows! But she asks me at the dinner table, so I can't say what I'd like to say. One Christmas I was so tired of it, I said, "Mom, I like cock more than you do, so stop asking me about women." Everyone was mad at me for saying it in front of the children. I left and went to a movie."

"Wow. What about your Dad?"

"He doesn't say anything. He drinks."

"Oh."

"I suppose every family has some drama."

I shrugged. "I wouldn't know."

"That's right . . . do you have any aunts and uncles, or cousins?"

"None that I know. My father had a brother who died when they were kids, and my mother's brother lives in Virginia or West Virginia. I'm not sure. He didn't come to their funeral, so I don't know anything about him. Maybe I have cousins somewhere."

"Don't you want to find out?"

"What for? They wouldn't mean anything to me."

"Still, I'd be curious. Family is important."

"Even if you don't like them?"

"I think so. Did your parents ever talk about their families? What about your grandparents?"

"All dead, I assume. I never asked because I knew they wouldn't want to talk about it. There were a lot of things we didn't talk about."

"That's too bad. It must have been . . . I don't know . . . lonely?"

He tapped into something I didn't understand yet. It brought tears to my eyes and he noticed.

"I'm sorry, Adam, I didn't mean to . . . I shouldn't ask so many questions."

"No, it's okay. I don't even know why I'm getting emotional. I don't know if it was lonely or not. I don't have anything to compare it to. I don't know what it was like in other people's houses. My parents were good to me. They loved me, and they loved each other. It was quiet. That's what I remember the most. It was so quiet."

"Hmm. It wasn't quiet at my house. There was so much going on."

"Were you always angry at your mother?"

"No, not when I was a kid. Everyone claims I was her favorite, but I was the youngest. I wish I could stop being angry at her, but she keeps pissing me off."

"You're lucky, in a way."

"Uh, how's that?"

"Well . . . at least you have a reason to be angry. I don't. I mean . . . I know I was angry about my parents' death and how unfair it was, but I think I was angry at them for a long time before that. I don't know why." I looked at Carl. "I'll have to talk to my shrink about it. I don't want to bore you with my . . . whatever."

"It's not boring. You don't show your feelings much."

"I used to have more control over myself before . . . I'm trying to get it back."

"Is that really the way you want to go?"

Before I could respond, the waitress came with our food. I love it when that happens. The steaks were thick and perfectly cooked. We had baked sweet potatoes and a ridiculously tall haystack of deep-fried onions. Carl wanted them but kept saying he shouldn't eat them. "I'll be paying for this for the next week." He shoved another forkful in his mouth.

"Why? You look like you could burn those off in no time at all."

"No, I used to be tubby, so I have to be careful."

"You were overweight? I wouldn't have guessed. You're so . . ." I was about to say "athletic," but it didn't capture the quality I had in mind.

Carl's smile made a dimple on one cheek. "So . . . what? Were you about to compliment me?"

I blushed and smiled. "Yes, but I doubted myself."

"Why?"

"I don't know. That's what I do." I tried to make up for it. "I like your shirt. You look very handsome. You are handsome, I mean . . . in whatever. You look good in whatever you wear. You're hot, okay? That's what I was thinking before I stopped myself. Are you happy now?"

Carl was laughing before I finished. "You're so damned cute. I'm glad we finally did this."

"Yeah, me too. I can't believe you're not in a relationship already. What is wrong with the gay men in this town? Are they stupid?"

"Don't get me started on that subject. I hate to say it, but I think a lot of them are stupid. And superficial and bitchy. Immature, no matter how old they are. I could go on and on. I've met nice guys who are already in relationships. I assume the rest of them are hiding out somewhere, like you were."

"Yeah, but I'm stupid and bitchy, too."

"You are not."

"You know I can be difficult."

"Yeah, I've noticed. I'm not perfect either."

"Okay, what are your weaknesses?"

"My weaknesses? Um . . . that's not what most people discuss on first dates. No one has ever asked me that. Let me think . . . uh . . . I'm a perfectionist."

"Pfft! That's your weakness? Come on."

"I'm a slob at home. Um, I don't read enough. I feel like I should read more, but I never enjoyed it much. I'm too competitive at sports and other things. Sometimes I take stuff too seriously."

I shook my head. "I'm not impressed by this list. I'm looking for serious character flaws."

"Tell you what . . . let's call my mother. She can give you a list." He smiled and put a chunk of steak in his mouth.

The reading thing was a disappointment, but Carl seemed like quite a catch. I felt lucky to be his friend, and whatever else he might be.

"So you had a good talk with Sam?"

Ugh! He had to bring that up. "It was brief. We didn't discuss much. It was more of an angry exchange, but at least we spoke to each other."

"An angry exchange? You had an argument?"

"Not really. It's hard to explain."

Carl looked down at the table and nodded slightly.

"Do we have to talk about him? I'm trying to move on."

"I know, but . . . you have to understand . . . I need to know things are resolved between the two of you before . . . I don't want us to move too quickly and then find out you're . . . I don't know. Do you know what I'm trying to say?"

"Yeah, I think so. I don't know what else to say to him. What is there to resolve? He had sex with other guys and he lied about it. I couldn't put up with it. I have *some* self-respect."

"I know, but he was an important part of your life. You should talk things out and part on good terms. You don't have to be friends, but you don't want to be angry at him for the rest of your life, do you?"

"I'm not angry. I mean, yes, I am, but . . . I don't know. I'm not sure what I feel about him anymore. I'd rather have that figured out before I talk to him."

"Or . . . talking to him could help you figure it out."

I sighed heavily. Once again, the waitress came to my rescue. "Are you finished, sir? Would you like a box?" I only ate half of my steak. Carl's plate was clean.

"I'll take it if you don't want it."

"Okay, I'll take a box." The waitress left with Carl's dishes. I knew he wouldn't let me off the hook about Sam, so I gave him what he wanted. "I'll talk to Sam. I promise. I know you're right, so I'll talk to him. We'll part on good terms. That's the way it should be."

Carl reached across the table to touch my hand. Startled, as always, by any gesture of affection, I almost pulled away.

"Hey, I saw you flinch."

"I'm sorry, I'm not good at this."

"You're doing fine. I wanted to touch you." He pulled back as the waitress returned with a box for my food.

We declined dessert and coffee, then argued about who would pay the bill. He put up a good fight, but I won. The drive back to his place was quiet. Carl looked at my CDs to see what music I liked. "Brahms' *German Requiem*? Is this what you're listening to?"

"Yeah. It's better than Christmas music."

"Is a requiem about death?"

"Yes, it's . . . um . . . it's a mass for the dead, but before you start thinking I'm listening to it because I'm depressed . . . it's beautiful and uplifting. Here . . . listen." I turned on the sound system.

"I wouldn't have thought that, but since you made such a point of it . . ." The music started. It was one of the livelier choral sections. Carl listened for a while. "It's nice. I've never understood classical music. Do you know what they're singing?"

"No. It's a bunch of Bible verses, but that doesn't matter to me. It's the feeling of the music that I like."

"You can feel this?"

"Yeah, it feels . . . it's comforting, I guess. I can't say why, exactly, but I think Brahms meant it to be soothing. I read about it a long time ago. I can't listen to Christmas music for a whole month."

"Huh. I like Christmas music. You can turn that off. I've heard enough to know you're not suicidal."

"Okay." We were close to his building. "Will you show me your place? I'd like to see how much of a slob you are." I was taking a risk, but . . . I felt like it.

"I don't know. I didn't have time to straighten up at all. I'd be embarrassed."

"Are you afraid to show me what you're really like?"

He smiled. "Now I don't have much of a choice, do I? Yes, please come up to see my place. I would *love* to show it to you."

I pulled into a parking space on the street next to his building. "Will my truck be safe here?"

"This isn't the 'hood.' It's a safe area."

"I'm only asking, not judging." I regretted not having a car alarm.

We entered the building, passed the elevator, and walked up four flights of stairs so Carl could start working off those deep-fried onions. Before he opened his door, he warned me again. "This isn't the way it would look if I knew you would come in."

I expected a pigsty. It was anything but. We walked into a large open space with tall windows and exposed brick walls. The central kitchen had stainless steel appliances, smooth wooden cabinets and black granite countertops. His furniture was modern, with steel frames and black leather upholstery. There were brightly colored accent pieces in strategic places. His condo looked like a suite in an expensive Scandinavian hotel.

"You're such a fucking liar."

"No, seriously, it's not as clean as it should be." He rushed to clear a few dishes off the gleaming countertop. There was a small dining area adjacent to the kitchen with a pile of half-opened mail on the table. In the living room, the seating was carefully arranged to take advantage of a view toward the harbor as well as the large flat screen TV on the wall. I noticed a beer bottle next to the sofa before Carl snatched it up and made it disappear.

At the other end of the apartment, the bedroom was partially hidden by a row of potted Ficus trees. I imagined how bright the room would be during the day. In a corner next to the bedroom he had a workout space with a fancy treadmill, a rack of dumbbells, and a punching bag suspended from a wooden beam. A steel mesh container held a variety of balls and equipment used for every sport I could think of. I could almost smell the testosterone.

"This is very nice, Carl. Not what I was expecting."

"What does that mean?" He stood next to me at one of the big windows.

"I pictured more of a blue-collar man cave."

"Is that how you see me?"

I turned to face him, leaning against the brick along the edge of the window. "It's not an insult. It's part of what makes you sexy. Having excellent taste and keeping a clean house is icing on the cake."

"Did you say sexy?"

"I know it's rude to ask, but how can you afford this on a police officer's salary?"

"Wow, that's incredibly rude." He was teasing. "I don't tell this to everyone, but I have a trust fund from my grandfather. He was a chemist at a pharmaceutical company."

"Oh?" I raised one eyebrow. "I'd love to peek at your bank statements."

Carl moved a little closer. "Is that how accountants flirt?"

"Apparently." My eyes focused on the golden chest hair visible through his open collar.

"So . . . why did you want to see my place?"

I hesitated before telling the truth. "I wanted to touch you." My face felt hot.

He stepped closer. "Go ahead."

"May I open your shirt?" He nodded. My hands shook as I undid the first button, the next, and the next. He wasn't wearing an undershirt. His body was everything I imagined. I'd spent more time imagining it than I wanted to admit. I placed my hands on his chest.

Carl smiled. "Your hands are cold, but that's okay." His nipples hardened, and goosebumps appeared on his tanned skin.

"Your body is so warm. It feels good." I missed the way a man's body felt. I slid my hands over his ribs and down to his waist. His flesh was softer than what I was used to, but pleasantly so. He tensed his abs, though it was unnecessary. He was muscular by most standards.

He leaned in and offered me a kiss that I accepted, clumsily. We tried again with a somewhat better result. I pressed my lips to his cheek, his jaw, and his neck. That felt better. He spoke softly, "How far do you want to take this, Adam? I'm not ready for . . ."

"Neither am I. I know this is a lot to ask, but . . . could I sleep in your bed tonight? I want to be close to you."

He kissed the side of my neck. "I'd like that, but I would have to put my arm around you. Would that be okay?"

"Sure. I can handle that. I'll even let you spoon me if we keep our underwear on."

He grinned. "That's very sensible, sir. Shall we proceed?" He took my hand and led me beyond the trees to his bed. "Why don't you get undressed while I set up the coffee maker and turn off the lights. The bathroom is right there." He pointed to a door and walked away.

I quickly ducked into the bathroom to pee and clean myself up a bit. I didn't like the way I looked in the mirror, but that was nothing new. I found a hook for my clothes and slipped into the bed as the lights in the other rooms went out. I pulled the covers up to my chest.

Carl walked in and touched a switch, leaving only the lights on either side of the bed illuminated. "You look good there." He tugged at the tails of his shirt and unbuttoned his snug jeans. Rather than hiding himself, as I had, he watched me watch him undress. He had no reason to be embarrassed. Everything he revealed was very attractive, including the bulge in his gray boxer briefs. Carl was handsome everywhere.

He crawled into bed and playfully lifted the covers to see me in my underwear. "I want to make sure you're following the rules. Big spoon, or little spoon?"

It hadn't occurred to me I could be the big spoon. I didn't want that. "Little spoon, please. You're too big to be a little spoon."

He beamed. "Thanks. I was nervous about . . . how I would compare."

Please don't say his name. "You're very well-built, Carl. Can I touch your chest again?"

He rolled onto his back and placed his hands behind his head. "Go ahead . . . treat me like a sex object."

I smirked and rubbed his fuzzy chest. "You are a sex object. You might as well own it . . . meat."

He laughed and covered his eyes with one arm. His big grin remained. "Thank you, Adam. Seriously, thank you for going out with me."

"Thank *you.*" I kissed his chest. "I needed this." I traced the trail of hair dividing his torso. "You'd better spoon me before I violate a rule."

"Uh oh." Carl switched off the bedside lamps and turned on his side. I rolled over and settled into a familiar shape. He wrapped his arm around me and shifted his body until it was pressed against mine. *He's not strong enough to move me.* I felt his breath against my neck. He hugged me tighter. "How's that?"

"Very nice." His arm wasn't quite long enough. It wasn't as heavy as I thought it would be. But it was nice. I was comfortable.

Carl smelled good, but it was nothing like *his* smell. He was warm, but there was nothing like *his* heat.

I couldn't keep the tears from coming. They fell onto the pillow, too quiet to be noticed. *He's sweet. I'm safe here. Carl is thoughtful and gentle . . . mature . . . stable . . . predictable. That's what I want. What more could I want?*

38

I woke up as the sun filled Carl's bedroom with warm, bright light. The smell of freshly brewed coffee encouraged me to roll over and stretch my arms above my head. Carl was in his workout space smoothly executing a series of pushups in snug gray sweatpants. He was shirtless. I propped my head on one hand and watched him until he finished. He stood up, shook out his arms and rubbed his pumped chest before he noticed me. "What are you looking at?"

"You know perfectly well what I'm looking at. Good morning."

He approached the bed. "Morning. Did you sleep well?"

"Yeah, I did." There was a flattering sheen of perspiration on his skin. "I suppose you have to get to work."

"I do. I'll jump in the shower. The coffee is ready, there's juice in the fridge, and feel free to eat anything that looks good."

I raked his body with my eyes. "Anything?"

Carl shook his head. "Why do you do this to me right before I have to go to work?"

"Come on! You chose to walk around shirtless."

He laughed. "I was going to wear the ribbed tank you like so much, but I thought it would be too obvious." He bent down and gave me a peck on the lips. "I have to get moving."

My eyes followed him all the way to the bathroom before I put my hand under the covers and stroked my erection a few times. A familiar question came to mind: *Why would a guy like that want to be with me?* I crawled out of bed and got dressed.

Carl's coffee was excellent, and his refrigerator was stocked with healthy food. I ate a cup of Greek yogurt after adding a lot of sugar. I sipped my coffee and wandered around looking at his stuff until he emerged from the bedroom as the handsome police officer who came to my rescue more than once. I kept trying to find something wrong with him, but he wasn't making it easy.

I stood at one of the large windows looking down at the street. "Carl, did I park my truck on this side of the building, or was it on the other street?"

"It's that street. There's no night parking on the other street."

"Okay. I don't see my truck."

"It's there. I'm sure it's there." He came over to help me look. "Huh."

"Do you see it?"

"No, but it must be there. You were parked legally, so it wouldn't have been towed."

"It's not there, Carl. I know what my truck looks like." I decided to have a little panic attack.

"Um . . . all right, let's see . . ." His face turned red. "Coincidentally, I'm heading to the police station where you could file a report about something that may have been stolen."

"Stolen?"

"Uh, I'm not sure what else would make a truck disappear. Unless David Copperfield is in town."

I was not amused. "I hate David Copperfield."

"Of course you do," he muttered. "We'd better go or I'll be late for roll call."

We took one last look when we got to the street, but my truck was gone. We got into his SUV to drive to the station. Country-western music blasted from the radio as he started the engine. *There it is. I found something wrong with him.* "Will you file the police report for me?"

"No, you'll have to talk to the desk clerk. I have to report to the sergeant for the start of my shift."

"Should I say I was at your place?"

"Um . . . say you were on State Street near Maple. Or you were visiting a friend."

"Okay. How will I get home?"

"They'll probably ask me to take you since you live in my patrol area."

"Oh, that's good. Do you want me to pretend I don't know you?"

Carl hesitated. "No . . . I don't think so. They don't need to know we slept in the same bed. They know I'm gay, but . . . they don't need . . . we're friends. If anyone asks, we're friends."

"Okay. That's what I thought." The whole situation was stressing me out. It was hard enough to deal with my truck being stolen without these other complications.

Carl was all business at the station. He seemed as nervous as I was. He pointed me toward the reception desk. "I'll see you later." I couldn't say what changed, but he was different. Maybe it was my imagination.

I gave my information to the woman at the desk and filled out a form. After everything was done, I asked her if I could get a ride.

"I'll take him," said a man standing behind me. The desk clerk nodded.

I turned around. "Detective Mansky." *Shit!* "Maybe I should wait for . . ."

"No, I'll take you. It'll give us a chance to talk. Come on."

Reluctantly, I followed him as Carl came out of the back room with a group of uniformed officers. I made a face and shrugged. He gave me the slightest of nods and looked away.

Mansky saw him. "Did you come in with Hanson?"

I sighed. "Yes."

"Was your truck stolen from your house, or somewhere else?"

"Somewhere else."

"Was it in the West Harbor neighborhood?"

"Yes." I rolled my eyes.

"Uh huh." We got into Mansky's unmarked sedan. "Fasten your seatbelt."

I muttered, "It's going to be a bumpy night." *Brought to you by the gayest part of my brain.*

"Bette Davis, right?"

I was astonished. "Uh . . . yeah."

"My wife liked that movie."

"You have a wife?"

"Not anymore."

"She divorced you? That's a shock."

He paused. "She died."

Oh, for fuck's sake! Can't I catch a break? "I'm sorry, that was rude."

We drove in silence for a few minutes before he spoke again. "Look, I know I'm an asshole. Everyone says it, and I don't blame them. I'm not trying to change, either. It works for me most of the time."

"Hmm. I suppose it would."

"I'm sorry I arrested you, but I had reason to believe you were at least an accomplice. You were right about a lot of things. The coroner listed accidental strangulation as the cause of death, but I'm sure Verdorven killed Bergdorf. His personal accounts were cleaned out. All his money is gone, plus the funds from Ellis. But it would be hard to prove it was murder if they ever track him down and bring him back here.

"Can't the financial transfers be traced? The money had to go somewhere. Henry's not carrying it in those tight pants he wore."

"The department doesn't have anyone with that training and the chief won't come up with the money for it. Maybe Jasper Ellis will hire a forensic accountant."

"What about Zipinski? Shouldn't he try to figure it out? He should be held accountable."

"It's funny you should say that. He thinks you should be held accountable."

"You mean that crap about my job description? It's bullshit! I was never told to supervise Henry's work. Everyone knew Henry was in charge while Zipinski was gone. That fucking job description wasn't written until right before I was fired! Did you know that?"

"It doesn't take much to crank you up, does it?"

"Yeah, well . . . you'd better not arrest me again."

"Don't worry about it. Your friend at the office has your back. She's an impressive woman."

"Donna is happily married."

"I know. To Kevin Gilson, owner of Gilson Electrical Contracting. He does a lot of work for Ellis Industries."

"He does? Why were you checking up on Kevin?"

"It's my job. Do you mind if we stop at the doughnut shop?" It was the place where Sam bought his doughnuts. "My treat."

"We're not on a date."

"Do you have a lot to do today? Ten minutes won't kill you." Mansky parked near the shop and I followed him in.

The shop owner knew him. "Hey! It's Officer Mansky! I'm sorry . . . *Detective* Mansky. Congratulations! It's good to see you." I was surprised anyone would be happy to see Doug Mansky.

"How are you, George? I was in the neighborhood and I had to get one of the best doughnuts in town. I miss this place."

"You can't have one. How about a dozen? On the house, for our old friend."

"My doctor says my heart will explode if I don't cut back."

"That's not a problem here. Our doughnuts have no fat, no sugar, only healthy stuff. Doctors write prescriptions for our doughnuts." George was quite a character. He finally noticed me. "Hey, you're the little guy from the neighborhood association."

"Yes, but I'm not little." *Dammit.*

"What happened to the big guy, your friend or whatever you call him? He hasn't been here for weeks."

"He hasn't? He was out of town for a week. Are you sure it's been longer than that?"

He called out to one of his employees. "Hey Cindy, when was the last time Prince Charming was here? Was it two weeks? Three weeks ago?"

"Four weeks. Right after Halloween."

When we broke up. "I'll take home a dozen for him. Put some of those chocolate cream thingies in there, and . . . do you know what else he likes?"

Cindy volunteered, "I've got it."

Mansky told her, "I'll pay for those and an apple fritter for myself."

George waved his hands. "No money from you! It's on the house. I wish you were still patrolling this neighborhood. Officer Hanson . . . nice guy, but he won't touch a doughnut. A policeman who doesn't like doughnuts! He won't even let his partner have one!"

"Oh yeah?" Mansky laughed and looked at me. "I wonder where he learned to treat his rookie like that? These young guys are too worried about how they look. But Hanson's a good cop. He learned from the best."

George agreed. "That's right." I tried not to roll my eyes.

Back in the car, Mansky told me, "Don't tell Hanson what I said about him."

"You mean that he's too worried about how he looks?"

"No, the other part. That he's a good cop."

"Why? Would it kill you to compliment him?"

"It's not the way we do things."

"Well, it's stupid."

"Yeah, probably. Does your boyfriend know what you're doing with Hanson?"

"Yes. No, wait, he's not my boyfriend anymore, but he knows about it. But I'm not doing anything with Carl. We're friends. I stayed at his place last night, but we didn't . . . why am I telling you this? It's none of your damn business!"

"You're fucking both of them."

"NO! I'm not fucking either one of them!"

"No wonder you're so tense. Don't gay guys usually have sex three times a day?"

"Shut up! Maybe you need to get fucked!" I probably shouldn't have said that. We arrived at my house and pulled into the driveway. Sam's truck was there.

"So, we're even now?"

"Even for what?"

"For arresting you. I gave you a ride and I bought you doughnuts. Now we're even."

I blinked at him. "The doughnuts were free. You're an asshole."

He shrugged. "I told you. I'll see you around. Stay out of trouble."

"You too, Doug." I used his first name to bug him. "And we're not even." I closed the car door before he could answer.

I tried to get into the house before Sam saw me, but he came out of his apartment and ran down the stairs. "Where have you been? Where's your truck? And who was that?"

"Do you seriously think you can question me?"

"I was worried about you!"

"Why? I'm an adult!"

He stopped himself before saying something else. He turned around, then turned back. "You know what? I'm not like you! I can't stop caring about someone at the drop of a hat! I still care whether you're alive or dead!"

"Where's your coat? It's freezing out here." I considered inviting him into the house. "I suppose you want to talk."

"YES! I've been asking you for weeks! Why are you being such a dick?"

I was surprised he called me that. "All right, let's get this over with." I unlocked the back door.

"Wow, are you sure you can risk letting me in the house?" He was more sarcastic than usual. I didn't dignify his remark with an answer.

"I bought doughnuts." I set the box on the table and went to the coffee maker before taking off my coat.

"Why did you do that?"

"I don't know. We were at the doughnut shop and the guy asked why you hadn't been there for a while. So I got a dozen. That's what you do at a shop."

"This is another one of your mixed messages."

"What? It's a box of fucking doughnuts!"

"The first time I came into this kitchen, you did the same thing! You talked like you wanted to get rid of me, but you gave me coffee and cookies. You're doing the same thing now!"

"You're reading way too much into things. I wanted a treat. I had a rough morning."

He opened the box of doughnuts. "These are all my favorites. You couldn't be more transparent." He was getting on my nerves with his . . . *truth* shit. Just like Agnes. "Will you tell me where you were, or not?"

"My truck was stolen. I had to file a police report."

"Stolen? From where? I know it wasn't stolen from here because you weren't home last night."

"I was at Carl's place."

Sam's expression spoke volumes. "You didn't waste any time, did you?" I glared at him until he yielded. "But I'm in no position to judge." He lowered his eyes and bit into a doughnut. I hung my coat in the back hallway and returned to the coffeemaker, silently cursing it for not giving me what I wanted immediately. With an edge in his voice, Sam asked, "Did you enjoy yourself?"

"Yes, I did. Carl has a beautiful condo."

He waited until I looked at him to say, "I know, I've been there." He knew how to push my buttons.

"That's right. Before you were in a monogamous relationship." I put air quotes on "monogamous." *Take that, motherfucker!*

His jaw clenched. He took a deep breath and moved on. "Who was that in the car?"

"Detective Mansky."

"What? Why would you get in a car with that asshole?"

"I needed a ride and he offered. It wasn't as bad as I thought it would be. He apologized for arresting me." The coffee was finally done. I poured a cup and sat down.

"Have they found Henry?"

"No. They don't have the people they would need to track him down." Sam got up and made himself a cup of coffee. He took two plates from the cupboard and placed one in front of me, then put a chocolate cream doughnut on it. "I have a feeling Zipinski will be charged with something. I'm sure Donna will nail him if she can." I picked up my doughnut and welcomed the puffy, gooey sweetness into my mouth. "God, these things are good."

"I know, I haven't had one for a while."

"They asked why you haven't been to the shop for a month."

"I haven't been eating as much."

"I can see that. You're not as . . ."

"I know."

"Is that an old shirt? It looks too small for you."

"I haven't gone to the laundromat. You used to like it when my shirts were too small."

I changed the subject. "What did you want to talk about?"

"Are you kidding me? We need to talk about everything! Like, why didn't you respond to any of the messages I left? I was going out of my mind!"

I felt guilty about that. "I'm sorry, I didn't listen to them until after you went to see your parents."

"Why not?"

I shrugged. It was hard to tell the truth. "I was afraid if I heard your voice . . ." I couldn't finish, and I couldn't look at him. I felt too much.

"All I wanted was to hear your voice. It would have helped."

"I was protecting myself."

"I don't want to hurt you."

"No, you never wanted to hurt me, but I still got hurt! How much was I supposed to take?"

His face flushed. "You're right. I know you're right. I guess I was hoping . . . I could change. Do you think I can change?"

I shrugged again. "Should you change? Maybe it's not realistic. Maybe I should change. Dave thinks I should be more . . . flexible."

"I don't care what Dave thinks. What does he know about relationships?"

"Probably more than I do. I don't know what the hell I'm doing."

"Neither do I, but we were figuring it out. I thought you could teach me how to control myself. You're so disciplined. I saw that from the beginning. You had everything under control."

"You say that like it's a good thing."

"I think it is. I need some of that."

"I'm not so sure. You're young, you should enjoy yourself. I wish I had done more at your age. I don't want to hold you back." I stood up to get more coffee.

"It never felt like that, Adam. I wanted to be here. I still do."

"We're at different places in our lives." I poured more coffee into his mug. I set the carafe in the sink and retrieved an envelope from one of the drawers. "I have your father's letter. It was beautiful." I gave it to him. "Thank you for letting me read it."

Sam looked at it sadly. "It was a good letter."

"How was your visit?"

He shook his head. "Not good. It was great to see my dad. I didn't realize how much I missed him. But my mother wouldn't let me stay in the house. I had to sleep in the barn with the animals."

"Oh, that's awful."

"I don't know what I was thinking. She was afraid of me when I left, and now I'm bigger. This beard didn't help." He rubbed his short black facial hair. "I should have known better."

"Did things get better after the first day?"

"No, it got worse. One of the neighbors saw me and he told the preacher. When my parents went to church services, they were shunned. That's a serious thing up there."

"But why? Your parents didn't do anything wrong."

"That's not the way they think, Adam. They were told to banish me if I didn't repent. My mother was a mess. My dad was torn between me and her. I agreed to leave so they could tell the preacher they threw me out."

"Do you think they would say that?"

"Dad claimed he wouldn't, but I don't think he'd have a choice. My mom . . . I don't understand her. I always felt closer to my dad, but I know she used to love me. I tried to show her I'm still the same person I was when I was a kid but . . . it's like she doesn't see me anymore. My own mother."

"God, that must hurt."

Sam nodded. He was trying not to cry. I remembered how his feelings made me uncomfortable with him at the beginning. *I should teach him how to shut that down. It would be so much easier for him.*

"Adam?"

"What?"

It took him a while to ask, "Do you still see me? Am I still the same person you loved?"

Oh my God. I had to stop breathing. *This is why I didn't want to talk to him. How can I stand up to this?*

I knew how he felt. I remembered what it was like to become invisible, when there was no one left in the world who really knew me. I should have wrapped my arms around his head and let him soak me with his tears, but I wouldn't. I protected myself. I pretended I wasn't strong enough.

I had to give him something. "Yes, I see you. You're still the same person." I went a little farther. "You're a good person."

Sam let a few tears fall. He wiped them away quickly and smiled. "Thank you. I needed to hear that." He swallowed the last of his coffee and sat upright. "I should go."

"Are you sure?" *Don't go.*

"Yeah, I should." He stood up and turned away.

"Take the doughnuts." I closed the box and pushed it at him. "You were right."

"I was?" He picked up the box.

"About the doughnuts. I got them for you."

He let out a small laugh but wouldn't look at me. "Yeah. You were never that good at hiding your feelings." He stepped into the back hall as though he couldn't get away from me fast enough. "Hey, um . . ." His voice cracked. "Do you think we could be friends again? Like when I first moved here?"

Is that all? "I don't know. We could try."

"Okay." He nodded. "Okay, um . . . thanks for the doughnuts. And for letting me talk to you. I'll see you later."

He left quickly, and a cold draft took his place. I folded my arms on the table and laid my head on them. I stayed there for quite a while.

***

Carl called me later that afternoon. "Hey, I have good news." My truck had been found on the other side of town, damaged but mostly intact. Someone had taken it for a joyride, ran it into a signpost, and abandoned it. The police department had it towed to a city lot so they could dust it for fingerprints. When they were finished, I could have it taken to the dealership for repairs.

"What happened between you and Mansky," Carl asked.

"Not much. He apologized for arresting me, then we stopped for doughnuts and he brought me home. It could have been worse. He told me not to tell you this, but he thinks you're a good cop."

"Are you sure he was talking about me? And it wasn't a joke?"

"No, he meant it. He was talking to the owner of the doughnut shop."

"Oh, that guy. I don't think he likes me."

"Would it kill you to eat a doughnut? Or take one home and throw it away."

"That's a good idea, I never thought of that. Those things are like poison."

"The one I ate tasted great."

"Well, good luck with your heart disease." Carl was a little too strict about food.

"I had a talk with Sam today, like I promised."

"How did it go?"

"Fine." *I fucked it up.* "We agreed to be friends."

'Good for you. You must be relieved."

"Uh huh." *Not really.*

"Will he be moving out soon?"

"I guess so. In January, if he finds a place." *What's the rush?*

"That'll be more comfortable for both of you."

"Yes, it would be." *More comfortable for Carl.*

"When will I see you again?"

"Whenever you want. I'm not busy."

"What would you like to do?"

"I don't know. Whatever."

"You don't sound too excited."

"I'm sorry, I'm thinking about my truck. Could we talk later? I'm too distracted."

"Sure, no problem. I'll call you tonight."

***

For the next few days I had to deal with my insurance company to get the repairs on my truck authorized. Staying in the house for days on end never bothered me until I felt trapped by my lack of transportation. I went out with Carl one night, but I was still stir-crazy. It was so bad, I called Donna to ask when we were going Christmas shopping.

Understandably, she asked, "Are you feeling all right?"

"Yeah, but I need to get out of this house. Could we go tonight?"

"I suppose, but the mall is only open until nine and by the time I get out of the office . . ."

"Why don't you pick me up after work and take me to that Thai restaurant, and if we run out of time we can skip the shopping."

"Oh, I should have seen that coming. Well, I need to talk to you about something anyway, so let's do it. I'll pick you up at six. We can go shopping on Saturday."

"Sure. We could do that."

While I drank a cocktail decorated with a little umbrella and stuffed my face with Pad Thai, Donna brought me up to date on the latest developments at the office. "You can't tell anyone else about this, but Jasper Ellis is about to sue Zipinski for ten million dollars."

"Good, he deserves it."

"Zipinski doesn't have ten million dollars. Even if he settles the lawsuit, it'll ruin him."

"Don't tell me you feel sorry for him."

"No, he can rot in hell, but a lot of people will lose their jobs."

"Oh, yeah. I wasn't thinking about that. Including you, I suppose. That sucks."

"That's what I wanted to talk to you about. We should open our own accounting practice."

I nearly choked on a noodle. "What?"

"We could start our own business. The two of us."

"I thought we couldn't do that because of our contracts with Zipinski."

"Zipinski won't exist after Jasper is done with him. Someone will have to service all those accounts. If we establish ourselves as soon as possible, we can start picking up the clients who abandon Zipinski."

"What makes you think any of them would trust us?"

"If we land one high-profile client, others would follow. We only need enough to keep the two of us busy. If we want to expand later, we can do that."

"Whoa, whoa. Slow down. That's a lot of ifs."

"I already have Ellis Industries."

I stared at her for a full minute. "Okay, I need to ask you . . . what's the deal with you and Mr. Ellis? Why does he have so much confidence in you?"

She shrugged. "I've known him for a long time."

"How long and how well?"

"Adam, don't be rude."

"Donna, I'm not agreeing to anything unless I know what I'm getting into. What's your history with him?"

"Haven't you known me long enough to trust me?"

"I'm not in a trusting mood lately."

"By the way, have you talked with Sam yet, or are you still . . ."

"Don't change the subject."

She rolled her eyes and sighed. "This is not a good time to tell you about this." She played with her food. "It was a long time ago, and I'm embarrassed to admit it." She twirled a paper umbrella. "I had a brief affair with Jasper. There's nothing like that between us now."

I suspected as much but hoped it would be something else. "Was this after you were married?"

She nodded. "Not long after Colin was born. When I returned from maternity leave, I was assigned to audit one of the Ellis accounts. I had to retrieve records from their offices, and I met him there. He was an impressive man . . . rich, influential, distinguished. He took an interest in me immediately. I wasn't feeling very good about how I looked after having a baby, but my breasts were still swollen from nursing and . . ."

"I don't need the details. Cut to the ending."

"Fine. It only lasted a few weeks. Kevin knew something was wrong and eventually I confessed." She stopped there, but I knew there was more to the story - the part that was difficult to tell. "Given your recent experience, you know how Kevin must have felt."

I was retrieving some of those feelings as she spoke. "How could you do that to him?"

"It wasn't directed at Kevin. It's not like I had a plan. The first time was completely unexpected. I assumed that was the end of it. When Jasper approached me again, I told myself it wouldn't make any difference because the mistake had already been made. I thought each time would be the last, that he would get bored with me and move on to someone else. I didn't have any illusions about a real relationship with him. He lived in a different world. I got tired of it, I felt guilty . . . so when Kevin asked me what was wrong, I told him."

"Was he angry?"

She shook her head grimly. "I wish. It's awful to discover how much you can hurt someone who loves you."

I wondered if Kevin's reaction was like mine. It was difficult to imagine. I knew there was at least one difference. "He forgave you."

"Yes. It was terrible."

"Terrible? What do you mean?"

"I wanted him to punish me. It's not easy to be forgiven like that. No one could possibly deserve it, and I'm not that lovable. But Kevin thinks I am. So I try to live up to it. Where I would be without him?"

"And where would he be without you?"

She smiled, perhaps the warmest smile I had ever received from her. "Thanks. Years later, I realized . . . that's when I truly made a commitment to Kevin . . . when I took responsibility for his heart."

I thought about it. Accepting another person's love is an awesome responsibility, not to be taken lightly. I wondered how often I had hurt the people who loved me. Maybe that's what Flora meant when she hoped I would pull my head out of my ass.

"How did you continue to work with Mr. Ellis after that?"

"I told him Kevin knew what we had done, and that he forgave me. Jasper was very impressed. Obviously, he hadn't been a very good husband to either of his wives. He tracked Kevin down to apologize and asked for his advice on how to be a better man. That's the type of guy he is. Later, Kevin said he understood why I was seduced by him. They went to a bar and talked for a long time about a lot of things. Kevin wouldn't tell me everything they discussed, but Jasper became a patron of Kevin's contracting business. Kevin got a lot of work from him, for Ellis Industries and from Jasper's friends."

"And you were okay with that?"

"Why wouldn't I be?"

"I don't know. It all sounds a little too cozy."

"It's not like we all hang out together on the weekends. The only contact we had with Jasper was through our work. Until I went out to lunch with him on your birthday."

"And Kevin knows about this?"

"Yes, I told him what I was planning to do. He trusts me."

"Okay, and what was your plan again?"

"First, to help Jasper destroy Zipinski. Then to step over Zipinski's corpse and take whatever accounts I can get and ask you to go into business with me."

I stroked my chin and thought about it. "It's hard to dislike a business plan that includes stepping over Zipinski's corpse."

"So you're in?"

I nodded. "Yeah, I'm in."

"Good! Gilson and Evans Accounting Services . . . how does that sound?"

"Why not Evans and Gilson?"

"It sounds better the other way. And it was my idea."

"Shouldn't it be alphabetical?"

"Ladies first. I'm older. I've landed more accounts than you have."

"One account!"

"A big one!"

"I'm regretting this already." I felt like my life was getting back to normal. "Hey, we should pay for dinner and get over to the mall so you can do some shopping tonight."

Donna gave me a funny look. "Are you sure you're feeling all right? I thought you didn't want to go shopping."

"I don't, but you do, and . . ." I played with my paper napkin, tearing off pieces and making a little pile. "You've done . . . stuff . . . for me."

"Oh."

It was very quiet in the car on the way to the mall.

***

My truck was in the shop for more than a week. I was running out of food, so, reluctantly, I left a message for Sam asking if I could borrow his truck to go to the grocery store. He called me back a while later.

"I got your message. I need to buy a few things, too, so we could go tonight after I get home."

"Together? Um, I need to get a bunch of stuff. You might not want to stay that long."

"I don't mind."

It took me a little too long to respond. "What time?"

"Around five? Do you want me to knock on the back door?"

"No, I'll be ready."

When Sam pulled into the driveway, I rushed out the door to meet him, feeling nervous. He tried to make small talk on the way to the store, but I kept bungling it with one-word answers. Eventually he asked if I was looking for a job. I told him about Donna's plan to open an accounting practice, but I quickly ran out of things to say about it. *He's so much better at this than I am.*

He told me something new. "I've been talking to Pastor Fletcher about my problem."

"The woman at St. Paul's? From the neighborhood association meeting?"

"Yeah. She's very nice and I felt like I needed . . . I know this will sound dumb, but . . . I wanted a second opinion about what God thinks of me."

"Didn't you get enough of that growing up?"

"I know, but she has a different way of looking at things. I told her I wasn't sure I believed in God, and that didn't bother her. I told her everything."

"Everything? You mean . . . you talk about . . . sex and stuff?"

"Yeah, everything. Even Henry."

I found that hard to believe. "And she's not . . . what does she say?"

"She asks me questions and I tell her a little more about . . . whatever I'm telling her, and she . . . I don't know . . . she makes me feel more normal."

"That sounds like my psychologist. Are you figuring things out?"

"Yeah. A little."

We were quiet for a while. "I can't believe you talk to her about sex."

He offered a small shrug. "She's fine with it."

I grabbed a cart at the grocery store while Sam picked up a hand basket. "Won't you need something larger than that?"

"No."

"You could eat more in one meal than that would hold."

"I'm not eating that much anymore."

"Do you have enough money for food?"

"Yes."

"If you need any . . ."

"Are we shopping, or not?"

"Fine, let's go." *I was trying to be helpful!* "You don't have to stay with me. You can go your own way."

"Are you afraid to be seen with me?"

"No, I'm just saying, I won't be offended if you want to go in another direction."

"Can't I walk with you?"

"Yeah, that's fine. Whatever." *Why does this have to be so difficult?*

We walked up and down the aisles without much conversation. Sam asked me a few questions about how to cook things. I felt guilty about buying the ingredients for recipes I knew he liked. It seemed silly for him to be eating in his apartment while I had plenty of time to cook for both of us. I thought about inviting him to join me for dinner again, but I didn't think he would be comfortable.

I went through the checkout first and waited near the door for Sam. A woman who looked vaguely familiar approached me.

"Adam? Adam Evans?" She smiled.

"Yes." I looked at her suspiciously. "I'm sorry, do I know you?"

"It's been a long time. We were in high school together. I'm Grace Lorbecki. It's Grace Franklin now, but back then . . . I don't know if you remember . . . you took me to our senior prom."

"Oh." *Oh God.* "Yeah, I remember. You sat next to me in English." She was quiet and liked books, like me. "How are you? What are you doing now?"

"I'm fine, I'm married and I have two kids, a boy and a girl. I teach English Literature at Lincoln High School. How about you? You became an accountant, right?"

"Yeah, how did you know that?"

"Well, I saw you at . . . I saw the thing on the news about your parents and . . . I was at the church for the funeral but . . ."

"I'm sorry, I don't remember . . ."

"No, it's fine, I didn't talk to you or anything. I stayed in the back. You looked so . . ." Her expression changed. Before I knew what was happening, she had her arms around me. "I'm so sorry, that must have been a terrible time for you. You looked so lost up there. I wanted to give you a hug at the time, but I didn't want to intrude."

I stood there with her arms around me, too paralyzed to reciprocate. Sam stood behind her, keeping his distance but watching the little drama unfold. I felt something raw and frightening rising within me.

Grace let go of me and took a step back, brushing a few tears from her face. "I'm sorry, you weren't expecting something like this at the grocery store, were you?"

"No, but I appreciate . . . I mean it was a long time ago already, but still." I looked her in the eye briefly. "I've never been good at this stuff." I looked down at the floor.

"It's okay, Adam. I know how you are. I had such a crush on you back in high school. You were sweet."

I snorted. "Sweet? Seriously? That's not what I remember." My eyes were getting wet.

"Yeah. You were quiet and smart. Everyone liked you as far as I know."

"I shouldn't have asked you to prom. I can't believe you were stuck with me."

"I wasn't stuck with you. I was glad you asked me. We had a good time."

"I mean afterward." Much to my surprise, I was becoming a tearful, sniffling mess. "I'll never forget the way I left you on your porch, crying. I felt like a piece of shit."

"Oh, no! You mean the handshake? Don't worry about that. Sure, I was disappointed you didn't kiss me. I didn't understand at the time, but I got over it. When I heard what other girls went through with some of their dates, I felt lucky I was with you."

I tried to clean up my face with the back of my hand. "I didn't know what to do with girls. I didn't know what to do with anyone."

She pulled a few tissues from her purse and handed them to me. I felt like everyone in the store was watching. "You weren't that bad. We were all confused back then. Trust me, I work with high school students." She watched me wipe snot off my hand. "Are you waiting here for someone?"

"My friend." I moved my head to indicate Sam who was patiently leaning against a wall.

She turned to look at him. "Wow! Are you sure he's only a friend? If you're trying to decide whether to kiss him or not, I think you should kiss him."

I smiled and shrugged awkwardly. "We've done more than that. He's my first."

Grace nodded and wiggled her eyebrows. "Good for you. I'm glad you found someone. Could I give you my number? I'd love to get together so we could talk more."

"Yeah, sure, that would be interesting. But I'd better give you my number because I'll never call you."

She laughed. "I appreciate your honesty. That's what I liked about you. You were more vulnerable than most guys." She handed me a scrap of paper and a pen.

"Vulnerable? Are you sure you're remembering the right guy?" I wrote down my number.

"Yes, I know who you are. I'm glad I ran into you. I'll definitely call." She started to walk away.

"Grace?" She turned back. "I think I owe you a kiss. Do you mind?" She looked like the shy girl I remembered. I leaned in and kissed her on the cheek, then gave her a real hug, like Sam taught me. His eyes met mine briefly.

Grace's eyes glistened. "Thanks, Adam. I feel like I'm in high school again. I'd better go. I'll call you." She turned and walked into the store. I watched her until she disappeared down one of the aisles.

Sam stood next to me. "Are you okay?"

"No, I need to get out of here." I felt disoriented. *Is it dark already?* I forgot it was already dark when we arrived. The chilly air helped to clear my head, but something inside me seemed to be moving, like tectonic plates shifting against each other. I loaded my groceries and climbed into Sam's truck.

He didn't say anything until we were on the street. "Who was that?"

"A girl from high school. We went to prom together."

"You went to prom?"

"Yeah, it was stupid. Such a stupid, stupid thing to do." I was angry. "But they told me I should ask someone, that it wouldn't look right if I . . ." I was more than angry. "They *knew!* They knew I was gay and they told me to ask her to prom!"

"Who?"

"My *fucking* parents!" I surprised myself. I'm sure Sam was surprised as well. "They sat there and told me it would be the right thing to do. They were *so careful* about how they said it. I thought they accepted me, but . . ." I slammed the heal of my hand against the dashboard and sat back again.

"Whoa!"

I yelled, "They didn't teach me ANYTHING! They didn't teach me how to make friends, or how to talk to people! They didn't even teach me how to talk to THEM! They sat on their dead asses and read their fucking books! All those goddamned books! Was I supposed to learn about relationships from Jane fucking Austin?" I slammed my hand into the dashboard again. It felt good, so I did it again, and again. Then I started kicking.

Sam pulled over to the side of the street. "Adam, calm down before you hurt yourself!"

I didn't care. I kept pounding and kicking. "What kind of parents don't . . . they didn't give me a normal life! I was a fucking emotional CRIPPLE! God, I HATE them! I fucking HATE them!" Snot and tears ran down my face. "How could they DO that to me?"

Sam put his hand on my shoulder and rubbed it gently.

I held my head and rocked. "I need to talk to Flora and Agnes. They were there, they know what happened."

He pulled out his phone and dialed. "Hi, it's Sam. I'm fine. Adam needs to talk to you. Can he come over? Yeah, kind of. Five or ten minutes? Okay, thanks." He ended the call and put the phone in his pocket. "They'll be there." He put the truck in gear and drove toward home.

I continued to cry, thinking about all the subtle ways my parents taught me to be ashamed of who I was. In a house where so few words were spoken, every movement in their faces was meaningful. I knew what was allowed and what wasn't. Certain hand movements were unacceptable. Ways of talking. Specific words. *Don't draw attention to yourself. Don't sit that way. Don't wear that color. Don't talk. Don't feel.*

Sam pulled into the driveway. "If you give me your keys I'll put your groceries away."

"Are you sure?" I dug into my pocket.

"Yeah, just go. They're waiting for you." He held out his hand.

I put the keys in his palm and held his hand between my hands. "Thank you." He nodded slightly.

I jogged down the driveway and crossed over to Flora's front sidewalk. Before I could even ring the bell, Agnes opened the door. Flora stood next to her. "Honey, what's wrong?" I burst into tears and she opened her arms.

***

I don't know how long I was there. I cried and yelled, pressed my face against Flora's soft, warm body, and paced restlessly. They listened and comforted me, patting and squeezing my hands. When I could sit still, Agnes fed me. She brought three glasses of port and refilled them until I felt warm and full and a little sleepy. By the time I left, my life made more sense to me, though I can't say what I learned. It was too big to put into words, but it meant enough to change me.

I crossed the driveway in the peculiar, cold silence that only exists on winter nights. It makes the world feel peaceful no matter what happens during the day. My kitchen light was on, the door was unlocked, and my keys were on the kitchen table. Sam had put my groceries away and washed the dishes I'd left in the sink. I missed having him in the house.

I went upstairs, planning to crawl into bed and sleep as long as possible, but I saw the light in Sam's apartment. I picked up my phone and stood at the window. He came out of the kitchen as soon as the phone rang.

"Hi."

"I saw your lights. I wanted to thank you . . . for everything."

"No big deal. How are you feeling?"

"Better. We had a good talk. Difficult, but good. How are you?"

"Um . . . I'm fine." He raised his free hand to scratch the back of his head. He was wearing blue sweatpants and a plain white t-shirt.

"You look good."

"I do?"

"I can see you from my window."

He turned toward the house and approached his window, looking up. "Are you spying on me?"

"Is it considered spying when you leave your blinds open?"

"Oh, there you are. I didn't know there was a peeping Tom in the neighborhood."

"Adam. A peeping Adam."

"Uh huh." He pressed his hand against his window. I spread my hand against the cold glass on my window.

"Come over here, Sam. Sleep in my bed. The house feels empty without you."

I heard him breathing. "That's not a good idea. It wouldn't be right."

"Why not?"

"I can't keep hurting you."

"I don't care anymore."

"You should care."

"My feelings for you haven't changed at all."

"Neither have mine, but . . . it would be a mistake."

"I miss you."

"I miss you, too." His voice quivered. "But I can't give you what you want."

"I only want to be with you again."

"That's not enough. You want more than that, and so do I. Maybe, with enough time . . . but you can't wait for that."

"I want to."

"Don't. I can't promise you anything."

"Okay." I sniffled. "I understand. I'm not angry at you anymore."

"You probably should be, but I won't argue with you." We stood and looked at each other. Despite the distance between us, he felt closer than he had for a long time. "I should go to bed. I have to get up for work tomorrow, unlike some people."

"All right, I'll let you go. Thanks again." I took my hand off the window. My fingers were numb from the cold. "Good night, Sam."

"Good night, Adam." He ended the call and turned away from the window. He didn't close the blinds.

Faced with the prospect of sleeping alone again, I thought about Carl, briefly. It was too late, or I was too tired. *I'll call him tomorrow.* I undressed and dragged myself into the bedroom. I lay there looking around the room before I turned off the light and fell asleep.

The next day, I called an antiques dealer to talk about selling my parents' Victorian Gothic bedroom furniture.

39

Sam and I . . . we never had a conventional romantic relationship. We became friends when I was trying to hide my attraction to him and he was trying to make himself more attractive to me. My nearly impenetrable defenses may have made Sam think he needed to try that hard. But I realized, much later, that he didn't see himself the way I saw him. He was more insecure than I ever would have guessed. He couldn't tell whether I thought of him as more than a friend until my defenses were finally breached and my feelings manifested themselves with all the grace and poetry of a nervous breakdown.

I did the opposite with Carl. As often as possible, I let him know how wonderful he was. We dated the way most people do, with dinners and movies and other activities. Carl came up with most of the ideas. Bowling was more fun than I expected, but paintball made me irritable. A word of advice . . . never agree to play paintball with a cop. Still, I liked the effort he put into things, and told him so every time.

Though we pretended not to be bothered by Sam's lingering presence at my house, we spent our nights together at Carl's place. He was a decent cook, favoring low-fat grilled meats and stir fries, with fresh organic vegetables and whole grains. My colon fell madly in love with him. After dinner, we kissed and cuddled in front of his modern fireplace, where blue flames flickered on a bed of pebbles. During long conversations, we shared our stories and got to know each other in a way men rarely do when they're out of college and sober. Our intimacy advanced with measured steps, not too quickly and not too slowly, until it felt like we were at the threshold of a commitment.

I felt comfortable in Carl's bed and became more familiar with his body, and he with mine. One night, while I lay on my side exploring his well-built physique, I told him, "You're the type of guy I lusted after when I was in school. If I'd been in class with you, I would've sat a few rows behind you so I could look at you without being obvious about it."

He grinned. "Seriously? Don't you think we would have been friends?"

"No. No way. I stayed away from good-looking guys as much as possible. Gym class was the worst. Were you out in school?"

"Not until I was in college. I was pretty sure I was gay, but I still dated girls in high school."

"Did you have sex with any of them?"

"With a few. I wanted to have kids, and I knew life would be easier if I was straight. I was hoping I could make it work, but it wasn't what I wanted."

"What type of guys did you like?"

"Some of the athletes were hot, but the guy I had the biggest crush on wasn't someone I thought I would be attracted to. He was a pitcher on the baseball team at my high school. Tall and lanky, nice looking, but nothing special. He was smart and quiet, and he had a dry sense of humor. Once in a while he would say something in class that got me laughing so hard I couldn't stop. I had to serve detention once because of it. I thought it would be nice to be with a guy who could make me laugh."

"Did you ever tell him how you felt?"

"No, he was straight. That didn't stop me from thinking about him."

"I know what you mean."

After a pause, Carl asked, "Do you ever think about having kids?"

"My therapist asked me a question like that recently, and I realized I never thought about my future after I finished school. Once I had a decent job, I'd met all the goals I had for myself. Apart from financial goals . . . paying off my student loans, setting up a retirement account and another savings account for . . . whatever. A house, maybe? But I didn't want to leave my garden. When my parents died, I inherited the house and all their savings. From then on, all I did was go to work and think about the garden." I rolled onto my back and looked at the ceiling.

Carl turned over and laid his arm across my body. "You never thought about meeting someone?"

"No, I shut everyone out. I wouldn't have known how to have a relationship, but I knew what to do with my garden. There was always something to do, something to plan. I knew what I wanted it to look like, and every year I got a little closer. Unless something unexpected happened. Gardening must sound boring to most people, but no matter how well you plan, there are challenges like insects, or bad weather. Or someone burns down your shed. Some plants don't thrive, and others get bigger than expected. I took a few risks that paid off. You hope for the best, and if it doesn't work, you try again until you get it right. You have to stick with it."

Carl furrowed his brow. "It sounds like you *were* in a relationship . . . with your garden."

"It is like a relationship. I never thought of that."

"And you never thought about having kids?"

"No, I never got that far. I was just getting used to the idea of living with . . . someone." I almost said Sam's name. "I don't know if I would be a good parent."

"You don't give yourself enough credit." He kissed my chest. "Now, what were you saying earlier about lusting after someone like me?"

I smiled. "I don't remember."

"Are you sure?" He crossed his leg over mine and pressed himself against me. "Let's see if I can jog your memory."

My body responded enthusiastically. In all the right ways, Carl was hard and soft, hairy and smooth, strong and gentle. He knew what he was doing. When protection was needed, he provided it without interrupting the flow of our intercourse.

I knew he cared about me. I would even say we loved each other. Nevertheless, I began to wonder . . . if I couldn't love him the way he loved me, how I would tell him? I wanted to be honest. I was haunted by a melancholy spirit . . . by something I couldn't give him, and by someone I couldn't forget.

***

Christmas was rapidly approaching. As president of the neighborhood association, I felt obligated to decorate the outside of my house. I couldn't continue to be the curmudgeon of Eden Place, so I had to make a trip to Dave's Nursery.

I hadn't been there since the day I found Sam and Greg in the shed. It was very different in the winter. One of the greenhouses was filled with poinsettias and the shop shelves were stacked with light sets and manufactured decorations. The lot next to the main building was lined with racks of evergreen wreaths and garlands. Beyond it was a small forest of cut trees. Dave was there to greet me.

"Adam! It's good to see you." He shook my gloved hand. "I was hoping you'd come back someday. I would have understood if you didn't, but I wouldn't have been happy about it."

"Come on, Dave. I have exacting standards. Where else would I go?"

He smiled and hugged me like he used to do. He slapped my back to reassure everyone in the area that it was entirely platonic. "You're a good man, Adam. I felt bad about the things I said at Thanksgiving."

"It's all right. You gave me your honest opinion. That's what friends should do."

He cocked his head to one side. "Do you know he's working today?"

"Yeah. We're talking now, so it's okay."

"Oh, that's good news. I'm tired of looking at his mopey face. Some of the customers noticed the change in him."

"Well, don't get too excited. I didn't say we were getting back together."

"Yeah, I know. But there's hope."

"Is there?"

"Sure there is. Can't you be optimistic for a change? I wish he would get rid of that beard, though. I think the ladies liked him better without it."

"I think it looks great on him."

"Crap. That means he'll keep it."

I scoffed. "You think he'd keep it because I like it?"

Dave made a face. "Yeah . . . he would. You don't get it, do you, kiddo?"

I didn't want to hear it. "I haven't told him anything about the beard. Where is he anyway?"

"He's back there somewhere. Why don't you look around? I bet you five bucks he'll find you, even if you try to hide from him."

"Stop it. Are these garlands fresh? They won't turn brown on me, will they?"

"You're goddamned right they're fresh! Who do you think you're talking to?" I liked Dave's brand of customer service.

I looked at the boxwood wreaths. I liked a narrow category of tasteful holiday decorations, and boxwood wreaths were in that category. A variegated holly wreath would have been better, but they were expensive and hard to find. Fir garlands were unacceptable; only cedar would do. I had my standards.

"Hi, Adam. I thought I saw your truck." It was Sam. Dave's bet would have paid off. "I was wondering if you would decorate for Christmas."

I looked up and was caught off guard, once again, by his extraordinary handsomeness. His shaggy hair stuck out from under a knit cap. With his smooth, dark facial hair, flannel shirt, and well-worn barn coat, he looked like a young lumberjack. "Damn, that beard looks good on you."

He grinned and stroked his face. "Thanks, I'm glad you think so. Dave doesn't like it."

I waved my hand dismissively. "When was the last time Dave was right about anything?" Forgetting ourselves, we smiled at each other like awkward high school sweethearts. Then he remembered to act like an employee.

"Can I help you find anything?"

"I'm wondering how many garlands I need for the front porch."

He thought for a moment. "Probably six."

"That's what I was thinking."

"I like the cedar better than the fir."

"Okay, I'll trust your judgment. And I want a twenty-inch boxwood wreath."

"Did you see the holly wreaths in the greenhouse? They're expensive, but . . ."

"He has holly wreaths? Where are they?"

"Come on, I'll show you." We walked through the shop to get to the greenhouse. "I assume you'll want one of our oversized inflatable lawn decorations. We have a giant teddy bear holding a jack-in-the-box that's very nice."

I made a face. "One night, I'd like to go through the neighborhood with a butcher knife and puncture those stupid things. That's my idea of a merry Christmas."

Sam laughed. "I can see you doing that. But think of all the sad children the next morning."

"That's the part that makes me cheerful."

He laughed again. "You're such a Scrooge." He pointed at the holly wreaths.

"Wow, those are nice. Sixty bucks? Jeez, is it worth it?"

Sam shrugged. "You'd spend that much on dinner at a restaurant, and it would be gone in an hour. At least this would last for a few weeks. You could put it inside the house where you can see it, and put the boxwood wreath on the front door."

"Huh." *He has such great ideas.* "All right, why not?"

"Let me get a box while you pick the one you want." I made my choice and watched him reach up to unhook it from the wall. I could have watched him all day. *I used to watch him all day.* "I should have worn my gloves; this holly is sharp. Could you hold the box while I put it in there?"

I stood next to him - very close to him - while he situated the wreath in the flat box. It was nice to feel his warmth again. I confess that I leaned on him more than I needed to. He didn't move away. Not until I asked a poorly timed question.

"Have you heard from Greg?"

Sam stiffened and leaned away. "No. Did you think I was still seeing him?"

"I wasn't accusing you of anything. You were good friends."

"Well, I ruined that. I'm sure he's still angry. There's probably a support group somewhere for all the people who are mad at me."

"I don't think so. He told me you were his only real friend."

"That was before." He put the lid on the box and cut a piece of twine to tie it shut.

"You could talk to him. Do you want me to call him?"

"No!" Sam looked at me like I was an idiot. "Why would *you* call him?"

"So he knows I'm okay with it."

"Look, *I'm* the one who fucked everything up! I need to fix things on my own. You're being too nice again."

"No one has ever accused me of being too nice."

"I have!"

"That's ridiculous. Why can't I offer to help you? Greg apologized to me because he wanted to help you. That's what friends do."

"This is different. I mean . . . you know damned well what I mean."

"You called Carl about me before you went to visit your parents. What was that about?"

"He told you that? He wasn't supposed to say anything!"

"He thought it was a classy thing to do. You impressed him."

"That's not why I did it."

"I know; you did it for me. Maybe I'll hang out with Greg if you won't be his friend anymore."

"Yeah, right! Because you have so much in common. Stay out of this. I'll call Greg when I'm ready to call him."

"No, you won't! You're punishing yourself. You think you haven't suffered enough. That's the religious guilt they fed us as kids. You have to do your penance!"

"Shut up!" He shoved the box at me. "Here's your wreath. Do you need any help with the garlands, sir?"

"Sir? Sounds like I touched a nerve." I took the wreath. "Yeah, I do need help with the garlands."

"I'll get someone for you."

"Why can't you do it?"

"Because you're getting on my nerves."

"I said you should call your friend! Is that so terrible?"

"What if I don't trust myself around him? Did you think about that?"

"What will you do? Stay away from all men, forever?"

"Maybe I will! I knew you would go soft on this! I need you to be strict with me!"

"What? It's not my job to keep you in line. I'm not your mother." Dave came into the greenhouse.

"Then butt out, Adam! Mind your own business!" Sam glanced at Dave and stormed off.

Dave watched him go. "What the hell happened?"

"I don't know. I told him he should call Greg and he got all weird about it."

"Greg? Why would you tell him to call Greg? That idiot was part of the problem."

"I don't think so. Greg's not perfect, but he cares about Sam, and Sam should have friends his own age. He can't spend all his time with senior citizens."

"Who are you talking about? You're not that old."

"Dave . . . are you over sixty? Sixty-five maybe?"

He narrowed his eyes. "The kid was right . . . mind your own business."

"I'm the youngest friend he has right now and I'm twelve years older than he is."

"I hate to tell you, but that didn't look like a friendship a minute ago."

"That was nothing. He's angry because he knows I'm right."

"Every time the two of you have an argument, my sales go down ten percent."

"Oh, bullshit! You talk like he's the only person who works here. Greg was good at selling stuff and you didn't think twice about losing him."

Dave grumbled, "I liked you better when you were quieter."

"Well, too bad I'm not lonely and miserable anymore!" I realized, *Hey . . . I'm not lonely and miserable anymore!* Even though Sam and I weren't together, my life had changed a lot. I had friends . . . friends who took care of me whether I wanted them to or not. "Look, Dave . . . this isn't about us. Sam doesn't have a family anymore, so he can't afford to lose friends. If you happen to see Greg again, could you try not to scare him away?"

He frowned. "I don't scare people."

I raised one eyebrow. "Um . . . okay."

"All right, I won't punch him. I hope you're buying more than that wreath."

"Yeah, I want garlands, but your employee walked away from me."

Dave shook his head. "I don't understand your relationship."

"Sam and I aren't in a relationship. We're just friends."

He scoffed. "Like hell you are. Come on . . . let me help you spend your money. You need any lights? I've got the best lights . . ."

After loading my truck, I pulled out my phone and searched through my contacts. My call went to voicemail, so I texted Greg. "You owe me a favor. Call me."

***

Donna called me one morning while I was still in bed. "Zipinski just laid off most of his employees, including me. He's filing for bankruptcy."

"Bankruptcy? He's putting all those people out of work a week before Christmas?"

"He's such a dick. He must have found out Jasper was planning to sue him."

"Or maybe he's being charged with a crime. Have you seen Detective Mansky lately?"

"No, but he has enough evidence for a criminal charge. I made sure of that."

"What about me? Can I be accused of anything?"

"The worst Zipinski could say is you should have known about the account Henry set up. But his secretary knows you were out of the loop while Henry was in charge. She hates him as much as we do. She worked for him for more than twenty years and probably knows where all the bodies are buried."

"Well, what's the next step in your plan? Is there something I should do to get our business going?"

"I'll get Kevin's lawyer to take care of the legal stuff and a partnership agreement. We should rent office space somewhere. Do you know of anything that's available?"

"I might. Let me look around and see what I can find. You're probably busier than I am."

"You mean you're not spending all your time decorating for Christmas?"

"Believe it or not, I pulled the artificial tree out of the attic and I'm putting it up today. And I'm thinking of baking cookies."

"Were you visited by three ghosts?"

"That's the second time I've been compared to Scrooge this week, but when Sam said it, I was asking for it."

"How is Sam? I haven't talked to him for a while."

"You should call him. He needs his friends."

"He needs . . ." She stopped herself. "Never mind, that's none of my business."

"What isn't? What do you think he needs?"

"No, I'm not telling you. I should have kept my mouth shut."

"You haven't given me any advice about Sam since I broke up with him. You must have an opinion."

"I have a lot of opinions. That doesn't mean I should share them."

"I never thought I'd hear that from you."

"This is an unusual situation. I care about both of you, so it's difficult. Are you sure I shouldn't invite him to Christmas dinner?"

"No, it'll be awkward if people keep treating us like a couple. I'm sure he feels the same way. Flora and Agnes want him to spend Christmas day with them."

"As long as he has a place to go. What about Officer Hanson? He's welcome if he wants to come."

"Carl will be with his family."

"How is he?"

"Fine."

"How's the relationship going?"

"Fine."

She waited. "Is that all I'm getting?"

"What did you expect? Photographs?"

"Is that an option? I bet he's super-hot."

"Donna . . . you just lost your job. Shouldn't you call your husband?"

She sighed. "I suppose, but he won't be bothered. We were expecting this. What kind of cookies are you baking?"

"Gingerbread. Maybe sugar cookies."

"Can I come and spend the day with you? We could talk about our business plan."

"Um . . . I guess you could."

"Great! I'll be there in fifteen minutes."

"No! I'm still in bed! I haven't taken a shower yet!"

"Okay, twenty minutes. See ya!" She hung up before I could say anything else.

Dammit! I jumped out of bed and ran to the bathroom.

***

On Sam's day off, I asked Greg to show up at the house in the morning. Sam knew nothing about it. Unfortunately, Sam went out before Greg arrived.

I heard Greg's voice while I was drinking coffee and reading the newspaper. He stood on the driveway shouting, "Muffin! Hey, Muff! Where are you? Come out here so I can kick your ass!"

I opened the back door and asked him to stop yelling. "Greg! He's not home. He probably went out to buy doughnuts. You can wait for him in here."

He hopped up the stairs and came into the house. "Thanks, dude. It's cold out there."

"Thanks for coming."

"No problem. I can't wait to see him. I miss his ugly face."

"Do you know he has a beard now?"

"Yeah? I bet Dave hates it. He has a thing about facial hair." He hung his coat on the back of a chair and sat down.

"Yeah, Dave hates it. I think it looks good on him. Do you want some coffee?"

"No, I already had six cups. I'm cutting back."

No wonder he has so much energy. "What are you doing these days? Have you found another job?"

"Not yet. No one's hiring during the holidays and I don't know if Dave would give me a good reference. I'll have to depend on the Muffin for that. Do you know anyone who might hire me?"

"I don't know many people. The other day I told Dave you were a good salesman."

"You mean I'm a good bullshitter."

"Something like that. Hey . . . I thought of something. My friend next door owns O'Neill's Automotive. The last time I was in there, the manager asked if I wanted to try selling cars. That's the last thing I would want to do, but I could probably get you an interview if you want."

"You think I could sell cars?"

"Sure. Especially to women."

"You're right, they can't resist me." He didn't seem to be kidding. "It's worth a try. I don't have any other leads."

"I'll call him. Do you mind if I give him your number?"

"No, that would be awesome, I appreciate it." He looked at me curiously. "You pretend you hate people, but you don't, do you?"

I shrugged. "Meh." I had a reputation to maintain. Greg seemed more mature since the last time I saw him, and not a moment too soon.

We heard a vehicle pull into the driveway. "Is that him?"

"Probably. Let's see."

Greg pulled on his coat and beat me to the door. He was outside before I could put on my coat. "Hey, butt face! Why haven't you called me?"

Sam was caught off guard. "What are you doing here?" I stepped onto the porch.

"Dude, you told me Adam wouldn't want us to see each other, but you're a lying sack of shit! I'm here to kick your ass!" Greg took a boxer's stance and put up his fists.

Sam threw me an angry glance. "Go home." He pulled a box of doughnuts from the truck.

"I'm not leaving, bro. I'm gonna kick your ass and eat your doughnuts." Greg bounced around Sam, making it difficult for him to get to the stairs. "You better put that box down before I get your blood on it."

"Knock it off!" Sam swatted at him, but Greg stayed out of reach. "You know you can't win."

"You look kinda scrawny, Muff! I think I'll beat you this time." He lunged, then bounced away. Sam was irritated. He knew Greg wouldn't give up, so he set the doughnuts on the stairs. Before he could straighten up, Greg jumped on his back. "I've got you now, bro! I'm taking you down!"

Anyone else would have been toppled by someone as solid as Greg, but he may as well have been a squirrel on Sam's back. He stood up and tried to remove Greg. "Get off me, you crazy bastard!" I wasn't worried. They had done this so many times, pretending to dislike each other when they obviously felt the opposite. *I'm glad I'm not like that.* Unable to free himself from his tenacious friend, Sam threw himself into a large snowdrift, making sure Greg landed beneath him.

"Fuuuuuuck," Greg moaned. "How much do you weigh, dude?"

"More than you, dumbass!" They wrestled in the snow. Sam let Greg think he had the upper hand before using his superior strength to immobilize him. "Stay down, dammit!"

Greg ignored his obvious defeat. "You give up? Is that all you can take?" He was never one to concede.

"Fine, I surrender." Sam stood up and extended his hand. Greg grabbed it and threw snow in Sam's face, then ran away. Sam chased him around the yard until he tackled him and rubbed his face with a handful of snow. They were satisfied, or tired, so they stood up and brushed themselves off.

I quietly slipped back into the house and listened. "I don't like to punish you, bro, but it had to be done." Greg opened his arms. "Come on, let's hug it out." Sam finally smiled. They threw their arms around each other. Greg's feet left the ground. He slapped Sam's back until he was released. "Shit, Muff, you didn't have to crack my ribs!"

"I forgot how weak you are."

"What kind of doughnuts did you get me?"

"They're mine. You can have *one*."

"That's okay, you're still my best bro. Even when you're selfish." Greg followed Sam up the stairs to his apartment.

I poured myself another cup of coffee and caught myself humming a Christmas carol.

***

Flora and Agnes were having dinner at my house on Christmas Eve. It was my way of thanking them for everything they had done for me. Carl didn't have any family obligations that night, so I invited him to join us. We couldn't spend all our time at his place without admitting that Sam was still a barrier between us. I wanted Carl to feel comfortable in my home.

Though we agreed not to buy each other presents, he showed up early with a small gift. "Carl! Dammit, I thought we had an agreement!"

"I know, I know, but I couldn't show up empty-handed. It's not a big deal. Open it and get it over with."

I carefully tore the wrapping paper. It was a three-disc recording of Bach's *St. Matthew Passion,* a choral masterpiece I didn't own. "Carl . . . this is great! How did you know I would like this?"

"I wasn't sure. I told the guy at the music store about the requiem you were listening to. I asked if he had anything like that. I made sure it was something serious. You know I don't understand classical music."

I was touched that he bought me something he wouldn't enjoy. Unlike the things people buy more for themselves than for the recipient, this was an unselfish gift. It was a small thing, but it made me love Carl a little bit more. I thanked him with a kiss that was better than most of our kisses. He noticed the difference. "I did well, didn't I?"

"You did very well. I wish I had something for you, but it would be hard to match this."

"Don't worry about it. I'm happy to be with you." His sincerity made my heart ache. "Whatever you're cooking smells great."

"It's all comfort food, and I don't want to hear any talk about calories or triglycerides."

"Okay. Do you want to kiss my abs goodbye? You probably won't see them for a month."

"That sounds sexy." I smiled and rubbed his firm belly. "Can you stay here tonight?"

"I'd better not. I want to get to my parents' house early tomorrow to watch the kids open their presents."

"That's too bad. We could have cuddled for three and a half hours and listened to these CDs."

"Hmm . . . that sounds . . . nice."

"I'm kidding."

"Oh, thank God. I thought you were serious."

I laughed. "Scared you, didn't I?" I kissed him again. "Do you want a beer? I got your favorite."

"Sure. I'm a little nervous about this dinner. I feel like I'm meeting your parents for the first time."

"You already met Flora and Agnes."

"Yeah, when you were still with Sam. Do they approve of me?"

I hadn't thought about that. "They don't approve or disapprove as far as I know. They want me to be happy." I handed him a bottle of beer.

"Are you happy with me?"

"Sure, why wouldn't I be? Haven't I been telling you how wonderful you are?"

"All the time." He looked out the kitchen window. "That shed looks great now that it's fixed up. Did Sam do all the work himself?"

"Yes, he did."

"Is he home tonight?"

"I don't know. I don't think so."

The doorbell rang. *Perfect timing.* Agnes and Flora arrived with a gift basket and a large tin. "What's all this?"

"Nothing to fuss over," Flora replied. "Agnes has been baking, and there are a few other items for your enjoyment, barely worth mentioning." The basket held wine, cognac, pâté, a tin of caviar, crackers, two kinds of cheese, chutney, a Christmas pudding, hard sauce, Irish tea, shortbread, mince pies and pralines. It was like a luxury hamper from Harrods.

I clicked my tongue. "You two . . . honestly . . . you're too generous but thank you very much."

Agnes presented the tin to Carl. "Happy Christmas, Officer Hanson. Shortbread and mince pies. I hope you enjoy them."

He was surprised. "Thank you. Merry Christmas. Please, call me Carl. I'm not on duty tonight."

Flora extended her hand. "It's lovely to see you again, Carl." It was all very polite. I was counting on Flora to ease the tension. "Dear me, I had forgotten how handsome you are!" *That's a good start.*

Carl blushed. "Uh, thanks." He smiled and looked at the floor.

I put my arm around his waist. "You'll have to get used to Flora's compliments. She likes to flirt."

"It's true, I do! One of the privileges of old age is that I can get away with anything."

"You've been doing it for forty years, ma'am." Agnes' expression was blank, as usual.

"I need to finish our dinner, so why don't the two of you sit down with Carl and ask him a hundred questions about every aspect of his life."

"My heavens, you make it sound like an interrogation!" Flora took him by the arm and led him into the parlor. "I am curious to know, Carl . . . is it difficult to be a homosexual in the police department? I'm sorry, I should say 'gay.' Is it difficult to be a gay police officer?" Carl looked at me over his shoulder as I went to the kitchen.

The dinner was relatively simple – green salad, pork shoulder, roasted beets and rutabagas, and au gratin potatoes. For dessert I made gooseberry pie, one of my favorites. It turned out to be a hit. Even Agnes was impressed.

Inevitably, Flora mentioned Sam. "Adam, it was very sweet of you to restore Samson's friendship with Gregory. I know they're both grateful."

"Gregory? I don't think I've ever heard him called that."

"It suits him better than Greg. I told him it's more of a grownup name."

"You met him?"

"Yes, Clarence brought him over to meet me after he interviewed for a sales position. He has such wonderful energy, although Agnes wasn't as fond of him, were you dear?"

"Hmph. All noise and movement."

"He tried to charm Agnes, which is so often a mistake." Agnes looked sideways at Flora. "But Clarence was impressed by his effort and agreed to give him a chance on our sales staff. We need to bring in younger people."

"I've seen him in action. I think he'll do well with guidance."

Carl interjected. "Is this the guy who worked with Sam at the nursery?"

"Yes." I kept my answer brief.

"Isn't he the one who was with him . . ."

"Yes, that's him."

Carl looked as if he couldn't believe I had forgiven Greg. "That *was* generous of you to get them back together." His tone suggested I was crazy. "And you recommended him for a job?"

I was about to explain myself when Flora asked, "Carl, do I remember correctly that you knew Samson before he met Adam?"

Boom! I held my breath.

Carl was blindsided. "Uh . . . yes, I knew him from . . . I'm a member of the health club where he used to work, so . . ."

"Did you have a professional relationship, or were you friends? I can't recall what I heard."

Carl's face went completely red. "Um, we were . . . acquaintances."

"Well, that's all in the past." Flora waived her hand and smiled sweetly. "It's lovely to see how much you care about Adam. I'm so pleased you've become part of our little family. We're a motley crew, aren't we?"

I nodded. "Yes, we are." Flora was amazing. "You and Agnes are the glue that holds us together. I wanted you to come tonight so I could thank both of you for everything you've done for all of us." I lifted my wine glass in a toast.

Carl followed my lead and raised his glass. "Thank you for including me in your crew." There were no more questions about Greg.

After a quiet pause, Agnes moved her dessert plate in my direction. "I wouldn't refuse another wee piece of pie."

"All right . . . does anyone want coffee?"

One of Agnes' eyebrows moved. "I could show you how to make a proper pot o' tea."

"I'm sorry, would anyone like tea?"

"I would." Agnes stood up and went to the kitchen.

Flora chuckled. "I'll have tea as well, dear."

The evening ended at a reasonable hour. The women left first, perhaps assuming Carl would stay the night. Before he left he asked, "How did I do?"

"You were fine. You're part of the family now."

"That was nice of her to say, but I'm not sure she meant it."

"Flora means what she says. She's very forgiving, and very wise. So is Agnes."

"After facing the two of them, I should be ready for my mother tomorrow."

"Good luck with that. Don't forget the goodies Agnes made for you." I gave him the tin.

"I won't eat any of this. Why don't you keep it?"

"Are you sure? You could share it with your family."

"I'd have to explain where I got it, who made it . . . it's not worth the trouble."

"Okay, I'll take it to Donna's house tomorrow."

"Can we get together after Christmas?"

"Sure. Let me know when."

"I will. Good night." He kissed me. "Merry Christmas."

"Good night, Carl."

I watched him walk to his car, then turned off the porch light and went to the kitchen. As I filled the sink with soapy water, I saw Sam on the stairs to his apartment. He turned and saw me, so I gestured for him to come over. I dried my hands and let him in the back door. "Hi, how are you? I have a lot of cookies and stuff. Do you want some? I can't eat all of them."

"I suppose. What have you got?"

"Agnes made shortbread and mince pies."

"She gave me a box of those this morning. They were awesome. I never had that mince stuff before."

"They're gone already?"

"Well, yeah."

"You can have this batch she made for Carl. He didn't want them."

"Why not?"

"He's strict about his diet. He's afraid he'll gain weight."

"You used to be like that."

"Yeah, but that was different."

"No, it wasn't."

"Yes, it was."

"Sure. What kind of pie is that?"

"Gooseberry. Do you want to try it?"

"I love gooseberries! We had those on the farm. Do you mind?" He took off his coat and grabbed a fork.

"Leave a piece for me."

"Uh huh." He started eating out of the pan.

"I mean it."

"I know, I will. Mmm! This is good! You make the best pies."

"Thanks. Agnes had two pieces."

"Wow!"

I got started on the dishes. "Where did you go tonight?"

"Greg invited me to his family thing. I had a great time." Sam became more animated as he talked. "They do this gift exchange where you pick something from a pile of packages or you can steal one from someone who already opened one."

"I've heard of that."

"But they get super competitive about it. They're all yelling at each other and laughing. You won't believe this, but Greg is one of the quieter people in his family."

"Oh my God."

"And he's the youngest, so his brothers and sisters spoil him and tease him. It was interesting to see what a real family is like. And there was a ton of food." He carefully isolated the last piece of gooseberry pie and ate everything around it. "How was your dinner?"

"It was fine. Carl was interrogated."

"How did he hold up?"

"Pretty well. They were nice to him."

"Why wouldn't they be? He's a nice guy." He finished eating and smacked his lips. "Can I help with the dishes?"

"That's not necessary."

"I want to."

"All right. Suit yourself."

He pulled a towel out of the drawer and started drying the glassware. We worked together in silence for a few minutes. "Thank you for calling Greg."

"You're welcome." I was proud of what I had done. It worked out better than I expected. "He'll be selling cars at O'Neill's?"

"Yeah, he's excited. Thanks for that, too. He thinks you're the best guy in the world."

"Well . . . he's not wrong." Sam nudged me with his elbow. "I heard he met Flora and Agnes."

"Yeah, it was part of his interview. Clarence told him to keep Agnes in a conversation for as long as he could. Can you picture that?" He laughed. "Imagine trying to sell a car to Agnes!"

"Impossible." I smiled at the thought.

"I know! She'd be, like, "Give me what I want, or I'll beat you with a ladle!" Greg called her "young lady." God, I wish I had been there!"

"Yeah, me too. At dinner she said he was "all noise and movement." Isn't that perfect?"

"It is. There's more to him than that, but I know what she means."

"Yeah, it takes a while to see it. He's a good guy."

We were quiet again for a while. The dishes clinked and the water sloshed. I kept thinking there was something I wanted to say, but I couldn't remember what. I thought of something else. "I put up the Christmas tree. I haven't done that since my parents died."

"Do you mind if I look at it?"

"No, go ahead." He left the kitchen. A few minutes later, I took a break and followed him.

He stood close to the tree. I joined him there. His face was lit by the warm light from the tiny bulbs. "It's beautiful. Where did you get the ornaments?"

"My parents collected them over the years. Some might be from their families. I'm not sure."

"What about this one?" He pointed to a flat, crude thing made from pieces of glass, plastic beads and toothpicks.

"I made that in school. It's supposed to be a crown."

"I see that. They kept it all those years?"

"Yeah. Every Christmas my mom would say it was the prettiest ornament we had. It was a joke."

"Are you sure?"

I shrugged. "It was weird to go through this stuff. There are a lot of memories here."

"I bet. Thanks for letting me see it."

"No problem." *You should come over and hang out in the evenings. We could sit and look at the tree, and talk, or read, or whatever.* I said none of that.

"We should finish the dishes. It's getting late."

"You can go if you want. I'll finish up."

"No, there's not much left. It's the least I can do."

We went back to work until everything was put away and the tables and countertops were wiped clean. Sam put his coat on. I stacked containers of food into his hands. "Wait, I should give you some of the cookies I made."

"This is enough, Adam. I'll get those later. I won't starve."

"I hope not. That would be a sad Christmas story in the newspaper: "Young man dies from cookie deficiency." It could happen."

He grinned. "I don't think so."

"Let me get the door. Your hands are full." We maneuvered around each other in the tight space of the back hall until the door was open and he was heading out.

"Good night." He bent his knees and was about to kiss me before he realized what he was doing. He straightened up. "I'm sorry. I didn't mean . . . I wasn't thinking." He looked rattled.

"I understand. Don't worry about it." It was awkward. *And nice.* "Good night. Enjoy your Christmas dinner next door. I envy you."

"Yeah, but you get to be with Donna's family. That should be fun."

"We'll see about that." I closed the door, locked up, and shut off lights. The Christmas tree was the last thing I left on. I spent a few minutes looking at it before I went to bed, thinking about all the quiet Christmases I spent with my parents. I listened to the wind outside. The house creaked.

In bed, waiting for sleep to come, I thought about the kisses I got from Carl that night. I couldn't remember how they felt. The kiss I *didn't* get, however . . . I could feel that. My lips parted . . . my neck stretched . . . and my heart beat faster.

***

Christmas day at the Gilson house was an entirely new experience for me. They opened their presents before I arrived, and there was torn wrapping paper and empty bags and boxes everywhere. Colin and Mike threw wads of paper at each other while Sarah played with her new tablet computer. When the boys threw something at her, she did her best to ignore them. The house smelled like bacon and burnt toast.

Donna said, "Welcome to the real world. Do you want to start drinking?" It was 11:00 am.

"Sure. What have you got?"

"Pink Moscato."

"Perfect." I followed her into the kitchen. There were dirty dishes and pans everywhere. "Did you just finish breakfast?"

"A few hours ago. Why?"

"No reason. Your house is very . . . it feels . . . lived-in."

"It's a pigsty. You can help me clean up if you want."

"I suppose. Is that your plan for the day? We clean this place up, and I go home?"

"No, we play games in the afternoon and then have dinner." She gave me a huge glass of Moscato.

"Do I need to be drunk for some reason?"

"It won't hurt."

"What are you making for dinner?"

"We'll order Chinese, and I made a cheesecake for dessert. We love cheesecake."

"Sounds good. Where do we start with this mess?"

"Let's see if the dishwasher is empty." She opened it. "Of course not. I think these are clean." She checked a plate and decided they were washed. "Rinse those dishes while I put these away."

Kevin came through the back door smelling like cigar smoke. "Adam! Merry Christmas, it's great to have you here." He shook my hand. "I was getting some fresh air."

"Yeah, I can smell the freshness all over you. Merry Christmas."

He laughed. "My wife lets me have a cigar on holidays, but I have to smoke in the garage. She has you working already?"

"The minute I walked in the door."

"Get used to it. She'll be your new boss."

"Partner. We'll be partners."

He patted me on the shoulder. "Sure you will, buddy. Good luck with that."

"Ignore him," Donna said. "I don't need to be in charge of everything." Kevin and I broke into snickers. "Shut up! Kevin, make sure the kids aren't killing each other."

"Come on, babe, they're old enough to be trusted." He went into the other room. "Mike! Put that lamp back on the table! What are you trying to do? Get over here!"

"Let me know when you need more wine."

I smiled. "I'll be fine."

After the kitchen was cleaned up, we gathered around the dining room table to play games. One of the chairs was held together with duct tape. Mike asked me, "Where's Sam? Is he coming later?"

"No, he's with Flora and Agnes today. Do you remember them?"

"Is that where the swimming pool is?"

"Yeah, that's it."

"Why didn't he come here?"

"Um . . . we decided to do things separately. I'm sure you'll see him soon."

"Yeah, we will," said Donna. "Now, who wants to tell Adam how to play Spoons?"

They all talked at once. As far as I could tell, Spoons was a card game that involved violent conflict, and the goal was to have a spoon in your hand. They argued about how to position the spoons on the table. They measured the length of each person's arm and the distance between each player and the spoons. This didn't make sense until we started to play. I was shocked by the dirty tricks they played. When they pretended to reach for the spoons, I fell for it. But not again. I wasn't prepared for their level of aggression, so I was the first player out. I sat back, drank my wine, and watched the conflict. The noise level was deafening, but it was fun.

We took a break after the game, and everyone went in a different direction – to the bathroom, the kitchen, or the garage. I looked at their Christmas tree and the uneven arrangement of ornaments. Many were obviously made by the kids. While I stood there, a cat came and rubbed up against my leg. I crouched to pet it.

"She doesn't usually like strangers. I'm surprised." Donna brought me a fresh glass of wine.

"Is it my personality, or do I smell like tuna?" I stood up and shook the cat hair off my hand. "What's that picture on the wall?" I gestured toward a child's painting of a simple evergreen tree with a black background.

"Colin made that when he was in kindergarten. They were supposed to paint something for Christmas and that's what he did. I came to pick him up and his teacher was worried about him because of all the black around the tree. I asked Colin what it was, and he whispered, "It's a Christmas tree in a bear's cave." Like it was the most obvious thing in the world. I told him it was beautiful and had it framed. It's one of my favorite things."

I looked at the painting again. The story behind it touched me. Young Colin could imagine a lonely bear making the best of his situation by putting a Christmas tree in his cave. Or . . . maybe the bear liked being alone. I don't know, but I had to fight back tears.

Donna noticed. "Are you okay?"

I nodded. "Yeah. It's a good painting. I like it a lot."

"It must be hard for you to be around all this noise. I know you're not used to it."

"It's fine. I've had enough quiet to last a lifetime."

"I'm glad. I was afraid the kids would get on your nerves."

"I like your kids. I like your family. Thank you for inviting me."

"I've been inviting you for years. I'm happy you finally came."

I laughed. "That's true, you have been inviting me for years. I didn't understand what I was missing."

"We'll call the Chinese restaurant soon. Do you want anything in particular?"

"Something spicy, like Szechuan. But I like all Chinese food. It doesn't matter."

"Okay. The kids are starting a different game if you're up for it."

"You bet I am. I'll win this time." I didn't win, but I enjoyed playing.

Dinner was good, too. I never would have ordered takeout food for a holiday, but it allowed Donna to relax with her family. While we ate, Sarah asked about Sam and whether we would get back together. I told her I didn't know, because it wasn't only my decision. She thought we should get back together and planned to tell Sam the same thing. I thanked her for her input.

Colin said, "You guys don't seem like you would fit together, but you do. It's weird."

"I know what you mean. Hey, whatever happened with that girl and the poem you gave her?"

"She thought it was creepy, but she broke up with her boyfriend right after that."

"I'm sorry it didn't work out."

He shrugged. "One of her friends read the poem and asked me about it. Now we're hanging out."

"They're dating," said Sarah.

Colin's made a face. "Old people go on dates. We're hanging out."

"Whatever that means," said Kevin.

Sarah said, "I think it means sex."

Donna looked at Colin. "It better not. Do you hear me?"

"Yes! God, Mom, how many times do I have to tell you, we're not having sex!"

"As many times as I ask. You need to focus on school."

"But not only school," I offered. Donna glared at me. "All I ever did was focus on school. I should have learned more social skills; don't you agree?"

"Yeah, Mom. I need social skills."

Donna conceded, grudgingly. "Yes, social skills are important. As long as they don't involve sex."

I raised my fist to Colin and he bumped it. I smiled like an idiot.

Later in the evening, as I was leaving, Donna took me to the door and slipped a wrapped gift into my hand. "Donna, you didn't need to do that."

"It's nothing. I didn't spend any money on it. Don't open it until you're at home, okay?"

"All right. Thank you."

"Oh, wait! I have something for Sam, too. Can you give it to him?" She ran into the kitchen and came back with a plastic container. "We made cookies for him."

"Great. He needs more cookies. Why don't I get any?"

"Because you baked your own and Sam doesn't know how. Maybe he'll share them with you."

"Fine. Thanks again. Good night."

When I got home, Sam's apartment was dark, but Flora's house was brightly lit. It wasn't very late and they were obviously still together. I would have to give him the cookies later. I turned the thermostat up a couple of degrees, lit up the Christmas tree, and put the *St. Matthew Passion* into my CD player. The music made the house feel less empty. I settled into my big leather chair and unwrapped Donna's gift.

It was a well-worn copy of a children's book, *The Velveteen Rabbit, or How Toys Become Real*, by Margery Williams. I'd heard the title, but I never had children's books as a child. I only read grownup books. I opened it. Donna's name was written inside the front cover in a childish scrawl. It was a thin book, so I started reading: *"There was once a velveteen rabbit . . .*

Early in the story, I read this passage:

"When a child loves you for a long, long time, not just to play with, but REALLY loves you, then you become Real."

"Does it hurt?" asked the Rabbit.

"Sometimes," said the Skin Horse, for he was always truthful. "When you are Real you don't mind being hurt."

"Does it happen all at once, like being wound up," he asked, "or bit by bit?"

"It doesn't happen all at once," said the Skin Horse. "You become. It takes a long time. That's why it doesn't happen often to people who break easily, or have sharp edges, or who have to be carefully kept. Generally, by the time you are Real, most of your hair has been loved off, and your eyes drop out and you get loose in the joints and very shabby. But these things don't matter at all, because once you are Real you can't be ugly, except to people who don't understand."

I was hooked. I kept reading, and when I finished I was a blubbering mess.

At the end, inside the back cover, Donna had written, "Sam made you Real, not just to him, but to everyone. Please don't let him go."

I wiped my face on my sleeve. *Stupid children's book!* But I knew it wasn't stupid. It was one of the most grownup things I had ever read about the transformative nature of love.

I couldn't sit still. I started pacing. I paced all the way to the kitchen and looked out the window. The lights were on in Sam's apartment. I paced a little more and put on my coat. I grabbed the container of cookies and took my keys, locking the door behind me as I left. I went up to his apartment and knocked.

He came to the door wearing a bright red sweater. "Adam!" I knew right away he had been drinking. "Do you like my new sweater?"

"That's a great color on you. But you look good in everything."

"Come in!" He gestured broadly. "What's that?"

"Donna and the kids baked cookies for you." I gave him the container and closed the door.

"Aww, that's so nice." He pulled off the lid. "Snowmen, and colored sugar balls, and . . . whatever these things are." He put one in his mouth. "Mmm, good! Come and sit down." He sat at the kitchen table.

I took off my coat but remained standing. "Did you have wine tonight?"

"Yep. I feel it a little, but I'm okay. I had a very good time. How about you?"

"It was great. We played games, it was noisy. I had a lot of fun."

"I love games. Your eyes are red. Are you tired?"

"A little, but I'm fine. Can I have a cookie?"

"Sure, help yourself. I'll have another one." As we bit into our cookies, he looked at me. I hid nothing from him. He smiled a little. "It's good to see you again."

"It's good to see you, too." I moved closer. "You have crumbs in your beard."

"Do I?" He raised his chin. I lightly brushed it with my fingertips. Sam closed his eyes. "Are they gone?"

"Not quite," I lied. I rubbed his beard with both hands. "I like this."

"That feels good." He seemed relaxed and happy.

"It's so soft. I don't know why I'm surprised." I gently touched his moustache. "I've never kissed a man with a beard."

He took a breath. "Would you like to try it?"

I was as close to him as I could be. "Yes, please."

"Okay."

I kissed Sam as if we had never been apart. I rubbed my cheek against his beard and kissed his throat. "I like it. I could get used to this."

"Adam . . ." I pulled away. Sam gazed into my eyes and shook his head slightly, but his hands were firmly planted on my waist.

"Don't send me away." I kissed his lips again. "Please don't."

"We'll regret it."

"No, we won't . . . I won't. Let's love each other . . . forget everything else . . . let's just love each other tonight."

It didn't take long for him to surrender. He stood and picked me up, holding me in his arms and kissing me with a wild hunger. We paused long enough to undress. His body had changed, but I wanted him more than ever. He carried me to his bed . . . pressing against me . . . surrounding me. I loved him . . . I loved him . . . I loved him. I loved most of his hair off and made him loose in the joints. He made my eyes drop out. He loved me shabby.

***

When I woke in the morning, I saw Sam's bare, broad back. He was sitting on the edge of the bed. I knew something was different. I knew him well enough to know.

"Good morning."

"Good morning." He sniffed.

"What's wrong?"

He didn't turn around. "I don't know if you'll understand."

"I'll try." I waited. "Trust me."

He sniffed again. "I need to figure things out. But I can't think about those things when I'm around you."

"Okay. I can understand that."

"Dave has a spare room . . . I can stay there as long as I need to."

I swallowed hard. "That's good. He'll take care of you."

"I don't know about that." There was a long, long pause. "I'm afraid I'll lose everything." He put his head in his hands and sobbed.

I crawled across the bed and knelt behind him, rubbing his back. "That won't happen, Sam. I won't let it happen."

He stopped crying after a few minutes. "You have Carl now. He's solid . . . you can count on him."

I kept my hands on his shoulders. "I know I can, and I will, in some ways. But . . . it won't work with Carl. He's a great guy, and I hope we'll be friends. I just don't see us together in the long run."

"What will you do?"

"I'll tell him . . . soon."

"No . . . I mean after that. What will you do without him?"

"Oh . . . I'll wait for you."

"What?"

"I know you'll argue with me . . ."

"I can't promise you anything! You *know* that!"

"I don't need a promise, and you don't have to be perfect. I'll take my chances with you, Sam. I trust you."

He turned to look at me with tears in his eyes. "Are you out of your mind?"

"Maybe. I don't know."

He let out a long sigh and shook his head.

"I know . . . I'm difficult." I kissed his shoulder. "Could you stay in bed with me for a while? I'd like to make this last a little longer."

Sam nodded, followed my lead, and shifted to the center of the bed. He lay on his back with one arm around me. I put my ear against his chest and listened to his heart while I explored his body, reading and memorizing him, preparing to be away from him. My hand came to rest on his belly. For the first time, I felt a layer of softness. "This feels different. Have you noticed that?"

"Yeah. Too many cookies, I guess."

"Huh. Maybe you're like the rest of us after all. I like it."

"Me too." He stroked my hair. "It means someone is taking good care of me."

***

I met Carl at his apartment after work, with sushi and sashimi from one of his favorite restaurants. We ate and talked about his time with his family on Christmas day. I told him about Christmas with Donna's family and coming home to listen to the music he gave me while I sat in front of the tree. I didn't tell him the rest.

"Will you stay with me tonight? I like having you in my bed."

"Sure, I can stay." I screwed up my courage. "I need to tell you something first."

"Okay."

I rehearsed my speech many times but couldn't decide how to start. I opened my mouth, then stopped. I tried again, but nothing came out.

Carl made it easier. "You're still in love with Sam, aren't you?" He didn't sound angry.

I nodded and started to cry.

"Don't cry, Adam. You don't need to cry." His voice was kind and understanding.

"It's not fair to you. You're a great guy, and you've been so good to me."

"I know. I'm glad I had my chance with you, but I think we want different things in life. I've known about Sam for a while. Probably from the beginning, if I'm honest."

"Why didn't you say something? You could've called me on it."

"Why would I? I like being with you, and I know you like me. This is the best relationship I've had in a long time."

"You deserve so much more."

"I know, but for now, this is nice. Can I tell you something, though?"

"What?"

"I liked you better when you were with Sam. You were different . . . more alive or something. I can't quite put my finger on it, but now you're . . . kind of dull. Too polite. Sam was good for you. You were good for each other."

"You think I'm dull?"

"Is that all you heard?"

"No, I heard the other parts, but . . . I don't want to stop spending time with you. You're awesome."

"See what I mean? Too polite."

"Well, you're too fucking rigid! I can't believe you didn't take the desserts Agnes gave you! Do you know what it means to get food from her? All you can think about is your goddamned abs!"

Carl grinned. "There he is! That's the Adam I'm talking about. By the way, I hate your furniture. I couldn't live with that stuff."

"Shut up! Prick. I rehearsed a whole speech for this!"

"I bet you did. Was it good?"

I shrugged. "There's one thing I promised myself I would say, even though it won't be easy."

"Uh oh."

I had to say it before I choked. "I love you, Carl. I really do. I only have a few friends, and most of them are women. I'm so fucking proud that you're my friend."

Carl rubbed his hand over his face. "God dammit." He was trying to hide the little tears in his eyes. "Why did you have to say that?"

"I wanted to make a cop cry."

"Fuck you!" He stood up to collect the sushi containers. "Get your ass into my bed."

"You still want me to stay?"

"Yeah. Don't you like having sex with me? I know I enjoy it."

"But . . . if we're not . . . if this isn't going anywhere . . . why would we still do that?"

"Because we like it. We like each other. We both know where we stand. I work hard on my body and I'd like to share it with someone, preferably a friend. You like my body, don't you?"

"Yes, I love it."

"All right, then. Let's go."

"But . . ."

"But, but, but . . . get yourself undressed and we'll see where it goes. It's just sex, dude. Or maybe you're too rigid for that."

My mouth opened, but I didn't have a comeback. *Just sex? Can I do that?* I stood up and went to the bedroom, unbuttoning my shirt as I walked. *Is that what I've been doing here?*

He turned off the lights and joined me, slowly undressing on the other side of the bed. "I guess I can tell you now . . . I met someone recently. He's very attractive and he's gay." Carl pulled off his jeans. "We only talked once, but . . . I felt like, maybe . . . I don't know." He rubbed his thick chest. "He's probably out of my league."

"Who could possibly be out of your league, Carl? Look at you!"

"This guy is a doctor."

"So?"

"I'm a cop. Why would a doctor want to be with a cop?"

"Oh, please! Can we talk about this later? I'm feeling very flexible on the issue of casual sex. I'd like to enjoy your body now." I crawled into bed.

Carl grinned and raised his arms into a long, tall stretch. He ran his hands down his torso and flexed his abs. All six were present and accounted for. "I still have 'em."

"Yes, I'm impressed." I pointed at his crotch. "Is that package for me?"

He laughed and quickly removed his briefs. "All right, smart ass, you asked for it." He pounced on me like an animal. It was the best sex we ever had.

***

Sam moved out of the coach house at the end of December. Greg helped him load things into his truck while I stood around feeling helpless. I tried to put on a brave face for Sam, but we were both struggling. I retreated to my kitchen and waited for the end, when Sam came to say goodbye. He brought his keys and the beautiful vase he gave me for my birthday, the one I gave back to him.

"Please keep this, Adam. It reminds me too much of that day." His eyes were wet.

"I shouldn't have given it back. I was angry."

"I know." He shifted awkwardly. "We'd better get this over with. I won't last much longer."

"You're right. No point in dragging it out." I stood up. "Will I see you at all?"

"I think so, but I don't know when. I might be a mess for a while."

"Yeah, me too. Remember, my friends are your friends, too. That doesn't change. Call them as much as you want."

"I will."

"And me . . . I'll be here."

"Thank you." He opened his arms. "Let's do this."

We had a good long hug. This is where I would usually shut down my feelings, but I wasn't as good at that anymore. It hurt like hell, but it was the good kind of hurt.

I'm kidding . . . it hurt like a motherfucker.

We pulled ourselves together as well as we could and went outside.

Agnes showed up with containers. "Mrs. O'Neill would have been here, but she had a prior engagement. I made a few things so you won't go hungry." She gave the containers to Sam, who passed them to Greg, who tried to pry the lid off the first one. Agnes glared at him. "Don't!" Greg stopped and tiptoed away like a cartoon burglar.

She continued to talk more than usual. "There's more food where that came from. Don't be a stranger. And don't let that man give you bad manners!" She meant Dave. "You've always had good manners."

Sam stole a hug from her so she could stop talking. "Thank you for everything, Agnes." When he released her, she swatted him on the arm as if he had misbehaved, then pulled out a handkerchief and turned away from us.

Greg came back and opened his hand to Sam. "You'd better let me drive, bro. You're a wreck." Sam gave him the keys. Greg hooked his thumb toward the front of the truck. "Get in. I'll be right there." Sam kept his eyes on the ground and did as he was told.

Greg waited for him to close the door. "C'mere." He embraced me, hard. "I'll kick his ass every day. Stay strong, bro." He let me go, and all I could do was nod.

Greg pointed at Agnes with his most charming smile. "And you . . . one of these days I'll call and take you out for a nice dinner, maybe a movie," he backed away, "and who knows where it might lead?" He wiggled his eyebrows and ran to the truck.

I stood next to Agnes as we watched them pull away. "Do you think I did the right thing?"

"Aye, 'twas the only way, as hard as it was." Her soft hand took hold of mine and squeezed. "I'm right proud of you."

40

"Donna, stop. Come on, it's a holiday. You promised me you wouldn't work."

"I'm doing one little thing before I forget."

I stood next to her desk tapping my foot, trying to get on her nerves. "I don't think you're able to stop."

"Do you think I'll fall for that?"

"Fall for what? I don't know what you mean."

"Reverse psychology. Did that ever work on me?"

"Yes . . . many, many times. I'm so good at it, you didn't realize what was happening."

"Uh huh. Why don't you go? I'll be out in a minute."

"That's what you said half an hour ago."

***

It had been five months since we established Gilson & Evans Accounting Services and we were getting more work than we needed. It was a good problem to have. Rather than taking on more partners or employees, we decided to stay small, choosing the clients we wanted and referring the rest to former colleagues who had set up their own practices after the demise of Zipinski and Associates.

Alvin Zipinski had been ruined in every sense of the word after being charged with several counts of fraud. He tried to shield his assets from the lawsuits filed by Jasper Ellis and other clients who found irregularities in their accounts, but he didn't succeed. After the local newspaper ran a series of articles about former Zipinski employees who had been sexually harassed and were paid to keep quiet, Mrs. Zipinski filed for divorce and moved to Arizona. To top it off, Zipinski was asked to resign from the parish council at the local Catholic church. He withdrew from public life but would be making court appearances for years to come.

Whenever Donna and I read about the latest development in Zipinski's downfall, we asked ourselves whether we should feel a little bit sorry for him. Then we laughed. It was one of our favorite jokes.

Henry Verdorven had not been found. I was tempted to think our lives would have been better if Henry hadn't existed. He hurt Sam when he was vulnerable and ill-equipped to deal with his anger and aggression. On the other hand, Sam might not have sought refuge with me if Henry hadn't messed him up. Henry seduced me into helping him take control of the accounting firm, harming many employees and clients in the process. But it also put an end to Zipinski's abusive and unethical behavior. Perhaps Henry played a necessary role in the great scheme of things.

Still, it would be difficult to argue that Robert Bergdorf benefitted in any way from his association with Henry. He must have hoped for a better future based on whatever lies Henry told him. I developed an obsession with Bergdorf while I had a lot of free time. I searched for anything I could find about his life, his family, his work, and his education. It surprised me that someone could exist with so few connections to the world, but I had to admit, I was the same way a year earlier. That's part of what fueled my obsession. If things had gone differently, I might have been Henry's victim. I felt guilty about my involvement in the events leading to Bergdorf's death. I thought I owed him something, and I couldn't let it go.

You'll probably think I'm an idiot, but I asked Detective Mansky for information about Bergdorf. I hated his smug expression, so I reminded him how much I had contributed to his promotion to detective. That wiped the look off his face. He gave me more information than he should have about his attempts to find Henry. He tried not to sound like he was asking for my help, but he kept suggesting I 'follow the money.' He pretended to be called out of the room and left me alone with several folders full of financial records related to the Bergdorf case.

Did I look at them? Hell, yes! Mansky knew what he was doing. I was hooked. By the time he came back, I had a list of ideas and unanswered questions, and that smug look was back on his face. He's such an asshole.

Jasper Ellis was happy to give me access to his company's records when I talked to him about Robert Bergdorf. Donna was already serving as his outside accountant and auditor, but he asked if I would be willing to comb through financial records and investigate paper trails that might lead to Henry. "It could require what I would call 'creative' methods of inquiry. Are you comfortable with that?"

"Yes." I didn't even blink.

"It would involve travel if you plan to follow the money. Will that be possible?"

"Yes." I noticed his use of the phrase, 'follow the money.' "Did you talk to Detective Mansky about this?"

His face revealed nothing. "Are you interested or not?"

"Yes, definitely. But it's my ethical duty to suggest you hire an experienced forensic accountant. This isn't my area of expertise."

Mr. Ellis frowned. "Can't you take a class?"

"I suppose I could."

"Donna Gilson trusts you. That's good enough for me." When he mentioned the size of my expense account, I probably had drool on my chin. I shook his hand and we understood each other. Whatever it would take, we would find Henry and make him pay for his crimes.

***

Donna still hadn't torn herself away from the computer. When we converted the apartment in the coach house into an office for our business, I thought I would be the one who would spend too much time working. After all, it was right there behind my house. But Donna was so happy to be her own boss, she was becoming a workaholic. Kevin nagged her, the kids nagged her . . . what else could we do? Some people are compulsive. I'm glad I'm not like that.

It was Memorial Day, and everyone was coming over for a cookout. The weather was warmer than usual for the end of May. My garden looked great from the window of the coach house. The huge lilacs were in bloom and the peonies were already opening. Our first guests had staked out sunny spots in the yard.

"Hey, Donna?"

"What? I'm coming!"

"Colin went into the garden shed with his girlfriend. I don't know what they would be doing in there. It's pretty small."

"That's not funny, Adam. I told you, I'll be out in a minute."

"I'm not kidding. They closed the door."

"I'm not falling for it. Isn't Kevin out there?"

"Yeah, but Mike is stuck in the hedge, so Kevin is busy. Flora is talking to Sarah. She would probably encourage them to make out anyway."

"Dammit!" Donna shut off the computer and banged things around, closing drawers and putting things away. She stomped to the door and pointed at me. "They had better be in that shed or I'll wring your neck!"

I grinned at her ridiculous threat. I wasn't bluffing - Colin did go into the shed with his pretty girlfriend. I felt bad about ratting them out, but I don't like it when people touch my stuff. I locked the door to the office and followed Donna down the stairs. Kevin freed Mike from the hedge in time to see his wife marching across the yard. He asked me, "What's going on?"

"Colin went into the shed with his girlfriend."

"Good for him. Don't tell Donna I said that. Colin stands up to her more than I do. They're so much alike."

"At least it got her to stop working." We watched her drag the kids out of the shed. The girlfriend was embarrassed, but Colin had a smile on his face.

Kevin looked happy, too. "Hey, I've been thinking . . . I could put a wireless remote override switch on the heating and cooling system in your office. You could keep the remote controller in the house. That would allow you to shut the system off when it's time for her to stop working. When it gets too hot or too cold, she'll quit. What do you think?"

"Sounds reasonable. Go ahead and install it when she's not working. At night, maybe. I suppose she'll be angry."

"Oh yeah. I can handle it if you can."

"Sure, let's do it." Kevin rewired the whole building when we remodeled the space, so this would be an easy fix. Something had to be done.

Donna marched back to where we were standing. "Kevin, why weren't you watching them?"

"Why weren't you? I was busy with Mike. So . . . is she pregnant?"

I stifled a laugh.

"That's not funny!"

"Come on honey, loosen up a little. Colin isn't stupid."

"Yeah, but his penis might be."

"Ooh, baby, I love it when you talk about penises." Kevin put his arm around Donna's waist and nuzzled her neck. "Maybe we should go in the shed for a few minutes."

Donna slapped his arm, but her smile showed Kevin's tactic was working. "All men are alike."

I put my hands up. "Not me . . . I think girls have cooties. I need to find out what's happening in my kitchen. I can't believe I left him alone in there."

Donna jumped at the chance for payback. "Come on Adam, loosen up! What's the big deal?"

I waved my middle finger as I walked away. I *was* loosening up. I had gone through a big adjustment after years of having the house to myself. I climbed the porch stairs and went into the kitchen. "How's it going? Do you need any help?"

"No." Carl was preparing ribs for the cookout. "I know what I'm doing. I've been grilling since I was ten years old."

"All right, just asking. That's a lot of ribs. It's a good thing we bought a second grill. How much did you buy?"

"Twenty pounds. You can't have too much meat at a barbecue. Everyone loves meat."

"You should sit next to Colin. It'll be fun. You know, we'll have lots of other food."

"Yeah, but the ribs will be gone in no time. People love my ribs."

"Colin won't. He might have a few things to say about the meat industry. Agnes is grilling portabellas for him."

"Okay, whatever. Any other warnings? Because I don't know how to handle tricky situations. I'm only a cop."

"Point taken. I want you to be comfortable. You seemed tense earlier."

"Well, it's the first time . . ."

"Carl!" We were startled by Sam's greeting. Wearing a bright polo shirt and shorts, he was freshly shaved, and his hair was damp from the shower. He approached Carl and wrapped his long arms around him from behind. "How are you, buddy?"

Yeah, Sam came back. Did I not mention that? I'm sorry, let me back up.

***

It took longer than I expected, which was fine. If Sam was coming back, I wanted him to be sure about it. I didn't hear from him at all for a couple of months – no visits, no calls, not even a text message. I respected his wishes and didn't try to contact him. It was hard, but at least I received regular reports from friends who saw him or talked to him. "He's figuring things out," they would say. "He'll be okay."

I'm sure Donna let Sam know how I was. Greg would call me to brag about his success as a car salesman or to tell me about his new girlfriend. He asked transparent questions like, "Have you met anyone new?" or, "How's your love life?" I told him the truth – there was no one else, and I wasn't looking.

I had sex with Carl a few more times. He helped me understand the difference between a 'fuck buddy,' as he liked to call me, and the relationship I had with Sam. It gave me some insight into Sam's sexual activities. It also cemented my friendship with Carl. I could talk to him about anything. Our honest conversations made it clear we wouldn't be compatible as a couple. When he started dating Liam, the young doctor he'd met, we discontinued our sexual relationship and talked on the phone more often than we saw each other.

At the same time, Donna and I were remodeling the coach house and setting up our business. It was good for me to stay busy. I signed up for a forensic accounting class online. I found a new project for the neighborhood association. And there was always the garden. Though our separation was supposed to be for Sam's benefit, it also gave me time to realize that, even without him, I was happier than I was before I met him. I could live without Sam, but I didn't want to.

After I stopped wondering when I would see him, Sam sent me a text. It was formal, but sweet: "Would you do me the honor of letting me buy you dinner?" My heart did a somersault. With trembling hands, I replied, "Yes yes yes! When?"

He took me to a seafood restaurant downtown and wore the dress shirt and tie I gave him. We were nervous, as though we had just met and didn't know what to talk about. I broke the ice. "Tell me about yourself, Sam. What do you do?"

He looked down for a moment. "My business partner and I run a garden center and landscaping service called Dave and Sam's." He looked up and smiled.

"Dave made me his partner. We're changing the signs and everything." I was so proud of him, I thought I would burst.

He told me about living with Dave. "It's not a bad house, but I don't think anyone else had been in there for years. He had piles of stuff everywhere, like one of those hoarders. I told him I couldn't look at that crap every day." Sam helped him clean the place up and throw things away. They tore out carpeting and painted all the rooms, put blinds on the windows, and replaced some of the furniture. "He hadn't gone to a doctor for ten years! Can you believe that? I made him go in for a checkup. Then he was pissed off because he was perfectly healthy and I wasted his time and money."

"I'm amazed you got him to do any of those things."

"It wasn't easy, but I wouldn't give up."

"Yeah, I know. You're good with people who are set in their ways."

I told Sam about my work with Donna and my conversation with Jasper Ellis. He was excited about the idea of trying to find Henry and made it sound like I was becoming a private detective. I treated it as a joke, but it was a fantasy of mine. My head was filled with dramatic scenarios in which I brought bad people to justice using my accounting skills and a few well-placed karate chops. I have never studied karate.

We didn't talk about our relationship that night. He drove me home and politely asked if he could kiss me. I agreed, of course. It was a simple peck on the lips, but it felt like so much more because it had been so long. "You'd better go . . . quickly." I knew what he meant. Things would have progressed rapidly if we hadn't stopped there. As Sam pulled away, I noticed a silhouette in the window next door and saw the curtains move. Flora, or Agnes, or both had been watching us. I waved in their direction before going in the house.

A couple of weeks later, I treated Sam to prime rib at a restaurant known for it. He told me what he was learning about himself. None of it was surprising, and much of it resonated with me. His early life was filled with shame and loneliness. He was angry and felt guilty about being angry. No matter how much sex he had, something in him was never satisfied. He knew what he needed, but he wasn't ready to accept it. He didn't know why.

I told him how things turned out with Carl, including the sex. I think he was relieved because, in a way, it evened things up. It was also important for Sam to know it was over. We both treated Carl badly at times. Despite our behavior, he was a reliable friend. We felt lucky to have such good friends.

After the weather grew warmer, I went out to clean up my flower beds one morning. The crocuses had already come and gone. The daffodils and tulips were about to bloom. Spring is the most exciting time for a gardener, filled with the promise of things to come. I put in my ear buds and clipped dead stems and cleared away debris. I didn't know Sam was there until I saw his boots. I pulled out the ear buds and looked up.

"I was in the neighborhood. You want some help?"

"Sure. Start at that end and we'll meet in the middle." We worked for fifteen or twenty minutes without saying much until we were next to each other. He rested on his haunches and waited for me to finish. I sensed he had something to say, so I paused to look at him.

"Adam . . . I'd like to come home."

I felt a surge of emotion but didn't want to make a scene. Not in the front yard. "I was hoping you would say that. It hasn't been the same here without you." I cut down the last of the stalks and gathered them in my hand. "You'll have to move into the house."

"Is that okay?"

"Yes, that's what I wanted. Did I tell you I sold my parents' bedroom furniture?"

"No, I thought you loved that stuff."

"It was beautiful, but I felt like I was sleeping with ghosts. The bed I bought is more comfortable. King size, so you can stretch out. I got two nightstands and two big dressers."

"Did you know I would come back?"

"I was optimistic." I threw the handful of dead stalks into my wheelbarrow.

He was quiet for a minute. "I need to say this before I chicken out." His face flushed. "Sometimes I like to get aggressive during sex. Not always, but . . . I did it with other guys because I thought it was wrong and you didn't deserve to be treated like that."

"Even after I said it was okay?"

"Yeah. I was ashamed of it. And I thought you were fragile. I thought I was protecting you, but you're stronger than me in some ways. I think you could handle anything."

It was a great compliment. "We'll need to test that hypothesis. A lot." Sam smiled. "But we should probably eat lunch first."

He leaned forward and kissed me. "I love you so much. Why did I stay away for so long?"

"It was the right thing to do. You needed to figure out what you wanted."

"Yeah, well . . . I figured it out."

***

"Damn, you're solid as a rock." Sam had his arms around Carl as he stood at the counter preparing the ribs. "Are you overdoing it at the gym?"

"No. Stop touching me, I'm trying to work." Carl was still adjusting to Sam's affection.

Sam hugged him tighter. "I love you, man."

"Great. Go away." Carl blushed.

Sam didn't move. "You have to say it back to me first."

Carl sighed. "Fine. I love you, man." It wasn't enthusiastic, but he probably meant it. Sam finished him off with a pat on the butt. Carl squirmed and looked at me. "Do you encourage him to do that?"

"No," I lied. "That's the way he is with everyone."

Sam looked out the window. "Colin brought his girlfriend, huh? Good for him. Shouldn't one of us be out there with our guests?"

I shrugged. "They're more like family. We can neglect them."

"Okay. Why are you letting Carl do the cooking? You never let me cook for company."

"Carl offered to bring the ribs, and you can barely fry an egg."

"I can scramble."

"Besides, Carl wanted to show off for Liam."

"Not true," Carl objected.

"Oh!" Sam jumped right on that. "Are you demonstrating your caveman skills for your brain surgeon boyfriend? That's adorable."

Carl shook his head. "First of all, he's a pediatrician."

"Same thing."

"And he already knows I can cook."

"Yeah, but cooking for a party . . . that's a different skill. Am I right, Adam?"

"Absolutely. It's an important part of the application."

Carl made a face. "What application?"

"To become a doctor's husband. You'd be entertaining his doctor friends."

"Oh, fuck off! He's not a pretentious prick, he's a regular guy . . . who happens to have 'MD' after his name . . . and makes four times as much money as I do." He muttered, "I still don't understand what he sees in me."

I reassured him. "It's your abs, Carl."

He hung his head and grumbled, "Why do I even talk to you?"

I spoke louder to get through to him. "Carl! You're handsome, and smart, and sensitive, and generous."

Sam chimed in. "You do a lot for the community. The work you do with those kids is awesome. You're a loyal friend. You forgive people like me for being assholes."

"Okay, you can stop now."

"And he's good at accepting compliments," I added.

"He never has bad breath." Sam nodded and paused. "Hey, Carl?"

"What?"

"Can I touch your butt again?"

Carl grinned. "Get the fuck out! I'm never coming back here. Jerks."

"All right, stop torturing him." I pushed Sam toward the door. "Take some of the kids next door to see if Agnes needs any help?"

"Agnes never needs help."

"I know, but it's polite to ask. Besides, you need to practice telling Colin what to do if he'll be working at the nursery this summer."

"Fine, I'll go. Besides, I want to be out there to greet Liam with a big hug when he arrives."

Carl reacted as expected. "Stay away from him!" Sam was already gone. "He wouldn't do that, would he? Liam is shy."

"Don't worry about it. He'll probably tell him what a great guy you are. I suppose you won't like that either."

He thought about it. "That is true. I'm nervous about having him meet everyone."

"I can tell."

Carl went to the sink to wash his hands. "Sam can be . . . overwhelming."

"I know."

Carl took a long look at Sam through the window. "He's like a big friendly dog that jumps up on people. If you're not used to that . . . you know what I mean?"

"Uh huh. Are you putting those ribs in the oven?"

"Yeah, then I'll finish them on the grill."

"Can I have my kitchen back now?"

He rolled his eyes. "Yes, you can have your kitchen back."

***

Our guests arrived gradually. Sam introduced people and wove them into the group that was already there. He had social skills I would never acquire. Meanwhile, I made sure everything we needed was where it should be. Donna provided snacks for the afternoon, and Kevin set up a croquet course for those who wanted to play.

Greg showed up looking better than ever, wearing classic Ray-Ban sunglasses with his preppy clothes. He brought his girlfriend, Kate, an attractive elementary school teacher a few years older than him. Due to her influence, Greg enrolled in classes at the community college while continuing to sell cars at O'Neill's Automotive.

Kate had a beautiful tattoo of a flowering vine that started somewhere under her dress and ended with a tendril wrapped around her right forearm. Greg caught me staring at it. "Dude, are you crushing on my girlfriend? That's so not cool." Kate quickly won me over by pulling me aside and showing me the hidden parts of the vine.

Sam liked Kate but was jealous of the time his friend spent with her. He talked to me about his complicated feelings for Greg. It wasn't all that different from what I felt for Carl. Discussing it helped us understand our boundaries and expectations of each other. We chose to be monogamous, but it was a commitment we had to make every day.

I was pleased that Joe came over with his daughter, Susan. We hadn't seen him much since his house was fixed up, but Sam faithfully cleared the snow from his sidewalks throughout the winter. "You guys have been so good to us, I figured the least we could do was to come over and eat your food."

"You should come more often to visit your old shed. It looks different now, doesn't it?"

"It sure does. Sam did a fantastic job. I like the angel on top."

"That's the only thing left from the shed that burned. Will Susie be okay with all these strangers?" I looked around to see where she had gone. "She can go in the house if she needs a break."

"She's getting better around people."

I saw Susie walk up beside Sam and take hold of his hand while he was talking to Kevin. "Look at that. I thought she was afraid of him."

"Of Sam? No, why would she be afraid of him?"

"Didn't she say he was too big?"

"At first, but she got used to him. By the way, I think her pediatrician will be here."

"You mean Liam? Carl's Liam?"

"Yeah, we call him Dr. Conroy. I guess their relationship is getting serious."

"Did you introduce them?"

"Not directly, but I had something to do with it. I told Dr. Conroy about Carl and his volunteer work at Susie's school, the work on the house, and the program for troubled kids. I may have mentioned Carl was gay and single." Joe smiled. "Next thing you know, Dr. Conroy was volunteering to provide medical care for the kids in the program."

"What a coincidence."

"I feel good about it. I've never done anything like that before."

"You should be proud, that's great. Carl is head over heels for the guy. I can't wait to meet him. Do you want something to drink? We have snacks."

"I'll help myself after I say hello to Mrs. O'Neill. Do what you need to do. I can jabber with anyone."

I decided to start drinking. I went to the box of wine in my refrigerator and filled two glasses with the stuff that was too cheap and sweet for most guests. Returning to the garden, I offered the second glass to Donna. She took it as though she expected it and continued her conversation with Kate.

Dave and Clarence arrived while I was busy with other things. They were talking about Greg, in front of Greg, who looked less than comfortable. Sam was nearby but did nothing to rescue Greg even after I gestured to him. I would never understand that aspect of their friendship. I stepped in as Dave remarked, "He wasn't the hardest working employee I ever had, but at least he didn't steal from me."

"Hi Clarence. Hey Dave. I hope you weren't talking about Greg."

"Yeah, I was saying good things."

I made a face. "Were you?" Greg's eyes expressed eternal gratitude. "I bet your customers missed him this weekend."

"Yeah, some of the ladies were asking for him. And a couple of guys." He looked at Greg. "I told them where you work now."

"How's he doing at the dealership, Clarence? Was I right about him?"

"He's doing great! He sold more than some of our senior staff during the slowest season of the year. We're glad to have him."

Dave barely hid his surprise. "Huh. Well . . . I taught him everything he knows about sales. Keep it up, kid." Greg smiled and puffed himself up.

"I'm going next door to check on Agnes. Do you want to come along, Dave?"

"Yeah, sure. I could do that."

"See you later." I led him away. "Jesus, Dave, was that the best you could do?"

"I was trying to be nice, but I never liked the guy."

"Clearly."

"I promised you I wouldn't punch him, and I kept my word."

"I'm giving you credit for that."

"Hey, I saw that white peony. I told you it would bloom if you gave it a chance."

"Yeah, it's beautiful. You were right."

"Of course. I sell the best plants and I give you the best advice, don't I?"

"The best advice about plants, yes. Do you miss having Sam around the house?"

"Honestly, no. It was like having a wife. I had to hide my old porn magazines in the garage to keep him from throwing them away."

"That's terrible."

"He helped me with a few things I was meaning to do for a while. He's a good kid, but I see enough of him at the nursery. I like living alone. I'm set in my ways."

"Hmm. It was nice of you to give him a place to stay. It was good for both of us, and I'm glad to have him back."

"He's so happy, kiddo. He loves the hell out of you. I was glad to help."

"And you made him your business partner. He's so proud."

"Yeah, if I don't live forever, I wanted someone who could take over. I figured he was ready."

"He's ready. I'd still like to see him go to college, though. Part time."

"College? What does he need college for? He can make a good living from that business."

"It's not about making a living, Dave. He's smart, and he lived a sheltered life. It would expand his world and develop his mind. I hope you won't discourage him."

Dave grumbled. "He wouldn't have to go in the summer, would he?"

"Fall and winter, and only if he wants to. Can I count on your support?"

"Yeah, all right."

"Let's see what Agnes is cooking." I tapped on the patio door and pulled it open. "I came to check on you."

"And you brought trouble, I see. What am I supposed to do with him?" Her expression was blank, as usual.

Dave smiled. "I'm here to help you, woman! Have you got any of that whiskey?"

"On the table." There was a full bottle of Macallan and two crystal glasses. Dave broke the seal and savored the smell of it before pouring a few fingers into each glass.

"All right, I think Dave has what he needs. What are you cooking?"

"Sirloin kebabs and grilled vegetables."

"That sounds good. Did you know Carl is grilling ribs?"

"I've been told. I'm afraid he'll be taking most of them home."

"It's not a competition, Agnes."

"I'm certain it won't be."

Dave understood her meaning and laughed quietly as he handed her a glass.

"Whatever. Do you need any help?"

She put one fist on her hip. "Do you know how long I've been cooking for parties?"

"Sorry, I shouldn't have asked." I tried not to smile.

"I'll text Mr. Colin when I need help carrying things." She must have seen a shadow of doubt in my expression. "I know how to text! Get back to your guests." She dismissed me with a wave of her hand.

I looked at Dave. "Are you good?"

"Yep."

"Okay, see you later." As I walked back to my house, I thought about all my friends' quirky personalities. Among these people, I felt normal.

On the other side of the hedge, Carl stood with an attractive guy in a t-shirt and jeans. He had red hair and a neatly trimmed ginger beard. "There you are. Adam, this is Liam Conroy."

"Hello, Liam." I shook his hand and noticed his pale blue eyes. "I've been looking forward to meeting the guy who turned Carl into an insecure teenager."

"Adam!"

"Carl, no matter what I say you'll be embarrassed." I turned back to Liam. "He's been nervous all day. I don't know what he thinks we might do."

"I don't know either, but he's been nervous for at least a week. It made me more curious to meet you all. I've heard a lot about you."

"I promise you, we're very dull." Carl was holding a pie. "What's that?"

"Liam made it. He's a good baker."

Liam smiled and stroked his beard. "It's a cherry pie, but you should take it away from him. The last time I made one, Carl ate half of it in one night."

I raised my eyebrows and watched Carl turn red. "Is that right? He never used to eat dessert. Here comes my partner, Sam. Prepare yourself, Carl."

"Liam, ignore him! Pretend he's invisible. He'll like that."

"Hi guys! You must be Liam. I'm Sam Engel, Adam's faithful servant."

"Partner."

They shook hands. "Hi Sam, nice to meet you. Carl told me to ignore you, but I couldn't pull it off. You're very tall."

"Thanks. Being tall is the one thing I'm good at. Right Carl?" He put his arm around Carl's shoulders and jostled him. "Is that a pie?"

"Liam made it. Stop touching me."

"Mmm, let me take that." He lifted the pie out of Carl's hands. "I know exactly what to do with it." He licked his lips and grinned.

Liam addressed Sam. "I understand you're the one who created this beautiful garden. You're a professional landscaper?"

"No. I mean, yes, I do landscaping, but Adam is the gardener. This is all his work. I can't take credit for any of it."

"The shed is your work. You can take credit for that."

Liam apologized. "I'm sorry I got it backwards. Your garden is incredible. It must have taken years to get it to this point."

"Yes, more than half my life. I started when I was about fifteen years old. This was my parents' house."

Carl stopped me. "Adam, I need to get the ribs on the grill. Could you introduce Liam to everyone?"

Sam offered, "I can do that. Adam has other work to do."

"Uh . . ." Carl looked nervous.

Liam laughed. "Would you relax? I can handle myself. Go take care of your meat."

Sam covered his mouth and snickered. *Poor Carl.*

"Liam, for God's sake, don't give him more ammunition. I knew I would regret this."

"Come here." Liam gestured for Carl to come closer. He whispered in his ear for a minute. "All right?"

Carl calmed down. "Really?"

"Yes, really. Give me a kiss." They kissed and gazed into each other's eyes for a moment. "I'll see you later."

I took the pie from Sam. "That's not safe with you." Sam led Liam away. Carl wiped his eye with one finger as we walked toward the house. "What did he say?"

He cleared his throat and blinked a few times. "He said it didn't matter what anyone would say because he already loves me."

"Awww. It's so obvious you're in love with him. He's beautiful. His eyes are like swimming pools." Carl nodded. It was rare to see him so emotional.

Carl took the ribs to the grill and Donna came into the kitchen to get more wine. "Do you need help with anything? I can have Kevin come and help you. I know you don't want me to work too much."

"Everything is ready to go. I'll wait until Agnes brings her stuff over. We have too much food."

"That usually happens. Everyone thinks there won't be enough and then we're begging people to take the leftovers. It's something to keep in mind now that you'll be entertaining a lot."

"I don't know about that. We'll see."

"I never imagined you would be hosting something like this. I would have been surprised to see you show up for something like this. Who made the pie?"

"That's from Liam, Carl's boyfriend. Did you meet him?"

"Yes, he's adorable! I wanted to squeeze him like a stuffed animal, but Kevin stopped me. I think Sarah already has a crush on him."

"I thought she wasn't allowed to look at men."

"It's okay as long as they're gay. I'll encourage her to date gay men until she's finished with graduate school."

"You'd better start a trust fund for her psychotherapy."

"Education comes first. Kevin is stricter with her than I am. He'll let Colin get away with things, but not his daughter. He'll be one of those fathers who happens to be cleaning his gun every time her boyfriend comes over."

"By the time Mike is dating, you'll be more relaxed about these things."

"We'll be lucky if Mike lives that long. I'm amazed he hasn't broken any bones yet. Maybe Liam could be his pediatrician so I could see him more often."

“Yeah, that's a good reason to change doctors.”

“Are you happy for Carl? They seem like a good match.”

“Yeah, he’s perfect for Carl.”

“I'm surprised it took him this long to find someone. He's such a hunk.”

“You should tell him. He works hard to look that good, and he loves compliments.”

“Sam looks healthier than he did a few months ago.”

“Yeah, he's eating better. He actually had a little belly fat during the holidays.”

“Don't tell me you think he's overweight! Why do gay men have such impossible standards? You need to let go of this idea of physical perfection. Sam is as close as it gets.”

“I know! Calm down. I don’t mind if he gains a little weight.”

“Then why are you complaining about it?”

“I’m not! You don’t listen to me. I was saying . . .”

“You should have more of this.” Donna raised her wine glass. “It'll help you relax.”

“You know what? I think I do need another drink. Let's go outside so I can check the beverage supply.”

Donna followed me and stopped at the grill to squeeze Carl's arm and tell him what a hunk he was. She left him red-faced and smiling and proceeded to do the same to Greg. I decided to hide the box of wine when I returned to the kitchen.

I saw Flora sitting by herself at the edge of a flower bed. I sat down next to her. "Why are you alone? You're usually the center of attention."

"Don't worry about me, honey, Clarence was here. He went to get us another drink." She reached over and took my hand. "Look at all these people, Adam! You've come such a long way since last year. I hope you see that."

"I do. But I wouldn't have any of this if it weren't for Sam."

"Give yourself some credit, for heaven's sake. If it hadn't been for you, he wouldn't have all of this."

"I never think of it that way."

"Well, you should. You're an extraordinary young man, and you're only getting started. Who knows what adventures lie ahead? By the way, did you check in with Agnes?"

"I did. I left Dave there to keep her company."

"Well done. She was in a peevish mood today. Did they open the whiskey?"

"Yes, immediately."

"They might keep us entertained this evening. Perhaps there will be fireworks."

"Or they might get mellow and stay quiet."

"That is possible. I'll vote for fireworks."

"Me too. I like fireworks."

As if on cue, Agnes came marching through the opening in the hedge followed by a band of young people carrying food.

"Look at her! I'd better get my stuff out of the fridge."

"All right, dear. It's been a lovely day so far."

Agnes showed the kids where to put things, then went straight to the grill to assess Carl's ribs. I stopped nearby to listen. Carl stood with his tongs raised, waiting for her to say something. Agnes took a long look at the sizzling meat, she sniffed the air, glanced at him, glanced at his supplies, and said only two words. "Bottled sauce?"

"It's from Texas! Everybody loves my ribs!"

Agnes took one last look. "We'll see." She went off to take care of her steak kabobs.

Carl looked at me, incredulous. "Is she challenging me?"

"It's not a competition, Carl."

"Oh, it's *on!* You'll see!"

"Carl . . ."

Liam was behind him, smiling and stroking his beard. He settled him down with a dry remark. "That's right, boo. You can take that old lady."

Carl cracked a smile and went back to turning the ribs.

By the time everyone finished eating, no one cared who ate what or how much was left over. People sat and talked in small groups. Colin and his girlfriend occupied a single chair. Greg told Kate about the poem Colin asked us to read. Mike lost two croquet balls in the hedge, but no one bothered to look for them. Dave and Agnes traded barbs. There was a lot of laughter. Sweaters were retrieved from bags and cars. Fireflies appeared.

I went back and forth to the kitchen, packing up leftovers and putting things in the refrigerator. As I was heading out, I met Sam on the back porch. "Hey." His eyes sparkled. "I feel like I haven't seen enough of you today."

"I was thinking the same thing. I wish these people would leave so we could be alone."

"Next time we'll make sure they don't enjoy themselves."

"That would be my approach."

He wrapped his arms around me. "Are you as happy as I am?"

"No, I think I'm happier."

"That's impossible. I've never been so happy."

I smiled. "It's not a competition."

"But I would win."

I stroked the hair on his forearm and looked at the garden and our friends. A year had passed, and I saw that it was good. "I never thought I would have a family, but this is nice. No babies required."

"I agree. Greg will probably have a few we can borrow. We can stuff them full of candy and send them home dirty."

"I'm sure Carl and Liam will have kids, too."

"Definitely. If they could make a baby with their eyes, they would be pregnant already."

I laughed. "You're funny. I forgot that about you."

"We both forgot things for a while."

"We'll have to keep reminding each other."

My heart beat steadily. It felt larger than before. Large enough to hold him, and them, and love's perfect ache.

***

That's my story, the way I remember it. It may not be entirely accurate. I was raised with books, so my imagination takes over sometimes. I never thought I would have much of a story, but that year was quite an adventure. I wonder what would have happened to me if my tenant didn't get transferred to Chicago, or if Sam wasn't looking for an apartment, or if I refused to rent to him. Like many stories, it depended on a lot of things being just right.

My hero, Sam, had to be just right. I was lost, and the only hero who could save me had to be handsome enough to stop me from thinking too much. He had to be strong enough to tear down my walls. He had to be big enough to hold me when I wanted to run. But the most important part, the tricky part . . . was that he had to need me as much as I needed him. Sam was perfect.

I hear him in the bathroom. I hear his footsteps crossing the landing and coming into the library. "Adam, why aren't you in bed?" His voice is sleepy. "I hate it when I wake up and you're not there."

"I'm sorry. I wanted to write something before I forgot."

He sits where he always sits when he finds me here, in the soft chair next to the desk. His long, strong limbs fold gracefully as he rakes his hair and rubs his eyes in the shadowy light from the lamp. He's beautiful. He's everything I described.

He stretches his neck to smell the white peony in the vase on the desk. "What are you writing about?"

"Us."

"Again? Are you writing good things?"

"Yes, it's a good story. It has a happy ending."

"I hope so." He's serious.

"What if it didn't, Sam? What would you do?"

He takes a breath and lets it out in a weary sigh, resting his head on the heel of his hand. "I would try again. We would write a better ending." It's the answer he always gives.

"That's right. No matter how long the story gets."

He looks at me for a long moment and nods slightly. "I'll give you five minutes before I carry you back to bed. Why do you do this to me?"

I smile. "I'm sorry, I should be more considerate. But I like it when you carry me to bed."

His mouth curves up on one side. His eyes sparkle under their heavy lids.

I type . . .

THE END

Made in the USA
Middletown, DE
18 May 2021